A TALE
OF THE
WIND

A TALE OF THE WIND

*A Novel of
19th-Century France*

KAY NOLTE SMITH

VILLARD BOOKS
NEW YORK
1991

All rights reserved under International and Pan-American
Copyright Conventions. Published in the United States by
Villard Books, a division of Random House, Inc., New
York, and simultaneously in Canada by Random House of
Canada Limited, Toronto.

Villard Books is a registered trademark of
Random House, Inc.

Library of Congress Cataloging-in-Publication Data

Smith, Kay Nolte.
A tale of the wind: a novel of 19th-century France by
Kay Nolte Smith.
p. cm.
ISBN 0-394-57835-X
I. France—History—19th century—Fiction. I. Title.
PS3569.M537554I6 1991
813'.54—dc20   90-50666

Manufactured in the United States of America
9 8 7 6 5 4 3 2
First Edition
Book design by Chris Welch

For Phil, again. And always.

Acknowledgments

I am grateful to some dear friends: Joan Mitchell Blumenthal for insights into the mind and techniques of a painter; Dr. Allan Blumenthal for help on issues musical, medical, and psychological; Arthur Silber for perceptions on matters operatic, legal, and otherwise. I am grateful to many strangers: scholars who have written vividly and in absorbing detail about the arts and society in nineteenth-century France. To single out Frederick Brown's *Theater and Revolution,* Jerrold Siegel's *Bohemian Paris,* and Volume Four of *Histoire de la vie privée,* edited by Michelle Perrot, is only to neglect dozens of other works that also helped me re-create the period; any errors in that re-creation exist despite them and are of my own making. Finally, I am grateful to my agent, Meredith Bernstein, whose support and enthusiasm never wane, and to my editor, Diane Reverand, who first suggested that I turn my love of this time and place in history into a novel, and knew just how to help it happen.

PART ONE

1827–1835

On the day when Christianity said to man: You are a duality, you are composed of two beings, one perishable, the other immortal, one carnal, the other ethereal, one enchained by appetites, needs, and passions, the other lofted on wings of enthusiasm and revery, the former bending forever to earth, its mother, the latter soaring always toward heaven, its fatherland—on that day, the drama was created. Is it anything other, in fact, than this contrast on every day, this battle at every moment, between two opposing principles that are everpresent in life and that contend over man from the cradle to the grave?

—VICTOR HUGO,
Preface to *Cromwell*

Chapter One

When he looked back and tried to understand how it happened, for surely a man should be able to explain the things that altered the course of his life, he could say only that he had felt pierced by the sight of her, on that street corner, in the dawn. The feeling had come at him like a spear thrown slowly and surely, and when he tried to lift his hands to pull it from his heart—his magic hands, which he had worked hard to train—they had failed him. He had simply stood, unable to move, staring at her face in its prison of rags and grime.

That night he had been working at one of the smaller theatres on the boulevard, doing his magic act four times a day and changing scenery as well, for the extra money. After the last performance, he declined to go with some other stagehands for a drink and a bite; they shrugged, accepting that he sometimes preferred to go off alone. "Nandou wants the night to himself," one of them said as he walked off. His colleagues liked him for his wry observations, his knowledge, and his devotion to hard work, but they could not forget his singularity. No more could he.

Leaving them, he had walked out onto the boulevard, which was still crowded, audiences milling about after the various performances like a great, noisy beast unpenned into the night. Some of them wore silks and velvets so soft that one longed to stroke them, for all Paris, rich and poor, came to the boulevard theatres. The boulevard was where they found theatrical life—not the arid, stilted neoclassical dramas of the Théâtre-Français but mime and magic, dancing and animal acts, and, above all, melodramas. Not long before, one of the journals had counted up the crimes committed on boulevard stages over the past twenty years—stabbings, poisonings, assassinations, seductions, abductions, drownings, and on and on—and they had added up to a total of one hundred and fifty-one thousand, seven hundred and two. They had earned the street its nickname: the Boulevard of Crime.

Nandou straightened his shoulders, pulled on his cap, and pushed his way through the crowd to a side street where the noise was only a distant hum and the darkness was thick. Apart from the central squares, few streets had light once the sun had gone down and the shops had closed. Sometimes an oil lamp flared and swung in the wind, or the rare passerby carried a torch, its glow revealing the fear in his face as he scurried to his destination, but most streets were as black as coffins, and as narrow—breeding places for footpads, the highwaymen's city cousins, who robbed people on foot rather than on horseback; but Nandou carried a stout stick, and his wit and his voice, and a love of the dark because it granted the peace of invisibility. Although his shoulders were broad and his belly flat and hard, the daytime throngs could halt his progress or jostle him into the gutters, and the omnibuses were a thundering menace.

Angling and circling through the night streets, he stopped before a café he often visited and peered through its windows at the tables crowded with artists and students. They would argue late into the night, cheeks hot with wine and defiance, demanding freedom and denouncing tradition, as artists and students have always done. France had lived through a revolution that began with cries of liberty, equality, and fraternity but had turned into a reign of terror and ended, not with a republic, but with Napoléon as emperor. After Napoléon's abdication, the monarchy had been restored; for the students of 1827, the word *liberty* was still a battle cry. But in their conversations new words had also begun to rise, like arms lifted in rebellion: *individuality . . . Romanticism . . .* and the name of the young poet who was becoming the embodiment and symbol of their desires, *Victor Hugo . . .* Nandou stood for a while at door of the café, but then moved on.

By night he liked to roam widely, embracing Paris and the violence of its contrasts. Left Bank, Right Bank. Down alleys the width of a rat's tail, and along the expansive Champs-Elysées to its end, where they were building an Arc de Triomphe that would reach the sky. To the Seine, where he stood staring, sometimes thinking that a thousand pails of slops were flung into it by day, sometimes seeing only its night magnificence, all blemishes erased by the dark, the currents breaking the moon into rocking pieces of silver. To the Louvre, where slept treasures that took his breath with their beauty—and into the filthy, choking slum that stood between the Louvre and the Tuileries courtyard. Saint-Honoré, where the garbage held silk scraps and scented handkerchiefs, and Montmartre, where the open sewers closed his throat and set his eyes streaming.

When he finally stopped and leaned against a building to rest, it was first light and he was far from home. Above his head, between the angles of the roofs, floated rags of pearl-colored clouds. In the distance lumbered one of the sewage wagons that appeared with the morning, great dripping beasts come to empty the cesspools and cart their stinking contents out of the city.

Down the open gutter in the center of the street came a white cat, barely more than a kitten, picking its way, lifting and placing its paws as elegantly as the ballet dancers who performed at the theatres. It stopped in front of Nandou, stretched, and yawned. There was a splotch of black on the tip of one ear, and the inside of its mouth was rimmed with a line of black, as if it had taken a sip of ink. Nandou knelt; the animal regarded him gravely, then began to rub against his leg with delicate insistence, its fur a white impossibility in the filth of the streets. He reached down and felt bones sharp with hunger beneath that fur. He made a soft *tsking* sound; the animal stood still. In his jacket was a roll he had bought that afternoon. He broke off a piece and set it down. "Here, little beauty." But the cat ran. He chased it to the corner, where it scuttled into an alley. "Why do you run away when I am being kind?" he shouted, knowing it was foolish. "Come back and look at me!" At the end of the alley he saw a flash of white, but when he got there the cat was gone.

"Damn you," he muttered. He peered in several directions to get his bearings, and saw a small group of figures moving from one heap of garbage to the next—ragpickers. All over Paris they came with the light, like the sewage wagons, and formed another grotesque creature of the dawn: its humped back made of huge bundles, its single yellow eye the lantern they held above the garbage, its deformed hand the large metal hook with which they dug for objects.

He headed toward them. There were six, but he could tell neither age nor sex because their postures were bent and their clothes a gray, indistinguishable lot, probably hooked from the trash. They stopped their slow rooting among the heaps of garbage and moved aside to let him pass. One of them lifted its head: a man with dulled eyes and a thin mouth that curled down at the sight of Nandou. Nandou inclined his head, half in irony, and moved on. Then he stopped.

Another figure had lifted its head, and a face was looking at him from beneath a moldy scarf. A young face, thin, with a grimy smear on one white cheek, but perfect. Her dark eyes were large, the hair escaping her scarf was black and curly, and her mouth was two small, sweet red fruits, one protruding a bit above the other. Eyes locked to hers, Nandou waited numbly for the hint of contempt, the turning away. Instead, the two little fruits parted in a smile, and then in words: "Good morning, monsieur."

"Jeanne! Get on with your work!" said the man whose eyes were dull. In contrast, his voice snapped like a whip.

"Yes, Papa." Before the girl turned back to the garbage heap, she smiled at Nandou again and wrinkled her nose in a way that would have made him laugh if he had been able to make a sound. If he had not been speared.

Finally he managed to walk away a bit, to slip into a doorway and look back, watching her work. It wasn't just that she was beautiful and that beauty always caught at his heart; it was that she existed in the filth, and so defied it. She was a pearl made even more rare by its setting of squalor.

She was young, he thought. Twelve? Thirteen? Still straight when she stood up, but how long before her body acquired a permanent crook? And what if she avoided that fate by doing something else with her body; what if she went on the streets?

He groaned and forced himself to look away, at the other five people. They seemed to be a family: mother and father, bent, gray of skin as well as hair, and four children, of which she was the youngest and the only girl. He watched them fish out scraps of lace, a brass button—he knew it was brass because he heard her tell one of the others—some cigar ends, a shoe. He wanted to throw things into the heaps for her to find: gold pieces, and a dress of blue velvet, and a paper cornet filled with chocolates. He was standing there, planning how to do it—he would have to steal the things, but it didn't matter; he despised thieves, but if he had to become one, so be it—when the feeling came over him, the strange sense of hopelessness and power that had marked other moments of his life.

The first time, he had been very young. His mother, a fritter-vendor, had taken him with her while she worked the Boulevard of Crime. He had stood beside her while she shaped and filled the dough and tossed pieces into a pan of hot fat, where they spat and sizzled, first angry but then accepting their fate and swelling into the crisp fritters she hawked in a voice like a bad wheel—*Hot and sweet, oh buy them hot, eat them sweet*—yelling loudly to compete with the other vendors and with the actors drumming up trade by acting out scenes in front of the theatres. He had stared at the flames writhing beneath the fritter pan, and the actors gesticulating, like flames themselves; his heartbeat had swelled to the loudness of a drum, and he had had a surge of awareness that he was unique and glorious among God's creatures. His mouth had opened in wonder, and then twisted to one side as the other part of the feeling came: a strong undertow of futility, of not knowing how or where to spend his marvelous power of mind and soul. "Why the hell're you looking like that?" his mother had said. "Aren't you ugly enough as it is?"

Nandou clenched his walking stick in both hands. He had been acting as if he could talk to the beautiful girl hooking through the piles, could know her, give things to her. But what could a man like him be to such a creature?—even if she was a ragpicker's daughter. He slumped against the doorway.

After a while he felt something against his foot, and looked down: the cat. So thin and delicate, so white amid all the filth. It gave a small mew. He mewed back at it softly, a perfect imitation. It gazed up at him. For several minutes the two of them regarded each other, motionless. "You like me?" he said. "I am the handsomest fellow you have ever seen?" With a swift motion, he reached down and picked it up, tucked it inside his jacket, and strode away.

Jeanne lifted her head and watched him walk down the street. Never had she seen anyone like him before, or any eyes like his.

"Little bastard," said one of her brothers. "Little son of a bitch."

"Half a man," said another. "That's all he is."

Her third brother said, "We know which half is missing, right?" The three of them laughed, loudly as always, as if they were showing off their laughter.

Behind them, her father swore. "Don't waste time staring after a dwarf."

That was what he was? Jeanne thought. A dwarf?

"Eyes and ears on the hook," her father said. Her brothers muttered. Her mother sighed.

Those were the sounds that defined Jeanne's life: her mother's weariness, her brothers' grumbling, her father's droning about the hook. A dozen times a day he told them to keep their eyes and ears on it. The words no longer held meaning, for he uttered them as reflexively as a dog growls at the sight of a bone, and the others had long ceased to hear them as anything but a series of sounds. Still, the words were true. One had to be alert, watching for what the hook uncovered, listening to what it might strike through the slime of kitchen scraps and grease, cinders and rotting cloth. The sounds were different from one another, even with similar things: glass duller than china, paper more hollow than leather, wood sharper than bones. Some things could fool one because they had no sound at all, like hair and horse droppings, and some couldn't even be felt, like feathers. So one had to watch carefully, and move along as fast as one's eyes and ears and legs could manage before the streets filled with people, and before the heaps could destroy their treasures, slowly turning everything, by some damp inner alchemy, into a grayish-brown sameness.

Some years earlier, the family had taken Jeanne out for the first time and shown her how to work the garbage heaps. She had begun to do it, and was doing it still; anything that had happened before the time of the heaps had slid from her memory. The days became nights, which became weeks and months, marked off from one another only by heat or cold, or by finding something special in the streets—like the Day of the Coin. It had been lying by itself on the cobbles, as new and shiny as dawn, and Jeanne had spotted it first. Her brothers had been beside her in an instant, whooping and tearing the coin from her fingers. Her father had demanded it, of course, and that evening the family had had a large piece of cooked mutton from the Saint Honoré market and a bottle of real wine, smoky and red and quite unlike anything Jeanne had ever tasted.

Sometime later had come the Day of the Plate. It had been wrapped in paper, which Jeanne particularly liked to find, especially if it had printing, even though she couldn't decipher the strange marks. This wad of paper, half-buried by bits of string and food, had not only printing but illustrations, and even more wonderful, inside it was a beautiful little plate, unbroken, with violets painted on it, and gilt edges: a miracle of porcelain. She had stuffed it in her dress, determined to keep it to herself for a while; she would pretend to find it in one of the piles in the next day or so. But that evening, when she took it out to finger the gilt and the delicate colors, her brothers caught her. She often fought with them, scratching and biting, but a fight would break the plate, so she had handed it over, swearing furiously. Her father had beat her, but by then it had been too late for him to run out and sell the plate, so it had sat all night on the top of the cupboard, where she could see it and try to imagine a house in which such treasures were consigned to the trash.

This would be another time to remember: the Day of the Dwarf.

She lifted her head again. The dwarf was at the end of the street, just turning the corner. When he walked, he pitched very slightly to one side. How strange to be a man half the size of her brothers.

"God, I'm hungry," muttered her brother Pierre, behind her.

"We all are," she hissed back. "Don't talk about it."

"You could earn us some real money if you wanted," Pierre said.

"I don't want to go on the streets."

"Little bitch."

"Big bastard."

Jeanne had seen girls who went on the streets, some no older than she: lips painted very red, hips pushed forward, voices too loud or too soft as they offered to do things men seemed to want them to do. It was the thought of their eyes that stopped her, eyes with no more life than things in the heaps. She had also thought of going into a convent, but who could tell if the eyes of nuns were any different, buried as they were at the end of the long white tunnel made by the wings of their head-dresses?

Her father slapped her shoulder. "Eyes and ears on the hook!"

She bent down again. The dwarf's eyes, she thought, were like no others she had seen, strange and dark but alive with a heart of light, as if each held a small sun. When they had looked into hers, the hunger had loosed its grip on her belly, the tiredness had stopped tying her to the ground. She would remember the Day of the Dwarf.

"You have brought the princess to me," said the man, with an imperious gesture. "You shall have what reward you wish. A bag of gold?"

"My master and I do not seek such paltry payment. You shall learn in time what reward we seek." Nandou bent low, his black velvet cloak sweeping the ground. When he straightened, he put on his feathered hat with a flourish and smiled so malevolently that there were cries out in the audience.

It was not an interesting role—only the evil gnome in a fairy play—but whatever the part, one must play it with conviction and concentration. That was the glory of acting, and the power. So, in the dressing room, as Nandou had put on the hose, doublet, and cloak and drawn black lines around his eyes and painted a cruel curve on his mouth, he had begun to feel the creature's dark desires curdle and heave in his belly: the hatred of all who made him bow, the greed for power, the cold knowledge that it could never bring beauty or peace . . . "My master Satan rewards his creatures with gifts greater than gold," he said. He turned, went swiftly downstage toward a wall, and walked force-fully through it.

On the other side of the "wall," caught and steadied by two stage-hands, he heard a roar of appreciation from the house. People knew an actor couldn't walk through a wall, but they loved to be fooled into thinking he had. They wouldn't want to know how it was accomplished: sleight of hand with wood, steel, and canvas. So why couldn't they be made to see a dwarf as if he were tall and well-formed—like Corneille's Cid or Shakespeare's Othello? Why was there no such thing as sleight of soul, to use on a ragpicker's daughter?

He had forgotten her, of course. Yes, he had gone back to stare at her half a dozen times, but that was finished. Yes, he had followed the family to their home near the Taxgatherers' Wall, in a street sunlight never seemed to reach, for the doorways to the hovels were moldy, and the faces of the old women leaning against them and of the children squabbling in the narrow passageways were dead and white, like mush-rooms. Yes, he had got a child to tell him the family name, Sorel; he had followed the father and the oldest brother on their circuitous way to sell pickings from the trash; he had crept up behind them and heard them talking about the francs a whore might bring home in the morning if she was young and pretty. His face had grown so hot in the chilly November air that he had had to open his collar. But what could he do? Offer to buy her services for a night, a week, a month, as long as his money lasted? But he didn't want her services; he wanted . . . He didn't want to know what he wanted. In any case, he would never have enough money to keep her off the streets forever. And if by some magic he did, when she became a woman, the most beautiful woman in the world, then no amount of money would be enough to keep disgust from her eyes, her lips, and her heart. No, he would not go to those streets again, to hide in doorways and watch her bend and dig but sometimes lift her head to stare at the sky. . . . He would forget her. In fact he had done so already.

His performance finished for the night, he made for the dressing rooms, skirting a line of painted flats and a pen to hold trained animals until they were needed. All week he had been playing the gnome, but soon the bill would change. No other dwarf roles were in sight at the moment, so he would go back to doing magic shows and working as a stagehand. Some years before, a giantess in a sideshow had wanted him to join her, but he would not display himself as if his size were all that mattered—"See the Colossal Woman and her Amazing Dwarf!" A gnome in a play was part of the theatre; a sideshow dwarf was only a freak.

He had seen his first play when he was seven, slipping away from his mother to hide behind the skirts of two shopgirls as they entered one of the theatres and scurrying after them up to the galleries. He hadn't understood much of what went on, but the lighted stage far below had seemed to be there for him alone, glowing, a frame in which pictures not only lived but changed. He had gone back often, sometimes for only ten minutes at a time, so that bits of the performances swam disconnectedly in his mind—swords flashing, a boat capsizing, a dragon roaring, a beautiful woman smiling. One afternoon, when he was nine, he had slipped back out of a theatre toward the fritter-cart and heard someone screaming. He thought the noise came from the corner where the "Puller of Teeth, Bad or Sound" had set up all week, but the man's chair was empty of victims. The man himself, with dozens of others, was standing, gaping, a few yards from the fritter-cart, where Nandou's mother was dancing and shrieking, unreachable inside a cloak of flames. Oil from the pan, people said afterward, must have spilled on the fire and ignited her clothes. She must have been drinking, they added. Nandou knew they were right but said nothing. The next day he had stood on the boulevard outside the theatres, catching at the coats of managers until one of them said yes, there was a job: an elf for an enchanted forest scene.

That had been long ago; now he was twenty-four. Still playing gnomes.

In the dressing room, where the spicy smell of grease paint fought the stale odor of costumes, four other actors had started a card game. They looked up, and one of them said, "Ho, Nandou, what's the house like?"

"Like your stomach, my friend. Big and loud."

They laughed. Another said, "Did you go see the English actors this week?"

"Of course." An English troupe had crossed the Channel to play at the Odéon and had become the talk of Paris. Even though he couldn't understand the language, Nandou had been to see them at least a dozen times, watching backstage courtesy of the stagehands.

"Is it true, then, what everybody is saying about them?"

"My friend," Nandou said, "it is more true than you can imagine. The English are so natural! No walking sedately about the stage in a toga declaiming in Alexandrine verse—they move like real men and women, full of passion. Ophelia's madness, her grief—they tear out one's heart. Even the Ghost of Hamlet's father is more alive than anybody on stage at the Théâtre-Français."

"You've been there this week too, I suppose?" said one of the actors. Everyone knew that Nandou went often. When he nodded, the actor said, "Tell us then, what is new at our great national theatre?"

"Ah, you mean what is old. You know that nothing new is permitted at the Théâtre-Français. One may do a copy of a copy of a copy of Racine or Corneille—who themselves were copying the Greeks, although they did it with genius—but if one should chance to try anything new, such as injecting a little life into the proceedings . . . " Nandou sliced his throat with a finger.

"Then why do you go to see those dreary tragedies?"

Nandou slipped off his black velvet cloak. "I see everything." It was the literal truth. If a play appeared on any stage in Paris, he had to see it. The theatre was his temple, and a priest had to know everything, good, bad, boring.

The actors smiled at him in easy friendship, shook their heads, and went back to their cards. Theatre people were the only beings Nandou had met whose gaze accepted him without comment. Theatre people, and the cat he had carried home, and the ragpicker's daughter. But he had forgotten her: how the two little fruits of her mouth parted when she smiled, how lively her eyes were—how, when she looked at him, he had felt he was seeing something about himself, the part that made him unique and wonderful among God's creatures.

He looked into the dressing-room mirrors at the other part of himself, the physical vessel into which some malevolence had poured him. It was a sublime irony that the thing he loved most, the theatre, forced him to do what he hated most, look into a mirror. He was tall for a dwarf—an inch over four feet—but who would be a king of ants? Although his torso was normal size, the legs supporting it were the length of a child's, and his arms hung only to his hips. The one miracle was his hands, on which the fingers were perfectly shaped and the joints able to move backward as well as forward. He had trained those hands well, to be like two sleek racehorses that could outrun the eye any time and could direct a gaze wherever he wished.

As he removed the makeup, the cruel red curve of mouth disappeared, and his own emerged, straight and rather full. The artificial whiteness of skin gave way to his natural swarthiness. His face—square, with strong cheekbones—might have belonged to any young man, except for the high, prominent dwarf's brow and the skin held tightly around his large black eyes, as if expecting a blow. His head was leonine, whether by its nature or in proportion to his stature was difficult to say, and his hair, thick and black, was worn to his shoulders. He had the look of a fierce, intent mind grafted to a mocking body.

He dressed, took his stick, bade the cardplayers good night, and left the theatre and then the boulevard, going anywhere except where he wanted to go: the streets near the Taxgatherers' Wall. He passed the café he had decided not to enter on the night he had first seen the ragpicker's daughter, and, because he had forgotten her and this night was different from that one, he went in. Some students called: "Here's our dwarf who knows poetry!" One night they had been arguing over a line of Lamartine's and he, knowing the poem in question by heart, had settled their dispute. He waved to them but took a table to one side, where he raised his hand and held it motionless. The waiter, a leathery old man usually slow to attention, shuffled over at once. Nandou ordered wine and sat watching the students, who wore motley clothes and left their hair long, in defiance of accepted fashion. They argued whether Delacroix would do more paintings like the one he had just shown at the Salon, full of violence and passion, and talked of their other idols: Géricault, Hugo, Walter Scott, Lord Byron. A boy in a dark-red doublet lifted his glass, cried "Shakespeare!" as if he were saying "God," and then added, "Let's ask the dwarf if he knows *Othello!*" "In English!" cried another. Everyone at the table laughed and cheered.

Nandou smiled at them but shook his head, tossed a coin on the table, and stood. In moments he was back on the dark streets. Yanking his cap low, he walked on, searching for nothing and no one. No cafés, no conversations, no calls for a dwarf to perform his literary tricks—only empty streets where he could become a pair of eyes that looked but sought nothing.

Approaching a street that was a tunnel of shadows, he heard someone call for help. He hesitated; it was not a night for human contact, especially not with a fool, and who else would be roaming in the dark? He walked on, but the sound of the man's voice tugged at him. One could not abandon people, however they might deserve it. He swung back to look down the street.

Dark shapes hovered near a building. He inched closer, made out two footpads and a victim, heard a rough voice: "Keep your mouth shut and hand it over."

Nandou lifted his stick and cracked it against a wall. "We are coming!" he cried. Then, using a different voice, throwing it to come from the opposite direction, he yelled, "Swords ready?" Another voice, another direction: "Let him go or we'll run you through!" He kept it up, banging with his stick.

The footpads cursed and ran.

In a moment the victim called, "Who is there?"

"A friend," Nandou said, and walked toward him. The edge of the moon slid around the clouds, and he could see that the man was tall and young, with a jutting nose and a high forehead that gleamed in the light. "Good God," he heard, and knew that the man had seen he was a dwarf.

"I have no one to blame but myself for walking this way so late and alone," the man said. "May I know to whom I should offer thanks for a rescue as clever as it was welcome?"

"I am called Nandou. Just Nandou."

"A name as unusual as the rescue. How do you come by it?"

"With respect, I never explain my name, though many have asked its source."

"Very well, then, Nandou, will you accept a reward? Some of the francs you have saved me?"

"Sir, your safety is reward enough. Shall I walk a way with you?"

The man laughed. "Very well. Thank you. My home is not far." As they walked, he inquired what Nandou did and asked a number of questions. A suspicion began to prickle along Nandou's arms. "Sir, you seem to know the theatre."

"I do," the man replied. "And I plan to know it even better. Ah, here we are. My home. So, Nandou, you will accept nothing but my thanks?"

The moon welled into view. Nandou's suspicion became certainty. "Monsieur Hugo," he said slowly, "I will accept a copy of the next work from your pen."

"You shall have it." The man bowed and went into his building.

Nandou stared after him, long after the moon had disappeared again.

He lay on the bed in his attic room, six flights up on the Boulevard of Crime, watching the late morning sun move by inches across his spare furnishings. In his ears was a faint, constant thud he had long before decided must be the sound of his heart. All his life he had heard it but hadn't known what it was until he learned to read and went to the public reading rooms to hunt for information about dwarfs. In a book about the human body, with its illustrations of perfectly proportioned males, he had learned about the heart and the circulation of the blood. The sound in his ears, he concluded, must be his pulse. He had asked one of the nuns who were teaching him, in exchange for his working each morning in the convent kitchen, whether she could hear her heart as he did. "Of course not," she had said, and told him his imagination was too lively to please God.

Another sound reached his ears: The cat had stretched along his thigh and was purring like a little saw. He had not intended to keep it—who kept a cat, except in a kitchen, to chase rats?—but somehow, that first day, it had stayed in his jacket all the way home, where he had given it some of the milk he stored on the sill and a piece of old cheese. He had expected it to eat, step out the window that overlooked the back court, and disappear forever over the roofs. But it had come back, again and again. He named it Fidèle, and let it sleep beside him, and told it to forget the ragpicker's daughter.

He heard several sharp knocks. Fidèle sat up, ears pricked. "Don't worry," Nandou said, "it's for downstairs." The knocks came again, on his own door. He got up, pulled on his trousers, and answered.

A messenger boy stood there. "Are you Nandou the dwarf?"

"Can't you see what I am?"

"I had to try half a dozen theatres to find where you live." The boy held out a parcel. "Compliments of Monsieur Victor Hugo, for the dwarf Nandou."

"Fidèle," Nandou said softly, closing the door, "I told you he had made me a promise. Victor Hugo—the hope of the future! The finest poet in Paris! Why did you have no faith? Why did you say he wouldn't remember? He has sent me a copy of the preface to his new play, *Cromwell*. Everyone has been talking about it. They say it is the manifesto of Romanticism!"

He sat at the table to read it, devouring the words. Hugo was attacking the neoclassical tradition for its artificial insistence on beauty and on the unities of time and space, for its demand always to "follow the rules!" How ridiculous that all the action of a play must occur on the same day, in the same place. How unnatural that anything ugly or violent must take place offstage and could only be announced by a messenger, in beautiful verse. But Hugo was saying more; he argued that there was a duality in man, in nature, which the drama must be freed to reflect. In Nandou's mind began to appear an image of the drama as a creature crippled in chains of rules, a creature like himself, even though Nature, not some academician's rule book, had imposed his own chains. Oh, to be free of them! To be able to play Othello or Hamlet, as the English troupe had done, or even the hero in a boulevard drama!

"Pay attention, Fidèle," Nandou said. He got up and began to pace and read aloud: " 'The modern muse will recognize that everything in creation is not humanly beautiful, that ugliness exists beside beauty, deformity alongside grace, the grotesque on the reverse of the sublime, evil with good, shadow with light . . .' " He struck his head with one hand. "Fidèle, listen! 'As a means to the sublime, as a contrast to it, the grotesque, in our view, is the richest source that nature can open to art.' . . . 'In the epoch called romantic, everything is witness to its intimate and creative alliance with the beautiful.' "

Trembling, he sank back into his chair and buried his face in the cat's fur. "Fidèle, if the ugly and the beautiful belong together in art, it is because they are together in nature. It is *natural* for them to be together." After a time, when he lifted his head again, he saw more clearly than he ever had. He could not free himself of the body to which Nature had consigned him. Nor did he have the power to free the drama. But there was one thing he could do, one creature he could free. Victor Hugo had seen what he was like, and had sent him this message: that he was not to be always alone, that he and the ragpicker's beautiful daughter should be together. Not as man and woman, of course—Beauty did not couple with the Beast. And what kind of mad thought was that? His appreciation of her was that of a sculptor or a painter. Of course it was. What else could it be? No, not as man and woman—for she was not yet a grown woman, and he never would grow to be a normal-sized man—but at least together.

He lifted his head, laughed, and seized the preface again. He hadn't dreamed it; it was there: ". . . 'the real results from the very natural combination of two types, the sublime and the grotesque, which intersect in the drama as in life and creation. For true poetry, complete poetry, lies in the harmony of opposites. . . . Everything that exists in nature exists in art.' "

That is what he and Jeanne Sorel would be, the harmony of opposites.

But how was he to free her? He looked again at the pages, where Hugo had written, "Let us take a hammer to theories, poetics, and systems." But there was no way to take a hammer to three hulking brothers and a suspicious father. He put his head in his hands. The cat rubbed against his fingers.

Chapter Two

Jeanne's mother always rose first, shivering in the black, to put sticks on the tiny, broken hearth, coax them into life, and hang the coffee to boil. When she had lit a candle, the others got up too, one by one, Jeanne's father groaning out of the low bed that creaked and groaned itself, as if in sympathy, and Jeanne rising from her rag-covered straw in the corner of the other room, which she shared with her brothers. The three boys slept on one large pile of straw, slumped together like bags of sand. Always last up, they rubbed their eyes, stamped their feet, and flapped their folded arms against the cold that found a hundred chinks to let it in. Pierre, the oldest, swore beneath his breath. Pierre was always half-angry, like a coal that never burned out. Jacques and Bertrand were coals that never caught fire.

Each week the family hauled water from a public well; some was left in a cracked basin, but it had grown a skin of ice during the night, so none of them wanted to splash it on their faces. They huddled around the table, the brothers jockeying for position on a bench, the parents on two ancient stools, Jeanne on an upended barrel from which rose memories of the fish it had once held. There was a rustling whenever any of them moved: sheets of newsprint they had saved from the piles and stuffed in their clothes for warmth. "Coffee," Jeanne's father commanded, and her mother filled their mismatched cups. The brothers' spoons dove into the sugar bowl like talons, and when their mother handed them their share of the bread, they tore at it with their teeth, looking in the dim light like wolves. Something in Jeanne rebelled at the way they looked, but she could not keep herself from tearing at the bread too, though it made little difference; her hunger only snarled and shifted position, already impatient for the other meal of the day.

When the bread was gone, Pierre said, "God, it's cold."

"Talking about it only makes it colder," she said.

"God, it's cold!" he shouted.

"Pierre, please," said their mother hopelessly.

Pierre grunted loudly, and Jacques and Bertrand did too.

"Why do you always do what he does?" Jeanne said to them.

They shrugged and drank coffee. Jeanne pulled her shawl tightly around her shoulders. Inside her blouse she felt the newspaper scrape against her breasts, which had begun to grow since the previous winter. She stared into the candle, thinking of the supper they would have: the soup in which the flavor of pork fat was always so faint that it was like a memory, the plate of lentils—or would it be rice tonight?—and the glass of vinegar-flavored water that had seemed even more sour since the real wine they had had on the Day of the Coin.

The six of them sat in a stupor, clutching their cups until her father shook himself and said, "Time." He and Pierre took the two lanterns and lit them from the hearth. Jacques and Bertrand took the chamber-pots out to empty them into the street. Jeanne rinsed the cups and spoons in a pail and put them in the cupboard, while her mother put out the fire. Against a wall slumped the hooks and empty bags, which carried the odor of the piles deep in their heavy fibers. The family picked up its loads and filed out into the cold. Above them the thinning blackness was still pricked by stars; around them bloomed the yellow lights of other lanterns, as more and more ragpickers emerged from similar hovels. Slowly, lanterns weaving, they would march together toward destinations all over Paris, a parade of convicts chained not at the ankle but at the shoulders, by the humps of their pungent bags.

Jeanne's father led the way, her brothers went next, and she and her mother came behind. Eventually they separated from the other marchers and moved alone toward their usual areas. Once Jeanne had asked why they did not try some new streets, perhaps across the Seine. "We go where we are supposed to go," her father had answered. In a street where the trash was piled high on both sides, barely leaving room for pedestrians, they began to work. Each day Jeanne found the hook harder to use because not only were her hands stiff with cold, so were the piles.

The dwarf had not appeared for many days. She didn't know how many because she had run out of fingers to count. After the first time, he had appeared again, silently, one morning; then three times more, always from nowhere. One moment there would be only the street, and the next, he would be standing by a building, half-hidden in a doorway, arms folded across his chest and his gaze burning out toward where they were working. But now it had been so long since he had come that she had begun to forget his face. Only disembodied pieces of it would come to her mind, like something broken and tossed into the trash: the glowing eyes, perhaps, or the broad cheekbones.

"Eyes and ears on the hook," her father said.

Icy orange light spilled over the roofs, predicting the sun. Jeanne toiled on, the time passing in a cold, gray string. Beneath a heap of eggshells she found a piece of brown cloth, torn from breeches. Her mother gave heavy sighs every now and then, as if the hook were pulling them out, and Pierre muttered under his breath in constant little explosions: "Goddamn hook . . . goddamned peelings . . . why the pissing hell is it so cold? . . . " Jeanne moved away, attracted by a glint in a neighboring heap: a buckle, but so badly bent that it wouldn't bring much. Then she saw a pair of shoes, perfectly good ones. She reached for them, but they were attached to feet and legs. She looked up. The dwarf was there, beside her.

Despite the cold he wore no cap. He had thick black hair, down to his shoulders. She smiled. "Hello, monsieur."

An expression crossed his face as if something were hurting and pleasing him at the same time. "Hello, Jeanne," he said.

She was not surprised; nothing about him was ordinary, so why wouldn't he also know her name?

"I am Nandou," he said.

She had never heard such a name, but it was right that he should be called something different from anyone else.

"How old are you?" he said.

She thought for a moment. "Just thirteen. And you?"

His black eyebrows rose in his high forehead, but he said, "Twenty-four. Tell me, are you hungry?"

"Yes. Always."

He reached into his pocket and handed her a bag. It was warm and greasy, and had come from a fried-potato vendor. The aroma filled her until she thought she might faint. She was going to cram potatoes into her mouth, but the dwarf was watching and somehow she knew he wouldn't like that. So she forced herself to take one at a time: crisp gold on the outside, soft and white inside, so each bite resisted for a moment and then gave in with a wonderful squish. The taste made her want to weep, but if she wept, she would have to stop eating.

"Hide the bag," Nandou whispered. "The potatoes are not for the others."

She wanted one more, just one, crisp and sweet and fat, but he was right. She tucked the bag into the folds of her rags, where it lay like a warm brick.

"Hey!" cried Pierre. "That damn dwarf is back. Talking to Jeanne!"

"Jeanne!" her mother called.

The whole family came to stand beside her. She heard Pierre mutter, "God-damned Half-a-Man." More loudly, he said, "Here, you, be off. We want nothing to do with the likes of you."

Her father glowered. "A dwarf! What the devil does a dwarf want with us?"

"Only to wish you good health and good morning," Nandou said, a smile curling his voice but not his face. "As one gentleman to another." He made a bow that was graceful, even if his arms and legs were short.

"Look here," Pierre said, "do you want something?"

"Of course," the dwarf said in a strange, light voice. "Everyone wants something."

Pierre gaped, swore again, and finally managed, "Well, what is it, then?"

"I want the world to be a richer place." Nandou lifted a hand, moved it in a strange, graceful pattern, plunged it into his pocket, and withdrew a fifty-sou piece. With a delicate turn of his wrist, he tossed it onto the pile where Pierre had been working.

Pierre scrambled for the coin, and the others ran to join him. But not Jeanne; she was thinking of what Nandou had said. *Everyone wants something.*

"Jeanne," he said softly, "I'd like you to come with me, to leave your family. Would you?"

"What do you want me to do?"

"Just . . . come to live with me," he said.

"Why?"

"So we can be friends. Will you come?"

Her family had come back to stand beside her again. Her father said to Nandou, "What do you want with my daughter?"

"I've come to take her away."

Her father blinked. "Away? What do you mean?"

"Away with me."

Her mother clutched Jeanne's shoulder with one hand. Her father cleared his throat loudly.

"You little bastard!" Pierre yelled. "My sister is not going off with no ugly little bastard like you."

"Why not?" Nandou said, smiling. He was so calm. She couldn't take her eyes from him.

"Why not?" Pierre yelled. "I'll show you why not!"

"Wait a minute, Pierre," her father said. "This dwarf has money to throw away. Maybe he has come to offer money for her."

"Maybe," Nandou said. "What price would you put on her?"

After a long silence, her father said, "Fifty francs." Jeanne turned in astonishment to look at him, but he didn't meet her eyes. Her mother gave another heavy sigh and increased the pressure on her shoulder.

Nandou put his head to one side, considering. "Too much," he said at last. "I am a poor man. Jeanne, you will have to come with me for free. Will you?"

She looked into his eyes, where the little dark suns shone. They were so alive. When she stared into them, so was she. She lifted her chin and said, "Yes, I will."

"She goes nowhere!" Pierre shouted. He lifted his hook. Bertrand and Jacques did likewise. "We will carve you into pieces," Pierre said to Nandou.

"Don't hurt him!" she cried.

Her words seemed to make Pierre even more angry. His hook snaked out, across Nandou's face. Jeanne screamed, but the dwarf neither moved nor spoke. In his dark skin, the gash was as white as a bone. Small, bright-red beads began to form at its edges, then to grow larger and run together. Nandou paid them no attention. He lifted both hands above his head, then thrust them forward in a powerful motion, his fingers aiming like knives. "Back!" he hissed.

Her brothers faltered and stopped, until Pierre shook himself and said, "Are we afraid of half a man?" They advanced again, but Nandou did not move.

"Do not touch the dwarf again," said a strange voice, thin but powerful. "If you touch the dwarf, you will die."

Jeanne looked around. So did her brothers, her parents. There was no one in sight; the voice had come from nowhere. Nandou was immobile, his hands still lifted and pointing.

"Touch the dwarf and die," said the voice.

"Who the hell is talking?" Pierre shouted.

"I am the dwarf's master," said the voice. "Do not ask my name. To learn my name is to die."

Jeanne's mother gasped, and her father, who never went to church, crossed himself. Nandou put one hand to his face, where a trickle of blood was running down his cheek, like a piece of ribbon getting longer and longer. His other hand began to make a circling motion in the air. Jeanne had to watch it; she couldn't help herself. Then Nandou moved slowly to the pile of garbage onto which he had tossed the coin. Never taking his eyes from them, he bent to the pile, and in an instant his circling hand had plucked something from it: a white rose, large and perfect, on a pale green stem.

Pierre's hook fell from his hand.

Nandou walked back to them and presented the rose to her father with a flourish.

"The dwarf is my servant," said the strange voice, which was now coming from the heart of the pile. "In my name, he gives you this rose, in payment for your daughter."

Her father took it; his fingers shook.

"Are you ready, Jeanne?" Nandou said.

She lifted her chin: "Yes."

He held out his hand. She took it. The two of them began to walk down the street. The top of his head was level with her shoulders.

"Jeanne!" called her mother, her voice high and hopeless.

"Don't look back," Nandou said. "Whatever you do, don't look back."

From inside her rags, Jeanne pulled out the bag of potatoes and ate them while walking around the room. She looked down at the small stove that was sending out some heat and up into the cupboard where food and dishes were kept. She inspected the table and its one chair, peered into the press at Nandou's clothes and into the alcove at the bed, and stood before the two shelves of books, motionless except for the hand that steadily put potatoes into her mouth and the jaws that accepted them. Nandou watched from the doorway, holding a cloth to his cheek.

"I will buy another chair this afternoon," he said. "And a cot for myself. The bed will be for you."

"Just me?" she said suspiciously. "Who else lives here?"

"No one else, except you now." Jeanne put her head to one side and regarded him, lids lifting and falling slowly. "And the cat," he added.

"What do you mean?"

"Fidèle?" he called. "Where are you? Come out, Fidèle." He clicked his tongue several times and then began to mew perfectly. Jeanne stared at him. Fidèle crawled out from under the bed and began to lick her paws.

"Cats don't live inside," Jeanne said.

"This cat does."

"Why?"

"Because I invited her."

Jeanne put her shawl on the chair and shivered. "Do you think they will come after me? Pierre and Jacques and Bertrand? And Papa?"

"They might if they thought I had money. But if they haven't left the garbage heaps by this time in their lives, they're not likely to do so now."

"I've never seen a rose in the heaps. How did you find one?"

"Perhaps I will show you one day."

Silence filled the room like a big pudding, thickening and fixing the two of them in its midst, each staring inward, thinking of the thing they had done. Finally Nandou shook himself and said, "Well. We must begin our life together."

"All right," Jeanne said. She raised her hands, took the newspaper out of her bodice, and began to pull off the bodice itself.

"What are you doing?" Nandou cried.

She went on taking off the layers of her ragged clothes, which fell around her like the petals of a dirty flower.

"Don't do that." Nandou's voice got higher and thinner with each word. "Stop! Stop!"

When she finally did, she was nearly naked, thick black hair hanging to the buds of her breasts but not covering them. "Don't you want to feel my tits and get between my legs?" she said.

Nandou turned very dark, as if the blood on the cloth had rushed back into his face. "No, I don't. Where did you learn such language?"

"I hear the whores on the streets. Isn't that what you want me for, to be your whore?"

"No."

"Why are you whispering?"

"No," he said loudly. "Why did you come with me, if you thought that's what I wanted?"

"I . . . don't know. I like your eyes."

Nandou scowled. "Put your clothes back on. No, wait. They are rags. We must get you some other things to wear. In the meantime . . . " He went to the press, took out a shirt and a pair of trousers, and handed them to her. "No, wait," he said distractedly, "it would be good if you washed first. Your face and your hands and . . . everything. I bought fresh water from a seller yesterday." He went to a low stand that held a pitcher and basin, got a bar of soap, and thrust it at her. "Here. I will go . . . I will be in the alcove." He went in, sat on his bed, and stared at the wall.

"We hardly ever had soap," Jeanne said. She lathered her hands and held them out as if they wore gloves. When she finished and called out that she was ready, Nandou saw that her upper body was drowned in his shirt but the trouser legs were too short. "I will get you some trousers that fit," he said. "And a cap. You can put your hair up under it when you go out."

"Why should I dress like a boy?"

"It will be better," Nandou said. "Believe me."

Jeanne shrugged. "What do we use to pee?"

"There is a *privé* under the stairs on the first floor."

Jeanne's eyes widened as they had over the soap.

"Do you have to go?" Nandou said.

"No. I wondered what to do, is all."

They looked at each other, looked away, then back again. "Nandou is a funny name," Jeanne said. "How do you come to have it?"

"I neither explain my name nor discuss it," he said.

The silence grew still thicker and heavier. Finally Nandou said, "Can you read and write?"

Jeanne lifted her chin. "No."

"Well, let us find out what you do know. Sit down, please. Yes, there, in the chair." He folded his arms. "Can you tell me who is our king?"

She hooked her legs around the chair rung. "King Charles."

"Where does he live?"

"In his palace, of course. The Tuileries."

"Why did Napoléon abdicate? The second time, that is."

She frowned. "Waterloo?"

"Good. Why did we have the Revolution?" She said nothing. "How did it come to produce the Reign of Terror?" When she didn't answer, only twisted her legs more tightly around the chair, he sighed and walked away.

"I guess I am fucking stupid," Jeanne said.

"Don't use that language."

"What language?"

Nandou sighed. "You are not stupid. Just ignorant."

"What's the difference?"

"To be ignorant is not to know. To be stupid is not to care that you do not know."

"Ask me some other questions."

"Very well. Who is Victor Hugo?" Silence. "Molière?" She flushed but said nothing. "Voltaire?"

"I know him!" she cried. "Voltaire is the man with a cane."

"What do you mean?"

"That's what the *saltimbanques* say. They yell it out in front of their booths. 'Step right up, come right in, see the Mandarin skeleton, see the cane that Monsieur Voltaire used!' "

"Dear Lord," Nandou said. He picked up Fidèle, as if for solace.

"I don't care who Voltaire is," Jeanne said.

"I will see that one day you do."

"I don't fucking care!"

They stared at each other in silence.

"I must go out," Nandou said abruptly. "For an hour or two."

"I'll come with you."

"No, no. Stay here. I'll let the cat go out. Come, Fidèle." He went to the window and briefly opened the shutters; Fidèle leaped up and onto the roof.

When Nandou was at the door, Jeanne said, "Can I have something to eat?"

"Take what you like. But try not to gobble it down. Eat slowly."

He left, propelled by the same feeling that had gripped him the night he had first seen her—uniqueness and futility, together. The reality of what he had done was so exhilarating that he felt he could walk as if his legs were normal. But at the same time he was pinned by its weight, for he did not know how to live with her—with anybody, but especially with her, with her questioning gaze and her manner as direct as a slap and her porcelain beauty that mocked him by its mere existence. He walked out onto the boulevard. Directly in front of him the woman with eggs was calling in a high, cracked voice—"Fresh in the shell! In the shell!"—and other merchants were loudly hawking ink and cocoa and oysters and licorice water, but he barely heard them over the drumming of his heart. He felt invincible and happy and afraid and ugly.

In the room, Jeanne took a bag of green apples and a wedge of cheese from the cupboard and ate all of them, each bite following hard on the next, until her stomach swelled under the waistband of the trousers. Even then she could not stop; she found a loaf of bread and a plate of butter and ate first from one, then the other, scooping the butter into curls with her nails, not bothering to look for a knife. When there was no food left, she sat in the chair. The room was quiet, the quietest place she had ever been. For the first time in her life she was alone.

When Nandou returned, she was still sitting there.

He caught her looking at him often and oddly; the fear that she thought of leaving began to branch and twist around his heart. He decided he must convince her that he wanted nothing from her, that his goal was only to help her. So, along with proper trousers, he bought her a copybook and pens and tried to teach her her letters, cautioning her all the while against going out alone.

"Why?" she asked.

"It is too cold."

"It is no warmer when I go out with you. Besides, ragpickers are used to the cold."

"You are not a ragpicker any longer. You are a girl who is going to learn to read and write."

"Why?"

"So you will have the means to become an educated person. If you are educated, you can become whatever you like. That is the glory of living in these times, when one no longer needs to be held to the state in which one was born."

"Why do you let the cat stay indoors?"

"Because it is not good to live one's life on the streets. As you will not have to do if you are educated."

"Why does the cat have a black line around the inside of her mouth?"

"Because there is a touch of evil in each of us, as well as good. And now, no more questions whose only purpose is to keep you from learning your letters. Recite, please, from the letter F."

"F. G. H. I. . . . I don't want to be an educated person."

"Yes, you do. Come, now. You can learn if you try. You are not trying."

"I don't want to read!"

"I don't believe you." He would look at her with his glowing eyes, and defiance would blaze from her. Then, despairing of success, expecting his dwarfishness to drive her away any day, he would try to mask those fears from her—and from himself—by speaking more and more coldly.

Before Nandou went to whichever theatre had hired him for the week, he gave Jeanne assignments. When he returned, they were rarely finished. Most of the time, ignoring his prohibition, she left the room as soon as he was gone. She ran lightly down the stairs and onto the boulevard, to see the jugglers and the trained rats and dogs and hear the organ grinders and singers, and to stare at the jostling crowds, especially at the dandies and the ladies in velvets and silks. On fine days the sun played coldly and brilliantly on the spectacle, striking sparks from the gold buttons on soldiers' tunics, from a merchant's tray of eyeglasses, from a tinker's pots.

One afternoon she heard the theatre barkers calling out about a "fairy play" complete with "an enchanted palace, a bewitched princess, an evil dwarf, Satan rising from the depths, the ballet of a hundred exquisite fairies . . . " The word "dwarf" attracted Jeanne; she decided to get in. Without money she could not queue for a ticket, so she made her way into the crowd, pulling at the sleeves of the well-dressed, begging. She had poor luck until two young men with beautifully embroidered waistcoats laughed and tossed her a few coins, with which she ran back to the theatre. She thrust the coins at the ticket-seller, not knowing what they had bought until she got inside and was directed, pushed, and shoved high, high up, to a place that nestled below the ceiling.

Crowded on every side, elbows and knees poking her like sticks, she watched the curtains pull apart and reveal a new world. The enchanted palace glowed with light and jewels, the hundred exquisite fairies danced as lightly as leaves on the wind, the princess was blond and lovely in a green silk dress; even the man who plotted to capture her was splendid in his black velvet evil, and the dwarf who served him was . . . She put her hands together in a single, silent clap and did not move for the rest of the scene. The cruel face, the cold voice, the wickedness clinging to him like mist to a rainy street—they made her forget it was Nandou even as she recognized him, and see instead an ugly gnome. "My master Satan rewards his creatures with gifts greater than gold," said the Nandou-gnome, and, impossibly, he turned and walked through the wall.

She stayed to the end of the play, over an hour later, through Satan's amazing appearance from the underworld, through the rescue of the princess by a magician and a dashing young man, through the spectacular ballet of fairies, wood nymphs, and dragons. When it was over, the audience cheered and applauded, but Jeanne's feeling was too deep for release in sound. She had known Nandou worked in the theatres—he had told her so—but she had assumed that what happened inside them was like what the *saltimbanques* advertised: If you paid, you could go into their booths and see the bearded lady or the giantess or the living skeleton. She hadn't known that inside the theatres was not a sideshow but a different world. When she emerged onto the boulevard, she was surprised to find the sky nearly dark, for inside her there was so much light.

At home, she ate bread and cheese and a rind of ham and then paced the room, lifting and looking at things as if she had not seen them before, repeatedly asking Fidèle why Nandou didn't come. Finally she fell asleep on the bed. Sometime later she woke with a start to find him looking down at her, holding a candle, his expression unreadable behind its light. "Nandou," she whispered. Then she sat upright. "Nandou! I saw you—at the theatre. Yes, in the play! You were the gnome who helped to capture the princess!"

He had been for one of his long, late walks; cold and solitude still clung to him. "You went out alone?" he said. "Were you wearing the trousers? And your hair up under the cap?"

"Yes, yes. Nandou, it was so wonderful. Why didn't you tell me what the theatre was like?"

He looked down at her—for she was still sitting on the bed, so her head came only to his shoulders instead of the other way around—and saw himself reflected in her gaze, not as he looked but as he had felt when he too stole into the theatres and sat in the galleries and gave his heart to the stage. He put down the candle and cleared his throat. "How did you get in to see the play?"

"I begged for money. How did you walk through the wall? How

did the castle sink into the lake? How did you talk that way? How did you make yourself so evil? I hated you, you know." She was gleeful. "I fucking hated you!"

He turned away.

"Don't be angry," she said. "I didn't mean to swear. It just came out."

"I'm not angry."

In a moment she burst out again. "It was so wonderful! I want to work in a theatre, too."

Nandou said nothing. He went to the two bookshelves, took down a book, and began to read aloud. Soon he was pacing the room, gesturing, his voice assuming half a dozen personalities. When Jeanne started to laugh, he stopped and said, "That is Molière. One of the greatest playwrights France has ever produced. A thousand times greater than the man who wrote the piece that excited you tonight." He held the book under her nose. "But you cannot read a word Molière has written. Not a word by him, not a word of tonight's play, not a word of anything. *Why* don't you want to read? Don't you understand that you *must* learn? That you cannot have anything you want in this life unless you first learn to read?"

Jeanne grabbed the book and tossed it to the floor.

Nandou screamed. Even in her shock, Jeanne could not help thinking that he had not made a sound when Pierre's hook slit his cheek. He picked up the volume and looked at her, his gaze burning. Then, in a voice that seemed worse to her than the scream, he said, "Why do you want to harm books? They have never tried to hurt you." She was silent. "You cannot live here and harm books," he said. "Do you want to live here?"

She said nothing.

"What do you want?" he said. "Can you tell me, Jeanne?"

She lowered her head. "I want to read. More than anything in the world."

"Then why don't you learn?"

"I am afraid," she whispered.

"Of what?" She said nothing.

After a moment his hand touched her shoulder. "Then there is no problem," he said gently. "Fear—that is not a problem. Fear is only something within you that can be put aside." She lifted her head. "All you need do is will yourself to do it. Yes, that is all! And the fear will have to obey you. Do you not see how wonderful that is? Nothing else in the world will obey you that way—not other people, not a horse, not even a cat. Nothing. Not your purse—can you simply tell it to fill itself, and watch it obey? Of course not. And not your body. Can you simply say to your body, 'Be tall,' and find the next morning that it has—" He stopped as if his voice had tripped on a cobblestone.

The two of them looked at each other for a long time. "Come, sit down," she said, and coaxed him to the table. She got a bottle of his beer from the windowsill, where the drafts kept it cool, and brought it to him, but he sighed and pushed it away. She sat on the floor beside his chair and tucked her legs beneath her. "How do you come to be a dwarf?" she said.

All Nandou's life he had stiffened his soul against that question. He opened his mouth to answer without emotion—"Ask God," just that, nothing more. But more came; he couldn't stop it. "I don't know why I am this way. My mother was normal size, and she said my father was too. I never knew him, but he must have been normal or else she would have screamed at him for being a runt, slapped him, tried to keep him hidden behind the cart while she sold—" Nandou stopped and swallowed. He started to reach for the beer, but his hand fell back. "So why are my legs half the length of a man's? Even of my mother's? Why do they look as if someone sawed them with a bad axe? Why do my arms bend out like handles on a jug? Why do I . . . Why am I . . . " He cleared his throat. "Ask God. But you will have to ask him yourself. I won't speak to him. If I am his handiwork, then he has made me this way either for sport or else for some terrible purpose, and for either reason, I reject him. And if I am not his handiwork, what kind of God is he, that he didn't stop my creation? Where is his mercy? His power?" Nandou put his head in his hands.

Gradually he became aware of a pressure on his hair and another on his leg. He looked down and saw Fidèle rubbing against his ankle. He looked up and saw Jeanne stroking his head. "I will learn to read," she said. "Then I will read all the plays in the house, while you act them out." Nandou managed a smile. Her fingers moved down to his face, to the fresh scar tissue over the slash from Pierre's hook. She said, "I was afraid you would send me away if I tried to read and you saw I was too stupid to learn."

Nandou clutched her fingers. "I was afraid you were going to leave."

"I will never leave, Nandou."

He cleared his throat again. "You like living with a cat and a bird?"

"What bird?"

"One day, when I was your age, I saw a book in the window of a printer's shop, a book with pictures of birds. There was one from South America—*un nandou.* It has a long neck, and a body so ungainly it can only run along the ground. One of Nature's jokes—a bird that cannot fly. So I took its name. It suits a man who cannot walk and stand like a man."

Jeanne stroked his hair again. "I want to live with a bird and a cat. I want to read so I can find myself a wonderful name in a book, too."

A strangled sound escaped Nandou, and turned into a laugh.

They fell into a habit: Each night, when her assignments and his work at the theatre had been finished, he would read something—Homer, Virgil, Dante, Byron, Lamartine, Hugo. One night he acted out for her the *Othello* he had seen with the English players. Another time he parodied a melodrama she had just seen, grimacing and lurching about like the villain until she shrieked with delight. When he finished, she would cry, "Bravo, Nandou!" and whistle and shout like the people in the galleries.

By summer she could read the simpler passages in some of the journals and grasp enough of their meaning to ask relevant questions. "If the Revolution was for liberty and equality and no more royalty, why did Napoléon make himself emperor? Why do they say King Charles wants to erase the Revolution? How could he do that?" Sometimes Nandou would feel he was not in Paris, speaking to a French girl, but was trying to explain things to savages in America. Her voice would be puzzled, and her eyes would fix earnestly on his face, and as he struggled to explain, he would see the foolishness and the sadness of things with new clarity, so that she began to seem the means of extending and honing his own perceptions. Sometimes he took her to the public reading room, where he himself had first read so many of the things he cherished. Whenever she had done particularly well, he took her to the theatre where he was currently working and let her watch from backstage. If anyone looked askance at her, he said, "My nephew Jean," and hurried her on.

The first night she saw a huge ornamented chandelier coming down from the ceiling with its gas jets at half flame so the lamp men could work on it, she cried out and leaped aside; after that, she begged to arrive early enough to watch it every time. She liked to station herself behind a row of flats or a rack of costumes, where she could see not only the performance but the endless comings and goings before it started: the firemen trooping in to their posts, from which they would stay ready in case of accident; the callboys dashing about at the stage manager's orders; the lighting master laying out the keys he would turn to adjust the flow of gas and thus create his effects; the men moving about on the catwalks in the flies—not only stagehands but also some spectators they favored by letting them sit up there ("But Nandou, why does anybody want to sit where it's so hot and dusty?" "Some people like to look down on the rest of us"); and the hired claques for the leading actors and actresses bustling in importantly to cross the stage and go through a special door to their center seats in the auditorium. ("But Nandou, if the actors are good, why do they have to pay people to applaud?" "Actors are always afraid there won't be any applause.") When the performance began, she would stand in the wings with her arms wrapped around her body and her dark eyes locked on the stage as if memorizing it.

She wanted to know how everything was done. Nandou showed her the device that permitted the trick of walking through walls: "The English invented it for *The Vampire,* so it is called the vampire trap. The wall is actually a flat with two panels, like shutters, painted to look like one solid surface. But see these steel bands? They make both panels snap back the moment you go through them. But you must go at a good speed." After she saw him doing magic, pulling a dove from a hat and plucking a bouquet from two scarves he tied together, she said, "That's the way you did the rose, isn't it?"

"Yes."

"And the voice that came from the heap? Did you do that too?"

Lips nearly closed, he threw his voice across the room and said, "Did you think I was God, to make flowers out of nothing?"

She stared, then said slowly, "No. I thought you were a man who could make flowers out of nothing. Isn't that better than God?"

Nandou looked away, so she could not see the expression in his eyes.

She heard some people at the theatres call him "Hugo's dwarf"—for the sobriquet had been coined after the day on which the messenger had gone to various theatres asking for him—and wanted to know what the name meant. He told her the story of the rescue and explained the preface to *Cromwell* by saying, "Victor Hugo wants the plays at the

Théâtre-Français, our national theatre, to be as free as the melodramas on the boulevard."

"Why aren't they?" Jeanne was sitting on the floor of the room, legs tucked under her, eating an apple in the exaggeratedly tiny bites she took whenever Nandou said she still ate too fast.

Nandou groaned inwardly, took a sip of beer, and began explaining the Classical insistence on beauty and on the unities.

"It sounds goddamn silly to me," Jeanne said.

"True, it is silly. You have gotten quite smart. But not smart enough, or you wouldn't keep using such language."

"Don't you want people to think I'm a boy?"

"I want them to think you speak educated French!" Nandou's voice was sharp.

"All right. I apologize. The rules you are explaining to me do not seem to embody . . . are not the most excellent embodiment of reason." Nandou suppressed a smile. "What if the play is about a war?" she said. "How can all the action take place in twenty-four hours?"

"The war becomes a very short one. That makes the foot soldiers happy and the generals sad."

Jeanne laughed, then leaned forward and said earnestly, "But *why* are there rules?"

"We all need guidelines to help conduct our business, isn't that so? The trouble comes when people take the fact of having a rule as more important than its content. Now, in the case of the theatre, in Greece, many centuries ago, there were certain ways of writing tragedies, which were very great plays. Centuries later, when Frenchman like Corneille and Racine came along, they followed the Greek way of writing. Ever since, the French Academy has insisted that plays—proper plays—must be written in that same way. But the theatre, like a man, cannot be held to the ground and simply made to repeat the past."

" 'Eyes and ears on the hook,' " Jeanne whispered to herself.

"The Greeks were great writers, as were Corneille and Racine, but they are dead, all of them. We must have our own great writers, who must be free to write as they want—as free as Shakespeare—and have their works performed at our Théâtre-Français. That is what Hugo and the Romanticists are fighting for—the freedom to follow, not tradition, but their own minds and hearts. Do you understand?"

"I think so," Jeanne said. "But I still don't see why there are such stupid rules."

Nandou sighed. "Why do we still have a king? Why did the Revolution fail? Some questions have no answers."

Jeanne finished her apple and held the core between two fingers like a spool. "Why did you want me to come live with you? Is that also a question with no answer?"

Nandou said nothing. The cat leaped onto the table, to his hand, which moved into its fur. "I told you the day you came. So we could be friends."

"Are we?"

"Don't you think so?"

"How can I tell? I never had a friend before. Did you?"

"No."

"Then you can't tell either."

"Yes," he said firmly. "Now, what shall I read tonight? Who shall it be?"

"You choose," she said. "I will like anyone you choose."

One night when he came home from the theatre, she leaped up as soon as the door opened and ran to him, her voice high. "Nandou, I have a wonderful thing to tell you!"

"What is it?" he said. "I am very tired." He pulled off his cap, looked at her closely, and frowned. "Why have you cut off your hair?"

"Because I have a job!"

He stared as if she had spoken some language other than French.

"I have a job at a theatre! I went out this afternoon and talked to some of the managers. It's good that you wanted me to wear trousers and call myself Jean Sorel—I see that now—because the job I asked about was callboy. I said I was the nephew of Nandou, and Monsieur Claude said he would take me on for a week, to see if I do well. I decided it would be easier to be a callboy if I cut my hair. Isn't it marvelous? A job in the theatre!"

Nandou's hands dug into his own hair, as if reaching for his brain. "Why didn't you speak to me first?" he said hoarsely.

"I wanted to surprise you. And I did, I can see it. I am going to work in the theatre, like you! Me, Jeanne Sorel, ragpicker. I mean Jean Sorel, callboy." She laughed and began to strut about the room with a ludicrously exaggerated boyish walk, her loose cotton nightshift flapping against her body.

"No boy walks like that. Thank God you didn't try to be an actor."
She laughed and kept strutting.

"Why do you want a job in the theatre?"

She stopped, put both hands on her hips, and looked at him in astonishment.

"Yes," Nandou said. "All right." He sat at the table. The cat jumped on his lap. He began to stroke it without looking at it, or at Jeanne.

"We need the money," she said. "You can buy a new coat."

Nandou sighed. "At least you will be working on the Boulevard of Crime. If you were going to be at the Vaudeville or the Porte-St.-Martin, it would be too dangerous. How would you get home at night? How could I come to get you?"

"I know the streets of Paris well, by their garbage."

"Promise me you will work only here, on the Boulevard of Crime."

"But, Nandou . . . " She faltered before his gaze. "All right. I promise."

From below came the sound of loud voices, a ball of unintelligible words rolling up. "Off, Fidèle," Nandou said. The cat leaped from his lap and he rose, with the small, effortful sound he always made when he sat or stood, without realizing he made it. Jeanne moved close to him, peering down into his eyes, trying to decipher them. "You have grown," he said. "When you came, my head was even with your shoulder."

"I thought you would be happy I have a job. Aren't you happy, Nandou?"

"I am a man in ecstasy, who is going out for a walk."

"But you said you were tired."

"Life has suddenly come coursing back."

"Don't talk like a play, please, Nandou. Let me come out with you. Take me with you."

"No," he said harshly. "Get back into bed."

"I could go out anyway. As soon as you leave, I could go wherever I like."

"Yes, you could. You can always do what you like. I can never stop you."

"Oh, Nandou," she said plaintively, "you know I won't leave."

Her words echoed in his mind all the way down the stairs. He recalled the sense of power he had felt the night he found her; it seemed only a mocking memory. He began to walk briskly, the tiredness in his body dispelled by agitation. His feelings for her seemed to be rising from the depths of his blood, where he tried to hold them, like objects under water, with no evidence of their existence except a thin stream of bubbles. He loved her, he thought—but only as a student, a friend, a daughter. He loved her, he thought—but only because she had learned to love the theatre as he did; what else could she have done, when he had taken her there so often and talked to her about it every day, as he would talk to himself? He loved her, he thought—and the bubbles burst up in a rush, making him lightheaded with what he had struggled so long not to know: the fact that he loved her as a woman, too, the woman she was becoming, whose existence had leaped at him that night. Her lovely thick hair had been cut off as crudely as if an axe had done it, but she had never been more beautiful; the long hair seemed in retrospect to have been a distraction from her eyes and mouth. How could he have failed to realize that she was becoming a woman? Her breasts were quite full and she had begun to bleed—taking care of it so matter-of-factly, telling him she knew what to do, she had watched her mother many times. She didn't need him for anything now, except her food and a place to sleep, and soon, perhaps, she wouldn't need those either. One night she would leap up and announce, not that she had a job, but that she was going to leave. He groaned and stumbled on, and reached the Pont Neuf.

The moon hung over the Seine, a cold white fire casting a thousand reflections. He craned down to see his own. Half a reflection from half a man, he thought. The actor who could play only gnomes. He was grotesque in spirit as well as body, a carnal animal in a turtle shell, who could not scrub from his memory the fact that she had been willing to sleep with him when she first came because she had thought that was the price. . . . No, the grotesque and the sublime could share a room, but never couple. The fact that he could even imagine such a thing was proof of his folly. . . . But as long as she did not know, perhaps she would stay. As long as he did not tell her what was in his black heart but kept it hidden from her forever, shoved it down, down, beneath the water . . .

He stared into the Seine and took a vow of silence.

Chapter Three

The young man put down his silver knife and leaned forward. "This is 1830, Uncle Claude. With respect, we cannot live by old ideas. The world is changing, and we must change with it."

"Humph," said the man to whom the remark had been addressed. He took a sip of Burgundy from a crystal glass. "Your son is young, Henriette."

Henriette Vollard put a damask napkin to her lips, touched them once, then laid the napkin down. "Yes," she said. "Louis is indeed young. And youth always thinks it must be radical, until it comes of age and discovers that society must be preserved, not attacked and destroyed."

"I am twenty, Maman," Louis protested.

"That is precisely my point," she replied.

There was silence around the table, where the Vollard family was gathered for dinner: Henriette and her husband, their two sons, and as guests, Vollard's brother Claude and his wife. The silver chandelier was so ornate it might have been shaped by a pastry tube, the table was polished cherry wood, the wine upon it was from an excellent cellar, and the beef on the platter came from a cow once pampered enough to grow rich marblings of fat. Most important of all, the meal had been prepared with the help of running water, for the Vollard house was one of the few in Paris not only to be connected to the public water supply but to have that water pumped above the first floor. The Vollard family belonged to the upper layers of the *bourgeoisie*—not quite *grande* enough to be involved in running affairs of state but well regarded in circles that moved below the highest circles. The family had once owned land in the country, whose forests had made possible a furniture-making establishment, which in turn provided capital for other investments. Olivier Vollard, Henriette's husband, had a fine, high-bridged nose that scented financial opportunity as others' did wine but poked itself into little else. In his brother Claude, who was also his partner, that nose had a slight but permanent flare of disdain, reflecting its owner's interest in artistic matters; he bought paintings from Salon artists and numbered several important playwrights among his friends.

Claude rolled a dark-red circle of Burgundy inside his glass. "Louis, you may be young, but you are old enough to see that your behavior is distressing your parents. Your father says you do not express interest in any of the firm's affairs but instead spend your time with poor art students—young men who live in attics and harbor the illusion that they are artists, although none of them have painted anything that could be shown at a Salon."

"They admire Delacroix," Louis said. "Delacroix has shown at the Salons."

"Humph," said his uncle. "He is the most violent, undisciplined painter in Paris. Unless one considers Géricault. Why would you take such men as models? If you want to study painting, I can recommend you to some of the finest studios in France, where you will learn the beauty of the Classical approach."

Louis flushed and his dark eyes glittered. Although he was the only man in the room whose hair was long, touching his shoulders, he was properly dressed for a family dinner, with a pale yellow *gilet* and a neckcloth folded up to the fashionable height. "It's kind of you, Uncle Claude," he said, his voice as starched as the cloth, "but I do not wish to paint the way people have done in the past. I am interested in the art of the future, and the future of art."

"Where do you learn such talk?" Henriette Vollard said sharply. "From those scruffy friends of yours?" Louis didn't answer. "I don't understand why they can't dress properly and cut their hair. What is the point of letting your hair hang to your shoulders or dressing like a court jester? Worse, a ragpicker?" She smoothed her gown, which was red silk patterned with black flowers.

"They are rebelling against their elders and betters," Claude said tersely. He ran a hand over his bald head and down his cashmere waistcoat.

Louis still made no reply. His brother Nicolas, two years older, said mildly, "Maman, they read English authors like Sir Walter Scott and Lord Byron and wear exotic and medieval-looking clothing to express their admiration for those authors' works."

"They should be reading French authors," said Claude.

"You mean," Nicolas replied, "like Voltaire and Rousseau?"

At the mention of those radicals, Claude's jaw tightened, like a trap ready to spring, but his wife intervened. "Nicolas, you don't join your brother in his associations with these persons?"

"No, Aunt Madeleine."

"Can't you get him to follow your example, then, and join you in learning the firm's affairs? Claude says you are doing splendidly in the office."

"My dear aunt, I never set examples for Louis, lest he do the same for me."

A look flashed between the brothers, a lighthouse signaling a ship. They smiled, an identical smile that was virtually the only similarity in their appearances, or their interests, and that served to cast the differences in relief: Louis was tall and elegant, with a high forehead, red lips, his father's brown eyes, and dark hair that curled naturally. Nicolas, though also tall, was broad-shouldered and solid, his face a square and his sandy hair cropped close to it, his eyes gray like his mother's. The brothers had always been good friends, as if the differences between them made not a chasm but a bridge.

"Louis," Henriette said, "perhaps you will at least tell us how long you plan to endanger your future by wasting your time as you are doing now?"

Olivier Vollard spoke for the first time since the main course had been served. "Louis will come to his senses sooner or later. Perhaps sooner, if we all leave him alone."

"Papa!" Louis clenched a fist on the gleaming white tablecloth. "With respect, my senses have not been lost or abandoned. They have been awakened, to the need for liberty—in art, no less than in life."

Henriette's hand went to the long chain looped around her throat. Her knuckles tightened. "In the search for liberty," she said, "whose lives are to be sacrificed this time?"

Louis's eyes met hers, then dropped. Although the Revolution had ended more than thirty years earlier, it still scarred his mother's spirit, for she had been the daughter of a vicomte. When the cry for "liberty, equality, fraternity" had become a scream for the blood of all aristocrats, her fearful parents had sent her to live with poor, untitled relations. Her parents' fear had come true; their necks had bowed to Madame Guillotine. When Henriette was twenty, the relations had arranged a marriage to Olivier Vollard, and her life with him had been a comfortable one. But there were not enough possessions in Paris, in the world, to make her forget that she had lost her birthright, or that her loss had been caused by passionate young men who claimed righteousness.

"I am sorry, Maman," Louis said. "My intention was not to distress you, and never will be. I believe the world must be shaped by ideas, not swords."

"Very pretty," Henriette said dryly, but her hand left its grip on her chains and settled back to the table. The family ate for some moments without speaking, working through the beef and the vegetables, knives and forks ringing occasionally against the porcelain plates, wine chuckling softly into the glasses as the servants refilled them. Then, gradually, as if restoring the conversation to its proper terrain, though without conscious intention of doing so, the four older adults began to talk of King Charles: his opinions, his decisions, his battles with a rebellious Chamber of Deputies. The two brothers listened without joining in, their faces expressionless except for occasional quick ship-to-lighthouse looks at each other.

Finishing a discussion about the presence of the French fleet in Algeria, Claude said, "The monarchy is the true protector of France's interests."

"And of her future," added Henriette.

"Precisely. That is why the monarchy must be protected." Suddenly Claude swung around to Louis and said, "Look here, do you know this young Victor Hugo?"

Startled but polite, Louis said, "Not personally, but I have read him, of course."

"This *Hernani* of his—you know what it is?"

Louis glanced around the table before answering cautiously. "I've heard a good deal about it. All Paris has."

"Pah!" Claude's explosion of breath rippled the wine in his glass.

"What's wrong?" Olivier asked.

"The Théâtre-Français is giving in to those Romantic upstarts, that's what. First they accept a play by that young savage from the provinces . . . Alexandre somebody-or-other . . . so that we have to watch, among other indecencies, a duke crushing his wife's hand with an iron gauntlet. An attack on the nobility, on the stage of the Théâtre-Français! And now . . . Dumas, that's his name, Dumas . . . now comes Monsieur Victor Hugo, who may be a splendid poet but who is worse than the barbarian Dumas. First he refuses to change his characterization of Louis Thirteenth. When the censors ban that play, back he comes with another one—this *Hernani.* They say the hero will be a bandit. A criminal for a hero! And the language, God only knows what that will be. If that play succeeds, believe me, it will be the end of all respect for the language, the drama, and the monarchy."

"Hernani won't succeed," Madeleine said. "We will all be there to see that it doesn't."

"Not I," Olivier said.

"Of course not, you haven't been to the theatre in twenty years. But the rest of us . . . "

Slowly the four adults turned to look at the brothers.

Nicolas's shoulders lifted. "I admit that I am curious about the play."

Louis's napkin was in his hands. He twisted it once, violently; it seemed like a thin white neck. Then he set it beside his plate and said quietly, "I will be at the opening of *Hernani.* With my friends."

Henriette's voice was quieter still. "With your long-haired friends, and against your family?"

"Maman, please. I have nothing but respect for you"—his eyes swept the table—"for all of you, but I have my own opinions about things."

"Romanticist opinions?" Henriette said. "Republican opinions?"

Her questions hung in the air like little daggers. Everyone watched Louis, waiting for them to fall.

Finally Olivier shook his head. "As you said, Henriette—he's young. He'll come to his senses. Let time do its work."

Louis shot to his feet. Nicolas looked up, narrowing his eyes in a plea for caution, but Louis spoke without looking at him. "Maman, Papa, Aunt Madeleine, Uncle Claude—I must ask you to excuse me. I am no longer hungry, and I have an appointment."

Henriette opened her mouth but then closed it firmly, compressing her lips to ink lines. Louis bowed to her, turned, and left.

The adults sighed, almost in unison. "He'll come around, Henriette," Olivier said. He speared a last piece of braised carrot on his fork.

"Nicolas," Henriette said, "thank Our Lord you would never behave as Louis is doing."

Nicolas sipped his wine, his gray eyes calm above the sparkling glass.

. . .

"Sorel!" called the stage manager. "Jean Sorel!"

A pencil clutched between her teeth, a list in her pocket, Jeanne ran up and heard him bark, "Dressers to Madame Duclos!" She was off again, cutting an intricate path around stagehands and behind scenery, hunting out the two dressers who were to help the evening's leading lady in and out of the next of her ten costume changes. Madame Duclos, one of the most popular actresses on the Boulevard of Crime, played a young orphan who was struck dumb when she secretly witnessed a murder and who regained her power of speech many twists of the plot later when about to be joined in a marriage of convenience to the murderer. At intermission Duclos's dressing room was full of admirers, most of them men: well-dressed bourgeois or sometimes even members of the nobility. They all seemed old to Jeanne, and foolish, bending over Duclos's hand and smiling until their lips must surely hurt. Men behaved strangely with women; in that regard, the theatre was no different from the streets. Jeanne had to help shoo them out so the dressers could get in and do their work. When they were gone, Madame Duclos said, "What a nice boy you are." She laid a hand on Jeanne's cheek with a grand gesture, then smiled and gave the cheek a soft pinch.

"Thanks, madame," Jeanne said and dashed out. She sped up to the catwalk and along it to the other side of the stage—sometimes that was the quickest way—smiling to herself. Nandou had said they would soon find out she wasn't a boy, but they hadn't, and already it had been two years. She wasn't as bad an actress as Nandou thought, although she had no desire to go on the stage. For the present she was content to be one of many nondescript moles scurrying about in the backstage chaos—and smiling often because never had she felt less nondescript. She could barely remember how it had felt to be a blind, yearning creature trapped inside a girl who dug through garbage, for the creature had pushed through the skin of the girl like a flower through dirt, and had acquired sight.

She ran down the stairs at the other side of the stage, to round up the urchins who had been hired for the night—for a few centimes each—to stand beneath some painted cloths and manipulate sticks so the cloths would look like waves. In the middle of Paris one wanted to see an ocean? Some lights, some cloth on sticks, some boys to wave them— and there the ocean was. When she was a ragpicker's daughter, she had hardly imagined anything, except having more food. But in the theatre one could imagine everything, because it could be made to happen.

"Hold the stick straight, like so," she told an urchin, patted his head, and raced back to the stage manager. Snatches of dialogue floated from the stage: the murderer was threatening to stab the orphan girl, who would manage to grab the knife and turn it on him. It was boulevard melodrama, not great literature—she had come to understand that—but the author had been free to write it as he liked.

The stage manager dispatched her on another round of duties, and another, until finally she heard the distant roar of applause; the play was over. She felt eyes on her and knew that Nandou was in the wings, waiting, watching her. He was doing magic four nights a week in another theatre and came to meet her afterward. When she had finished everything, including fetching more wineglasses for the crowd in Madame Duclos's dressing room, she ran over to him. He didn't want to go to a café, he said; it was late and he was tired.

"Oh, please," she said. "Dear Nandou, please let's go."

He scowled, but in the way that meant he was doing it only for show, and they left. The air was bitter cold; the theatre crowds had nearly all dispersed to their carriages or to a nearby restaurant. Jeanne wrapped her wool scarf all around her head and shoved her hands into her pockets. "Did you have good houses?" she asked.

"Fine. Everything went well for you? No one looked at you suspiciously?"

"Of course not."

"You're sixteen now," Nandou said. "You're a woman. You can't always dress like a callboy."

"Why not?" she said. "It's easier this way."

Once inside the noisy café, their cheeks and fingers stung with warmth that seemed to come as much from the animation of the crowd as from the air. Groups of students sat at most of the tables, talking excitedly. The faces could be different from one night to the next; the arguments, and the passion with which they were proffered, remained the same. The students wore a motley collection of exotic clothes—a long medieval robe cut from a blanket, a pilgrim's hat, shoes with pointed toes affixed to them—and their hair curled on their shoulders. "If they could," Nandou had once said, laughing, "they would drink their wine from skulls." Yet he wore his hair like theirs.

Several of them looked up and cried, "Hola, it's Hugo's dwarf!"

Nandou shook his head to stop them, but one corner of his mouth lifted, and he made his way to a small table close to theirs. He sat, the noise masking his little unconscious grunt of effort, raised his hand to summon the waiter, and ordered wine for the two of them.

At the table, someone shouted, "If the Théâtre-Français can be forced to do *Hernani*, then the king can be forced from the throne!" Everyone else cheered. Jeanne raised her glass too. "The Classicists have been spying on rehearsals," cried someone else. "There will be a plot against *Hernani*!" Excitement flushed the students' faces and, like a fire, reflected on Jeanne's.

Although Nandou seemed to be looking into his wineglass, she could feel him watching her, as she often did. She had felt it just that morning when she was lying on her bed reading and he was sitting at the table with Fidèle in his lap. She never knew what expression was on his face while he watched her because it changed as soon as she turned to him, almost as if he was trying to hide something. But Nandou did not hide things; he brought them to light. Still, as soon as she turned to him, she could see the look changing. But from what? She smiled at him. He gave a mock scowl and lifted his glass to drink. When he was sitting at a table, one would have to look closely to see that he was a dwarf. Or that she was a girl? They were an odd pair, she thought: the dwarf yearning to be taken for a normal man, the girl masquerading as a boy.

She realized she had just thought of him as a dwarf, something she rarely did if they were alone. At home his dwarfishness seemed to have little reality, like a mirror turned to the wall. But when they were with others, out in the world, his difference would be forced on her by its reflection from dozens of eyes. Did he feel the same way?

The thought held her in an uncomfortable grip; for a while she did not notice the hubbub near the door. But she could not remain oblivious; whoever had come in was creating excitement the way a ship threw up waves. "What is it?" Jeanne said. "Who is it?"

The answer swelled around her in excited whispers: "It's Nerval! Gérard de Nerval!" She recognized the name; Nerval belonged to Victor Hugo's circle, and was often mentioned in the journals. She and Nandou leaned forward to watch as Nerval moved through the café, stopping at many of the tables, talking to people. He was handing an object to each of them. Jeanne jumped up, trying to see what it was. Something small and red. "What is it?" she cried. But she forgot to care about an answer because her gaze had caught on a face across the room.

The most wonderful face she had ever seen: high forehead, dark eyes, pale skin, full red mouth. The man was not dressed like the students with whom he sat—his clothes were those of a gentleman, including a pale yellow *gilet*—but the students talked with him easily. Nandou tugged at Jeanne's sleeve. "What is it?" he said. "What is the matter?"

"Nothing." She watched Nerval approach the table where the man sat, talk to its occupants, hand out the small red things. The man with the wonderful face smiled and took one. *Who are you?* Jeanne wanted to cry. Instead she asked, "What is Nerval giving out? Nandou, please make him come over here!"

"Sit down," Nandou said.

Moving across the room, Nerval soon reached the table of students next to them. "Listen, all of you," they heard him say, "Hugo has refused to use the Théâtre-Français's hired claque for *Hernani*. They cannot be trusted. He has secured the usual claque tickets, and many more, for his friends, so I am recruiting young men for opening night. There will be a battle with the Classicists, and we must claim victory." The students cheered wildly.

The objects in Nerval's hand were squares of red paper. He counted them out and laid them on the table. "Your passes," he told the students. "Be at the Théâtre-Français, one o'clock on the twenty-fifth, the rue de Valois door."

He walked away. Jeanne grabbed Nandou's arm and whispered, "We must get passes too. Please! We must." Nandou nodded and lifted his hand, which didn't move but seemed to draw the air around it like filings to a magnet.

Nerval, twenty feet away, turned around, looked back, and came to Jeanne and Nandou's table. He studied the two of them and frowned, as if he didn't quite know why he was there. "You are not art students, are you?"

"No," Nandou said, lowering his hand to rest on the table. "We are a harmony of opposites. *Everything that exists in nature exists in art.*"

Nerval nodded. "A kindred spirit, I see. You know your Hugo."

"May we have passes too?" Jeanne said.

Nerval looked at them closely. Then he held up a red paper square, on which a word was stamped. "Do you read this?" he asked.

"Hierro," Nandou said. "Spanish for iron?"

"Right. That is what each member of our army must be. Courageous, independent, quick. Like the sword." Nerval's gaze fixed on Nandou, registering his short legs, his size. "I don't know. We must have dependable men."

"No one is braver than Nandou!" Jeanne cried. "Why, one night when thieves tried to—"

"Quiet, Jean!" Nandou said harshly. To Nerval, he added, "Forgive my nephew. He is too excitable."

Nerval smiled. "Then he had best come in your charge." He laid the red square on the table and placed another beside it. "Be at the Théâtre-Français at one. Be of iron." Then he moved on.

"Bravo for the dwarf!" cried someone at the table next to theirs.

"Yes," cried the others at the table, "three cheers for Hugo's dwarf!"

Nandou shook his head to silence them. The students laughed and turned back to their own discussion. The thought in Nandou's eyes was as clear to Jeanne as if he had spoken it: They couldn't remark his bravery, or anything else about him, without tying the word "dwarf" to it, like bells to a leper. She wanted to take his hand but could not do so in public. And if she did, he might look into her eyes and read them, as she had read his; he would see that now she had a reason for wanting to see *Hernani* that had nothing to do with the theatre, Romanticism, or Victor Hugo. She glanced across the crowded room, where the man in the pale yellow *gilet* was laughing at something, his face like a painting in its frame of dark, curly hair.

Loudly she said to Nandou, "Isn't it splendid that we're going to fight for the theatre?"

On the day, the Seine was frozen solid, as it had been much of the winter, and the weather so cold that Fidèle didn't even make her morning journey out the window. Jeanne and Nandou found their way to the Théâtre-Français, feet ringing on the icy cobbles like hammers. As befitted members of the Romantic army, they had dressed outlandishly, in costumes from the theatres' racks: Jeanne in a brightly colored Bedouin robe with a long yellow scarf wound around her head, Nandou in a black Spanish cape lined with red velvet, which on him hung to the ground, and a big red velvet cap. The rue de Valois was a sea of young, long-haired men dressed in a rebellious riot of colors, as if pots of paint had run amok in the street. They were stamping and shouting— jokes, anti-royalist slogans, Hugo's verse—breath steaming in the air. Nerval was there, with other captains. As Nandou and Jeanne moved toward him, holding up their red squares, someone called, "It's the dwarf! Hugo's dwarf!" and they were folded into the ranks. Pushing and pulling, jostling and being jostled, Jeanne struggled not to lose her yellow scarf, and to rise on her toes to see whether the young man was somewhere in the crowd. But she couldn't spot him.

Passersby had stopped to gape at the crowd. Half a dozen urchins, eager for action, ran to the debris in the gutter and began throwing it—food scraps, rags, horse droppings frozen into rocks. The Romanticists raised their canes, their fists, their voices. Jeanne swore with them: "Stop, you little bastards! Damn you!" She looked at Nandou and laughed, her eyes daring him to criticize her language. A scowl twisted his face for a moment, until he shrugged and hollered: "Hey, stop, you little sons-of-bitches!" Jeanne screamed in delight—at him, at the bright, clear afternoon, at the knowledge that others were scrabbling through the garbage of Paris while she was fighting for the theatre.

A roar of excitement; the Théâtre-Français had opened its doors. She and Nandou swarmed in with the rest of the Romantic band, the red circle of the sun still burning in their eyes as they entered the theatre's gloomy cave. When their vision adjusted, they found seats in the pit, and the hours of waiting for the curtain to rise began. As each captain led in his troops, swaggering down the aisles, everyone shouted approval. Eventually there were people in all sections of the theatre—four hundred in all, someone said. Behind Nandou and Jeanne a voice began the Revolution song "Ça ira": "The aristocrats to the lamppost, the aristocrats, let them hang." Soon the whole house was singing, to deafening applause. Joining in, Jeanne looked into the rows to the left and right of them. In front of her someone rose and shouted—no words, just shouting for the joy of it. "Bravo!" she cried, and peered into the rows ahead of her. Someone began reciting a passage from *Hernani*. "Bravo!" she cried, and peered into the row where the speaker sat.

"What are you looking for?" Nandou said.

"Nothing," she said. She leaned over, touched his hand, and said, very close to his ear, "Thank you for this wonderful day, Nandou. For all my days." He squeezed her hand until it began to ache. She couldn't pull back to see what was on his face. By the time she could, he was smiling.

All sense of time drained away; there was only the rise and fall of voices, and emotion, for one song or cheer or luminary after another. Names Jeanne knew only from the pages of journals or café gossip were shouted out, then materialized as splendid figures going down the aisles: Balzac, a stain on his face from a rotting cabbage some urchin must have thrown at him outside; Théophile Gautier in a scarlet waistcoat and silver-gray pantaloons; and Dumas, his hair a frizzy dark cloud, his arms raised in a gesture of victory.

Everyone had brought food; as the bundles were produced, the odors of garlic, wine, and ham began to rise. Nandou, opening their own packet and cutting chunks of cheese, pointed to the statues of Corneille and Racine in the wall niches and said, "Watch their stony nostrils—do you think they're going to flare in outrage?" Nandou was smiling and laughing as Jeanne had never seen him do; it was as if, for this one day of his life, the world held no mirrors and his dwarfishness did not exist.

A bit of greasy sausage wrapping sailed past her; people were tossing debris to all sides. She turned her head to watch, saw a figure come hurrying down an aisle, and was unable to move. "What is it?" Nandou said. "Nothing," she told him. Later she said, "Off to the left, about a dozen rows—who is that man with curly dark hair and the bright-green waistcoat?"

Nandou craned his head. "I don't know," he said. "I don't think he's anybody. Have a piece of chocolate." Jeanne took one, bit off a corner, chewed. After a moment she looked down at the portion still in her hand, surprised because the dark richness she adored had failed to register on her tongue.

At length, to a huge shout from the crowd, the great chandelier came slowly down from the ceiling. The footlights brightened; the candelabra in the stage boxes were lit. "Here comes the enemy," Nandou cried, as the traditionalists and the academicians began to take their seats. In every possible way they were a contrast to the Romantic army: largely elderly, the men wearing sober gray or black pantaloons and pale cravats, faces cleanshaven and hair cropped, if they still had any, for there were many bald skulls gleaming like bulls'-eyes. When they saw the debris on the floor of the boxes and the orchestra—the greasy pieces of paper, bits of sausage, empty wine bottles—collective mutters of disgust rumbled from them like belches: "Appalling!" "No decorum in life or in art!" "No respect for property or tradition!" "Long-haired barbarians!"

"Don't you like our manners?" Nandou shouted, and people around him took up his cry. One elderly gentleman raised his fist. "Don't you like our hair?" Nandou shouted, pulling off his red velvet cap and lifting it high. "*Vive* Hugo!" Soon the whole pit was rocking and clamoring, while the loges and the orchestra growled and snapped back. *"Vive Hugo!"* Jeanne shouted, and saw with sudden clarity that the shouting, the struggle, indeed the whole night, were about something much larger than Victor Hugo or even the theatre. At stake were not just rules about a play, but ways of living. Was the past always to be sacred, as those graying, disdainful men at whom she was shouting would have it be; was one always to do things as they once had been done? The old men had created the world into which she had been born, and had not created it well; they had destroyed a revolution and restored a king, and they would keep her as she had begun—a ragpicker's daughter; they hated change and freedom and passion. *"Eyes and ears on the hook!"* she heard herself shout. She laughed and shouted more loudly, "You are the appalling ones, not us! *Vive* Hernani!"

Without her willing it, her eyes turned to the left: A dozen rows away, the man with the wonderful face was on his feet too, shouting, raising a defiant arm. Everything she was feeling in that moment grafted itself onto his person, took him as its image and expression. She would have shouted his name, if she had known it. *"Vive* Hugo!" she screamed.

The prompter's three knocks boomed around the theatre, signalling the start of the play, sounding this time like cannons. The curtain folded back slowly on a bedroom, an old female servant, the sound of a knock, and the first lines:

Could it be he already? Another knock. *Yes, that's the private Stair. . . .*

Hisses rose like steam from the loges and orchestra. Already Hugo had defied Classical tradition, which required that a thought always end at the end of a line. But this one—with its overflow of beats, as everyone could hear—had brazenly spilled over into the next: as the Romanticists had spilled into the theatre, and into the future. They yelled, to silence the Classicists' hissing. The actress, obviously frightened, was finally able to continue, but only for a few more lines. More hisses, more shouts to drown them. There were interruptions after every other line; the audience tugged on the play like a rope that carried its hostility from one side to the other. Everything that enraged the traditionalists thrilled the Romanticists: a king who talked like a commoner, an attempted seduction, a poisoning, a vendetta, a murder—and lyrical language passionately expressing love and hate. One scene engendered such fury in the orchestra and loges that fights broke out and the actors could not go on. Nandou was beside himself; he struggled out into the aisles, shouting, fists raised, his normal dislike of crowds forgotten. An elderly man tried to pummel the top of his head, but Nandou roared and kicked him in the shins. Jeanne was on her feet, shrieking hoarsely, fists clenched. It was ten minutes before the hubbub died and Nandou came back to his seat.

The final curtain fell. Pandemonium. People leaning out of boxes, shouting, weeping, cursing. People thronging the aisles, so that she and Nandou could not squeeze out for a long time. Some way ahead of them, Jeanne saw the man with the bright-green waistcoat. With no more conscious decision than she had had about shouting during the performance, she pushed and wormed her way ahead and got close enough to hear him say to his companion, "It's not over, you know. We must come back again and again." With a great shove, she plowed between two people, placed herself next to the man, and cried, "Haven't we won, then?"

He angled his head to look down at her and smiled. "Not yet, I fear."

"Will you be back, then?" she shouted.

"Yes!" He laughed. "Will you?"

"Yes! Yes! When will you be back?"

He laughed again, teeth white against his red lips. "Tomorrow night, lad!"

"Come on, Louis," his companion shouted.

"I'm not a lad!" she called, but he had been pulled away in the crush.

She hung back until Nandou came up beside her. "What a night," he said, when they had breathing space. "What a glorious night for the drama and for France." His hair hung disheveled from under the red velvet cap, his cape was askew. He took her hand—in public, although he had always cautioned her not to do so—and his eyes fixed on hers, the small suns glowing yet trembling, as if they would burst with light. "Ah, Jeanne . . . " he said. "Jeanne . . . " He crushed her hand in his and seemed unable to say more.

She smiled down at him. "People say the fight isn't over. We must come back. Tomorrow night."

"That would be splendid," he said, "but I have to work. Don't you?"

"I will have to tell them I can't. I must come back, Nandou. I must."

Chapter Four

Streaks of dark gold lingered in the purpling sky, and the brisk, early April breeze was losing warmth, though not energy. In the open window, Fidèle stretched along the sill and stared down into the rear courtyard. During the day children played there, voices shrilling, and lines of washing hung at odd angles to one another, shirts and blouses agitating in the wind like headless victims of the Terror, but now the shapes of children and wash lines were surrendering to shadows. Noises drifted in and flicked the cat's ears: sparrows' late chattering on the opposite rooftops and the faint clamor from the boulevard, where the theatres were drumming up trade for the seven o'clock shows.

Suddenly the cat's ears swiveled toward the door: shoes were clacking up the wooden stairs, faint at first, then rising slowly.

The door opened. Nandou peered into the darkening room. "Jeanne?" he called. No answer. "So, Fidèle," he said softly, "she went out?"

He walked to the table. On it were a loaf of bread and two oranges with a note stuck between them: "Dear Nandou, I will be having supper with Louis. I may be late." He read it, eyes narrowing, then threw it down. From a large pocket in his coat he took a bottle of wine and a folded newspaper. He got a glass from the cupboard, lit the lamp on the table, and sat down, with his unconscious grunt. The cat jumped from the sill to the table and rubbed against his arm. He took a drink, laid out the paper, and read an article about tension between King Charles and his Chamber of Deputies. When he finished, his brain had absorbed nothing. He drank again. "I have news tonight, Fidèle. We are going to move. I have found a bigger place—two rooms and a little fireplace. Still five flights, but we are not rich enough to live any lower." He lifted the glass but put it back untouched. "She will like it. She'll have more space to herself. So will I. It will be easier to prepare our food and to . . . " His words died away. The normally faint thud of his heart grew louder in his ears. Perhaps, he thought, his heart was too large for his body, mocking him by being normal. Why couldn't it be dwarf-size and silent? Why must he listen to the sound of his inner being?

He retrieved Jeanne's note and reread it. His posture did not change, but he spoke so violently that Fidèle's head jerked. "If I hadn't made her learn to write, she couldn't leave me notes. I wouldn't have to know where she is!"

He put his head in his hands. "She tells me everything. It never occurs to her that I might not . . . that I might feel . . . "

When he hadn't been able to return with her immediately to *Hernani,* she had gone by herself, despite his cautions. "I will be fine, Nandou. Don't worry. I will find someone to sit with." When she came home late that night, her face had been a little lamp of excitement: "I waited outside the theatre, Nandou, and someone I had seen the night before got me a pass. His name is Louis Vollard, and he is studying painting, but he's not poor like his friends, I'm sure of that. He's going to get me a pass for Wednesday night, too." She hadn't even tried to keep her eyes from shining. Why should she? She was only sharing things with Nandou. With the dwarf Nandou.

Immediately he had learned all he could, from a wigmaker who knew the man's mother's dressmaker: Louis was the younger son of Olivier Vollard, whose various enterprises included Vollard et Cie., furniture makers. Louis was twenty and handsome. And tall. Nandou said nothing of this knowledge; he merely stroked Fidèle and listened to Jeanne, her eyes like black jewels while she talked and her fruited mouth ripe and eager. "Do you know that on opening night, while Louis was sitting with us, his uncle was with the Classicists? Yes! The family was furious and forbade him to go back to *Hernani.* But Louis went anyway. They don't want him to spend time with his artist friends either, but he does. Louis defies his own family! Isn't that splendid?"

Forgetting that he meant to say nothing, Nandou had said, "You are also splendid, for you too defied your family."

She had waved it aside. "What does it mean to defy a ragpicker? But Louis's father is an important man, and Louis's mother was a vicomte's daughter."

So Nandou had shrugged, and dug his hand into Fidèle's back, and watched Jeanne put on a skirt to go to meet the man, and listened to her in silence when she returned. "Louis thinks the future of painting lies in embracing Nature." And "Louis can read Goethe in the original German." And "Louis has a little studio where he paints every morning, at least two or three hours." And everything else Louis said and thought and did, which she could not tell without saying his name a dozen times, as if the pronoun *he* had been banned from the language. Louis, Louis, Louis, until Nandou wished for the heart of a giant, whose thundering beat would drown out those two syllables.

One day Jeanne had said, "Do you think I should bring Louis to the theatre to see you?"

He had answered cautiously, "You have told him about me, then?"

"Yes. Well, no." She flushed. "Louis knows I live with a friend from the theatre, that is all. But I think perhaps you should meet each other."

I am not your father or your brother, that I have to meet the man you are falling in love with! Don't make me see you together! Nandou had choked with the need to say it. To silence himself, he had had to fetch a knife and a roll of sausage and cut a slice. He had coughed and eased his throat inside his collar, and his voice had come out as raw as a crow's. "I would advise you not to tell Louis Vollard about me."

"Why not?"

Yes, tell him about the dwarf, let him leave you in disgust. He had coughed again and said, "I don't think Monsieur Vollard would understand."

"He would! You think that just because Louis is rich and well brought up, he can't—You are wrong. I will show you that you are wrong."

"I don't think a poor man would understand either, or anyone who isn't in the theatre. Or isn't a dwarf." He hadn't been able to suppress a mirthless laugh. "I advise you not to put Monsieur Vollard's friendship to such a test."

Please argue, please insist. His whole being had concentrated on making her do so, the way he focused himself when he did magic, so that the audience's will would surrender to his commands. She had looked dubious for a moment, and he thought he had won.

But then she had kissed him on the cheek and said, "Perhaps you're right, Nandou. I won't do it now. But soon. You'll see."

Nandou lifted his head. Wind flickered the lamp, sending his nose and mouth in and out of a cave of shadow. The cat yawned, the ink rim of her mouth framing her arching pink tongue.

"I know, Fidèle," he said. "I vowed to make her see me as a friend, nothing more. I have succeeded. Bravo! Encore! The dwarf is a good actor!" He laid his hand on the cat's body, which seemed to tremble with him. "If she would worry that I might be jealous, and try to hide what she is doing . . . if she would grant me the stature of a rival . . . a hopeless one, but still a rival . . ." He groaned, knowing that it would be worse if she did try to hide things, for then he would have to imagine what she was doing: laughing with Vollard, looking up at him, Vollard resting his hand on her shoulder, or reaching for her hand, or even . . . He groaned again, cursing his actor's imagination. "Yes, my friend, I am suffering," he said to the cat. "But even so, I am glad. It is better to suffer and love her than to feel nothing."

The cat mewed, protesting the increased pressure of his hand. He relaxed it. "Sorry, my friend." He poured more wine. "Shall I go out walking till dawn and not have to know what time she comes in? Or shall I stay to be here—the friend to whom she can tell everything? Eh? Which shall it be?"

The cat left his hand and went back to the windowsill. Once again it looked down into the courtyard, where the motions in the shadows had become those of tails and paws. Nandou stared into the lamp, burning the shape of its light into his eyes.

"Yes, the battle of *Hernani* is won," Louis said, "but now the fight is beginning in reality. This king—who once offered amnesty to political prisoners—now he is swallowing the liberties of Frenchmen every day!"

He drank off his wine and poured more for both of them, although Jeanne had barely finished her first glass. They were dining in a little restaurant near the Palais-Royal, after a walk through its bustling arcades and then along the quais. They had poked along, smiling at nothing and everything: the merchant of provisions who sold tiny larks, the man who gave pedicures, and especially the shacks of the bookshop-publishers, where bibliophiles rooted among the wares, sending up little puffs of dust. At twilight the colors of the sky deepened so subtly that before one could name them, they had changed, and Notre Dame rose into their midst like lace transmuted into stone.

"Hey, little one," Louis said softly, "are you listening?"

"Of course," Jeanne said. "And you are right. The situation can't go on." It wasn't that she hadn't been attending to what Louis said or that she didn't care what the king was doing. It was that sometimes when she was close to Louis, sitting across from him at a café table or walking along the street with his hand touching hers, his presence would suddenly cast everything else into the background, even what he was saying. She would stare at his face, held by its constant paradox: Though its features were achingly familiar, she always seemed to be discovering them for the first time.

"You weren't thinking of the king at all, were you?" Louis said. He made a fist and put his knuckles gently against her cheek for a moment.

"No," she said. "I was thinking of a much more pleasant subject than a Bourbon monarch who works every day to turn back the clock in France."

"Really? And what might that subject be?"

"Oh, a man I know. A splendid man who is handsome, clever, and a Republican, of course."

Louis' gray eyes narrowed. "And his name would be?"

"I don't think I will say." Jeanne pursed her lips, to pinch off a smile. There was a perverse pleasure in acting as if she thought about any man other than Louis. If she had no choice about loving him, she could choose to pretend she didn't. "I will say only that he has the same name as a king."

With mock severity, Louis said, "I have a rival named Charles? After our fat, white, sleepy king?" He puffed his cheeks and nodded his head to one side.

Jeanne laughed and clapped. "Charles is not the king this man is named after."

Louis took her hand. "You have the most enchanting laugh in Paris. In Europe. In the world."

The game faded away. They looked at each other, her breath forgetting to go in and out, her world bounded by the shape of his face.

She had felt that way from the beginning, from the time she had gone back to *Hernani* alone and had waited outside the theatre in the crush until she spotted Louis and his friends, and, in her best callboy voice, asked if he could get her a pass. "I'll try, lad," he had said, and smiled, his teeth white and even. She had tagged along behind them—if you wanted something, you had to go after it; Nandou always said that—and had managed to sit next to Louis. He was intrigued to hear that she worked in the theatre—"What an enterprising lad you are"—but his manner had been impersonal and hearty. He had gotten her a pass for two nights later, and that time, when the crowd swelled out into the street, where the usual post-performance fights were breaking out, he had asked her to join him and his companions at a café. She had had two glasses of wine and tried not to look at Louis all the time. His eyes glittered while he talked and his hands made quick, square gestures and Jeanne had thought she could feel the excited beating of his heart. He had turned to her frequently—"More wine, lad?" "Do you know Géricault's *Raft of the Medusa,* lad?"—until she couldn't bear it any longer. She had leaned so close to him that her cheek muscles tightened as if his hair had touched hers, though it hadn't. "I have something to confess," she had whispered. "I'm not what I told you I was, a callboy at the theatre. That is, I have the job, but I am not Jean Sorel. I am Jeanne." He had pulled back and stared in surprise—but also in relief, she was sure of it. Then he had begun to smile and finally to laugh until the others had called, "What's the joke?"

"Nothing." Louis had put a comradely arm around her shoulder and whispered, "I'd like to keep it our secret, wouldn't you?" There was a prick of disappointment—why didn't he want to tell everyone?—but she had nodded. Ten minutes later he had leaned very close to her and whispered, "Do you know how much I would like to see you in splendid gowns instead of these callboy trousers, so I could lose myself in contemplating your beauty?"

From that night, he had wanted her to meet him alone, for suppers or for walks, and she had moved in the strange but welcome confines of the skirt she had laboriously sewn for herself. Nandou's eyes had gone quite wide when he saw her working on it, but all he said, softly, was "Such industry." Sometimes, as she and Louis strolled, she would think that now she must tell him about Nandou, but each time something within her said no, something from the core of instinct that was the heart of her being. All Nandou had taught her, and all she had learned as a result, was precious, but nothing could deny or replace the power of her wordless feelings, which had succored her through the early years of her life and then had led her out of them. So she remained silent.

Louis's hand, and his eyes, were still holding hers. "Are you still hungry?" he asked softly.

"No." Even in that moment, with her entire being focused on him, Jeanne knew a flicker of amazement that it could be so—that she was not hungry.

"I am," Louis said. "But not for food. You have reduced all my appetites to one—the desire for your smile, your laugh, your face. For all of you. Jeanne, sweet Jeanne . . . Will you go with me to my studio? Now?"

For a moment, as plainly as if he were only at the next table, she could hear Nandou saying, *Everybody wants something.* "Yes," she said. "I'll come with you."

Louis kissed her fingers. "You are so direct. I love that."

There was no sense of passage from one place and image to another. One moment they were in the restaurant; the next, in the street, her hand in Louis's, the April wind tugging at her bonnet, a crowd bobbing at the edge of her vision. Neither of them spoke a word, nor did the sounds of the street impinge on the silent communion of their hands. Somehow, after a while, they were in the houses of the place des Italiens; they were entering one of them; they were climbing to the top floor and two small rooms that looked out on a court. A lamp. A table and chairs. Louis hanging his coat on the back of one of them. Louis smiling and saying, "Do you know that I used to be afraid of you?"

"What do you mean?"

"I was drawn to you from the first moment, but you said you were Jean Sorel, callboy. I thought something must be terribly wrong with me, that I could find a boy so attractive."

Louis's face, very close, his eyes as large as the whole of the world. His hands. His whisper: "Sweet Jeanne, I don't want to frighten you, now." And her answer: "I'm not afraid, Louis. Not at all."

Outside, the roofs had begun to stir with sparrows, and the sky with color. Jeanne stepped along delicately, lifting her skirt above the grime in the streets. Louis had said he didn't want her to leave, ever, but she had to get home so Nandou wouldn't worry; her note, after all, had said only that she would be out to dinner. Louis's arms and words had pulled her back a dozen times, but finally she had made herself leave. "I'll be back soon," she had promised, and crept down the stairs.

In the distance lumbered a sewage wagon. Near a corner, something atop a pile of trash caught her eye: a cracked plate, porcelain, with gilt edges and violets painted upon it. She stopped as if an arrow had pinned her. The plate was like the one that had marked a special Day in her life as a ragpicker. She stared; between the mornings when finding a pretty object in the trash had been all she could hope for and the mornings with Louis that now stretched before her lay a chasm too wide for her mind to cross. She could only reach out and lift the plate, as if it contained the wonder she felt. She remembered the brutish noises that had sometimes come from her parents' room at night; the first time she heard them, she had sat up in fright on her straw. Pierre had said, "Ah, it's only the two of them screwing." When she didn't understand, he had explained it was like the dogs when they mounted each other in the streets. Could those sounds, those actions, bear any relation to what had now happened to her? Pity for her parents, even for her brothers—for all creatures who could not feel as she did—flooded her, and she wanted, for the first time since she had left her family, to see them again; to run through the streets and find them and say, "Look what I have become, see how happy I am, can you be happy for me?" But even as she thought it, she saw her father in her mind: the gray, suspicious face, the bowed back, the lips that had licked together and then opened to say he would sell her for fifty francs. He was nothing to do with her any longer; none of them were. Her family was Nandou and Fidèle, who would understand and be happy for her. She looked at the porcelain plate, about to throw it back on the pile of trash, but decided to keep it—because now no one could tell her not to keep it. She walked on. Above her head the roofs angled toward a faintly blue sky, and a swallow sailed in high circles.

When she climbed the stairs and opened the door, she saw Nandou asleep at the table. She took off her bonnet and went softly toward him. Beside him lay a newspaper, a half loaf of bread, an empty wine bottle on its side, and her note, crumpled. His head rested on his muscular arms, black hair spilling over them, and his short legs sprawled beneath him as if they were boneless. The window was open, the air in the room chilly but fresh. A wave of tenderness wrung her; the caring she usually felt for Nandou seemed intensified a dozen times, as was everything else this morning—magnified and clarified as she imagined it must be when one stood on a Swiss mountain peak. "Good morning, Nandou," she said, trying to hold her voice quiet, hearing joy beat within it like wings against glass.

Nandou's head raised slowly. He looked at her almost as if he didn't know her and said in an odd, hoarse voice, "You look very beautiful." She was surprised, and he seemed to be too; he never said such things to her. For a moment they regarded each other like strangers. Then he groaned and staggered up, and she could feel the memory of wine in him, heavy against her weightlessness.

"Have you been out on one of your walks?" she said.

"No." He pulled his hands through his hair as if punishing it, then dragged them down his face. "I was sitting here waiting for you, to tell you some news. I fell asleep."

"You shouldn't have waited. Are you all right?"

"Of course. Are you?"

"Yes. Oh, yes." The three words came out as one.

Nandou straightened the wine bottle. "You had a nice dinner, then?" She nodded. "So nice that you tucked a plate under your arm as a souvenir?"

She had forgotten the plate; she pulled it out, laughing. "It's not from dinner. It's something I found . . . something that makes me . . . " She set it on the table. "Something I used to wish that I . . . " She clasped her hands, unable to suppress the words any longer. "I have some news, too. Wonderful news."

"Yes, I see that you do. What has happened?"

"I have . . . I am . . . Louis and I love each other!"

"Ah. Well. Having heard you extol Monsieur Vollard's virtues for weeks now, I am not entirely consumed by surprise."

"I have never felt like this in my whole life, Nandou. I didn't know it was possible to feel this way."

Only after Nandou's face had failed to become a mirror of her own did she realize she had wanted it to. His face didn't change at all; he merely nodded several times. Then he went to the basin and splashed water on his eyes and cheeks. When he turned, his hair was damp and his eyes blank; his will was preventing her from reading them, as he had been doing more and more often of late, closing himself off from her and becoming as remote as a character in a play.

"Are you angry?" she said.

"Of course not. Why would I be?"

"I don't know," she faltered. "Where is Fidèle?"

"Out all night. Like you."

"You *are* angry."

"I have no reason to be. I am not your father or your brother, to order your comings and goings. I am only . . . Why should I be angry?"

"You do want me to be happy, then?"

"Of course not. That's why I wanted you to leave the garbage heaps—so you would never be happy."

"Dear Nandou, I'm sorry. I know you want me to be happy. You are the one who taught me life is nothing until one learns to love something." She took off her shawl, laid it on the back of a chair, and sat, watching his face all the while. "You have done so much for me, Nandou. You shouldn't have to look after me any longer." She reached for the loaf of bread and broke off a chunk, but instead of eating it, she began to tear it into smaller pieces. "You should have this place to yourself again—no more stockings on the chair or apple cores on the table, no more worrying that I will grow up stupid . . . "

"You are leaving." Nandou's words were stones dropping into water.

"Louis has a place where the two of us can live and be together."

"The two of us?" he said, bewildered, almost as if she meant himself and her.

"I love Louis, Nandou. Can you understand that?"

"Of course not. What would a dwarf understand of love?"

"Don't say such things. Someday you will fall in love, too. I know you will, and then you will understand why I must be with Louis."

Nandou picked up the porcelain plate and studied it. "This is cracked and dirty. A misfit. No one would want it. No one. Why did you bring it home?"

"I don't know. It reminded me of something." She put down the bread, scooped the crumbs and flakes into a neat pile, and leaned forward. "I wish we could all be together—you and I and Louis and Fidèle."

"Don't be foolish." Nandou put the plate back on the table with such force that it broke in two. Both of them stared at the pieces.

"You don't want me to go," Jeanne said. "Do you?"

She could see a vein swelling on each side of Nandou's throat before he spoke. "I don't want you to be hurt," he said. "I have seen these young bourgeois, who find a girl to live with for a while in the place des Italiens, and then go back to their lives in the faubourg—"

"Not Louis. Louis loves me."

"No doubt. When you are together, when you . . . No doubt he means what he says at such times. But later, when he—"

"Louis loves me!" she cried.

Nandou eased his throat in his collar as if it were sore. "Remember the night you announced you had a callboy job? I told you then: You can always do what you like."

She remembered the response she had made that night: *Oh Nandou, you know I won't leave.*

"You must be happy," he said. "That is what matters. Will you keep working on the boulevard?"

"Not for a while. Louis thinks it would be . . . not for a while." She lifted her chin. "You haven't told me your news."

"It's nothing. I have found a larger place for us to— a larger place. That's all."

"Oh," she said faintly. In the silence, she tried to force her gaze into Nandou's, clenching her hands with the effort, but his broad face was closed and his eyes unreadable.

She turned away, to the window. "Look," she said with relief, "here's Fidèle come back." She ran to the window and took the cat in her arms. "Fidèle, I am going to live in a place of my own. Two rooms, with a skylight and a window on a court. But I will come and see you, you and Nandou, because I love you, and we'll talk about the theatre, and Nandou will read things and act them out while you and I listen. So you mustn't be upset that I am leaving, because I will come to see you often. Very often! And we will play and talk as we always have done . . . "

She went on chattering, holding the cat, stroking it. Nandou went to his cot and stretched out. He raised one short arm, stared at it, clenched his fingers, then put his arm over his eyes.

At the grand piano in her drawing room, Henriette Vollard frowned at a Mozart sonata she had once played easily. She hadn't tried it for many months, and motions once automatic had been forgotten by her fingers. She flexed them, removed and laid on gleaming wood the sapphire ring with which her husband had remembered her forty-fifth birthday, and attacked the sonata, mouth tight with resolve. Velvet drapes were pulled to allow afternoon light into the large room, which was papered in red brocade and furnished with a divan and sofa of kingly proportions. At the other end, balancing the piano, was a huge fireplace.

Henriette was not preparing for any concert, private or public, nor playing simply for pleasure. Music was a skill, that was all, and skills should not be allowed to rust. Many years before, she had mastered the piano, along with everything else required of a young woman. There had been no daughter to whom she could pass on either the skills or the authority with which she deployed them, but she reminded herself that sons were better guarantors of the future.

She was leaning closer to the page of music when the door opened; Louis slipped into the drawing room and sat on the sofa. Her mouth tightened, but she made her determined way to the end of the sonata.

"Bravo, Maman," Louis said.

She lifted her hands from the keys and reached for her ring. "We haven't seen you in four days."

"Sorry, Maman. I've been busy. But I came as soon as I knew you wanted to see me." He smiled at her brilliantly.

As she had a thousand times, Henriette thought that he was extraordinarily handsome, in a way his father was not, nor his brother, nor certainly herself. For an instant, no longer, she allowed the thought to please her, then consulted the watch pinned to her belt on a long chain and went to pull the bell. "I am glad to learn I still have the power to make a request that you will honor."

"Maman, please believe that it was painful to go against your wishes in the matter of *Hernani*. But the play is no longer being performed. That battle is over. Can't we be finished with it, too?"

"Ask your Uncle Claude."

"I have apologized to him most sincerely for not sharing his aesthetic views. I thought he had accepted the apology. Am I mistaken? Is that why you wished to talk to me?"

"No," Henriette said curtly. "Since your appearances here have become so few and so perfunctory, I asked your brother to find out what you have been doing lately."

Louis sat erect. "And what has he told you?"

The doors opened and the maid came in, her entry properly unobtrusive. "Please ask Monsieur Nicolas to join us here at once," Henriette said. The girl bobbed and left.

"What has he told you?" Louis repeated.

Henriette made a steeple of her fingers and looked over it at her son. "That there are things more serious than running with ragtag art students and cheering a defiance of theatrical tradition. Among them are the fact that for some months now you have had rooms in the place des Italiens. Why are you surprised? Nicolas says there was no difficulty in finding it out."

"And nothing wrong in doing it. I need a place where I can paint."

Henriette sat across from him, on the edge of the divan. "And the young person you have installed there? What need does she address?" In the silence, she saw that she had not only surprised her son but embarrassed him. Had he thought she would leave it to his father to discuss such matters with him? She leaned forward. "What are your intentions with regard to this person?"

"She has a name, Maman. Jeanne Sorel."

"I see. And what do you know of her background?—if she has told you the truth about it."

"It's something no one would lie about." Louis sat even straighter. "Jeanne is the only daughter of the ragpicker Sorel, who lives near the Taxgatherers' Wall."

"Dear sweet Jesus." The words came before Henriette could stop them, an occurrence so unusual that for an instant she thought someone else had said them. She ran her tongue over her traitorous lips and clenched her hands. "Insupportable, Louis. You must end the liaison, kindly and gently, of course, but end it, for everyone's sake, including the girl's. It could never survive such a difference of perspectives, backgrounds, and standards. In a few months you will look back and be glad it is over. In a few years you will scarcely credit that you were ever party to such a liaison."

She watched her son's face darken; nothing so angered young people as to hear that their passions would cool with time. But they would; everyone's did. Louis took a deep breath, no doubt gathering himself for some tirade that would reveal the folly of her attitude without being openly disrespectful.

"You do not understand, Maman, you don't know what—"

"I understand perfectly well. And I know more than you think."

The doors swung open again and closed behind Nicolas. "Maman?" he said, in the firm, quiet voice she sometimes thought he must have been born with, for she couldn't remember his sounding any other way. Surely he had once had a boy's piping tones? Perhaps not. Even when his cheeks were plump with childhood fat, the gray eyes above them had been thoughtful and discerning.

"Louis!" Nicolas said with real pleasure. "Are you here for dinner?"

"Not until I've taken my medicine, apparently."

Nicolas made a rueful face and went to sit beside his brother.

"I have something to say to you both," Henriette said. They looked at her expectantly, respectfully. "As young men, the two of you feel certain natural desires. This is a fact of nature, of your natures, and I would be foolish to deny it. I know that your father has shown each of you in turn the proper . . ." She made a steeple of her fingers again, studied it, dismantled it. ". . . The acceptable ways of dealing with these desires before you marry." They were acceptable only because one had no choice. Young boys, if left on their own, would gratify themselves, and a brothel was undeniably preferable to the horror of masturbation. Still, she hadn't slept on the night she knew her husband was taking a fourteen-year-old Nicolas to visit one and, two years later, Louis. And now that they were young men . . . Young men had affairs; that was the way of the world. But there were limits.

Her sons were regarding her without expression, though Louis's cheeks were flushed. She leaned forward. "But to set up housekeeping with some young girl who is known to sometimes go about in trousers and to have lived previously with a *dwarf*—that is not acceptable. No."

The color in Louis's face guttered and went out like a candle in the wind. "Maman, excuse me, but you're mistaken."

She turned to Nicolas. "Am I?"

Nicolas shook his head. "No." He put a hand on Louis's shoulder. "I'm sorry you have to receive information that is apparently a shock to you. I thought you knew. Look, Louis, I simply asked a few discreet questions. I was sure you'd rather have me doing it than someone Papa hired. They were determined to find out, you must realize that."

Louis nodded dumbly. "But . . . Jeanne always said she lived with a friend from the theatre."

"That's true enough—the man works on the Boulevard of Crime. I believe he is sometimes called Hugo's dwarf, but I do not know why."

Waching the struggle on Louis's face, Henriette felt something so brief that its passage left no trace and was only, yes, that's how it feels, why shouldn't he learn—replaced at once by the wish to tell him, *Don't let it hurt you.* She didn't, of course. That was how people learned—from being hurt.

Nicolas squeezed his brother's shoulder and took away his hand.

"She's beautiful and clever," Louis said, "the most beautiful girl in—"

"Her physical endowments are not at issue," Henriette said. "But our understanding with the Tissot family is. If the baron were to hear of this liaison . . . Worse yet, the baroness! Do you think they would still consider you a suitable candidate for the hand of their Edmée? A young man's affairs are one thing, everyone understands their nature and accepts their existence, but to live openly with the daughter of a ragpicker, who has been the mistress of a dwarf . . . " Henriette set her lips tightly, to prevent further treachery.

Louis leaped to his feet. "She was not his mistress! I know that she had never—" He stopped himself, then clasped his hands behind him as if they were being tied. "You are repulsed by Jeanne's background, Maman, but I admire her for rising out of it. I'm sorry, I know such things matter to you, but I don't care that there are no titles in her family. People can no longer be held facedown in the mud because they were born into it. They are individuals. They must be free to find their true natures and set their destinies, just as art must be free to reveal the truth. If Jeanne Sorel is my destiny, I must be free to love her!" He stood for a moment, flushed, eyes glittering and hair curling around his face in tiny dark banners. Henriette was gripped by two opposing sensations: weary distaste for the Romantic phrases he was spouting and admiration for the splendid figure he made while spouting them.

She turned the sapphire ring on her finger three times, slowly. "I assume your Romanticist friends teach you that nothing matters but feeling deeply and that because one's feelings are strong, they must be obeyed. It is in many ways an attractive idea. But the lesson of adulthood is that desire and action are separable and in fact must often be separated—that of the many considerations to be weighed in making a decision, one's emotions are often the least. No doubt you regard me as unfeeling for saying these things, but I say them out of experience and affection for you. There are reasons for the structure of society, and for its rules. Over the decades they have guaranteed the survival of our institutions, our culture, our families. By protecting the past, they make the future possible. I do not expect you to understand this, at twenty, the way I understand it, for I am of a different generation. What I do expect you to do is believe that I have your best interests at heart. Do you believe it? Look at me, Louis, and answer me."

His voice low, Louis said, "I do believe it, Maman. In return, you must believe that I wish to show you all the honor and respect owed by a dutiful son. But I cannot tear out my heart for you. Please do not ask it."

Henriette tightened her lips and shook her head.

Nicolas said, "Have you considered, Maman, that perhaps Louis cannot help himself?" He was quite calm. The ability to keep his reactions hidden, so like Henriette's own, should have been a bond between them; it was not.

"One can always help oneself in such matters," she said. "To think otherwise is self-indulgent." She went to the door, opened it, turned back. "Louis, if you hope to console yourself by thinking my opposition to this liaison will soften, I trust your brother to assure you of the contrary." With her right hand, she flung her skirts behind her and left.

In the silence, Louis sank back onto the sofa. Nicolas put an arm around his shoulder.

"I don't believe she was his mistress," Louis said. "She was not with anyone before me. I could tell. Anyone could have told. I mean . . . I don't mean that she would have let anyone . . . "

"I know what you mean."

"Thank God. You always do. Did you see her, Nico? Did you see how beautiful she is?"

"Yes. Very."

"Then you can understand how I feel about her. Can't you?"

"I think so. I also understand how Maman feels about you."

Louis looked into Nicolas's eyes. "What would you do if you were in my place?"

Nicolas squeezed his shoulder and stood up. "I never would be in your place, you know. Maybe that's better, maybe it's worse—it's just a fact. But, if I were trying to reduce Maman's wrath, I would be home for dinner more often. I would go to the office at least once a week and look interested, I would take Aunt Madeleine driving in the Bois sometimes, and, let me see . . . yes, I would cut my hair the way Maman likes it."

"Not that," Louis said. "The rest of it, I suppose you're right, but not that."

The brothers smiled their identical smile at each other. Then Nicolas added, serious again, "And I would stop neglecting my friendship with Edmée Tissot."

Chapter Five

Through the skylight at one end of the larger room, hot July sun poured over Louis's painting gear and paled the lines of a chalk drawing he had propped up. At the other end of the room were a sink and a small, shiny blue stove. There were two large presses for holding clothes and books, and a dining table with three chairs that one had to examine closely to notice they didn't quite match. The walls, on which glazed paper depicted a military scene with dubious accuracy, met at odd angles, for the place had been cut out of larger rooms. The tiny bedroom was almost the shape of a slice of pie, but it was sunny in both reality and spirit, papered in a pattern of leaves and bright yellow flowers. Both rooms were tidy and clean; the floor, in fact, was still damp and slightly swollen after the scouring Jeanne had given it. She sat on the horsehair sofa, in a blue calico dress Louis had bought her, her gaze confirming for the tenth time that morning that everything was perfect. Yet anxious twinges kept interrupting her reading like hovering insects.

It must be the political situation, she thought. The streets were uneasy, though quiet, the heat sitting on them like a lid on a pot. King Charles had called for new parliamentary elections, hoping to rid himself of liberal Opposition members, but the Opposition had been returned in even greater numbers. The people were edgy, wondering what Charles would do next. He had tried to rally them a few weeks earlier with a celebration over the Algerian capitulation to the French fleet, but they hadn't cared. Louis said hardly anyone had cried *"Vive le roi!"* when Charles drove to Notre-Dame in his gilded coach. The journal on Jeanne's lap held frightening, infuriating news: Charles was now considering signing some ordinances that would take away various liberties guaranteed to all Frenchmen by the Constitutional Charter of 1814. If he did, the troubled quiet in the streets could turn to violence.

A breeze sauntered in through the window behind Jeanne but did little except stir the heat. She picked up the journal, read another half page, felt another twinge. She put the paper down and ran her hands over her hair, which was growing but was still not long enough to pile very high, although it did make decent ringlets at the sides of her face. She remembered how it once had covered her shoulders like a collar of black velvet. One day it would do so again, and Louis would love it. She got up and walked slowly to the other end of the room, where he kept his papers and chalks and canvases, and the paints in the copper tubes he said were such an improvement over bladders. He had not worked much since she moved in: a few attempts to paint a horse, à la Géricault, and some chalk drawings of her that he scowled at before tearing up. The one he had left out was a profile of her, on which he had worked and reworked the mouth but still hadn't got it right. "How can it be so easy to kiss and so hard to draw?" Jeanne laughed, recalling the words, picked up a tube of paint labeled "Naples yellow," and put it to her lips. *Make him come today. Make him come.*

He was often kept away by what he called "family obligations," which involved being with his mother and father and brother, or others of what must be a large family. She imagined his parents and his brother sitting with him, wineglasses lifted, at a long table shining like ice in sunlight, the three of them looking like him except for a difference of hair and age, smiling gently and often because who would not smile to be living in a splendid house with Louis Vollard? She had never asked him to take her to meet them; instinct had warned her to wait for him to offer—as he would do now, of course. Then there would no longer be anything left unspoken in their conversations. No more hoping that if she said something like, "I walked away from my family without even looking back," he would say something like, "I really don't need to have dinner with mine tonight." She understood his devotion to them; to a Frenchman, family was sacred. She had read that somewhere. Perhaps everywhere. Only she and Nandou were different. His mother, who had burned herself to death because she drank too much, was buried in the common grave at Montmartre Cemetery. When Jeanne asked whether he had been afraid to be left alone so young, he had said, "Yes, but it was easier than being with her."

Nandou's face came into her mind: swarthy and broad, forehead rising high, long hair that he combed with his fingers when he was excited till it stood at odd angles, like black straw. She had seen him half a dozen times since moving out. Twice she had gone to the theatres to wait for him backstage, but that was hard: There she was in her trousers and cap, still pretending to be his nephew the callboy, with people racing by and calling, "Hello, Sorel, coming back to work?" and the smell, compounded of paint and glue and sawdust and makeup, seeping into her, pungent and loved—yet she was no longer part of any of it. She was on the outside now: a member of the audience, who sometimes attended plays with Louis but more often went on her own, wearing trousers because it was easier to be a man alone than a woman. Being backstage as an outsider was so disorienting that she couldn't quite think what to say to Nandou, and he seemed no better off than she, so they wound up talking about familiar things like strangers. But even those conversations were better than the ones they had when she went to see Nandou in his new rooms, where the furniture and objects she knew so well sat about at unaccustomed angles, looking different and shabby, like hems that had been lengthened badly. She had been there four times, and it was always hello, how have you been, how's Fidèle, did you see the story in the journals about whatever-is-the-latest-political-news, did I tell you I've been reading whatever-she-was-reading, did you hear that Hugo is at work on another play . . . The last time she had gone, she had played a game of string with Fidèle, the cat pawing and pouncing after it with an intensity that kept her laughing all the while. When she turned to Nandou, who was sitting at the table, to see if he was laughing too, his gaze had been unguarded for once. She had looked into his eyes and seen pain, hanging there, silent, unblinking, swaying, like a fish at the bottom of a pond. *Don't be hurt,* she had wanted to cry, *please don't.* But if she did, they would have to talk about why he was hurt.

"Are you all right?" she had faltered.

"Of course," he had said, eyes unreadable again. He had put his legs up on the rung of the other chair—awkwardly. "I have never been better off. At the theatres, a full week's work, and at home, plenty of space to stretch my legs." He had smiled as if his words were innocent and held no sarcasm, but she had been unable to stop thinking about the pain she had seen. She had gone on playing with the cat, pulling the string in automatic circles, barely seeing the pounces that had been so amusing a moment before because now her mind was fixed on the need to say or do something that would make Nandou feel better.

The thought had come as swiftly and sharply as the cat's claws: tell Louis about Nandou. She hadn't asked herself why that would make him feel better; she had simply known that it would. The prospect of doing it as soon as she got home had sustained her through the rest of the visit. She had asked Nandou to read something, and when he did, pacing the room, summoning up characters with his voice and a few gestures, it had almost seemed as if she had never left. But when she got home, Louis hadn't been there, and in the waiting for him, the urgency of telling him about Nandou had faded. When he did come, there hadn't been a good opportunity to tell him. She must do it, she thought. She must, and would. But not today. Today there were other things to tell him, if he came. She gripped the tube of yellow paint. *When* he came.

She looked down; she had almost squeezed the copper tube together in the middle. It made her think of Madame Duclos being fastened into a corset to play an ingenue. She tried to smooth out the tube a little, then put it down and took a breath deep enough to make her breasts rise and fall beneath the blue cloth of her dress. From nowhere a fat bluebottle lit on Louis's drawing of her and began to crawl proprietarily from her chin to the mouth that was not quite right. "Damn you!" she cried, as if the hapless fly were the cause of her anxieties. It buzzed and flew to the other end of the room. She ran to the sofa, grabbed the journal she had been reading, folded it into a weapon, and began attacking. "You bastard! Back to the heaps, where you belong!" With lazy dignity, the fly sailed to the skylight, where the sun was centered, and out. She stood looking up after it, the sun printing a white ball on her vision.

From street level, feet began to pound up the stairs. "Louis?" she whispered, not moving, counting the steps, waiting for them to stop at each landing. But they kept rising.

When the door burst open, her eyes still held the sun and he seemed to be framed in its corona. She ran to him, half-blind, saying his name.

He was waving a newspaper, which he held above her head while he put his other arm around her and kissed her. The excitement was so palpable in him that it forced the kiss apart. "What is it?" she cried.

"The ordinances are announced in the *Moniteur*."

Shaking her head to clear her vision, she grabbed the paper. It was what they had feared; it was madness. King Charles had issued four ordinances: He was suppressing some of the Liberal newspapers that opposed him, dissolving the new Chamber of Deputies before it had even met, setting new elections for September, and shrinking the number of citizens eligible to participate in them.

"This is tyranny," she said.

Louis nodded. "He is going to force his will on France in spite of the Charter. He has signed his own death warrant."

"Who will execute it?"

"The people," Louis said.

"How is it in the streets?"

"Quiet, so far. If there is fighting, Jeanne, I will be part of it."

They looked at each other, eyes brilliant, breath quickening, as if the upheaval coming to their world was felt already. Her cheeks began to grow warmer; she saw that his were too. Gazing at his high, pale forehead and the fullness of his lips, an awareness of his mortality, and her own, swept through her like a cold wind, and she cried out. "Yes," he said, and she knew he was feeling as she was. She reached for him; he took her hand, then her mouth, and then they were kissing deeply and moving by blind but sure steps to the bedroom. She had never known shyness or modesty with him, not even the first night, but now such a need came over her to be one with him, to be captured by his flesh and to capture it, that she could hardly tear off her dress quickly enough. In the sunny room, they fell upon the bed in a tangle of hands and cloth and buttons, talking incoherently, uttering sounds that were neither sobs nor laughter but something of each, while their bodies moved urgently, constantly, as if to deny the possibility that haunted them, of stillness.

Afterward they lay dazed. She was the first to stir, rising up on one elbow to look around the room, her small, pie-shaped island of security, and then at him. "I love you," she said. He smiled but did not open his eyes. She wiped beads of perspiration from his temples, then licked the sweet saltiness from her fingers. Now was the time to tell him, she decided, now when they were so close. She whispered, "Louis, we are going to have a child."

His eyelids trembled, lifted slowly. "What did you say?"

"I am pregnant. With our child."

"Child?" he echoed, as if it were a new word.

"I was wishing it hadn't happened so soon, but the way we are . . . " She gestured at the clothes strewn around them and laughed.

He sat up and put his hands to his mouth. "You are certain?" he said, voice muffled by his fingers.

"It's three months now." She watched the swell of muscles along the arch of his back. "Louis, tell me what you are thinking. Look at me."

Finally he did. "It's splendid news, of course, but it's so unexpected. I assumed you were . . . I thought that you . . . "

"Knew some way to prevent it? No."

"My clever little Jeanne, you weren't that clever?"

"No."

"You didn't know anybody who could have helped you? Actresses—surely they know about such things. Or maybe someone from your old life . . . ?"

"I'm not working at the theatres now, Louis, so I'm not talking with actresses. And my old life . . . You mean the whores we used to see on the streets at dawn? I suppose they've had abortions. Is that what you mean?"

"No." He sighed. "So, what shall we do, little one?"

"Become good parents," she said slowly. "Maybe this is the best time of all to have a child, Louis. If the future is a threat, now we'll have a weapon against it, the weapon of new life. Something we made together, out of our love, to shield us no matter what the future brings."

He nodded slowly, but his thoughts seemed far away.

"You will tell your family?" she asked, wishing it hadn't come out as a question.

He touched her cheek. "You say you can think of the future, Jeanne, but I can't. Not today. There may be fighting tomorrow, and I could die, so I—"

"No!"

"Yes. It's possible. So let's not think of tomorrow. Let's be happy while we can."

"But . . . *are* you happy. Louis? About the child?"

"Of course. I'm just surprised. You didn't give me any warning, you know, even though you must have been suspecting it for weeks."

"I wanted to be sure."

"Yes, I see. Besides, you like secrets, don't you?"

"What do you mean?"

His smile was so gentle that for a moment she didn't take in the words that followed it. "You told me you lived with a friend from the theatre. You never said the friend was a man. And a dwarf."

She could not make her mind produce any words except *Oh, shit,* which she dare not say because Louis hated her to swear. He kept smiling, so perhaps he wasn't angry, after all. Perhaps he would understand. She smiled back at him, hesitantly. "I know it was wrong of me, Louis, but I was afraid you might not understand. People in the theatre have unusual living arrangements. Just because men and women live together doesn't always mean they are lovers. Nandou was—is—my dear friend, but only my friend." Louis's expression didn't alter; she must keep talking until it did. "I told you I ran away from my family, and it's true, but Nandou helped me to do it. He came by and saw me and talked to me . . . he made me see . . . It's very hard to explain, Louis, that's probably why I didn't tell you . . . he made me realize I didn't have to spend the rest of my life as a ragpicker. He asked me to go live with him so he could teach me how to read and write and— No, don't raise your eyebrows like that, it's true. He knew I needed an education, Louis, so he gave me one, all by himself. He introduced me to the theatre. He's an amazing man, clever and intelligent. One night he even saved Victor Hugo from some thieves. That's why they sometimes call him 'Hugo's dwarf.' And he . . . I was wrong not to tell you about him, but now that you know . . . You're not angry, are you?"

"No." There was still no change in Louis's expression. That was the trouble; people's faces didn't stay the same for minutes on end.

"Louis, I would never have met you if it weren't for Nandou. He took me to the café where I saw you that first time, across the room, and to the opening night of *Hernani,* when I first talked to you."

"If he was so much a part of your life, how is it you never mentioned him?"

"I told you. I was afraid you would think that he and I—or that you would be upset because he is a dwarf. I should have known better. You wouldn't base your judgments on superficial things. Not you. Not a man who defies his family to study art and live with a ragpicker's daughter." She laughed; once her fears were put into words, they crumbled with the weight of their own foolishness. "Not telling you was an insult to you, I see that now. You of all people would understand my friendship with Nandou. How could I have thought anything else? No wonder you were upset—you thought I didn't understand *you,* and rightly so." She brushed back a curl of hair that clung damply to his forehead. "Can you forgive me for having misjudged the depth of your humanity and the fineness of your character?"

He looked at her in silence, his eyes as guarded as Nandou's. For a dreadful moment she was certain that everything was going to be different now, that the conversation was like a trapdoor in the stage floor, which would spring open, swallow her, and close behind her as if nothing had happened, but then he said softly, "Yes, I forgive you."

She kissed him. "I know you'll like Nandou. I want you to meet him now. You'll see how intelligent he is, how—"

"I'm sure he's altogether splendid, but enough about him for the moment." Louis got off the bed and pulled on his light-gray pantaloons. "I must see what's happening on the streets."

She scrambled up too and picked up her dress. "I'll come with you."

"Fine." He slapped her playfully on the buttocks, and before they left, he kissed her and called her "sweet Jeanne," as always, so surely everything was going to be all right after all.

But several hours later, when they had walked through streets that were hot but heavy with calm, so the air seemed like the sullen yellow that precedes a storm, when they had had eaten at their favorite little restaurant near the Palais-Royal and Louis had determined that no one inside that official structure seemed to know anything, he said he would take her home because he had to go see whether his father and brother and uncle knew anything. When they were back in the place des Italiens, he took her face in both hands and kissed her deeply.

Jeanne said, "I'll see you here soon," relieved it hadn't come out as a question. He nodded. "Be careful!" she called as he walked away.

It was impossible to sleep that night, for every sound might be gunfire, or gathering crowds, or his footsteps on the stairs, yet was none of them. In the morning, after a bout of nausea, she paced back and forth between the need to go out and learn what was happening and the fear that he would come and she would miss him. The need for action won; she pulled on trousers, shirt, and cap, and propped a note for him on the table.

At the corner café she choked down coffee and a roll and the news about the ordinances: In the name of the Constitutional Charter, forty-four journalists had put their necks on the block by signing a protest against the king's suppression of the press. Paris must wait to see if the blade would be lowered.

Jeanne left the café and walked up and down the streets, which were filling with people as restless as she. In the early afternoon word ran through the crowd that the police were now heading to rue de Richelieu and the offices of one of the Liberal newspapers that had been ordered to close. A surge began in that direction, and she joined it, swept along by cries of "Long live the Charter!"

A sea of people rumbled in front of the offices of *Le Temps;* its printers and editors had locked the doors and now stood in a phalanx confronting the Commissioner of Police, refusing to allow him and his troops to enter and break up the presses. When the commissioner tried to find a smith to unlock the doors, they thwarted his efforts, the crowd cheering them on. One of the editors produced a copy of the Napoleonic Code and in a booming voice read out the article prohibiting house-breaking. The crowd whistled and applauded. Despite the heat and the press of bodies, Jeanne began to feel as she had on that cold February day when she approached the Théâtre-Français. But this time the battle was not on stage but in earnest: Republicans against the monarchy, as Romanticists had battled Classicists, and for the same reason, their freedom. She kept standing on her toes, struggling to see into the crowd. Once she spotted the frizzy hair and imposing posture of Alexandre Dumas, so surely Louis must be there as well—face passionate, one arm raised in defiance, as she had seen him at *Hernani.* She was right; she spotted him yards away and began to wave and shout his name. But when the man turned his head, he was not Louis. She had printed on a stranger the face she carried always in her mind.

In the end the Police Commissioner prevailed over the editors of *Le Temps;* he got in, ordering his soldiers to clear the streets. As they advanced, bayonets fixed, Jeanne had no choice but to retreat with the crowd, anger rising in a sour clot. She forgot time as she moved with the throng, which was now forced along by walls of soldiers, for the Paris garrison was moving in to occupy the boulevards. Guns and soldiers in the streets—it was revolution! Around her people angrily yelled the garrison commander's name. Above her were shots, whip-cracks that sent people in all directions, shouting out news as they heard it: Three persons had been killed in the rue Saint-Honoré! Barricades had gone up in rue Richelieu and had been demolished! There were smoke, fury, and panic, but no Louis, no matter where Jeanne ran or how often she called his name.

She turned a corner and careened into the manager of the Vaudeville Theatre. "Monsieur Arago!" she cried. In the next moment someone had gripped her arm so tightly that it hurt—Nandou. "I went to the place des Italiens to look for you," he shouted. "Are you all right?"

She nodded, unable to speak, knowing that the difficulty he could have maneuvering in crowds had not prevented him from coming out to look for her. "Are you alone?" he said. "Where is Vollard?"

She struggled to lie, but his eyes forbade it. "I don't know," she said.

He set his lips for an instant. "You must go home, where you will be safe. I will take you."

"No! I won't go! I'll come with you. Where are you going?"

"With Arago. He closed the Vaudeville and now he is closing the other theatres. We are telling the managements to ring down their curtains and send the audiences out. There cannot be laughter on the stages while Paris is in tears!"

She heard shouts of "Sorel!" and saw familiar faces in the group behind Arago: stagehands, actors, dressers.

"Vive la Charte!" she cried, and joined them as they headed to the theatres near the Bourse. When they passed lighted windows or lamps, she stole glances at Nandou. He wore the workman's clothes in which he performed his stagehand's duties, and a soft brown cap. His face was dark with heat and exertion, except for the pale wire of the old scar from Pierre's hook. She wanted to embrace him, and all of them, because she was with the theatre again—and the theatre was leading a revolution.

Shouting "Stop the plays! Close the theatres!" they neared the place de la Bourse and stumbled on the body of a young woman. "It was murder!" someone shouted from a window. "She was only standing watching the urchins throw stones, and the soldiers shot her!" Nandou said to Arago, "Let us put the victim where the audience can see her." Several of them carried the body to the lighted steps of the Théâtre des Nouveautés, where it would bear powerful mute witness to the departing audience.

"Stop the plays! Close the theatres! They are killing people in the streets of Paris!"

They yelled it everywhere, marching, calling audiences to pour from the city's theatres, watching faces light with the same rage they knew to be on their own, inspiring people to tear up paving stones, erect barricades, hunt out muskets. And when they had succeeded in closing the theatres, they went to join those they had inspired. They built with stones, with furniture people threw down to them, with anything else they could find, so that sometimes Jeanne felt she was back poking through the debris of Paris. They sang and yelled their defiance of Charles and all tyrants, she and Nandou and the stagehands and actors and students, so that sometimes it seemed she was back at the opening of *Hernani*. They ate bread and cheese and ham, which seemed to appear magically, but refused wine or brandy because clear heads were needed and the battle was its own intoxication. "Long live the Charter!" "Down with the Bourbons!" Gradually, the night forged everything into a single passion: Jeanne was in the theatre and on the barricade, fighting the Classicists and the monarchy, defending the stage and the city, just as Louis must be doing, wherever he was, so they were united in the revolution for a republic and for liberty and, forever, in the child she was carrying.

They all slept in brief snatches on one another's shoulders and on the structure they were building. By morning they realized they badly needed weapons and stood about trying to find a way to procure them. "What about the property rooms?" Jeanne said. Nandou laughed, and everybody laughed, and soon there was a plan. "No," Nandou said to her, "you cannot go with us!" "You can't stop me," she yelled, "remember? I can do what I like!" He turned away. Soon she and he and nine others slipped from behind the barricade.

There were soldiers in the street in front of the theatre they had selected, but they walked to the backstage door easily, as if they belonged. Once inside, they collected swords and rifles and powder and stacked them by the door. When they were ready, Nandou said, "Give me three minutes to reach the soldiers, and then I will try to get you at least ten more." The quiet confidence of his words hung in the air after he left.

One by one, the group began to leave, loaded with weapons. Jeanne's arms and shoulders were slung with powder horns. As she gained the street, she could not keep from looking over her shoulder: The soldiers were gathered around Nandou, laughing, as he pulled a scarf from his pocket, then from his ear.

She hurried on. Glancing down a side street, she saw two men, clearly insurgents, not soldiers, standing before another who sat on the ground, slumped against a wall. She was ready to turn away, but something caught her gaze. The next moment she was running down the street, powder horns flying, screaming "Louis!"

The two men spoke to her, trying to stop her, but she pushed them aside with a strength she hadn't known she possessed and dropped to her knees beside Louis. His thigh was bleeding from the black mouth of a bullet wound. One side of his face was scraped raw.

She kept saying his name, over and over, until his eyes opened. He looked at her, puzzled. "Jeanne?"

"Yes. Yes, my brave and wonderful darling. I knew you would be fighting. I knew it. Are you in much pain? Don't worry, I'll take care of you. Everything will be all right, you'll be fine, I promise. We'll get you home, and I'll take care of you . . . " She went on, murmuring to him, touching him, gently pulling the torn cloth away from his wound, stroking the cheek that was not bloody. His expression turned to a frown. "What is it?" she cried. "The pain? Tell me, my darling." She saw that his eyes were not on her but on someone beside her.

She turned. Nandou stood there, his back to the sun but his eyes narrowed as if to avoid it. He and Louis looked at each other, their glance excluding her like crossed swords.

To say something was impossible; to be silent was worse. "Nandou, this is Louis," she finally managed. "We must help him."

"Of course," Nandou said. His gaze moved to her, and for an instant the suns in his eyes blazed like the one behind his head. He pulled a scarf from his pocket and held it out. "Tie this around the leg above the wound, to keep it from bleeding."

She did as he said, though her hands seemed as awkward as if they were someone else's. When she had finished, she said, without looking up, "Nandou, I must get Louis home."

"Home," Louis echoed, his eyes clouding.

She stood up. "Please help me with him, all of you. I must get him home while it's still fairly quiet."

"You know where he lives?" asked one of the two men.

"It's not far, just to the place des Italiens."

Louis's hand lifted, then fell back. "I must go . . . to rue du Faubourg Saint-Honoré . . ."

"No, Louis, I will take you home . . . "

"Saint-Honoré," he said, his voice stubborn despite its weakness. "Number thirty-nine . . . home."

"Louis . . . "

"Home!" His eyes closed again.

Jeanne moved away and leaned sideways against the wall. She pushed her body tight against the stones, until they dug into her shoulder and thigh. The nausea had come only because it was morning, only because of that.

Behind her, Nandou's voice said, "Are you all right?"

"Yes," she said fiercely. "Yes."

Chapter Six

After three days—*Three Glorious Days, as they came to be known*—the Revolution was over.

The people rushed into the Tuileries. They tore up the king's correspondence and flung it out the windows, to flutter into the gardens like birds. They stamped through the halls, into the chambers, and up onto the throne, on which they took turns sitting and shrieking with laughter. In the streets they sang and danced and cried *"Vive la République!"* and told tales that would circulate into legend: of the shopkeeper who, when a medical student took a bullet from his body, kissed it and said with his dying breath, "Take it to my wife." Of the twelve-year-old boy who was wounded while bringing down a Lancers officer but refused credit for his courage, saying, "Love of one's motherland turns a child into a man." The Three Days had produced heroes worthy of a play by Hugo, and victory worthy of those who had died for it: France would be a republic.

Yet when the presidency was offered to Lafayette, he declined. Instead, power passed to another Bourbon, Louis Philippe, and within weeks the Chamber voted to give him the crown. Once more France had a monarch.

Still, the new king swore to uphold the Charter. And he relaxed censorship in the theatres, so that managers rushed to mount new productions and to pile as much as possible into each performance.

In the dressing room one night, one of the actors said to Nandou, "I see your nephew has returned to work. Where has the boy been?"

Nandou put dots of red makeup in the near corners of his eyes, to make them look more brilliant from the audience. "Away," he said.

"I know that," laughed the actor. "Away where?"

Nandou squinted into the mirror. "Visiting his mother. In the south."

"Ah." After a moment the actor said, "Tell me, is the mother a dwarf like you? Or is she normal, like the son?"

Nandou narrowed his eyes and pulled down his mouth; ugliness bloomed in the mirror. "She is normal in every way," he said. "And very beautiful."

"Imagine! And yet she is your sister?"

Nandou scowled. "One cannot explain what happens in families."

"True," laughed the actor.

The next week, when Nandou was shifting scenery, one of the other stagehands asked him, "Didn't I see your nephew on the barricades with you during the Three Days?"

"You may have. He was there."

"Hard to believe he was capable of fighting. Look at him in the corner over there, pale and drooping. Is he ill?"

"Jean is perfectly well, only a bit tired today."

"Tell that to the stage manager," the man said derisively. "I say this only to be helpful, you understand. I know you don't want your nephew to lose his place on the callboy list."

"He is fine," Nandou said, and moved to tie off a counterweight line as if nothing were wrong, with Jeanne or with himself.

Whenever possible, he tried to work at the same theatres where she found jobs. He heard the stage managers calling: "Here, Sorel, move faster to line up that crowd!" "Now, where the devil is Sorel?" "I sent Sorel for the wigmaker two scenes ago, isn't he back yet?" Twice, at the risk of missing his own cues, he went looking for her. Once she was standing between two racks of ballet costumes, face buried in a bank of feathers and netting. When he reached in to her, she lifted wet eyes, then pulled away and said, "I am fine, Nandou!"

The second time she was in a corner by a pile of unpainted flats, retching into a pail that had held the pungent glue used to seal the canvas to its wood frames. He didn't move, though each spasm that began in her body seemed to end in his own and his heart suddenly drummed with the knowledge of what was wrong with her. When she stood up, he said, "I'll take care of it. Tell the stage manager you are ill and must go home."

She wiped her mouth and eyes and looked at him the way she had once refused to learn to read. "I'll clean it up, Nandou. It's my mess."

"Why won't you let me help you?"

"I'm not ill. It's only that the ham I had for breakfast didn't sit well. I'm fine now."

"Then come with me after the performance and eat something that does sit well."

"I can't. Not tonight. I'm sorry."

"Very well." He hesitated. "Are you cold?"

"No."

"Then why wear your jacket in this heat?"

She lifted her chin. "So no one can see that Jean Sorel has breasts. Don't you have an entrance in a moment?"

Why couldn't he say, *You are going to have a child, aren't you?*

Because she would either lie or tell the truth, and he could bear neither.

Since the day they carried Vollard to his home, she had come to visit only twice, her smile as bright and fixed as a clown's. I am fine, Nandou, yes, everything is fine. No, she couldn't come to live with him and Fidèle again because she was waiting for Louis to return to their rooms. Of course he would return!—as soon as his doctors said he might. It was only natural that he had wanted to be carried to his parents' home!—to take advantage of the treatment of fine doctors and the care of devoted servants. His decision had been proven correct, for he was recovering well. How did she know he was? Why, she went frequently to the house in rue du Faubourg Saint-Honoré. (That much was true, for Nandou had followed her there several times. But she never went inside; he had seen her speak to the servants who answered the door, and then turn away with a sag in her body that made him want to rush into the house himself and find Vollard and kill him. Ah, to kill Vollard . . . Why hadn't the garrison soldiers done it; why had a musket aimed for his thigh, not his heart?) Until Louis returned, she said, with the bright smile that never rose to her eyes, she was working in the theatres again because she had the time and the desire. Was there anything strange about that? Of course not. I am fine, Nandou, fine!

What could he do in the face of her determination to act as if all were well? Nothing, except tell himself that if she hadn't been determined and stubborn, he couldn't have rescued her from the ragpickers' world. Nothing, except shove his hands into his pockets and his thoughts to the back of his mind, and return to the wings to pull the cloak of character around him and await his cue. *Enter dwarf, smiling evilly.* And, when the performance was over, call good night to her as if she were a colleague, nothing more. And then follow her without letting her know, clinging to walls and doorways like some awkward butterfly of the night, to make sure she reached the place des Italiens safely.

When her step quickened as she approached the corner and her gaze lifted to the rear of the top floor like a plea, part of him rose in hope as well, but not for her reason. And when there was no light from the rooms and she stared at its absence, he wanted to caper in the street— because the lack of light meant Vollard was not there. Because now she was feeling what he had always felt: a love that could find no ease in reaching its object but must be choked back inside, unable either to find release or to stop growing.

But when her head sank and she opened the door and entered the building heavily, the rest of him would revolt against his gloating. He was despicable, unworthy, evil; no wonder she could not love him, for his soul had become a match for his body. He would move on into the night, thinking of her suffering and of the child she carried, his wicked glee draining away, his being filling instead with the desire to comfort her. He was more her creator than the ragpicker-parents from whom he had stolen her. She had been raised on all that he had taught her to love, and if she had chosen Vollard, it was because he, the dwarf, had taught her to love beauty and to cherish liberty and those who fought for it. If it were in his power to send Vollard to her, he would. Vollard had been wounded in the fight for a republic; one had to acknowledge it, even if, when one had seen him lying against the wall, bleeding, one had wanted the blood to keep gushing until that impossibly perfect face was as drained and still and white as plaster—not because Jeanne loved him, but because he was hurting her. Her pain was not to be borne; he would kill Vollard for causing it.

Oblivious of the sounds and smells of the night, his thoughts trailing him like hungry dogs, he would walk on and on, until he found himself back at the place des Italiens. Standing against the building next to hers, he would crane up toward where he imagined she slept, glad she slept alone, despising his gladness. Then he would stump on again until he reached his own rooms, where he would take up Fidèle and whisper his thoughts, often clutching the poor cat so tightly that she whimpered.

One day, when he had managed again to work at the same theatre as Jeanne, he saw that something was different. She executed her chores as usual, but each time she was alone, a smile bloomed. Nandou was doing sleight of hand after a pantomime, and when it was over he went to find Jeanne, who was counting out swords for a patriotic spectacle next on the bill, smiling. "What makes you so happy tonight?" he said.

The smile vanished. "Nothing." It returned. "I am feeling good, that is all."

"Splendid. Perhaps, then, you will come with me to one of the cafés?"

"Yes," she said. "All right."

He had prepared himself so well for refusal that at first he didn't take it in. Then he grinned, and kept grinning as he walked away and all through the remaining hours, so that people looked at him and said, just as he had said to Jeanne, "What is making you so happy tonight?"

He chose one of her favorite cafés; he urged food and wine on her and sat watching her consume them as greedily as if the body being nourished were his own. She had cut her hair again, like a callboy's, and it hung to just below her ears like two black, blunt wings. In the lamplight her skin seemed even whiter than he remembered, and her mouth, with the lovely dominance of top lip, even redder. Suddenly he was terrified to learn what had made her smile all night, and began talking instead of impersonal matters: The new king walked on the streets daily, taking his constitutional, looking like any citizen, but was he to be trusted? Hugo was writing a new play. A manager wanted a play about Napoléon from Dumas, who was unenthusiastic, so the manager locked him in a room next to his own mistress, Mademoiselle George. " 'But my mistress is waiting for me!' Dumas cries. 'I sent her a bracelet to keep her patient,' replies Mademoiselle George. 'And I shall be your jailer. Don't make such a face. Be a bit gallant. Get to work!' A week later, the play is done!"

Jeanne laughed and clapped. "What a wonderful actor you are, Nandou."

The sound of her voice, as happy as it had been when he had used to strut around the room performing for her and Fidèle, undid his resolve. He put a hand on hers and said, "Tell me what is making you so happy tonight."

"Dear Nandou." Jeanne put down her wineglass. "A message came from rue du Faubourg Saint-Honoré. I am to go there tomorrow. It means Louis must be quite well. I knew he would send for me. I knew it."

"Ah," Nandou said. He took his hand from hers and drank deeply, to hide his face, before he asked, "Vollard himself sent you this message?"

"No, it came from his mother. I was surprised, because I have never met Madame Vollard, but then I realized what it means." The smile burst from her again. "Louis must have told her that . . . Naturally, she wishes to meet the woman her son will . . . I am to be there at ten-thirty tomorrow morning."

"You think the Vollards are ready now to accept you?"

"Why else would his mother send for me?" She lifted her head; the flame of the lamp danced in each of her eyes.

"I hope you are right," Nandou said. Part of him meant it.

From the street, the oak door with its brass hinges and knobs had an impossible air of solidity—more than the Taxgatherers' Wall or the wall around the Louvre, more than the door itself had had on the day they carried Louis up to it and he disappeared inside, as if into a fortress, leaving Jeanne with nothing but streaks of his blood on her hands and cheeks and clothes. She had returned to the door half-a-dozen times, in trousers, pretending to be one of his art-student friends asking after his health. If the footman answered, she got a stiffening of nostrils and lip and the tersest of replies, but sometimes one of the maids opened the door. They were friendlier. One of them had told her that Louis's leg was badly infected, and later, that his fever finally had broken.

Today a bonnet of leghorn straw hid her hair, and instead of trousers, there was a dress of pale yellow cotton, borrowed from a grisette who lived across the hall from her. It was too big but at least not impossibly tight for her waist, which had begun to thicken and which she covered by arranging the ends of a light shawl to fall over it. She stepped forward and lifted the brass knocker.

The footman answered. "Yes?"

"I call at the request of Madame Olivier Vollard. I am Jeanne Sorel."

"You are expected. Come." The man's teeth were as white as new gloves.

In Jeanne's imagination the house had been like a stage palace, light glittering from a hundred jeweled and mirrored surfaces. In reality her slippers sank into dark, thick carpets, her skirt brushed past furniture as solid as trees, and her nose caught a strong smell of wax. At length the footman halted, knocked, opened a door, and gestured her in as if delivering a parcel.

A woman rose from a small sofa as smoothly as if on a wave. Her eyes, which seemed to swallow Jeanne in one gaze, were gray, like her dress, and her mouth was fixed in a fractional smile. "Mademoiselle Sorel," she said calmly. "Thank you for coming."

"It was good of you to ask me, Madame Vollard."

The woman's lips pursed for an instant. "Please sit down."

Jeanne did so, on the small matching sofa opposite the woman's, and kept her face as expressionless as the one studying her. She had expected that face to be a master mold of Louis's, but the only sign of him was a similarity of chin. The woman's features were pleasantly proportioned, no more; on second glance her nose was too large; in fact, she was plain. Perhaps, Jeanne thought, she had come to the wrong address; perhaps Louis and a beautiful mother were waiting for her in the house next door. She could see the scene in her mind, clearly.

"You are a pretty child," the woman said.

"Thank you, madame. May I ask at once for news of Louis's health? It concerns me so deeply that I permit myself to mention it immediately."

The woman sighed. "You are a pretty child who speaks prettily. My son's health improves every day." She moved her hands; the chains and rings she wore gleamed in the sunlight spilling between the velvet drapes. "As you surely know, I have asked you here because of your former liaison with him."

The word "former" rose into the air and echoed in bat-like shrieks. Jeanne pressed her folded arms more tightly over her shawl and began the words she had prepared. "Madame Vollard, please allow me to confess my relief that the secrecy of my relationship with Louis is ended. I have longed to meet the mother of someone so dear to me, to beg her forgiveness for what may have seemed like haste on our parts, and to assure her of my—"

"Haste?" the woman said, as if she had never heard the word before.

"Yes, I mean . . . I should like to have met Louis's family before we . . . I am sure he has told you that we . . . "

"Mademoiselle, I believe you will find this interview less painful if you allow me to speak first."

"Painful?" Jeanne said. "Is it going to be painful?"

"My dear child, there are those who would not grant this interview at all, who would simply dispatch a letter to you, if they did anything. Fortunately for you, Monsieur Vollard and I are not among their number."

"Letter?" Jeanne said. Her mind could not produce any words of its own.

Madame Vollard rose. Her skirt seemed to hiss as she walked to a small *écritoire* and took out an envelope. "My son has written this to you."

Jeanne managed to say, "I shall read it later, when I am alone."

"I advise you to read it now. If you do not read," the woman added kindly, "I will be glad to help you."

The kindness was cold water that shocked Jeanne's mind back to life. "I need no help. In fact, madame, I have just been reading a volume of Ronsard that Louis gave me."

The woman's expression did not change. Jeanne took the envelope from her outstretched hand, opened it, and extracted two heavy sheets of paper.

My dear Jeanne,

Knowing what anxiety you must have been feeling on my behalf during these past weeks, I take this first chance my returning strength permits to tell you that my recovery now seems assured. I will have paid a price, however, for even though the doctor's fears have not come true and he has been able to save the leg, it will probably always be somewhat stiff and thus provide a permanent reminder of the vain glory of those three days when it seemed we might remake the world.

Alas, there are other scars from those days—chiefly, one accompanying my sad realization that I cannot live, as I had once hoped, free of all responsibility to my family. The concern they have shown for me, the expert medical care which their station in society has procured for me, and without which I surely would have lost the wounded limb, and the knowledge of how deeply I had hurt my mother by attempting to live outside her world and her wishes—awareness of all these things has come slowly but surely, beginning with the night when my fever finally burned itself out and left me once again in possession of all faculties save physical strength.

If I could create Louis Vollard solely in the image I wish for him, I would make him a creature as free as you, able to ignore the claims of blood and tradition. Alas, I have discovered those claims will not be denied—not without doing the kind of violence to my family that I cannot allow. But in accepting my responsibility to them, I do not deny what I owe to you. Our idyll is—must be—finished, but I want the setting in which it flourished to remain yours. So that you may continue to rent it, and provide for all your needs, you will receive a sum of money.

Your future will be brighter without me. You may not know it now, but I assure you it is so.

The recognition that the time we spent together has now ended does not diminish the pleasure of recollecting it.

Louis

Jeanne folded the sheets carefully and replaced them in the envelope. It had no weight, the room had no air, and her body had no feeling, except for a strange tingling in her lips.

Madame Vollard had sat down again and was regarding her calmly, hands folded in her lap, a blue ring glowing more intensely than her gaze. "You are upset. That is to be expected. May I offer you some coffee?"

"No. Thank you." Jeanne bit her lips. "I should like to see Louis."

"A natural desire, but one that cannot be fulfilled. The two of you will not meet again, the wisdom of which decision I am sure you will appreciate when you have had the time to reflect. These matters are best ended cleanly."

"Matters?" Jeanne cleared her throat. "Louis and I love each other. You must know that. You're his mother—how could you not know?"

"My child," said the woman, her voice still flowing with the honeyed poison of kindness, "I did not send for you in order to encourage, discuss, or in any form debate your liaison with my son, but to ensure your understanding that it is finished, and to confirm the financial arrangements indicated in his letter."

"Excuse me, madame, you know what Louis's letter says? Have you read it?"

For an instant, a line appeared at each corner of the woman's mouth, like a pleat. "Here are a thousand francs," she said, unfolding her hands and revealing a small blue velvet bag. "They will guarantee a much better future than you would otherwise have been able to anticipate. Louis wishes you to have this money, and because we are not unsympathetic to your situation, his father and I concur, provided you understand that the money represents the final encounter between you and this family. I think you will agree that we have been generous and that you have profited from your liaison, for not only do you now have a handsome dowry, with which to marry someone of your own class, but you have acquired useful knowledge, for my son has clearly taught you how to read and speak well. Should you care to leave the theatre world in which I understand he found you, and frankly I would advise you to do so, for you seem clever enough to be sensible, you could surely find work in some of the better houses in Paris."

The woman smiled, fractionally. The smile was a string pulling from Jeanne everything that had held her together while she listened—her clothes, her skin, so there seemed nothing left but her bones and blood and her heart fluttering as nakedly as a fish tossed on a riverbank. She felt something crying within her, and it seemed to be the child, which had never before made its presence known except in bouts of nausea. But now she could imagine its tiny fists beating below her heart, urging her to sit straight and keep her eyes level, telling her she did have something left: the child itself, and her pride—which were worth the loss of everything else and would be its recompense. She looked down and saw one hand clutching the envelope and the other still holding the two ends of the shawl, which now more than ever must hide the existence of the child from the woman's gray eyes. The child was hers alone, like her pride; it would know nothing of the Vollards.

She lifted her head and said, "You are mistaken, madame. I was quite able to read before I met Louis, and to speak well. Your son did not teach me either of those things, both of which I learned from a dear friend in the theatre, a wonderful man who is a dwarf." She had not planned to say the words—they had simply leaped from her lips—but the woman's nostrils flared when she heard them, and seeing it, Jeanne's voice grew stronger. "Please be good enough to give Louis a message from me. Tell him that I will have his belongings sent to him at once. Tell him also that nothing could induce me to accept the thousand francs, or any other amount from him, however large or small."

Madame Vollard rose, holding out the blue velvet bag, jangling the coins within. "I advise you not to be prideful and foolish."

"I am not foolish, madame. Nor have I forgotten what I learned as a ragpicker—it is unwise to take everything people toss away. One must be selective."

The woman sucked in her breath. "Your origins betray you. Only a ragpicker's daughter would reply to generosity with insult."

"You call it generosity?" An image leaped into Jeanne's mind: her father narrowing his eyes and telling Nandou he would sell her for fifty francs. She had not expected to find his moral equal in a place of velvet and silk and blue rings. Worse than his equal, for Madame Vollard was educated, and the daughter of a vicomte. Standing as tall as she could, Jeanne said, "A ragpicker would say you are only trying to buy me off. And I, his daughter, tell you I cannot be bought or sold. Permit me to wish you good morning, madame."

The expression that congealed on the woman's face was deeply satisfying to watch; Jeanne held it in her mind all the way out of the room and along the hall and until she somehow found the front door again.

Outside, a carriage was passing under a warm sun, and the leaves of a large chestnut tree waved in a breeze. Arms folded tightly over her shawl, one hand still clutching Louis's letter, seeing little of those who passed but a white blur of faces below dark hats and bright bonnets, Jeanne concentrated on walking, one foot at a time, until she reached the tree, then past it to the corner, then around the corner, one street at a time, along the walls of private gardens and before the houses that reared up beside them in disdain. What kind of creatures lived there, who offered her money to leave them alone behind their stately doors, as if she were merchandise from a shop, and then talked of being generous? If that was society's view of right and wrong, she preferred her father's. He had been more honest; he had merely demanded money. And he had not expected gratitude. Gratitude! How had Louis agreed to what they wanted? How could he? Louis *knew* her.

Almost panting, anger pushing her faster and faster, Jeanne finally stopped before a small church to catch her breath.

"Are you all right?" said a voice she would know anywhere.

She turned to him. "Did you follow me here?"

His skin turned even duskier. He shrugged and said, "I had to make sure everything went well for you."

Never had she wanted so badly to tell him the truth, to sink onto his broad shoulders and let his short, solid body be her bulwark. But he had said, *I have seen these young bourgeois, who find a girl to live with for a while in the place des Italiens, and then go back to their lives.* And she had scoffed and cried, *Louis loves me!* Ever since Louis had been shot, she had fought to keep Nandou from knowing how stupid she had been. The night before, in the café, she had been even more stupid. The ramrod of pride could not let her bend now.

She crushed Louis's letter deeper inside her hand. "I am fine," she said.

Nandou made a fist, as if he were crushing a letter too. "Are you going to be with them, then, with the Vollards?"

"No. I am not." She lifted her chin. "But that is no matter. I would not wish to live in such a place. I will be much better as I am."

Nicolas Vollard had just come home from the offices of Vollard et Cie. Hearing that Louis wished to see him, he went at once to the room where Louis was propped up in the bed that had been his since boyhood.

"Nico! Did you hear what has happened? Has Maman told you?"

"No, but it can't be good. You haven't looked this pale since you were first carried up here."

"Frédéric did not have my letter delivered to Jeanne! He took it to Maman instead. She had Jeanne come to the house this morning, and gave it to her, and Jeanne refused the money and insulted Maman."

"Good God."

"Damn Frédéric's butler's soul! And yours, too. If you had done as I asked and delivered my letter to Jeanne yourself, this would not have happened."

Nicolas sank into the small chair by the fireplace. "Louis, I am sorry, truly. I was afraid to place myself in a situation where I might have to answer the girl's questions, because I had no answers. But I did not imagine this could be the consequence."

Louis's shoulders moved inside his nightshirt as if itched. "It's a dreadful mess."

"Yes. Do you think you could—"

"It's more dreadful than you know," Louis said tonelessly. "Jeanne is going to have a child."

"Oh, Louis, no!"

The brothers looked at each other, as though for the first time they truly were doing so as adults; as though their mutual gaze, which had walled them inside their shared lives the way a fence protects a childhood garden, was no longer able to do so. The knowledge that one of them would be not only a son but also a father washed over them, confirming the irretrievable loss of their years of play. Nicolas's eyes narrowed. He nodded slowly, as if tasting a rough new wine. Louis fell back on the pillow. His body seemed to flatten against it.

Nicolas said, "The child is yours, I presume?"

"Jeanne said so."

"Do you have reason to believe otherwise?"

Louis's long fingers plucked at the coverlet. "I don't know. Those theatre people . . . That damned dwarf she lived with and never told me about . . ."

"I thought you were sure that you were the first to be with her."

"Yes, but why didn't she tell me about the dwarf? Why should I believe he was only . . . He was with her when they found me, you know."

"Does Maman know about the child?"

Louis turned away. "No. I was afraid it would make her angry at Jeanne."

"Now she's angry anyway."

"You don't understand, Nico. I had to beg Maman to give Jeanne a thousand francs. 'I warned you against such a liaison. Why should I now have to pay for the fact that you ignored my warning?' Imagine what she would have said if I had told her there was to be a child! And I certainly can't tell her now, because she would realize that I knew it all along but kept it from her. Damn it! Why wouldn't Jeanne take the money?"

Nicolas said, "Perhaps because she is proud."

Louis turned away, revealing two scabs on his cheek and one above his eyes, as big as a watch. "You disapprove of my behavior, don't you? You despise me."

"I can't imagine I could ever do that."

"But you are thinking something. You must be."

Nicolas touched the high points of his neckcloth. "Once you told Maman it would tear your heart out to give up this girl."

"I meant it, Nico. But what else can I do? I can never make her my wife, not unless I reject Maman and Papa. And how could I do that, after they have provided the care that saved my life?" Nicolas said nothing. "Part of me longs to continue the liaison with Jeanne, but what sort of future is that for her? To spend her life waiting for me to be able to spare an evening with her, perhaps a whole day if we are lucky? I cannot ask her to live half a life with me. She deserves a whole life of her own."

"Noble sentiments," Nicolas said.

"Are you mocking me? Are you thinking it is the oldest story in

Paris—to get a girl with child and then . . . Tell me what you think, Nico. Please."

"Louis, it doesn't matter what I or anyone else thinks. If you believe your action was right, then accept what you did. Make peace with it."

Louis sighed. "The things I said about the future and art . . . and Jeanne . . . I believed them, you know. Perhaps I still do. But they won't come true just because I believe them, will they?—any more than we were able to dethrone the king just by rushing into the streets shouting 'Down with the Bourbons!' "

"But Charles did abdicate."

"But we have Louis Philippe in his stead."

"A man who wears civilian clothes and refuses royal crests on his doors."

Louis's head dug deeper into the pillow. "I don't think Jeanne loved me too deeply. She'll soon return to her theatre friends and forget me." Nicolas was silent. "Why don't you say what you are really thinking?" Louis cried.

"Very well," Nicolas said. "I was thinking of the wooden soldiers Uncle Claude gave you for one of your birthdays—the sixth, was it? You would barely stop playing with them to eat or sleep. But then you snapped the leg off one of them during some maneuver, and wanted nothing more to do with them. You said they hadn't been good soldiers anyway, and you hadn't truly cared for them."

"That was only to make myself feel better."

"Exactly," Nicolas said.

Louis's hands lifted, then fell back. "Nico, promise me you won't tell anyone about the child, especially Maman. If she knew she was going to have a grandchild whose other grandparents are ragpickers . . . "

"You are never going to see your child, then? You abandon it?"

"I didn't say that." Louis leaned forward. "I'll make it my business to learn about the child. I'll see that it has whatever it needs."

"How?" Nicolas asked.

"Somehow. I will, I swear it. I'm not a bastard, you know." Even as he said it, Louis flushed at the implication of the words: that his child would be one. He sighed. "Nico, you never make a mess of things, do you? Why is that?"

It took Nicolas a moment to answer. "I could, you know. But nothing has yet tempted me to do so."

"Do I hear regret in your voice?" When Nicolas didn't reply, Louis added, "You haven't promised to keep the secret. Say you will, Nico. Please."

Nicolas lifted his hands. "All right, dear brother, I promise."

The child grew within her every day, it seemed to Jeanne, changing her body so that her breasts rolled like heavy apples inside her callboy jacket and her waist pushed hard against the trouser band. As the child grew, so did her feeling against its father, until it began to seem that one was the product of the other—that the thickening of her body came not from her days and night with Louis but from the hardening of her heart against him.

As soon as she had returned from her interview with Madame Vollard, she had packed up his painting gear, his clothes, and everything he had ever given her, and spent precious centimes to hire someone to deliver the lot to his parents' home. Then she had sat on the horsehair sofa, stared at the emptiness, and cried long and bitterly, until her face felt as if wasps had been at it. She had cooled it in the basin, and then begun scrubbing everything, even the inside of the stove; when she was finished, she had walked back and forth through the rooms many times, hugging herself as if cold, her gaze sweeping everywhere as if it were a brush, painting out all memory of him, her lips softly telling the child that its mother had been a fool but would never be one again.

In September, no longer able to hide her condition, she had to cease working at the theatres. She told Nandou she was going to do so, but only that, nothing more. They were in a café; when she said it, he pulled a hand through his hair, then cupped it over his mouth while his gaze searched her face like a torch, shining down the tunnels of her eyes. Then he said, softly, so she had to bend to hear him, "When will the child be born?"

"So you know, then."

"Of course."

"How long have you known?"

"For weeks. When is it due?"

You hid your knowledge from me, she thought. *Why can I hide nothing from you?* "In about four months, I think."

He nodded. "How will you live until then? And after then?"

She looked straight into his eyes; he had taught her that was how one made people believe in one's tricks. "I have money. Louis made sure of that."

"I am glad to hear it," he said. "How much money?"

"Quite enough." For a moment she almost believed it herself, hearing the jangle of coins inside blue velvet. The strange thing was that Nandou was the only one who would understand her action and the angry pride behind it; he would have felt and done the same, she was sure, perhaps even taking the bag but flinging it down with a grand gesture—*I do not seek such paltry payment.* Her grisette friend, Marie, had collapsed on a chair when she told her, crying "A thousand francs? How could you? How could you?" over and over, but Nandou would smile if he knew, Jeanne was certain, the way he had when she wrote her first proper sentence, one eyebrow and one corner of his mouth rising together in a salute and his eyes flashing with pleasure. But if she told him, he would know how bad her situation was and would insist on helping her. He would even understand why she didn't tell him; he knew all about pride.

"So Vollard is accepting responsibility for the child?" he said.

She kept her gaze locked on his. "Yes, of course." It was hateful, lying to make Louis seem honorable in Nandou's eyes. But perhaps it was just, for hadn't she lied to Louis about Nandou?

"I am glad," Nandou said, "for your sake, of course, but for Vollard's as well." He leaned back in his chair, releasing her.

In relief she turned aside. A man at the next table was staring at Nandou over a mug of beer, the eyes at once curious, condescending, and bold, as if they inspected not a fellow creature but something unable to feel their gaze. "What are you looking at?" she cried. "Keep your damned eyes to yourself!"

The man blinked and put down the mug. "Watch your tongue, son. Or do you prefer to step outside?"

"I prefer to pour your beer over your eyes!"

"What are you doing?" Nandou cried, one hand clutching her arm.

She shook it off and turned away from both of them, knowing in that moment that her anger was not for the stranger but for herself— because in his insolent stare she had just seen her own treatment of Nandou. Hadn't she promised herself a hundred times to tell Louis about him, but kept putting it off? Hadn't she pretended to do so for fear of Louis's jealousy? But that had not been the only reason, perhaps not even the chief one. She had done it because she feared Nandou's dwarfishness would shame her in Louis's eyes. In the stupid blindness of her passion, she had betrayed Nandou, who had done everything for her.

She could never let him do anything again. That was only just.

"What in the name of the gods is wrong with you?" Nandou said angrily. She was glad of his anger; she deserved it. But as they left the café, he said gruffly but protectively, "Your condition must be making you behave so oddly."

In October, to save money, and without telling Nandou, she packed her few belongings and moved across the hall, with Marie, who was glad for Jeanne's contribution to her expenses. Marie had come to Paris from the country, to seek work at sewing and lace-making and send whatever money she could back to her parents on their farm. Jeanne was trying to learn from her, so she could also apply to some of the same merchants for work, but her fingers would not move nimbly, like Marie's; they kept dropping stitches, or the needle, or sticking it into themselves like awkward duellists, until she swore it had been easier to learn to read than it was to sew properly.

Marie was in love with a young would-be poet. When he came to see her, a bottle of cheap wine under one arm, the three of them might have supper together, Marie laughing and blushing as the poet blew her kisses across the table and Jeanne pretending she did not think he would one day return to his solidly respectable family and never be seen again. So the lovers could be alone in the one room, she left after supper and spent most of the night on the stairs, huddled in the poet's coat. It was difficult to sleep, so, to keep from staring at the door of the rooms where she had once thought happiness would last, she made up scenes and acted them on the stage of her mind: The woman who escaped from prison disguised as her jailer. The woman who declined to sell her child for a fortune and reared it in the woods, with a lion. The woman who killed the lover who betrayed her by sewing him a shirt of poisoned silk threads.

In November, the poet disappeared, and Marie went back to her village in the Midi. Jeanne managed to pay the room rent alone; the merchants to whom Marie had introduced her gave her some work. But it took too long, for she had to do things over and over before they were good enough to deliver; she spent hours to earn each sou.

In December, two of the merchants rejected her clumsy laces and said they would give her no more work. She stretched her remaining money by reducing breakfast to coffee and supper to the same watered soup and lentils she used to watch her mother prepare. Although she was constantly tired—carrying water up from the public well sent her to bed for hours afterward—hunger often kept her awake. Sometimes she imagined that what gnawed at her from within was the child, already trying to nurse. Sometimes she imagined tales of dreadful obstacles and the huge banquets that rewarded people who overcame them. When she did fall asleep, she dreamed of the blue velvet bag. In the dream everyone she knew—Marie, Nandou, her parents, her brothers, even Madame Duclos from the theatre—stood in a circle around her and chided her for not taking it. Then she would awake with a start and place her hands on her bulging abdomen and taste again her hatred of Louis, who could have arranged for the money to be sent to her somehow, if he had wanted, even though she would have refused it again.

Once a week or so, for the child's sake, she would accept Nandou's invitation to dine in his rooms, where the ghost of the girl she had been when she first met him seemed to mock her. That creature had stuffed everything into her mouth at once and asked for more, but Jeanne Sorel must eat with decorum now and pretend she was too full to take any more mutton or peas. A dozen times she was on the verge of confessing everything to Nandou, but then her pride, and her guilt over him, would move within her, like the child; she would lift her chin and ask him how the trial of the former king's ministers was progressing and was it true that Hugo's new play would be going into the Porte-St.-Martin?

In January, after paying the rent, she had enough money for food or the midwife, but not for both. There was only one thing left to do, and no longer a choice about doing it. One dawn she rose in blackness, drank enough coffee to stop her shivering, put on her jacket and two shawls, and crept down the stairs, her body as unwieldy as if she were pushing a cart with her hips. Out on the street cold gripped her tightly, but there were bands of pearl in the sky and a tremor of orange. She began to walk north and west, away from the streets that had bounded her life in recent years. A band of sweepers passed, brooms slung over their shoulders like muskets. A mother and child huddling in a doorway looked up at her with old eyes. A dog slunk from an alley and pattered at her heels for a few blocks before giving up, dispirited. Her toes grew colder, barely moving within her shoes, but her cheeks started to burn. When she finally stopped, she looked around to make sure she was alone, rubbed her hands together violently, as if trying to make sparks, and began to dig through a pile of garbage at the side of the street.

For more than an hour she dug and moved on, dug and moved on.

Although her sticky, reeking hands were poor substitutes for the hook, she found a buckle that could be shined and sold, a beef bone to add to the soup, and a filthy but strong piece of blue wool. Each time before she bent over, she scanned the street, fearful of seeing other ragpickers. Yet, as time passed and her back felt more and more like a rusty knife that did not want to fold into its case, she began to wish she would see them. Perhaps she would even meet her mother, and talk to her for a moment. Her mother would know what to do when the child began to come. Her mother had screamed in pain when Jeanne walked away from them; she could hear the scream again, in her mind.

She realized the scream had come from her.

The insides of her legs were icy and wet, and the rusty knife had moved from her back to her front. She fell onto the garbage until the pain subsided.

Somehow she pushed herself up, wiped her hands on her shawls, and started walking again, toward home. Several streets later she realized the buckle, bone, and wool had been left behind on the pile where she had collapsed. Before she could turn back, another pain sliced into her, and when it was over, she knew she could go only in one direction—to the midwife's. Her legs needed to be pulled up for each step, like a marionette's, but her hands could not help because they held the globe of her belly. The sun had risen, high and cold, and a few people were emerging onto the streets. When the next pain struck, she sank into the covered doorway of a wineshop and knew she could not get up again. She wanted to curl in on herself, but the pain, and her bulk, would not let her. She sprawled across the doorway, panting, a shawl wadded behind her head and her feet pushed hard against the opposite wood, and tried to imagine a place where there was no pain, only chestnut trees in bloom, and sunshine.

Instead, she imagined that Nandou was looking at her, calling her name as if she were dying. She decided that she was.

Then she felt his hands under her shoulders. She opened her eyes; he was there. It was no use telling him she was fine; he would know she was lying. Perhaps he had always known. "It will be all right," he was saying. "I will take care of everything."

The pain was crouching, ready to spring.

"Let me help you," he said. "You must let me help you."

If she did, she thought, she would have to repay him. Somehow.

The pain leaped, and she screamed.

Chapter Seven

Edmée Tissot lifted the veil of English point and let it fall slowly over her face. In the mirror, her eyes shone at her from the veil's shadow, and the widening of her smile was visible, like sun through leaves. It seemed to her that the veil, the dress, the day itself, had been designed to reflect all that she felt: the April sun as bright and fresh as her hopes, the white taffeta and lace she wore rustling and trembling like the outward form of her excitement, the veil making her happiness all the more evident by being unable to subdue it.

Edmée had wanted to marry Louis Vollard from the first time she danced with him. Of all the young men at that ball, he had been the only one not to merge into a sea of earnest eyes and faintly sweaty palms. The others were too predictable in their claims to horsemanship, acreage, and lineage, their shifts between braggadocio and respectful attention. Perhaps they were too much like her, reared in propriety and comfort, sharing values she had always known, differing only by expressing them in a deeper voice and from a man's perspective. Although Louis had been quite proper in his manner and dress, from the moment he bowed to her, put his hand on her waist, and led her out in a waltz, she had felt there was more to him than to his peers. He did not ask after the health of her father the baron or compliment her gown; he said nothing at all for some time, merely danced with his spine as straight as a sword, his steps mechanically expert, and his dark eyes far away. Finally she asked, "The party is not to your liking, Monsieur Vollard?" Instead of breaking into apology, he had looked down at her, searched her face, and said, "Do you not think, mademoiselle, that there are too many parties in Paris, and too little to celebrate?"

Although Edmée's breath had flown out in surprise, she said, "I feel no surfeit of the one or lack of the other. But no doubt I am less well versed in the life of Paris than you are, monsieur."

"Paris has many kinds of life."

"Do you know more than one of them?"

"Perhaps."

"I, alas, know only the one in which I have been born and raised."

"Which has survived the Revolution virtually intact."

"Do you not approve, Monsieur Vollard?"

"Of which, survival or change?"

"Of either."

Maneuvering her smoothly in a turn, Louis had said, "There can be no life without change."

"Nor without survival, I presume."

He had lifted both dark eyebrows, but he could be no more surprised by her response than Edmée was herself. She did not have such conversations with the young men of her acquaintance, nor with her friends or parents. The talk she knew was of fashion and its changes, of music and riding and sewing and learning how to plan large parties and discipline servants. If, after dinner, there floated out scraps of the men's conversations about a crisis in the banks or the palace or the Chamber of Deputies or Algeria, those words had little more connection to her life than did the cigar smoke that accompanied them.

Moving in unison with Louis in the dance, she had looked up at him and asked, "Are your sympathies Republican, then, Monsieur Vollard?"

"If they were, Mademoiselle Tissot, would you smile more, or less?"

"I don't know." After several more turns, she had blurted out, "More."

"Indeed. In sympathy or scorn?"

"I . . . cannot answer until I know whether you are a republican or not."

But he had not told her. They had circled in silence for the rest of the dance, his tall figure the one stable point in a whirl of silk and scent and laughter and violins. Although he held her no more tightly or closely than the waltz required, for the first time she had felt she understood why some people said it was a lascivious and impure dance.

When the music stopped, he had removed one hand from her own and the other from the small of her back, bowed, and thanked her. In a moment she was led out again by someone else, whose face she could not keep in mind even as she looked at it, whose hand on her back had a sweaty, alien pressure.

On the way home she had tried to find out more about Louis, but her mother had merely said, "A handsome young man, but inclined to rebellious notions, I hear. Do not interest yourself in him." Edmée had smiled to herself and sunk back into the seat of the carriage.

The next morning she awoke knowing there was a void at the heart of her existence. She had had such a thought before, but only in the middle of the night, when she would sometimes wake for no reason, sit up in bed, and, in the silent darkness of her parents' huge house, stare at the gilt-edged mirror on the opposite wall and shiver because she could see nothing in it but a shadow without shape. The day after dancing with Louis was the first time she had such a feeling in the sunlight—when the image in the mirror was quite visible and familiar: her brown eyes too large and far apart, her thin face topped with pale gold hair. For several days afterward she had gone about staring at things as if she had never seen them before. Her mother had asked if she were ill. "Not at all, Maman, I am perfectly well," she said, and turned her gaze on her mother, whom she had always taken for granted and whom people said she resembled so much: a beautifully dressed creature who knew everything required to maintain a large house in Paris, a country estate, and a stream of chatter about the comings and goings of church, state, and society. Edmée had always known that she was being raised to live the same kind of life as her mother's—which of course was a very pleasant one. "For heaven's sake," her mother said, looking up with a frown from her morning coffee and letters, "why do you stand and stare at me? Can you find nothing to do?" So Edmée had wandered off. In the kitchen, one of the cooks was making *pâte feuilletée:* placing butter in the center of the dough, which she folded and rolled and turned with expert motions. The dough would rest for an hour or so, then be folded and rolled again, and rested—over and over until, hours later, worked into hundreds of the thinnest imaginable layers, it was cut and shaped and baked into dessert shells. Rich, flaky, light as air, and empty. But of course very pleasant. Despite the heat of the kitchen, Edmée had shivered, and when the cook asked, "Will you have a pinch of my dough, Mademoiselle Edmée?" she had cried, "No!"

She cried it again, amazed at herself, when her parents announced that they wished her to marry the younger son of a marquis with whom her father often hunted. "I won't do it," she said. Her mother ordered, threatened, cajoled, but Edmée declared she was ill and could not recover until the plan for her future was changed. Her father railed, but two doctors came, examined her, shook their heads, went away. "Very well," said her mother finally, "there will be no marriage discussions with the marquis." Edmée got out of bed, and concentrated her energies on maneuvering herself into places and parties where Louis Vollard was likely to be.

Soon she realized she had an ally in his mother, who smiled whenever she saw the two of them chatting or dancing. The Vollards gave a ball, to which the Tissots were invited; the favor was returned; there were invitations to dinner. Periodically Edmée's mother would frown and demur—she heard that Louis wasted his time daubing on canvases, with the riffraff of the art world; she saw that he wore his hair too long—but, on the other hand, there were no more staunch royalists than Monsieur and Madame Vollard, who, one must acknowledge, kept a handsome enough establishment. Besides, they were well spoken of by a bishop who was a particular friend of Edmée's mother. Edmée managed to keep her parents from learning that Louis attended the opening of *Hernani,* though when he told her about it, she trembled with love for him—not because she cared whether the Romanticists won or even had a clear idea why they were fighting but because, watching him describe the tumult, she was certain that life with him could not be empty at its heart. When he was wounded during the Three Glorious Days, she had known moments of terror, not all related to his health: Had he been fighting on the rebels' side? If he had, and her parents learned it, would they dismiss him as a suitor? Although she had secret doubts about the church, Edmée spent hours kneeling by her bed, half praying for Louis, half lost in dreams of nursing him to health. The news of his recovery had been followed by two other miracles: the pleasure her parents took in the crowning of a new king, which made them much less interested in exactly how Louis had been wounded, and some months later, when he was pale and thin and limping, the start of negotiations between the two families and finally the formal offer for her hand in marriage.

Edmée smiled at her reflection in the mirror. "Madame Louis Vollard," she said, the veil moving with the breath of her words.

The light through the window changed, muted by a passing cloud. Suddenly the girl in the mirror's long, gilded rectangle flung back her veil and looked out in consternation. Madame Louis Vollard—how could she become such a person when she barely knew the man whose name she was preparing to take? Louis often seemed preoccupied and distant—proof, she always thought, that there were rebellious, mysterious passions within him. But what did she actually know of them? She knew the things he had said to her and the sound of his voice while saying them, but nothing of his mind. She knew his face and the pressure of his lips in a few kisses, but nothing of his body. She clasped her hands, imploring her mirror image for reassurance, remembering that once, when Louis told her that he admired Rousseau and looked down with a challenging smile, she had replied, "I do not attack the past, but neither do I wish to be its prisoner." He had raised his eyebrows, said, "Well done," and laughed. But now she was to be a prisoner of the future, about which she knew nothing except the name under which she would live it. Her hands had gone damp; she ran them along her lace-and-taffeta dress.

Her maid came into the room with the crown of orange flowers. "Oh, Mademoiselle," the girl cried, "how beautiful you are!"

The words restored Edmée to reality. It was true, she thought: She, and the day, were beautiful—as her life with Louis would be, too. She had worked and schemed and planned to bring it into existence; to doubt it would be to commit treason against herself, and Louis as well.

She lowered her veil again, and the maid arranged the flower crown.

Nandou held out his hand.

The child grasped his index finger in one of her fists and stared at him with the intensity of a praying nun. In a moment he wiggled the finger. Her lips curled upward, and delight gurgled from her.

Dear God, he thought, she was wonderful. Each finger and toe a tiny perfection, the whole of them a miracle. Lashes set into soft lids with a jeweler's precision. Black hair lying on her skull like strands of silk over pearl.

Why had he not known a child could be so enchanting? He had always disliked children; they seemed to be mocking him, with their limbs soon to reach the length of his own and their piping voices reminding him he could never fully banish the higher tones from his own utterance. Children were loved for being humans in miniature, whereas he was mocked for the same thing. He had expected only to tolerate her, for Jeanne's sake, but in the perfection of her proportions he forgot the pain of his own, and was enslaved.

She had been born late on that January day when Nandou found Jeanne and brought her home with him. After the midwife left, Jeanne lay as pale and still as a figure on the tombs at Notre-Dame, the squalling red infant tucked beside her. She opened her eyes long enough to whisper, "Her name will be Solange," and then sank into sleep as if it were death. For nearly a week she had barely spoken—Nandou had had to do everything for her, sometimes even tell her to give the child her breast, and what did he know of such matters? Fearing he would lose both of them, he had had to learn. On the sixth day, Jeanne sat up, looked around with eyes that no longer were pieces of dark glass, and called him.

She lifted a hand to his cheek, touched the old scar from her brother's hook, then let her hand fall to rest on his arm. "Twice you have saved me, Nandou, and now my child as well. I have no way to thank you, except to promise you will not have to do it again."

He had tried to smile. "I shall do it as often as necessary."

"It will not be necessary again. I promise."

What did she mean, he had wondered: that she would not leave again? He could not let himself think such a thing. She had promised it once before, and he had believed it, but she had left. This time he would neither think it nor ask her to explain what she meant. He would simply take the days as they came.

His night walks had become things of the past; if he took them, he was too exhausted to spend the mornings with Jeanne and Solange. Each night he came straight home from the theatres, and while Jeanne made him a quick supper, sat by the cradle he had found on rue des Can-nettes—the shopkeeper's brows had risen in moons of bemusement, as if to ask, "For you to sleep in, Monsieur the Dwarf?"—and told the latest news from the journals and the boulevard.

Once Jeanne said, "Do they ever ask what happened to your callboy nephew?"

"I tell them that you—he—has gone back to his family in the Midi."

"You might better say he is dead."

"I see no reason to talk of death."

Jeanne sighed. "Perhaps not."

"Let us talk instead of how, when Solange is a bit older, you can come to the theatres with me once more. I can tell everyone that you are Sorel's sister."

"Perhaps." Again, Jeanne sighed. She often did so, stopping in the midst of cutting vegetables or washing the baby's clothes, staring into the distance as if hearing a voice and then opening her mouth to answer; but all that came was that heavy expulsion of breath, over which her lips closed regretfully. Once Nandou could not keep from asking, "Are you thinking of Vollard?"

"Certainly not." Then she had added, with the sudden, flaring intensity of one of the new phosphorus matches, "If I were, it would be only to hope he is suffering."

It had been Nandou's turn to sigh.

A few nights later he said, carefully, "Today there was talk of Dumas and his bastard son. It seems the mother failed to make proper acknowledgment of maternity when the child was born, even though the birth was registered. Two weeks ago Dumas acknowledged the boy legally, and since the mother had not established her claim, the court now says Dumas can take the child from her."

"You are not telling me this only because it is gossip, are you?"

"No. I think you should go to the Mairie and make a formal declaration that you acknowledge Solange as your daughter."

"Louis Vollard has no interest in Solange. Surely that is clear." After a silence, Jeanne added, "Still, you are right. I shall attend to it."

They did not speak of Vollard again, even on the spring day when, after long hesitation, Nandou brought home a journal and pointed to a paragraph headlined, MARRIAGE OF DAUGHTER OF BARON TISSOT. Jeanne read it, motionless except for her eyes, which grew wider and wider until they slammed shut.

"I am sorry," Nandou said.

After a moment Jeanne lifted her head. "Not for me, I trust." With more bitterness than he had ever heard from her, she added, "The one who deserves your pity is the Tissot child."

That "child" was a year older than Jeanne herself, according to the article. But Nandou said nothing, only watched Jeanne fold the paper and place it on the table. An hour later he saw her spread it out, open it to the article, and clean a fish onto it, biting her lip as the slashes of her knife showered scales over the print and her hands buried it beneath loops of entrails.

That night, when he had finished his supper, she said, "Would you read to me, Nandou, as you used to do?"

He went to the shelf and took down his most recent and precious purchase: Hugo's *Notre Dame de Paris,* which all Paris seemed to want to read; he had had to stand in line for hours to get a copy. He ran his hand over the cover, with its sketch of a beautiful young woman giving water to a grotesque creature, opened to the first page, and began.

For many nights he read, his voice taking them deeper and deeper into the story. If it woke Solange, Jeanne would pick her up and hold her, so that, each time he looked up from the page, he would see the two of them watching him. More than once, he saw tears running down Jeanne's face. "What is it?" she would say. "Why are you stopping?"

"Nothing. Something in my throat." That was true enough, for what rose to choke him was not only sympathy for the hunchback's plight but the desire to know whether Jeanne cried for the hopelessness of Quasimodo's love, or for the pain of Esmeralda's.

He would not ask; he mastered himself and read on. But when he put down the book and she made ready to sleep, when he lay on his own bed and could hear the rustling of her clothes and see fragments of her shadow cast on the far wall, he would allow himself to know two things: that his life now held more than he had ever dared to dream, but would never hold what he wanted most.

He had the child, though, from whom his love did not have to be hidden.

He began each day by bending over the cradle and saying, "Hello, Solange. Good morning, beautiful child." The first time she answered him with something more than shapeless sound—"Dou," she said one day, "DOU!" which had to be an attempt at his name—he capered around the two rooms crying, "Hear ye, hear ye, Solange is speaking!" Jeanne looked up and laughed, almost the way she had used to do, and Fidèle flattened her ears and raced under the table. He fashioned toy animals for Solange in the theatres' scenery workrooms. He sat for hours doing tricks for her, making a centime appear and disappear between his fingers or pulling a red scarf from behind her ear. He greeted her first steps with applause and cries of "Bravo!" and celebrated her first sentence with little cakes from the patisserie.

"You will make her feel she is the center of the world," Jeanne chided.

"Ah, but she is," he replied.

Although Jeanne made a face at him, in truth she doted on Solange too. Sometimes when the child was sleeping they would stand on opposite sides of the cradle smiling and looking down, and he would know that, just as he was thinking she would never stand on the boulevard selling fritters, Jeanne was vowing she would never hold a ragpicker's hook. As they stood watching, his smile would widen, but Jeanne's would fade into a bitter line.

On the Ash Wednesday after Solange's first birthday, when Mardi Gras revelers were straggling home after their debaucheries high on the bluffs outside the city limits, someone on rue Chauchat died of cholera. Within weeks the plague had swept the city. Corpses were stacked in the alleys like firewood. Funerary wagons could not keep up with them, and the air, acrid with smoke from crematory ovens, stung one's eyes and throat. Nandou begged Jeanne not to go out on the streets, where no woman ventured without veils, and for once she did not argue. His own face covered with a mask, he managed to buy the food they needed, although his money was shrinking; many of the theatres stayed open, but they were often nearly empty. Getting water was difficult; a rumor had spread among the poor that the cholera was not a disease at all but a lie put out by authorities who wanted to poison them, and mobs had carried off people spending time near wells and lynched them.

Each time Nandou neared the apartment again, he began to shake. He would be certain it was the cholera, for people were always stricken suddenly, collapsing wherever they happened to be. Then he would realize he was not ill, only terrified of what he might find at home. "Are you all right?" he would call as he opened the door. Jeanne would shout back, "We are. And you?"

One day there was no answer when he called. His heart deafened him and his legs failed. He closed the door behind him and slumped against it.

At length something penetrated his awareness: Jeanne was squatting beside him. "What is it?" she said, eyes huge and voice cracking. "The cholera?"

He could not produce a sound.

"Nandou! Are you ill? Is it the cholera?" She began shaking his shoulders. "God, please, I can't bear it if Nandou dies!" Tears filled her eyes but, instead of running down her cheeks, spattered on his face with the motion of her shaking, which also loosened her hair from its pins.

A curl flicked into his eye, and when he winced and pulled back, he regained his voice. "I am all right," he said.

She went on shaking him with blind, mighty strength, as if she thought he were dead and her action could restore him.

"Jeanne, stop, I am all right!"

Finally she heard him and sank back on her heels, panting from her exertion. They stared at each other, the reality each had imagined fading slowly from their eyes. "What happened to you?" she whispered.

"Where is Solange?" he asked.

"Sleeping. What was wrong? Why did you fall against the door?"

"Because you didn't answer when I called. I thought you had . . . left me."

"Didn't I promise you would never have to come after me again?"

He tried to smile. "I didn't believe you. In any case, you are too young to make such a promise. I would not hold you to it."

"I will hold myself. She touched his arm. "I will never leave again, until you ask me to."

"Why should I ask that?"

"Because you will want . . . Surely you hope to marry one day? To find someone like . . . someone who is . . . "

"Like me? Do you think I can love only another dwarf?"

She flushed. "No. I only meant that . . . that I will not leave, until you ask me to."

"I will never ask it." He touched her hand, his heart beating so strongly that he was sure she could feel it in his fingers. She smiled, then got to her feet and started pinning up her hair. He rose too, with a grunt, and walked away, to pick up Fidèle and bury his face in the animal's fur so that what he felt would not shine out into the room.

"Were you able to find bread?" Jeanne asked.

"Yes, but it's not fresh. Why didn't you answer me, then, when I called?"

"I didn't hear you. I was busy." Unaccountably, she blushed.

"With what?"

"Something."

"What?"

"Nothing."

"Jeanne, tell me," he said gently.

She shrugged, moved away, then turned back. "I was . . . I have been . . . " She took a breath, exhaled slowly, and went into the other room, where she slept. In a moment she came out holding a sheaf of papers against her breasts. "I have been . . . I want to earn some money. No, that's not true. I mean, it is, but money is not the only reason. I want to *do* something, Nandou. It's been burning in me for a long time, nearly since Solange was born. I want to write. So for weeks now, every time you go out, I have been working on a play." She clutched the papers even more tightly. "I think it is not too dreadful. Will you read it?" She looked down at him, her eyes as bright as if they reflected the gas lamps at one of the theatres.

"How can I read it," he said, "if you don't let go of it?"

She gave a small, embarrassed laugh and surrendered the papers.

"No more coffee for me," Edmée told the maid. "Monsieur may want some."

From behind the journal he was reading Louis said, "None for me."

He heard the maid place the silver pot on the huge sideboard and leave the room. He read on—news of the Bourse, which did not interest him greatly but of which he was required to exhibit some knowledge— becoming more and more certain that Edmée was looking at him. At length he put down the journal; she was. "Is something wrong?" he said.

"No. I merely like to look at my husband."

Whenever she made such comments, he felt she was saying what she wished to hear from him. "Are you feeling well this morning?" he asked.

She made a noncommittal sound.

Louis picked up the next paper in his pile and frowned. "What's this? I don't recall ordering this."

"No," Edmée said, "I did."

He read off the name. "*La Liberté, Journal des Arts.* My dear, do you know what this is? Have you read it?"

"No, but I understand it is a new publication that advocates complete liberty in the arts. I thought it might interest you."

"The editors are anarchists."

"Are they?" she said blandly. "I thought there might be some interest- ing commentary on the censors' closing of Hugo's new play."

"The play portrayed a king as a libertine. Naturally Louis Philippe was offended. He may call himself the Citizen-King but he is still a Bourbon. What more is there to say?" Edmée kept gazing at him. "Sometimes," he said, "I think you want me to revert to my earlier days."

"Sometimes I think you want to forget them. Why do you not keep on with your painting? You fixed up a room up as a studio, but you don't use it often."

"Painting should rule one's life," Louis said, "not be done in one's spare time. And I am kept busy with Vollard et Cie. and our social calendar."

"Louis, I would cancel every engagement, if that would please you."

"Don't be foolish."

"It is not foolishness. I—" Edmée stopped. Her eyes widened and she gave a small gasp.

"What is it? Are you not well?" She was pregnant, for the second time; she had lost the first child at four months.

"It is nothing," she said after a moment. "As long as the doctors do not order me back to bed, I shall be fine."

"You must do as they tell you."

"I know. But it is not always easy to do what one is told."

Louis gave a short laugh that he regretted immediately, but she merely took another sip of coffee and then said, "Soon I will be unable to go out, so our social calendar will be restricted. That is why I thought you . . . why I ordered the journal . . . I only want you to be happy, Louis."

He knew it was true. In their first year of marriage she had always deferred to him—sometimes too much, he had thought, the way a pillow would adjust and yield to one's head—though of late her gaze could sometimes be as surprisingly direct as a sword emerging from feathers. He took up *La Liberté,* wanting to read it and at the same time resenting its presence on the tray.

The next time he looked up, she was watching him again.

"What is it?" he said. "Why do you always look at me so intently?"

"I merely want to understand you."

"I do not think I am a puzzling man."

"You are in some ways."

It was not a subject he wished to pursue. He put down the journal and stood. "I may be late tonight."

"Very well," Edmée said gently. "Do not forget that tomorrow night we are dining with my parents. I think my father wishes to ask you about— Oh, dear." She put a hand on her abdomen.

"What is it? Edmée, what is it happening?"

She smiled as though he were across the room instead of only across the table. "I think you had better send for the doctor," she said.

An hour later he was in the library, waiting, with a bottle of brandy for company.

Outside, a harsh November wind had risen and was making the fire draw fitfully. Louis stood at the window, watching the afternoon darken, listening to the panes rattle, thinking that events had rushed at him like the wind against the glass. The fervor of Romanticism and revolt had swept him up; Jeanne had blown into his path and bewitched him; the lead from a stranger's rifle had plowed into his thigh. He had returned to his parents' house to heal himself, but they had behaved as if his return were permanent, and by the time he would have been strong enough to withstand the force of his mother's will, she had brought her vision into reality and he had been borne along toward his wedding and his honeymoon trip to Italy and his appearances, frequent though as brief as possible, at the offices of Vollard et Cie. He sighed and drank more brandy.

It was mid-afternoon when the library door opened and the doctor came in.

"Monsieur Vollard," he said, "I am sorry to have to tell you that your wife has again lost a child."

Louis nodded; he had felt certain it was going to happen. "But Edmée will be all right? She will be able to bear children in the future?"

"With rest and care, she will recover her strength, yes. But I must tell you, sir, that I have serious doubts she will ever carry a child to full term."

"What do you mean?" Louis said. "You told us she would very likely be able to give birth."

"That was indeed my hope after the one unfortunate occurrence. But now, after a second incident in less than two years . . . " The doctor raised his eyebrows as if deferring to a higher wisdom.

Without thinking, Louis reached for his glass. "What are you suggesting? That there will be no children?"

"I am forced to warn you that such an unhappy future is likely." When Louis said nothing, the doctor added, "Your wife is asleep now, so it would be best to wait until dinnertime before you go up to her."

"Very well." The doctor must have said a few more things, which Louis must have answered, for the next time he focused on the place where the man had been, no one was there.

He drained off his glass and stood, indecisive. He had a great desire to call for another bottle and lock the door, yet Edmée's family had to be notified, and his own. He remembered the day he had told his parents

Edmée was expecting, the first time. His father had embraced him, and then his mother had put her hands on his arms and looked up into his face. "I am pleased with you, Louis," she had said softly.

He had been unprepared for the surge of pride. "Are you, Maman?"

"Yes, Louis. Very pleased." She had leaned up and placed a kiss on his cheek, so brief and light he had wondered if their flesh actually touched.

How he was now going to tell her there would be no children, he couldn't imagine. The whole point of the marriage had been children, hadn't it?—to tie the houses of Tissot and Vollard with the strength of blood.

And what would life with Edmée be like if she had no children to . . . well, to distract her? Their relationship had settled into domestic and social routines, certain patterns of flesh and spirit, that gave her a good deal of time to herself; how would she fill it in a childless future, except to demand more and more of him? Those brown eyes, widely spaced as if to hold their questions in a more secure grasp, would focus on him even more often, wanting something from him he could never quite define. *I want to understand you,* she said. How could she, when he hardly understood himself? Why did he refuse to let Edmée express any admiration for the rebellious ideas he had used to hold? Why had he said "used to hold"? Why did he hate himself for having become respectable and yet not hate the respect with which he was addressed as the baron's son-in-law? Why had he started occasionally visiting a certain house where the women were no more beautiful, or willing, than Edmée, only more naked? The week before, one had greeted him wearing nothing but a huge false pearl in her navel; he had laughed and been aroused, yet he had despised her.

And, hardest question of all: Why had he abandoned his firstborn child if there could not be another?

With an oath, he put down his empty glass and strode from the library, limping only slightly.

The room he had converted to a studio was on the second floor. He had not been in it for several weeks, as there had been no need for Edmée to remind him, and he had never taken out the bundle of canvases and drawings at the back of the large cupboard. Jeanne had sent the bundle to his parents' house two and a half years before. At the time he had merely ordered it put into storage, and when his things were moved to the new house, he had had it sent along, again without looking at it.

But he had not forgotten. Its existence had remained a softly compelling pressure in the back of his mind, which he had always resisted, though he did not know what it wanted of him.

The first thing out of the bundle was a painting of a rearing horse. He put it on the easel. When he had finished it, he had thought it rather good. Now he saw that the animal's flanks lacked the heaving life that Géricault would have given them. But if he kept on working . . . He put the painting aside and lifted out a sketchbook. As he turned the pages, the hope with which he had filled them seized him again. They were good, weren't they? At least, not bad. That hand was excellent, that foot solidly planted on the earth . . . He came on a chalk drawing of Jeanne. It was his first sight of her since the day he had been wounded. A mistake leapt out at him; the mouth was definitely not right. As he stared at it, frowning, the lips began to move; they whispered, "Louis, how could you leave us . . . " The blood rushed to his face. He swung his head and reduced her to chalk and stillness.

He watched his hands tear the drawing into halves, then quarters. He picked up another, of her head at a different angle, and tore that as well. And another and another, until no drawings of her were left and she lay on the floor in fragments of chalk lines that could never come together again and reproach him.

His mother had been right about her, of course. Just before his wedding he had paid someone to find out whether she was living with the dwarf again. "She is there," the man had reported, "with an infant, a female. The father? That I cannot say, monsieur, although the dwarf behaves as if it is he."

"Does he, by God?"

Several times more Louis had sent the man to learn what he could, particularly after the cholera had claimed nearly eighteen thousand victims. The child had not been one of them. The child who was his. Neither had Jeanne, nor the dwarf.

He gathered up the pieces of torn paper and pushed them into a trash basket. As he bundled up the sketchbook and horse painting again, a memory came over him, so vivid and physical that it knotted his gut, of how happy he had been when he worked at them.

He would have that feeling back again. He swore it, then stood quite still as an idea of how he might do so began to come into his mind.

Chapter Eight

"He likes it?" Jeanne said. "He truly likes The Dwarf Lord?"

"Yes!" Nandou cried. "He wishes to produce it in the spring."

"I can't believe it. I don't believe it." Jeanne had been making a tart when Nandou burst in with his news; she looked at the half-peeled apple she still held in one hand as if it had materialized out of the air. "A manager actually wants to *produce* it?"

"What else would one do with a play?"

Jeanne yelled with delight and sent the apple sailing, the peel wobbling behind it like a tail. Fidèle howled, Solange jumped up and down, screaming, and Nandou laughed so hard he fell onto a chair.

When they all subsided, they looked at one another in silence. *"The Dwarf Lord,"* Nandou said in his deepest theatrical voice, and they all began yelling and laughing again.

Finally, gasping for breath, Jeanne said, "Tell me every word he said. I must know everything."

Nandou grinned. "He likes the idea of the torture that turns the hero into a dwarf. He thinks the gypsy and prison scenes will provide suitably spectacular effects. He likes the idea of the rescues, and the disguises, and—"

"Does he agree that you should play the role?"

"Does he know a dwarf who can act better than I? Who is not only willing to work on the special shoes but able to help devise them? And if he did, would I allow anyone else to have the role? I would kill first! But there is more. He especially likes the scene when the hero hides in the hollow tree and overhears his father confessing that he abandoned him. And . . . " Nandou raised one hand.

"Yes, yes?"

"He will pay the playwright Jeanne Sorel twenty francs per performance, plus two free seats."

Jeanne lifted her apron, threw it over her head, and shrieked. When she stopped, he said softly, "I haven't seen you this happy since . . ." He hesitated. "Not for a long time."

She put down the apron and smiled.

"I shall never be able to thank you as I would like."

"Dear Nandou, I want no thanks. For once, I have done something for you."

His laugh was strange, as if it hurt him, and when he spoke, his voice was as frail as silk in the wind. "You have done many things, Jeanne. You have given me . . . Since the first time I saw you, I have been . . ." The silk fluttered into silence, but his eyes remained on her, as if he could neither pull them away nor close them.

"What is it, Nandou?" she whispered, knowing in that moment that she did not want him to tell her.

He pulled his hands through his hair, wavered for a moment, then grabbed Solange, kissed her lips and cheeks, and buried his face in the child's neck.

In a moment he looked up and cleared his throat. "When the play opens," he cried, "we will have a party and invite everyone to supper, everyone who ever knew Jean Sorel the callboy. But tonight . . . Solange, tell your maman we will celebrate tonight, just the three of us, because she is a playwright and I have a magnificent role and you will be two years old next week. Tell her to put on her best gown. Tell her we are going to a restaurant—yes, you too—where the three of us shall have a splendid meal and bring home the scraps for Fidèle."

Soon they were ready, Nandou in his best gray vest and mother and daughter in frocks it had taken Jeanne many hours to sew. "Wrap up the baby well," Nandou said. "It is cold outside."

Jeanne smiled. "Of course it is cold. This is January."

Nandou laughed as if the remark was brilliant, and held out his hands. "I shall carry her. Come along, Solange, leap into your horse's arms!"

"Dou!" Solange cried, and was running to him when there came a knock at the door. Jeanne looked a question, but Nandou shook his head. "I'm not expecting anyone either," she said. "Maybe it's someone from the theatre. Maybe it's about *The Dwarf Lord*!" She ran to the door.

The man standing there was tall and expensively dressed, in black with spotless white linen: a stranger, yet to Jeanne something familiar seemed to cling to him along with the cold air from the street. He looked at her for a moment, eyes narrowing as if against the light, then

took off his hat and asked, "Have I the honor of addressing Mademoiselle Jeanne Sorel?"

"You do, monsieur. And you are?"

He hesitated. "A messenger."

"You do not look like one."

He smiled, and in that instant she knew who he was and why he
looked familiar. "No," she said, without thinking.

"I beg your pardon?"

"Whatever you have come to say or do, I am not interested."

"You know who I am, then?"

She lifted her chin. "Yes."

Nandou had moved to stand beside her. "What is it, Jeanne?"

The stranger looked down at Nandou as if he were merely another
man, not a dwarf. Even so, Jeanne said, "Please leave. As you see, we
are going out."

"If you would allow me only a few minutes of your time . . . "

"Monsieur," Nandou said, "state your business or do as the lady asks."

"Very well. I have been asked to deliver this to Mademoiselle Sorel."
The man took a letter from the pocket of his coat.

"I won't accept it," Jeanne said fiercely. "It's from Louis. He sent a
man with a letter last week, and the week before too. I tore them both
up."

She heard Nandou suck in his breath, but he said nothing.

"I know," the man said. "That is why I have brought this letter
myself."

"Does Louis never have the courage to tell me to my face what he
wants?"

"If you had not torn up the other letters, you would have read his
request to speak to you."

"And would have denied it."

"Then clearly what is lacking is not Louis's courage but your consent." The man's eyes, neither challenging nor mocking, regarded Jeanne
with a directness that was unsettling because it reminded her of Nandou.
He held out the letter. "Please do me the courtesy of reading this."

"I do not see that I owe you any courtesy."

"Not even that of normal civility?"

"Jeanne," Nandou said, his voice as deceptively mild as a March wind,
"who is this gentleman?"

"My apologies," the man said. "I am Nicolas, the brother of Louis Vollard. Do I have the honor of addressing Monsieur . . . Nandou?"

"You do."

"Will you not use your influence with the lady and convince her to read this letter?"

The three of them looked at one another in silence. Solange moved forward and buried her face in Jeanne's skirt. Nandou raised a hand, as if to signal a piece of magic, but instead he took the letter. "Jeanne, we cannot continue this conversation unless we invite Monsieur Vollard to enter."

"These are your rooms," she said coolly. "Invite whomever you like."

The table held a toy rooster Nandou had made for Solange and the apples Jeanne had been peeling. He cleared them away, handed Solange her toy, and placed the letter in the center of the table. They all sat around it as formally if they wore the red robes of justice and the heavy envelope bearing Louis's slanting script were evidence. Jeanne took Solange on her lap.

"I assure you, mademoiselle," Vollard said, "that it is in your interest to read this letter."

"Nothing your brother has to say could interest me." Jeanne smoothed Solange's dress, glad she had labored over it instead of doing her usual haphazard needlework, and put her hands in the child's hair, dangling the soft, black curls over her fingers. Solange was her shield against Vollard, yet at the same time she wanted to defy him by showing him the child's perfection. How could one's child seem like both a shield and a weapon? And why should Nicholas Vollard make her feel she needed them?

"Jeanne, please," Nandou said. She saw the question in his eyes: Why had she not told him Louis had been sending her letters? The answer made no sense: Because she had not wanted him to look the way he was now looking. "If you want to know what is in the letter," she said, "read it."

His brows rose in his high forehead. "I don't know what you mean."

"If you want to know what is in the letter, you will have to read it to me. Yes, why not? Read it aloud."

His tongue ran around his lips. "I don't want to do that, Jeanne."

She shrugged. "Very well. I shall tear it up, as I did the others."

"Jeanne, please . . . "

"Monsieur," Vollard said, "if the lady will hear the letter no other way, I implore you, for her sake, to read it as she asks."

Nandou's eyes beseeched her but he said, "Very well." He broke the seal on the envelope, pulled out two sheets, and began, his voice flat and deliberate:

My dear Jeanne.

I imagine that you read these lines with conflicting thoughts and feelings. Let me assure you that I write them with the most genuine regard for you and the most devout hope that your life is a happy one. I regret your decision not to accept the money my mother offered you on my behalf, an offer made with the most sincere good wishes on her part as well as on mine.

Nandou's gaze swung to Jeanne, then back to the letter.

However, I cannot help but admire your strength. Nor can I help concern for the child, of whose existence I have been aware nearly since it began. It is my earnest desire that she have everything she needs. In short, I wish to provide for her.

Jeanne watched Nandou's hands gripping the edges of the letter, his knuckles as white as if he clutched for balance on the ledges of Notre-Dame.

I acknowledge that my offer is belated, but no less sincere for that. Its very lateness impels me not only to contrition but to the most generous recompense I can conceive. I am willing—and eager—to bring the child into my home, so that she may have every advantage I am capable of providing, because I—

"Stop!" Jeanne said. "No more. I do not wish to hear about the generosity of the Vollards."

Nandou put down the letter slowly.

In the silence, Solange banged her toy rooster on the table and said, "Dou! No stop. I like you to read. You read so nice." Nandou did not smile.

Vollard leaned toward Jeanne. "Hear the whole letter before making a decision. Louis knows you are a proud woman, who has been hurt by his actions in the past. He believes any attempt to explain or apologize would insult you both, so he wishes only to make an offer for you to consider." Vollard neither pleaded nor argued; his voice was calm and steady, yet there was power in it, like a plank laid over rushing water.

"Did Louis tell you to say those things?"

"Louis asked me to be his representative in these discussions, knowing you would not speak to him if he came himself, and that even if you did, certain feelings might interfere with the factual matters to be discussed."

"Tell Louis I no longer permit my feelings to compel my actions; he has cured me of such behavior. Tell him we no longer have any matters to discuss. Whatever words he uses, or delegates you to use, their meaning is that he wishes to take our—my child away from me. Tell him I will never allow it. Never."

Vollard folded his hands. They were large, the fingertips square and the nails trimmed to the same shape. Then he turned his gaze to Solange, who had begun squirming. "What is your name, child?"

She bounced up and down on Jeanne's lap and said her name three times.

Vollard smiled. "A beautiful name for a beautiful child. Where did you get that rooster you clutch so tightly?"

"Dou makes it. Dou!"

"I see. Do you know what it says—what sound our national symbol makes?"

She waved it in the air and reproduced the crow Nandou had taught her: *"Cocorico!"*

Vollard's smiled widened. His mouth and square jaw, Jeanne thought, were nothing like Louis's. His eyes were the gray of his mother's but held no condescension. "Permit me, mademoiselle," he said, "to tell you something that may soften your heart toward Louis. He and his wife have learned that she will not be able to bear children."

Jeanne covered Solange's hands with hers. "Therefore I am now to suffer?"

"I assure you Louis does not wish you to suffer."

"Whatever Louis's wishes may be, they no longer concern me."

"Mademoiselle, with all respect for the pleasant rooms you have here, for Solange's little frock and her plain wooden rooster, do you really believe you can give her the advantages that her—that Louis can? Do you think it fair to deprive her of the things that every mother would surely wish for her child?"

Jeanne held Solange tight against her, remembering the day when she had been summoned to the Vollard house and had first felt the baby's presence beneath her heart. "Your mother," she said, "was willing enough for Louis to be deprived of what he said he wanted—me."

She had aimed the words carefully, but they seemed to have reached Nandou instead, for he gave a small grunt. Vollard merely said, "I see."

"Did your brother not tell you to offer money to me? To try to buy my child, as he once told your mother to buy me?"

This time she knew she had reached Vollard; he winced, and hesitated before he answered. "There is no question of that. Louis simply wants to offer his daughter what he can."

"Indeed? Perhaps to raise her to be a servant in his house."

"He wishes to make her his daughter. To give her his name."

After the thudding in her ears subsided, Jeanne could feel Nandou shifting beside her, as if pressures were building beyond his control. She raised one hand to stop him. With the other, she held Solange tightly, and looking at Vollard over the child's head, she said, "There are many things my daughter might do, for I still believe in the ideas Louis used to say he espoused—that we are all free to become what we can. My daughter might be an actress, perhaps. An author, a singer, a shopgirl, even a grisette. A wealthy man's mistress or a courtesan in the fau- bourgs—neither of those would please me, but I could accept them. But there are three things she will never become, monsieur, not while I am alive to prevent her: a ragpicker, a whore in the streets, or a Vollard."

Her words had grown louder, battering against the steadiness of Nicolas's gray gaze, but he made no move until she finished. He shook his head slowly, almost sadly. "As a Vollard, mademoiselle, I naturally regret your answer. But there seems nothing left except to convey it to Louis and tell him of the conviction with which it was delivered." He stood, and lifted his hat, the sleek, black bourgeois top hat that Louis had once despised but probably now wore.

Solange pointed at him. "Look! The man goes up, up, up."

He smiled. "Adieu, Solange." Then he turned to Nandou. "Mon- sieur." Although he towered above him, Vollard bowed as if their eyes were level.

The door closed behind him. Jeanne was still staring at it when Nandou spoke. "Bravo," he said softly. "Bravo."

She turned, more pleased than by anything he had ever said to her, even about *The Dwarf Lord.* A smile burst from her heart; she could not only feel it on her own face, but see it reflect on his and then grow, as if she were the magician for once and he the helpless spectator.

Yet as they looked at each other, something that had not happened for a long time began to do so: His dwarfishness slithered into her mind. She saw not only the brilliant eyes but also the forehead cantilevering above them, not only the clever hands but also the arms that reined them in. . . . It was happening because of Nicolas Vollard. She did not know how or why, for he had not registered that dwarfishness by word or gesture, yet she knew he was making her see it anew. But she would triumph over him; she would keep smiling at Nandou and not think of Nicolas Vollard again. She would not let her smile die.

When the moment was over, and she had won, she said, "Do you think that he . . . that they . . . Do you think he will be back?"

"I think Vollard came prepared to offer you money but soon realized with whom he was dealing."

"I hate him," she said.

"Do you?" Nandou's voice was mirror-smooth.

"I hate all men named Vollard. I'm sorry I made you read Louis's letter."

"It does not matter, not after what you told the brother."

"I should have told you about the other letters from Louis, but I—"

"Don't explain, please. There is no need." Nandou ran his hands through his hair and cried, in a different voice, "Solange! You are beautiful, adorable, and wonderful; your mother is in her best dress, I am in my gray vest, and we were on our way to celebrate. Let us continue!"

The gaiety that had risen as easily as a balloon before Vollard's visit now had to be held up with their hands. When Nandou requested a table at the restaurant, the most expensive Jeanne had ever been to, the headwaiter looked down at him in amused exasperation before shrugging and leading them toward a far corner—so far that they seemed to parade endlessly behind the waiter's back. As they passed, the diners looked up and murmured. "This is Paris!" Jeanne wanted to cry to them. "One sees everything in the streets of Paris! Have you never before seen a woman, a child, and a dwarf come out to dinner?" But she walked in silence, chin as high as she could hold it, inches above the top of Nandou's head.

He ordered wine and roast chicken and new potatoes and conducted two conversations simultaneously, one with Solange about the lights and the food, the other with Jeanne about the play. He lifted his glass in many toasts—to Jeanne, to the first-act opening, to the second-act curtain, to Solange's birthday, to Solange's cleverness—until his eyes shone too hotly and his broad cheekbones turned pink. Jeanne chattered and answered and smiled and kept tucking a napkin back into Solange's collar, but her mind did not stay at the table. It wandered to the foolish innocent she had been when she met Louis, the girl who had thought being in love with a man, and with art, was not only ecstasy but safety . . . to Nicolas Vollard, who had answered her tirade with dignity instead of the disgust she had expected. . . . When she forced her attention back to the restaurant, the huge room seemed to be made of mirror-shards, hundreds, then thousands, all glittering from chandeliers and silver platters, from silk and satin gowns, from sleek napkins and tablecloths, wineglasses and diamonds, starched aprons and embroidered waistcoats, and above all from eyes, eyes at every table; shiny gazes darted in their direction like shoals of little fish or else swung to them openly, gapingly—staring at Nandou as if he were a sideshow, and at her in quite another way, especially the men, who looked as if they wished their gazes were hands. She shivered.

"What is wrong?" Nandou asked.

"I do not like to be stared at."

He smiled wryly.

She cursed her thoughtlessness. "I mean, I do not like men to look at me."

"Don't you?" he said. He flinched, as if something had been thrown at him and he could not step aside in time. She realized that she herself had thrown it; for he was looking at her, and he was a man. His eyes had been telling her so over dinner all night; no, since that long moment, after he came home with news of *The Dwarf Lord,* when he had had thanks on his lips but something else in his gaze. No, since before that, long before. She had known it without knowing, always. Without wanting to know.

He seemed about to speak. She clenched her hands in her lap.

Instead he took out a small cigar, something he rarely did, and lit it. Solange had been growing sleepy, but her nose wrinkled and her eyes widened.

"Give me one too," Jeanne said.

He frowned. "Why?"

"So they will find something worth seeing when they look at us."

Wordlessly he handed her a cigar and lit a match, his motions as graceful as if he were doing magic.

She pulled smoke into her throat and managed not to cough or choke. "To the man who will be *The Dwarf Lord*," she said, lifting her glass.

He raised his as well. "To the woman who makes it possible."

On Louis's easel was a head portrait of Edmée. She had volunteered so eagerly to pose for him that he could not have refused, and indeed, the hours while she sat had been pleasant ones; not once had he felt unstated emotions hanging in the air like threats of rain. He laid out fresh colors and began with determination, working on the highlights in her hair, but the thought of the two men he had hired kept halting his brush in midair. He had been clever to find them, Louis thought; in fact, the entire plan was clever.

By mid-morning his excitement and tension were so great that he had to find something else to distract him. Edmée was lunching with a cousin, so he decided to go to the firm's offices. His father, pleased, waved him into a discussion he and Nicolas were having about their recently established bank. Even if the House of Vollard was only one of several hundred private banks in Paris, they were determined to make it one of the more powerful. "Investments are the future," Nicolas said. "Not just state loans and short-term speculation, but capital for the development of an entire railway system!" Louis usually felt alien in that setting, but he was struck by something familiar: the intent look on Nicolas's face. It reminded him of what he himself felt when he was involved in painting. He had always assumed that within themselves he and Nicolas were as different from each other as storm from calm. How could the present conversation have induced the expression on Nico's face?

Their father wanted them to lunch with him, but Louis said, "Papa, many thanks, but I must discuss something with Nicolas." Olivier Vollard nodded as if that were what he had wanted all along, and the brothers went out alone. The morning frost had not melted, and the refuse on the streets offered their shoes a filthy, treacherous crust. When a snowflake sailed onto Louis's cheek, his tension reared again; now there was the weather to consider as well.

When they were seated in a busy restaurant, with talk to their left

of shipping coal by railroad instead of steamer and to their right, of the
new credit restrictions imposed by the minister of finance, Louis said,
"Nico, do you find pleasure in contemplating railroads and factories and
discount rates?"

"An odd question. I merely tend to the family's business in the best
way I can. It is true that I find a certain challenge in what I do, but
to say that I . . ." Nicolas stopped, cocked his head as if listening to some
surprising inner voice, and laughed. "You are right. I do take pleasure
in it. Sugar-beet factories in the provinces? Railroads covering the entire
country—why not? I will tell you the truth, Louis. Sometimes it seems
as if I am still a child playing with toys. But in these games, there are
no soldiers or muskets or death." He leaned over the table and touched
Louis's hand. "From the smear of yellow ocher on your thumb, I deduce
that you have begun painting again and so are taking more pleasure in
life these days. Good." He sat back. "But surely it is neither my pleasure
nor yours that you wanted to discuss?"

"No." Louis hesitated. "I must ask you again. Are you positive Jeanne
Sorel will never give up the child?"

"Have I not said so a dozen times? Napoléon would have given up
his crown more willingly." Nicolas raised an eyebrow. "Why should
that statement bring a look of approval to your face? Is it possible that,
despite everything, you admire her stubborness?"

"Perhaps." Louis laid his hands on the white cloth, thumbs tucked in.
"Thank you again for your answer, Nico, and for having gone to see
her."

"You have thanked me for that ten times in as many days—many
more times than I deserve, since I returned with no good news."

"Nonetheless, you went."

"How could I not go, when you said it was my refusal to see her
the first time that brought about the debacle with Maman. But that
sounds harsh. I do not mean it so. For your sake, I was more than willing
to see the woman."

"Before you went," Louis said, "you referred to her as 'the girl.'"

"Did I?" Nicolas looked into the distance for a moment. "I was
wrong. She is a woman."

Louis paused while the waiter put several dishes in front of them. "Do
you not think it unforgivable for a mother to keep a child from its
father?"

Nicolas made a steeple of his fingers and laid it against his lips. "I think the situation is complicated when the father has abandoned the mother."

"You are on her side. I knew it. When you came from seeing her, I saw she had started to bewitch you. Each time we discuss it, I am more certain."

"That I see her side, Louis, does not guarantee my taking it." Gently Nicolas added, "What point is there in continuing to talk about it? Jeanne Sorel's position is clear, and there seems nothing you can do to change it."

Louis pushed at the vegetables on his plate. "I do not like to think that my child might believe the dwarf to be its father."

"I can only repeat that she did not call him 'Papa.' " Nicolas leaned forward. "Louis, you must stop berating yourself over the past. You chose to leave Jeanne and the child, you chose not to keep her as your mistress, you chose to marry Edmée. Can you not—"

"Do not speak so easily of choices! What choice did I have that day, lying there bleeding, afraid I might die without seeing any of you again? I had to rejoin the life I had with you, I had to see you all. . . . And then I was so weak from fever, and Maman so strong—" He clenched his hands in his lap.

"I do not mean to upset you," Nicolas said. "I only want you to enjoy the life you now have. Edmée is beautiful, she loves you, you should take pleasure in what you have instead of looking back at what you relinquished."

"Did Jeanne convince you to come back and say that to me?"

"Certainly not. I say it because I do not want you to ruin your future."

"But I am not, Nico. You will see." Louis took out his watch. "Now I must leave you."

"Without finishing your lunch?" Nicolas said in surprise.

"Yes. I have an appointment for which I cannot be late."

He had hired a carriage, for he could not use his own. As instructed, the driver brought blankets, a copper warming pan, and a flask each of brandy and chocolate. The snowfall had grown thicker, the flakes like heavy lace. Even so, Louis feared he might be seen, and ordered the driver to take the narrow side streets, not the Champs-Elysées. The carriage rolled over frozen mud and garbage, rocking as if to shake his purpose from him, but he clung as tightly to it as to the side rail. At last the vehicle lurched into the Bois de Boulogne, now empty of the fine carriages that used it as a showplace in good weather. Louis directed the driver to a spot near the pond, under cover of some trees, where he had first met the two men and made arrangements with them.

They were to arrive by four if possible. By four-thirty, the snow was heavier, and Louis's tension had grown so much that the carriage seemed to be still moving. The horses swung their heads and snorted, giving off trails of steam. Each time they did so, the driver would shift on his seat and clear his throat, as if a question were stuck there, but he had been paid handsomely to keep his mouth shut, during as well as after the proceedings.

At ten minutes until five, the driver cleared his throat again and half turned in his seat. "We are staying," Louis said sharply, more to himself than to the man. The warming pan was barely tepid, and above the trees dusk was settling in icy gold streaks. Louis had forced himself to leave much of the brandy in the flask, but now he drank off half an inch. The horses snorted again and shifted their great bodies.

Suddenly the carriage door was pulled open. One of the men backed in awkwardly, then held out his arms. The other placed in them a large bundle, wrapped in a filthy blanket, and climbed in after it.

"You are late," Louis said sternly, reprimanding his own fear.

"We did the best we could," said the man who had come in first. He thrust the bundle into Louis's arms.

Louis pulled back a corner of the blanket and saw two frightened eyes. The reality of what he had done struck him for the first time. His throat seemed to fill with a huge bubble.

"Where's our money, then?" said the elder of the men. Obsequiousness covered the hostility of his manner like a scarf over a footpad's face.

Louis forced himself to stop staring at the bundle and hand over the bag of coins. "As agreed. And do not forget the rest of the agreement: No one must learn of your role in this endeavor. Never doubt that if you betray me, I will discover it, and you will suffer."

"Yes, my lord," the man said sullenly. He had opened the bag and was ready to pour the coins into his partner's outstretched hand. "Get out," Louis hissed. "The money is there, all of it. Out! At once!" The tone of his voice sent the two men stumbling from the carriage, to spill coins on the cold ground and mutter curses at each other. "Go!" Louis ordered the driver. "Now!"

Despite the jolting of the carriage, despite the whimpering that came from the filthy blanket, he managed to pull it off and replace it with one of the fine English wool plaids he had had the driver bring. He was able to open the flask of chocolate but spilled most of it on the wool. So he simply cradled the bundle, steadying it against the motion of the carriage, murmuring comfort to it, and to himself. The snow streaking the windows made the streets even more treacherous, but as they slid along, his certainty grew that he had done the right thing. The bubble in his throat became a tingling in his veins, as if his own flask had been filled with champagne, not brandy. His thoughts rushed along in such a blur that when the carriage finally stopped at his door, the stillness was the greatest jolt of the trip. He stepped out with his bundle into wet, swirling snow. The carriage swayed off.

Jeanne was waiting in the wings. When Nandou came hurtling through the vampire trap, she ran to him.

"What is it?" he said, as two stagehands helped steady him after the strenuous exit. "What is wrong?"

"It's Solange, Solange is gone, they came and took her—"

"What?" Nandou grabbed her shoulders. "Who took her? When?"

"I was working on the new scene for the second act and she was playing with Fidèle, I heard them come in and speak to her, but I couldn't believe it, they said they only wanted to see her, and I was so surprised, I stood there and started to ask how they were, and suddenly they grabbed her up and ran out, and when I chased after them into the street, I couldn't see them, and she was gone, Nandou, Solange is *gone!*"

The red dots of makeup in the corners of Nandou's eyes quivered like blood. "We will find her. I promise. The Vollards cannot have her. They will have to kill me first."

"No, not the Vollards. It was Pierre and Jacques. My brothers!"

A wagon of flats was advancing toward them. Nandou pushed Jeanne out of the way and said, "Tell me everything, exactly as it happened."

While the child was being fed, washed, put to bed, Louis waited in the library. He ordered coffee instead of brandy but did not touch it, for his exuberance still propelled him. He rubbed his hands before the fire as if their action were kindling it, then paced back and forth, barely conscious of his limp. He felt as if he were still in the carriage, cradling the bundle, whispering to it, "You will see, everything will be fine, your new mother will love you, she will be happy, and I will paint pictures of you, many pictures, everything will be splendid, you will see. . . . " It seemed to him that by reclaiming his child, he finally was freeing himself from the life he had known with Jeanne—cutting the last of his ties to it by taking his daughter from it. No longer would memories haunt him; no longer would Jeanne's voice wake him in the night to ask why he had behaved as he had; no longer would he need to drown those words in a glass, or bury them in the blind flesh of women who inhabited red-velvet rooms. Yet, even as he felt he was freeing himself from that other life, he also felt he was recapturing it. Once more he would know the passion and dedication for painting he had used to feel; he would regain the sense of himself that he had lost. Although the things he felt were contradictory and should have canceled each other, they ran parallel in his mind, like two sets of wheels supporting one carriage without ever touching.

When Edmée finally came in, he smiled brilliantly at her, kissed her on both cheeks and on her mouth, and seated her in a chair before the fire. She was wearing a pretty green gown, and, though her manner was as smoothly composed as her hair, her cheeks were flushed and her eyes very bright. "The child says her name is Solange," she said.

"Yes." Louis took the chair next to hers.

"Ah. You knew that." Edmée folded her hands. "She fell asleep after eating some supper. I left Marthe with her. She is beautiful, Louis, and friendly too, once I managed to calm her fears somewhat. But who is she? Why have you brought her here?"

"Because I cannot bear the thought of your facing a childless future."

"There is still some hope. The doctor has not ruled out all possibility."

Louis leaned over and touched her hands. "You have suffered two losses already, my dear. To help you forget their pain—to help us both—I have brought Solange to be ours."

"What do you mean? Is she an orphan? Or a foundling?"

"Neither of those. But she is ours to care for."

"Oh, Louis . . . " Tears rose in Edmée's eyes, then in her voice. "But I must know more. A child does not appear from nowhere, like a bird at one's window. Solange has a Maman, whom she asks for, and someone else whose name I cannot quite make out. Whoever they are, they have

obviously cared for her well. I cannot believe they have abandoned her."
Louis withdrew his hand but was silent. "Have they died, then, and
Solange has come into your care?"

"There has been no death."

"Louis, you are frightening me by not telling me who she is. You
make me fear there is some dreadful secret in her life or background."

"I intend only to please you, not to invite your censure."

"I did not say I was not pleased. If I could have a daughter, I might
indeed wish her to be like this girl. But I do not understand why you
went out to find us a child without telling me, or for that matter, why
you decided the child should be a daughter, not a son. There must be
something more, which you are not divulging."

Edmée's gaze, gentle but steady, drilled into Louis's exuberance. Why
could she not simply share it? Why did questions come more easily to
her mouth than smiles? "Can you not simply trust me and take Solange
to your heart?" he said.

"Can you not trust me and tell me in whose heart she has lived until
now?"

A log popped loudly behind the firescreen. Edmée started, but her
eyes did not leave Louis's. He turned away and, without realizing, began
to knead the old wound in his thigh. Speaking more to the fire that cast
patterns on his cheek than to his wife, he said, "Solange is mine."

"What do you mean?"

"She is my daughter."

Edmée gasped, but by the time Louis lifted his head to look at her,
the sound had been suppressed and one hand covered her throat, as if
forbidding its return. "Who is her mother?" she asked.

"Someone who worked in the theatre."

"Has she given Solange into your care, then?"

"Solange is my daughter. I have reclaimed her, so she may have the
advantages her mother could never provide." Louis saw his wife's lips
begin to tremble and her fingertips lift to press them into stillness.
"Edmée, I know I have not been the best husband to you. But consider
that I have been tortured by not acknowledging my child and bringing
her to share my life. I told myself I would forget her because I would
have other children, with you. That is apparently not to be. But if you
can accept Solange, and love her, as I beg you to do, if you allow her
to fill the empty place in our lives . . ."

After a silence, Edmée said, "Does the wound cause you pain?"

"I could lie," Louis said slowly, "and tell you I felt very little, even at the time. But I wish to be truthful. I did love the woman."

"And now?"

"I have not seen her for two and a half years."

"I see." Edmée lowered her hands to her lap. "I could lie, too, but I shall not. I shall confess that my question was directed to the wound in your thigh, not to the one in your past."

Louis stared at her in dismay, then down at the fingers still digging into the cloth of his trousers.

"Two and a half years ago," Edmée said flatly, "you were asking for my hand. Was the woman your mistress at the time?"

"She was not. I swear it."

"But three years ago, and three and a half? During all the time you were dancing with me, and telling me I was beautiful, and coming to dinners and staring at me as if you—"

"Edmée, please!"

She pressed her fingers against her mouth again, but the words pushed their way through, and her hands fell to her lap, twisting around each other. "I do not think you can know much I loved you, Louis. You have always made me afraid to tell you. I loved you as if you were a god, because I thought you saw a treasure in me that I barely knew existed. I thought you could save me from myself, from my empty *pâte-feuilletée* life, but all the time I was loving and adoring you, you loved someone else. Now you bring me her child and ask me to love it for your sake."

"For both our sakes. And Solange is *my* child too, Edmée." Louis covered her hands with his own. "You are indeed beautiful. If you do not believe I think so, then the crime is mine for not telling you often enough. Never say I do not love you—only that I have not loved you as much as your beauty and goodness deserve. I have had nothing to do with the child's mother since before you and I married. But part of my heart has been with the child, I confess. If the three of us can now be together, you and she and I . . . " His eyes flashed in the firelight, dark curls hung on his pale forehead, and he spoke with a passion born of his need to silence her questions and make her believe—to ensure his vision of the past and the future by convincing her to accept it. "Help me keep the child, Edmée. Please. It will not be easy. I learned recently that it is possible to acknowledge a child without having the mother know, and I have done so. But when the notary drew up the necessary

documents, he discovered the mother had made her own formal acknowledgment soon after the child was born. Her declaration has prior-
ity over mine. She could not have known such details of the law. She
must have been acting on the advice of that—of someone she knows.
But now Solange is in my possession. The courts will honor my claim,
I know they will. They must! Help me, Edmée, if you love me, please
help me. We must let no one know that Solange is with us, not even
my mother or yours, until the court has ruled and Solange is ours.
Nothing matters about the past, Edmée, I swear it to you. Only the
future matters." Louis sank to his knees and buried his face in Edmée's
lap. "Do not punish the child for my sins. Take her into your heart. Help
me keep her. I beg you most desperately."

Edmée looked down at the long fingers crushing the fabric of her
dress. Her hand hovered over the curly black hair, then touched it.

The Dwarf Lord was forgotten. So were hunger and thirst, and the cold,
and the filthy slush choking the rat-tail passageways along which they
walked. Nothing mattered but the ache for Solange, and the fear.

Jeanne had demanded to come, despite Nandou's insistence that he
could do better without her. But when she actually stood in front of
the door, the door that had not changed in six years, she did not think
she could go in. Then she felt Solange's cheek against her own, as real
as if the baby were in her arms. She lifted her chin and opened the door.

Inside, her gaze raked the bare walls, the sacks thrown against them,
the rag-covered piles of straw, the table, the sagging bed, the small
hearth where a pot simmered but gave off no aroma. Over that hearth
huddled the room's only occupant, who turned and squinted. "Who is
it?" The words whistled through bad teeth. "Who is there?"

"It's Jeanne."

"Jeanne? What Jeanne?" The woman put a thin hand to her face.
"Jeanne is gone. Many years ago."

"She is here now."

Blinking, the woman came closer. Her back was as round as if a large
stone grew under her skin, her face as gray as cinders. Perhaps it always
had been. She stank of mold and mildew and things rotting in the heaps.
Had they all smelled like that? Jeanne wondered. For a moment, in a
little square cut out of time and pasted on the wall, she saw herself
working in the heaps and Nandou smiling at her, saying, *Come to live*

with me. She glanced over at him, standing by the door with his arms folded across his chest and his face hard with the need for Solange. "Is it you, then?" the woman said.

The present returned in a gulp of anxiety. "Yes, it is me." Although it felt like a lie, Jeanne forced herself to add, "Maman."

Her mother's arms rose partway, in a memory of embrace, but fell back to her sides. "Jeanne," she said. "You went off with a damn dwarf. He put a spell on you. But you got away, did you?"

"He's with me, right there by the door."

Her mother squinted and acknowledged Nandou's presence by a lift of her shoulders. She turned back to Jeanne. "Are you rich?" she asked incuriously.

"No." Jeanne realized she had no idea of her mother's age—forty-five? fifty? sixty? In her face the evidence of years had blended into a cracked, unreadable grayness. "How have you been, Maman? You look . . . Are you all right?"

"I had the cholera. It took Jacques, you know."

"No, I didn't. I'm . . . I am sorry."

"Yes, Jacques is gone. And you, too." She might have been calling off street names, not the loss of her children.

"Where are the others?" Jeanne said. "I must talk to them."

"Papa's out selling the haul. Pierre and Bertrand . . . " Her mother frowned. "Didn't come home last night. Or the night before."

"Did Pierre and Bertrand tell you where they were going?"

"Never tell me what they do."

"Did they have any money?"

"Papa keeps the money. You know that."

"Could they have left Paris?"

"Left Paris?" Her mother seemed unable to comprehend the idea.

"The last time you saw them, was there a child . . . Did they say anything about a child?"

"What child? Pierre's got no wife, nor Bertrand. We need extra hands, but they don't find a wife. Neither one."

"They've taken my child," Jeanne said. "Pierre and Bertrand found where I live. They came and stole my Solange, my lovely—" Pain and rage rose into her throat like a fist stopping her air. She gulped and cried, "They stole my daughter, Maman!" and put her hands on her mother's arms, searching her face for some sign of recognition and concern. She saw only a blinking of eyes and a wetting of lips. A dozen feelings were churning within her, but she could detect none in her mother. Yet they must be there. "When Solange was born," she said, "I thought of you. I wanted you there. She's your granddaughter, Maman. When I find her, I shall bring her to you. I want you to see how wonderful she is, how beautiful . . ."

"Ain't she a dwarf, then?"

Jeanne stared. "What if she were? What would it matter? She's my *daughter.*"

From his post at the door, Nandou said, "Let us go, Jeanne. She doesn't understand."

"How can she not? Maman, do you remember what you felt when I went away? When you lost *your* daughter? You cried out as I walked away—I heard you! You must have felt something! Tell me you did!"

Her mother's face knotted for a moment. "Long time ago. Long time. Papa and the boys were mad as pissing hell. It was hard. Yes."

"Then please, Maman, in memory of what you felt then, please tell me where Pierre and Bertrand have gone."

Her mother pulled out of her grip. "Can't tell you. Don't know." She started to move away.

Jeanne clutched her sleeve and said, "Maman, did you love me?" She had come prepared to say or do anything to find Solange, to lie or threaten or grovel, but that question had come without calculation or purpose. She had not even known she wanted to ask it.

"Oh yes," her mother said. But she kept shuffling back to the hearth.

"I see," Jeanne said, although she did not. "When Pierre and Bertrand return, tell them I was here. Tell them I shall not rest until they return my daughter to me."

Her mother nodded, bent to the odorless pot, and reached for a spoon, her hand like the claw of a bird. Suddenly Jeanne felt it was her own hand clutching the metal like a perch, her own guts beseeching the pot for aroma, sustenance, life. "Maman," she cried, "come with me now, come with us while we find Solange, and live with us for the rest of your days. It's not too late. You can become anything you like, if you try! Look what I have become! I will help you, Maman. Will you come? Will you?"

Her mother turned to look, then shook her head slowly, not quite regretfully.

Nandou said, "Come, Jeanne. It is best to leave."

She knew he was right.

If only there had been a Nandou for her mother, she thought, as they made their way through the festering alleys. But her mother wouldn't have recognized him. She would have seen only a dwarf.

Chapter Nine

Outside the Taxgatherers' Wall, roadside inns clustered like piglets at their mother's teats. They paid no toll on wine, so they could serve it cheaper than places inside the city limits. As a result, they were crowded every night with people from the working-class areas that surrounded bourgeois Paris, and loud with the sounds of darts, bowling, and singing.

Nandou straightened his cap, clutched his stick, and pushed his way into his eighth inn of the night in his search for Jeanne's brothers.

He and Jeanne had reasoned that they had kidnapped Solange in order to sell her, and since they had not taken her to their hovel, they probably had sold her already. Therefore, they would have money, although Jeanne didn't know where they would go to spend it. "I never saw them with anything more than a few sous," she had said when they stopped at a corner outside the ragpickers' quarters and stood beneath an oil lamp swinging in the wind. Its light had moved capriciously over Jeanne's face, consigning her eyes to shadow one moment and illuminating them the next, so that her pain and fear leaped at Nandou, disappeared, leaped again. With all the confidence he could muster, he had said, "Your brothers will have gone after whores and wine. I will take you home and then search for them." "I am going with you!" she cried, but he had argued that her presence would only complicate his task and could even prevent its success. Besides, what if the brothers had not been able to sell Solange after all and decided to demand money from Jeanne for her return? What if they went to the apartment and Jeanne was not there? "Very well," she had said reluctantly. Then, lifting her chin in the defiance he had first seen on the day he brought her into his life, "But I will go home alone. I know the streets of Paris as well as you. Do not waste a moment. Start looking for them at once!" He had understood; she needed to do something on her own, if only to find her way home, so despite his fear for her he had agreed. Long after she walked out of the light's fitful embrace, his vision held the way she had straightened the dispirited sag of her shoulders.

He had searched most of that night without success, gone home for a brief sleep that never came and food he did not taste, and set out again to comb the streets farther north and west. At a shop called "Two Maggots," one of the new kind that sold an entire range of goods, he learned that two men matching the brothers' description had come in the previous day to buy trousers and coats, but that information was his sole achievement. When night came, he had headed through one of the gates in the Taxgatherers' Wall, reasoning that the brothers might seek drink cheaper than it was in Paris.

"Hey, it's a dwarf!" someone cried as he entered the crowded inn, and others ogled him. A man with a small cap and huge hands boomed, "Aren't you out pretty late, little fellow?" and made as if to pet him, but Nandou raised his stick and bared his teeth. The man pulled back, cursing and jeering, inciting others to do the same. Nandou set his teeth, lofted his stick, and waded into the jeers to make a full circle of the place. The brothers were not there.

He left and pressed on, thinking that the whores to whom he had spoken earlier had been more civil than the inn crowds. The whores had flicked their eyes indifferently over his stature—except for one, no more than thirteen, he would wager, who had lifted her ragged skirt when she saw him approach and said, without malice, "Say, is your prick a dwarf, too?" Angry retorts had sprung to his mind, but how could he be angry with a scrawny, gray-faced child who had managed to retain a flicker of curiosity and life? "No, it is not," he had said, almost gently. Like her sisters, she did not recall seeing or servicing anyone resembling the two Sorel men. "But I never look at their faces," she said.

In the next inn a singing club was meeting in the rear, voices enthusiastic though not all inhabiting the same key. A waiter frowned at Nandou and a woman pointed a fat, drunken finger, but others let him pass without comment. He scanned the tables of singers and was turning away when something at the edge of the room caught his eye: a coat lying under a table. He squeezed by some singers and went closer. The coat was new. On the table above it were three empty bottles and two pairs of arms, on which lay two heads. Nandou lifted one by its hair and looked into Pierre Sorel's face. It did not look back; the eyes rolled upward like stones and the mouth hung like an empty bucket.

Nandou lifted the other head. Bertrand Sorel was also drunk but retained a degree of sentience; he groaned and his eyes fluttered once.

Nandou's hands tingled with desire to slam the heads together like cymbals. But he lowered them and made himself think. If he waited until the place was empty, and if he had the innkeeper's help . . . He went to find the man, offered him some coins, ordered a large glass of beer, and returned to sit near the brothers and bide his time.

Could the two sodden creatures really be connected to Jeanne? If they shared the same clay, what spark had animated hers while never reaching theirs—or her mother's? The wretched woman had barely seemed alive—drained of caring, as a vampire's victim was of blood. It had wrenched his heart to see how bewildered Jeanne was, how unable to accept what she saw and heard. Standing against the wall of the hovel, watching, he had thought of his own mother, livelier than Jeanne's, yes, by a hundred times, but drowning that liveliness in wine, as if needing to hear its dying sizzle again and again. No more than Jeanne's could his mother have been the source of his own spark—that exhilarating sense of uniqueness, which his dwarfishness could mock and stifle but never extinguish. One night he had thought to tell Jeanne of the feeling: "Do you ever look at the stars and know that only you can see their true fire?" But he hadn't said it. To let her see one of his deepest feelings might open the Pandora's box of more dangerous ones. Yet he was certain she too knew the exultation of uniqueness. It was the passion at the heart of their passionless union. Solange would know it, too—as her joint heritage from the two of them, who were joined in no other way. Solange was truly his child, although he never dared utter the thought aloud. He stared at the backs of the brothers' heads, thick with unkempt hair, and whispered, "Where have you taken my daughter?"

His eyes widened with a fear he hadn't permitted himself to know until that moment: If Solange were gone permanently, would Jeanne leave too?

When the singing club finally disbanded and began making its way out into the night, the innkeeper did what Nandou had paid him to do: He brought a pitcher of water, and he lugged the dead weight of Pierre Sorel several yards away. Nandou took two lengths of cord from his pocket and tied Bertrand's hands behind his back. He doused the man with water until he sputtered into awareness. Then, gripping the man's hair from the back and holding the walking stick under his throat, Nandou said into his ear, "Bertrand Sorel, you are guilty of a foul crime—stealing a child from its parents. For this evil, you will suffer the agonies of hell through eternity." The man struggled to turn his head, but Nandou's grip prevented him. "Nothing can save you but your confession. Tell me where the child has gone, while there is hope."

"Who are you?" the man croaked. "Where is Pierre?"

"I am Justice. Your brother is answering for his part in the crime, as you must also do. Tell me where you took the girl!" Nandou increased the pressure of the walking stick.

Bertrand cursed, thrashed his legs, sobbed, and finally said, "We took her to the man."

"What man? His name, damn you, his name!"

"Don't know." The pressure increased again. "Don't know!" More pressure. Sobs. "He wouldn't say his name. But he was rich. Must have been a duke."

"Fool! What duke would deal with you?" Thrashing of legs. "How did you find him?"

Gasps. Choking sounds. "He sent for us."

"How?"

"Some brat come looking for the Sorel boys one day, took us to meet him."

"Came to where you live, you mean?"

"Yes."

"What did this rich man tell you he wanted?"

"His daughter. Said our sister had her and he'd pay us to get her back."

"I don't believe you!" For a moment Nandou almost lost his grip on the stick. "You are certain he spoke of your sister?"

Gasping and thrashing. "Yes. Told us where she lived and all. Said—"

"And you took the child to him?"

Bertrand nodded and whimpered. Nandou released the walking stick, but instantly took out a scarf and tied it around the man's eyes. "Someone will untie you soon," he said. "Until then, sit and smell your rottenness."

He started to leave, determined to control himself, but his stick cracked on a table. Vollard again, curse his soul! First the mother, then the daughter! It wasn't enough that he snatched Jeanne from Nandou's life as if he had droit du seigneur, and returned her with haunted eyes. It wasn't enough that, when years had passed and she finally was smiling again, he had sent his brother to plead for him—and her eyes had stayed on the damned brother too long . . . too long! as if they could not help themselves. And when the smell of that visit had barely been scrubbed from the rooms, Vollard had hired two vermin to steal Solange. A thousand curses on his soul! The stick cracked across a chair.

"Ho!" cried the innkeeper, approaching. "Spare my furniture!"

Nandou grunted. "I have finished my work. Here are twenty francs more, to untie my friend in ten minutes and, if he has the wit to ask you, to say that the one who tied him up was six feet tall."

The innkeeper grinned and saluted.

"Louis!" Jeanne cried. "Louis got them to take her?"

"Yes." Nandou sank into a chair, cradled a mug of coffee, and watched as she clasped her hands and looked into space.

"I knew it. I knew it!" she said in a voice that might better have suited a moment of triumph. She began pacing around the table, the muscles near her eyes knitting and clenching.

Abruptly she stopped and came to Nandou. "I fear he will try to acknowledge her legally and apply to the courts for custody."

"It is possible," Nandou said.

"Is it possible the judges would give it to him?"

"Do you think judges dispense nothing but justice?"

"But the declaration I made . . . Thank God you had me do it, Nandou."

"Let us direct our thanks to Alexandre Dumas."

She did not smile. "Louis's position is stronger now that he actually has her." She put her head in her hands, then lifted it suddenly. "I shall appeal to Nicolas Vollard."

"No!" The word cracked out before Nandou could stop it. More quietly he added, "Surely that would be a mistake."

"He seemed a humane man, and he must have some influence over Louis."

"Then why did he not prevent the kidnapping?"

"Perhaps he does not know of it. Perhaps I should tell him."

Carefully Nandou said, "After all your experience with that family, how can you entertain the thought that any of its members might have your interest at heart?—particularly the brother of the kidnapper. Blood is a powerful tie."

"It did not tie me to my brothers."

"That is true, but . . . Jeanne, I shall get Solange back. I promise."

"How?"

"I have a plan," he said, although he had none, and no hope of one.

She looked at him, and suddenly her face seemed to break into pieces, like porcelain struck with a fist. She fell into the chair beside his, weeping and calling Solange's name.

He raised a hand above her head and finally let it touch her hair.

The chimney sweepers arrived on a crisp, sunny morning when icicles hung from the roofs in rows of dripping glass. The footman, expecting the sweep who always came, shrugged on hearing he was ill and led the two newcomers to the library, where the draft had been very bad for several days. They put down a large basket and removed ropes, brushes, shovels, burlap bags, and soot cloths. "My guess," said the older man to his helper, a boy, "is we'll need you on the roof." The footman uttered dire cautions about soot on the carpets and left them to their task. They moved the fan-shaped firescreen, struck a light to check the draft, and worked in silence. Through the doors came household noises: maids moving, silver clinking, the arrival of the post and the butcher. After much scraping, poking, and brushing, which covered them with filth, the boy looked at the heavy clock on the mantel. "Time for the roof, Pa," he said.

"Watch the ice." The father shoveled ashes and caked creosote into a burlap bag.

The boy wiped his shoes on the soot cloth and pulled his cap even lower on his forehead. He hefted a coil of rope with a bag of sand attached, went to the kitchens, and asked the best way to the roof. One of the maids led him up the inner staircase, its walls hung with watercolors and each landing furnished with a table holding a metal pot of flowers. "Some house," said the boy. "Who lives here?" "Monsieur is associated with the House of Vollard, and Madame is the daughter of Baron Tissot." The boy whistled approvingly. The maid told him to stop walking so slowly.

Once on the roof, by means of an upstairs window and some very cautious climbing, he uncoiled the rope and let it down the chimney. The sandbag at its end struck and dislodged an obstacle and sent it all the way to the hearth, where the older man picked it up. The boy let the rope slide down the chimney and wormed back in through the window. The maid had not waited, for he had said he would be on the roof at least half an hour. Adjusting his cap, he went down the stairs and stopped on the second floor. There were four doors. He opened one slowly: the mistress' boudoir. Next was a bedroom where a maid was working; he barely shut the door before she turned to look. The third door opened on another bedroom, empty; the fourth, on a startled face. A nursemaid in a high starched cap said in a voice to match, "Who are you? What are you doing here?"

"Oh, mamselle," he whined, "please help me. I'm the chimney cleaner's boy. It's my first time out with Pa. I was on the roof and I lost my way back down."

"Didn't you come down the stairs? Go out this door at once, turn left, and you will—What are you doing? You must leave this room, not come farther in!"

"You're such a pretty lady," the boy said softly, though she was as plain as a plate. "I never seen a lady like you."

"I don't know what you mean." The nursemaid smiled uncertainly. "You are a strange-looking boy. Your legs don't seem—"

"They're bent. From being up the chimneys all the time. And Pa beats me on the backs of them."

"Oh dear," the nursemaid said faintly. "How can people . . . "

The boy pulled a scarf from his pocket and waved it in a slow, elegant pattern. Before the nursemaid knew what was happening, he pushed her into a chair and tied her hands behind her with the scarf. She started to scream, but he whipped out another scarf and tied it over her mouth.

He heard a whimper of distress, spun around, saw a child on a miniature chair at a tiny table. He ran to her.

She was frightened; his clothes were strange and his face a mask of soot. She began to sob. The nursemaid twisted and thumped the floor with her feet. "Please, my darling child," he whispered, but she could not hear him through her howls, which grew louder when he tried to take her arms.

He pulled something from inside his filthy blouse. The child hiccuped, grew quiet, and stared—at a wooden rooster whose comb had been knocked off during the climb on the roof. He put it in her hand. "Dou?" she said hesitantly.

He nodded. "Quiet, my princess," he whispered. Loudly, so the nursemaid could hear, he said, in his boy's voice, "A scarf over your mouth too, little brat." But instead of gagging her, he whispered, "We are going home to Maman and Fidèle. But we must play a game. Will you be good and do just as I tell you? You must not speak or make a sound until we get home, not a sound. I will hold you tightly, with your face in my neck like this, my filthy neck, but that is part of the game. Here we go, home to Maman." Clasping her in both arms, twisting as if he were struggling to keep her quiet, walking sideways so the nursemaid would see little other than his back, he got to the door, opened it, and peered into an empty hall.

Once out, he spoke softly in his normal adult voice. "Now we must go downstairs and find a special carriage to take my princess home."

"Dou!" she said in a little peal of happiness. "I don't know why they—"

"Sssh, not a sound, remember? Be like Fidèle, who moves so quietly. Here we go. . . ." He moved down the stairs, stopping on each to check for noise. On the first floor, the butler was talking to someone, but they both went toward the kitchen. Nandou tapped on the library door, which was opened at once by his "father," a fellow stagehand. "Thank God," said the man. He reached into their basket, which was part of the stage trick of the disappearing Turkish slave, and opened a hidden compartment at its bottom. "Here is your magic carriage," Nandou told Solange. "You must lie in it without a sound until we are well out in the street." She whimpered and said, "Don't like it, Dou." The stagehand rolled his eyes and implored God's intercession, but Nandou cajoled until finally she curled up in the space, clutching her rooster. Hurriedly the two men piled their tools on top of the compartment. They could not fit in the object Nandou had knocked down the chimney: the obstructing ball of twigs, cloth, and glue that had forced the household to send for the sweeps. He had made it and then placed it in the chimney three nights before, walking over neighboring rooftops in the dark and on the ice to do so. "We'll have to leave it here," the stagehand said. Nandou nodded and laid it on the hearth. "Let's go, my friend," he said.

Carrying the basket between them, they stepped out into the hall and saw the lady of the house at the front door; she had just cleaned her shoes after coming in. From the other direction, blocking the path to the kitchen, a maid advanced to meet her.

"I see the sweeps are here," said the mistress. "Did they fix the problem?"

"I don't know, madame," the maid said. "I think they've just finished."

Edmée moved toward them and peered through the open library door. "They haven't cleaned up properly. What's that filthy thing on the hearth?"

"I'll get the footman to deal with them, shall I, madame?"

"No, I shall handle it." Edmée gave the maid the slender fur boa she wore over her pelisse and untied her bonnet. "Take these along, please. Now," she said to Nandou and his friend, "put down your basket and fetch that . . . that object you've left behind. Well? Why do you stare at each other? Do you not understand me?"

The stagehand hesitated. "Yes, madame."

"I'll get it, Papa," said Nandou in his boy-voice. The two of them set down the basket carefully, and he went to the hearth. Edmée watched, frowning. "What on earth is it?" she said as he brought out the filthy ball.

"Don't know," he said. "It come down the chimney."

"It seems odd. How could such a thing get into a chimney?"

Nandou shrugged and placed it on top of the basket, which the two of them lifted again. From within it came a whimper.

The three adults froze.

"Dou? Maman!"

"Set that basket down!" Edmée cried. "At once!"

The stagehand looked at Nandou, who cast a longing glance at the front door, then gritted his teeth and said, in his adult voice, "Permit us to do so inside the library, madame."

Edmée gaped. The two men moved into the library. "Release the child at once," she said, following them. "At once!" She started toward the bell cord. "How dare you try to take the child? When her father learns of this, he will see that you are punished. He will be—"

"I come from her mother," Nandou said.

Edmée turned slowly to him.

He opened the basket, pulled out the tools and cloths, unlocked the compartment, and lifted out Solange. One cheek was smeared with soot, and her eyes were red with confusion and distress.

"Solange, dear child, are you all right?" Edmée said, starting toward her.

"Dou," she whimpered, clinging to him.

"She is fine," Nandou said, smoothing her hair. "Sweetheart, do not worry. Your carriage has broken a wheel, so we cannot go home as quickly as we would like." To his stagehand colleague, he said, "Many thanks for your help, my friend, but I do not think you should become any more involved in this affair. Be off." The man looked uncertainly at Edmée. "I assure you," Nandou said, "the matter is now between madame and me. Is that not so, madame?"

"I believe it is," Edmée said.

The man shrugged, muttered that he would see Nandou later, and left.

"But you are not a child," Edmée exclaimed. "You are a dwarf."

Nandou bowed. "And you are the wife of Louis Vollard. Did he not tell you about me?"

"No."

"Perhaps there are other things he did not tell you."

"Perhaps there are." Edmée slipped the fur-lined pelisse from her shoulders and laid it over a chair. "If Solange's mother has sent you for her child, why did she allow Louis to take her in the first place?"

"She did not allow it, madame."

Edmée's hand went to her throat.

"Your husband made several requests for the child, which she refused. He then sent two men to kidnap her. I was thus forced to try to kidnap her back. As you see, I have nearly succeeded."

Edmée turned away. When she looked back, a red circle stood out on each cheek as if pasted there. "Please sit down."

"Madame, my clothes are filthy."

"It does not matter! Sit, or I shall ring for the butler after all!" More gently she said, "Solange, are you hungry? Shall I send for one of cook's apple tartlets?" Solange's head swung in a slow negative. "Very well. Will you come and sit by me?" Solange regarded her gravely but did not move. Edmée moistened her lips. "Monsieur," she said, "do you know Solange's mother well?"

"Maman!" Solange cried.

"Yes, my little cabbage, I hope you shall see her soon. Madame, I know her very well. I have known her since she was thirteen."

"Did you know of her . . . Were you aware that she and my husband had . . . "

"I was witness to their affair, madame."

Edmée looked down at her folded hands. "I have thought of her constantly since the day I learned of her existence. Yet I do not know her name or what she looks like."

Nandou glanced at the door, as if he might try to run to it. But he said, "Jeanne is very beautiful, madame. As monsieur your husband is handsome."

"Did she love him?"

"Passionately. Helplessly. Totally."

"Ah. And he loved her in kind?"

"I never spoke to him about her."

"You must have had an opinion."

Nandou hesitated. "It would be colored, madame, by my failure to understand how any man could not help but love her."

"I see," Edmée said slowly. "Does she know how much you love her?"

"I cannot tell her."

"Sometimes one cannot. That is true."

They looked at each other over Solange's head. Without intending to, they were entering into a complicity of revelation. Nandou had meant only to manipulate Vollard's wife, she had wanted only to get information from him, but instead each was tasting the relief of saying things felt so deeply that no one but a stranger could be trusted to hear them.

"Do you know why they parted?" Edmée said.

"Monsieur Vollard left Jeanne, after being wounded during the Three Glorious Days."

"But why, if he loved her?"

"Is it not true that men seldom marry the women they love?"

"Or love the ones they marry." Edmée sighed.

"Madame, I must call to your attention that time is passing, and—"

"When Louis left Jeanne, did he know there would be a child?"

"He knew. He left anyway. I have thought it was *because* he knew."

"But he at least provided for the child?"

"No. I have done so." Edmée made a sound like an abandoned kitten, then pressed her fingertips to her mouth. Nandou said, "In his name, madame your mother-in-law offered money to Jeanne. She refused it. She is very proud. And desperate to have the child back. As am I. Madame, please, if you would—"

"My husband's daughter is important to him, terribly important. That is why I agreed to . . . I cannot give him a child."

"I am sorry, madame."

Softly, almost to herself, Edmée said, "Nothing was as I thought. From the first waltz to the wedding to the . . . All pretense. I shall not forgive him for it. I shall see that he—" She shook her head, as if emerging from a trance. "He may be home soon. If he finds you here . . . "

"We are at your mercy, madame, Solange and I. And her mother."

Edmée put her hands to her temples and closed her eyes. For a long moment she stood, fingers pressing deep into her skin, as if some answer lay near the bones. Then, firmly, she said, "Leave at once."

"Both of us?"

Edmée opened her eyes. "Yes. As you had planned. Can you carry the basket yourself?"

"Not without leaving most of its contents."

"Leave everything, then."

Nandou did not move. "What will you tell your husband, madame? If you say that a dwarf took his child, he will know who it was, and where to find me."

"I shall say that a chimney sweep and his boy took her. Hurry, please! Before I change my mind! I shall go upstairs and in five minutes pretend to discover that Solange is missing and send at once for my husband. That is all the time I can give you. Hurry! No, wait a moment," she said as Nandou started to put Solange back into the basket. She ran to the child, put her hands around her face, and kissed her. "Remember that I was fond of you," she said.

Just as Nandou reached the front door, sounds of a hubbub came floating down the staircase: The nursemaid had finally been discovered. "Wait . . . " Edmée said, but Nandou heaved the basket to his shoulder and ran down the front steps, lurching on his short legs toward the corner.

They made two decisions, one terrible, one merely difficult.

First Jeanne had to embrace Solange until they were both breathless; then she had to hear the story of the escape many times, even though she had helped to plan it. "So, Louis had not told the truth to his wife," she said. "What else could one expect of him? It serves him right that you tricked the woman into letting you go." Nandou said that he hadn't exactly tricked her, it had been her decision, but Jeanne waved her hand impatiently. "I am glad you made Louis's wife act against him. That is even better than what we planned. How clever you are, Nandou. But Louis can be clever, too. He will find another way to take Solange. Don't we have to . . . hide her? Shouldn't we send her away?"

They tried to convince themselves it was not necessary. Nandou argued that Edmée Vollard seemed like a woman who would keep Louis from further abductions, but Jeanne gave a short, disbelieving laugh. Jeanne spoke again of appealing to Nicolas Vollard to restrain his brother, but Nandou scowled and asked why she now thought any Vollard could be trusted. In the end they agreed they had to send Solange away, at least until they could be sure of Louis's intentions. An actor friend of Nandou's had a married sister who lived about ten miles northeast of the city; he was certain she would take Solange to live with her. They decided to leave immediately, though it was close to Mardi Gras, on the grounds that in the chaos of carnival it would be easier to leave the city unobserved.

They made arrangements: Jeanne sewed a coat for Solange and mended the clothes she had been neglecting. Although Nandou had already been absent from the theatre a good deal, he requested more time, explaining that the final version of *The Dwarf Lord* could not be delivered yet, due to the author's illness. Despite the heavy carnival demand for them, he managed to rent a cart and horse.

The day of the journey was bright and crisp. As they headed uphill from the Boulevard of Crime and through the city gates, Solange bounced and babbled about the horse, the basket of food and wine, the pole-full of Mardi Gras masks stuck in the ground in the courtyard of an inn, the sight of Fidèle burrowed into the straw in the back of the cart. After an hour, Jeanne climbed up to sit beside Nandou and said, "If she continues to be known in the country as Solange Sorel, it will be that much easier for Louis to find her again."

His eyes narrowed. "Yes. It would be wiser to call her something else."

They sighed and made their second decision.

After half a mile Jeanne said, "How can I call her anything but Solange?" She wiped her eyes and glanced at Nandou. In profile, his strong, straight nose and high, slanting forehead were drawn against a canvas of brilliant blue sky. His cap lay beside him, and his black hair blew in the breeze like snakes. Wonderingly she said, "Is Nandou your real name? I have never asked you."

"That is true." Half his mouth smiled.

"I ask you now."

He slapped the reins, and some chain of memory flicked across his face. After a silence so long it seemed he would not answer, he said, "Gabriel."

She tried to graft this new information onto the man she looked at, half-expecting his visage to change in some way. How could she have lived with him for most of six years and never asked his real name? She had simply accepted that a dwarf would take the name of an awkward, strange bird—one of Nature's jokes, he had said. She thought of the character she had written for him: the prince who was tortured until he became dwarf-like but learned to strap special fifteen-inch-high devices to his shoes, so he could enter a room as a "normal," though stiffly moving man and then, when alone, remove the devices and scuttle about doing deeds no one could suspect him of or blame him for. Suddenly she felt she knew nothing of Nandou at all. How deep did it go, the pain of being a dwarf, which she saw and heard only in an occasional sardonic twist of his mouth and turn of phrase? Why was he content to live with her, when he could have sought someone who would want him as a man? "Is there more?" she asked, meaning more to his name but half-hoping he would answer her unspoken questions.

"My name is Gabriel Corday." He shrugged. "No relative of Charlotte's, but I admire her for killing the tyrant Marat."

They rode on, Solange bouncing and chattering behind them.

"Let us call her Gabrielle," Jeanne said. "Gabrielle Corday."

He drove in silence so long that she feared she had angered him; she saw only a tightening of his mouth and a heave of his shoulders. Then something rolled down his cheek, glittering in the sun. He wiped at it angrily, as if at a fly, and cleared his throat. "That would please me. If you are certain."

"I am quite certain."

Jeanne pulled Solange onto her lap, and they told the child about the new game they were going to play, in which she would have a lovely new name for living in the country and no one must know her old one, that's right, no one. She did not understand and looked as if she would cry, but Nandou said they would come and visit her as often as they could. "And Fidèle can stay with you all the time, and you can whisper your old name to her sometimes, if you like."

It was dusk when they reached the farm. The actor's married sister was a plump, sun-weathered farm woman with three young children of her own. She gave Nandou a long, curious, but not malicious stare; while hens clucked and strutted at her feet, she read the letter they had brought from her brother. Within ten minutes, they had agreed on the terms of the boarding. "Look, Sol—Gabrielle," Jeanne said, "you will have a real rooster, not a wooden one." The child clutched her toy even more tightly.

Jeanne and Nandou stayed for a supper to which they contributed chocolate and several bottles of wine from their basket. After seeing "Gabrielle" to bed in the room with the other children, they minded all of them while the woman and her husband went into the nearby village for carnival and a grand procession led by the local King of the Young. They stayed the night in the straw above the horses, and planned to leave by sunup, to avoid the crush that would come later in the day when Mardi Gras festivities began. But in the morning, though it was a holiday, there were still chores to be done; they offered to help so Jeanne could see how Solange reacted to the animals. Then Nandou wanted to tell her one last story, to remember that night when they were gone; then it was ten o'clock, and they knew that if they did not leave at once, they would snatch "Gabrielle" away and never return.

"Goodbye, my little sweetheart, my cabbage, my angel," Jeanne said, holding her as if to press the imprint of the small body permanently into her own.

"Goodbye, my Gabrielle," Nandou said. He pulled a coin from behind her ear, tried to laugh, then stroked her cheeks and ran his thumbs over her silky little eyebrows again and again. He turned away and picked up Fidèle. "My dear old friend," he croaked, "do not forget me. And do not let her . . ." He plunged his face into the cat's fur.

On the road, heading back to Paris with the farmwife's gift of eggs and sugared almonds for Mardi Gras, they were both silent at first. Then, looking far over the fields to the horizon, Jeanne said, "When she was born, I said you would never have to save me again. But now you have saved her. How can I tell you what I feel, what thanks roll from my heart in waves—"

"Let us have no more talk of thanks," he said brusquely. "Not between us."

They rode on. "I shall never forgive Louis," Jeanne said. "Never. I shall raise her to hate the sort of man he is. I swear it."

After another distance Nandou flicked the reins and said, "How brave she is. Kidnapped, then hidden in the bottom of a basket, then thrown into a new life, even her name changed . . . "

"Remember when she had the colic?" Jeanne said. "I thought she would never stop crying, and one night you began reading Lamartine to her and she stopped."

Nandou nodded. "Remember when I had just carried up a bucket of water from the well and she dropped two fresh loaves of bread into it?" They drove on, each listening more to inner words than to what the other said, soaking themselves in their separate memories.

Soon revelers began to appear around them, singing and shouting, faces hidden behind every kind of mask while their bodies, freed of burdens for this day above all others, weaved and danced beside the road and across it. Beneath the mask and crown of a princess, a fat shape wobbled in its gown like custard on a plate. Below the horns and grimace of a demon capered a bent back and shanks as thin as slats. Many of the figures traveled in carts and wagons or rode horses; an ancient nag came plodding along with two drunken Pierrots, one slumped over his neck, the other flopping over his rump. The road shrank with its traffic, which grew louder and heavier as Paris came nearer. By dusk, it was clear they would be in the thick of the crowds that gathered each Mardi Gras night in Belleville, to drink and carouse in the taverns there. Early on Ash Wednesday morning, as they had done for centuries, the crowds would carom down the bluffs to the Temple district in the "descent from la Courtille."

Torches appeared in many hands, flames leaping in an endless, frenzied effort to free themselves from their sources. But it was the crowd that grew freer. Two masked figures clambered onto the cart, each waving a bottle of wine. "Here's a beauty!" cried one of them, throwing his other arm around Jeanne. "Hey!" Nandou yelled, but Jeanne laughed and pushed away the arm. The man fell on the straw in the back of the cart and lay spread-eagled. His companion cried to Jeanne, "If you can make his cock wake up and crow, he's yours," raised her skirts, and leaped back down into the crowd.

"Since we are stuck in this," Nandou said, "you had better make yourself a mask."

"How? From what?"

He pulled out his knife. "Cut a piece from your shawl."

"This is good merino. I would have to be earning many more francs for *The Dwarf Lord* before I would cut it up." She lifted her skirt, hacked a piece of cloth from her petticoat, cut two large holes in it, and tied it over her eyes. "Shall I make you one as well?" she said.

He shook his head and said sardonically, "No dwarf needs a mask."

"Oh, oh, oh," a voice bawled at Jeanne from beside the cart, "how I would love to climb up and pick your two lovely apples!"

"Asshole," Jeanne said good-naturedly. "Your eyes are bigger than your brain." She hadn't sworn in Nandou's presence in years, but after all, it was Mardi Gras, and people behaved as on no other night of the year.

Someone was playing a flute; people held hands and moved along, dancing the farandole. One's body could not help rocking to the rhythm; Nandou swayed in his seat too. When they neared a courtyard tavern in Belleville, he said, "I am going to dump our passenger here." He maneuvered the cart to a spot beside the tavern, watered and fed the horse, and hauled the unconscious reveler from the straw. The effort made his back and shoulder muscles bulge beneath his jacket. Jeanne clapped and shouted "Bravo!" He made an elaborate stage bow, and an equally grand gesture toward the tavern.

The tavern, adjoined by a garden with an arbor, was a *courtille* like the one that had given its name to the traditional Ash Wednesday descent on the city. Expensive carriages as well as rough carts were clustered around it, for on this night certain elements of fashionable Paris came to the haunts of the plebeians. The garden was already filled with dancers and drinkers, flute and guitar players. In its center swayed a woman in a jeweled mask and a silk gown, the low bodice revealing the bulging fruit of her breasts and the little stems of their nipples. While the onlookers urged her on—"Show us more!"; "Shake that basket!"; "Feed the animals!"—she undulated toward a man in a black velvet suit and a lion mask, her breasts rolling like melons in silk. He leaned over her, bit, then lifted her and half-threw her toward another man in a wolf mask, who bent her backward, slowly stroked her abdomen, then sent her weaving back to his friend. A King Charles spaniel with a jeweled collar ran at their heels, then trotted off to relieve itself beneath a bush. But a Pierrot sat there, embracing a Columbine. People applauded the dog and urged it on.

Inside the tavern the music was louder and four masked women on the top of a long table lifted their skirts and kicked their legs in a dance from Revolutionary days, the cancan. Men whistled and clapped, and other women fought to climb up on the table. Beer foamed up to painted mouths, wine ran down the fronts of costumes. Hands reached to touch Jeanne as she passed, and when she pulled away, voices called, "Hey, look what she's with" and "There's the best one yet—a dwarf." But the voices were not mocking, and when Nandou lifted his stick high to answer them, it was in triumph, not anger. For one night in his life, Jeanne thought, he was normal. When all the world was in costume, his body was only the cleverest of all disguises.

He bought wine for the two of them, drank his first glass with barely a pause, and told Jeanne to hurry or he would take hers, too. He ordered sausages and bread and more wine; he laughed when one of the cancan dancers fell off the edge of her table and applauded when her replacement kicked even higher; he pulled a red scarf from the open mouth of a sleeping drunk at the next table, to the applause of half the room. The wine reddened his cheeks and gave his eyes the sheen of glass. Jeanne watched and ate and drank, and forgot everything except how to laugh and clap and hold out her glass.

A shout went up; the sun had appeared, and now the descent would begin. In the tavern garden, couples straggled from beneath and behind the shrubbery, their warm breaths misting before them in the chill air. The woman with overripe breasts, one now spilling freely from her bodice, was supported by her male companions and trailed by the panting spaniel. People clambered into their carriages and carts and mounted their horses, or rushed out onto the road to join a procession that seemed to have begun farther up and to have no end. Pulsing down the bluffs toward Paris, it turned into an avalanche, and spectators lined the road to watch its twisting growth. People in the vehicles threw sugared almonds and eggs at the spectators, and handfuls of flour that dusted their caps and faces like snow. Jeanne reached into their basket from the farm and tossed out a fistful of almonds. "Eggs!" Nandou cried, "Eggs!" When she gave him one, he threw it with his free hand, right on the pate of a tall, burly man who howled and laughed at the same time; so did Nandou. "More eggs!" he cried, and she obliged, and they rolled on downward, no longer Jeanne and Nandou but only part of the avalanche. To be in its heart was to forget everything but its forward motion, to feel all else merging with the wind from that motion—the loss of Solange, the rage at Louis, the anger at her brothers, the specter of her mother; all of them were fleeing to some purgatory of the spirit, while the flesh was free to careen down a bluff with the sun rising behind her and Paris rising ahead. She heard a voice call her name—not someone in the crowd but Nandou, who shouted "Jeanne" into the din around them as if he wanted no answer and needed only to shout. He looked like a demon, hair streaking into the wind, mouth parted in a rage of ecstasy.

As they neared the Temple district, where the descent traditionally ended, Nandou turned the cart aside, maneuvering it out of the stream with difficulty. "Where are we going?" she said, but he shook his head as if pursuing some private goal that made speech impossible. They stopped in a street she did not know, in a small square near what looked like a convent. Above them the bare branches of a huge tree crisscrossed the brilliant sky. The noise of the revelers was clearly audible, yet far away, and the bells of Paris's churches were ringing in their many voices. "Why are we here?" she asked. Nandou said nothing, only stared ahead, his teeth sunk deeply into his lower lip as if to stop the trembling in the rest of his body. "Are you all right?" she said, and put her hand on his shoulder. He jerked as if her hand were heated iron. "Ah, God, I can't any longer," he cried, and flung himself into her lap, his cheek against her stomach, his hands around her waist. "Don't move for a moment, just for a moment," he said. "Close your eyes, don't look at me. Stop up your ears, don't listen, just let me stay here for a moment, like this, close to you, part of you, as if I belong where I am. I'll stop in a moment, I'll go away, but not just yet, not yet. Don't say anything! No, please! You don't need to, for I know what you will say. It's not your voice I want to hear, it's my own, saying what I've ordered it never to say, never. I love you. I love you. I love you!" he shouted into the empty square. Then, softly, "I want you with a need so deep it has eaten me away. There is nothing left within me but hunger. I am a shell—a turtle shell." He laughed. "Step on me. I will crack beneath your foot, and you can push the pieces into the gutter, where they belong . . . " He groaned and then shifted, and his hands crept up from her waist, toward her breasts, stopping where their fullness began and digging into her ribs like a drowning man clutching at a raft. "I despise myself," he said. "I know what I am, how grotesque, yet it makes no difference—I want you. I am an animal that can never be satisfied. It is not enough that you write for me the best dwarf role in Paris, that you stay with me, that you share my life, that you let me share the joy of your child—no, I want more. I want your body as well, every lovely inch of it, within my hands, beneath my mouth . . . " He slid down and pressed his lips into her skirt, into the triangle of her thighs. It seemed to her that she could feel his heartbeat, that all of his body had become a thudding heart, transmitting its rhythm into her own, holding her immobile even while it leaped against her.

Suddenly he lifted his head, sat up, and looked at her in terror. "What am I doing? What devil has . . . No, don't speak, please, not a word, in the name of any friendship you feel for me, you must be silent, please, I beg you to say nothing while I run from your sight, like the animal I am. The Dwarf Animal." He gave a strangled laugh, then grabbed his stick and jumped down from the cart. She put her hands over her mouth, to make herself grant him the silence for which he pleaded. He pulled on his cap, looked up at her as if punishing his eyes with the sight, and then walked off, half-running, his broad shoulders heaving and his short legs pitching him from side to side. She watched, wrung with the desire to do anything in the world for him, except what he wanted most.

After the hours it took her to return the horse and cart, she went back to the apartment, but he was not there. Nor was Solange, nor Fidèle. She feared she would not see him again, ever. It seemed that all of her life had disappeared with one stroke, as if it were nothing but the scenery in a fairy play. She wandered aimlessly through the two rooms, back and forth, touching Solange's little chair, looking into the cupboard where her clothes had hung, staring at the partition behind which lay Nandou's bed. She slept a little, but when she woke, his wretched words were in her ear. She wandered, tried to think about *The Dwarf Lord*— but what if the dwarf never returned?—ate something, tried to read, slept again.

When he came in, she had just lit the lamp. He stood in the doorway not quite looking at her, his shoulders drooping. The light flickered on his broad cheekbones and then seemed to disappear into the caverns of his eyes. He cleared his throat and said, "I shouldn't have left you with the cart."

"It's all right. I took care of it. Would you like some supper?"

"No. I am not hungry." He winced, as if hearing the echo of the hunger he had earlier confessed to her. "I am very tired. I shall go to bed."

"Very well," she said.

He started to move but stopped. "I was drunk, Jeanne, very drunk. You will forget my words, please."

"Did you not mean them?"

"Of course not." He shrugged, the bravado of the gesture belying its falsity. "Carnival brings out the beast in all of us. Except in you."

"You are not a beast!"

He sighed. "I'll say good night, then."

"Good night," she said.

She waited, hearing him remove his clothes and sink on the bed. For the first time since Solange's birth they were alone in the apartment.

She pressed her hands together, and her lips, and sat thinking of the girl she once had been, who had come alive through art and then, discovering love as well, had simply followed the call of her body, believing that no man who shared her love of art could possibly betray her. There were losses, she thought, which changed one forever—like the loss of faith in love.

At length she rose, put out the lamp, and slipped off her own clothing. The moonlight lay cool across her breasts. She moved to the partition.

When she sat on the edge of his bed, he reared up and said harshly, "No, Jeanne! I do not want your pity, or your gratitude, or—"

"Ssh." She put a hand over his mouth. "Let us pretend that carnival is not over."

Chapter Ten

The manager's expectations, admittedly rather modest—perhaps a run of several weeks—had already been exceeded. Night after night he watched crowds line up and jostle into the auditorium; act after act he heard the applause crescendo and saw the box-office receptacles bulge with coins. Who could say exactly why? Anyone who knew the secret of what made a play a hit would long ago have retired with his riches. Perhaps it was the effects, which were particularly skillful; perhaps the performance of the title role, which was even better than the manager had anticipated; perhaps, most likely of all, it was the eminent critic who had come to the boulevard and decided to call the attention of Paris to what he saw:

> A king's enemies prevent his only son from succeeding to the throne by capturing the boy and keeping him for years in a fiendish device that prevents his legs from growing and, in effect, turns him into a dwarf. The young prince's revenge upon his captors, his leading of a band of renegades who help him regain his throne and fortune, and the astounding means by which he achieves these things, form the heart of *The Dwarf Lord,* a new melodrama on the Boulevard of Crime by a new author, J. Sorel. In the title role is an actor billed simply as "Nandou," who is himself a dwarf and is equal to every challenge, histrionic and physical, of the text . . . It is wondrous to watch M. Nandou maneuver on and off his "stilts" and execute the tricks that permit him to become the instrument of vengeance and justice not only for himself but for others. Yet there is more to his performance than physical novelty and dexterity. A simple lift of his hand can express the weight of a full heart, a brief greeting contain a wealth of venom. . . . And, despite a childlike rapidity of action reminiscent of M. Dumas, there is more to Sorel's play than amazing effects. . . .

In addition, certain facts about the author and the dwarf had made their way from greenroom gossip into the journals: that, despite her obvious beauty, Sorel had worked on the boulevard for several years as a callboy, and still on occasion went about dressed in trousers, behavior made all the more tantalizing by being illicit; that she appeared to take no lovers and, in fact, lived with the dwarf—in what manner no one was certain, for both were silent about their private lives, thus increasing speculation about them. Fed by the twin fires of gossip and success, *The Dwarf Lord*'s box-office receipts had gone from good to better. Melodrama was at its peak, and if the manager had neither Dumas and *La Tour de Nesle* nor an actor like the great Frédérick Lemaître, he had a play and a star that not only filled the galleries to bursting but brought more and more carriages to the doors each night, to disgorge their elegantly dressed loads. Only one cloud hung in the sky: What future was there with a dwarf? Could there be another starring vehicle for him? Presumably the answer rested with the Sorel woman, and if she tired of the dwarf . . . The manager decided not to think of such matters but to count his blessings, and his receipts.

"I refuse to believe, mademoiselle, that you are the playwright. You are too young and beautiful to have acquired such skill."

"May one ask, monsieur, which skills you think it appropriate for youth and beauty to acquire?"

"Let us say those of giving and receiving pleasure."

"But have I not done so with my play? It has given you pleasure, or surely you would not be here, and also allowed me to receive it, in the form of my percentage of the box-office receipts."

An appreciative murmur came from the crowd in the dressing room—Nandou's dressing room, which Jeanne visited during intermission and after the final curtain whenever she came to the theatre, usually once a week. She stood quietly in the wings and moved from one spot to another to get the best view of each scene. Somehow word would get about the theatre that she was there, and by the second intermission, the dressing room would be filled, mostly with men: *lions* from the Right Bank in their fashionably bright waistcoats, bourgeois in black suits and crisp white linen. Sipping wine from glasses the callboys brought, they would speak to Nandou and then turn their attention to her. "Do they come when I am not here?" she asked Nandou. "Without you," he said, "my dressing-room crowd is much more plebeian."

In time-honored theatrical tradition, the young gentlemen, and some not so young, paid compliments and issued invitations to supper. The compliments were accepted with a disarming smile and, at the same time, acknowledged in phrases that rendered them hollow. *For me, the performance cannot be complete unless mademoiselle consents to supper afterward.—I would be honored, monsieur, but alas, there is no place in the final act of the play for the spectacle of eating.* The more sweetly she mocked their flattery, the more eagerly it was offered. *With a mouth shaped so exquisitely, mademoiselle should be on the stage herself.—You think so, monsieur? But if I were on the stage, I should have to mouth the words of others. Or perhaps that is what you prefer a woman to do?* While she chatted, Nandou sat at his dressing table, touching up or removing his makeup, drinking water by the bottle and watching, sometimes in the mirror but sometimes directly, when he would swing his chair around, fold his arms, and follow the conversations without moving, only his eyes sliding back and forth as if he were at a tennis match. On his right index finger, like an unblinking third eye, glittered a large black oval ring that was an important prop in the play but was not fake; he had bought it himself.

Why would such a beautiful creature as you, mademoiselle, go to supper often with the dwarf but never with me?—Because, monsieur, he never wastes time telling me I am a beautiful creature.

One night Jeanne turned away from such a conversation and then stopped at the sight of someone who had just edged his way in and stood near the dressing room door. She looked at Nandou, who lifted both eyebrows but was silent. She moved across the room, stopping several times to chat with more animation than usual, and finally stood before the recent arrival, who was immaculately and conservatively dressed and carried a *Dwarf Lord* playbill in one hand. He bowed and said, "I hope I am not unwelcome."

"I confess that seeing you here amazes me."

"I have come to congratulate you, both of you, on your success." He lifted the playbill. "You have written something ingenious and compelling, and the performance of it is altogether amazing."

"You were in the audience tonight?"

"I was."

"I did not think a man active in the financial world would have time for melodrama."

"If I were immune to the lure of the Boulevard of Crime, I should be virtually alone among Parisians."

They looked at each other in silence, unsmiling but intent.

"Has your brother dared to come with you?" Jeanne said.

"I am here with friends, mademoiselle. I do not know Louis's whereabouts this evening."

"I wonder whether you knew of Louis's actions eight months ago."

"I beg your pardon?" When Jeanne did not answer, Nicolas Vollard said, after a moment, "How is your delightful daughter? I trust she is well."

Jeanne's eyes widened. She turned and called to the room at large, "Ladies and gentlemen! Nandou and I regret that we must ask you all to leave." To Nicolas she added quietly, "Not you, if you please, monsieur."

Amid good-natured grumbling and protestations, the visitors filed out. When the last had left, Jeanne started to speak, but Nicolas had already gone to sit near Nandou. "Monsieur, permit me to join all Paris in saluting the extraordinary things you do in this play."

Nandou inclined his leonine head.

"The physical feats may command one's attention most strongly, but the conviction with which you utter the Dwarf Lord's thoughts and feelings will, I believe, remain even longer in the memory."

"Thank you, monsieur," Nandou replied. "But the credit for my character's thoughts and feelings must go to his creator." He indicated Jeanne with a grand wave of one arm.

"I would never wish to minimize Mademoiselle Sorel's creativity, which impressed me greatly this evening. But I suspect she is giving one voice to ideas the two of you share."

"That is true," Nandou said.

Jeanne said, "Nandou and I both believe in the ideals for which the Dwarf Lord fights. I might remind you particularly of his commitment to justice."

Nicolas looked puzzled. "I do not see how I could forget it." When Jeanne did not reply, he said, "I wonder if the two of you would join me for supper?"

"No." Nandou's reply was quick and light, but firm. He offered no explanation, merely looked steadily at Vollard.

"A pity," Nicolas said. "I should have liked to learn how you—"

"Monsieur Vollard asked me how my daughter was," Jeanne said.

"Did he indeed?" Nandou lifted his hands, moved his fingers as if shaking water from them, and folded his arms. The black ring glittered.

"He trusts she is well," Jeanne said. She turned to Vollard. "Have I quoted you properly, monsieur?"

"The words are correct, but not the tone in which you repeat them. I assure you my interest in your daughter is genuine. I know that you do not like to remember it, but she is, after all, my niece, and I found her to be a charming child."

"So charming," Jeanne said, "that you would like to know her whereabouts, of which you would then advise your brother?"

Vollard frowned, looking from one of them to the other. "I do not particularly care where Solange is, only that she be well. You seem to be imputing some other concern to me. May I know what it is?"

"Monsieur, when is the last time you saw my daughter?"

"At your apartment nearly a year ago."

"You do not know that she was—"

"Jeanne!" Nandou said.

Jeanne bit her lips. "You have heard nothing of her since that night?"

"No indeed. What should I have heard?"

Jeanne turned to Nandou, but he was watching Vollard, his folded arms one straight, tight line, his mouth another. "Monsieur," he said softly, "why did you come here tonight?"

"You may like to think that I have no regard for your struggles, but the success you have both achieved interests me, even pleases me. I had thought to come tonight and pay it my respects."

Nandou cocked his head and said, as if it were an abstract consideration, "Are you sincere? Or are you a good actor?"

"As one whom I believe to be both, you must decide that for yourself." Vollard rose and turned to Jeanne. They looked at each other, appraising and challenging at the same time. Then he bowed. "Mademoiselle, may fortune continue to reward your talents." To Nandou he said, "Monsieur, your presence enriches the stage greatly." He went to the door, opened it, turned back. "In a month or so, you may read an announcement in the journals, for which I had thought to prepare you. My brother and his wife Edmée expect their first child in January."

In the silence, sounds drifted through the half-open door: actors and stagehands calling good night, the final thump of a scenery wagon, the slap of a coil of rope.

"His wife," Jeanne said, "who could not bear a child? So that he had to send you to try to take mine?"

"Apparently miracles happen," Vollard said. "I thought the news might ease your mind."

When neither of them responded, he stepped through the door and closed it behind him.

Jeanne walked about the dressing room slowly, hands clasped under her chin. "Louis was lying, then. Pretending he could never have a child, to justify his attempts to take Gabrielle."

"I have no desire to defend Louis Vollard," Nandou said, "but when I spoke to his wife, she told me she was barren. I believe she was sincere."

"She was lying to justify his taking Gabrielle! Do you think Louis would marry a woman who wouldn't lie for him?"

Nandou shrugged. "Perhaps you are right. Or perhaps it is Nicolas Vollard who lies."

"About the pregnancy? That would be folly, when the truth could so easily be proven. No, I believe him."

"Very well. But then consider—if Louis Vollard's wife is now pregnant, he will have a child from his marriage. Perhaps he will no longer try to take Gabrielle. Perhaps we can bring her home."

A smile crept upward, relaxing Jeanne's features. Nandou crossed his arms over the back of his chair and watched her for several moments. "Since we took her to the country," he said, "there has been no sign of a search. Do you not think she can return to us?"

"When Louis's child is born, and is well, we will talk of it." Jeanne put her hands to her hair, which was shaped too severely for fashion, without ringlets or coiled braids. "Let us go to supper," she said. "Somewhere fashionable and crowded."

"If you like."

When they reached the steps of the theatre, Jeanne said, "Why did you refuse Nicolas Vollard's invitation?"

"Do you not always refuse their invitations?—no matter how they plead or how much they declare they admire you?"

"I do not regard Nicolas Vollard as an admirer."

"Would you have preferred to dine with him, then?"

Jeanne hesitated. "No. But I do not think he is like the others who come, who believe they can flatter and lie their way into any pleasure they wish."

"And for whom you can show your contempt by dining with a dwarf instead of with them."

She turned to him. "Do you think that is what I am doing?"

"Yes. But I never refuse to go, do I?"

Nandou held out his arm. She rested a hand on it, and they started off.

"Long life to my brother!"

"To Papa!"

"To Olivier!"

"To my husband," said Henriette Vollard, finishing the toast.

They were seven in all, the entire family—except for the new grandson, Marc, who was home with his nursemaid, one of the finest in Paris, a woman who once had worked for the duchesse de Lessert. It was Olivier's sixtieth birthday, for which Henriette had arranged a supper at one of the most elegant restaurants in Paris: oysters, kidney with purée of shallots, *boeuf à l'Anglaise,* boned and sliced pigeon on conserve of leeks, petits fours and *millefeuilles.* Olivier would have been as happy dining at home, but what was the point of wealth and position if they were not sometimes displayed?

He sat at the head of the table, looking rumpled despite the newness of his waistcoat and trousers and the care with which his servant had dressed him. He would never look elegant, Henriette knew; his careless manner suggested that fine clothes were rather foolish and hardly the equal of the old dressing gown into which he slipped as soon as he was in their rooms. She watched him talking with Claude and Nicolas. There was little need to hear the words, for the animation of his face revealed their subject: the success of the House of Vollard, the banking arm of the firm, and plans for expanding it. "One day," Olivier had said to her, "and the day is not far off, to be the head of a great banking firm will be more important than having a title." Financiers as the aristocracy of the future? It was an ironic prospect—that the birthright she thought had died on the guillotine could be restored to her by means of financial transactions. But perhaps no more ironic than a monarch who called himself the Citizen-King and went about Paris carrying an umbrella.

She took a sip of her champagne and looked around the table at the others. There was her achievement, she thought: the solidity of the family. Father and sons, daughter-in-law, Claude and Madeleine. Not that the latter two were her achievement in the literal sense, for she had inherited them when she married Olivier, but how tirelessly she had worked—exhaustedly would be the better word—to refine Madeleine's tastes, to suggest the circles she should cultivate, to ensure that neither wavered in loyalty to the monarchy—and all of it having to be done firmly but subtly, with allowance made for Madeleine's high opinion of her own penchants and Claude's proclivity for thinking of himself as an art expert.

"My dear," Madeleine was saying to Edmée, as she spooned up a candied violet, "little Marc will want a brother, won't he?"

"I haven't asked him," Edmée said, with the dryness that had crept into her manner sometime in the past year, unnoticed, until one day it was there, like a fingernail scraping on slate.

"Of course you haven't asked him, what a notion. But he will be delighted, as will we all."

"You speak as if I were carrying another child, Aunt Madeleine. I assure you I am not."

"But now that the spell has been broken and the doctors proved wrong—you have noticed, I am sure, that their certainty is in direct proportion to their inaccuracy—there is no reason Marc cannot have a brother. All boys want brothers, and all families want boys, in the plural." Madeleine laughed at her words and patted Edmée's hand.

Edmée's eyes narrowed slightly, but she smiled. Even, white teeth; graceful shoulders and smooth bosom revealed by a peach-colored gown; blond hair Watteau would have approved. By look and lineage she was the perfect daughter-in-law. On the day of their wedding, Henriette had met Louis coming along the hall from his bedroom, dressed and magnificently ready to begin the life she wanted for him. The sight had brought such a surge of love and pride that she had had to lean against the wall for a moment. "Are you ill?" he had said, in concern. She had clutched his hand and replied, in a shamefully weak voice, "It is only that this is a happy day for me. And the start of happiness for you."

"Because I am doing the right thing?"

She had nodded, and they had stood looking at each other, as immobile as figures on a wedding cake, she unable to say either less or more, he flushed with some emotion she would not ask him to name.

He was looking at Edmée across the table, his fine red lips and brown eyes motionless, his whole face quite still—in fact, as if his only role at the dinner were to observe. "Louis," Henriette said, with a sharpness she neither intended nor cared to examine, "do you not think your wife looks especially lovely this evening?"

His gaze swung to her. "Especially, Maman? It is difficult to say. Edmée always looks lovely. I have concluded it is part of her character."

"As probity is of yours," Edmée said dryly. Their eyes met as coolly as goblets touching in a toast.

"Perfection, my dear, is a goal one may honor without achieving." Louis lifted his glass and drank, the motions executed with the physical grace he had had since boyhood yet somehow as empty as the glass when he put it down.

Very well, Henriette thought, there were tensions in the marriage. That was only normal; men and women, by their natures, grated on one another. At least Louis was behaving properly. At the beginning of the marriage, though she would admit it to no one, not even Olivier, she had feared Louis might fail to discipline the passions that had ruled his adolescence and would do "something foolish," as she put it to herself. But the interchange she had just witnessed confirmed that finally he had accepted his situation and responsibilities. He was, however, drinking too much. She took a last sip of her own champagne, and with that motion, quite unbidden, came a memory of Louis as he had so often used to be, fire flaring in his eyes and coloring his cheeks—a memory so vivid that she waved her hand in front of her face to dispel it.

"Is something the matter?" Edmée asked.

Henriette collected herself. "Nothing at all. When will you bring my grandson to visit me again?"

"One day next week," Edmée said. "Perhaps you would like to have him for an afternoon while I see Madame Palmyre about some new gowns."

"That would be delightful," Henriette replied.

At the other end of the table she heard Nicolas talking about railroads, a subject that always made his voice rise and his gestures quicken. How strange it was that as they got older, Louis become more detached and Nicolas more involved, reversing the pattern of their earlier years. Still, there was one place where Nicolas retained his usual inscrutability: marriage. There was a young woman Henriette considered highly suitable—the daughter of a wealthy wine merchant and a titled Englishwoman. Nicolas was attentive, but only to a point. If Henriette asked him what was wrong with her, he would say only, "She is handsome enough, but there is a certain tightness of the eyes." Tightness of the eyes? What did that signify? As long as her father did not have tightness of the purse strings. But Nicolas was Nicolas; he could not be moved and molded like his brother.

When the last of the coffee was finished, the family patted its lips with damask and rose like one body stretching many limbs, the men looking expansive and the women standing even straighter than usual to keep their corsets from pinching. They proceeded in a slow line from their private room, through the main dining area, where waiters maneuvered with trays and noses held impossibly high and corks seemed to pop continually, like toy drums in an odd symphony. A gratifying number of diners lifted their heads to observe the family's passage, and near the door, where parties waited to be seated, a banker of the men's acquaintance hailed Olivier and offered his felicitations on the event.

The street door opened, a cold breeze swept in, and before Henriette realized what had happened, her family had halted. She started to ask "What is the matter?" but the words stuck in her throat because she saw that, although the person who had come in was wearing trousers, it was Jeanne Sorel, accompanied by a grotesque little person. A dwarf.

Henriette saw color leap into Louis's face, but she could neither speak nor move toward him. A friend had once described seeing her husband struck with paralysis—"as if he was turned into a statue in the midst of asking for his morning journals"—and that very thing seemed to be happening to Henriette. The word *no* came into her mind but, unable to escape through her mouth, boomed inside her head.

Nandou saw him just before Jeanne did, but there was no time to warn her. Her entire body stiffened, and she blurted, "Louis!" as if in shock.

"Jeanne?" he said. "Is it you? I wasn't . . . You look different."

They stared at each other. Then she gave a defiant tug on her waistcoat and said, "But I have not changed. Still wearing trousers, as you see, and incidentally, still believing in the ideas for which you once fought."

And Vollard was still as handsome, Nandou thought, watching him flush at her last words. His wife stood behind him, eyes wide. They flicked in Nandou's direction; he prayed she would give no sign of recognizing him. As if she heard his thought, her gaze went back to Jeanne.

"You have had a great success, I hear," Vollard was saying to her.

"Thanks in large measure to my friend Nandou, whom I believe you have not seen since a certain violent day in July."

Vollard turned to him. "And whom I am certain I failed to properly thank for his help."

"Monsieur," Nandou said curtly and inclined his head; it was all he could bring himself to do.

"I hope you have been well," Vollard said to Jeanne.

"Do you?" The two words were ice, dripping scorn.

Vollard flushed. "I shall always wish the best for you."

"You will understand if I am not fully persuaded of that."

"Jeanne, I do not—"

"Because of you, Louis, I have had to send my daughter away from Paris. I shall never forgive you for that. Or for other things."

Vollard was obviously startled; perhaps he had thought she would not dare to speak of such matters in this setting? How little he knew her, then.

She went on. "Never try to approach her again, Louis. Never."

"Do you threaten me?" he said.

"Do I need to?" When he did not reply, merely tightened his lips, she said, "Will you not introduce me to the lady who accompanies you?"

Vollard squared his shoulders and, with a dignity Nandou had to admire, although grudgingly, said, "Edmée, my dear, allow me to present to you Mademoiselle Jeanne Sorel, an old friend who has become a playwright."

She had no chance to respond; an older woman Nandou had not seen before, her color high, suddenly pushed Edmée aside and stood beside Louis. "What is happening here?" she said.

"Good evening, Madame Vollard." Jeanne spoke with honeyed civility. "Since we last met, I understand you have celebrated the birth of a grandson. Allow me to congratulate you. I presume he will be taught to uphold the Vollard honor like his father before him."

The woman looked in silence from the top of Jeanne's hair to the bottoms of her velvet trousers before saying, "I am unclear in what manner you now wish to be addressed. Mademoiselle? Or is it monsieur?"

"In any manner you choose, madame, as long as it is a just one."

"Ah. To do that, I think, will be to leave you to your present company and bid you good night."

Nicolas Vollard appeared beside the woman. "Maman," he said, smoothly but firmly, "before you go, allow me to present to you Monsieur Nandou, one of the most excellent actors in Paris, whose performance as *The Dwarf Lord* I have had the honor of seeing."

"Madame," Nandou said, bowing regally.

"Monsieur," she said, shortening the word nearly to a hiss. "You will excuse my family and me. Our carriages are waiting."

Nandou bowed again.

The woman snapped her skirt behind her and headed out the door. Louis took his wife's arm and said, "Come along, my dear. I think it is not proper for us to remain here any longer."

Jeanne said nothing, merely turned to watch them leave. Behind them filed three older persons, looking puzzled. Nicolas Vollard stayed to the last. "Mademoiselle," he said to Jeanne, "I wish there were not such enmity between you and my family."

"But there is," she said softly. They looked at each other.

"Good evening, Monsieur Vollard," Nandou said.

Nicolas turned to him. "It is a pleasure to see you, monsieur, even under such awkward circumstances." He bowed and left. All the Vollards, finally, were gone.

They did not stay in the restaurant; Jeanne said she had no appetite left. All the way home she spoke only once—"*Not proper,*" said in a low, bitter growl that stiffened the cords in her throat.

They had taken a new apartment, many blocks from the old one, before bringing Gabrielle back from the country: a larger place, on a lower floor. Each of them had a bedroom, including the child. A young student, who lived at the top of the house, was large and strong, and knew how to use a knife, came down to look after Gabrielle in the evenings. He said she had been fast asleep for several hours.

After he left, Nandou said, "You told Vollard you had sent her away. Are you hoping to make him think she is still out of Paris?"

"Yes." Jeanne took off her jacket. "I cannot stop being afraid for her. Perhaps we should send her to a convent school."

Nandou was silent, watching her slip off her waistcoat, which was a bright, Romanticist red. "I would be happy if you never again wore such clothes."

"Why? Do you think they are *not proper?*"—said as bitterly as before.

Nandou tried to answer lightly. "I think you are a splendid woman, but only an indifferent man."

"Perhaps, but at least all the journals know my name."

"You could be arrested for dressing in that fashion."

"I am not worried."

"I am." Then, still trying to sound light, "Why make yourself a freak? One freak in this household is enough."

She cocked her head. "You know me. Don't you understand why I do this?"

"Yes." Nandou took a deep breath. "You do it to deny your beauty. I do not like to see such a thing—I, who would sell his soul for a scrap of beauty if only Satan would present himself and offer it to me."

Jeanne undid her neckcloth, not taking her eyes from him. "Have you considered that I may do it because I wish to make myself more like you?"

"A hundred times. But I cannot accept such a reason. I permit myself to live with illusions only on the stage." He rubbed the huge black ring on his right hand. "I think you believe it is only your beauty that attracts men—men like Louis Vollard. So, by denying that beauty, you punish him and all his confrères. Especially him."

She seemed astounded. Then her eyes flared. "If Louis Vollard should be punished, it is not because he found me beautiful but for other reasons, which you know quite well."

"You think I am wrong, then?"

"Indeed you are. If I sometimes dress in men's garb, it is only to show my disinterest in appearances—of all kinds—which so often trap the unwary and reward the undeserving."

"Elegantly phrased. Yes. But not so different from what I said, is it?"

"There is every difference. I do not see how you can—"

"Maman? Nandou?" Gabrielle had come down the hall from her room and stood in her nightdress, rubbing her eyes. At nearly four and a half, she was lovelier every day, her hair like silk and her face, without its baby fat, revealing a perfection of line that presaged great beauty.

She ran toward them; Nandou was ready to reach for her, but Jeanne grabbed her hands and pulled the child onto her lap.

"Come, my sweetheart, my precious, sit with me, give me the largest embrace in the world, arms around my neck, squeeze hard, harder—yes, that was strong and lovely, it has left me quite breathless. Shall we tell Nandou what we think? Yes, I believe we should. Let us tell him that the world is run by men—a kind of men whose name we don't care to say in this house but who have the power to do as they like. Not men like him, for no one is like Nandou, but men who pretend to love art and liberty, who swear their undying passion, but then abandon what they had claimed to love. We shall never forgive them, never. But we shall have our revenge on them, my sweet and beautiful little one, yes, we shall. You will grow up to have as much power as they—not because you are beautiful but because you will be an artist, such a superb artist that they will have no choice but to honor and admire you and make you the toast of Paris. Gabrielle Corday! everyone will shout—even the cats and dogs and the roosters. *Miaou! Oua-oua! Cocorico!* Bravo Gabrielle Corday!"

At the sound of the name, his name transmuted into hers, Nandou could never keep from smiling. Gabrielle settled more deeply into Jeanne's embrace and soon was sleeping, her black hair and delicate profile lying like a drawing against the white of the shirt Jeanne still wore. Nandou rose. "Shall I put her back in her bed?"

"No," Jeanne said. "I want to sit with her like this for a while. Just sit and hold her."

He nodded. "Good night, then."

"Good night."

He went across the hall to his room. Fidèle, on the bed covering, was grooming herself. She was older now, a little less eager to leap out onto roofs but still as white and soft as new snow. He watched her for a moment, envying the love of her own body that made her endlessly wash it, then removed his trousers. The boy-legs were naked, pale in the light of his lamp, bent as if trying to become crescent moons. They ached; the Dwarf Lord's time upon his special shoes sent arrows of pain into his arches and up his calves, which could last for hours after the final curtain. He had told no one, not even Jeanne. Nothing worth having was achieved without cost, and for *The Dwarf Lord* he would have paid any price. Fidèle knew, of course. He had told her when she and Gabrielle returned from the country, and strangely, the pains had eased a bit. He put out the lamp and sat on the bed, working his fingers into his soles and calves. The cat came to nestle against his hip, purring in sympathy.

When the pain receded, he lay down and pulled up the covering. After a while he heard Jeanne go along the hall, to put Gabrielle back to bed, and then across to her own room.

But it was not her door that opened; it was his own.

She came to sit beside him. "Shall I stay with you tonight?"

One could choke on the irony, the unimaginable irony, of her asking such a question, as she had done a dozen times since that Ash Wednesday night. "No," he said.

"Why, Nandou? Why do you pretend that you no longer desire me?"

"It is not pretense," he growled.

"Yes, it is," she said. "You could hide things from me when I was younger, but no longer."

More than life, he wanted to possess her again. "Very well, I still desire you," he said lightly, as if he were playing comedy.

"Then why do you never wish me to be with you? Please tell me."

"Because . . ." The words were loath to come out; they were pebbles trying to pass through a needle's eye. "Because you do not desire me," he finally said.

She turned away, as he had known she would; how could she deny what he said to her?

"I do not blame you," he said, "not in the smallest degree. But neither do I wish to have . . . to take . . . to be part of your 'disinterest in appearances.' "

"What do you mean?" she asked slowly.

"I mean . . . " He could have said a dozen things, more or less innocuous, but some weary devil in him did not want to dance so close to the edge of truth only to retreat from it. "I mean that if you sometimes wear trousers to show your contempt for Louis Vollard's world and what it has done to you, then you can sometimes offer to sleep with the dwarf for the same reason."

He felt as if the words were tangible, as if they lay on the bed between the two of them like knives that either could pick up.

"You believe that?" she said softly. "You think I came to you that night because I felt contempt?"

"Yes." He felt cold; a shiver had started in his midriff and threatened to shake his entire torso. "But that night I didn't care."

"And since then?"

"I have not wanted to be a surrogate for your hatred of Vollard." She was silent and immobile for so long that it tore other words from him. "Do you deny that that is what I am?"

"Yes, I do."

If only he could see her face; if only the lamp were still lit, and he had something to guide him other than the beguiling sound of her voice.

"Nandou, you are the only being in the world who understands me, whom I can trust, who knows me better than I sometimes know myself. You have done everything for me, seen everything that is in me. No one has ever been closer to me, nor ever will be."

"But you do not desire me," he said, as softly as she had spoken. Then, almost shouting, "Do not lie, Jeanne!"

The silence was long, long, like a skein of silk unwinding inch by inch.

"No," she said finally. "But I love you, Nandou, as if you were part of me. Can you not accept that I wish to make you happy?"

The silk unwound another length. "It would not make me happy."

"I am sorry," she said.

She leaned over, kissed his cheek, and left.

PART TWO

1848–1858

O I am well aware that the prime requisites of a play are laughter, tears, passion, emotion, involvement, curiosity, the leaving of real life at the cloakroom; but I maintain that if, having those elements at my command and sacrificing nothing of what is essential to a theatre work, I can exert some influence on society; if instead of dramatizing effects I can show causes; if (to take one example from a thousand), while portraying, dramatizing, and ridiculing adultery, I can find a way to make the public discuss it and legislators revise the laws about it, I will have done more than act as a poet; I will have acted as a man.

—ALEXANDRE DUMAS
fils, letter to
A. M. Sarcey,
in *Entr'actes,*
First Series

Chapter Eleven

*I*n the year that Gabrielle turned seventeen, everything began to change.

On her birthday, in January, her mother and Nandou gave a small dinner for her, with a few theatre friends—"dear and trusted," Jeanne said, toasting them over roast capon. There was the usual sort of conversation: about the struggle for artistic truth, the failure of Hugo's last play (did it prove Romanticism was dead?), the way Louis Philippe became more of a Bourbon each day and less of the Citizen-King he called himself, about the future of drama, of Paris, of France. Jeanne spoke in her quick, musical voice, like a flute racing to the end of a passage, scattering brilliance as it went. Nandou was silent for long periods, leaning forward now and again to unleash a flow of words that made one want to applaud: "Suppose you were asked to put this king of ours upon the stage. How to do it?—for you would have to walk on the streets like any citizen, but not hear the discontent of others. You would have to claim to see a peaceful future, yet be blind to the insurrections rising all over Europe. You would have to claim you speak to the people, yet have nothing to say to the rumbles of workers and the threats of Communists. My friends, since the drama is forbidden to offer demeaning portraits of a monarch, you would be unable to play the creature called Louis Philippe, for he is deaf, blind, and dumb."

At the end of the dinner, Gabrielle's mother gave her gold hoop earrings, in which a treble clef of seed pearls swung like a bell, and said, "Dearest Gaby, you are even more beautiful than I imagined you would be, and more talented, for that voice will make you one of the nightingales of the world." Applause, laughter, and tears in Jeanne's eyes. Nandou gave her a gold brooch: a rooster with a crest and beak made of coral. While everyone admired it, he said, "*Cocorico*" and poured her another glass of wine, in proof she was no longer a child. She could not drink, for a choking wave of love filled her throat.

Yet barely a month after that dinner, there were barricades in the streets, and blood and death. The somnolence of Paris under Louis Philippe, and of Gabrielle's own life, gave way to upheavals.

It began one morning late in February. Nandou appeared at the school where she studied voice with an Italian master and said she must leave with him at once. Wiping rain from his cheeks and shaking it from his felt hat, he said, "There is going to be revolution again in Paris. You must come home." She tried to argue, for she was comfortable and happy at the school and had made friends with the other singers, but his brows knitted until they formed a single rope, from which his eyes were suspended like lanterns. "When Paris is sane again," he said, "you will sing. We all will. Now hurry. Your mother is worried." So while Signor Martinelli twisted his hands and expelled soft, unhappy breaths—perfectly placed, nonetheless—and while Nandou told of the Garde Nationale and the angry crowds near the place des Victoires, Gabrielle packed her scores and notebooks. When she was ready, Nandou took her down the hall and told her to stay while he fetched the cab he had paid to wait for them. Music case at her feet, she heard the rain drum as if summoning her and the scales and solfège calling from behind her. Would revolution keep her from making her debut that year? Sixteen or seventeen was the proper age, and she was eager to step into the world that would bring her success and excitement and . . . she did not exactly know what else; it was simply the world lying at the end of her girlhood.

All her life, so that the words were like the heartbeat that cradles the unborn, her mother had said, *You will be an artist.* What kind had been unclear until she went to the convent school where Nandou once worked in the kitchens. Some of the older nuns knew him and told stories about him: how he peeled potatoes so fast and furiously they jumped from their skins, and how he would then sit motionless under the courtyard tree for hours learning his letters and numbers. When Gabrielle was ten, Sister Marie-Thérèse asked to hear her sing. In the bare classroom, heart thumping, she had performed three little songs. Sister nodded, her coif swaying like a single wing that could never fly, and said, "You have a bird in your throat, child." Gabrielle had begun to imagine it: a silver bird with a gold beak, on a perch in the cage of her throat, which would bring her wonderful things if she fed and cared for it properly. Sister had given her daily singing lessons of an hour, then two. For a year she had studied at the Conservatoire, learning that the silver bird was her master as well as her slave, and then had moved to Martinelli's because he was noted for coaching in the Italian repertoire and his school was smaller and more intimate. "That way," her mother said, "we can know who your fellow students are."

The street door opened, revealing not Nandou but the parents of one of the other singers—the Vérons, who owned a splendid shop in rue de Rivoli. They greeted her while closing their umbrellas. "We are taking our Amélie to the country," said Madame Véron. "Paris is no place to be now. Someone has come to fetch you, Mademoiselle Corday?"

"He has just gone for a cab."

"I hope he finds one," Monsieur Véron said. "I saw the only vehicle in sight being commandeered by, of all things, a dwarf."

Gabrielle swallowed. "I am sure there will be no trouble."

"Mademoiselle, you speak with the certainty of the young. But I assure you that when the working class begins rioting in the streets, when the Socialists dare to challenge the order that has been so carefully established by our—"

The door banged open. Nandou stood there, wind whipping the rain around him like a cape. He held an umbrella and wore a red cravat—bourgeois and revolutionary symbols incongruously joined. "Come, Gabrielle, quickly," he yelled.

Madame Véron's eyebrows made steep little roofs. Monsieur looked as if someone had dropped ashes into his cognac. Gabrielle's voice felt caught, like a skirt on a branch; she smiled while trying to pull it free. If only she could say, "This is Nandou, a famous boulevard actor," but he had forbidden her to introduce him that way—and sternly. "Do not think to make people behave differently by waving before their eyes whatever small fame I have. If they wish to stare, let it be for what I am in reality, not on the stage."

"Gabrielle!" he said. "Why do you not come?"

If only she could go to him in silence, take his hand as she had done when she was a child, and disappear with him into the rain. Let it wash her back in time and size, to the days when he had been the most wonderful person in the world because he knew everything but was no taller than she.

"Mademoiselle," said Monsieur Véron, "do you know this person?"

She wanted to say no. She went cold with shame, which gave her strength to tug her voice free. She could almost feel the *ping* of release in her throat. "Monsieur and Madame Véron, I have the honor to present my father to you."

"Your father?" monsieur repeated, amazed but not malicious.

"Yes," she said firmly.

"Monsieur Corday," Véron said, with a stiff nod. As if he had poked her, his wife echoed, "monsieur." Their faces wore the look Gabrielle had seen often: curiosity and pity and disdain, all twined in a nostril-flaring knot.

"It is an honor and a pleasure to meet you," Nandou said. "Unfortunately, both must be cut short by my desire to hurry Gabrielle away, out of concern for her safety." He spoke in his most silkily elegant voice, in such contrast to his wet, bedraggled person that Gabrielle wanted to laugh.

"Gabrielle?" he said. She mumbled good-by to the Vérons and stepped into the downpour. Nandou took her music case and handed her an open umbrella, which she held over them as they ran to the waiting fiacre, both awkwardly, she because of her skirt and he because . . . because he always ran that way. When she was small and her mother talked of "when you grow up," she had assumed Nandou would grow up with her; she would become an artist and help Jeanne take revenge on bourgeois hypocrisy, whatever that was, and he would grow tall and be able to run like the wind. "No, my sweet," her mother had explained one day. "Nandou has grown as much as he can. He will never change." "Why not?" "No one knows," her mother had said sadly. "It is the way he was made." Gabrielle had run to her room and wept. When Nandou came home, he had coaxed her out to sit on his lap, in the crook of his short arm, while he read her the tale of Petit Jean, the pint-sized giant killer. "You see?" he had said. "One need not be tall to do great deeds." She had put her arms around him and hugged him until he pretended not to breathe. The same feeling wrenched at her now.

Yet she hoped the Vérons were not watching him.

When they were settled in the fiacre and it began to move, Nandou said, "You did not have to introduce me to those people, Gabrielle."

"Yes, I did," she said fiercely.

He smiled as if he understood exactly what she was feeling—everything.

Despite the rain, the streets were busy with nervous, angry life. Skirting the Concorde, the fiacre passed large groups marching toward the place and shouting, faces determined, hair and workmen's caps plastered above those faces by the rain. Gabrielle took Nandou's hand. "What do they want?" She neither fully understood nor much cared about political matters, but the sight of such strong feeling on so many faces was mesmerizing.

"They have had some very lean years," Nandou said, "what with bad harvests and railway failures and credit freezes affecting so many of their jobs. They believe the answer is to be rid of all the ministers, perhaps even the king."

"And then what?"

"Ah. That is always the question in France. After the Revolution, what?"

Gabrielle tucked her hand deeper into his, as if it were a muff, and settled against the seat, her eyes darting to the windows every few minutes, watching the needles of rain and the march of determined faces.

The carriage swung wide to circumvent an area where people were shouting and tearing paving blocks out of the streets. "What are they doing?" she cried.

"Building barricades."

The horse reared, and the carriage ground to a halt. In a voice as nervous as a whinny, the driver said, "Let us pass, my friends, please."

"Down with private carriages!" "Good citizens take the omnibus!" "We can use the wheels and seats to build our barricade!"

"Please," the driver said. "Please!"

"What will they do to us?" Gabrielle asked.

"We will be all right," Nandou said. "Be alert and cautious, but not terrified. Terror stops the mind." He squeezed Gabrielle's hand, then put his head out of the window. *"Vive la République!* In the name of liberty let us pass."

"In the name of justice," a rough voice shouted back, "why should we?"

"Because liberty and justice cannot be in opposition!"

"Then come down and fight with us! Get your hands dirty and your feet wet!" The carriage rocked suddenly, whether from the wind or the actions of the crowd Gabrielle could not tell. A matching spasm of fright went through her body. Her eyes clung to Nandou, but saw no fear in him.

"I fought for the Republic in the July Days," he cried, "but now I must see that my daughter gets home safely. Let us pass!"

"Let your daughter come and fight, then!" a woman cried. "Is she too proud to soil her hands?" Gabrielle clenched them in her lap.

The carriage rocked again. Nandou reared farther out of the window, exposing the upper half of his body. "Each man fights in the way he thinks best. Each woman too." His voice rang through the rain like a whip. "My daughter will uphold the cause of liberty and justice in her own fashion, but now she must get to her home. Let us pass, my friends!"

Rumblings and mutterings. Then a voice called, "Hey! It's the Dwarf Lord! It's Nandou!" Others shouted his name; some whistled approvingly.

He grinned, lifted a hand, and shouted, *"Vive la République!"* The fiacre began to move again. He pulled himself back into the seat, dripping rain, and gave Gabrielle the smile from childhood: a little pleat in one corner of his mouth and a sideways dance of his eyes, as if the two of them alone shared a secret. "The plebs always loved *The Dwarf Lord,"* he said, wiping his face with his hands. Then he added, almost wistfully, "I wonder if it will ever be revived again." Gabrielle did not know how many revivals there had been. The first time she had seen the play, when Nandou had suddenly appeared on the stage looking almost like other men, she had felt as if hundreds of painless needles were piercing her from head to toe.

"No," he said, swinging his head so that rain sprayed her cheeks. "I doubt I still could handle the shoes. In any case, the theatre is changing. But the plebs remember, as you heard."

"You told them I would uphold the cause of liberty and justice in my own way. Do you truly believe that?"

"Don't you?"

"Yes," she said, with more certainty than she felt. Things were expected of her; she knew that. Yet at the same time Jeanne and Nandou treated her as if she needed protecting. She had always been cautioned not to tell people her address, her name, or anything about her family, and if she went anywhere by herself, her mother became nervous. How was she then to uphold the cause of justice or become one of the world's nightingales? It was confusing.

When they got home, Jeanne came out of her room in a dark-red dressing gown, her hair loose, and held her in a long embrace. "You are here," she said, "we are all together, and we shall stay together until this is over."

"Will we have to leave Paris?" Gabrielle asked.

"Let us hope not." Jeanne went into the kitchen, put on an apron, rummaged in the cupboards, and came out with bread, cheese, pears, and a butt of ham, which she put on the table in her typically haphazard manner. Nandou got out a bottle of red wine, and the three of them sat down to lunch.

"They are putting up barricades," Nandou said.

"So it happens again," Jeanne said softly. She cut a pear into quarters and ate one of them in small, elegant bites.

"What do you think will happen?" Gabrielle asked her.

"Fighting, singing, dying. When it is over, things will be different—not a great deal, but somewhat. That is what happened before and will happen again, until finally France is free of kings and their tyrannies. Each time, of course, one hopes things will change completely. One always hopes."

"Do you think the workers are in the right, then?"

Her mother cut slices from the ham, which came out in different sizes, for she talked all the while she was cutting. "I know what it is to be a worker. I have worked as hard as anyone marching in the streets today. But do I think the government should be turned over to the workers and private property abolished? No. I do not think Communist ideas will be the salvation of France, or even of the workers. Heaven knows that wealth is abused in France, but Nandou and I have struggled too hard for these possessions"—she waved her knife at the red cloth and candlesticks on the sideboard, the framed prints, the piano—"not to know that work deserves the reward of owning its fruits." She speared a slice of raggedly cut ham onto Gabrielle's plate. "But I agree that this government should be toppled. No matter how much Louis Philippe talked of republicanism when he took the throne, no matter how many bourgeois cling to the tails of that frock coat he affects or how often he calls himself 'citizen,' he has made a mockery of the word. Look at the power he has allowed the censors to take back into their nasty hands. Look at the changes I had to make in *The Black Galleon* before they would approve its production! When I think of those long censorious noses, pinching in disapproval because I gave certain speeches to a queen . . . In my dreams I see those noses, and there *I* am the one who does the pinching, I assure you." She gave Nandou a slice of ham. "Will it be like the Three Glorious Days, I wonder?"

"Even if it is the same," he said quietly, "we will be different."

They regarded each other above the rims of their wineglasses. Jeanne said, "Remember how Arago closed the theatres?"

"Remember your plan for getting munitions to the barricades?"

"And how you didn't want me to come with you to help execute it?"

"And how you did what you wanted anyway?"

They smiled, but suddenly there was challenge between them as well, flaring out of some cavern in their past. Gabrielle watched her mother's chin lift and Nandou's left hand rake through his hair. She could never grasp all that passed between them in their silent exchanges, which seemed almost physical and made her want to stand between them and hold out her hands to intercept what she could not see. "Were you on the barricades in 1830?" she asked.

"We were," Jeanne said. "Everyone who believed in liberty was on the barricades. Even some who would later become pillars of respectability."

"How did they let a woman fight?"

"They thought she was a man," Nandou said. "She was wearing trousers, and her hair was cut short."

"If I was born in January of 1831," Gabrielle said carefully, "then when you were on the barricades, Jeanne, weren't you . . . pregnant?"

Her mother seemed startled but answered matter-of-factly. "Yes. I was."

"Then I was on the barricades, too!" She clapped her hands. "Tell me about it. Please."

"Pah!" Nandou frowned. "There is little to tell. We sang, we fought, we won, at least for the moment. Now others will do the same."

"*Vive* Hernani!" Jeanne said.

"*Vive la République!*" Nandou threw his voice to one side of the room; from the other came "*Vive la France!*" He jumped on a chair, lifted a piece of ham on his fork, and waved it like a tricolor. Jeanne laughed and began to march around the table singing the "Marseillaise."

Their laughter and their passion were irresistible, as always. Gabrielle began to sing the "Marseillaise" too, marching behind Jeanne. But gradually, instead of being in the room with them, she began to feel she was outside, nose pressed against the glass: looking in on a dwarf who waved food about and a woman who was beautiful, yes, but who sometimes went about in trousers or smoked a cigar, who swore like a footpad when she was angry. . . . Why must they behave so flamboyantly? Why keep such odd hours? Why hold "salons" for boulevard actors who lived from hand to mouth but swaggered about as if they owned half of Paris, posturing and emoting—with Nandou smiling and excusing them: "That is boulevard theatre—poverty in velvet and grand gestures." What would life be like with a normal-looking father and a mother who wanted to be called "Maman," not "Jeanne," and who dressed and acted properly?

Parents like the Vérons, perhaps?

Abruptly Gabrielle stopped singing; never had she had such a thought before. Yet at the same time it seemed to have lain within her for years, waiting for release. The Vérons, she told herself, were probably guilty of a thousand instances of bourgeois hypocrisy. She went to the window. The rain had slackened, and at the corner she could see a file of indistinguishable figures. Rebels? Workers? The agitation in the city seemed a reflection of her own.

Behind her was sudden silence. "What is it?" Jeanne said. "What is wrong?"

"Nothing," she said, her back still to them.

"I don't believe you," Jeanne said.

"Gabrielle Corday," Nandou said in a mock-severe voice, "turn and face the tribunal of truth."

"My lord, I obey," she said, matching his tone. And when she did turn around, they were as they had always been: precious to her, both of them, Nandou strong and wise and wonderful in his exotic dwarfishness, her mother a haven in her beauty and idiosyncrasy. She wanted them to smile and sing again so she could absolve her guilt by joining them, could plunge between them and let the familiar extravagance of their voices and gestures flow over and around her, and into her. "I want to go out into the streets," she said, "to help the workers fight. I want to be on the barricades, only this time to know that I am there because I have been born. I want to see it all. We can do it together, the three of us, can we not?"

"Yes!" Nandou cried. "To the barricades!"

"Gaby! Darling!" Jeanne came across the room with her arms spread wide. "You cannot fight in the streets." Gabrielle was enfolded in the dark-red dressing gown, her cheek flattened by Jeanne's soft one. "You will fight in your own way, with your voice. Remember that power and glory lie with art, not with a Citizen-King and his hypocritical bourgeois supporters, who speak of liberty and justice but only want to be safe. Art is the weapon of revenge against them, against the respectability that destroys the soul . . . "

So familiar a litany, almost soothing. Gabrielle put her arms around her mother and smiled over her shoulder at Nandou. He did not smile back. "I shall go out," he said. "The Citizen-King cannot topple without a push from me."

"Be careful," Jeanne said. "You are not a young man any longer."

"Nor am I an old one." He grabbed his umbrella and pierced the air.

He returned hours later, muddy and sodden but his face agleam, crying, "He has abdicated!"

Workers died; soldiers died. The mob attacked the gates of the Tuileries Palace and rushed into the gardens. The king cut off his whiskers, disguised himself as a shabby Englishman named "Mr. Smith," and was smuggled across the Channel. The new Republic was inaugurated in the place de la Bastille.

Actors sang the "Marseillaise" and the "Chant du Départ" to their audiences. Jeanne added explicitly republican passages to the play she was working on, for managers were eager to find works with such sentiments, either new ones or old ones exhumed from the first Revolution. In the journals, political caricature was permitted again. "Look at this," Nandou cried, over a Daumier cartoon: An urchin sprawled on the throne as if he owned it, saying, "Boy, what a soft life." A dozen times that day Nandou recited the caption, and laughed, his broad shoulders shaking.

He took Gabrielle back to Martinelli's. Politics, she found, had invaded even there. The signor talked about similar uprisings in Venice and Milan—and all over the world, it seemed—and the other pupils, those who had not left Paris, worried that their futures would be affected by the growing economic crisis. All over Paris one saw groups of workers smoking, playing cards, reading the revolutionary papers, making speeches. Were they heroes or terrorists? No one seemed to have a clear answer, not even Nandou and Jeanne. No one could be certain whether a day would be peaceful or filled with new turmoil.

For Gabrielle the turmoil lay within, not on the streets. Now that she had begun to see her parents in a new light, she could not stop; the need to understand them obsessed her. Why did they fling themselves into everything with such intensity? How had they come to be together? She had the idea they had met in the theatre but did not recall whether they had actually told her so. A dozen times she vowed to ask them but was stopped by the knowledge that she really wanted to know something else and the fear that it would escape her lips: Jeanne, how did you come to choose a dwarf? Do you love each other . . . physically?

She looked at her mother, at the skin as fresh as her own, the red lips held in a composed line. If I come into a room where you are alone, Gabrielle thought, why do I sometimes, for an instant, surprise a look of such sadness and stillness in your face, before it springs back to the life I know, that I want to hold you as if you were the child and I the mother? Why does Nandou sometimes go out walking all night, with a trembling in his face that I can feel though I cannot see it because his features are set over it like a carving? What is it that happens between the two of you?

She shivered. "What is wrong, darling?" Jeanne said at once.

"Nothing."

Nandou looked at her over his soup, with the childhood smile.

At Martinelli's the next day she asked her friend Amélie Véron if she believed her parents shared the same bed. "Not for years," Amélie said airily. "My father has a mistress, you see. Maman pretends not to know, but he's had her for ages. He takes her to the Opéra every Thursday. So if they want me to make my début on a Thursday night, it will be difficult." She laughed, and so did Gabrielle, but without amusement. That night at dinner she told the tale to Nandou and Jeanne—the part about the mistress. "Do you recognize it for what it is?" Jeanne said. "A typical example of bourgeois behavior. You will find, Gaby, that it is a story repeated all over Paris."

"Not only by the bourgeoisie," Nandou said. "The nobility have a long and honorable history of extramarital expertise."

"They are not so hypocritical," Jeanne said firmly. "They make no pretense of being virtuous. For true hypocrisy, nothing equals the bourgeois mind."

"Unless it be the mind of a king," Nandou said.

Or of your daughter, Gabrielle thought, recalling the time Jeanne had told her they were not married. With a hollow worse than hunger growing in her stomach, Gabrielle had asked why not. "Because," Jeanne had said, "too much hypocrisy and cruelty are perpetrated in the name of that institution." But Nandou and Jeanne were not hypocritical or cruel, so why had they not married?—especially when she herself was born. Was her mother ashamed to be wife to a dwarf?

Into Gabrielle's mind, like a fist, came the knowledge that her mother never felt such shame; only she, Gabrielle, did. "Oh, Nandou . . . " she cried.

"What is it?"

"It's . . . It's only . . . I love you, Nandou. And Jeanne. I love you both."

"You are the treasure of my heart," Nandou said.

"And of mine," Jeanne said.

Did the Vérons ever say such things to Amélie?

Would the inner turmoil never end? Or the outer?--for in May there was another attempt at revolution, which failed, and in June, when unemployment was even more severe, the streets were suddenly filled with thousands and thousands of armed insurgents: workers, old soldiers, ex-convicts, and riffraff, all spearheaded by the Communists. Jeanne and Nandou were truly worried, and there was no question of Gabrielle's even trying to get to her classes. From inside the apartment they listened to the roaring of guns and voices and saw a barricade going up at the end of the street. Jeanne watched it with a strange, long-ago expression; then she lugged two chairs and an old cupboard to the door and would have taken them down the street to add to the pile if Nandou hadn't stopped her and done it himself. He insisted on going out—"for bread and news, because we must have both to live"—and returned with word that the archbishop of Paris had been killed while pleading for peace and the defending troops were now in the hands of a general as ruthless as Genghis Khan. From the windows Gabrielle saw men lying in the street, arms and legs at strangle angles, like the marionettes Nandou had made her when she was a child. "Close the shutters," Jeanne said, but Gabrielle could not help staring down. Passion for their cause had once moved those men about frenziedly; now it had tossed them to their death. Passion was frightening if it could lead to that flat, odd-angled lifelessness. Yet her parents were not frightened by it. They reveled in it. Would she ever feel it? Did she want to?

After four days the violence stopped. But barely a few weeks afterward, with the paving stones still bearing traces of blood, another scourge came: the cholera.

If the windows were open, the stench floated in—perhaps bringing the disease with it—so they kept them closed and tried to fan themselves into some degree of comfort. Jeanne wore only a petticoat and an old blouse. Nandou tied up the tails of his shirt so that his flat, muscled belly showed. Gabrielle tried to stay at the piano, coaxing the silver bird, working on *La Sonnambula* and *I Puritani,* to be ready for the new and wonderful life that music would bring her. Jeanne made changes to her new play, in which Nandou would have an interesting though not major part, for a dwarf role of some sort had become the trademark of her melodramas and people looked forward to seeing what she had devised. Nandou read the manuscript aloud, and they discussed the truth of the characters and debated the future of French drama. It all should have been soothing in its familiarity. Yet when Gabrielle looked at Nandou, the nakedness of his belly seemed to accentuate the shortness of the arms that hung on either side of it. And when Jeanne hitched up her petticoat to cool her legs . . . Why couldn't they behave differently? Why couldn't she stop having such disloyal thoughts? "Oh, I want to go out!" she cried.

"You will," Jeanne said. "The cholera will pass. We survived it before, and we shall do so again."

"Was I alive then?"

"You were two years old. I was terrified you would become ill, and even more terrified that Nandou and I would, for then what would happen to you?"

One day a messenger, masked against the cholera, came to the door with a letter from Martinelli: The Théâtre-Italien would resume its full schedule now that the cholera was subsiding. Regrettably, two of the sopranos engaged there had succumbed to the disease. If Gabrielle would report the next morning to the director, she would have the virtual guarantee of an immediate engagement.

Gabrielle's hands went numb. "Maman!" she called. "Jeanne!" in such a shriek that they both came at once, her mother with pen in hand, Nandou from a nap with his eyes and hair storm-wild. After Jeanne read the letter aloud, he grabbed Gabrielle and danced her around the room in the strangest polka that ever was, so she could not stop laughing. When they lurched to a halt, Jeanne stood with the letter held against her breasts. "We must come to our senses," she said. "It is a splendid opportunity, but you cannot take advantage of it."

"What do you mean? Of course I shall."

"My darling," her mother said, "how can you go out while the cholera is still raging?"

"It's not raging, it's subsiding."

"It is not over. It has killed two sopranos—Martinelli himself tells you. Am I to learn it has killed another, named Gabrielle?"

"It would not dare, not when I have an opportunity like this. Sir Cholera, I defy you!"

"Do not joke, Gabrielle. Nandou, tell her what it is like to see bodies turning black and stacked in the streets like cords of wood."

"I do not need to see bodies. I know the cholera is dreadful, but if I allow it to stop me, won't that also be dreadful? Surely this is the opportunity you have always told me to prepare myself for."

"Nandou!" Jeanne turned to him, but he simply gave an odd smile.

"You always seem afraid for me," Gabrielle said. "I do not know why, but you cannot always protect me. If I am to make my reputation as a singer, I must go to the Théâtre-Italien tomorrow. You cannot stop me."

"The pissing hell I can't!"

"Maman, I am going."

"Jeanne," said Nandou gently, "do you not recognize your own voice when it comes from your daughter's throat?"

Jeanne threw down Martinelli's letter and sank into a chair. "Very well," she said finally. "But on the streets she must wear a veil against the cholera, a heavy one. I shall make it myself."

That night Gabrielle fell asleep with difficulty and woke after only a few hours, not knowing why. Gradually the sound of voices slid into her awareness. Nandou and Jeanne were talking in the kitchen, the words only a murmur but their intonation sharp. She got up and went silently along the hall.

"She is seventeen," Nandou was saying. "Have you forgotten that at her age you were already a mother?"

"Do you think I want her to live as I did?"

A chair creaked. "You cannot protect people from life, Jeanne."

"I am speaking of death. Death from cholera."

"No, you speak of life. Do you not think I wish to protect her from its perils—as I once wished to protect you? I could not do it, nor can you."

Silence. The knowledge that a look was passing between them, the need to see what it was—perhaps to catch its content for once—drew Gabrielle toward the kitchen like an actor to a light.

Her mother said, "I cannot forget how close I came to losing her."

"She is not in danger from him now." Nandou's voice rose, a knife starting to slide from its sheath. "He has been silent for years, except in your anger. Can you not forget?"

"Do you expect me to forgive the bastard?"

"No. I pray for you never to think of him again."

Her mother gasped and cried, "Gaby!" Gabrielle saw that, without realizing, she had stepped into the doorway. "What are you doing?" her mother said.

"I heard you." She could think of nothing else to say.

Nandou was at the small table, her mother near the cupboard. Nothing moved but their shadows, swaying on the wall with the flame of the lamp. "What kind of danger was I in?" Gabrielle said. "Did someone do something bad to me?"

Jeanne looked at Nandou, who raised his eyebrows and folded his arms but was silent. "There was a time," she said slowly, "when someone tried to steal you from us. I can never forget it. Perhaps it makes me too protective, but I cannot help it."

"Steal me? Do you mean . . . to kidnap me?"

Jeanne nodded. "Do you have any memory at all of being in a very big and elegant house? Or being carried out in a large basket?"

"No." In its newness and strangeness, the thought of a kidnapping was intriguing, although clearly her mother would not care to hear her say so. "Who tried to kidnap me?" Gabrielle asked. "And why?"

Jeanne pushed back her hair, made a knot, and held it in both hands. "Someone I trusted, whose hypocrisy was revealed soon enough, who thought to solve a problem he had brought upon himself by taking you away from me."

"It was a man, then?"

"The particulars need not concern you, sweetheart, nor do I wish to discuss them. But if I despise the hypocrisy of respectability, it is because I have suffered from it, and if I tell you no man is so despicable as one who betrays what he claims to value, it is because I have witnessed such betrayals."

Light flooded Gabrielle's mind and seemed to fill her body. Finally she understood why her mother always spoke of respectability and the bourgeoisie in such scathing terms, as if she wanted to dip the words

in salt: One of them had betrayed her in some awful way. The sound
Gabrielle made was half relief at comprehending and half rage that
anyone should have hurt her mother. She ran to Jeanne and embraced
her. "I shall see that you are avenged," she said. "I shall fight the
hypocrisy of respectability, and all those who do not care about liberty
and justice but wish only to be safe."

Another idea burst into light, but she kept its comfort to herself. *And
if I do as I have just said, perhaps I shall atone for my dreadful thoughts.*

Behind them Nandou said, dryly this time, "Jeanne, do you recognize
your voice when it comes from your daughter's throat?"

She made her first appearances in light opera. The critics noted the
"purity and silvery brightness" of her voice, her "charming appearance,"
and the "convincing manner" of her portrayals. She loved the backstage
flurry, the hush before the first notes from the orchestra, the ease with
which the silver bird performed, the applause—but not the terror of
waiting to go on, the sweat and makeup caked on the costumes, the
tyranny of the conductors. Jeanne's new play had opened well, although
it was not as successful as *The Dwarf Lord*—none of them had been—
and often Jeanne or Nandou, or both, came to watch her from the wings.
Afterward Nandou said, "Not bad," and told her which gestures and
movements had been best. Her mother embraced her and whispered,
"Dear Nightingale."

The glimpse of the past Gabrielle had pried from them stayed in her
mind, coloring everything, as a drop of ink tinges a basin of water.
Applying makeup in some tiny dressing room or standing backstage
waiting for a cue, she tried to imagine how her mother had been
betrayed, the events of the nights' libretti weaving themselves into her
scenarios. Perhaps her mother had known a penniless young man who
pretended to be heir to a title, and when she told the truth about him,
he tried to punish her by kidnapping her child. Or perhaps there was
a crime in his past, which her mother discovered, and to prevent her
from revealing it, he tried the kidnapping. Or perhaps he had loved her
mother, and when she chose to share her life with Nandou he had been
so heartbroken and puzzled and yes, offended, that he had tried to steal
the child she had with Nandou and put a changeling in its place. That
last scenario held a guilty fascination. Sometimes it even entered Gabrielle's mind when Nandou was coaching her. Part of her listened—

"Always look for the truth of the role, and if the author has given you none, find your own"—and watched his amazing demonstrations, for by some alchemy he became the characters: His dwarf body seemed to elongate, his fluttering hands were a young girl's, and a fresh beauty lit his swarthy face. But as she watched and learned, questions slithered into her mind: Had he been the reason Jeanne was betrayed? What if she herself had a child that was born a dwarf? How could she bear it? Why could she not free herself of such thoughts?

As the months passed and she sang more frequently and confidently, bouquets of flowers began to arrive at her dressing room, with the cards of men she had never met, followed by the men themselves. She was not surprised, for she had seen it happen often in the theatre, and her mother, who had seemed to resign herself to letting Gabrielle make her own life and decisions, had predicted it would happen to her as well. "They will say they are in love with you—will beg you to smile at them, come to supper with them, come to a small private room with them, just for an hour. Smile as radiantly as you like, my dear, but do not believe them, for their declarations are hypocritical, aimed only at assuaging your fears of that very hypocrisy. You are not meant to be exploited for their pleasure. If anyone is to be exploited, let it be them. Let them watch you from the audience and suffer the pain of not being able to win your love or to come any farther into your life than the door of your dressing room."

Once Nandou entered the room as Jeanne was speaking. She did not see him, and as he listened, his face flushed so dark that the whites of his eyes gleamed like milk. "Don't tell her such things, Jeanne," he said.

"Why not?" Jeanne swung around to him. "Have you forgotten that they are true? Do you wish her to learn that truth by the same means I did?"

Nandou's gaze thrust against hers like a lance against a shield. Then he shrugged and left the room.

"There are some things even Nandou cannot understand," Jeanne said. She patted Gabrielle's hand. "No one can, except another woman."

Gabrielle smiled. Her mother had called her a woman; she would earn the title.

In her room, Gabrielle slept deeply, a dream of success flickering behind her lids, the silver bird silent in her throat. In her room, Jeanne lay half-awake, pieces of a plot floating in her mind, a smile holding its shape on her lips even though the thoughts that had summoned it were gone. In his room, Nandou stared up into the darkness, hands clenched at his sides, thinking that if Fidèle were still alive, it would be all right. She would settle against him and soothe him in a warmth of purring, which was like his own heart lodged in another body. But years earlier Fidèle had crawled into a corner of the room on shaky legs and died. He had taken the precious white body down to the courtyard and buried it, then walked till dawn, to the street, still choked with filth, where a kitten had danced around his feet and led him to Jeanne.

Without Fidèle, nothing lay between him and the terrible need except his will. Sometimes it would leave him and float into the darkness, taunting him with its absence. Finally he surrendered and went to her door.

"Jeanne," he said in the choked voice she had heard for the first time on the morning after that long-ago Mardi Gras.

"Come in," she said softly.

The moon was as bright as a lantern. He closed the shutters before he would go to the bed, and he said nothing; for him it had to be an act of silence and darkness. She dared not speak either, for fear he would answer and talk of such things as contempt.

Afterward he sat on the edge of the bed, hating himself, and said, his voice as flat as if he held it beneath a paving stone, "It is not right for you to live this way, Jeanne. Why do you not take a lover?"

When she didn't answer, he said, "The Lord knows there is no shortage of applicants."

"Then the Lord should also know I am not interested in taking a lover."

"Why not?"

"I . . . don't know," she said.

"It is the way of the world. Every woman in Paris has a lover."

"And every man a mistress. They say Victor Hugo has hundreds. So why do you not have one, then?" Silence. "We are not like every man and woman in Paris, are we?" Silence again. "If I did take a lover, you would claim I did so only to show my contempt for the world to which he belongs. But I cannot sleep with a man for whom I feel contempt."

Nandou groaned.

"I must enjoy a man's conversation and wit, you see. I must admire his courage and steadfastness, find something pure in his soul. I do not know why, but it is so. Perhaps all those years with the refuse of the streets have disinclined me to that of the spirit."

He was afraid that through the inches of bed between them, she would be able to feel how he was trembling. When she reached for his hand, he took his clothes in silence and left the room, vowing never to go to her again, knowing he would be unable to keep the vow.

Chapter Twelve

With a hand that he noted was perfectly steady, Louis Vollard reached for the brass knob to the breakfast-room door, opened it, and went in. "Good morning," he said to Edmée, who was drinking coffee and looking fresh and crisp in a dress of the peach color that suited her well.

"Good morning." Her voice was cool and dry. "I did not hear you come in last night, so I assumed you would not be down this morning."

"As you see, you are wrong."

"Yes."

Louis poured coffee from the sideboard and brought it to the table. "Let me ring for some food for you," Edmée said.

"No, thank you." He repressed a wince. In silence he drank the tepid, strong coffee, while she watched him.

When he finished, she said, "Why is Nature so kind to you, Louis? No matter what excesses you inflict upon yourself, you remain as handsome as ever."

He shrugged. In all the years of their marriage, the eighteen years in which they had retreated to separate islands in the river of daily concerns, joined only by love for their son Marc, she had never stopped asking questions that had no answers. At least she no longer seemed to expect them, as she had in the beginning.

She sighed and consulted the small gilt notebook beside her cup. "We have opera tickets for Wednesday, and Thursday we are to dine with the Girardins. There will be music afterward—she had hoped Chopin could play, but I gather he is too ill. Shall I have the pleasure of your company on both occasions?"

"Of course." Louis half rose from his seat and made a mock bow, which he immediately regretted. The best way to deal with the subject of his past failures to accompany her was to behave as if they had not occurred, and to seek neutral territory. "From that schedule," he said, "I take it you are glad to be back in Paris." She and Marc had just come from an extended stay at her parents' country place, to avoid the political winds that had shaken the city. Order seemed to have been restored at last, though by a means that surprised many: Bonaparte's nephew, Prince Louis Napoléon, had returned from exile and recently been elected president of the new republic.

"It was good to leave," Edmée said equably, "and good to return."

"You will find that the paving stones have been put back almost everywhere and the gaslights repaired. The city has returned to a nearly normal state."

"And the state of the republic? My father said the insurgents were thieves and murderers and had to be put down just as they were. When I said I did not countenance their means but had sympathy for their plight, he called such ideas mad."

"I do not see any point in your arguing with your father, Edmée."

"It was not an argument. I hope I know the futility of arguing."

For the first time since he had come into the room, they looked at each other directly. Usually, by unspoken agreement, they avoided doing so, their glances sliding away like the midair kisses women give one another. But sometimes, as if they had a compulsion to remind themselves why it was better not to do so, their eyes would lock, and he would see in hers the cool disdain and the resignation that, in its way, was worse than hurt and anger.

Didn't it mean anything to you, then? she had cried years before, the first time he had stayed away for several days and nights. The memory of where he had spent them trailed him up the stairs like a vapor that soon would be gone. She must have been working at her desk when she heard him; she had come to the doorway of her boudoir, wearing something pale yellow, holding a letter opener. *All the talk of your life being changed by the child and your renewed dedication to the sacred ideal of art—none of that was real?* Although her voice had stayed low and composed, she had begun working the letter opener between her hands, the hilt in one palm, the point in the other, twisting and twisting—*Is brandy the great reality for you now?*— until suddenly red began dripping on the pale yellow skirt and her voice cut off in midword. *God, Edmée, let me help you . . .* But she had screamed *"No!"*—the first time he had heard her scream, except when she lost their first two babies—and shut the door. He had gone into his own dressing room, regarded the face above a cravat that he vaguely recalled had been tied around a naked thigh, and loathed what he saw. *I shall never again do these things. I shall drink only wine with dinner, I shall paint every day, I shall be Louis Vollard again . . .* And he had been. He had been!—for months at a time; once for over a year, which would have become a permanence if his father had not died and his mother had not expected him to spend even more time at the House of Vollard. And if he had not come to realize that he would never be able to say *I am leaving, I am going to paint and paint only*—because he was not good enough to say it. Finally the pressure of the unsaid and the need to keep his sanity had forced him to return to his usual haunts. There had been more scenes—always at some door, it seemed, where Edmée would stand watching him approach, voice cooler each time until finally it froze and she merely stood and watched before she turned away and closed the door behind her.

He broke the lock of their gazes. She lifted her coffee cup and drank.

"Will you be going to the offices this morning?" she said.

He had been determined to go; perversely he said, "I doubt it."

"What will you do, then?"

"I have not decided."

"Very well." Her voice was like freshly laundered linen. "I must call on your mother today, and Aunt Madeleine if there is time."

Louis rolled his eyes. "I would have thought it impossible for Madeleine to grow even more boring and tiresome, but between them, age and illness have accomplished it."

"True, but one feels a certain pity for her."

"Because one is saintly."

"I wish you would not say such things, Louis."

"Why not?"

"I assure you I am not saintly. And I do not think you mean it entirely as a compliment."

"I am envious, that is all."

After a beat of silence she said, "I think we should have Nicolas and Joséphine to dinner."

"Why? You do not particularly care for Joséphine, and I see Nico all the time at the office."

"It would be rude and hurtful not to invite your brother's wife occasionally."

And I am not rude and hurtful, as you can be. She was thinking that—must be thinking it. Why in hell didn't she say it? Anger filled

Louis, not only at her probity but at the fact that she denied possessing it. He could never tell her to stop flaunting her virtue because she never did; as a result he was a hundred times more aware of it than if she had talked of it incessantly.

"Are you quite well, Louis?" she said.

"Certainly." But in fact the room seemed too hot, or too cold, or his cravat too tight.

"Would next Sunday night suit you?"

"For what?"

"Nicolas and Joséphine."

"Whatever you wish." He pushed aside his cup. "Where is Marc?" There was something he must do for his son, something he had been putting off for weeks.

At the mention of the boy, a smile lit Edmée's face and erased half her years. "Still sleeping, I believe. He goes back to school in two days, you know." Marc was enrolled at a boarding school in Paris, in the classical program, which would prepare him to study one of the professions.

"I shall go up to him," Louis said.

"Do. He will like that." When he was nearly at the door, she said, "Louis?" He stopped. "You are a good father."

He would not have thought the words would please him so much. But the pleasure was canceled by his anger at experiencing it. "Marc is a good son," he said.

He went back upstairs quickly, except for the small hesitation over each step that his old wound demanded, and opened the door to Marc's room with caution. But the boy was sitting in bed cross-legged, still in his nightshirt, a book on his thighs. "Papa!" he said in surprise.

"Good morning. Your mother thought you were still asleep."

"I woke early. At school I hate doing it, but I can't seem to stop."

Louis took a deep breath, for the room always seemed to him to be filled with fresh air, and sat beside Marc on the bed. He was a quiet, private child, with eyes like Edmée's, curly light-brown hair framing an Andrea del Sarto face, and an air of intensity beyond his years. "What are you reading?" Louis said.

"*The Three Musketeers.* Papa, it is a wonderful story. To have friends like that . . . to be with them all the time . . . Did you know that Monsieur Dumas's son used to attend my school?"

"I did not. Will you be glad to get back there?"

"It's all right." Marc stretched out his legs and wiggled all his toes. He was still part child, Louis thought, though his body had thinned into gangliness and his voice had begun to change. "I like school, actually," he said, "though most of the fellows don't. They say I am too serious about it."

"Are you?"

"I don't know. But I do not think I can change. It is the way I am."

"So, you are a fatalist already?"

Marc leaned forward, his gaze suddenly intent. "Papa, do you think a person can change the way he is?"

With effort, Louis kept his expression neutral. Was the question directed at his own behavior? Could a mere boy go straight to the heart of things: Is one forever bound to the cycle of making vows and then breaking them? To the knowledge that one could be better than one is, so much better, if only one could . . . Marc's gaze was clinging to his face like hands to a rock. "It is difficult to change," Louis said slowly. "But if one does not give up, if one holds to the belief that it is possible . . . You do not look as if that is the answer you wanted."

Marc sighed. "I wanted the truth, Papa." He turned away and reached to put the book aside. Some papers fell from it, which he started to shove under the pillow, but Louis stopped him. "Let me see. Sketches? Of what?"

"Only some scenes from the book. And one of the fellows at school."

Louis looked carefully at everything. "Some of these are quite good, Marc. Perhaps those days in my studio were not a waste. Do you remember them?"

"Oh yes." Marc smiled, the brilliant smile that crowded all seriousness from his face.

"I remember them too," Louis said. A little boy beside him on a short stool, one leg dangling, chin in both hands, asking about the palette, the brushes, the chalks, keeping the tubes laid in neat rows. . . . In those years Louis had spent a good deal of time in the studio, mornings and weekends, and the child's presence had made him feel renewed, revitalized—purified in a way he had not bothered to understand, so happy had he been to experience it. But all too soon Marc had been swept off, by a governess, then to school; and in the cold light of solitude, the canvases had been too lifeless; and then his father had died; and one day the need to disappear for a while had been overpowering.

"Listen, Marc," he said, "I could show you some things, if you like.

In the studio, and as soon as the weather is fine, we can go into the countryside."

"Please," Marc said. His eyes were clear and shining. So clear. "Please, yes. How old were you when you started painting?"

"I do not recall exactly. Uncle Claude took me to a couple of Salons, and when I was around fifteen, I should think, I met someone who studied at the Académie but had rather Romanticist ideas. He introduced me to the painter in whose studio I worked for several years."

"Why did you not show something in the Salon of 1848? They would have—" Marc stopped.

"They would have had to accept it, you mean?" For only the second time in its history, the Salon had been open to everyone that year; over 4,500 paintings had been submitted, an impossible number. "I did not show anything because I would not pretend to a mastery I do not possess."

"But Papa, you are—"

"Enough of that," Louis said. It was time to get on with what he had come for. "At your age, I had been introduced to other aspects of life than painting. My father took me, and later your uncle Nicolas, to a place where we learned the . . . where we learned what it is to be a man." In a red-velvet room, from a woman named Ninette, to whom Louis's father had said, with a strained nonchalance quite unlike his usual manner, *Ninette, ma chérie, this is my son. I have chosen you to be his governess tonight.* Above the woman's bodice and between her red garters, flesh had puffed like dough. Years later, after his marriage, Louis saw her again: raddled, painted, sweeping up at a place where her younger incarnations now reigned. "I must now do the same for you," he said gently to Marc. "Do you understand me?"

"Yes." Marc blinked several times, rapidly, and a flush spread across his cheeks.

"You have not yet been with a woman, have you?"

"No."

"We shall go tomorrow night, then."

"Tomorrow?" The boy's voice was high and thin.

"Are you afraid, son?"

"I . . . yes, I am."

For a moment Louis was tempted to say the hell with the authorities. But that would not be fair to Marc. It was a father's duty to keep his son from the evil of self-gratification, and there was only one way to do it: introduce him to the pleasures of gratification with the opposite sex. He had put it off long enough already, for no reason except a reluctance he had neither examined nor understood. "It is natural enough to be nervous," he told Marc. "But there is no need for fear. You will see."

He chose a place where he went infrequently: rooms above a restaurant near the boulevard Saint Denis. "Your son?" madame said. "His first time? Charming. We shall take excellent care of him." She summoned a woman named Arlette, not Ninette, but the white flesh was the same, and the red bodice and garters, and the bright rouge on her lips and cheeks. When she saw Marc, the professional allure of her smile was softened by a touch of maternal protectiveness.

The four of them sat in the parlor drinking brandy and chatting. Three of them chatted, that is, for Marc was as silent as the satyr in the corner, who held stone grapes above stone lips. There seemed to be a permanent flush on Marc's cheeks, and he stared fixedly at Arlette with what would have been rudeness in other circumstances. She kept adjusting the lace on her well-filled bodice and tossing her head so that her red hair brushed back and forth on her bare shoulders. At length madame gave a quick nod. "Marc," said Arlette, "will you come with me now?" She stood, one hip canted, and held out her hand.

Marc gave Louis a look of such entreaty that Louis heard himself say, "Tomorrow we shall begin work in the studio, if you like."

"Please," Marc said. "I would like."

"Why do you think of tomorrow," Arlette said, "when the night is only starting? Come." She took Marc's hand. As he left the room, his shoulders lifted and straightened.

"Do not worry," madame said. "Arlette is very good with the shy ones. She will make him feel like a prince."

Louis held out his glass for more brandy.

"May I suggest someone for you?" madame said. "I have a new Swedish girl, a blonde, who has the most—"

"No," Louis said. "Not tonight."

Madame nodded approvingly, and even though Louis knew it was her business to seem to approve, no matter what folly or peculiarity a client confessed, he was soothed. "Will you join me in a game of cards while you wait?" she said.

They retired to her chambers, papered and decorated in pink, with an ormolu clock so ornate that Louis could barely make out the hour. Madame's cards made crisp little snaps when she dealt or laid them down; the noises flicked against Louis's nerves like whips. Telling himself there was no reason to be agitated, he studied his cards through drifts of smoke from madame's excellent cigars, tried to listen to her polished chatter, and lifted brandy to his lips only half as often as he wanted, for he was determined to be sober when Marc emerged.

At four o'clock, or perhaps five—it was difficult to tell through the cupids twining about the clock face—one of six little bells on madame's wall rang. "There," she said. "Your son has finished."

Louis laid money on the table. Madame took it with a motion so swift that her hands were folded again before he knew the notes were gone.

Even in the glow of the pink-shaded lamps, Marc seemed pale. Arlette sat on a sofa adjusting her lace and her hair. "Good night, mademoiselle," Marc said to her. She smiled and patted his arm.

Outside, the sky above the rooftops was pale yellow, streaked with white. Somewhere a lone carriage was clattering. "From now on," Louis said, "you will not need me to—" He stopped, for Marc was stumbling to the gutter in the middle of the street. He bent over it for a moment, then began to retch. Louis ran to help him, but the boy sobbed "No" between his convulsions, so fiercely that Louis retreated and waited.

Finally Marc stood, wiped his face with a handkerchief, and came slowly back to Louis. His eyes were red and wet. "I am sorry, Papa. I must have had too much brandy." A tear welled onto his cheek.

"No doubt," Louis said. Suddenly he felt tears within him, too, but for what reason? Marc seemed to be wordlessly beseeching him for silence, so he granted it, and they went all the way home without speaking.

The theatres were busy every night, the cafés filled with laughter, the gaslights brilliant on the boulevards. Once again, Gabrielle felt that the city was matching her mood, for she had been given some important roles: Marie in *La Fille du Régiment* and Rosina in *Il Barbiere di Siviglia,* on which she had worked as if her life was at stake. Neither Jenny Lind nor Henriette Sontag needed to fear her, the critics said, but they admired her arpeggio passages and staccato notes and praised the neatness of her figure and the beauty of her oval face and large dark eyes. She was going to be a success, as her mother had promised.

If the work was hard, other things were easy: to smile at someone who presented himself at a dressing-room door; to cock one's head and slide one's gaze toward his; to have supper with him once or twice, if one liked him; and finally, when his eyes were filled with pleading, to say with regret that one could neither share his feelings nor go to supper with him any longer. They were often young, those adoring men; sometimes Gabrielle felt that all of them, herself as well, were playing a game not far removed from the schoolyard.

The best part of the game was telling her mother about it. "It happens just as you said it would. They call me the most beautiful girl in Paris, they send flowers—one night there were four bouquets of roses—they beg for smiles and suppers and swear they are in love. Then, when I tell them I hear the hypocrisy in their declarations and will not be exploited for a few nights' pleasure before they return to their respectable lives . . . oh, the look on their faces!"

"I know," Jeanne would say. "I know." And she would take Gabrielle's hands and squeeze them.

One night a bouquet appeared with neither young man nor card attached, only a note in a fine hand: "Your performance gave me extraordinary pleasure. Please accept these flowers as the smallest of repayments, from An Admirer Who Prefers Not to Sign His Name." A week later came another bouquet and note. "I cannot describe the effect that the purity of your voice and person has on me." After half a dozen of them, Gabrielle's curiosity was aroused. When she told Jeanne, her mother gazed into the distance for a moment, then said, "This man is cleverer than most, that is all. When he finally does appear, he will assume you have already fallen in love with him. All the more reason to relish telling him his efforts have failed."

Weeks went by with nothing but more flowers and brief notes. Gabrielle began to think of the author as "Monsieur X" and to wonder whether his was among the pale blur of faces toward which she directed her arias. Or had he seen her at some private concert—even spoken to her there? Then, after a performance one night, as she ran back to her dressing room for some forgotten gloves before getting into a carriage with Amélie Véron, a man stepped from the shadows by the stage door. "Mademoiselle Corday," he said, "I find I can no longer remain an anonymous voice that addresses you only in the silence of an occasional note. The spell of your artistry and person has defeated me."

He was a good deal older than she, and very handsome. She found herself agreeing to have supper with him the following night, then three nights later. He said he would not tell her his name unless they were to become good friends. He said she was the incarnation of the two things most precious to him, innocence and beauty, and took her hand and kissed the wrist. She looked down at the scattering of silver that gave such distinction to his thick black hair and decided to agree to one more supper, to prolong the pleasure of telling him he would not see her again—and then of telling her mother what she had done, for she knew, in a way she did not fully understand, that she was at last going to help avenge the betrayal her mother once had suffered, and pay for her own guilty thoughts.

She allowed the man's carriage to take her home. When she stepped out, he leaned from the window, caught her hand, and kissed it again.

The carriage moved off. She went toward the door of the building, certain she had finally entered the world of adults, smiling because she was no longer one of the girlish innocents she portrayed in the world of opera. But her smile sagged as her arm was gripped tightly above the elbow.

"Nandou," she cried, "you are hurting me. What are you doing out here?"

"Watching something I cannot believe I have seen."

There were only two sounds in the bedroom, where Jeanne had let the fire die: the scraping of her pen and the ticking of the clock, one as erratic as the other was regular. Alternately she scratched out phrases, stared into space, laid down the pen, snatched it up again. Each time she stopped writing, she heard the minutes marking their passage in small military clicks, impervious to the nature of what they measured and anyone's need to hurry it or hold it back. She wrote because she could not sleep until Gabrielle was home; because Nandou had gone out for one of his solitary night walks; and because writing was necessary to her, a voice of self with no other mouth.

She slid her hands into her hair, which hung long and loose on the shawl she wore over her dressing gown, then lifted the pen again and wrote so heavily that she seemed to be trying to reach the desk through the diary page: "I do not know if there is another play within me. At times a setting comes into my mind, or a passage of dialogue floats in like a phrase of music, but they prod nothing else to life. I should like to do something more than another melodrama, however exciting or ingenious—or profitable—another might be. But what? I feel I am changing, like the theatre itself, perhaps, and do not yet see the direction of those changes. The spirit of the great Romanticists has always guided my small efforts. I shall never accept that it is dead, but it may be true that its mind and flesh have grown corpulent. What, then, without its guidance? If I were a poet . . . but I can only make the language serve my practical needs and advance my plots. Nothing more. Perhaps I came to it too late."

She put her pen between her lips and looked into the distance, past the daguerrotype of Gabrielle, the shelf of books, the dresser with its enameled hairbrushes, the washstand painted with lilies, back to the day she had begged a few coins on the Boulevard of Crime and gotten in to see a fairy play. Then she shook her head and wrote again. "Still, could I have dreamed then of what I have managed to do? Eight plays on the boulevard. One a huge success, none a failure. If I write a hundred, each time I shall be amazed that I have done so—that the visions of my mind can be transferred to the minds of others. It is a communication more personal than physical intimacy, for one's body can be given without involvement of the spirit, but one's inner visions cannot."

She stared at what she had written, threw down the pen, and rose. Clutching the shawl about her with both hands, she began to pace the bedroom, teeth holding her lower lip. Her glance flicked several times to the desk, as if she might return and cross out what she had written. But she did not. *I have everything,* she thought. *A daughter, a measure of success, a man whose devotion and understanding could not be greater.* She sank onto a corner of her bed. *Yet I do not have. . . .* Her head fell into her hands; her hair swung beside her face like two black curtains. She hated times like these, when suddenly, for no reason, her body ceased to be the silent handmaiden of her spirit and became a place of aching voids; when the pleasures it once had known whispered along her veins, and the desire to be consumed by love, to feel her flesh and spirit drowning in it, made her skin chafe against the confines of her clothing.

If only those pleasures, and that drowning, were not tied to one face and body. She did not still desire Louis; she hated him. But what she had known with him, had been known with him alone. Lacking any other guise, it invaded her dreams in his person, even after so many years. Hatred of him was the only way to exorcise the memories, but always they returned, a hydra-monster of longing. For that above all she hated him.

She rose from the bed as if it had pushed her up, went back to her diary, and dipped the pen in the inkwell. "Why does the body refuse to obey the will?" she wrote. "Why, if one has decided that certain things are right and desirable, can one not be content in their acceptance?"

Why do you not take a lover?

She gave a little moan and sank back in her chair.

In truth, as she had told Nandou, she did not know why. Something within—in the wordless heart of her being where the great decisions of her life were made; where she had decided to follow him out of the heaps, to live with Louis, to refuse Vollard money, to commit herself to her present life—had simply refused to consider any of the men who had made clear their desire for her over the years.

She could be only with Nandou. And he did not satisfy the aching voids.

If she could speak when he came to her, if she did not know that he needed the cloak of silence, she would tell him that his physical being filled her with tenderness—that she wanted to shield it from the mocking stares of the world and soothe it of the scars they had raked across his spirit. But she could not say that, not to a man as proud and private as he. She could answer only with the warmth of her own body, and yearn, in silence, for him to treat it as his equal—as something he might stir to greater response if only he would not assume she could feel nothing for him. It was his contempt for himself that stood between them, more than anything on her part. But how could she say such a thing to him? The night he had asked why she did not take a lover was virtually the only time they had spoken after being together; and just as she had reached for his hand, hoping she might be making a crevice in his armor, he had left.

The next day he had been formal and distant, until gradually they returned to their normal relationship. Each time, that was the way.

Never was he more impersonal than when he had just been with her: as if the physical intimacy he permitted himself required the atonement of spiritual distance.

If only he would not despise his need for her. If only he would accept what she was able—and happy—to give him, without torturing himself because he could not make her give more.

If only she herself did not want more.

On the open diary page, she saw she had drawn something without realizing it: a rose. A bouquet of white ones had arrived on the opening of each of her plays after *The Dwarf Lord,* with a card attached. "Permit me to offer my compliments once again." Or, "With admiration for your continuing success." Or, "May you and your work continue to grace our theatres." But always the same signature, in a sloping hand: "Nicolas Vollard." Twice he had come backstage as well, to ask briefly after "your charming daughter" before kissing her hand and leaving.

Why do you not take a lover?

As if it belonged to someone else, she watched her hand write the sentence in her diary and draw thick curlicues beneath it. The other hand lifted her hair, then slid to rest along her neck, where her pulse beat against her palm.

She dipped the pen again and with deep slashes inked out both the sentence and the rose.

"So be it," she wrote, and drew two thick lines under the words. "I must get to work once more. Work is the great fire that burns away all else. I must seek inspiration for another play. Let me think of an exotic setting—the Orient, perhaps, or even America??? Or—what if the setting is not exotic at all? What if everything were to take place in Paris, and not the Paris of long ago but of our—"

She stopped; the apartment door had opened. Voices: Nandou's and Gaby's, sounding odd. She blotted the page and locked the diary back in her desk.

Going down the hall, she heard Gaby say, "Your shoes are filthy. Why do you go out walking when they have just covered the paving stones with tar?"

"I go when I like, modernization or not. Do not change the subject."

"Very well. You grabbed me so tightly that it hurt."

"I did not mean to hurt you. It was the shock . . . to come back from walking and find you like that . . . "

"You would forbid me to see a man, is that it?"

"If you ever see that one again, I shall take you away from Paris and never allow you to return. I swear it, Gabrielle, by the fact that I love you. Do you promise never to see him again?"

An angry pause. "No. I am nearly nineteen, and quite capable of—"

"What is it?" Jeanne cried, running into the room. "What has happened?"

They turned and looked at her: Nandou in the old trousers, jacket, and cap in which he still roamed the streets sometimes, his breathing as heavy as if he had carried a stone up the stairs. Gaby in a dress of ivory silk, bonnet still in her hand and her pretty lips held as tightly as a fist. They seemed fixed in their poses, as if they had been painted. "Tell me what is the matter at once," Jeanne said, "or I shall conclude something worse than it could possibly be."

"You would be right," Nandou said, folding his arms.

"What, then?" she cried.

Gabrielle threw her bonnet on the table and began undoing her cape. "Nothing is wrong except Nandou's odd behavior. I allowed an admirer to drive me home, that is all. I have told you about him, Jeanne—the one who kept sending bouquets but never made himself known. Finally he did appear. I have had supper with him several times. He is behaving precisely in the manner you predicted, and I shall soon be doing just what you would wish. I shall tell him I could not possibly care for him, and dismiss him and his hypocritical bourgeois respectability." She ran her hands along the smoothness of dark hair that swept over her ears and back, and looked at Jeanne as if she were already receiving the praise she clearly expected. "I see no reason for Nandou's actions."

Nandou said, "Ask her who the man is."

"I have told you that I do not know his name."

Nandou's chest heaved. "It is Vollard. I saw his face quite clearly in the lamplight."

Only one thought came into Jeanne's mind, the words rattling like pebbles in a bowl: She should have known. The flowers—she should have known. No doubt he sent them to many women. While she was drawing his white roses in her diary, he had been driving her daughter home and pressing his suit upon her.

She looked at Gabrielle as if seeing her for the first time: how fresh and prettily colored her skin, how delicate the lines her brows drew above the shining eyes. How young she was. "How did you meet him?" Jeanne said.

"One night he was waiting at the stage door."

"Has he asked you to become . . . intimate with him?"

Gaby's chin lifted; Jeanne felt the angle in her own throat.

"Do not worry," Gaby said. "I shall not do it. I wish only to—"

"For God's sake, Jeanne!" Nandou cried.

"Were you not the one," she cried back at him, "who said she must be allowed to live as an adult?" She pulled her shawl tighter and said, more quietly, "It would not be wise for you to see the man again, Gabrielle."

"Why not? Who is he? What is wrong with him?"

"He is . . . He is a bourgeois, a banker, whose fortune is considerable by now, I would imagine. He lives in rue—"

"Not Nicolas," Nandou said. "It was his brother."

"Louis?" The name sounded odd to Jeanne's ears, as if she were not pronouncing it properly. She cleared her throat. "Louis." No, that was not right, could not be. "Louis," she said, more loudly, and then her mouth closed around it in a snarl, and the name felt right. "God damn him to hell!"

"Maman," Gaby said in concern, and started toward her.

"No," Jeanne managed. Gaby stopped, confused. Jeanne took several gulps of air and said, "Let there be no question about this. You cannot see him again, for any reason, under any circumstance. Ever."

With a look settling over her face that Jeanne had never seen there before, Gaby said. "I think you had better tell me why. You are extremely distressed, and for that reason alone, I must know who this man is and what he has done."

Jeanne's lips were dry and salty. "No. Believe me, Gabrielle, I know what is best for you in this matter. Just accept that you cannot see him again."

"Surely you will not start treating me like a child again. I do not need protecting any longer. I thought you agreed to that."

That was why she seemed different, Jeanne thought: on her face was the look of one woman to another, not a daughter to her mother. "My darling," she said carefully, "has this man told you he has a wife?"

Gabrielle blinked. "No. But I have assumed it. Isn't that the point of such men—that they pose to the world as virtuous when they are not?"

"Yes."

"I have never seen you like this," Gaby said. "I do not believe the sole cause can be the fact that he is married. What else do you know of him?"

Jeanne's throat was as dry as her mouth. "The details do not matter."

"No?" Gaby swung around. "Nandou, you will tell me, then."

He shook his head. "The decision is your mother's."

Gaby made a steeple of her hands, put it beneath her chin, and paced the length of the room. Then she stopped and turned to Jeanne. "Is he the man who tried to kidnap me years ago? Who betrayed you in some way?"

Jeanne looked at Nandou, beseeching, but for once he seemed helpless. Yes was as perilous as no; she swung between them until she felt almost dizzy.

Watching her, Gabrielle said, "I think he must be."

Jeanne sighed and nodded.

A smile began on Gabrielle's face, and would not stop growing. "Why then," she said, "I can be the instrument of revenge."

"No, no, no. It's out of the question."

"But don't you see—it's quite perfect, almost like something you might have written, Maman. The child grows up and avenges both her mother and herself. When I see him again and refuse him, in the most humiliating way possible, I shall tell him who I am. I should think you would appreciate the—"

"No, Gaby, no!"

Gabrielle folded her hands and said, "Then I must know why."

The only refuge was silence.

"If you do not tell me," Gaby said, "I shall ask Monsieur Vollard himself."

Silence. Gabrielle turned to Nandou. His broad face was still, except that a muscle jumped in his cheek, near the old scar. "Nandou," she said, "you know what happened, you must know. Please tell me."

He lifted a hand, and the wild hope came to Jeanne that he would lift the other as well and wave them both and make everything disappear. But he only pushed his fingertips into his cheek, where the muscle jerked.

"Do not ask it of him," Jeanne said. "If anyone tells you, it must be me."

"I am waiting then, Maman."

Jeanne made a slow knot of her hair. "Very well." She let the knot unwind. "Louis Vollard is your father."

At first Gaby did not seem to react at all. Then she swallowed and turned slowly back to Nandou. "You . . . are not?"

"No."

"I don't understand. You always acted as if . . . you never . . . I have always believed . . . "

"In my heart you have always been my child," he said.

"But . . . " She looked about ten years old, ready to cry.

"Oh, sweetheart," Jeanne said, running to her. But when she got there, the child was gone, replaced by a woman who did not want to be embraced. Who said, "Then you have lied to me all of my life, both of you. You talk of the need for truth on the stage, yet in reality you have denied it to me. Why?"

Papa? The child-voice had said it, years before, when they had brought her back from the farm; naturally the children she lived with there had addressed their father by that name. *Papa?* she had said, in her sweet bird-voice. Hearing it, Nandou had lifted his eyes to Jeanne's, struggling not to plead. She had made a decision, and said to the child, "We shall not use the names 'Papa' and 'Maman' in this house. Now that you are Gabrielle, I shall be Jeanne, and Nandou will be as he always has been. Do you know where your new name has come from? From Nandou, for his true name is Gabriel Corday. Yes, just like you."

They had never actually denied or confirmed that he was her father; they had simply allowed her to assume it.

"Why?" Gabrielle repeated.

"Because I loved you," Nandou said. "I wanted you to feel safe in that love."

"I did," Gaby cried. "But I . . . " Her gaze jerked from one of them to the other, like an animal's when it scents danger. Then her shoulders collapsed with a sob and she ran between them and down the hall to her room. The door slammed.

She would not open it to either of them, all night. In the morning, when Jeanne rose early, she was gone.

Louis and Edmée were dining alone at the long table that reflected candles and wineglasses like a dark mirror.

After they had eaten the soup course in silence, Edmée said, "What a shame the Palais-Royal could not have been made ready in time for this year's Salon. Where will it be held, do you know?"

"No," Louis said. "I believe they plan to push it into early '51 and make it serve for both years. I do not think it is a wise decision."

"Who will be more disappointed, the painters or the public?" Louis shrugged. "Whenever it happens," Edmée said, "we will take Marc, shall we? The three of us can attend together."

"If you like."

"Wouldn't you like?"

"Certainly. A splendid idea."

Edmée leaned forward. "It has been wonderful to see him in your studio, Louis—to see both of you there."

Louis smiled. "The boy has talent. A good deal of talent."

"Then . . . what about his attending an art school?"

"It will mean a struggle with his grandmother. With both grand-mothers."

"Surely that is not a reason to deny his wish. If he is truly good, he should work at painting full-time, not merely steal an hour here and there."

Almost to himself, Louis said, "I never expected you would align yourself against my mother, Edmée."

"I will do anything for those I love. Do you not know that?"

In the silence, the butler entered and approached Louis. "I beg your pardon, sir, but a letter has been delivered and the messenger claims he was ordered to place it in no hands but yours."

Louis laid down his napkin in annoyance and went out into the hall.

When the man handed over the letter, he broke the seal, which he did not recognize. The message was short. He read it three times.

"Are you all right, sir?" the butler asked. He repeated the question.

Louis stuffed the letter into his pocket. "Bring my coat, and tell madame that I have had to go out."

"Very good, sir. Do you want the carriage?"

"No. I shall walk."

Three hours later, sitting on a red velvet sofa, quite drunk, Louis shouted for matches and an ashtray. When a seminude girl brought them, he took the letter from his pocket, put it on the tray, set it aflame, and watched it fade to a shell of ashes, which collapsed under the touch of a finger. But the words would not fade from his mind: "Louis.

Gabrielle Corday's true name is Solange Sorel. If you ever attempt to speak to her again, I swear I shall kill you. J."

The ashtray tumbled from his hand to the carpet. He fell back on the sofa and tears slid over his cheeks and ears onto a red satin pillow.

Chapter Thirteen

"I don't know which is worse," Jeanne said, "to have her kidnapped, or to know that she left of her own will because she hates us. No, here is the worst thing—knowing that one man is the cause of both."

"She does not hate us," Nandou said. "That is not possible."

"Are you sure?"

"Yes," he said uncertainly.

Jeanne put her arms on the table, laid her head on them, and cried, her shoulders lifting and twisting as if they carried the tears and the tears were made of lead. Nandou stood with one hand on her hair, unable either to comfort her or to cry himself. His pain was as tight as a fist, and would not uncurl.

They went through it again and again, each day, every night.

"What we did was best for her," Jeanne said, "whether she knows it or not."

"Of course it was," Nandou said. "We were thinking only of her."

"What should we have done—let her grow up knowing she is illegitimate?"

"That would have been cruel."

"And how could I have told her about Louis?"

"You could not." Muscles bunched in Nandou's jaw. Jeanne cried again.

What we did was best for her, whether she knows it or not. They put the thought in a dozen different ways, to make it seem like a dozen reasons for doing what they had done—to reassure themselves they had done the right thing.

But how could it be the right thing when she was gone—again?

Nandou went to the Théâtre-Italien and tried to catch her when she came out after performances, but she looked at him as if there were nothing between them more personal than air and said, "I do not wish to speak to you now." He bowed his head and watched her go off in carriages that seemed to roll over his heart.

"Why did I tell her the truth?" Jeanne wailed. "I should have found another reason for her not to see . . . him again. For my plays I can invent explanations for anything. Why could I not invent one for my own daughter that night?"

"I was too hard on her," Nandou said. "I grabbed her too roughly and hauled her up here like a jailer. I threatened to banish her from Paris if she did not do as I wished. I behaved just like the father we let her assume I was." *You . . . are not?* The sound of those words, like three drops of rain hanging on a bare branch, swelling but not falling, would not leave his ear.

Jeanne wrote her a long letter: "Life is empty without you . . . I never meant to hurt you, only to protect you . . . I will never hurt you again, I swear, if only you will come home, please, my darling Gaby, I ask it with all my heart and breath and soul . . . " The boy who took the letter to the Théâtre-Italien brought it back unopened, saying Mademoiselle Corday would not accept it.

Jeanne went to her room, stared at the daguerrotype of Gabrielle, and cried for an hour. Then she dried her eyes, splashed them with water, and went out to announce, "I shall not run to her and beg. She is the one who left us."

"I would beg," Nandou said, "if only she would talk to me."

Piece by piece they began to resume their lives. Hours went by without their speaking of her, then days; once an entire week. But they thought of her every night, separately and privately, Nandou on his bed, Jeanne on hers, each staring up into the dark.

Nandou thought of how he would catch Gabrielle some day or night and make her talk to him; how he would convince her to return to them, or at least to be one with them again; how the fist of dry tears inside him would finally relax.

Jeanne thought of Louis: how sweet it would be to take revenge on him for stealing her daughter twice, if only she could think of some way to achieve it—some way that would not only hurt him as he had hurt her but would punish him for the terrible hypocrisy of his actions, of his life . . .

In January of the new year, 1851, she thought of a way. If it worked, it would take time—months—but by fall, surely, it would be finished.

And when it was, she would be all right again. Fall at the latest; only nine months. She smiled into the dark. A revenge that might take as long as a child to grow, but with this wonderful difference: When it was born, the pain would not be hers. She would be able to breathe again, for the pain would be Louis's.

Nandou attended the performance of *Il Barbiere di Siviglia* dressed as elegantly as was possible for him. He did not like the clothes, which required height and grace of their wearer and seemed to call even more attention to his lack of such qualities. A dwarf in evening dress was like a boy in his father's clothes. *Isn't that a sweet little suit?* he heard a woman say during one of the entr'actes, a creature on whom jewels and flesh both hung pendulously. Still, he thought it best to see Gabrielle in the finest clothes he could muster. "Where on earth are you going?" Jeanne had asked him. When he told her, hope had leaped in her eyes, then sunk into caution.

As Gabrielle sang Rosina, he tried to see her performance objectively. It was difficult for him to judge her singing; her trills and other vocal acrobatics amazed him, but he knew that many sopranos could execute them. She had a facility for comedy that one could bring out with careful coaching, she was spirited, and a quality of sweetness pervaded all she did. Rosina, in fact, seemed the perfect role for her. But did she come onto the stage and seize the audience with the power of her personality? Did her voice make one feel one was hearing something extraordinary, unforgettable? The answer, he feared, was no. But was she beautiful? Did he love her so much he did not care whether she was good or bad, a great artist or only pleasingly talented? Yes, a hundred times yes.

After the performance, he posted himself in the shadows by the stage door. He had discovered where she was living by watching at that door and chatting with stagehands and porters. Not far from the Théatre-Italien was a large, somber house where a number of singers lodged. Amélie Véron was one of them, and Gabrielle was staying with her, in second-floor rooms. Twice he had gone there, but Amélie Véron answered and said Gabrielle could not speak with him. This time she would, he had sworn it. If she went home, he would follow and stay until she let him in. If she went to supper, he would be on her doorstep when she returned. He rubbed his hands and stamped his feet, for warmth as well as determination, and gripped his ebony walking stick with gloved fingers.

The stage door opened; some orchestra musicians appeared against the light like cut-outs. Instruments held as carefully as children, they moved down the street, grumbling about the recently imported custom of performing in evening dress. "Let the English keep their notions to themselves." "Or send us a better one—their wages. A Covent Garden violinist would be insulted to play for what I earn!"

If it were not for *The Dwarf Lord,* Nandou thought, he too would still be caught in the hard partnership of art and poverty. He lived carefully, reminded of the perils of theatre life by the plights of the colleagues he and Jeanne fed and entertained, but the chronic fear of destitution had been removed. Because of Jeanne. Once he had thought he was rescuing her from poverty. It was not the only irony in their life together, he thought.

The stage door opened again. A young woman appeared in the light, and Nandou's heart thudded. But it was a stranger, who moved toward the bank of carriages waiting down the street. A door opened on one of them; a hand stretched out to help the woman in.

When Gabrielle had alighted from a carriage that night, when Vollard had leaned out and kissed her hand, it had seemed to Nandou that the hand and the face were Jeanne's. A hallucination, he had thought—a mocking one, conjured out of the desire for her that drove him to walk the streets. Then his vision cleared, and he had seen that it was Gabrielle, not her mother—but it was still Vollard.

If only he could explain to Gabrielle how he had felt, he knew he could make her understand. But it was the one thing he could not explain: the jealousy of Vollard that still haunted his life because Vollard, damn his soul for eternity, had made Jeanne feel a passion that he himself—*Dwarf,* he thought, *dwell not on such matters.*

Another shaft of light from the stage door. A man emerged lugging a cello.

But directly behind him, calling good night to someone over her shoulder, was Gabrielle. She wore a plain blue frock beneath her shawl; clearly she was not dressed to go to supper or to some party. Nandou gripped his stick, waited until she set off along the street, and followed at a discreet distance.

That she should walk alone!—no matter how close were the lights and noise of the Grands Boulevards or how short the distance she had to go. He bit his lip to keep from calling out and stayed ten paces behind, unable actually to see her walk but seeing it anyway: the straight back, the steps that were precise and careful yet did not fully repress a rebellious sway. . . .

What we did was best for her, whether she knows it or not.

She turned into the narrow street where she lived. A bright full moon, high above the roofs, was the only light. Nandou stayed behind until she neared the door of her building, then ran to her. She turned and saw him. The small purse from which she had taken a key closed with a snap.

"Gabrielle, you must talk to me," he said.

"Why must I?"

"Because we have loved each other for nineteen years. Or did you not love me after all?"

In the moonlight, beneath the shadow of her bonnet, her eyes were dark holes with unreadable silver glints. "I have nothing to say to you, I think."

"Then I will do the talking." He had meant it as a joke; it came out as a command. "Let me at least say that you were good tonight. I saw the whole performance from the house. Quite good. Do you recall how we worked on the role?"

"I do not feel well tonight, Nandou. That is why I have come home right after the performance."

"Have I not looked after you a hundred times when you did not feel well?" She said nothing. "Shall I beg you, Gaby? On my knees?" He lowered himself to the rough cobbles and held the walking stick before him with both hands. "Please, dear girl who is not my daughter but who will always be the daughter of my heart, please talk to me about what has happened."

"Get up, Nandou. You will ruin your good clothes."

"I will get up when you say you will talk to me."

She sighed. "Very well. We will go upstairs and speak for a short while."

When they entered a large, pleasantly furnished room, a young woman rose from a sofa by the fire, where she had been reading, and stopped short. "May I present Mademoiselle Amélie Véron," Gabrielle said. "Amélie, this is Nandou."

He bowed. "Mademoiselle has spoken to me at the door several times. I am delighted we now meet under more pleasant circumstances."

"Nandou fell in the street. That is why his clothing is muddy."

"I am sorry, monsieur," Amélie Véron said. "Are you hurt?"

"Not in the slightest."

"Amélie, Nandou and I need to speak privately for a moment."

The young woman murmured some polite phrases and withdrew, closing the glass doors behind her.

"She is the daughter of the Vérons?" When Gabrielle nodded, Nandou said, "How do such respectable persons allow their daughter to live on her own?"

"She too has decided to leave her home."

"I see. And what is she rebelling against? Respectability?"

Gabrielle removed her bonnet and gloves in silence and unfastened her jacket. The hope seized Nandou that she would be wearing the rooster brooch he had given her. She said, "I suppose you want to explain why you and Jeanne lied to me. Very well. But do not tell me, please, that it was for my own good."

First point to Gabrielle, Nandou thought. How self-assured she had become. But she was at the age of omniscience; never again is one as clever as one feels at nearly twenty. She slipped off her jacket; she wore no jewelry.

With a little grunt, Nandou settled into a chair and looked up at her. "You have caught me out. I did come here to tell you that Jeanne and I behaved as we did for your sake—for your good. It is true, but you do not wish to believe it, and I understand. It is difficult to accept that others might know what is best for one. So, instead, I will tell you something else that is true, perhaps even truer." He watched her run her hands over her hair in the gesture she always used when composing herself. "Why did you tell your friend I fell in the street," he said, "when that is not the truth?"

Two angry circles appeared on her cheeks; even as a child, her feelings had risen easily to her skin. "You suggest the situations are comparable?"

"No, no. I merely ask why you told a small lie to your friend."

"Because I did not wish you to be embarrassed!"

"A man who looks as I do could never be embarrassed by so simple a thing as muddy trousers." Gabrielle blinked and then set her lips. "Were you not the one who would have been embarrassed?" he said. "By having your friend see you with someone so little concerned with appearance that he deliberately sinks to his knees in the mud of the streets while wearing his best clothes?"

Gabrielle sucked in her breath and stared, as she had used to do when she was a child and he did magic tricks for her.

"Gaby, I mean only to make you see that, at heart, one lies for one's own sake. However much your mother and I considered your interest when we lied to you, we also lied for ourselves. If she let you believe I was your father, it was not only to spare you the knowledge that your actual father had abandoned you but to spare herself the pain of having to confess it to you. And if I let you think you were my daughter, it was . . . to hide from myself the pain of knowing you were not."

She lifted her chin, as Jeanne might have done. "You have just admitted that you were thinking more of yourselves than of me."

"I accept that," he said. "We should have worried more about how you would feel if the truth ever came out."

"Maman was Louis Vollard's mistress, wasn't she?"

"Yes. But he left her soon after learning she was going to have a child."

Gabrielle looked as she had when he told stories of specters and shades: afraid to hear more, unable not to. "Is he the one who tried to kidnap me?"

"Yes."

"Then you have lied again. Only a moment ago you said he abandoned me. He didn't! He tried to get me back."

"Only because he thought his wife was childless! And with no regard for your mother's feelings, none at all! Gabrielle, it was a painful situation and not a simple one. It cannot be reduced to arithmetic: he did this plus this minus that. If it could be, we might have told you long ago."

There was anger in her face, of a depth and kind he had not seen there before, tightening the muscles around her eyes and mouth like a winch. "How could you have believed that lying to me would be best for me? You who say the truth means everything? All my life I have believed you told me the truth about things, about everything. But all the time you were lying to me, making me . . ."

"It is easy now to see that we were wrong. Do you think we would not have spared you the pain and humiliation of your . . . encounter with Vollard if we had known such a thing would occur? No vision is ever perfect, except hindsight. Can you not understand how we felt when you were only a child, a child we adored? And when you were older, we felt . . . we did not know . . . Can you not take pity on us and forgive us?"

He thought she might be going to scream. But when she spoke, it was a whisper—"You lied, you lied"—repeated with the blind intensity of nuns at their rosaries.

"Can you never forgive us, Gaby? Is that what you are telling me? You no longer love us?"

"I still love you," she cried as if she hated him. "But all these years I have been . . . you have made me . . . Oh, I can't explain it to you. I can never explain it to you!" She put her head in her hands.

He got up, went to her, touched her arm. "Try, Gaby. I will understand. I promise."

"No!" she cried, pulling from his grasp. "No! Go away, Nandou. Please!"

"For how long?" He managed to keep his voice steady.

"I must make my own way now."

"I understand. You wish to be on your own. That is . . . admirable. But you will come to see us?"

"I do not know!" Her voice climbed. "But I do not wish to see you now."

"Very well." If he could take nothing else with him from this night, at least he would keep his dignity. "If you should need money . . . "

"I have all the money I need," she said.

He did not believe that could be precisely true; she had not become a star and was probably earning only modest sums. But he said, "I am sure you do. But I know how precarious a performer's lot can be. If you should need anything, anything at all, you know that your mother's arms, and mine, will be open for you always." She said nothing. He went to the door, pulled the knob, turned back. "Was it so terrible, then, believing the dwarf was your father?"

A strange little squawk came from her, as a bird might make when it falls to the ground. Then she shook her head, again and again—but for yes or no?—and fled into the depths of the apartment.

He was out in the street and several blocks away, walking steadily, mechanically, when the fist inside him sprang open. He stopped, leaned against the rough comfort of a wall, and cried as he had not cried since the night Fidèle died, and for the same reason: tears were for that which was irrevocably lost.

When he finally lifted his head, the moon swam in mist and the street was a blur. Down its length, there seemed to be a vague shape moving

toward him. A white kitten? Or a child, laughing and calling "Dou"?
He wiped his eyes; there was nothing. The street was dark and empty.

"It is no use," he told Jeanne when he got home. "She is very angry.
The moment she starts to feel something for us, she calls up the anger.
I believe she still loves us, I know she does, but that too makes her
angry."

Jeanne's body sagged. "Was she wearing the earrings I gave her? No?
Do you think she ever wears them? Will she never come to us again?"

"Jeanne, please do not torture yourself."

"You are tortured too, yet you never weep or scream."

"Do not be so certain. People do not care to know what a dwarf is
feeling. He does best to keep such things to himself."

"I am not 'people.' I am Jeanne."

"Yes. You are Jeanne." He laid his hand on her shoulder. She put her
own over it. As he stood there, in the shadow of her warmth, desire came
over him. He moved away from her and said, "I am going to bed." She
nodded.

He lay in the dark, struggling with himself. He had heard that before
battle a soldier needs a woman more keenly than ever, to assert in the
face of death the fact of still being alive. Because he had lost Gabrielle,
he had to know that Jeanne was not lost to him as well; he could know
it only by possessing her. No matter how he would loathe himself
afterward. He heard the bells strike two, then three. At four he crept
along the hall to her door.

He heard a faint "Come in." When he went to her, she started to
speak, but he put his hand over her mouth, then let it trail along her
skin. He drowned himself in the scent and feel of her, knowing a
pleasure so intense that it drove out all else, even the shame of experiencing it. But for so short a time. So short. He left as he had entered, in
silence.

I won't do it, Edmée Vollard told herself. *Of course I won't.*

She sat alone in her boudoir, half-dressed. Around her murmured the
familiar sounds that made up the days of her life: servants washing,
dusting, polishing, grooming the house as carefully as if it were a person

or a horse. So much activity put in motion by nothing more strenuous than words from her lips—and after uttering them, what had she to do but find ways to fill her days? Through her windows came a warm summer breeze and the flute-song of birds in the garden. *If I did it,* she thought, *I could be jeopardizing all of this.*

If she did it, she would be a model of discretion. To see the knowledge of one's activities held in the eyes and smiles of half of Paris, like reflections lying in puddles everywhere—no, she would make certain that such was not her fate. On the other hand, that fate would not be up to her alone, would it?

She opened one of the little concealed drawers in her desk and took out a note. Elegant handwriting. Exquisite paper.

Lady, pity my thirst, which consumes me day and night and grows greater for being denied. No wine can satisfy it, for in that pale satisfaction it finds only the sorrow of lacking its greatest need. May I never drink from the glass of your lips? Must I live forever in the desert of your refusal?

She had met him at the Opéra one spring night, when she was attending with a couple who often invited her to join them in their box while Louis was elsewhere. No one had noticed when an usher came up and discreetly pressed a note into her hand. It spoke of an admirer who had been observing her from afar and was unable to stop himself from asking to come closer—to meet her. If Louis had been with her . . . if he had not come home the night before reeking of brandy, breaking yet another of his vows . . . if the chestnut trees had not just come out in a green that took one's breath, if the skies had not been so fresh and blue, with the swallows sailing them like little paper ships . . . if a hundred things. She had met him in one of the arcades near the Palais-Royal. They had looked in shops, at books and jewelry and ivory pieces, and talked of music and poetry. He had light-brown curly hair and chestnut eyes with crinkles at their edges, and he spoke with an appealing intensity. He reminded her of Louis—not the Louis of her present life but the one she had loved before she married him. How curious it had been, to feel a dull anger toward Louis, to think of how much he had hurt her, at the same time that she was dallying with another man because he reminded her of Louis.

Edmée put the note back in the drawer and stretched her hands above her head. Her arms and breasts were still firm; within her chemise and corset, her figure still trim. *I would like to do it,* she admitted, relieved to be allowing the desire into consciousness, and leaned back with a sigh. His name was Henri. After the first meeting there had been another, in the Tuileries Garden, and then others in the Bois, at the Louvre, in the Jardin des Plantes, all very discreet. Once she had seen him on the boulevards while she was strolling there with Louis. She had gone lightheaded with a sensation of rebellion, although what rebellion was there, in fact?—for she and Henri had done nothing except talk. Wonderful talk, however. He loved music as much as she had grown to do and was a passionate advocate of the new sounds against the Classical school of the past; the future, he thought, lay with Liszt and his colleagues at Weimar. Meyerbeer he dismissed with a wave of a graceful hand; the Italian Verdi would eclipse all of them. "If I had one wish," she told him, "it would be to have a true gift for music, to do more than play the piano like any other Parisienne." He had smiled slowly, touched her cheek, and said, "And if I had one wish . . . "

He had a reputation as a seducer; she had found that out by asking around, subtly, of course. Still, he read his poetry to her with such feeling. He did everything with feeling. Sometimes she imagined herself a vampire, wanting to suck from him some of that life-giving intensity. When he prophesied that "our prince-president" who "cannot forget that his uncle Napoléon made himself emperor" would find a way to abolish the Republic and deprive Frenchmen of their liberties once again, his chestnut eyes flashed. And when he told her how beautiful she was, how the sight of her standing against the hedges in a pale coral frock was like the benison of sunrise. . . . *I would like to do it very much,* she thought, *but what if things went wrong?*

If she met him, it would be at three, in his rooms near the boulevard des Italiens. To that, she had agreed. But she had not decided if she would meet him.

She extended her legs in front of her, berating herself for lacking courage while studying the long, slim feet that showed beneath her pantalettes. If she had any vanity, it was for her legs: the calves with just the right fullness, the slim ankles. A foolish thing over which to be vain, for no one ever saw them but her maid and Louis, and he barely looked at them anymore. Yet when she was dressed to go out, it was the secret knowledge of her legs' shapeliness that made her confident. Marc's legs were much like hers; too bad men's fashions so resolutely avoided knee-breeches. She smiled; Marc himself would never have such a thought. Or would he? She knew little of the inner life beneath his quiet, intense manner, except that it centered on painting, not politics or girls or the House of Vollard, only painting. She imagined him working, lower lip caught in his teeth, eyes narrowed in concentration and passion.

Without warning she was crying, the tears as warm and slow as summer rain, crying for nothing. Or perhaps for everything: for a marriage that had curdled so young, leaving her breasts, her whole body, heavy with unwanted love; for the illusions that had finally died on the day when she learned that Louis had kidnapped his little daughter and so had lied to her all along; for the sad little rebellion she had staged; for the years of watching Louis's weakness, which was impervious to both screams and silence; and, strangely, for the good father Louis had become. For the Louis-that-might-have-been.

When she heard his voice call her name, she jumped from her chair. "What is the matter?" he said, entering the room.

She grabbed her peignoir with one hand and dabbed at her eyes with the other. "Nothing. It is so warm, and I was . . . I thought you were at the offices."

"I was. I decided to leave."

Say you came home to paint, Louis. If you do, I will not go to Henri.

"Nicolas has gone to Rouen to see about a manager for the new office, and there is nothing requiring my urgent attention." He said the last words mockingly.

Say you came home to take me out, and I will not go to Henri.

"Where do we dine tonight?"

"At the St. Cyrs'. They are planning a séance, remember?"

"Ah, yes." He made a face. "Is everyone in Paris going to hold one of those damn things?"

"Did you want something, Louis?"

"Want? No. Well . . . I suppose we might go for a drive."

She stared at him; he never said such things. "A drive?"

"Yes, if you like."

It took her a moment to realize what she was feeling: anger, because he had failed to give her an excuse to go to Henri.

"Are you all right?" he asked.

"Yes." She heard herself add, "I am afraid I can't go, Louis. I have an appointment with the dressmaker at three."

He shrugged. "No matter. It was an idle thought. I won't disturb you then." He turned and left the room.

At four o'clock, when she was half-lying on a sofa and Henri was kissing her throat, it came to her clearly why she had been angry with Louis: not because he had failed to give her an excuse but because she had needed him to provide one. And always had. *Why should I require an excuse at all?* she thought. *Isn't my whole life with him an excuse? Why can I not have the courage simply to do what I want?*

"Adorable one," Henri said, "my lips can read your skin. They tell me that you are thinking. You must leave the realm of thought before you can enter the kingdom of the senses."

"You are right," she said. She stretched out a leg, in a cherry-and-white stocking, wrapped it around his, and pulled his head down so that his lips could find her breasts.

In the fall, everyone returned from country houses and seaside, and a hint of crispness in the air seemed to make the lights glow more brightly and the horses' hooves strike the paving stones with a sharper ring. Social calendars filled with balls, receptions, days at the races, theatre and opera dates—filled nervously, in anticipation of the dictatorship that everyone agreed was coming. There had been many signs from Louis Napoléon, including his asking Parliament to revise the Constitution to extend his term as president of the Republic. Parliament had refused; a coup seemed inevitable.

"And quite necessary," said Henriette Vollard, at a family dinner. "This Republic has done nothing but create financial disaster."

Joséphine Vollard, on Henriette's right, cut into a breast of roast partridge. "We must have stability if there is to be prosperity." She turned to her husband. "That is what Nicolas believes. Isn't it?"

Nicolas rubbed the spiderwork of lines in the corner of his right eye, the only visible sign that he had passed into his forties, and said, "It is true there can be no economic progress when the ship of state is rocking from side to side."

"There you are, then," Joséphine said, as if someone had been disputing her. She was a fine-boned woman who would have embodied the vogue for china-doll delicacy except that in her perfect complexion a small mouth sat like a purse with a snap.

"And who is rocking that ship?" Henriette said. "The workers. They cannot be allowed to upset everything we have built."

"Does stability have to mean dictatorship?" asked Edmée, who was generally rather silent at family affairs. No one answered her. "Does it, Nicolas?"

"I don't like to think so," he said slowly, "but we French don't seem to understand how else stability is achieved."

"Does anyone?" Edmée said. "What about the Americans?"

"The Americans!" Joséphine cried. "They are the very opposite of stable, with their constant westward migration and their factions arguing over slavery."

"I think we French comprehend stability very well," Henriette said. "We have been the heart of the civilized world for centuries of monarchy."

"But things cannot remain as they have always been," Edmée said.

"I hope I know that better than any of you, after all I have lived through. But change must be change for the better. Disruption is not progress."

Nicolas turned to Edmée. "If I were president of the Republic, and God forbid that it should be so, I would find it difficult to reconcile the needs that a banker has, for example, with those of a worker in a sugar-beet factory."

"Would you try?" she asked.

"I would believe it to be my duty. But could I succeed?"

Edmée looked at Louis. "You have nothing to say on a subject like this?"

He had been drinking his wine and following the conversation with darting glances. Putting down the glass so firmly that the ruby liquid rocked, he said, "I have more important things on my mind than politics."

Silence. Joséphine gave a tight little laugh, like pebbles thrown down marble stairs, and began talking about the latest antics of her five-year-old son Denis.

After dinner Nicolas took Louis aside and asked, "What is the matter? You have been giving Edmée the most burning stares all evening."

Louis gripped Nicolas's arm, released it, paced in a circle, came back and peered into his brother's eyes. "Can I trust you, Nico?"

"Need you ask?"

From his pocket Louis took a letter that had been crumpled and then smoothed out. "I received this two days ago."

Nicolas read it silently: "To Monsieur Vollard from One who Wishes Him Well. If you follow madame on her afternoon outings, you will discover they often take her to the arms of another man." When Nicolas looked up, Louis's mouth was so tight that it seemed to be sewn. "This appears to have been written by a public scribe," Nicolas said. "Have you any idea who sent it?"

"What does that matter?"

"I take it you have followed her, then?"

"Yesterday afternoon. His name is Henri Foucher. A poet, of Republican sentiments, better known for his numerous seductions than for his verses."

"Ah. I am sorry, Louis. You had no suspicions?"

"Of Edmée the virtuous?" Louis gave a short, bitter laugh. "I swear to you, Nico, I shall kill her."

"I know you have had a shock, but please do not speak so foolishly."

"My words are neither foolish nor idle."

Nicolas put a hand on his brother's arm. "I do not believe you mean that."

Louis pulled away. "You are wrong."

"I would expect you to be angry at first, but are you not reacting more strongly than is warranted? Forgive my speaking frankly, but you have never been truly in love with Edmée. Nor have you been faithful to her. Your pride is hurt, certainly, but—"

"Do you defend her conduct?"

"No. I only ask you to consider—"

"Suppose you had received such news about Joséphine?"

After a pause, during which Louis stared into his eyes as if to strike fire in them, Nicolas said, "Let me be honest with you, brother, as we always used to be. I wish it were not so, but I would not particularly care, so long as she was discreet."

Louis turned away with a soft explosion of breath.

"Have you talked to Edmée? Does she realize that you know?"

"No."

"What are you planning to do?"

"If you cannot understand my feeling, I do not care to discuss my action."

"Louis, you are alarming me. Please let me—"
But Louis had left the room.

For two days he walked around with anger choking him like a clot that
no amount of reasoning, or brandy, could dissolve. What Nico had said
was true—he had never loved Edmée and had betrayed her many times,
with many women. What Nico did not understand was that none of
that was the issue. The issue was . . . He did not know what it was. He
knew only that the anger in his throat could not be swallowed.

He spent an entire morning walking up and down the street where
Foucher lived, thinking he should challenge the man. But it was not the
man he wanted to challenge. It was . . . He did not know. What he felt
in the pit of his stomach took him all the way back to boarding school,
to a holiday when he had preferred to stay by himself and sketch rather
than visit a brothel with some of his classmates. When they came back,
they had taunted him and tied him over a chair. Pulled down his trousers
and pinned two of his sketches to his underpants, one on his rear, the
other above his penis. His stomach had gone as soft as custard; they had
not only made a fool of him but reduced him to pap . . . Yes, he was
a fool . . . relinquishing the passions of his youth, embracing respectability and a proper wife, only to have her mock him by abandoning the
virtue that had reproached him for years . . . Her lover was not only
a Republican but a poet—anyone but such a man!—who lived less than
two blocks from the studio he himself had once had, damn her for that
mockery above all . . . A fool, soft and wet, who did nothing right.
Who tried to warm himself in admiration for an exquisite creature
because she was so pure, so innocent, so unlike any Ninette . . . or
Arlette . . . Admiration was all he had intended, all!—but she had mocked
him too, and shamed him by turning out to be his own daughter.

Nothing turned out to be what one expected. Especially one's life.
One must fight back, somehow.

On the third day Edmée said she was going to rue de la Paix, and
Worth's. But when he followed, she went to Foucher's address. From
down the block Louis watched her, throat hard, stomach quivering.
When the hem of her lavender dress and the ribbon flying from her hat
had disappeared inside the door of the building, he turned and walked
briskly down the street.

An hour later, there were stentorian knocks on the door of Foucher's apartment and voices demanding immediate entry. When Foucher answered, still scrambling to tie a dressing gown around him, five policemen burst in. Their leader produced a warrant for one Edmée Vollard, who was known to be on the premises, sorry, monsieur, but we must satisfy ourselves as to whether the lady is here, that door leads to the bedroom?—ah, madame, apologies, but you are hereby under arrest on the charge of adultery, please dress as quickly as possible so you may accompany us.

Edmée, as white as the lace on the chemise she had managed to pull over her breasts, stood clutching her dress in front of her, seemingly unable to put it on or to move at all, except for her eyes, which kept blinking in refusal to accept what was happening. A policemen opened the door again and said, "If you do not dress at once, madame, we will take you as you are."

"Henri!" she cried, through the open door.

"Do not worry," came his voice, too thin to be reassuring.

When Jeanne emerged from her room for lunch, Nandou was sitting at the table, waiting for her.

"Is it going well?" he asked.

"I have created nothing today except a large pile of crumpled papers."

"Do not worry," he said. "It will come again."

"Will it? How can you be sure? I should be surprised if I have written ten good pages since . . . since Gaby left."

He nodded. "She is always in the mind. Her presence was so light, her absence so heavy."

"Will she ever come back?"

It was not a question that either tried to answer any longer, but they could not keep themselves from asking it sometimes, as if to stop would close off all possibility of her return.

In silence they began eating the cutlets and salad the maid had prepared.

After a moment Jeanne said, "Something happened this morning, didn't it? You look as if you are waiting to tell me."

"I used to be able to hide things from you if I wished."

"You will again, when I am able to write again, and for the same reason." He gave a grunt that was also a sigh. "Well, what is it?" she said.

Nandou pulled his hands through his hair. "I heard some gossip in the café this morning. Louis Vollard has had his wife arrested for adultery."

Jeanne's fork fell from her hand and clattered to the plate. She looked down at it, picked it up, placed it on the cloth. "Arrested?" she said.

"Is that not an irony, in light of his own behavior?"

"Yes."

"You do not ask who was the man in question."

Jeanne reached for her glass and took a sip. "Who was he?"

"One of your admirers, I believe. Henri Foucher."

"Was he arrested as well?"

"He was taken to the district Commissary of Police, but apparently charges against him were dropped. Madame Vollard is in Saint-Lazare prison."

"Prison?" Jeanne said faintly.

"You know how serious a charge adultery is for a woman."

"Yes. But I did not think . . . " Jeanne pushed her plate away. "I am not hungry."

"What is the matter?"

"Nothing."

"Then why do you look as if someone is walking on your grave?"

"It is a shock to learn what Louis has done, and to hear that Henri Foucher was involved with Louis's wife. That is all."

"I believe there is something more."

"I do not wish to discuss it."

"Why not?"

"I do not wish to discuss it!" She pushed back her chair and left the room.

Chapter Fourteen

O n the night of December 1, Paris went to bed as usual. On the morning of December 2, it woke to learn that the coup had finally occurred. Opposition leaders had been rounded up and jailed. Placards everywhere announced the dissolution of Parliament, the imposition of martial law, and the imminent holding of a plebiscite. Louis Napoléon was now in total control. He had chosen the date for its precedents: It was the anniversary of the Battle of Austerlitz and the day his uncle Napoléon I had been crowned emperor.

In the Vollard home on rue Faubourg Saint-Honoré, where Henriette had been living in lonely splendor since Olivier's death, her sons faced her in the drawing room. It had changed little since their childhood, except that the brocade wallpaper had been replaced by a striped one. They sat on the sofa, as they always had when summoned for serious conversations. The very feel of the sofa, like thin fur over thick bones, presaged some kind of reprimand or confrontation.

"What is happening in the streets?" Henriette asked.

"They are quiet," Nicolas said. "Thousands of men are massed in the central quarters, but no shots have been fired. We do not yet know what price will be paid for this coup."

"There is always a price for achieving order," Henriette said.

"I wonder if those arrested last night might not consider it too high." Nicolas spoke with his habitual calm, but there was something restless within it, like a fish moving below ice.

"The situation could not be left as it was. Do you want the House of Vollard to suffer still another year of uncertainty and losses?"

"I want only to understand. The Revolution was over before I was born, yet I have lived through three uprisings in which people died by the thousands in the streets of Paris. Is there to be no end to blood and barricades and death?"

Louis, who was sitting rigidly on the sofa, staring ahead, turned to his brother in surprise. Henriette raised her eyebrows, stretched her hands, so that her sapphire ring winked in the glow of the fire, then, queen-like, laid her arms on the arms of her chair. At sixty-six, her hair had turned a soft and flattering gray, but her posture had not given an inch. "We can do little, and certainly nothing at the moment," she said, "about what is happening in the palace or the streets. The point of this meeting is something that is within our control. Yesterday, when I asked you to come here this morning, I did not even know the coup would take place, although I confess I am not sorry that people now have something to distract them from thinking of Louis's mad action." She settled her gaze on her younger son, who reacted only by clasping a hand on each knee. "Are you going to persist in charging Edmée?" she asked.

"I am doing what is right," he replied tonelessly. He looked as he always did—properly dressed, unself-consciously elegant in bearing— except for his eyes, which had the fixity of glass.

"Edmée's behavior is a sin before God. It shocks and offends all decent people. But how can it be right to subject the Vollard name to public comment and ridicule? To have the journals speak of matters that belong within our walls—that, Louis, is unacceptable."

Louis shook his head violently but so briefly that he was still before Henriette could be sure he had moved. "What is unacceptable is Edmée's conduct."

"I have said I agree."

"Then you should want her to receive the punishment the law provides."

"I want the punishment kept within the family. You made the crime public by your impetuous rush to the police. Now our goal must be to remove the situation from the public eye, which will happen if you drop your charges at once, before the fortuitous distraction of the coup is over, or at least request that she be detained in a convent, not in a prison."

"That is your goal, Maman, not mine."

Henriette leaned forward. "What is your goal then, in the name of heaven?"

Louis's eyelids beat for a moment. "I want justice."

After a silence Henriette said, "I know you are hurt, Louis. Do you think I do not feel it when one of my sons is suffering? But if you persist, you will only hurt yourself still more. Remember the scandal of a few years ago, when that foolish Biard found his wife with Victor Hugo and had her arrested for adultery. Do you not recall how Paris laughed and criticized and gossiped?"

"Biard is not a foolish man," Louis said. "He is a fine young painter."

Henriette clicked her teeth. "You talk as if you were still twenty, being led through life by your passions."

Louis smiled, not the smile that gave his mother secret pleasure but one that held his mouth nearly motionless while the flesh around it twisted. "To the contrary, Maman, I have been led too often by your view of what is right. But not this time."

"Do not make it sound as if you have lived your life on my terms."

"Now that you put it in those words, I believe that is exactly what I have done. Yes. Your terms."

"That is absurd, Louis! I have merely tried to make you see the wisdom of certain courses of action."

"How is it, then, Maman, that after following those courses, I end with a wife who commits adultery?"

For an instant it seemed Louis's words had reached her, but then Henriette's chin rose higher. "Do not lay your failures at another's door. It is up to a husband to keep his wife from straying outside the marriage bonds."

Louis shot to his feet. "You blame me? Me? When I have always done what you wished? Married the woman you wished? Joined the firm as you wished? Given up what I—" He stopped, choking on the words. "By God, for once in my life I shall do as I wish!"

They stared at each other, Henriette rigid, Louis trembling as if his body held not only his own agitation but all that hers refused to allow.

"Is it your wish, then," she finally said, "to disgrace us all?"

"It is my wish to make Edmée pay for what she has done! I would prefer that others not be affected, but as you just observed, there is always a price for achieving order."

"Nicolas," Henriette said, "you must make your brother come to his senses."

When he did not answer, both turned to look at him. "Surely," Henriette said sharply, "you are not on his side in this matter?"

Nicolas made a fist and lowered it to the arm of the sofa. "I think, with you, that Louis will hurt everyone involved, himself perhaps most of all. And I very much do not want to see him suffer."

"There," Henriette said to Louis. "Your brother—"

"But I do not understand you either," Nicolas said. "You say that what Edmée has done is shocking and deserves to be punished, though privately. Yet adultery is committed every day and night in the highest of circles, including that of Louis Napoléon. Isn't the duc de Morny, his own half-brother, illegitimate? How many cocottes and so-called actresses attend balls at the Elysée Palace? You know these things, Maman. All Paris knows them—much of Paris is busy doing them itself, with no cries for punishment. The hypocrisy would be amusing if it did not also destroy one's desire to laugh."

"If you will not discuss this matter sensibly . . . " Henriette said.

"And if there is any punishment," Nicolas continued, "it is only the woman who suffers. When Biard charged his wife with adultery, her lover was released because he is the famous Victor Hugo, a peer of the realm, while madame went to prison. Do you not see the hypocrisy? No? Louis, you must see it."

Still standing, Louis said doggedly, "The laws of France allow a wife to be punished for the crime of adultery."

"Whereas for a man it is not even a crime, unless he keeps the mistress in his home. In which case the true crime would be his foolishness."

Henriette sighed and suddenly seemed old, on her face the look of disorientation in a changing world that the elderly often wear. "I do not understand you, Nicolas. You know a banking house is sensitive to scandal. I count on you to safeguard the firm's interest."

"But not to be concerned with the plight of my sister-in-law?— whom, as it happens, I like."

"Do you defend her action?"

Nicolas hesitated. "I do not want her sacrificed to Louis's obsession."

"Obsession!" Louis cried.

Nicolas rose to face him. "Forgive me, brother, for you know I love you, but that is how it seems to me. Besides your anger at Edmée, I sense something else in you, driving you to neglect all other considerations. Forget the House of Vollard, forget the scandal that Maman fears . . . ask yourself, in the name of the happy life we shared in this house, if the destruction of Edmée can truly ease the soul of Louis."

Henriette watched something pass between her sons, too strong to interrupt. Often she had seen their gazes lock and a mirror-smile bridge their differences, but neither smiled now. Each pair of eyes struggled to control the other; it was like the game they had played as children, when they stood face to face, arms rising higher and higher as each tried to put his fist atop the other's.

"I shall not change my mind," Louis said at last.

"I shall not help you do this thing," Nicolas replied.

"Give it up, Louis," Henriette said. "Think of the firm, and the scandal!"

"Think of Marc," Nicolas said. "And of yourself. Give it up."

Louis turned and left the room.

"No more work today," Belloc told his pupils. "I must go out into the streets and see what is happening. Clean up and clear out, all of you. If you have families, they may be worrying about you."

Marc swallowed his disappointment. He had hoped to spend the day at Belloc's, a drafty barn of a studio on the fringes of Saint-Germain-des-Prés, where he had a special arrangement: He worked on Saturdays and whenever else he could get away from his regular classes. Belloc had refused at first; then he looked at examples of Marc's work, grumbled, and assented. Massive and hirsute, Belloc looked as if he worked on a farm or a railroad; he had a huge appetite for food, drink, and women; but he revered painting. No typical studio behavior was allowed: no initiation rites that had new pupils prancing about naked to the jibes of their seniors, no crude and stupid joking while they worked.

When news of Edmée's arrest appeared, Belloc had placed a paw on Marc's shoulder and said, "Vollard, I sympathize, but you must not let your parents tear you in half. A painter must be a whole man. Two men, in fact. One to paint like a demon, another to stand aside and tell the demon what to do."

Marc left the studio and began to walk. There seemed to be few insurgents, but everywhere he saw troops: bullet eyes and well-fed cheeks above tight jaws. He almost took out his notebook but decided it might invite trouble to stand on a street corner, sketching. He wondered if his mother knew what was happening, in her cell in Saint-Lazare prison. Was it dark? Noisy? Dirty? Was she able to comb her beautiful hair, that was like long strands of honey? He forced himself to stop picturing her. Belloc had found the right words, he thought: He did feel torn in half. In truth, though, even before the arrest had cut into his life like an axe, he had found it easier not to be with both his parents at the same time. The love he felt for each, the experiences he had with each, were as different as chalk and oil and could not occupy the same frame.

He had realized as much, and forcibly, at the last Salon, when they had insisted that he attend opening day with both of them. The three of them had struggled through the huge crowd and the air filled with dust. On one hand Marc had the fellow-painter's conversation of his father, on the other, the loving but naïve comments of his mother. "I think the still lifes you do are as just good as that one," she had said—pointing to a canvas alive with subtleties of color Marc could not yet summon. Finally he had run away, moving far ahead to look at things by himself, especially the Courbets. "Ugly," people were calling the hard-faced peasants and weary stonecutters; "shocking," they said; he knew only that they were raw, somber, and so striking that he was still in their grip when his parents found him. For some minutes he didn't hear a word either of them said. And when he did hear, how to balance between his father's reaction, so much like his own—and for such things he would always love his father, no matter what he did— and his mother's wondering why anyone would choose to paint such unpleasant subjects? He had wanted them to leave him alone, both of them, everyone, leave him alone with his chalks and oils and the visions in his head struggling to be born. He had made some inadequate excuse and walked away, to consider what made the Courbets so powerful.

He realized that his nose and ears were cold; he had walked the whole way home. At the door, he squared his shoulders, both to shake off the reluctance he felt and to strengthen his determination not to show it.

As soon as he went upstairs, his father came out into the hall. "How are you, son? Did you have trouble getting here?"

"I saw troops everywhere, but no one tried to stop me."

"You had better remain here until we know that order is being maintained." Marc's face must have shown something, for his father said, "You can paint here, you know." A room had been converted into a studio for him, next to his father's. Neither of them used his room very often; Marc preferred to work at Belloc's, and his father . . . who could tell his father's reasons?

"What are you doing, Papa?" Marc asked, for Louis's hands were dirty and his cravat askew.

Louis hesitated. "I am bundling up all your mother's things."

"Why?"

"Because I do not want the servants to do it."

"I mean . . . what are you going to do with them?"

"Give them to the ragpickers," Louis said, with a strange satisfaction.

Do not try to talk to him about her again, Marc told himself, running his hands through his curly brown hair as if to cage his thoughts. *Keep quiet.* But his voice seemed to have its own will. It said, "Papa, please don't do it."

"You expect me to leave everything as it is and welcome her back some day?"

"I don't mean that. I mean . . . withdraw your charge against her."

The look Marc dreaded came over Louis's face: a child's stubbornness mixed with an adult's determination. "Marc, you must accept that she has hurt me in a way I cannot forgive. She has to pay."

Don't remind him he is hurting you. Don't! "But you are hurting me."

"I regret that, deeply. But it is not my doing. She should have thought of you before behaving as she did."

"Papa, she is in *prison.* How can you want that to happen?"

"You do not understand," Louis said. "One day you will, when you have learned more of women and their ways."

No, Marc thought; he would never understand his father's kind of passions. No more would his father understand his.

"I am only doing what must be done," Louis said.

Marc looked at the man before him, elegant in spite of his disarray; who suddenly seemed as alien as an Indian from the Americas. *You are wrong, Papa,* he wanted to cry. *Yes, she was wrong too, but no matter what she did, it is not right to treat her this way.* But the words would not come. Who was he to call either of them wrong when his own soul was unclean? When he lived with a darkness deeper and heavier than either of theirs could ever be?

"I know this is very difficult for you," Louis said. "Would you like to leave Paris for a while? Go to Italy and do some painting? You could stay as long as you liked. I would arrange it with your school." His voice was gentle, his eyes concerned; he was Papa again.

"Thank you very much, but no," Marc said. "Excuse me, please, Papa, I must go to my room now." He started to his door, then turned and said, "I cannot leave Paris while Maman is in Saint-Lazare."

His father nodded and said, "I understand." The strange thing was, Marc believed that he did.

. . .

All day Jeanne and Nandou watched the sight of soldiers on the street, drawn to their windows as to a magnet. They broke away only to be pulled back and finally lured down the stairs and outside to learn what they could. After making certain Gabrielle was safe—Nandou's discreet inquiries at the Théâtre-Italien told them she was attending rehearsals, which were going on as usual—they walked the streets for several hours. Everywhere they heard evidence of the smoothness of the coup and the foresight of Louis Napoléon: All printing plants were in the hands of his garrisons. All the National Guard's drums had been burst so there could be no *appel* calling its citizen soldiers to defend the Assembly and the Republic. There were differences from earlier revolts—chiefly the fact that this time there was no revolt, only suppression—but the phalanxes of soldiers, the hard gleam of rifles, the immediate muzzling of the press were all painfully familiar.

Back in the apartment, everything was painfully strange.

In the four days since Nandou had brought word of Edmée Vollard's arrest and Jeanne had refused to discuss it, they had spoken to each other like characters in a play—worse, like actors just starting to rehearse those characters, still in their own *personas* but with others' words and motions laid over them like ill-fitting clothes. At meals they had discussed politics like strangers sharing a café table: "Louis Napoléon has the support of the industrialists and the bankers." "The middle classes seem too apathetic to oppose him." "And the liberals and radicals lack strong leaders." Jeanne spent more time in her room, at her desk; she opened the drawer where her diary was hidden but just sat looking at its Morocco leather cover. Nandou took books down from the shelves at random and read the same pages again and again. The corners of the apartment filled with the pressure of unsaid things—not only of the immediate situation that Jeanne had refused to discuss but also, as if one kind of silence made another less tolerable, of matters between the two of them that had had no tongue for years, if ever, of longings expressed only in things done in darkness.

The coup was in fact a welcome distraction. But when they returned to the apartment, they had said everything there was to say about it until new developments should occur.

"I shall try to work," Jeanne announced. "I do not want any supper."

"Nor I," Nandou said.

They went their separate ways in their small world of five rooms.

In the hours before dawn, when he was staring up into blackness, Nandou heard a sound so muffled that it might have been the pumping of his heart or the sighing of wind against the panes. But his heart was quiet for once, and there was little wind. He sat up, rose, went slowly down the hall, stood outside Jeanne's door for many minutes. The sound was louder. He pushed the door open and saw her at her desk, a lamp very low, her head in her hands and the curtain of her hair swaying with the motion of her shoulders. He said her name twice before she heard and looked up. Tears ran over the dam of her fingers.

"What is wrong?" he said.

"Everything."

"Tell me."

"I cannot."

"Is it Gabrielle?"

"Yes. No." She struggled between sobs and words. "She is gone and nothing I write is good any more and I . . . I . . . that woman is in prison."

"Vollard's wife?" She nodded. "Why should you care about her? What has she to do with you?"

"Nothing! That is what is so . . . I never meant to harm . . . I never imagined Louis would . . . "

"Tell me what you have done." Nandou's voice was so calm with the assurance she would do so that she looked up as if mesmerized.

She wiped her eyes. "I persuaded Henri Foucher to try to become the woman's lover."

"How?"

"He has asked me often to become his mistress. You must know that." Nandou folded his arms. "Yes."

"I told him there was a woman more challenging to conquer than I. I told him that if he were successful . . . "

"You would succumb?"

"No. I did not say that." She looked away.

"Did you allow him to assume it?

"Yes."

"Go on."

"He told me he did succeed. He said he had begun to fall in love with her. I . . . " Jeanne shivered and pulled her shawl tighter over her dressing gown. "I sent a note to Louis anonymously, saying his wife was unfaithful."

"Why?" The syllable hissed like a blade through air.

"To make him pay for what he had done to Gaby."

"By involving his wife?"

"He pretends to be respectable. I wanted to shatter that respectability."

"By shattering the woman?"

"I thought that if she could be seduced, she deserved to be."

"She is the one who let me bring Gabrielle home when he had kidnapped her. Did you think of that? Did you think of the woman at all?"

"I have thought of nothing else since I learned she was in prison."

Nandou seemed not to have heard. "No. No, you thought only of Louis Vollard. Dear God!" His voice was suddenly so harsh and loud that Jeanne pulled back in her chair. "For how many years will you think only of Louis Vollard? How long will you pull his shadow over our lives like a shroud? After all that I—Why does the man who abandoned you still have your heart, while the man who rescued you—" He stopped as if he had run headlong into a wall but must not show the pain.

"He does not have my heart," Jeanne said, "only my hatred!"

"And where has that hatred led you? Have I ever been in your bed without finding him there as well, without knowing you compare the dwarf to him and find the dwarf wanting?"

"Why can you not forget you are a dwarf when you come to my bed?"

"Ah, God! Can *you* forget it?"

"I could, yes, I could, if only you—"

"Do you not know that I am never more a dwarf than when I am touching you? That this prison of a body, which drives me to you against my will, never closes its bars on me so tightly as when I most want to be free of it, with you?"

"Then why do you come, if it makes you wretched?"

The laugh he gave was part croak.

"How do you think I feel, knowing I have made you wretched? Nandou, I have prayed that God would turn me into a dwarf too, so that we—"

"No!" he cried. "Never!"

They looked at each other as if the floor had become a catwalk with no railing.

Groping for a foothold, Jeanne said, "I don't care that you are a dwarf. Why can you not believe me?"

"Because you fell in love with Louis Vollard, not me."

After a silence she said, "I cannot help what I am, Nandou."

"No more can I." He lifted his hands, then dropped them to his side as if they held lead weights.

"I was wrong to try to punish Louis through his wife. I have been realizing that for days. Perhaps all that I have done has been wrong. Except for one thing . . . taking the hand you offered me so long ago. You believe that too, don't you, Nandou?"

The sigh he gave seemed to drain not only the anger from him but all other feeling.

"You must believe it," she said. "If you didn't, I would— You must."

"I do. You know that. But I did not bring you out of the heaps, I have not loved you all these years, to watch you become a destroyer of other lives."

She bit her lip but didn't reply.

"I am tired, Jeanne," he said. "Very tired. I shall go back to bed."

She watched him return to the door. "Would you . . . " she began. He stopped. "Would you stay with me for the rest of the night?"

Far away, down in the street, someone was shouting something unintelligible, except for the word "liberty." The two of them listened until the voice faded.

"No," Nandou said. "Tonight I do not wish to stay." He left the room.

On December 3 both sides moved: The troops were sent back to their barracks, to give the insurrection time to develop if it dared, so that it might be put down decisively and the coup justified. The republicans formed a Committee of Resistance, which organized the erection of a few barricades. But the fighting was desultory; the workers who had been crushed so brutally in 1848 were not eager to offer their necks again, and the bourgeois seemed little perturbed.

Nandou went out in the afternoon, an old brown cloak wrapped about him and his stout walking stick in one hand. Beneath winter clouds the city had an air of unreality, for shops were open, restaurants were busy, and *flâneurs* strolled the boulevards as usual. Could Paris become a tyrant's empire again with so little protest? Where was the fire of 1830? Could his desire for Jeanne fade in one night—in one conversation? He angled over to the Boulevard of Crime, past the building where he had once lived. When he had taken Jeanne up those stairs for the first time, frightened, grimy, defiant, he had not known what to do except wash away the dirt and ignorance and pray the girl beneath them would not look at him and be repulsed. That young dwarf would have found it inconceivable that one day she would beg, "Stay with me," and he would not want to—that her hatred of Vollard would finally exhaust him, and the revenge to which it led her would fill him with such anger and sadness that he could feel nothing else.

But what would he do without his desire for her, which had driven him mad and kept him sane all at once? For twenty-four years it had been a part of him, inseparable from his capacity to feel. It was his tie to the world of normal creatures, the worship of beauty that made bearable his own apostasy. In it, and through it, he was not the figure of fun that all mirrors revealed but a man as serious as any other. Without it, he was naked—a bird stripped not only of the capacity to fly but of feathers as well.

He walked on and on, wrapped in his cloak and his thoughts, until the sight and noise of a crowd drew his attention outward. He saw that he had gone all the way to the Bastille. Soldiers and police were guarding the dark and ugly fortress, and talking to them, haranguing them, was a tall, dark man with a high brow and a passionate voice. *"Louis Napoléon Bonaparte is a traitor . . . has violated the Constitution . . . come join with the people . . . "* Nandou went closer and smiled, for the man urging the soldiers to change sides and fight the tyrant was Victor Hugo. Hugo, who had stood up in the Assembly to which the people had elected him and had delivered a speech of scathing criticism against the prince-president—*Because we had Napoléon the Great must we now have Napoléon the Little?* Nandou watched and listened, his hands clenched. No, Paris would not be cowed easily, not while men like Victor Hugo existed.

The fire of 1830 could be ignited again, but not if one stood on the sidelines. He must take action, Nandou thought, as Hugo was doing. He must try to help rouse the citizens. Then he would go home and tell Jeanne how he had seen Hugo and been inspired; her face would light with the flame that always stirred him. He clutched his stick and walked toward the crowd. "Come, my friends," he cried. "Let us do as Monsieur Hugo has urged. Let us fight the tyrant. *Vive la République!* Down with Louis Napoléon! Let us march to the place de la Concorde and gather strength as we go!"

But the crowd looked at him with more curiosity than passion, and only a few straggled after him, no matter how he waved his stick and exhorted them. When he reached home, dispirited, Jeanne was not there.

On December 4 there was activity. Barricades rose in the Faubourg Saint-Antoine and rue Montorgueil; one on boulevard Saint-Martin, near the theatre, reached third-floor height. Musket fire skittered along the embattled streets, and cavalry regiments swept down them, followed by infantry.

Nicolas Vollard watched and listened from his office, near the Bourse. In the 1848 insurgency he had stayed in the office, believing, unreasonably, that his presence there could help safeguard the interests he worked so carefully to build. It did not, of course. The number of bank failures surrounding the 1848 crisis, the political unrest that had been its harvest, and several seasons of actual bad harvests—all had made the financial world as shaky and cautious as an old man on ice. Since his father's death and even before, Nicolas had made railway financing the most significant investment of the House of Vollard. Were those long-term railway loans safe? How were the railways to keep growing if bankers could not keep them alive with such loans? Nicolas had had more than one nightmare in which the specter was named illiquidity. Stability was imperative, and Louis Napoléon promised to provide it. But at what price?

Suddenly he knew that, this time, he could not stay in the office and watch, like some slaveowner who profited from his slaves' labor but did not know how they lived. If the Republic was being abolished in the name of stability and security, he should at least be witness to the act.

Hatless, wearing a coat he had been ready to give to one of the porters, he walked toward the boulevards. In the gray-white afternoon, familiar sights thrust themselves forward as if new: blue and rose bottles holding gilt artificial flowers in a shop window, dirty scabs of ice on the sludge in the center gutters, mud splattering and coating his shoes. The sky disappeared and re-emerged as he went from narrow lanes to

squares where the whole of heaven seemed to open above him. He passed
the school where he and Louis had been sent as boys—where his own
son Denis presumably would go in a few years. He felt no nostalgia;
his strongest memory was of wanting to leave and join the world of
adults. Denis would do well there, he thought, for the boy was not only
intelligent but good at two other things required for school—taking
orders from superiors and giving them to juniors. Suddenly, hearing his
thoughts, Nicolas stopped short; should a man be so detached about his
own son?

He heard the crack of muskets and the drumming of boots and
hooves; the boulevards were near. When he emerged onto them through
a passageway of shops, the blood left his cheeks—just as it was draining
from the wounds of the corpses piled before a glovemaker's. One old
man was still lifting his umbrella in a threat now powerless and lifeless.
Farther down was a shop where a little boy lay on a pile of toys; Nicolas
ran in, but the child was dead, veins showing blue in thin eyelids.
Nicolas sagged against a wall, unable to move. The feeling seized him,
unreasonably, that the boy had been taken to punish him for his imper-
sonality about his own son. But he loved his boy, he thought. Surely
the things he felt added up to love: pride, concern, a certain tenderness
when Denis came from the bath with his hair curling around his ears
and his skin rosy. Nicolas pushed himself away from the wall, took off
his coat, and laid it over the dead child.

On the boulevard troops filed past. Yet people hung from the windows as if watching a parade. Nicolas went on, his thoughts fixed on
the track on which the dead child had launched them. Sometimes he
almost forgot he had a son and a wife; they seemed to belong to some
other man—and life—to which they would be returned, like parcels
sent to the wrong address. His thoughts and energies were with the firm,
which posed a hundred challenges and pitted his brain and judgment
against others'. His life was lived at the House of Vollard, not the
Nicolas Vollard house. Joséphine understood. He had chosen her because
she was clever and, trembling on the far edge of the marriageable age,
had a forlorn little droop to her upper lip that touched him. And because
it also touched him that she was one of the poor relations of the wealthy
family whose name she bore. If he had to marry someone, let it be a
woman to whom the title Madame Vollard could give some pleasure.
If she would keep a good house, he would be a good provider. Were

those not sufficient reasons for their union? They were the only ones he had had. No, to be fair, he had also chosen Joséphine because she was not his mother's choice. How could he have known that the two of them would find so much common ground and become good friends? That the sad little lip would grow thinner instead of smiling, and would cease to touch him?

He passed a restaurant; through its plate-glass windows diners were visible. A dandy lit a cigar. What kind of day was it—what kind of city?—when death and foie gras shared the afternoon?

Someone called his name. When he turned and saw Jeanne Sorel, she seemed an apparition. But she was real, moving toward him, a heavy brown shawl pulled tight, a bonnet hanging by its ties around her neck. Of all the strange things he felt on this unreal afternoon, the strangest was the desire to take her by the hand, pull her into some doorway or building, and possess her.

"Why are you alone?" he said, as if no greeting was necessary.

"I thought I wanted to be." Her eyes were large, and she sounded as if she could not quite catch her breath. "Everything is so . . . unreal."

"I have been thinking the same thing."

"Corpses are piled near the Théâtre des Variétés, but people don't seem to . . . In 1830 everyone was . . . " Her sentences, unfinished, floated in the wind.

"Were you on the barricades in '30?"

"Yes. With Nandou."

"Where is he today?"

"I do not know. He is out on the streets, I am certain, but we did not . . . "

"Please allow me to see that you reach your home safely."

She swung her head; the bonnet bumped along her shoulders. "Why have you come out today?"

"To watch the death of the Republic."

"Are you one of its mourners?"

"Yes," he said, and found he meant it.

"But you did not fight to keep it alive?"

"I fear I did not."

She regarded him steadily before speaking again. "I wanted to see you. If the coup hadn't occurred, I would have come to your office two days ago."

"You surprise me greatly. Why?"

"To ask you to persuade Louis to drop his charges against his wife."

"Now you amaze me. Such a matter can have nothing to do with you, surely."

A loop of dark hair had escaped from the coil at the back of her neck. She tucked it behind her ear. "Louis has cruelty to one woman on his conscience already. I do not wish to see him be cruel to another."

"You hate Louis. Why should his conscience concern you?"

"Perhaps the conscience in question is not his."

"I do not understand."

Jeanne hesitated. "You must know that I have wanted revenge against your brother for twenty years. But revenge can have its dangers, its innocent victims."

"I understand less than ever now."

"I cannot explain. I can only beg you to make Louis drop his charge."

"I have tried," Nicolas said. "We have all tried, and failed. He is bent on doing this; it is as if his life depended on it."

"Ah."

"I am sorry. I do not need to understand your motive in order to regret your obvious desolation."

"Thank you."

"Do you think," he said, "that we shall ever meet for a reason other than to speak of Louis?"

"I cannot say." Her gaze reached deeply into Nicolas's. Then darkness settled in her eyes like sediment drifting down in a bottle of old wine.

"What makes you feel you can come to me for help?" he said.

"What makes you send me white roses each time a new play of mine opens?"

"The hope you will find the same pleasure in receiving them that I take in sending them."

She smiled faintly and then, as if she regretted having done so, moved away from their strange encounter as quickly as she had entered it. Nicolas could only watch her go.

On December 20, a plebiscite approved the *coup d'état* by well over seven million votes.

On New Year's Day, 1852, a Te Deum was celebrated in Notre-Dame in gratitude that France had been saved for a Bonaparte. Above the carved portal hung a huge red tapestry with the total vote embroidered in gold.

In January of 1852, a new constitution was drafted, giving Louis Napoléon dictatorial powers.

Chapter Fifteen

Several events in early February pleased the government, for they gave the public something sensational to discuss and distracted its attention from the zeal and speed with which thousands of Socialists and republicans were being sent into exile or jail.

One event was a new play, Dumas *fils*'s adaptation of his novel *La Dame aux Camélias*. The censors had banned it for over two years, not only because its heroine was a courtesan—an aspect of life never shown on stage, unless removed to the safe, rosy distance of historical Romantic dramas—but because it portrayed her as noble and self-sacrificing. Louis Napoléon's half-brother, the duc de Morny, had the sense to see that it would make an excellent diversion because it was controversial; after covering himself by procuring a certificate of the play's moral soundness signed by three writers, he got the censors to release it. As he hoped, it was a wild success: defended for its honesty, attacked for its immorality, wept over nightly.

The second diversionary event, which also had a woman's conduct at its heart, was the trial of Edmée Vollard.

In the courtroom, the three justices presided from an elevated platform in their red robes. The prosecutor also wore red; the defense black. Edmée Vollard entered in a high-collared dark frock without ornamentation, which drew all color from her face and diluted the gold of her hair nearly to white. During her two months in Saint-Lazare with prostitutes and other adulterous wives, dark hollows had grown beneath her eyes, which still held the disbelief that had begun with her arrest, muted now by weariness. She sat behind the defendant's rail, looked all around the courtroom, gazed for a long, barely smiling moment at her son, and from then on stared straight ahead.

The proceedings opened with the customary *interrogatoire* by the presiding justice, who could ask the defendant as many questions as he liked. This justice intended to use the prerogative fully, and made his view of Edmée's conduct clear from the beginning. Each question was preceded by a flare of his nostrils and delivered with a cold moral authority refined for more than twenty years. The spectators leaned forward, many hoping for weeping, cajoling, and diatribes of contrition or justification, but Edmée disappointed them, answering briefly in a soft voice, sitting motionless except for a white lace handkerchief twisting in her hands like a living thing.

Were you given to willful behavior as a child, madame?

No more than others, I believe.

As a young woman, were you taught respect for the institution of marriage?

As much as others, I believe.

The spectators murmured, wondering whether this was confidence or insolence.

In the second row Marc Vollard sat as straight as his mother; invisible lines seemed to link his posture to hers. With each question a shiver passed across his face, as if he might speak. He did not, only bit his lower lip and studied his mother with the intensity he directed toward a canvas in the studio.

How many years have you been married, madame?

Twenty.

How many children have resulted from this union?

One. The white handkerchief twisted.

Marc turned to look at his father, who sat many rows behind him, his head bowed. Nicolas had just come in and stood near the door. Besides Marc, they were the only members of the Vollard family present. At a dinner for Marc's eighteenth birthday, just passed, his Vollard grandmother had behaved as if there were no impending trial. His father had looked as if he could think of little else, but had not mentioned it. None of Edmée's family, the Tissots, were in the courtroom.

What have you to say, madame, about the charge against you?

I have nothing to say.

You attempt no justification?

I ask the court's mercy.

Could her hair have gone whiter? Marc wondered. Was that possible in so short a time? He always pictured her as a creature of peach and soft gold, who was somehow at odds with the house and the life she inhabited. Despite her warmth and kisses and the charmed circle her arms had made for him when he was a child, he had sensed something sad, or alien, or . . . he did not know; he could not find words, only images. He thought of her as a creature of sunrise colors who lived in the wrong light.

What led you, madame, to commit this act, which you do not deny?

I cannot say.

You cannot say, madame? Or you will not say?

I cannot.

When he had visited her in the prison, she had been in no light at all. She had put a hand through the iron grille and run it over his face as if she were blind and said she was so desperately sorry. There was no answer to that except "I love you, Maman."

"And I love you, Marc. I must try to explain, to make you understand why I did what I—"

"No, Maman. Please. I do not want to hear." It was true. He did not want to know what sexual passions might have driven his mother, or anyone. Including himself. Especially himself, for the Darkness would reign if he allowed it.

She had begged him not to attend the trial, but he could not abandon her to face it alone. No more could he sit with his father in the courtroom, as if sanctioning the charge. He could only sit at a point between them, as the apex of the triangle made by his mother's suffering and his father's angry pain.

Did your husband deny you any material comfort, madame?

No.

Did he provide a good home for you? The handkerchief twisted, trying to get away. *I cannot hear your reply, madame, please speak up.*

Marc shivered. Would she talk about the times his father stayed away from home, times when she tried to pretend otherwise but it was clear she did not know where he was? Suddenly it occurred to him that she might have known after all: about the women with their red lips and the easy postures that seemed designed to guide the eye to the triangle between their legs. He did not know if it would be worse or better if she had known about them.

Yes, madame? Your reply was yes? The home you have violated is a comfortable one?

It is. It was.

Silently Marc called to her, Tell them. Tell of the unquiet silences between the two of you, the conversations like cracking ice, the stale, sharp reek of drink that sometimes would hang in the air after Papa had been in the room. . . .

Have you had other lovers, madame?

The handkerchief convulsed. *No.*

So the transgression that brings you before this court is the only one in an otherwise blameless life?

I do not say I am blameless.

Indeed, madame.

The spectators rustled. The nostrils of the presiding justice made lofty arcs.

Marc turned to look at his father. Louis had lifted his head, and his face seemed torn between anger and wretchedness. In his own way, Marc thought, his father suffered as much as his mother. He looked at her again. The white handkerchief was now a ball in one hand, but she was still erect. Leave her alone! Marc cried silently, teeth biting deeply into his lower lip.

Gabrielle missed the first day of the trial because of a rehearsal, but on the second day she arrived early at the Palais de Justice, head low so no one might chance to recognize her. She managed to sit a row behind Louis Vollard and some distance across. He was the reason she had come: not to speak with him—she was not ready to do so yet, if ever—but to see him again.

The prosecution witnesses began with a policeman. The prosecutor paced in his red robe like a lumbering flame while the man spoke.

On the afternoon of November fourth, a gentleman presented himself at the commissariat and stated that if we went to Number Four, place Vendôme, we would find a lady engaged in adulterous conduct . . .

He was followed to the witness bar by other police officers and the concierge, who said Madame Vollard had come to the address in question at least six or seven times.

Gabrielle paid only sporadic attention to them. By angling her head, she could see Louis's profile around the edge of her hat. She thought she saw something of herself in him, some reminiscence of nose and lip. *You remind me of someone,* he had told her once; but she put that memory out of her mind. The suppers with him had not happened; they belonged to the days of illusion, when she had thought success would simply drop into her outstretched hand like ripe fruit. The conversations with him had no meaning because neither had known who the other truly was. But then, what kind of person was he?—the father who had abandoned her, then tried to kidnap her, and who later had approached her in a way no father would approach a daughter. She looked at him again and again, hoping to read his nature on his face, finding only that he was pale and tense.

The defense lawyer, an elderly man in a black robe, called his few witnesses: people who had worked for Madame Vollard. Where were her friends, Gabrielle wondered, and her family? The woman now at the bar had been her maid for many years.

In your observation, was Madame Vollard a good wife and mother?

My lord, she was always affectionate and dutiful to monsieur and very loving to their son.

You were aware of her movements, where she went every day?

Yes.

Did you know her to have lovers?

Never while I was with her, my lord. Never.

Louis Vollard had had a mistress, Gabrielle thought—her mother. And had he not meant to ask Gabrielle herself to be another?—albeit without knowing her identity. Why did no one speak of his conduct? The answer came instinctively: bourgeois hypocrisy. She looked at him again. One hand covered his left cheek, and his eyes were narrowed. He did not look righteous or smug, only unhappy.

At length the red-robed prosecutor positioned himself to give his summation, the *réquisitoire*.

"You are here confronted," he told the jury of twelve men, "with a case that is simple but grave, for it strikes at the sanctity of the family, which lies at the heart of our French nation and society. We deal here not with someone ill-educated and therefore possibly less aware of the obligations of her sex, but with a woman whose upbringing and education were of the finest and who was accepted into an excellent, respectable family. Her behavior should have been governed by the high principles to which she had been exposed throughout her life. Instead, she betrays those principles and violates the sacred roles of wife and mother. The husband who had trusted her, the child who should have been able to look to her for guidance, both are forgotten as she abandons the virtue that should have been her constant guide and inspiration and allows herself . . . "

The prosecutor stopped, for a young man sitting near the front of the court had shot to his feet.

"I am Madame Vollard's son," he said in a voice that was firm yet trembled, like a bridge in a high wind. "I wish to inform the court that she has been, that she is, an ideal mother. Never has she neglected me for even the smallest period of time. She has showered me with love and paid attention to every need I have expressed to her. I can only wish, for all persons in this room, that they have a mother as devoted as mine."

Everyone stared at him; mutters rose from the spectators as well as the court officials and jury, but he continued. "My mother . . . Madame Vollard . . . has been the greatest influence for good in my life, and whatever transgression may have brought her to this courtroom and its judgment, I consider her moral character to be above reproach." He glanced over his shoulder—at Louis, Gabrielle was certain—and sat down.

Red and black robes swirled around him, voices clashed. But Gabrielle was barely aware of the fuss. Until that moment she had not considered that Louis Vollard had a son. She stared at his proud back and curling brown hair, his words resounding in her ear as their meaning sank deeper. What would it be like to be torn between one's parents in such a painful way? As a new thought struck her, she stifled an exclamation. If the man was Louis Vollard's son, he was her own half-brother.

She barely listened to the defense lawyer's *plaidoirie*, except to note he was asking for mercy, because she was so rapt in the discovery of a sibling. Especially one whose situation sent vibrations of sympathy coursing through her, as if she were a tuning fork. To have a mother whose action must have grieved him . . . even shamed him . . . yet to defend her before the world, to declare openly his love for her . . . Where did he find the courage? Did he hate himself for being ashamed of her? Could she try to speak to him when the court adjourned? But what would she say?

The jury retired to deliberate.

Murmuring, rustling, debating what verdict would be returned and how long the wait would be, much of the audience rose for a break and pushed its way toward the courtroom doors. Gabrielle rose with it, struggling to keep Marc Vollard in the line of her vision as journalists descended on him. "Excuse me," she said to her left, then her right, barely seeing the people she jostled and was jostled by.

A hand gripped her arm. She turned angrily to its owner, and met her mother's eyes.

"Gaby, dear," Jeanne said, almost shyly, "it is so wonderful to see you." Behind her stood Nandou, dark eyes intent in his dwarf's brow.

Gabrielle could not move, not even if a spectator pushed her; she was helpless, while a net of emotions fell over her as she stared at them. Never had she imagined they would attend the trial. Her mother, properly dressed, so beautiful. . . . "You look well, Jeanne," she said carefully. "How are you?"

"I miss you."

Through the cloth of her jacket, Gabrielle imagined she could feel her mother's naked hand—the warm, thin fingers, one with a little bulge on the side from holding a pen. She wanted to smile at her mother, but she would not. Her mother, who had lied to her about Nandou, who had told her she would be a great artist. . . . And Nandou . . . magical hands hanging at his sides, but only to a little below his waist . . . who had let her live with the lie . . . He was going to say nothing, she knew it; he was only going to look at her with a gaze that slid into her brain as easily as a knife into butter. Someone in the crowd bumped into him, nearly ruining his balance, and Gabrielle felt the old love rising in her throat, as it had the night he had followed her to her apartment, and the old shame. She feared she would choke. If she had not spent the first nineteen years of her life believing he was her father—if they had not made her believe it—she would never have had shameful thoughts about either of them. She would not have roiled with guilt for having those dark feelings or struggled to push them back into the inner cesspool from which they kept rising.

"When the verdict is in, will you come and have dinner with us?" Jeanne said.

She could feel that struggle tearing her again, right there in the courtroom. She shook her head.

"Just a coffee, then?" Jeanne said. "Please."

They had lied to her and made her feel ugly things. They were doing it to her still. It was easier not to see them. It was better. It was just. This was the palace of justice, was it not? She looked at the sunken panels in the walls depicting the sword and scales. "No," she said, "I cannot."

Jeanne released her arm. Gabrielle turned and pushed her way out.

.   .   .

Nandou raised an eyebrow when Jeanne asked for more wine—normally she drank very little—but he made no comment, merely signaled the waiter, who brought another bottle.

She refilled her glass and drank half of it at once. Nandou cocked his head but said nothing. Around them, in a café where they had sat a hundred times over the years, arguing plays and politics, conversations buzzed, many of them about the trial. Several theatre colleagues had hailed them when they came in and waved them over, but Jeanne had told Nandou, "I can't, not tonight," and they had settled in a quiet corner well away from the windows and the door.

"Why did the woman say nothing?" Jeanne said. "Not a word in her own defense, nor about Louis's conduct. He must have had many mistresses over the years. Every judge in that room, every man on the jury, has had mistresses. It is bitterly unfair. How could the woman have remained silent?"

"Perhaps she knew it would not have helped her cause to denounce her husband's conduct, or that of any other man."

"But a year in prison! And the justice dared to call it merciful because it was not the maximum sentence of two years." Jeanne lifted her glass, looked into the wine, and said softly, "I cannot forgive myself." Nandou was silent.

She drank. "I loathe the presiding justice. I shall put him in a play and make him the villain." Nandou smiled.

After a moment she said, "Why doesn't the wine do its work? The courtroom seems printed on my vision forever."

"Wine has its own will. If you badly need your wits, it clouds them. If you are desperate to drown a memory, wine will keep it bobbing in front of you."

"Then why do people drink so much of it?"

"We always hope happiness will lie at the bottom of the glass."

Into Jeanne's mind came the memory of a drunken carnival night. Was it in Nandou's mind too? His will forbade her to know, as it had done many times in the past. In that respect, nothing was different between them. Yet nothing was the same. It had not been the same for weeks and weeks.

The change had begun after the night she confessed her role in Edmée Vollard's fate. Nandou had been angry with her—rightly—but when the anger left, something else went with it. She had realized its absence only gradually; it was like becoming aware of a new silence but not knowing what had stopped: a clock? a street noise? a distant bell? She would find herself looking around and frowning without quite knowing why; then Nandou would come home and the silence would seem more pronounced, even though they were talking as usual. Something was different when he looked at her, although the large black eyes were as intent and probing as ever. One day he had read aloud an act of a play she was working on; it was not right, and he had put his hand on her arm in sympathy. In the casualness of that gesture, she suddenly had understood: What was gone was his desire for her. The desire he had always struggled to hide, even on those nights when it defeated him—it was not there any more.

She ought to have been glad; how many times had she wished he would not suffer because of it? She was glad for him, certainly she was, but for herself . . . how different life was. She could not seem to find her balance. On the surface, everything stayed the same, but within, some support was gone that she had not even realized she leaned upon—almost, she thought, as if the sound that had stopped was her heartbeat.

She put her hands to her temples, then clasped them in her lap. "Did you expect Gaby to be at the trial?" she said.

"I did not. But it is not so surprising. She would no doubt be curious about Vollard's wife."

Jeanne sighed. " 'Hello, you look well'—that is worse than if she had said nothing. It is not even true. I have looked dreadful ever since she left. If she wants only truth in her life . . . She was not staying to speak to Louis? You are certain of that?"

"Positive. I saw Vollard leave with his brother."

"Ah." Jeanne had not known Nicolas was there until nearly the end of the session. Her cheek had begun to tingle, as if someone were staring at her; when she looked in that direction, she saw him. He had lifted his shoulders, as if in apology. The distance had reduced his face to the essentials of a drawing: gray eyes, straight nose, square jaw. She had turned away and not looked back.

She drank again. "Gaby would not even come to eat with us. No more begging or pleading with her, Nandou. Ever. We have our pride. She knows where we are. If she wishes to see us, let her come to us. Let it be as she wants it."

"I do not think we have a choice," he said.

"We shall simply go on without her, shall we not?"

He smiled, but as if at a memory.

"Jeanne! Nandou!" She looked up to see a man advancing on them, a poet who often came to their salons, a gifted man who had been out of Paris for some months. He kissed her hand, told her she looked tired but as beautiful as ever, seated himself at their table, and said, "And to what have I returned? The Republic dead, Hugo in exile, and Henri Foucher taking himself off to Italy while one of his mistresses is tried for adultery? You must tell me all the news."

Jeanne cast a mute plea at Nandou; she could not sit there and pretend to gossip about Edmée Vollard.

"Let's see," Nandou said. "Hugo says he will not return until Louis Napoléon is gone, so the Bonaparte is depriving us of literature as well as liberties. Dumas *père* is bankrupt, but Dumas *fils* is thriving. He has turned his novel into a play that is brutally real and therefore is shocking those who go to the theatre to avoid life. But they have found other means of escape—the latest craze is table-tipping sessions to commune with the dead."

Nandou had understood her silent plea, Jeanne thought; at least that had not changed. She listened as he led the conversation to the poet's travels in Germany, but she said little, for his words had planted the seed of an idea in her mind. She retreated behind a fixed smile and watched the poet's mouth move as he described the peculiar music of Richard Wagner and the lucent beauty of the valley of the Rhine.

The mattress was straw, the single chair lacked half the cane in its seat, the drinking pot was chipped and scarred as if with the pox. Still, in recognition of Edmée's position in the world outside the prison, she was allowed a pillow and coverlet from home, a folding table, paper and pen, and a pile of books.

She did not read them, although she tried many times, opening to a page and bidding her mind to concentrate. Her eyes would obey and take in the words, but as separate beads that would not come together in a string. Writing was little better. In the first month after her arrest, she had tried to record her thoughts and feelings, but if she managed to write a paragraph, she found no ease in having her wretchedness stare back at her from a page. "They say that centuries ago Saint-Lazare was a leprosarium," she had written one day. "Am I one of the lepers of our time?" In a moment she had added, "I deserve all that is happening to me." That day was the last time she had used the pen.

For much of the time in her cell she drifted, mind swinging like a hammock between two poles: the thought of Marc and the memory of her boudoir; Marc's large, clear, loving eyes, his visits, the words he had cried to the court, and the cool, soft sheets on her own bed and the lavender scent that hung in the air. She seldom thought of Louis, because when she did, incredulity and anger would surge up and threaten both the hammock and its moorings; or of Henri Foucher, whose disappearance from her life had taken with it all sense of his reality. If she recalled the behavior that had brought her to the cell in Saint-Lazare, her partner was someone faceless and voiceless. But she tried not to recall it, for then a cold awareness of her own folly sank on her.

When she went for obligatory walks in the courtyard, she was aware of her fellow inmates. At first she remained aloof, for most of them were prostitutes, but she grew curious about the kind of creatures to whom society had declared her a virtual equal. She talked with a thirteen-year-old who had never been to church or school, a streetwalker who plied the Grands Boulevards and boasted of the fine parties she had attended, a crone who sold her sagging body for loaves of bread. They loathed the police, who required them to go for medical examinations and to carry the white card they called *la brème* because of the fish it resembled. They spoke of what they would do when they were outside again—the money they would earn, the children they would see, the spittle they would lavish on the police. They had more hope than Edmée did. For her the most forbidden thought of all was the day when she would be released. She could not go to her parents, who had paid for her lawyer but had granted all too eagerly her wish that they not attend the trial. Perhaps she would end up like the women in the courtyard.

One day a warder came and said she had a visitor, her sister. Edmée started to object that she had no sister, but something stopped her tongue, and she followed the man in silence to the room where inmates could see callers from behind an iron grille. Something was faintly familiar about the woman who waited there, but her face was partially hidden by a lace veil draped over her bonnet.

When Edmée was seated, the woman pulled back the veil. "I am Jeanne Sorel," she said. "Do you recognize the name?"

"Yes," Edmée said slowly. "You are Louis's . . . you were . . . "

"That is right." The woman's dark eyes moved over Edmée's face. "You have been treated unjustly. I was at your trial. I understand what you must feel."

Edmée put her hands to her cheeks; she must be on the flat, prickly bed in the cell, dreaming this encounter. But why dream of Louis's former mistress?

"You should not be here," Jeanne Sorel said. "You are guilty of no crime."

"Perhaps I deserve to be here." Edmée did not know why she confessed such a thing to this stranger; perhaps because it was a dream.

Jeanne Sorel leaned closer to the grille. "I want to help you escape."

"I beg your pardon?"

"I want to get you out of Saint-Lazare. Are you willing?"

"But . . . how? Why?"

"I am told that years ago you allowed my daughter to be returned to me. Did you also prevent Louis from making further attempts to kidnap her?"

"Yes, I was able to stop him."

"There is my reason, then. If you would like another, consider that we have both been misused by the same man and therefore are sisters by experience. I have still other reasons, which I may tell you one day if the escape succeeds. I repeat, are you willing to try it?"

The woman's directness was overpowering, a magnet that drew answers almost before one's mind had formed them. "I am willing," Edmée said.

"You have courage. You will need it, for if we fail, you will be worse off than you are now." Jeanne Sorel leaned very close to the grille. "Here is my plan." She whispered at length.

As Edmée listened, she pressed the nails of one hand into the palm of the other to see if she was indeed dreaming. She felt five little points of pain. "But I do not think I can do that," she protested.

"I watched you stay as proud and straight as the obelisk during your trial. Anyone who could do that can do what I propose, and more."

Edmée did not believe it, but the woman's intent gaze seemed to make disbelief irrelevant, as if Mesmer himself were telling her what to do. "Very well," she said. "I will try."

. . .

Carnival was at its peak. At night, sounds from the street came faintly into Saint-Lazare and made the inmate population more restless than ever. In his quarters, warder Mulot growled his disapproval and busied himself in preparing things: the table cleared and scrubbed, three chairs placed around it, the oil lamp trimmed and burning low. He took a little extra wine to fortify himself and sat down to wait for nine o'clock.

He was an old, lonely man who had seen every kind of rogue and wretch in his years of working in the prisons of Paris. All that remained to him of the ardor of his youth was a visceral belief in the corrupting nature of money and power and a corresponding tenderness for the one creature he believed to be both innocent and pure, his only grandchild, Georges.

The thought of speaking to the boy again made the mug tremble in Mulot's hand. He hoped he was not about to do something foolish, but what could be the harm in trying? If it did not work, he had lost nothing but the hope that it might. But if it did work . . .

He had met the man in a restaurant where he often had his suppers. They had fallen into a conversation about the sorry lot of the working class, during which the man, whose name was Jean, seemed in the grip of a powerful preoccupation. Finally he confided it to Mulot: He worked for a vicomte, and one night the servants had imitated what their employers had done earlier in the evening and staged a séance. It turned out that the pastry cook was a good natural medium, as hunchbacks often were, did Mulot know that?—so they had held more séances. As a result, Jean had been in touch several times with the spirit of his dead wife. As he talked, the joy of speaking to her had lit Jean's eyes, and the wish had come into Mulot's mind, and somehow slipped out on his tongue, to talk once again to his grandson, little Georges, who had been taken by the cholera in '48. Jean had been doubtful that the pastry cook would perform the service outside her own kitchen, especially in a prison, but had said he would ask her. Several nights later Jean had come to the restaurant again and said the woman wanted to try, for criminals sometimes had strong occult powers, as Mulot was perhaps aware?—but not during Lent, for doing such things in holy season might offend the Lord. So a session had been arranged for two nights before the end of carnival, and here was Mulot, putting down his mug to go admit the two of them at the entrance he had told them to use, sweating and worrying as if he were confronting a dangerous inmate for the first time.

When he opened the door, the shouts of carnival revelers pierced the night like hunting cries. In the shadows stood Jean and the woman, Berthe, whose hump bent her very low. Mulot led them silently back to his quarters. Berthe looked up at him and, in a thick, droning voice asked if he was a good Christian and then if he had wine, which she said might make her more open to the spirits. Mulot pointed to the bottle on the table. Now that the time had actually come, he found it difficult to say anything.

Berthe took off her bonnet and shawl and began to fuss about the table: too large for good contact among their hands, too high for her to feel comfortable, and so on. "We must humor her," Jean whispered, "or the whole thing may be a waste." Mulot nodded and fetched a smaller, lighter table from his bedchamber. Once more Berthe fussed: It should be placed a few feet more to the left, a pillow on her chair would be helpful, so would a little drink of wine, and so on. At first Mulot found her irritating, but as she muttered and *tsk*'ed to herself, touching and tapping everything with agile fingers, rather like a large insect testing a leaf, her motions and sounds began to comfort him. At length they were ready, the three of them seated around the table, hands outspread, fingers touching. After a long silence, during which Berthe's breathing grew heavier, she called out, "Is anyone there? Is anyone there? One rap for yes, two for no. Is anyone there?"

Again, long silence. Then a tilt and sharp knock from the table. An echoing knock from Mulot's heart.

"Is it a man?" Berthe said. Silence. Two knocks.

"A woman?" One knock.

"Does she have a message for Monsieur Mulot?" Two knocks.

"Is the message for me?" Two more knocks.

"Is it for Jean?" One knock.

On Mulot's left, Jean let out his breath as if he had been holding it for minutes. "Is it Marie?" he whispered. "Dear Marie, is it you?" A long silence. A gentle knock. "Ah!" cried Jean. "My wife!"

"Let us hear the message," Berthe said, her voice thick and throbbing, as if a bee were buzzing in honey.

The message was a long time coming, for it had to be spelled out, one thump for each letter of the alphabet. Mulot found himself counting with the intensity of a schoolboy at his sums.

jean I love you as ever be kind to louise

"Yes, yes!" Jean cried. "Louise is her sister, with whom she quarreled shortly before she died!"

The three of them closed their eyes and concentrated again, but there were no more knocks. The table was lifeless wood. Finally Berthe broke the circle of hands, fluttered her fingers like wings, and said they should have some wine before continuing. Mulot poured three mugs but barely drank his. Berthe sipped away, telling some long tale about her daughter's traveling to Languedoc, until Mulot finally asked to return to the table-tipping.

But despite Berthe's renewed calls to know if anyone was there, the table sat like a coffin. Mulot's brow ached with the effort of willing it to move. Finally Jean said they might as well stop, and Berthe gave a low assenting murmur, but then came a slight tilt and a soft rap.

"Is someone there?" Berthe called. One rap. "Is it a man?" Two raps. "A woman?" Two raps. "Is it a child?" A long pause. Then one rap.

"Oh!" Mulot said, in spite of himself.

"Do you have a message for someone?" A gentle rocking of the table. "This is unusual," Berthe whispered. Then, louder: "Do you wish to speak to someone here?" More rocking. "Do you wish to speak to someone here?" One feeble rap.

"Georges, little Georges," Mulot said, "is it you?"

One rap. Mulot groaned; he could not help it. Long silence. Then something spelled out in raps: *too weak need help*

"We do not understand," Berthe said.

weak Silence. *grandpapa bring help*

"Do you know what he wants?" Berthe whispered to Mulot.

"No," Mulot croaked.

Berthe's droning honey-voice addressed the spirit again. "I cannot bring you through clearly. Do you need some help?" One rap. "What help?"

lady has power Silence. *please*

"I do not understand," Berthe whispered. "I cannot tell what to do." More loudly: "What lady?"

Slowly, with a growing wait between each of the letters, the raps spelled out: *vollard*

"What does that mean?" Jean whispered.

"I do not know," Berthe said.

Silence.

"Do you know someone named Vollard?" Jean whispered.

Slowly Mulot said, "A woman in this prison is named Edmée Vollard."

Jean asked, "Is she a medium?"

"I have never heard so. She is serving time for adultery."

The table began to rock, as if it were nodding.

"Little Georges," Berthe said, "tell us, could the Vollard woman help you speak to your grandfather?"

One rap. Mulot felt cold but also flushed.

"Mulot, can you bring her here?" whispered Jean.

The table rocked again.

Mulot stood. "I will do it."

"Good," Berthe said. "While you are gone, we shall not move. We shall keep the spirit channel open."

Mulot took his keys and left. At once the reality of dank walls and sharp odors reasserted itself; he wondered if he was dreaming, or a fool, or both. But when he neared Edmée Vollard's cell, she rose from her pallet, came to the door, and before he could speak, said, "The child sent you for me. I feel it."

If the man did not soon drink the wine, Jeanne thought, she would take the mug and pour it down his throat.

But it sat on the other table, still untasted, holding the powder they had put into it while he went to fetch Edmée.

When Mulot returned, the last of his resistance was gone; one could tell from his eyes, which watered and quivered helplessly. By contrast Edmée had herself under tight control, her nervousness banished to the left corner of her mouth, where a small muscle hopped like a frightened rabbit. Seated at the table, her hands part of the circle and her head thrown back in a pseudotrance, she was doing a creditable job of emitting a childlike voice. But she had used up the scraps of information about the dead grandson that Jeanne had gleaned from Mulot during their conversation in the restaurant. For the past ten minutes Edmée had been reduced to innocuous avowals of love for "Grandpapa" and of the peace and happiness in "heaven." Neither the banality nor the slowness of the responses seemed to bother Mulot, who was caught in a fever of grief and remembrance that needed little fueling. One might feel sorry for the man, walled off by his work from much of human feeling and thus an easy prey when his Achilles heel was struck, if one's liberty, and Edmée's, and Nandou's, did not hang on his taking a drink of his wine and falling into a stupor that would allow them to leave the prison.

"Georges," Mulot said, "do you talk to your grandmother in heaven?"

Long pause. "Yes," Edmée piped. "Dear Grandmama is happy."

Jeanne cast a despairing glance at Nandou, who was unrecognizable beneath the false hump and inside the fussing, droning character of "Berthe." Even in her anxiety Jeanne marveled at the powerful reality of the persona he had created. She had not wanted to involve him in the escape; her goal had been to do it on her own, then to present him with a fait accompli of which he would surely approve. Using her own sources, she had gotten information about the warders at Saint-Lazare, but she had soon realized she could not do the rest without Nandou. On her own she was not a good enough actor to convince Mulot that the séance was real, nor was she strong enough to manipulate the table with her feet and hands. She had planned it, however, all of it, and when she broached it to Nandou, his eyes had held a familiar glow and he had said, "I see you have written me another splendid role." For a moment she had felt as if everything would once again be the same between them; as if she had never plotted the revenge against Louis for which the escape would help her atone. They would do it together, as they had done so many other things, in sign and symbol of the rightness between them. But the moment had passed.

"Grandpapa, I growing tired," piped Edmée. The desperation in her voice was so clear that only someone as self-blinded as Mulot could fail to hear it.

Quickly Nandou-Berthe said, "She is losing her ability to maintain the necessary spirit force. We must release her."

"No," Mulot begged. "Not yet."

"Then she must be allowed to rest and drink wine to refresh herself. Let us all stop and drink some wine."

"I want no more wine tonight," Mulot said. "Not while my little Georges is with me."

"Oh," moaned Edmée, and slid to the floor.

Chapter Sixteen

A huge chandelier glittered above the heads of the guests. *Another* seemed to have been broken into a hundred pieces and re-shaped around the necks and arms of the women. The furniture was gilt, and the wallpaper too, so that the room offered the light a thousand surfaces on which to replicate itself. Draperies, double and even triple, hung in thick swags at the windows, concealed doors and cupboards, and by their number hinted at the substantial income of their owner, who was a banker. The pets decreed by fashion were in evidence: A King Charles spaniel sat on a basket beside a sofa, and in a glass bowl four tiny tortoises from Africa bore witness to the presence of a family friend in Algiers. Most of the tables had been pushed against the wall and the chairs and settee arranged in a large semicircle before the piano for the musical part of the evening—its raison d'être featured a violinist, a pianist, and selections performed by Mademoiselle Gabrielle Corday.

She sang arias from Donizetti and Bellini and ended with the sentimental ballads requested by the hostess. At some salons the music was truly artistic—once, at the beginning of her career, Gabrielle had performed with Liszt—but, more typically, people preferred the ballads. "Your brow is marble, fairest one, your cheek a blushing rose, How long must I be banished from their sweet presence?" As Gabrielle sang, the silver bird trilling and soaring, she was quite detached, thinking that although she sang constantly of the joys and sorrows of love, she had yet to know either. When men admired her, then adored her, she no longer felt she and they were playing a game; the experience with Louis Vollard had cured her of that forever. Now she felt little except twinges of contempt for the sameness of their words, their eyes, their lies, and the satisfaction of knowing they would never be able to trick her and use her. "Must I remain forever in shadow," she sang, "never allowed into the splendor of your light?" Most of the audience was visibly relishing the song; several young ladies in the front rows dabbed their eyes.

It was a curious experience, being in the heart of wealthy, respectable society, behind its very doors. Perhaps these people were foolish, even silly, but, Gabrielle thought with a certain defiance, they were not peculiar and unpredictable and oddly dressed, as her mother and Nandou's guests would be. They lived in such ease, and so easily, with their jewels and gold and beautiful clothes and manners; above all, with the sense, almost palpable in the room, that such things were taken for granted.

She finished her last song and bowed to the applause. Rising out of that bow, she saw, near the back of the crowded salon, the figure of Marc Vollard. She moved through the room, on the lookout, as one had to be, for patrons and fellow musicians who might advance her career— but not for husbands, like so many sopranos she knew—accepting compliments, smiling at those who might hire her for a soirée of their own and bantering with the knot of young men who tied themselves around her like a cravat, but her goal was to reach Vollard. He was with a young woman; occasionally they talked with others but seemed to keep to themselves. When Gabrielle prevailed on one of her admirers to introduce her, the man said, "That is Marc Vollard, whose father charged his mother—"

"Yes, I know. I should like to meet him."

Marc Vollard bowed over her hand. "You sang beautifully, Mademoiselle Corday. I particularly enjoyed the Donizetti."

He was good-looking, she thought as she thanked him, although not in the way his father was. *Their* father. He had a strong, fine nose, rather small lips, a jaw strong with resolve, and brown eyes that were both intent and wary.

His companion turned out to be a cousin who had recently moved to Paris; her father had left his other interests to become an active part of the House of Vollard. "And you, monsieur," Gabrielle asked Marc, "are you also a banker?"

"Not yet," he said—politely, although she thought she heard in it the wish not to answer such questions.

"If our friends will excuse us," she said, smiling charmingly at her admirer and the cousin, "I have something particular to say to Monsieur Vollard."

His expression was puzzled as they moved away. It tightened when she said, "I should have liked to speak to you at your mother's trial. No, please—my purpose is not to monger scandal or distress you. I only want to tell you how much I admire you for speaking out for your mother. I know it took courage. I imagine it also must have been painful."

"It was," he said stiffly.

She waited before adding, "It must be dreadful to love your father and at the same time be angry with him."

He looked at her intently. "Can you understand such a thing?"

"I can."

His eyes grew wary again. "Your conversation is not like that of most young women I meet."

"Perhaps because I do not want from you what other young women want."

"Will you explain that, mademoiselle, or leave me to wonder?"

"Whether they acknowledge it or not, other women look at you as a potential admirer, suitor, even husband. I do not."

His eyes widened. "Mademoiselle, I do not understand."

"I want to be your friend, but only your friend."

He looked so bewildered that she laughed. The laugh made him smile, a captivating, brilliant smile. "I have never had such a proposition," he said.

"Perhaps you do not believe me?"

"I believe you, but I do not understand."

"One day I shall explain. When we have become good friends."

"Very well," he said. He held out his hand, still smiling, and she shook it.

From the street, faintly, rose the cry of a water-carrier. As if answering, sparrows flew past the window in a burst of chatter. Edmée opened her eyes. For the first time in days, she felt that her mind belonged to her again. Small, contented awarenesses came to her: The room, with its yellow curtains, was cheerful, the day was bright and crisp, a tantalizing odor of chocolate was in the air. She swung out of bed, regarded her legs with a pleasure she had forgotten, and began to make her toilette.

At first it had been like trying to wake from a bad dream: She could only stare in confusion at those who awakened her and try to sort memory from reality. Everything had blended in her mind, like flour and butter joining in a roux: The séance ran into the carnival; the warder's face, with the pleading, watery eyes that had nearly made her pity him, melded into one of the masks on the revelers with whom they had merged after leaving the prison; the fear in her throat became the cries of harlequins and shepherdesses on their way to and from dance halls and masked balls. When the twisting and singing through the streets had ended and she followed Jeanne Sorel and the dwarf Nandou into an apartment, she could not have said whether she was still on her straw prison mattress, imagining everything, or attending some carnival ball with two other masked figures. Had she really acted in a séance and fainted when she could see no way out of it, or of Saint-Lazare? Had she come around because Jeanne, in male attire, slapped her face and shook her? Had the warder really been lying unconscious in a corner? Was she really now in the home of the woman Louis had loved and the dwarf who had stolen back his child? For several days she had found herself constantly touching things—a wooden chair, a china plate—to ground herself in the comforting reality of ordinary things. If she asked, "Why are you bothering to help me?" Jeanne or Nandou, or both, only smiled and said, "Do not worry about such things now. You must rest." It was true; an hour after waking she would fall back into a sleep as heavy and gray as cotton wadding.

But this morning she was restored to herself. She put on one of the two frocks Jeanne had lent her and glanced again around the room Jeanne said was her absent daughter's. Smiling, Edmée thought of the child Solange she once had sheltered for a week and to whom she had said, "Remember that I was fond of you." It was pleasant to have that tie with Jeanne and Nandou.

In the kitchen, they were talking at the table. "Nothing has been properly cleaned for over a week," Jeanne was saying. "We must have the *bonne* back, if only for a day."

"Good morning," Nandou said, seeing Edmée.

They smiled at her. She smiled back, ready to say "Good morning" in return, but she was pinned in place, eyes stinging, by a rush of feeling for the wonderful ordinariness of things—the pot of chocolate, the plate of rolls, the checked cloth, the wall of copper pots—and for the two people presiding over that reassuring kingdom, who were wonderful precisely because they were not ordinary: the strangely proportioned man, the exotically beautiful woman.

"What is it?" Jeanne asked. "Are you all right?"

Edmée held up both hands and shook her head. "I was merely thinking how grateful I am to be here. You risked so much for me, both of you, when there was no need for you to do so, no—"

"Please," Nandou said, putting down the journal he had been reading, "I cannot bear speeches of gratitude."

"I would do anything rather than offend you," Edmée began, "but you must allow me to tell you how grateful—"

"No," Jeanne said, "we will not. Besides, you gave us something in return: Nandou a splendid role to play, and me the chance to write a kind of scene I truly enjoy. So let us hear no more about it."

Nandou waved a hand above the table. "Sit down and have breakfast." As if summoned by a magic force, Edmée did.

Jeanne handed her a cup. "You look much better this morning."

Edmée sipped the chocolate; never had it seemed so rich and dark. "I am certainly enough better to learn what they are saying about me in the papers."

"There has been nothing for several days," Nandou said. "The story has faded. All stories fade except those that are invented."

"But immediately after the escape, there must have been something."

"There was indignation from some quarters about the inefficiency of Saint-Lazare, and a rehashing of sentiments over your verdict."

"Nothing about the police trying to find me?"

"Yes, unfortunately," Nandou said, "there were such stories as well. The journals insist on mitigating our pleasures."

"Oh, dear."

"The police will not find you," Jeanne said. "If you could get out of Saint-Lazare, you can stay out."

Edmée broke a roll in half and buttered it. "I cannot remember all of it. How did Mulot come to be lying on the floor?"

"That was a bad moment. When he declined to drink the wine we had prepared for him—you must recall that, it is why you fainted—we all rushed to prop you back in your chair. In the shuffle, the good Berthe"—Jeanne bowed to Nandou—"took out the small sandbag hidden under her skirt and used it on Mulot. Your fainting turned out to be opportune, you see."

"Was Mulot killed?"

"Heavens," cried Nandou. "I hope I know how to use a sandbag without killing a man."

Edmée nibbled at her roll. "How do you come to know such things?"

"That one I learned from a footpad. But the idea that I should carry a sandbag at all was Jeanne's. Where did you learn about it?" he asked her. "In the theatre?"

"From my brothers."

Edmée considered her own lessons: music, English, cooking, horsemanship. How could she feel perfectly at ease with people who were so different from her?

"Wasn't Nandou splendid?" Jeanne said. "If you had not known the plan in advance, would you not have believed completely in Berthe the pastry cook?"

Edmée laughed. "I believed even though I did know the plan. Just as, the first time I met Monsieur Nandou, I believed in the chimney-sweep's boy."

"Please," he said. "You must call me Nandou."

"Very well, I shall. Nandou." Edmée looked at him fondly. The angles of his face and the squatness of his body, once one grew used to them, had a crude harmony, as a piece of rough-cut stone might lie pleasingly against the earth.

"Did you ever see him as *The Dwarf Lord?*" Jeanne asked.

"Indeed, yes. Louis did not want to go, but I—" Edmée stopped and felt her face flushing. "I insisted," she added firmly. "It was wonderful, both the play and the performance."

Nandou lifted his cup and drank; above it, his eyes glittered.

"Look," Jeanne said, "the name of Louis Vollard is going to come up between us. You must not feel awkward when it does."

"Thank you." Edmée found the words in her mind coming from her lips: "What am I to feel, then?"

Jeanne looked at Nandou, who regarded her blandly above the rim of his cup. "You must feel comfortable," she said, "for you are with a woman who understands that one can begin by loving Louis Vollard and end by hating him. I myself loved him for one year, then hated him for twenty. If you ask my advice, I will tell you not to let hatred of him consume you. But if you cannot take that advice, I am not one to condemn you."

"Now you give me even more cause to be in your debt, but I still have no idea how to repay you—or indeed to understand your concern for me."

"In that case," Jeanne said, "do not waste your time in trying. Come, have some more chocolate."

"No, thank you. I think I should begin making my preparations."

"For what?"

"Why, for leaving."

"Leaving?" Jeanne said.

"I cannot continue to accept your charity."

"There is no charity. You are here as an honored guest."

"Please do not speak of honor to me. I have dishonored my name, my family, and myself. I must now prepare to begin a new life."

"Where will you go? The police are surely watching to see if you go to your parents or your son. If you contact either, you need to be certain they would be willing to hide you."

"I know my son would, but I would never place such a burden on him. I shall appeal to my parents. They will help me," Edmée added firmly, for if she did not believe that, to what else could she cling?

"They will take you in and keep the police from learning where you are and returning you to Saint-Lazare?"

In spite of herself, Edmée shivered. She could see her mother sitting in her drawing room, icily beautiful, laughing with the bishop and pouring him coffee in a china cup as thin as a bird's wing. "I hope they will help me to leave France and find a new life elsewhere," she said. "In England, perhaps."

"Do you wish to live in England?"

Edmée sighed. "No."

"And if your parents decline to help you?"

"Then I shall . . . " The words faded. Edmée could think of no others.

Jeanne pushed up the sleeves of her red dressing gown and leaned on the table. Her arms were white and firm. "You have been convicted of adultery, which means you are ruined, both socially and financially. You have escaped from official justice, which means that if you are discovered, you will be returned to prison, perhaps for a longer sentence. I speak candidly not to upset or alarm you but to make you realize that the only sensible thing is to stay here for a while longer and let us continue to hide you."

"I have already intruded too much into your lives."

"We do not regard it as an intrusion."

"I am a virtual stranger. Why should you disrupt and endanger your lives for my sake? It is not enough to say we have both suffered because of Louis."

"It is enough for me."

Edmée turned to Nandou, who was watching Jeanne as closely as if he were going to sketch her. "You say nothing, yet my presence here must concern you."

"In this matter," he said slowly, "I wish all decisions to be Jeanne's."

"And I wish you to stay," Jeanne said.

Edmée considered for a moment. "I cannot pretend I would not like to stay, or have no need to do so. But I could stay only on one condition—that you allow me to earn my keep." She started to stack up the breakfast things.

"What are you doing?" Jeanne said.

"You have been able to have your *bonne* in only rarely, to keep her from discovering my presence. If I myself am the *bonne,* the work will be done every day, and I will no longer need to remain locked in my room when the girl comes."

"That is ridiculous!" Jeanne said. "You cannot be my servant!"

Edmée smiled. "I thought you had Republican sentiments."

"Please do not joke. It is out of the question."

"Why? Perhaps you think someone of my station does not know how to do the work. Ah, but you are wrong." Edmée picked up the plates and cups. "I have had many servants. I know exactly what their duties are."

Jeanne leaped to her feet. "Put those things down at once!" she cried, so vehemently that Edmée could only obey.

Jeanne pulled her hands through her hair, which hung loose. "I will not allow you to wait on me. Even if you did not feel uncomfortable, I would, and exceedingly so."

"No more than I would if I stayed and lived on your charity."

"It is not charity, I tell you! It is only what I owe—" Jeanne stopped and locked her arms over her breasts.

"Are you still thinking of how I let Nandou escape with your daughter? But that was long ago, and if you wish to speak in terms of payment, anything I did then has been more than recompensed by your arranging my escape from prison. I will not hear any talk of what you owe me."

A look crossed Jeanne's face that, in another woman, Edmée would have identified as helplessness. "On this point I am adamant," Edmée said. "I cannot, will not, remain unless I can do most of the cooking and cleaning. Since you refuse, I must leave. I ask only one last kindness—to borrow this dress, and a jacket and hat, all of which I shall return to you as soon as I am able."

"You will not be able," Jeanne said. "If you go out into the world as you are now, you seal your doom."

"Perhaps that is what I deserve."

"Do not say foolish things or contemplate doing them. You must stay here."

Edmée drew herself up. "If I am foolish, I am also proud. I cannot accept charity, especially from people who, however much I have enjoyed their company since we met, were strangers to me before then and whose generosity I did little to merit and have heard less to explain. I shall prepare to leave at once."

"God damn it," Jeanne said, followed by a string of other oaths.

"You shock our guest," Nandou said.

"Help me, then," Jeanne pleaded.

"It seems you have met your match in stubbornness," he answered quietly.

Edmée watched the gazes of her two benefactors meet and go deeply into each other, until Nandou gave a slight shake of his leonine head and said, "It is your decision, Jeanne." He sat back and folded his arms.

With both hands, Jeanne made a knot of her hair. "Very well," she said, as if to herself. And then to Edmée, letting the knot untwist slowly as she spoke: "I will tell you why there is no question of charity. I owed you your escape from prison, and I owe it to you to hide you here as long as need be. It is because of me that you were imprisoned. I sent Henri Foucher to seduce you. I informed Louis, anonymously, of the affair. Let me give you two other facts, in the hope that if you can take any small comfort from them, you will do so. One is that Henri ended by falling in love with you. He told me so himself. The other is that I would never have acted as I did if I had foreseen the consequences. I meant only to punish Louis for . . . something he did to our daughter. I ended by ruining your life. That is why I owe you something. Everything."

An irrelevant memory came to Edmée: Louis's telling her that when he was wounded in the Three Glorious Days, he felt nothing at first, only numbness. It was the same for her: There was no feeling in her body, which began to sway as she watched it from a distance. Nandou surged from his chair and caught her. She put up a hand and clung to his arm, feeling the muscles beneath his shirt. "Brandy," he said.

Jeanne ran to a cupboard and brought back a small glass. Edmée sipped the stinging, golden liquid. "Why?" she said. "Why did you do it?"

Jeanne's eyes lifted to hers slowly, as if weights lay on the lids. "Because I hated Louis. I leaned on that hatred for support, but now I have seen what poisonous fruit it can bear. Love may be blind, but hatred is blinding."

"Poor Jeanne," Edmée said. "You thought it would punish Louis if I had an affair? He does not care what I do."

"He must, or he would not have had you arrested."

"I assure you he was moved by rage and frustration, not by wounded love."

"Do his reasons matter? No more than mine, I think. All that matters is what was done to you. I cannot ask you to forgive me, only to allow me to continue to repay you in whatever inadequate ways I can find."

Tears stood in Jeanne's eyes. Edmée turned to Nandou, but he was watching Jeanne, his broad face as strained as if he too wished to cry.

On the recently macadamized boulevard des Italiens, carriages and omnibuses rolled smoothly. At its edges, pedestrians promenaded in lively streams, wanting to see and be seen: black suits and silk dresses, *lions* with wild hair and insolent gazes, a provincial *curé* in a shovel hat, grisettes, comtesses, drunkards, dandies. The weather was warm enough to serve ices on the terraces of the cafés, and within their white and gold and red interiors waiters proffered platters of oysters, pheasant, and quail as if they were trays of jewels.

Gabrielle and Marc sat near a window, at a table with a snowy cloth. Around them rose animated conversations about the Bourse, the Salons, the literary and musical scenes, the couturiers, the court; in such places, the whole life of Paris seemed channeled into rivers of glittering words. Gabrielle listened, contented, then clasped her hands beneath her chin and said, "Do you often come here?"

"Not to this café, but I am out on the boulevards often. I sit on one of the benches and study the light and the people."

"What do you study about them?"

"Everything I can. How shoulders and chins announce whether their owners are arrogant or confident or hesitant. Noses and the kinds of shadows they cast. Eyes, which are the most difficult for me. But *you* must come here often. At least three people nodded to you when you came in."

"There are always musicians here," Gabrielle said.

Marc pushed aside his soup. "Would you rather think about music than anything else?"

Gabrielle laughed. "I have little time to think about it. I am too busy worrying about finding places to sing it. But if you ask the question seriously . . . " She considered. "Sometimes I believe I sing the best when I do not think at all but simply let the voice come as it wishes."

"You are lucky. If my hand is going to do as I want it to do, I must concentrate for all I'm worth. Even then, I am rarely satisfied. To see something so clearly in your mind and not be able to make your hand produce it—that is my lot most of the time. I imagine you do not have such experiences."

"Not often," she said. "Perhaps I am too contented with what I have already learned to do. Perhaps that is why I shall never be a great singer."

"Do you worry about such a thing?"

"In a way. Someone once told me I would be, and I believed her. But she told me other things that were not true, so . . . " Gabrielle shrugged and filled her heavy silver spoon with soup. "I like to sing, and I believe I sing well, but I shall not go into the history books."

"I think you sing beautifully."

"Truthfully, I often think so myself. Still, to be a great singer I think one must care about nothing else in the world. I do not have that kind of passion. I am not sure I would like to have it."

"I think I do," Marc said.

"You have it, or you want it?"

"Both."

Despite the difference in attitudes they had just revealed, they looked at each other appreciatively. Neither had discussed such subjects before with anyone. In the half dozen times they had met since the musical soirée, they had discovered an ease neither had known with a contemporary of the opposite sex. Gabrielle did not need to view Marc as a potential enemy; he felt no pressure, subtle or overt, to engage in flattery and flirtation. Cautiously at first, then naturally, they found themselves saying things they actually meant—in conversations as unlike the banter to which they were accustomed with members of the opposite sex as gas lamps are from the sun.

"What are you thinking?" Gabrielle asked.

"I was wondering whether I truly care about anything but painting."

"You care about your mother, for one thing. I heard that in the courtroom, and I know her escape must make you feel—" She stopped suddenly and sat back.

"It's all right. I do not mind talking about the escape. Not to you."

"You have no idea how it happened?"

"None, although God knows I have wished her free a thousand times. I know only what the press reported. The warder was entertaining people in his quarters. They turned out to be impostors. They overpowered him and got my mother out into a carnival crowd, in which all of them disappeared." With a savagery that made diners at the next table turn to look, Marc added, "I wish people would stop talking about it."

"I should not have brought it up."

"I do not mean you," he said more quietly.

"Has she attempted to contact you?"

"No. The police are watching to see if she does. I am sure she realizes that. She is so clever. And so beautiful." He gazed into the distance for a moment, then shook his head. "Your mother must have been beautiful too. Or did she die too young for you to remember?"

Gabrielle lifted her chin. "She was beautiful. But I do not think of her any longer."

As if the waiter had heard her silent prayer for distraction, he swooped upon their table and bore away the soup plates like trophies. When he left, she said, "Could your father have arranged the escape?"

"My father? Who sent her there in the first place?"

His voice was so wretched that Gabrielle regretted the question and hurried to erase its effect. "Does your father encourage you to be a painter?"

"Very much. Papa could have been a painter himself, but he never pursued it fully. My mother encouraged me as well. But neither of my grandmothers considers it to be quite respectable."

"What will you do?"

"I shall never stop painting," Marc said firmly. "But I do not know what else I shall do." He turned to look out the window. In a moment, he took a notebook from his waistcoat pocket, opened it, and proferred it. "I did this after I saw you in *La Fille du Régiment.*"

Gabrielle looked at a sketch of herself as Marie with one hand on her hip, her posture and the tilt of her head caught nicely, her mouth so convincingly open that one might swear she was indeed singing. "It's wonderful," she said. "May I have it?"

"If you like." He tore it out.

"Thank you." She rolled it up and put it in her purse.

"It is strange, but I feel as if we have been friends for a long time."

"I feel that too," Gabrielle said.

"Do you have many men friends?"

"I do not like most men. So I would not care to be friends with them."

"I do not care for most young women I meet."

"Do you ever wish you had a sister?"

"I have never thought of it."

Gabrielle aligned her knife and fork. The wish that had been peering from a corner of her mind like an urchin from an alley would be denied no longer. She said, "I have a secret I do not wish to keep to myself any longer.

"A secret? What is it?"

"I cannot tell unless you swear never to discuss it with another soul."

"I swear," Marc said. "By my love of painting."

Gabrielle lifted her hands, adjusted her hat, took a breath. "Very well. Like you, I believed I had no siblings. But I learned that years ago my mother had had an affair. She did not suffer for it, like your mother, but she had a child—me. Afterward she lived with someone else, a man I always thought to be my father. But he was not, as I learned."

"That must have been a great shock," Marc said.

"Dreadful. Then I learned my true father long ago married another woman."

"Have you met your true father?"

"I . . . " Gabrielle put her hands to her cheeks. "No. But I learned that right after his affair with my mother, he married another woman, with whom he had a son. Therefore, I have a half-brother."

"Your history is full of shocks. Have you met the half-brother?"

"Yes. But I have not told him of our relationship. I wondered whether you could help me."

"I?"

"If I were to tell someone he has a half-sister whose existence he never suspected, how should I begin? What should I say?"

"I should look him in the eye," Marc said slowly, "and tell him straight."

"Very well. I am looking you in the eye."

"You and I . . . ?"

"Now you know why I said I wanted us to be friends, and only friends."

"My father and your mother . . . ?"

"Your father never hinted at such a thing?"

"Never."

Gabrielle leaned forward anxiously. "You must never tell him you know, or ask him about it. If he has chosen not to tell you, I cannot be responsible for your violating his silence. Do you promise? I shall die if you do not."

"I . . . Very well." Marc looked grave, but a smile began to tug at half his mouth. "So it is not strange that we became friends so easily."

"No." She too began to smile. "I could not bear to be the only one of us that knew."

When the waiter arrived, they were grinning at each other so broadly that he had to set down their *perdrix aux choux* with an extra flourish in order to capture their attention.

"You will let it rest now, won't you?" said Nicolas Vollard. "After this last police report, there will be no more of it?"

Louis stood by a window in the firm's offices, looking out at a stately procession: Louis Napoléon, just crowned Emperor—on December 2, as his uncle had been years earlier—was making his way to the Tuileries. Without turning around, Louis said, "I shall do nothing more to distress the House of Vollard."

"I am not thinking of the firm," Nicolas said. "I am thinking of you."

"I know." In silence Louis watched the unison grace of horses and the flashing of gold braid and bronze helmets. "What must it be like," he said, "to change from president to emperor simply by issuing a decree? To transform oneself into something different by an act of sheer will?"

"Do not forget that people had to be killed, and the formality of a new constitution and a plebiscite had to be observed."

"Poor Nico. You disapprove of your emperor and your brother. Yet you must live with both of us." Louis sighed. "The emperor, at least, will be good for business."

Nicolas moved behind him and touched his shoulder. "So are you, when you make an effort."

"Do not pretend. I know that several important customers of the bank withdrew because of the scandal, and we lost Tissot's partnership in the railway bonds. You thought I was blind to everything but Edmée's fate, but I was not."

"Yet still you persisted."

Louis turned to face his brother. "I apologize for nothing, except for being made a fool of once again by her escape." Anger lit his eyes but went out at once, like a faulty match. "Do not worry—I have said I will do nothing further. The police have not found her after all these months, and even if the matter is not officially closed, it might as well be. I am beaten and I know it. That is the sign of the weak, is it not?—to know they are beaten. The last rebellion of Louis Vollard is over, may he rest in peace. To rest in a place, however, one must first be able to find it."

Nicolas gripped his shoulders. "Do not say such things. Even if what you do is misguided, as was your charge against Edmée, I can recognize my brother in the action and love him while I am furious with him. But when you pity yourself, when you declare you are weak and talk of—"

"But I am weak, Nico! Do you not know that, you who know me so well?"

The brothers stared at each other, faces as close as lovers', profiles as different as strangers'.

"Do you not know that knowing I am weak is what drives me mad sometimes?"

"Ah, Louis . . . " Nicolas broke his grip and stepped back. "Forget Edmée. Forget the firm, and everything else but the two things that matter to you—your painting and your son. If you do that . . . "

Louis smiled sadly. "I will become strong?"

"You may find some peace."

Louis turned again to the window. "That is what our new emperor promises, does he not?—*The empire is peace.*" He sighed. "I presume you and Joséphine will be attending one of the celebration balls?"

Nicolas nodded, and set his lips. The brothers stood in silence, watching the imperial procession pass.

Chapter Seventeen

The apartment was noisy with chatter. *After some months' hiatus,* Jeanne and Nandou were holding a salon. There were many actors, including some from the original cast of *The Dwarf Lord,* who greeted Nandou as if they had not seen him in years and studded their conversations all night with dialogue from the play; occasionally they burst into entire scenes. There were writers and painters, dressers and stagehands, including the one who, years earlier, had helped Nandou rescue Solange by acting the part of the chimney sweep. Two young performers, just arrived in Paris and eager to make their fortunes, presented a program of ballads and arias by the new Italian composer Verdi. A poet who looked as if he slept in barns recited verses to anyone who would listen, and a tall, burly playwright stood by the cold buffet on the large dining-room table, working away at its contents, denouncing the emperor and the censors between bites.

If Nandou moved about, he had to crane his head to speak with people, so he preferred to sit on the red plush sofa, feet on a fringed ottoman. People came and went, clustering beside him on the sofa and leaning over its back, but all the time he chatted with them—about Hugo's writings in exile or Flaubert's novels—his eyes kept silent track of Jeanne. In a rose silk dress, hair coiled on the nape of her neck, she moved easily about the room, introducing people to the woman at her side. "My dear, you must meet my cousin Aimée," he heard her say. "She has come to live in Paris and work in the theatre. She sews magnificently, and has started to work on costumes for Claudel. You must see what a splendid gown she designed and made for the new play at the Gaîté . . ."

"Aimée" smiled and held out her hand and asked polite questions and tilted her head charmingly while she listened to the answers. It would not occur to anyone that she was too regally gracious for a costume mistress, for the room was full of people to whom a manner grander than their station was both a tool of the trade and a compensation for its many hardships.

Jeanne had worked hard to help create "Aimée," inventing an entire life history for her, which included a vanished husband, a demanding mother who had died and freed her, and other particulars Nandou did not bother to remember. His part in the affair had been to devise the physical person: change the hair to a reddish brown and arrange it differently around the face, thicken and straighten the eyebrows, paint the mouth wider. Because Edmée's features were delicate, not strong, a few subtle lines could alter the balance among them. Her eyes still dominated her face, but if need be, she could wear spectacles. He had showed her how to alter her voice a bit and speak with the accent of the Midi; she could not maintain it, but she might manage it for long enough if confronted by someone from her old life, or by the police. Most important, he had managed to procure some papers to document her new identity.

She had been eager to embrace it. True, she had little choice, but she had abandoned "Edmée Vollard" with scarcely more regret than an old frock. Could he have done the same? Nandou wondered. If he had to become someone else, would he be so willing? The answer shot from within him like a leaping fish: No, he would not.

Not even, he thought, not even if he could become someone of normal height? No. He would not.

He was so astounded that his mouth fell open. After all the years of railing against the turtle shell of his body, he would choose not to leave it? *Dwarf,* he thought, *dost love thy dwarfishness?* But neither love nor hate was the question. In fact there was no question; he was what he was, and could not be separated. The turtle shell had shaped him—had been part of the exultation of uniqueness he had known since childhood. Even though it also made futility come with the exultation, that was inextricably part of him as well.

He was sitting, bemused, when Jeanne came up to him, flushed, smoking a small black cigar. "Why are you shaking your head?" she said.

"I have discovered I am still capable of having thoughts that surprise me."

She smiled. They were so friendly to each other, so polite. No anger, no fighting. No passions. Not since the night she confessed to him what she had done to Edmée. "I am going to introduce Aimée to Jules now," she said.

"I shall come in a moment." Jules, the stagehand who had acted the chimney sweep, was the one person in the room who had known Edmée Vollard. Now over sixty and ill, he sat in a corner, rocking a bit from side to side and smiling merely to be present. Although he was unlikely to remember Edmée after so many years, it was a test that, successfully passed, would give her confidence.

Nandou watched the two women move toward Jules. One in rose, the other in pale yellow, they were the most brilliant creatures in the room. There was a bond between them, undeniably. Sometimes he thought it was solely because of Louis; two women wronged by the same man could lessen their chagrin by sharing it. Sometimes he thought the bond came, perversely, from Jeanne's role in causing Edmée's situation: perpetrator and victim joined in a union like that of creator and creation. But whether one explanation was true, or both, something else was involved. Perhaps it was simply that they liked each other.

He slid from the sofa and walked toward them. Edmée—he must think of her as Aimée—was talking to Jules: "Forty-eight years on the Boulevard of Crime! You must know how everything is done. The new play at the Théâtre-Lyrique, for instance—how do they make the heroine disappear from the palanquin?"

Jules gave her the whole complicated explanation: pulleys, counterweights, a false top, trick painting. She asked intelligent questions, expressed admiration, and had instinctively known it would give Jules pleasure to talk of things he no longer had the strength to perform. His eyes were bright, and he stopped rocking. Clearly Jules had no memory of seeing her before. "A nice woman," he said when she moved off with Jeanne. "From the Midi, did she say?"

Across the room voices hailed Nandou. He made his way to a group clustered around a new arrival. "Look what Etienne has brought from Brussels!" The object was produced: a pamphlet on thin paper. *Napoléon le Petit* by Victor Hugo, said to be a diatribe against the new emperor that exposed him as a grubby, scheming, inept scoundrel. Hugo had written it in exile and financed its printing himself, for to publish him in France now meant risking imprisonment. Copies were being smuggled in inside hollow busts of Napoléon III, and the authorities had not yet discovered the ruse. "Let us hear it," cried one of the actors, and others took up the chant. The owner turned to Nandou and handed him the pamphlet with a flourish. Everyone clapped and cleared space near the piano.

As Nandou took the space and began to read, the feeling came upon him once again: the glorious awareness of his uniqueness, the undertow of melancholy. His voice flowed without effort, obeying every command of his mind, and if it could not descend to the richness of bass timbre, he loved it for that also—for its tenor nimbleness and grace, for its acid and honey, and the smoothness with which it moved from one to the other. He read savage phrases and knew their aim was made even more sure by the language of his body; he read with a passion he knew originated with Hugo but was also part of himself: "First, Monsieur Bonaparte, you must learn something of the human conscience. In this world there are two things—news to you, no doubt—called Good and Evil. We must reveal their natures to you: to lie is not good, to betray is bad, to assassinate is worse. Such things may be useful, but they are forbidden. By whom? you will ask. We shall explain. . . . Monsieur Bonaparte, one may be a master, one may have eight million voices to approve his crimes and twelve million francs for his smallest pleasures . . . one may have armies, cannons, fortresses . . . one may be a despot, all-powerful; but one day some obscure creature, some passerby, some unknown, will stand up and say: 'This, you shall not do.' That someone, that mouth speaking in shadow, which one can hear but not see, that passerby, that unknown, that insolent creature, that is the human conscience."

In the silence that followed, he heard and felt his heart, drumming with the knowledge that he was as he was: grotesque and grand at once. So be it.

The room burst into applause.

When the guests were gone, and any food remaining had been pressed into the pockets and purses of those who needed it most, the three of them tidied up.

Jeanne and Edmée bore dishes to the kitchen; Nandou, an apron around his middle, rinsed them at the sink, greeting each load with a different persona: a wicked troll, a saintly young girl, "Berthe" the pastry cook. They laughed, toasted the successful emergence of "cousin Aimée," and went over every aspect of the evening. At length Edmée said she was exhausted and must go up to her apartment: two tiny rooms on the fifth floor, which she had managed to procure only the month before. She started to leave but came back into the room and stood, face flushed and hands clasped as if she were about to make a confession.

"What is it?" Jeanne asked.

"I . . . " She shook her head, swallowed hard, and said, "Tonight I feel I have found something I always searched for. When I was Edmée Tissot, I thought my life was empty, like a pastry shell. I married Louis because I thought he could show me how to fill it—I thought he was a rebel against much that seemed empty and foolish to me—but he was too occupied with his inner demons to be a rebel. Edmée Vollard did nothing worthy with her life but raise her son. I miss Marc terribly, I must find a way to see him, but here, with you, I feel I have discovered the kind of life I always wanted. I do not mean being a seamstress and working in the theatre. I mean . . . not having to dress and act and speak and live so that people will think I am proper. I mean not caring what people say, not at the palace or in the journals, or in anyone's drawing room or opera box. . . . Tonight I said and did nothing important, I may never say or do anything important, but tonight I said and did it because I wanted to, and for no other reason." She looked at them, twisting her hands. Then she darted to Jeanne and kissed her. "Never say again that you ruined my life. You may have helped me to find it." She turned to Nandou, bent, and kissed his hand. "You are a magnificent actor. More important, you are a wonderful man." Again she went to the door. "Good night, my good friends," she said, and was gone.

In the silence Jeanne put her head in her hands.

"What is it?" Nandou said.

Her eyes lifted slowly to his. "Do you think I have paid for my crime?"

He heard the plea in her voice. In fact he thought she had paid. He had watched her set about making amends with a single-minded determination. He had witnessed her agitation and anger in the courtroom, her meticulous and clever planning for the escape, her constant concern for Edmée's welfare, her agony at having to confess her guilt, her careful creation of "cousin Aimée."

"Nandou?" she said. "Have I paid?"

"Yes." Why could he say nothing more than yes?

He saw the same question in her eyes.

After a moment she said, "Indeed, it was a good evening. If only Gaby had been here as well . . . But it was good."

"Yes." Hateful word; it hung in the air as limply as a flag with no wind.

In a briskly different voice, she said, "I have some news. I have torn up the play I was working on."

"Have you? I am sorry."

"But you know it was not good." He nodded. "Last week I began a new one."

"Bravo."

"It is not like any of my others. No castles or kings or lost treasures. It is about real things that are happening today in Paris—in fact, the kind of situation Edmée lived through."

"How is it going?"

"Well. Very well. For the first time in two years, I am truly excited. I feel almost as I did when I was writing *The Dwarf Lord,* except that there is no role in it for you."

"It does not matter," he said.

"It matters to me."

"Please, Jeanne. I well realize there are situations into which a dwarf cannot be made to fit."

"If you were God," she said, "would you make yourself like other men, or would you have all men be dwarfs?"

Did she know he had been thinking such a thing earlier in the evening? Did she know everything he thought? "I would be as I am," he replied slowly. "So I would never be God."

"Do you never wish you had wanted to be something besides an actor?"

"No."

"We cannot choose which things to love, can we?"

In the glow of the lamp, her face was soft. Her black hair was pulled away from it in the fashion of the day, her eyes were naked, and her mouth, with the slight overbite that had always stirred him, was soft and red, like fruit ready for picking.

"Nandou," she said, as if the words came against her will, "have you forgiven me?" He nodded. "Then tell me so," she said. "Say it."

"I have forgiven you." It was true, although he did not know precisely when he had done so. His anger had dissolved gradually, replaced by admiration for her efforts, but nothing more. He put a hand to her cheek, praying she would not see into him. For if he had forgiven her, why was everything not as it had been before? Could he live the rest of his life with her in a state of placidity, nodding and smiling like someone too old to be stirred by the wind or roused by the fire?

"I have been thinking," he said. "It was my fault as well as yours."

"You had nothing to do with it. I hated Louis, I planned a revenge."

"True. But my jealousy fed your hatred."

"Now you frighten me," she said. "You would not say such a thing if you still felt . . . if you were . . . " She looked at him so searchingly that he feared he was hiding nothing. Then she stepped back, smoothed her skirt, and said, "I am tired, Nandou. I think I shall go to bed."

On a Saturday in January, Edmée cleaned her shoes on the bootscrapers outside the church of Saint-Sulpice, opened the huge wooden doors, and walked into the immense interior. Pearl-gray light fell through the stained-glass windows and the panes high overhead. The quiet was so vast that whispers drowned in it and a footfall ringing on the stone floor was a bell from the bottom of the sea.

Edmée made certain her shawl covered her hair and shielded her face, then went to the large, shell-shaped font. Automatically her fingers dipped into the water and made the sign of the cross. Peering nervously into the rows of prie-dieux, she walked up the left aisle to stand before the huge figure of Christ crucified, held up by carved wooden garlands, which had always affected her like the touch of a cool hand. Then she went to the tenth row from the back, genuflected, and moved in. On her knees, she put up her hands as if to pray and closed her eyes. Despite all her years of questioning them, the attitudes of her childhood, which had been stirring since the moment she entered, settled on her like a veil released from its pins. She felt herself once again awed by the pageantry and mystery and cowed by the crisp black-and-white authority of the nuns who had educated her, the priests who had officiated every Sunday morning, the bishops who had come to tea and dinner, counseling and gossiping with her mother. They stood in soldier-ranks in her memory, staring at her, dozens of eyes pronouncing her guilty of mortal sin. She shook her head violently to throw off their gaze.

"Maman?" said an uncertain voice.

Edmée sucked in her breath and opened her eyes. "Marc?" When she turned, there he was. She rose from her knees and sat beside him.

They looked at each other in the pale light. Together they smiled, tentatively at first, then with a joy fed by seeing itself on the other's face.

"Oh, my dearest boy," Edmée whispered. "Am I truly with you again?"

Marc whispered back, "I knew there would be a message from you one day."

"I was afraid you might not still be working at Belloc's studio."

"I go several times a week." He grinned, as if at something splendid.

"I knew you would come. Are you all right, my darling?"

"I am fine, Maman, especially now that I am seeing you."

Edmée stroked his cheek, then frowned. "What is this? A little cut?"

"It is nothing. Only from shaving."

"Yes, you are fully a man now. I must no longer think of you as my boy."

Marc said nothing. One of his hands rested between them. Edmée covered it with her own. "It was a man who spoke out for me in court. That was the proudest moment of my life, but also the worst, because I had given you the reason to do it."

"I wanted to kill them. Truly, Maman—to aim pistols at their heads. I have never had such a feeling before."

"I pray you never do again. At least I can promise that your foolish mother will not be the cause. Never again will she need such defending. I swear it."

"Do not speak of it, Maman, please. There is no need. I would rather speak of other things. Wouldn't you?"

Edmée squeezed his hand. "Yes. Are you happy, my darling?"

"Why, yes," Marc said. "I suppose I am."

"You are painting?"

"Every day I manage to do something, if only to work in my sketchbook."

"Then you are happy."

Marc seemed about to laugh but stopped himself and looked around to make certain no one was watching them. The church was largely empty, and the few souls kneeling in the pews or waiting near the confessional were as deep in their own worlds as dreamers, if not as peaceful. "You look quite different," he whispered. "At first I was not even certain it was you."

"I have had to change everything," Edmée said. "My life, and my-self."

"That is what I want to talk about. Where are you living? What are you doing?"

"How I would love to tell you! But I have sworn to my new friends, who endanger themselves by helping me, that no one from my previous life shall know where I live, or under what name. No one. I must respect that oath. Besides, I would not put you in the position of having to lie about me, and for me."

"I do not care a damn if I have to lie for you."

"Ssh, Marc, no such language in this place, although I love you for the sentiment it contains. But I refuse to turn you into a liar." Edmée lifted a hand to his face again. "Do not look so unhappy. I will not leave you. We will meet often. Let us say that we meet each Saturday and each time agree on where the next meeting will be. Would that not be a good plan?" She smiled. "I am becoming rather good at intrigues and schemes." Then, realizing what other meaning could attach to her words, she bit her lips. "One day, perhaps, the police will cease to care about me and everything will be different. For now, be content with the fact that I am content, and have good friends."

"Did they help you escape from the prison?"

"My dear, I cannot tell you anything about that either. Someday, perhaps, but not now."

"How I cheered when the news came that you had gotten out!"

"What did your father do?"

Marc squared his shoulders. "We have not spoken of it to each other, but I know he was unhappy."

"I should not have asked you. Forgive me. Poor Marc. Between us, Louis and I have pulled you in two, have we not?"

Marc hesitated. "I suppose you hate Papa?"

She sighed. "I suppose, though I try not to. And I don't want you to hate him. He has always loved you, Marc. Always. You don't hate him, do you?"

A very old woman who had been moving slowly up the aisle neared their row, her steps like whispers because her feet were wrapped in rags. Marc waited for her to pass before he said, "Papa is too unhappy to hate."

"Ah."

"Sometimes I think I should hate him, though. He has done such a terrible thing to you."

"What I did was also wrong."

"I do not care. What does it matter if people have affairs?"

Edmée shifted on the seat. "Do not say such a thing in this place."

"But I think it, Maman."

"You do not fully understand. You cannot. When you yourself have fallen in love and married . . . Has it happened to you yet, my dear? In all the months since I saw you last, have you met a young woman who stirs your heart?"

Marc lifted his gaze to the ceiling, so high above them it was like a stone sky. Edmée watched his profile, saw his jaw clench, his lips tighten. Then he lowered his head. Speaking even more softly, so she barely could hear, he said, "A young lady has become a good friend."

How shy he was, Edmée thought. How handsome and splendid and shy. "I am so pleased," she whispered. "Tell me about her."

"She is a singer, a fine one. She is clever and beautiful and very understanding. We spend hours talking together. But we do not . . . We are only friends. That is all we will ever be."

Edmée smiled. "Do not be so sure."

He turned to her. "I am positive, Maman."

"Well, we shall see. But why do you frown? She sounds wonderful. Who is she?"

"Her name is Gabrielle Corday."

"Oh, Marc!" The words came out as a cry, which faded slowly into the vastness of the church like a bird over rooftops. "Do not speak for a moment," Edmée said. "Please, my dear." She knew he was looking at her oddly, but she needed time to absorb the name, and the fact, of "Gabrielle Corday." Of all the young women in Paris, why had he come to know the one who was Jeanne's—and Louis's—daughter? How could one be free to control one's destiny, as Jeanne and Nandou believed, and had almost made her believe, if Fate were to intrude its caprices?

She forced herself to ask quietly, "How did you meet Mademoiselle Corday?"

"She sang at a soirée to which I had taken cousin Sophie."

"I see. And you have become strongly attached to her?"

Marc put his hands on the seat before him and gripped its back.

"There is something I must confess to you, Maman. You are the only one I could ever tell. But it is difficult."

She put a hand on Marc's arm. "Do not say any more."

"But I must, Maman. I need to tell someone and you are . . . I have been . . . "

She looked at his face, its symmetry broken by wretchedness. Why was he so unhappy? Why was he not elated to be in love? Why did he not—Her thoughts stopped and crashed into one other, halted by a new, dreadful one: He believed Gabrielle Corday was of his blood. In the instant of thinking it, Edmée knew she was right. Louis had told Marc who Gabrielle was. And he, poor boy, was devastated. To fall in love with a beautiful girl, only to learn she was your half-sister and thus forbidden to you, forever . . . Edmée reached up, took Marc's chin in her hand, and turned his face to hers. "Do you love her so very much?"

"It is so hard to tell you what I feel . . . If I could marry anyone, I would wish it to be her. But I cannot, because I . . . "

"Yes, yes, I understand," Edmée said, stroking his cheek and soothing him as if he were five years old again. But the skin beneath her fingers was rough with the tiny pins of whiskers. She pulled gently on the lobe of his ear, as she had done so often when he was small, calling him her little monkey; he would laugh with a pleasure as pure as a mountain stream.

"Maman, when I tell you what I feel, you will hate me, as I hate myself. But I must tell you anyway. If you could only not hate me, just for an hour . . . "

"Ssh." She put her hand on his arm and looked past him, at the huge stone columns that anchored the church into the earth. Must a mother not do all she could to help her child? She thought of her own mother, who had neither attended the trial nor visited the prison, who had come to her only as a scent of violets, wafting from the notes on her exquisite stationery in her perfect handwriting: *Your father and I cannot understand how you could permit such a thing to happen. Of course we shall see that you have a good lawyer and shall pray for you daily. Can we have failed to raise you properly? I think God will witness that we gave you everything in our power. I counsel you to trust yourself to Him . . . .* Edmée looked up toward the Christ. The deep, carved lines of his face were serene in their pain. Suddenly everything was clear: If a child was suffering, a mother must stop his anguish. No matter what the cost. She had no choice—none that would please Him. It was simple, once one saw clearly.

"You do not need to tell me anything," she said to Marc. "I understand it all." His eyes widened. She took her hand from his arm. "I know what you are feeling. You have learned Gabrielle Corday is your sister. Is that not so?"

"Yes," Marc said wonderingly. "How did you . . . "

"How I know does not matter. Before you choke on the shame of confessing you love your own sister and cannot stop loving her, let me tell you something that will cure your pain, though it will cause you another kind." Edmée sighed. "You may love Gabrielle as freely as you wish. She is not your half-sister."

"What do you mean? Papa is not her father?"

"Yes, he is."

"But then . . . we must be . . . what are you saying?"

"You and Gabrielle are no relation to each other."

"I do not understand," Marc said slowly, as if he did.

"You are shocked. How could you be otherwise? Let me explain, so you may understand." Edmée looked toward the altar, which blazed with gold and candles, put her palms together, and lifted her hands to her chin. It would be easier if she imagined she was telling, not her son, but the priest who was genuflecting as he passed the cross. She closed her eyes. "When I learned that Louis had loved another woman and had a child by her, I was deeply, bitterly hurt—less because of the existence of the woman and the child than because he had lied to me about . . . something that happened concerning them. I saw then that Louis was not the man I had assumed him to be. I believe now that it was my own fault for having created in my mind a man I wanted rather than looking at the one who actually existed, but I was too young at the time to think of anything except my own pain. I wanted to do something rebellious, something to prove I could take things into my own hands. So I . . . oh, my dear, how difficult this is to say . . . " She opened her eyes and put up her hands as if to smooth her hair, but her fingers touched only the cloth of her shawl. She lowered them again and folded them tightly in her lap. The priest, she thought. Think of the priest. "I had an affair with someone who once had been a suitor of mine. You are shocked again, I know, but it is true. Now you know the worst of me, the thing known by no other creature save the man himself—that the transgression for which I went to prison was not the first of its kind in my life. It was only . . . a very different one. Often in prison I felt that I was paying for both of my sins and that it was right I should do so . . . But let me speak only of years ago. At that time, I had the foolish idea that defying Louis by having an affair, even though he would never know of it—and he never did, I never told him—would make me feel better. But of course it did not. It only made me guilty and wretched, and within a short time I broke it off. Soon after, I learned I was with child. I was terrified at first. Then I began to think that God might have forgiven me, because I was able to carry the child. I did not lose it, as I had lost two others. And when the child was born . . . " Slowly she touched her son's hand. "Marc, my dear, it was you. You were so precious, so wonderful, so healthy, that I dared to think I had been forgiven, and could only feel blessed beyond all hope of blessedness. I have loved you since the instant of your birth, loved you totally. And so has your father. I mean Louis. Of that I am certain. Whatever has passed between us two, he has always been your loving father. You know that, do you not?"

It seemed that Marc's head would never turn to hers. But at last it did. "Maman . . . how can you . . . Can you be sure Papa is not my . . ."

What a child he still was, she thought. What a wonderful, beautiful child. "A woman can be sure," she said gently. "But in every other way, Papa has been your father. If he were now to learn that he is not, which I pray you will not allow to happen, for I can see no possible good in such a thing, only pain and danger . . . but if he somehow were to learn, I am certain he would love you no less. You have been, you are, the finest thing in his life. You must continue to love him, Marc, for if you do not . . . "

Edmée stopped, drained of emotion and words. She wanted to sink to the stone floor and sleep in the peace and silence of the church; her bones ached with the need to do so. But she had to find more words, to stop the look on Marc's face, which had grown as tight and strained as if something were clawing behind his ears. "Forgive me for telling you," she whispered. "If there were any other way to reassure you, I would have taken it. Try at least to find comfort in knowing that you have done nothing wrong and that your feelings for this girl need not be denied but can become the foundation of your happiness."

He said nothing but put his head in his hands. Around them was only the echoing stillness. "Marc?" Edmée whispered. "Will you not speak to me?"

He looked up at her. "Why did you not let me make my confession before you made yours?"

"But my dear . . . What have you to confess, except a feeling you can now cease to regard as shameful?"

He laughed soundlessly, his mouth a sketch of so much bitterness that Edmée put a hand to her own. "I may indeed love Gabrielle, Maman, but not in the way you think. I do not love any woman in that way. I never shall. I cannot. I am one of those dreadful men who can love only . . . their own kind, though I have never allowed myself to do so. That is what I needed to tell you, for I must tell someone or go mad."

"Oh . . . " said Edmée, a cry that stayed trapped in her throat, echoing. The two of them stared, both struggling to disbelieve what they had heard yet each certain it was the truth.

For hours Jeanne had been writing furiously, the thoughts coming faster than she could shape into words, her pen going in and out of the inkwell like a thirsty cat's tongue lapping water. Finally she blotted the last page, stacked all of them, and read them over. Nodding in approval, a smile growing, she changed a word here or there, then took up the stack and went along the hall and into the dining room to show it to Nandou.

He was sitting with the lamp turned low, his shoulders slumped, his dark eyes fixed on space.

Her mood shifted to meet the one inherent in his posture. She went to him and said, "What are you thinking of?"

He stirred and answered without looking up, "Times that are gone."

As if by magic, she was plummeted back through the years: Gabrielle was laughing under the table, playing with Fidèle, and the room was warm with their love for one another, all of them, cat, child, woman, and dwarf, with Nandou's special love for her smoldering at its heart. Somehow he had transferred the images from his mind to hers; such a thing was not supposed to be possible, but she was certain he had done it.

He shook his head slowly; the images faded from hers.

"What have you there?" he said, indicating the papers.

"The new play. I had a wonderful idea this afternoon. I have created a role for you, after all."

He looked pleased but said, "You did not have to do that."

"Yes, I did." It was true. The thought of a play by her in which he had no role had been troubling her on every page, its weight heavier than regret, almost like a premonition of disaster. "Here is the first scene in which you will appear." She held it out.

He turned up the lamp and read silently. As she watched him, his head bent over the pages, the light striking the cheek that still bore a faint scar, she became possessed by the hope that the scene—the character she had created for him—would restore the times that were gone: Gabrielle would come back, laughing and saying how foolishly wrong she had been; Fidèle would appear on a sill one night, reincarnated, giving an ink-lined yawn; and when Nandou's eyes lifted from the pages, they would burn as they had used to. She clasped her hands tightly, for they wanted to touch his coarse, dark hair, as thick as when she had first seen him.

He lifted his head. His eyes glowed with pleasure and appreciation, but nothing more. "This is splendid, you know, Jeanne. Splendid. I shall love playing this man."

"I shall love watching you."

"How much you have given me," he said softly. "How rich you have made my life."

Without thought, she knelt beside him, covered his hand with her own, and allowed the words beating in her mind to escape. "Nandou, will you ever again want to come to me?"

"Jeanne, I . . . I cannot say."

"Ah." She withdrew her hand. "I am sorry. That is a question one should not ask."

He turned away, then said, his voice quiet and desperate, "Why do you not take a lover?"

"That is another," she said.

Chapter Eighteen

The play opened in the winter of 1854 and quickly became a success. The "House Full" sign began to appear in front of the theatre each night. Inside, in the boxes where jewels sparkled and fans moved as skillfully as the women who deployed them, and in the crush at intermissions, everyone chattered eagerly about it. How delicious! or How shocking! depending upon one's fondness for gossip, one's tolerance for the tendency of new plays to concern themselves with social issues, and one's view of what was or was not moral—for despite the censor's requirements the author's compassion for the central character showed through. As a result, some members of the public considered the play so scandalous that they would not endanger themselves by attending. A critic wrote: "Our world may contain sordid facts, but there is no reason to portray them on our stages. If it is possible for decent women to engage in adultery, their actions must be condemned, not made the sympathetic subject of drama." But such voices did nothing to stem the rush for tickets, and at supper parties all over Paris—many of them given, and attended, by courtesans—people found themselves in difficulty if they had not yet seen *The Trial of Louise Bernier* and could discuss it only in embarrassingly general terms.

Adding to the deliciousness was the belief that the play was based on an actual incident, the publicly revealed adultery and imprisonment, several years earlier, of Edmée Vollard. It was true that some of the drama's characters and events had no counterparts in that reality: "Louise Bernier" had a daughter, for example; there was a newspaper reporter who fell in love with her and tried to help her, and there was also—the playwright's trademark—a dwarf character, this time one who hawked newspapers near "Louise's" home and became her confidant. Moreover, "Louise" died in prison. Still, if there was anyone in society who did not think the play was based on the Vollard case, he or she kept that opinion secret. A final dollop of pleasure to the scandal, like the *crème Chantilly* ladled from silver bowls to top the cakes at the glittering boulevard cafés, was the fact that Edmée Vollard had still not reappeared, in society or anywhere else. "We still hope to find her," an official from the Department of Justice told one of the journals. "Our forces made every effort at the time she disappeared, and though no new information has come to light in the nearly two years since her trial, we consider the case still open."

The playwright made no comment on her sources of inspiration except to say, "It is true, I have always written of exotic locales and fantasy kingdoms. But do you not think the Paris of today is the most exotic, fantastic place of all?"

What most delighted, or antagonized, people was the central fact of the drama: At the very time Louise's husband was enraged by learning she had a lover, he himself was keeping a mistress, with the full knowledge and approval of those who called Louise immoral. In a scene that had all Paris talking, after the husband had Louise arrested for adultery, he went to his mistress for consolation, while in the street outside her apartment, the news-vendor–dwarf commented sardonically. ("Whom can a man look farther down upon than a dwarf? Ah, yes—a wife who does as the man himself does.")

When the playwright was asked if she meant to suggest that women should enjoy the same status and privileges as men, she said she believed in two things: equality between the sexes and a good after-dinner cigar. Well, really, people said, after they had laughed, what else could one expect from a woman who was known to cohabit with a dwarf?

"You may be angry at the author if you like," said Joséphine Vollard to her mother-in-law. "I am angry as well, of course, but the person I shall never forgive is Edmée."

Henriette Vollard drank more of the tea the two women often shared in the late afternoon, in the English custom Joséphine admired. "I did not say I had forgiven Edmée," Henriette said. She had grown frailer, assigning some of the duties of an arthritic hip to a silver-headed cane and allowing a family of cousins to move into the house and help manage it, but whenever she and Joséphine spoke of the play, as they rarely seemed able to avoid doing, her voice was as strong as lye. "If Edmée had not behaved as she did," Henriette said, "Louis would not have been driven to the foolish action that has haunted us ever since. Never think I forgive her. But once her trial had faded from the headlines, it did the same from people's minds. This play, however, this abomination by that *creature* . . . " Henriette's anger seemed about to crumple her in upon herself, but she gripped the head of the cane at her side and restored control. "The play could exert a much longer and stronger hold upon the public imagination. No doubt that is precisely what the Sorel person intends. She wrote the play deliberately to have her revenge upon us. I am as certain of that as of the fact that this chair is upholstered in silk."

With curiosity, for she had been told only the essentials of the history between Jeanne Sorel and the Vollard family, Joséphine said, "Years ago, when she came here and declined your offer, such a generous offer, did you see in her any signs of the vindictiveness she now displays?"

Henriette took a moment to answer, gazing at the two gilded bronze fish that formed the base of the covered sugar bowl in front of her. "She had a pride in herself and an arrogance of spirit that one would have expected to find only in those who have been bred to such attitudes."

Joséphine's brows lifted. "If I did not know better, I might almost think you admired her."

"I am not afraid to acknowledge an enemy's strength. At the time, the woman had qualities to which I would not have objected in a daughter-in-law, if her background had been suitable. She had more strength than Louis, in fact. But never did I anticipate she would use it against us, and certainly not in the venomous form she has now chosen."

"I cannot understand how the censor allowed that drama to be put on the boards," Joséphine said, "or why he cannot now be made to take it off."

Henriette made an exasperated sound. "There appears to be a growing body of support for this kind of thing in the drama—this Realism, as they call it. The Lord knows that I have spoken to everyone I know, and everyone Olivier knew, who might be in a position to influence the censor, but so far without success."

Joséphine pursed her lips; beneath her small felt hat, copied after the fashion of the new Empress Eugénie, her doll-like face became ten years older. "I shall speak to Nicolas again," she said. "He must make an effort to help in this matter. He cannot remain indifferent to his mother's peace of mind."

But when she broached the subject to him four hours later, at dinner, after they had discussed certain expenses in conjunction with Denis's schooling, Nicolas was as firm in his refusal as he had been all along. "I do not want Maman to suffer," he said, "but it is out of the question."

"She does suffer! An old woman, nearly seventy, to have to endure such a scandal?"

"Maman survived the Revolution. She is not going to be destroyed by a drama on the boulevards."

Joséphine regarded him silently for a moment. In their fourteen years of marriage she had never been able to predict on which issues he would be completely malleable—"Do whatever you like," uttered with a lift of his thick, straight brows that perfectly mimicked a shrug—and which would make him intractable. "You are cold, Nicolas," she said. "Cold."

"Perhaps." He laid his knife and fork on the plate like neatly crossed swords. "But I will not try to enlist my colleagues or customers in an effort to influence someone in court circles on the subject of that play. For one thing, it would be an admission that I believe the play to be about us, and for another, I do not think it would do any good."

"What is the point of having money and position if they cannot be used to exert influence?"

"They can be. I do not choose to use them on this issue, that is all."

Joséphine touched her hair, which descended in waves from a straight center part to form two long sausages on her neck. "I simply cannot understand you. Do you like to have everyone in Paris thinking of your brother, of the Vollard name, when they go to see that play?"

"You credit it with too much power. Many people in Paris have not seen it and never will. Like you."

"I would never lend my presence to such a disgusting event."

"Then how can you be sure it is disgusting?"

Joséphine leaned forward. "I hope you are not defending it?"

"I think it is well done, and raises questions about our society that thoughtful people would do well to consider."

"Are you saying you have actually been to see it?"

"Yes."

Joséphine put both hands to her forehead and looked at Nicolas through the cage of her fingers. "I don't believe it. How could you? Why would you—when it attacks your own family?"

"I assure you it contains no mention of us, and there are a number of references and characters that can have no connection with us."

"Do not be naïve. You know everyone assumes it is about Louis and Edmée."

Patiently, as if explaining to his young son rather than his wife, Nicolas said, "It was Louis who first made his and Edmée's actions the property of the public. If those actions inspire a good deal of comment, and even a drama, I do not think Louis can complain, nor can we do so in his stead."

"I thought you loved Louis," Joséphine said bitterly. "I thought you would want to protect him from the consequences of his action."

"Love does not keep one from recognizing weakness, or knowing it has to be paid for. Louis, and Maman—and you and I and Marc, all of us—must go about our lives as if the comments, and the play, have nothing to do with us."

"Oh, that is so easy for you to say—and do. You always go about your life as if nothing has anything to do with you." Joséphine held up a hand. "Do not tell me I have no understanding of what is required for you to maintain the family's interests. That is precisely the point: I do not understand. You plunge yourself into the House of Vollard, you work day and night, but not because you care about being rich. I knew that from the first. I always assumed you made yourself a slave to the firm because of your concern for the Vollard name and reputation, for the position in the world you were earning for yourself and your son, if not for me. Now I see that that is not the reason either, for you refuse to try to ban this harmful play by this dreadful, vindictive woman— Why do you do that? Why do you stare at my mouth when I am talking? You have done it before—often. I find it very disconcerting." Joséphine put the tip of her tongue out to touch her upper lip, then pulled it back.

"I was thinking of when I first met you," Nicolas said.

"What does that mean?"

"No more than it says. I was thinking of our separate reasons for desiring this marriage. I believe yours have been fulfilled, adequately if not amply." Nicolas rose and tossed his damask napkin down beside his plate.

"Where are you going? To the library to work, I suppose."

"No! Thanks to our peaceful, stable empire, I have enriched the House of Vollard sufficiently this week." The savagery in his voice startled Joséphine because she had not heard it before. In an instant his square face was smooth again, and she doubted the storm she had seen sweeping across it. "Do you not even care how all this is hurting Louis?" she said. "And Marc?"

"More than you can know."

"Then how can you possibly refuse to . . . " She stopped, for Nicolas had already reached the door.

In their home five streets to the west, Louis and Marc were also dining.

Although Marc spent much time away from the house, he stayed in to dinner with his father several times a week. Sometimes they ate in a silence in which every chink of the cutlery echoed as if in a cathedral. Sometimes they talked of art; they had closed off so many other subjects, either by mutual consent or separate decision, that art had become virtually the sole carrier of their communication. They never mentioned Edmée, of whom no trace was left in the house except for a daguerrotype in Marc's bedroom, and they had referred only once to *The Trial of Louise Bernier:* Marc had asked his father if he intended to see the play, and Louis had said, "No" in a tone that forbade further comment. They had always talked of art easily, but now their awareness of prohibitions lent an undertow of intensity to everything they said about it.

"Photography is splendid, of course," Marc said, "but I do not think it will ever do away with living models."

Louis raised his knife as if it were a brush. "You dispute Delacroix? He once said a photograph is the only way to represent the exact truth and so one should work with photographs of predetermined poses."

"I am working on a female nude at Belloc's, and I could not get the foreshortening of the leg without the woman there before me, in the flesh. You need a live model to capture truth with the brush. If truth is your goal."

"But can you ever find a living model that is exactly what you want?" Louis said. "They all have flaws, or if not, they are so different from your original idea that you find yourself changing it."

"What is wrong with that, if the change is a good one?"

Louis shook his head. "The true conception must be in your mind, not in the woman you are looking at."

"Are you not then refusing to see what is before you? That is the greatest sin for a painter, not to see. To allow himself to be blinded by some predetermined—" Marc stopped, then added rather lamely, "Of course I do not dispute that one must have a mental conception." He loaded his fork with lamb and lentils and shoved it into his mouth like a cork.

Louis nodded, but the pleasure had gone out of their conversation as quickly as air from a balloon. They finished the main course in silence. When it had been cleared, Louis looked at the empty white cloth in front of him and said, "Your grandmother complains that you have not been to see her in two weeks."

"Regrettably that is true. I shall try to go within a day or two. But I . . . "

"Does she keep asking when you are going to settle down and accept some responsibilities at the firm?"

"Yes."

Louis sighed and finished his wine. "She asks me whether there is any hope that she will see great-grandchildren before she dies."

"What do you tell her, Papa?"

"I say I hope so. I say that you escort various young ladies to balls and dinners and salons, but there is no sign yet of your desiring to marry one of them. Is that not the only answer to such a question?"

"Of course. Do you wish there were another answer?"

"I distinctly do not wish you to be pressured into marriage. I assume you take your pleasure, like any young man, as you look about for a suitable mate."

With two fingers, Marc spun the crystal water goblet in front of him. "Suppose I were never to marry?"

"What do you mean? Why would you not marry?"

"I . . . It was only an idle question."

Silence fell again, heavily.

"Papa, if you will excuse me, I will go upstairs to my studio."

"To paint by gaslight?"

"Not to paint. To think about painting."

"Of course." Louis seemed unperturbed, but as Marc reached the dining room, the question that had chafed within him for months, that he had always managed to rein in, burst forth. "Have you seen her," he said, "since . . . since . . . "

"Seen whom?"

"Your mother."

Marc hesitated. "Yes."

"Then you know where she is?"

"No, Papa, I do not."

Louis clenched his fists, but another question bolted from his grasp. "If you did know, would you tell me?"

Marc gazed at him steadily. "No. I could not do that. As you must understand."

"Of course," Louis said. Doors slammed shut between the two of them again, sealing the questions, and the subject, behind them.

"Good night then, Papa."

"Good night, my son."

Louis watched him go, thinking that he had broad shoulders, more like Nicolas's, really, than his own. And Marc's del Sarto face held little hint of Louis's own. So where was the father in the son, except in the love that he had poured into him, like rain into the ground, which left no trace of itself except for the beauty it allowed to flourish . . . Marc's eyes, so clear, brown, and questioning, they were hers. In Louis's mind, Edmée's name was never said anymore. She had been reduced to pronouns, which, like prison clothes, wrapped her in grayness and nullified her power—the power to act, enrage, humiliate. *Forget her,* Nico had said, *forget the firm, and everything else except your painting and your son.* The odd thing was, Louis could not forget the firm. He had given up so many things in its name; if he turned his back on the House of Vollard, how would he justify . . . what would he have to show for . . . He did not finish the phrases. He never did.

Not, he thought bitterly, that he did much for the House of Vollard, or did it as often as he should. Nico was the guiding, deciding force; and their cousin Blaise, who had come to Paris three years before to work in the firm, had more responsibilities than Louis. His work involved no major projects, only quiet things; lately he had toured some Vollard holdings and enterprises in the countryside. Outside Paris people were not so aware of the scandal, if at all. It would go away eventually. In fact it had died to embers until the cursed play blew life into it and made him . . . He did not finish that thought, either.

Half an hour later, without quite remembering what chain of mental or literal steps had brought him there, he was upstairs in his own studio, sitting on a stool near the corner, staring at the easel and a painting on which he had not worked in six weeks: a head of a young woman. A live model, one of the maids. But she was not there, and he had no photograph. No way to truth. Still, he had not gone out, had he? Had not hailed a cab and gone off, perhaps to the Bal Mabille, where there were so many mirrors that one's reflection drowned in a sea of others, where no one gave a damn about scandal, and afterward to a private room with one of the dancers . . . He had stayed in the house—in his studio, like Marc. Because of Marc. What a comfort the boy was. What an inspiration. *Not to paint. To think about painting.* Perhaps the head on the easel was not so bad, after all. Gaslight was kind to it. As it was to women in the rooms to which he had not gone. Because of the boy. Bless the boy. *To capture truth with the brush* . . . No, one could not work in gaslight, not properly. Even so, he reached for the table on which he kept his painting materials.

Half an hour later, when he looked down, he saw that the object in his hand was no longer a brush. It was a bottle of brandy from the drawer in the table.

"Oh Jesus," he whispered. "Dear Lord Jesus."

Jeanne was in her bedroom, at her desk, her feet up on a little blue velvet stool. She was not writing, or even trying to, but she had spent so many hours of her life at the desk, dreaming, imagining, writing furiously or laboriously, that part of her seemed ingrained in its honey-colored wood and she gravitated to it even if she wanted only to read or stare into space. *It knows the best and worst of me,* she would think, smiling at the conceit.

The clock read nine-thirty, its ticking audible because the rumbling of wheels out in the street had modulated by that hour. All Paris was at dinner or the theatre or the opera, Jeanne thought—all of Paris that had francs enough to eat and to entertain itself. Somewhere in the city Gabrielle might be singing at a private concert; the journals did not show that she was performing on a public stage at the moment. She had not yet become one of the nightingales of the world. "I doubt she ever will," Nandou had said. "She does not want it badly enough."

It had been nearly four years since she left. Her absence no longer screamed from the corners, and often Jeanne could sleep all through the night instead of waking with a start and falling back on the pillow to twist until dawn between hope and anger, remorse and wounded pride. It would almost be easier if Gabrielle had died, God forgive such a thought. One could come to accept death. But how to accept a situation that could change and must change, yet never did change?

Jeanne wrapped her arms around her knees and put her head down, staring at the tips of her slippers, which rested on the footstool beneath the hem of her skirt. She was alone in the quiet of the apartment, for Nandou was performing in *The Trial of Louise Bernier* and would not return until nearly midnight.

The first time he read the entire script, he asked whether she had written it for Edmée.

"No. Her story inspired me, certainly, but she never asked me to use it. Nor is she discouraging me from doing so. I wrote this because I want people to see the hypocrisy in the way women are treated."

"Ah yes. The bourgeois hypocrisy. Perhaps you have also written this to punish Louis Vollard?"

"Yes? Supposing I have?"

She had only said it to make anger flare in Nandou's eyes, as it once would have done. But he merely shrugged.

How foolish to think that anything so simple as a play might restore the times that were gone. If everything she had done for Edmée had not restored them, then nothing else would—not even the play that was, in a way, the last of her acts of atonement.

What irony in it all—her rage at Louis, which had so filled her that she could barely force her food down to join it, had led her to befriend Louis's wife. Her feeling for Nandou, which she never could coax from her heart into her flesh, had started to creep there without her will as soon as it had no chance of being satisfied. She should take out her diary and write about the irony that filled their lives, but she had not made an entry since a week after the opening of *The Trial of Louise Bernier,* when she had simply written, *"Succès de scandale."* Next week she would write something; next week she would be forty years old. Surely she would find something to say about such an event.

She lifted her head and rubbed her hands along her arms. It had grown cool in the room; April nights could be chilly. She decided to undress and get into bed, burying her thoughts beneath the duvet. She stood, stretched, and took the pins from her hair, which was shaped over her ears and coiled on her neck. How sartorially tame she had become, styling her hair fashionably, wearing multitudes of petticoats beneath skirts with layers of flounces—leaving rebellion to poor Mrs. Bloomer, who was bringing the wrath of English society upon herself for daring to suggest that women wear baggy trousers beneath a knee-length skirt. It had been several years since Jeanne had gone out in men's trousers or smoked a cigar in public, although she still liked one now and again at home. Nor did she hold court in Nandou's dressing room during one of her plays, baiting the foolish bourgeois who hoped to take her to dinner and then to bed . . . None of those weapons, she had found, were as satisfying as words could be.

The knocker at the apartment door rapped loudly. It would not be Edmée, who had been down to share supper and then gone up to bed early. Could it possibly be Gabrielle? Hope seized her like a fever; it must be Gabrielle. She jammed the hairpins in her pocket and ran to the door.

"Hello," said Nicolas Vollard. "I hope I do not disturb you."

She stared, clutching the hairpins as if they could assure her she was not imagining his presence.

"No," he said, "let me correct myself. I do not care if I disturb you. I want to disturb you. I must speak with you."

She motioned him to enter. He was unlike the man she remembered him to be; in place of the calmness and steadiness she had noted and liked since their first meeting was a tension that kept him moving, circling the chairs and sofa, swerving to avoid the ottoman. "Let me turn up the light," she said. When she had adjusted the gas and could see his face more clearly, his gray eyes were keen with an excitement she could not decipher. "May I take your coat?"

He shook his head. "I shall not stay long." But he took off his hat, laid it on the table, ran both hands through his sandy hair, and searched her face as if looking for some kind of sign.

"What is it?" Jeanne asked. "Have you come to chastise me for the play I wrote?"

"Why should I do that, when I sent you white roses for its opening?"

"Has something happened to Louis that you think I should know, for some reason I cannot imagine?"

"No. For once let us not speak of Louis. His concerns are the last thing I came to discuss. He has nothing to do with us."

"Us?" Jeanne said.

"Yes." Nicolas stopped behind the sofa. "Do you deny that there is an attraction between us and has been from the first?"

She could not help sucking in her breath, but then she laughed because he had been so direct. "I do not deny it," she said.

"Good." He put both hands on the back of the sofa and then pushed himself away. "I have denied it to myself, however, many times. I no longer intend to do so."

"What do you mean?"

"I did not think my life had room for such a thing as love. I did not know what it was—perhaps I still do not know. But if to think of someone more and more each day, to wish to be with that person, to make love to that person—if that is love, then I want to make room in my life for it . . . for you."

Slowly Jeanne said, "Are you asking me to be your mistress?"

"I . . . if it would please you. Yes."

"I think I must sit down," she said.

"Forgive me if I do not join you. I feel like something wound on a spring. You know almost nothing of me, of course, except that I am a Vollard and therefore a member of the family, and the kind of world, that you seem to despise."

"I know that you have built the House of Vollard into an important bank."

"And care for nothing except making money?"

"I do not say so."

"I do care for making money, not so much for what it can buy as for the pleasure of deciding how to make it, of balancing a dozen considerations against one another. How to gauge the effect of a flow of goods on the supply of money, how to weather political storms, how to finance railways without endangering our capital—I am . . . content . . . when I have such matters to deal with. But they are not enough. Being content is not enough. I want to be . . . " He stopped, his large hands opening and closing as if groping for words.

"Happy?" Jeanne said.

"Yes," he answered, and shut his eyes.

She sat watching him. A frozen inner motion seemed to grip his whole body. "How long have you been planning to come and ask me this?"

"Perhaps since the first day we met. Perhaps not until this evening, when I suddenly felt I could no longer . . . " Nicolas shook his head and resumed his restless moving. "I have never been a man of impulse, but I have envied those who can feel something so strong it overrides all else. Perhaps I have been waiting all my life to feel the impulse that has brought me here."

Jeanne watched the line of his cheek and jaw as he moved in and out of the field of the lamp. "A liaison with me," she said, "if discovered, would invite a worse scandal on your family than any your brother has caused."

"I do not care about scandal. Scandals have no longer a life, and no more meaning, than fashions in dress."

She smiled. "I suspect they mean a good deal to your mother."

"I do not act deliberately to hurt my mother, nor do I arrange my life to suit her wishes. But let me be clear in what I am proposing to you. I do not ask you to conduct an affair with me in secret. I have no wish to hide it."

Jeanne shook her head slowly. "To take as a mistress someone your mother . . . and Louis . . . must regard as an enemy . . . "

"I would have you as my wife, if divorce were not outlawed."

"I cannot understand your considering such a thing."

Nicolas smiled briefly. "Marriage is the only adventure left to the cowardly. Is that not what Voltaire tells us?"

"Are you cowardly, then?"

He came to stand directly in front of her. "I hope not. I would leave my wife if it would make you believe how serious I am."

"You have just succeeded."

He was looking down at her with a gaze as passionate as any she had ever seen directed at her, or wanted to see. "Even if I could," she said, "I would not ask marriage of you, or of any man. I do not desire marriage."

"But you do desire me?" He put out his hand and touched her cheek. *"Why do you not take a lover?"* she murmured.

"What are you saying?"

"Nothing."

He pulled her to her feet. The longings she had stifled for so many years rose up too, and became a roaring in her ears. He bent to kiss her, and she put her arms around him with a cry. She wanted him to do whatever he liked, to lay his tall body against hers and let her feel its power and urgency.

"Not here," he said, moments later.

"Yes," she said. "Here. Now. Please."

They sank to the floor, pulling and tugging at clothes, finding each other's flesh and digging their fingers into it like starving people at a feast. They rolled on the floor, scraped against the legs of chairs, and finally fused themselves into one body with a single purpose, which was, at last and at glorious length, fulfilled.

It was a long time before Jeanne felt her heart and her breathing slowing to normal, so long that Nicolas had stood and adjusted his clothing. He reached to help her up, but she shook her head, picked up her petticoats, and got to her feet by herself.

"I did not intend for things to happen this way," he said, not sounding in the least remorseful.

"Nor did I. I am sorry. But sometimes one is powerless not to obey an impulse—as you yourself were in coming here tonight."

He laughed. "Do not apologize. I will find a place where we can be together. Tomorrow. I will find it tomorrow."

She shook her head. "Do not do that."

"Why not? Ah, I understand. I presume too much. You have not yet decided how our relationship is to progress." His face was open, relaxed. Happy.

"Nicolas, we cannot be lovers, or anything else. We cannot be together again. I am sorry."

His face changed; how should it not? "I do not understand," he said.

"I do not think I can explain in any way that will satisfy you. I only know that, except for this night, I must be faithful to my dwarf."

The performance had gone well: a full house, murmurs of appreciation or disapproval at all the key places, and in the final act, when Louise Bernier dies in prison, the absolute quiet in the audience that comes only from its total involvement.

Afterward Nandou declined to join some of the other actors and set out to walk home, moving on the edges of the crowds still thronging the boulevards, gliding in and out of the cafés. Two dandies lurched into him, looked down in surprise, then doffed their hats in a courtesy so elaborate it was bereft of sincerity. "Good evening, gentlemen," he said equably. They were young fools who thought pleasure and wisdom lay in a bottle, but he was a dwarf who knew otherwise.

The night was bright and so clear it seemed one could see all the way to the Butte of Montmartre. Eddies of spring wind carried the scent of lilacs, and a three-quarter moon hung high, bathing Paris, turning roofs into silhouettes and trees into clumps of rustling silver. Smaller moons, the white globes of gas lighting, hung on branching candelabra along the major streets—part of the emperor's plan to rebuild the city. Louis Napoléon was revealing himself to be a master showman: dazzle the spectators so they will not notice the real nature of what is happening. He had married the Empress Eugénie in ceremonies of astounding glitter—the state coach regilded, white satin roses attached to the bushes in the Tuileries gardens, the interior of Notre-Dame hung with velvet and ermine, five hundred musicians playing the coronation march from *Le Prophète*. He created offices with such imperial titles as Lord High Steward of the Palace; he dressed his servants in green and gold liveries and silver chains; he gave balls and banquets and receptions for eight hundred guests; he had begun a massive rebuilding that was to give the city new and broader boulevards and beautiful parks. And lighting and paving and new water systems—all things that Paris needed, to be sure. But they were also part of the master-showman's act: everything glittering and shining, so no one would remember the absolutism of his power or recall that the liberties of French citizens had been swept under the expensive royal rugs.

Nandou turned into his street. It seemed as if the July Days had never occurred, nor the revolt of '48. *Plus ça change, moins ça change.* Was there something in the nature of Frenchmen that made them embrace revolution and monarchy in turn, with seemingly equal fervor? He had asked the question with increasing frequency as he grew older; now, at fifty-one, it seemed the answer must be yes. Perhaps that was what it meant to be French: to live at the heart of contradiction. Did he not live there?—a man who said he had desired one thing above all and when he was offered it, did not take it?

He went into his building and started up the two flights of stairs. In truth, even though he yearned for things to be as they once were, there was the compensation of a strange peace—of not loathing his dwarfishness, as he always had in Jeanne's bed, where the touch of her body seared him with the abnormality of his own. Never did Beast so feel his beastliness as when he embraced Beauty.

He let himself into the apartment and was surprised to see her sitting in the living room, with the lamp on, as if she were waiting for him. Ah, God, but he loved her, he thought—loved her more, almost, than when desire had consumed him, as if its absence were a purer, colder fire. He stood, simply looking at her. The angle of her posture, half in the pool of light, half in shadow, and the cascade of her hair, and the slope of her cheek all came at him like a wind-full of lilacs. He remembered exactly how it had used to be: how he would burn to touch her, possess her, even knowing he would suffer for it. For love of the fire, one could endure a sheet of flame.

"Jeanne," he said, surprised at the softness in his voice. She turned to him. "You are very beautiful tonight. Every night." He moved toward her.

She was silent, her red mouth quite still. No, a tremor moved it. "What is it?" he said. "Tell me." She raised one hand, and though it fell back onto the arm of her chair and did not touch him, he could feel her fingers, thin and warm, as clearly as if the arm of the chair were his own.

"Has something happened?" he asked. "Is it Gabrielle?"

She shook her head, so slightly that her hair barely swayed.

"Yes, something has happened. You are upset."

"Do I seem upset?"

"No," he admitted, his mood evaporating. "But you are. I can feel it." His gaze swung around the room. "Someone has been here tonight."

"Yes."

"Who was it? What happened?"

"Nicolas Vollard was here."

Nandou felt the hairs on his arms rise in a tiny chorus of warning. "What did he want?"

"Me," she said.

"What do you mean?"

"He wanted me to become his mistress."

From a distance, as if he had thrown it to the corner of the room, Nandou heard his voice: "What did you tell him?"

"I told him no."

He swallowed. "Why?"

"I do not know. I found I . . . could not."

"Did you want to go with him? To sleep with him?" If she said yes, he would know that his desire was gone forever.

"Yes," she said.

He sank into a chair and put his head in his hands. "You should have gone. I cannot give you what he offers—not the embraces, not the money, not the complete revenge upon his brother that you would have by accepting him."

"I want nothing more to do with revenge. Do you not believe that?"

"Yes, I do. I am sorry."

He felt her hands pulling his fingers from his face. "Did I not tell you I would never leave you?"

He groaned.

"Was I wrong? Am I a fool, Nandou?"

Chapter Nineteen

*A*t *twenty-four a young man should be thinking of starting a home.*

I do not understand, Marc. You have been introduced to some of the most beautiful and marriageable young women in Paris.

What shall I make of a grandson who interests himself very little in the firm and less in marriage? One of them at least, Marc. One of them at least.

The voices kept coming between him and the painting. It was of a head of a woman, wearing a hat that cast its shadow across her brow; her eyes looked a direct challenge, her hands were clasped beneath her chin, and the light, the hat, the shadow, the eyes, and the fingers all formed an irregular oval that was beginning to hold the feeling Marc wanted: strength and frailty combined. There was a chance the painting might turn out as he hoped, if only he could surrender fully to it—could "have the fever," in the phrase they all used to describe a burst of inspiration. But as he stepped back and forth from the canvas, judging the effect of a brushstroke, then dipping the brush again into the patches of color on his palette, the voices kept buzzing through his concentration—his grandmother, his aunt, his cousins, even his father once, although only once—like a cloud of gnats. Sometimes he felt they would swarm onto the canvas and settle on the colors. Nothing should stand between him and his vision. His life was a struggle to clear that path, to make his eyes see more deeply and his hand more truthfully execute what they saw.

He was working alone. Belloc, who had become a friend, was in Barbizon for a month painting landscapes. He had tossed Marc the key and a challenge: "See what you can do with a live model while I am away, and if the result is not too disgusting, I shall let you buy me dinner when I return."

Occasionally Marc still worked in his small studio at home, copying prints of works by the masters, trying to learn from their genius, but there he never felt as free or inspired as he did elsewhere. Yet he did not clean out the room and move away. The odd thing was that since his mother had made her confession, he felt more like staying on than he had while he believed Louis to be his father. Knowing there was no blood tie seemed to strengthen the tie that did exist, for whatever else Louis was and had done, he was still the man who had first put a brush into Marc's hand and showed him how to use it; still the man who could stand before a painting for half an hour without speaking, and when he did speak, say the right thing.

"What keeps you in that world?" Belloc would ask. "Why maintain the fiction that Marc Vollard will become a banker one of these days? Or years?"

He could not explain it, even to Belloc. Even to himself, not fully.

He knew only that the life of his family, of normalcy and respectability, kept him safe. If he moved out of his father's house and surrendered completely to the world of art, he would be lost. The sweet, tantalizing evil that lived in his flesh, the Darkness, would demand freedom, and he would be helpless to deny it. That, he could not allow. He would live his life as a monk. The Monk of Art. Monks loved nothing but God. And the greatest of gods was art.

He filled his brush with color and dabbed it on one of the fingers of the woman on his canvas.

His aunt: *I know a dozen young women just waiting to return a smile from Marc Vollard, if he would ever give them one.*

His grandmother, throwing up her hands: *You must start to pull your weight at the firm. We must find a wife who will speak sense to you.*

He stepped back from the canvas. The finger looked to him as mechanical as a metal pipe. "Damn," he muttered. "Damn!"

"What is wrong?" said the model on the chair. She was an Italian he had found in the model market, held every morning near one of the fountains. He had liked her direct manner and the wonderful colors in her skin.

He put down his palette and brush. "That is enough for today."

"It is only three hours," she said.

"No matter. I shall pay for four, as agreed." Marc pulled five francs from his trouser pocket and handed them to her.

She tucked them into her blouse and peered at the canvas. "My nose is not so straight like that."

"It has to be, for my purposes."

She shrugged, pulled an apple from her pocket, and began polishing it on her skirt. "You want me to make supper for you tonight?" When he shook his head, she shrugged and asked, "So, I come tomorrow morning?"

"Yes. I don't know. I shall send word."

"*Ciao* then, Marco." She squeezed his arm, bit into her apple, and sauntered out. He listened to her footsteps fade down the stairs, *clop, clop, clop,* like a spirited filly's. Belloc, and most other painters he knew, would have been happy to accept her offer of supper, and that which was likely to follow. He reached for the taboret containing his supplies and began cleaning his brushes. When he was painting women, he loved their bodies, which had a wonderful pliancy and satiny grace he yearned to capture on canvas, although he had not yet done so to his satisfaction and often despaired he ever would. He was stirred to passion by women: the passion of needing to see all the subtle tones of their skin, which were so elusive, and find the shapes of their quick little gestures. But when he tried to look at them in the other way—and God alone knew how he had tried, telling himself he wanted to kiss their mouths and touch their breasts—he could not make himself feel anything. When his father had taken him to the brothel to initiate him into the pleasures men took for granted, he had been unable to respond, let alone to perform, until in desperation he let himself imagine that Arlette was not a woman. After it was over, the shame of what he had done—not with his flesh but with his mind—had roiled and curdled within him until he vomited in the street, like a common drunkard. Why had God filled him with such Darkness? Why could he wish only for passion that was forbidden, and dream only of the kind of lean body that would . . . He caught himself up short, palms clammy with danger. If he permitted such evil thoughts . . . He must guard against them, constantly. If he acted on them . . . The world had sent his mother to prison for a crime much less evil.

He still could not believe he had told the truth to his mother. The words had come from him like blood from a knife wound. She, her brown eyes huge and stricken, had struggled to bind it but could not heal him. No one could. Still, the relief of saying it, aloud, just one time . . .

He could not even tell Belloc, whose appetites were so flagrantly normal that their energy filled the studio even in his absence. Marc had brought Gabrielle around to meet him, and when Belloc assumed they were sleeping with each other—"She is gorgeous, my sly friend, one could paint her all day and revel in her all night"—how much easier it had been not to challenge that assumption. Marc shook his head and swung back to look at the easel. At once he saw something wrong with the nose. But what? He stepped closer, back, closer again.

His aunt Joséphine: *There is a young woman you must meet, Marc. She and her parents will be at our affair on Friday evening.*

His father: *What harm can it do to attend Joséphine's functions once in a while? One of her young ladies might even take your fancy.*

His mother: *You know I will always love you. But you must try not to let this . . . this illness destroy your life . . .*

"Please," he whispered. "Let me work." He took up his brush again, even though he had just cleaned it.

On a splendid May day, with the sky cloudless and limitless, Gabrielle waited at the northern end of the Luxembourg Gardens, twirling a parasol on one shoulder. She wore a rose frock she particularly favored, over one of the new crinolines, which replaced yards of soft petticoats with a single huge one, built over a hoop: a fortress of fabric that kept everyone at more than arm's length while making the waist tiny and giving a lovely sway to the walk. She looked as sleek, contented, and carefree as the Second Empire itself, but in fact she was "at liberty" in terms of singing engagements and had been for longer than she liked. After performing in one of Offenbach's productions at his wildly successful theatre, the Bouffes-Parisiennes, she had hoped to be doing another but had not been cast. Weeks loomed before she was to go into rehearsal at the Italien; she would have to find some work to fill the gap. She became aware of her foot tapping restlessly beneath her skirt, and stopped it.

She had turned twenty-seven in January, on a day spent steaming her throat and sipping honey because she had a cold and the silver bird had to be coaxed back to health. Ten years earlier her mother had announced to the guests at her birthday dinner: *That voice will make you one of the nightingales of the world.* But it had not. Nothing had turned out as she expected. She was singing, yes, but not every week and not all over the world. She enjoyed singing, but to it was attached the albatross of hunting constantly for engagements, of trying—

"What takes you so deep into thought?"

She saw that Marc had arrived. "Nothing important," she said and smiled.

"I am sorry to be late. I was early, in fact, so I sat on one of the benches to do a little sketching—there was a wonderful Spanish face—and the next thing I knew, I was late."

Gabrielle laughed. "Do you ever think about anything but painting?"

"Certainly."

"You think about where to find models and buy paint."

"More than that," Marc said gravely, refusing to join in her little joke. His face seemed flushed, and minnows of light darted in his brown eyes.

"Is anything wrong?" she asked.

"No. But I have something to ask you. Let us walk a while first." They set off on one of the paths through the formal garden. On both sides was the discipline of trees, shrubs, and flowers. Between them swept Gabrielle's skirt, in its own trained shape. High above, the swallows drifted free.

"Have you heard from the Bouffes?" Marc asked.

"Not yet. No doubt I shall do so before long."

"No doubt." There was a small, rare moment of awkwardness between them, which Marc pushed aside with a question. "Do you ever think of what you will do when you retire from singing?"

"Retire!" she cried. "Why do you ask that?"

"Don't singers have to retire at some time in their lives?"

"Yes."

"Well, then?"

"I shall go to Italy and live in a splendid house on one of the lakes." Gabrielle shifted to allow another couple to pass them on the walk, the woman in a skirt as wide as her own.

"By yourself?" Marc asked.

"What do you mean?"

"Will you live alone on your lake shore?"

"Why do you want me to picture myself as a lonely old woman?"

"I don't, Gaby, but I worry about you. You have no family. You show no indication of plans to marry. You never tell me you are in love—only how foolish or disappointing some man has been."

Gabrielle shifted her parasol to screen the sun's probing. It was true; she had not fallen in love—only sung about doing so. Several times she had thought herself genuinely attracted and had actually begun two affairs. The men were generous and attentive, but the feeling that she was only an interlude in their lives—a dalliance with a singer, not a proper alliance—had grown more and more intrusive and uncomfortable, like a blister on the heel, and she had ended by kicking off the shoe. *You are not meant to be exploited for their pleasure. If anyone is to be exploited, let it be them.* She shut out her mother's voice and said, "I shall be fine. There is no need to worry about me."

"Do you think you will marry?" Marc asked.

"Like so many of my female colleagues, who scheme to find a man rich enough to support them when they stop singing? I doubt it."

"Is that what your friend Amélie Véron did?"

Amélie had left singing to marry the owner of a number of lace and textile factories. Gabrielle went sometimes to Amélie's for lunch or tea; it was pleasant to be away from the frenzy of practicing and dressing rooms and callboys, sitting in a grand, spacious house where society left its cards and "Madame" was treated with greater deference that most conductors—or tenors—had shown her. "Amélie does not say, but I should be surprised if there is true love in her marriage. However, as you know, I do not think I understand the word."

"There are many kinds of love," Marc said.

"You know what I mean."

"You mean something that consumes one, like a fire. Like art."

"I suppose so."

They walked in silence for a while, heading toward the large water basin in the center of the gardens, rimmed with urns.

"Gabrielle, do you think we love each other, you and I?"

She angled her head and spun the parasol. "I like to be with you, more than with any man I know. As different as we are, I feel you understand me. I never worry that you want something from me, or would merely use me, like other men. I feel comfortable with you, and safe—is that strange?"

"Not at all."

"I think perhaps I do love you." She smiled and added, in a rare mention of the actual nature of their relationship, "Dear brother."

Marc slowed almost to a halt. "I have been thinking of marriage."

"Have you?" She turned to him, surprised at the force of her astonishment.

"May we sit over there and talk?"

After she had arranged her skirt to make room for him on the bench, he leaned toward her, his eyes now shoals of light, and said, "I have an idea you may think is madness. But I am quite serious. I suggest that we marry."

"Marry whom?"

"Each other," he said.

"Can you be serious?"

"I have just told you that I am."

"But ..." Gabrielle's hands lifted and fell back into her lap helplessly.

"If we married, you would not have to worry about the future, or the present. You could have all the security of being Madame Vollard. You could sing as much or as little as you like—do whatever you like, in fact."

She tried to pull her thoughts around her, but they slipped from her grasp like scraps of silk. "But how would . . . why would we . . . I cannot . . . " She took as deep a breath as if she were preparing to sing a high D. "Have you forgotten that I am your half-sister?"

His pale skin grew even more flushed. "It does not matter whether we are related or not."

"How can you say that?"

"You are right. I am explaining badly because I am nervous." A smile shivered on his lips. "I do not mean that we should ever be more to each other than we are now. Friends, only friends—who share the same house and name. I would never ask you to be a party to . . . to . . . anything but friendship."

"Then you speak of a marriage in name only."

"Yes. One in which you could do as you like. *Whatever you like*, Gaby." He gave her a look that left no doubt of his meaning.

"But . . . why, Marc? Why do you want such a thing?"

"A man must have a wife, is that not so?"

"But surely he wants a wife with whom he can have . . . a wife who will . . . "

"I have not found a woman to my taste. Yet my family is beginning to insist that I marry."

"Even if I were willing, your father . . . our father . . . would never allow it. How could he?"

Marc's hands opened and closed like silent mouths. "I believe I shall be able to make him allow it."

Gabrielle looked away, at a little boy and girl running around the water basin in a laughing circle. In the distance were the twin towers of the church of Saint-Sulpice. Were they signs, she wondered, messages to her that twoness was desirable? She was looking for signs from outside herself, she knew, because within her was nothing but confusion. She looked down at Marc's hands, which were now gripping the edges of the bench. The hairs on their backs were so light they were nearly invisible. She raised her eyes to his, which were burning. "Why?" she repeated. "I must know why you want it."

"Since I met you, I have thought that if I were ever to desire marriage, I would wish the woman to be you."

"You speak so strangely. *Do* you desire marriage?"

"I think it would be best for me."

"But you do not desire it?"

"No." A pulse beat in his throat, above his collar, and his eyelids beat, too, but in a different rhythm. He looked wretched, and afraid. "I do not desire women . . . "

She waited for the sentence to continue. It did not. She realized that it was complete, and, with a long, slow intake of breath, she understood.

She thought that she should be shocked, and was not, for it explained several things: his failure to confide any love affairs to her, as she had with him; his detachment in speaking of a woman's beauty, which she had attributed to an artist's detachment. "I understand what you are saying," she told him.

"Do you?"

"Yes."

"Are you . . . revolted?"

"No," she said. "I have met such men in the opera and the theatre."

"I do not want to be this way," he whispered. "It is wrong. Wrong. But I cannot help it. I can only vow never to . . . do anything about it."

"Poor Marc. What a terrible time you must have been having."

"If we were married, people would leave us alone. In peace. We would be safe, both of us. I would work, and you—"

"Would you work at the House of Vollard?"

"As I do now—some of the time. Enough so they do not disown me."

"And painting?"

"The rest of the time. I would see that you had anything you wanted, Gaby. Anything. It could be fun. We get along so splendidly . . . Will you do it?"

"I must think about it, Marc."

"Of course. Of course." Hope flickered in his face but lacked the courage to lodge there. He turned away.

She felt as if her mind and feelings were being rocked from one side to another, like a carriage with its wheels caught in mud. To have the position and security of a family's name and wealth, to be mistress of a grand house rather than the slave of a tiny silver bird, to stop bowing to the demands of composers and conductors and struggling for ways to keep one's name before the public; instead, to give orders to a houseful of servants . . . No, it was madness. To marry her half-brother—even though they lived without sharing a bed—could there be a more unnatural domestic arrangement? . . . Yet why not? Would it be any more unnatural than her mother and Nandou's? She shook off that thought; the carriage rocked to the other side. To live in the same house with her father—as his daughter-in-law! Forbidden. Scandalous. Unthinkable. Yet . . . she would be able to know her father at last. She would have the name that belonged to her—Vollard. Madame Vollard . . . something her mother had not been able to achieve . . . Had she ever met a man she liked better than Marc? Who was more concerned about her? Kinder? If people found out, though, how shocked and disgusted they would be. Or would claim to be. But they would never know who her father was . . . Or her mother, for if the Vollards ever learned she was the daughter of the author of *The Trial of Louis Bernier* . . . She closed her eyes. She wanted to be respectable, she thought, wanted the comforts, the orderliness, the security, the peace . . . She waited for the inner challenge that should meet such heresy. There was none. Only relief, as if she had been struggling uphill against a wind and magically the wind had died down. Marc needed respectability too, she thought, though in a different way. Perhaps, without ever saying it, they had understood that need in each other. Perhaps it had helped to bring them close. She looked at Marc's profile: the aristocratic nose, the mouth that could leap into an irresistible smile . . . She was very fond of him. In fact she did love him, as a brother. In ancient Egypt, a king and queen had often been brother and sister . . .

"Look there," he said.

"What?"

"Look at that dwarf."

"Where?" Gabrielle cried.

He inclined his head toward a female dwarf coming along the path, gait truncated in the familiar way, arms bowed, hands reaching no lower than her waist. Gabrielle bit her lip.

Marc took a notebook and crayon from his pocket. "What must they think and feel," he said, "those creatures whom God made in so different an image?"

"They must find it difficult to love him," Gabrielle said slowly.

"Then I can understand them." His voice was bitter.

But in a moment, lower lip caught between his teeth, fingers racing over the page as his gaze darted between the sketch and its object, he seemed to have forgotten their conversation. Art would always be the most important thing to him, she thought. Always.

"May I see it?" she asked when he finished. He shrugged and held out the notebook. In a few dozen lines he had captured the whole sense of dwarfishness, the disproportion of head, the density of upper torso, the strange swing of arms, and, in this particular woman, a frowning concentration as she marched along. She would be wishing she could go faster, Gabrielle thought, and, if there were a crowd, taking care not to be jostled. "I would like to have this sketch," she said. "May I?"

"Why on earth would you want it?"

"I am not sure," she said truthfully. "I only know I would like it."

"But I need to—oh, very well." Marc tore it carefully from the notebook. "I said you could have anything you wanted, didn't I?"

"Thank you." Just as carefully, she put it inside her purse. She stood and said, "I shall consider it a betrothal present."

"Gaby!" He shot to his feet. "Do you mean it?"

She nodded. He tried to kiss her on the cheek, but her skirt was a bulwark between them, so instead he took both her hands.

"No!" Louis cried. "It is out of the question. I will not allow it."

"But Papa," Marc said, "you must."

"Why must I?" Louis was pacing back and forth in their library, between two plant stands.

On the sofa, watching him, Marc said, "You want me to marry, do you not?"

"Some day, yes, but not her. Anyone but her."

"She is the only one I ever could marry."

Louis stopped, pounded his fists against his thighs, resumed his striding. "It would be a dreadful misalliance."

"Because Gabrielle has no family? That should not matter nowadays. Didn't the marquis de Villette marry a horse-dealer's daughter? The old ways are coming down, just like half the buildings in Paris."

"It will matter a great deal to the Vollard side of the family, and to the Tissots as well, I should think."

"I do not see how Grandmother Vollard or Aunt Joséphine or any of the cousins can object. They have made their desire for me to marry quite clear. But if they are difficult, you could help convince them."

Louis made two swings of the room in silence. "I did not even know you were seeing Gabrielle Corday. How long has it been going on?"

"We have been friends since she sang at the Mirmonts, over five years ago."

"God! That long!"

"I have had ample chance to be certain, you see." Marc watched his father pace; in every step was a slight dip, a small, jerky reminder of a wound from the July Days of 1830. Impossible, sometimes, to believe that the man before him had fought on the barricades. Or had loved a woman and with her had a child who became Gabrielle. He was still handsome, hair as dark and curly as ever, but his skin seemed rougher and his features subtly thicker, as if he were not drawn in ink on fine white paper but rendered in chalk. He was still tall but, in recent years, somehow less solid. An ancient memory surfaced: hugging his father's legs and looking up, feeling he was hugging a great tree of a man.

Louis stopped and swung around to face him. "I shall have to tell you the truth. There is no choice. You cannot possibly marry this woman. This girl. If I had known that you were . . . She is your half-sister."

They regarded each other, Louis's breathing the only sound.

"You say nothing? You do not look shocked, even surprised?"

"Papa, I have not been honest with you. I was going to be, but— Forgive me. I know who Gabrielle is. I have known for some time."

"How do you know?"

"Gabrielle told me herself."

Louis lifted both hands and rubbed his palms into his eyes, as if they were burning. "She told you everything?"

"I do not know what everything is, Papa."

"Please tell me what you do know."

"Only that you and her mother had an affair before you married Maman."

"Did she tell you who her mother is?"

"Only that she is dead."

Louis's hands fell to his sides. "Dead?"

"I see you did not know it. I am sorry if the news upsets you."

"That is not what is upsetting me."

"Gabrielle dislikes speaking of her early life. I know only that she is alone in the world." Marc waited, but Louis said nothing. "One has only to look at her to know that her mother must have been very beautiful, but I should like to know something more of her, Papa, if you would be willing to tell me."

"It all happened over twenty-five years ago. I have no wish to relive it."

"I understand."

"Gabrielle has told you nothing more?"

"No. Is there something more?"

"No, no." Louis began to walk again. He hesitated when he passed the bell pull—*Do not ring for a drink, Papa, please*—but moved on, to the fireplace, where he stopped and turned again to face Marc. "If you know she is your half-sister, how can you think of marrying her?"

Marc's hands rested on his knees; he dug them in. Now came the part he dreaded: telling Papa that he was his son in spirit, but not in the flesh. *I can see no possible good in telling him,* his mother had said, *only pain and danger.* But Papa was stronger now than when she had said it, less agitated, more at peace with himself, surely. "Papa," Marc began, "no one will assume there is a blood relationship between Gabrielle and me. People will think we are only . . . and they will be right to think it, because . . . "

Louis held up a hand and came to sit beside him on the sofa. He laid the hand on one of Marc's and said, "If you have fallen in love with Gabrielle Corday, I am deeply sorry, for I know the pain one feels in giving up the woman one loves. But it must be done. What you propose is wrong, Marc. Unthinkable. You know that. You are too intelligent, too good, not to know it."

"Papa, I must tell you—"

"It could ruin your life. I could not bear to see your life ruined, as mine—I could not bear it. You are the most important person in the world to me, more important than myself, for I am only a would-be painter who drinks too much. There, I have said it. I know you know it, but at last it has been said between us. Let me say something else as well, for I never speak to you of what is in my heart. Do I? I speak of it to no one, rarely even to myself. When I look at you, when I sit across the dinner table from you, even while we are talking about where to buy the truest colors or how anyone could conceive anything as magnificent as the Sistine ceiling, all the time we are speaking, part of me is looking at you and thinking how I love you, how the only good thing I have done in my life is to be the father of Marc Vollard. Flesh of my flesh."

Don't tell me this, not now, please not now, Marc pleaded silently.

But the soft pressure of Louis's hand, and his voice, went on. "In you I am reincarnated—born in a new and better guise. One day you will be the painter, and the man, I am not. So, my dear son, I cannot allow you to ruin your future with this marriage. That would be to fail in my duty as a loving father. And to fail myself as well, for you are the best of me, the only thing I have produced on this earth that has not—You understand, do you not?"

Wretchedly, Marc said, "Yes."

"I knew it." Louis squeezed his hand. "At first it will be difficult, but you will find other women to love. If you have not learned it yet, let me assure you that women are everywhere, warm and beautiful, waiting to be loved."

"If I do not marry Gabrielle, I can never marry anyone."

"You are speaking out of pain, not sense. I understand. But one day you will meet someone else who pleases you."

"As Maman pleased you?"

Louis flushed but said, "Yes. The two of you will marry, and if you are as lucky in your children as God has granted me to be, you will have as splendid a son as I do. Then none of the rest of it will matter."

"Papa," Marc said, "you must believe me. Either I marry Gabrielle, or I never marry anyone."

"That is a foolish thing to say at your age."

"She is my protection," Marc said desperately.

"Against what?"

"Against myself. I am . . . I do not . . . Have you never noticed that I . . . Papa, do you remember, the night before you took me to that woman named Arlette, I asked you if a person can ever change the way he is? I have never forgotten what you said—you sat on my bed and told me it is difficult but one must not give up, one must keep believing it is possible. But you are wrong, Papa. I have tried ever since that night, and before that night, I have forced myself a hundred times to try, but I . . . cannot . . . "

"What are you trying to say, Marc?"

It was the gentleness in his father's voice, and the love, that allowed the rest of the words to come.

When they were out, Marc sat in miserable silence and watched Louis's face become a battleground, disbelief struggling with acceptance, revulsion with concern. Then, to his horror, he saw tears on his father's cheeks.

"No!" Jeanne cried. "She cannot do it. We must stop her."

"But how?" Edmée asked.

"She is as headstrong as her mother," Nandou said.

They sat around the dining table in the apartment. Jeanne was in a dressing gown, hair loose and ink stains on her fingers, for she had been working at her desk when Edmée pounded frantically at the door and said she had just seen Marc and there was news, shocking news. Nandou had been asleep; his gaze was heavy, half-held by the world of dreams, and one cheek bore the mark of the creases in the bed linen.

"How can Louis allow it?" Jeanne said. "If he believes they are both his children, how can he permit it?"

Edmée put her fingers to her eyes. They encountered the spectacles she always wore for a journey out into the world. She pulled them off and folded them neatly in front of her. "Marc has told his . . . deepest feelings to both Louis and Gabrielle. It is understood by all that there will be no . . . physical side to the marriage."

"But Gabrielle knows only half the truth? She still believes Marc to be her half-brother?"

Edmée nodded. "Marc said he could never tell my secret to anyone unless he told Louis as well, which he is not willing to do. In that resolve, as you know, I have encouraged him."

Nandou groaned. "I must have some coffee."

"Let me get it," Edmée said. Neither Jeanne nor Nandou objected; they had long learned that she actually liked messing about in kitchens, as if it were some advantage of which her upbringing had deprived her.

When she was out of the room, they turned to each other. Their gazes met and fused, as they seldom had since Nicolas Vollard's visit, which had placed a careful wall between them, as invisible as the separation between actor and audience, and as inviolate. They watched warily from opposite sides of that wall, pretended everything was as usual, knew full well it was not, but were unable to change it. Many nights they lay in their separate rooms, staring at the same moon-cast patterns on the ceiling, each yearning to join their spirits as they used to do, unaware that behind their walls—both the wooden and the invisible one—they were in fact still joined.

"My poor Jeanne," Nandou said.

"She allows us to learn the news from someone else. She does not even come to tell us herself. How can she do that, Nandou?"

"She knows how we would receive it."

"Like poison," Jeanne said, as if she were tasting the word.

"It will ruin her life," Nandou said.

"I accept that she no longer cares how her mother would feel, but . . . "

"But how can she be indifferent to her own happiness?"

"Yes!" Jeanne cried. "What kind of physical love can there be in such a marriage? How can she live with a man who never wishes to—" The import of her words struck her instantly, and came to Nandou a second later. Their gazes separated like divers heading for opposite shores.

Edmée came in with cups and a coffee pot. "Look how I am shaking," she said as the cups rattled in her hand.

Nandou took one, filled it, and drank off half of it at once. "If we were to tell Gabrielle there is no blood relation between her and Marc . . . ," he said.

Jeanne finished his thought. "It might make her still more determined to marry him."

The three of them were silent. From the street came the clatter of wheels and the cries of a flower-seller and a water-vendor. Nandou finished his coffee in another gulp and poured more. Edmée lifted her spectacles, put them down, repeated the motion.

"God damn it to hell," Jeanne said softly. Edmée winced, and Nandou shook his head.

"I know what Louis is thinking," Edmée said. "He is terrified for Marc, and fears that he himself may have contributed to Marc's . . . to his . . . I cannot make myself say the word."

"Sodomy," Jeanne said dully.

"I cannot say it because he does not commit such acts! But it is the word that people would attach to him." Edmée shivered. "I never expected to have to speak of such a matter, much less accept it in my own life." She attempted a smile, which crumpled. "The two of you seem innocent in this regard. Do you not know the horror and disgust with which the world regards this . . . problem?"

"Virtue likes to feel disgust," Jeanne said, "in order to experience itself as virtue."

"Yes," Nandou said. "The world needs monsters, perhaps because we are so much easier to create than saints."

"Do not speak of yourself as a monster," Edmée said sharply.

A look of surprise crossed his broad face. "You are right," he said. "I apologize for using the world's ugly language."

"There is no need to apologize," Edmée said.

"Yes, there is. To myself."

Edmée locked her hands around a cup. "If I did not know the two of you, if I had not met people in the theatre who are as Marc is, I might be like Louis—willing to countenance a marriage that would camouflage such a . . . problem."

Jeanne asked, "There is no chance Louis knows Marc is not his natural son?"

"None. I have never told a soul except the two of you, and Marc. Poor Marc. He had to decide which truth to tell Louis. He chose the one he thought would be the least painful. I wonder if he is right." She shook her head. "I cannot believe Louis wants Marc and Gabrielle to marry, but I am certain he believes he is helping Marc. He must be tortured by the same thoughts as I am—did we do something, when Marc was a child, to push him onto this path, which he himself does not want?" Jeanne put a hand on Edmée's. Edmée looked at her searchingly. "I do not want our children to marry," she said, "but I share Louis's fear. What will society do to Marc if it discovers his nature? Six years ago society sent me to prison for a crime it would surely consider mild in comparison. And last year did we not see Flaubert and Baudelaire tried for no action worse than *writing* about matters of which society disapproves?"

"Down with society," Nandou growled.

"Edmée, my dear friend," Jeanne said, "I understand your distress. Perhaps it would be wise for your son to marry—I cannot judge such matters—but, for her sake, it cannot be wise for my daughter to be the woman. I must stop her."

"How?" Nandou said.

Jeanne rose, tossed her hair over shoulders, and folded her arms. "I shall go to her. I have waited all these years for her to come to me, because she was the one who left, who stuck a knife in my heart and turned against me. But now it is clear she is not going to come. If this impending marriage did not bring her, nothing will. So I shall swallow my hurt and pride, no matter how they bruise my throat, and go to see her."

Nandou said, "And if she refuses to talk to you?"

"I shall make her."

"How?"

"Somehow. Find out where she is now, today, Nandou, please?"

"Very well," he said softly.

Chapter Twenty

Marc took Gabrielle to a great house on rue du Faubourg Saint-Honoré, to meet his grandmother: silver hair, a cane, fingers bent as oddly as twigs, a sapphire ring gleaming on one of them. Announcing that she was "acting in place of the mother Marc no longer has," the old woman gave them tea and an *interrogatoire*.

"Mademoiselle Corday, I understand you have no surviving immediate family members?"

Gabrielle heard herself reply dispassionately: "My mother has been lost to me for many years, and I never knew my father."

"Where were you raised, and by whom?"

"In Paris, by my mother and a friend. For a while I was sent to board with farmers who lived outside the city."

"Your education?"

"It was in Paris, at the good hands of the Sisters of Mercy, who gave my voice its first training. Then I studied with Signor Martinelli. My teachers' excellence has enabled me to enjoy a modest success in the opera."

The old woman folded her hands over the head of the cane and studied Gabrielle like something a tradesman had brought for inspection. Marc sat on the edge of a chair as if it were painful. Gabrielle felt detached from both of them, and from herself. On the day Marc proposed that they marry, she had been doubtful one minute and excited the next, fearful and then happy, but since the wild swings of that day she had felt little. Once, backstage, she had tripped over a rope and sprained her arm; she had had it bound tightly so she could continue to perform. Hours later, when the bandage came off, her arm had been numb, like something no longer attached to her. Now her whole being felt that way. The arm had returned to blood and life with a slow, throbbing pain, but she put that part of the recollection from her mind.

Yet with the numbness there was also a certainty about what she was doing. It was odd to be both detached and certain.

When Madame Vollard ceased asking questions, she leaned back in her brocade chair, and said, with the grim air befitting a judicial pronouncement, "I must tell you, Mademoiselle, that I disapprove of Marc's marrying a . . . performer, even though I know you have sung at some of our most respectable homes and enjoyed the friendship of the Vérons while they were alive. I would prefer an alliance with a girl of established family. But the world is changing, and Marc informs me that if I wish to see him married, it must be you or no one, so I suppose I must accede." She gripped her cane with both twig-hands, stood, and said, "You may kiss me."

Gabrielle watched herself rise and move forward. It was like approaching one of the statues above the front door; when her lips touched the woman's cheeks, she was surprised to find the flesh warm.

She expected that meeting Louis Vollard would be much harder; it was not. She went to the house where he and Marc lived, several blocks from the old woman's and no less grand. When Marc took her into the salon, Louis rose at once from a fat sofa with squat, carved wooden legs. He came to her, said "Gabrielle," and bent over her hand as though expecting her to deliver a blow to his neck, which, if she did, he would endure.

"Monsieur Vollard." He looked up at her with gratitude. "I am glad to see you," she said calmly. He nodded and replied, "Welcome to our home."

That moment seemed to define and seal the manner in which they would take up their new relationship: Nothing was to be acknowledged or mentioned. They would simply assume the roles of daughter- and father-in-law. It was like stepping into the second act of an opera when the soprano who had sung the first act was taken ill; one simply pretended to have been there all along, and the audience accepted it, for what else could they do?

Later there was a dinner that a dozen Vollards attended in order to meet her: Marc's uncle Nicolas and aunt Joséphine, their son Denis, his cousin Sophie and her parents, various other cousins and their teenaged children. Gabrielle spent the entire afternoon dressing, setting out every gown in her wardrobe on the bed and chairs before she chose the most expensive: a white tulle with satin ruchings, which looked the most youthful and spread regally over a crinoline. At the last minute she took out the gold rooster brooch and pinned it to her décolletage with a defiance she cared neither to examine nor dismiss.

The evening seemed like a performance: everything bright and gleaming—glasses, china, jewels, faces—and a chandelier hanging above them like a cluster of theatre clouds that would part to reveal some divinity at the final curtain. She was as charming as she knew how to be—like Adina, Rosina, Amina; like every sweetly virginal part she had sung. When no one was speaking to her, she lowered her lids demurely and took quick glances at the splendid buffet, the heavy double drapes, the mirror-polished floor—all of which would be hers after the wedding. Unlike the people for whom they were the setting, they contained no hint of performance; they had the bulk and richness of reality.

The conversation centered on Baron Haussmann's rebuilding of Paris, to create the splendid city the emperor desired: an aqueduct to bring water from a hundred miles away; the Bois de Boulogne turning into a glorious *parc à l'anglaise;* the meat-and-produce market of Les Halles, which had stood near the Palais-Royal since the twelfth century, to be completely rebuilt; broad new avenues radiating from l'Étoile like the spokes of a shining wheel.

"The emperor's dentist is building a mansion on avenue de l'Impératrice, on land where they used to grow cabbages!"

"We must get our new carriage in time for Longchamp."

"My dear, have you seen how they are cleaning up the Île de la Cité?"

"Do you remember that vile little slum beside the Louvre? I can barely believe it was ever there, now."

"I wonder how many of the people who lived there have found another home?" That speaker was Nicolas—Louis's brother. He sat at the long, shining table as if he were not part of the family but an observer. A faint, aloof smile hung about his lips, even when he was not smiling. Each time Gabrielle glanced in his direction, he seemed to be studying her.

"Rothschild thinks Haussmann's methods of financing are dangerously unorthodox, but Nicolas admires them, is that not so?" That was his wife, Joséphine. To her comments, she often added a plea for his concurrence, which he ignored. Nicolas, it seemed, had himself invested heavily in the bonds Haussmann offered for sale to the public. He spun the stem of his wineglass and said, "I admire Haussmann for inviting all citizens of Paris to share in its rebuilding."

"If you were interested in architecture, Marc, instead of painting," said one of the cousins, "I am sure no one would object."

There was an uncomfortable pause. Gabrielle knew the official family view: that he would "soon" be working at the House of Vollard on a steady basis, with painting only a hobby. She looked at Louis, who said nothing, and at Marc, who raised a knife above the table, then dropped it heavily. She considered speaking up, in her role as the affianced, but before she could decide what to say, another cousin changed the subject, and the talk returned to the rebuilding that was raising clouds of dust over whole sections of the city and making the ringing of hammers and the rasp of saws as common as the cries of street vendors.

"Did you know the emperor himself has staked out some of the new paths in the Bois?"

"They are planting four hundred thousand trees—can you imagine?"

"And under rue Royale," said Nicolas, "they are digging a great sewer."

"Nicolas, dear," said Joséphine, "why speak of such matters at dinner?"

"I should think it is exactly while eating dinner that we had best be concerned with the disposal of wastes."

Everyone stopped, like mechanical dolls halted in mid-motion, and stared at him. Then Louis laughed with pure, boyish pleasure. Gabrielle saw a look pass between the brothers, as of a secret shared. Except for Marc, the dolls started up again as if nothing had happened, silver fork to mouth, crystal goblet to hand, damask napkin to lips. She joined them. The difference was that she knew she was a doll.

"What do you think of them?" Marc asked her later.

"They were very polite and charming to me, considering that they must regard me as an intruder."

"We are always polite," Marc said.

"Except your uncle Nicolas, perhaps?"

"He never used to say much at these affairs, but in the past few years he has been uttering disconcerting comments, as if he finds us all incomprehensible and a bit ridiculous. I like him very much, though when I was a child I was afraid of him. He was never anything but kind, in a formal sort of way, but I felt—I still feel—that there was something powerful and dangerous in him, which he kept hidden. The strange thing was, after I began to study painting, he took me to lunch one day, only the two of us, for the sole purpose of saying that if painting was what I wanted, I must stay with it, no matter what anyone said, and he would back me. I am sure he keeps Grand-mère from making even more difficulty about the scantiness of my attention to the House of Vollard."

"Would he approve of your marrying me if he knew the truth of it?"

Marc was silent.

She caught his arm and heard herself say, "Why do you not leave them? Why not live completely in the world of painters, which means so much to you?"

"I fear what I would become." Self-loathing scored his face like acid.

"Ah, Marc . . . " A sudden warmth for him broke through her detachment. She touched his clenched hands.

He opened them, gripped both of hers, and said, "Are we doing something criminally foolish, Gaby?"

"Perhaps," she said. "But we are doing it nonetheless."

"We do not have to. Do you want to change your mind? You can. I would understand. Why should you be willing to save me from myself?"

"Do you want me to change my mind?"

His eyes fixed on hers and became their mirror, seeking certainty in order to feel it. Her own swayed like a bridge in high winds; if he said yes, it would collapse. "No," he said finally, and released her hands.

"Then we proceed to the wedding," Gabrielle said, her confidence, and numbness, returning. "September the fifteenth, eighteen hundred and fifty-eight."

"Yes." He smiled, young and beautiful again.

The next afternoon she was at her piano when there was a knock at the door. She frowned, put down the score, and crossed the room. "Who is it?" she called.

Silence. Then a firm voice: "Maman." And another: "Nandou."

She took a step back, involuntarily, and placed a fist over her heart, which had given a beat as loud as a cry. "What do you want?"

"I must speak with you," Jeanne said.

"For what purpose?"

Silence. Then, "Gaby, please open the door."

"I would rather not."

"I shall not go away. I shall stay here, we both shall, until you have to leave the apartment. You cannot stay inside it forever, so you may as well open the door now."

All too well, Gabrielle knew that Jeanne would do exactly as she threatened. She moistened her lips, ran her hands over her hair, and turned the knob.

Ah, she was lovely—more than ever, because she had been so long away from the embrace of their sight. Black hair pulled away from the perfect oval of her face, color as high and fresh as a wind, dark eyes bright. Beside him, Nandou felt Jeanne's arms lift to reach for her but fall back in an agony of control.

"Hello, darling," Jeanne said quietly. Gaby flushed. "You cannot imagine how wonderful it is to see you," Jeanne added.

"You look well," Gaby said neutrally. "Both of you. But how did you get upstairs? I told the concierge I did not want to be disturbed this morning."

"Pah," Nandou said. "As if I could not get past any concierge in Paris when I want." To force himself not to keep looking at her and drinking in the sight of her, as Jeanne was doing, he glanced around the room, which he had not seen since the time, years earlier, when he had followed her home from the Théâtre-Italien and tried to explain his and Jeanne's behavior. The drapes looked new, and there were some handsome paintings framed on the wall. "Mademoiselle Véron no longer lives with you?"

"No. She has married."

"And left the stage?"

"She was not having any particular success." Gaby bit her lips. "Well, Jeanne? What is it you must speak with me about?"

"Ah, Gaby," Nandou said, "how cold and cruel. This is your mother, who loves you so dearly and has missed you as one would miss a limb torn from one's body. Do you take no pleasure in seeing her?"

Jeanne sank onto a carved wood chair. "She does not. Look at her face."

"True," Nandou said, "it is exquisite but hard, like marble. I think I understand. She must force herself to have such a look because if she does not—if she allows us to know how it thrills her heart to see us again—how could she explain the years that she has denied such a pleasure to all of us? The longer she stays away, the less she can admit that she wishes to see us."

"Nandou!" cried Gabrielle. "Stop telling me what I am feeling."

"Am I right, then?"

"No!" she said, louder still.

"Tell me how I am wrong."

Gabrielle turned aside. In profile they could see the muscles of her throat and mouth working, as if she were trying to sing a high C without opening her lips. She looked back at them and asked, "What is it you have come for?"

Jeanne leaped to her feet. "Should I not come when I hear that my daughter is going to marry? And marry a Vollard?"

"How did you hear? There has been no public announcement yet."

"I can always learn what I need to know," Nandou said.

Jeanne went to Gaby. "What does it matter how we learned? We know, just as we always know where you are singing and how you are living. Do you think that because you left my life you left my heart? You are still here, here!"—Jeanne pressed both hands to her breast—"and you always will be. Do you think I can let you enter into such a marriage without begging you not to do so?"

"Maman, you can no longer tell me what to do."

Jeanne inhaled deeply; her eyes glowed, as if the breath had fed coals. "No, I cannot. Perhaps I tried too many times in the past to tell you how to live and what to do. Today I am here only to plead with you. After all that has happened, all that you know, how can you marry into the Vollard family?"

Gabrielle gave a joyless smile. "I should have thought it might please you. Is it not just the kind of joke on bourgeois respectability that you would enjoy? Is it not the perfect revenge?"

Jeanne went so pale that her eyes and lips seemed drawn on chalk. "You cannot mean that is why you wish to marry him."

"Did you not tell me, all my life, that art is a weapon for revenge against bourgeois morality? I have simply found a better weapon than art—marriage."

"You cannot mean it. Cannot. And even if you do—how is it revenge to marry into the thing you despise?"

Nandou watched them, Jeanne's hands and lips clenching in a single motion, Gabrielle's chin lifted in unconscious imitation of the mother she defied. "Perhaps," he said quietly, "she does not despise it."

"Of course she does." But there was a worm of doubt in Jeanne's voice.

"The fact is," Gabrielle said, "that I wish to marry Marc Vollard because I am extremely fond of him."

"Fond? Fond!"

"We have much in common and we are great friends. We—" Gaby stopped, for, though it was suppressed at once, Jeanne had made a sound, almost a snort.

"Gaby, listen," Nandou said, for if he did not come between them, what might they do, the two women he loved? "Your mother and I wonder what you and Marc Vollard know of each other. Surely you can understand our concern."

"Perhaps," she said. "But after all, it is *my* concern. If you are wondering whether he knows we are half-brother and sister, the answer is yes."

Jeanne said carefully, "Does he know who your mother is?"

"I did not tell him in the beginning because I . . . because I did not. And how could I him tell once you had written *The Trial of Louise Bernier?*"

"Ah," Jeanne said. "He did not like the play?"

"I shall tell you the truth," Gabrielle said with an edge of righteousness. "He thought it exposed things that need exposing. But like everyone else, he believes it was based on his mother's trial. How could I tell him—how could he tell his family—that my mother is the woman who made them the further subject of gossip and scandal? Of all women in Paris, you are the one they hate most."

"I see," Jeanne said. "But at some point Marc must have wanted to know who your mother was. You must have told him something."

Gabrielle lifted her chin. "I allowed him to believe she is . . . dead."

Jeanne gasped. A silence descended on the room, heavier with each second, like velvet drapes sinking into water. If he did not stop it, Nandou thought, it would take them all down.

"Gossip and scandal!" he cried. "Does Marc Vollard tell them he is marrying his half-sister? And their father allows it? There is scandal for you."

He regretted the words instantly, for he well knew she was not Louis

Vollard's daughter and therefore not Marc's half-sister, even though she believed herself to be; he should never say things to her that rested on untruth. But she answered with dignity. "There are things about Marc I cannot tell you that affect our decision. But I can say this: You need not concern yourselves, either of you, that there will be impropriety in this marriage. It will be a marriage in name only. We are agreed on that. And Louis Vollard knows it."

"But then . . . why?" Jeanne said. "My dear Gaby, to marry a man whose life cannot join with yours, that is to court disaster."

"I do not see why. I have learned that the world is full of husbands and wives who have as little as possible to do with one another."

Jeanne pushed her hands into her hair, upsetting its neat shape. "Why must you *marry* Marc Vollard? Why can you not simply remain friends? Gaby, in the name of the love I have felt for you since you first began to stir within me, how can I allow you to marry this boy when you are . . . when he is . . . "

"He is not a boy, Maman. And it is not up to you to allow it or not."

"It could be, if I tell the Vollards whose daughter you are."

"If you do," Gabrielle said, "you will never see me again." There could be no doubt that she meant it.

Silence again, heavy and liquid. He would drown in it, Nandou thought; they all would. At least they would be together as they went down.

Jeanne went so close to Gaby that Nandou was sure they could feel each other's breath. "What has happened to your passion for truth?" Jeanne said. "You left us because we had not told you who your father was. You behaved as if that were a crime never to be forgiven. Yet now you plan to enter a marriage built entirely on lies."

"It is not a question of lies, only of some things we are not telling."

"Nandou and I could say the same! We did not tell you some things, that is all. How can you build your future on the very thing you crucified us for?"

Gabrielle pulled back as if she had been slapped. Then she drew herself up and turned away.

"No!" Jeanne took her by the shoulders and spun her around. "It is true that we did not tell you everything. There are things I have not told you to this day, but this day I shall. Better yet, I shall show them to you. Yes! I shall show you why the Vollard family would not allow your father to associate with me, much less marry me. Then you can know the sort of world you are planning to enter. You can tell the truth to Marc Vollard and see if he still wishes you to enter it. Nandou, will you get us a cab, please?"

It was useless to struggle, Gabrielle decided. Her mother's determination was iron, like her grip, and her eyes blazed.

"You do not need to hold me, Jeanne," she said. "If you let me get my bonnet and gloves, I shall come with you."

Ten minutes later they were clattering along, the noise of the boule-vards wrapping the cab's silent inner space. Gabrielle turned to the window, to the daily promenade: embroidered vests, canes with jeweled heads, monocles, and the turbans, fezzes, derbies, and other headgear of the foreigners who had descended on Paris with the 1855 Exposition and never ceased arriving since then. But the spectacle was a blur because she kept glancing sideways at the seat opposite.

One of Jeanne's feet, in a worn black slipper, tapped impatiently on the floor. Both of Nandou's dangled inches above it. Gabrielle wanted to reach across the space to them: to touch Jeanne's perfect little hands and Nandou's magic ones, emerging from the arms that were too short. When she was a child, she had thought, Why doesn't he use his magic to make himself like other men? Now she thought, with a clarity she had never before had, Why could he not have accepted his natural world, the circus and the fairy plays? Why did he have to yearn to stretch beyond himself and play the great Romantic and heroic parts? Why was God so cruel as to mismatch his body and his soul?

But to reach out to them would be to admit she had been wrong to leave them. And to be reabsorbed into their world, imperceptibly but surely, like the sea pulling sand from the shore. She would begin to see things as they saw them. They would talk of art, and liberty, as a holy crusade one could not abandon. They would marvel that she had not become a passionate creature, like them. They would not understand other desires: for an ordered life, for simple things like beautiful clothes, for the pleasure of being accepted. They were always in defiance: of the regime, of people's staring at them, of normal life and lives.

"If you marry," Jeanne said suddenly, "what will happen to your singing?"

"I . . . have not decided."

"You would not give it up?"

"I might.

"Think how you would miss it!"

"I shall never be one of the nightingales of the world, you know."

"You sang in London."

"Once. Two years ago."

Jeanne was going to say more, but Nandou put a restraining hand on her arm, and she fell back against the seat. They rode on in silence, off the boulevards, circling a section of streets torn open to the sky and filled with the rubble of demolition. They passed lumber and bricks stacked in naked piles, and men in caps and overalls working on scaffolds that clung to the sides of rising buildings. "The showman at work," Nandou muttered.

"What do you mean?" Gabrielle asked.

"The emperor rebuilds Paris to keep Frenchmen from remembering they are not free men but his subjects."

Gabrielle was silent. That was just the kind of thing she did not want to hear. Paris was in ferment; a new order was forming, of wealth and comfort and happiness. She wanted to be part of it, not to criticize it.

The cab stopped; the streets had grown too narrow for it to pass. Nandou told the driver to wait for them. "Where are we going?" Gabrielle asked.

"I am taking you to the place where I was born and raised," Jeanne said.

It was a silencing thought. Gabrielle knew little of Jeanne's early years and family. She remembered asking about them; Jeanne had said, "I grew up in poverty, in a wretched life, which I left when I was thirteen. I have wanted nothing of it since but to forget it." She had spoken with such finality that Gabrielle had not broached the subject again. If she ever asked about Nandou's origins, he would grimace and distract her attention with a toy or a story about Petit Jean. As children do, she had accepted the boundaries laid down by the adults in her life. Everything had seemed of a piece with her difference from other children; the lack of grandparents and aunts and cousins was somehow part of the fact that her father was a dwarf.

She walked slowly and carefully, trying to hold her skirt above the mud and refuse of ancient streets that grew narrower as she moved along them, until her skirt began to fill their width. The sun's light, even its name, seemed never to have entered those alleys. From their mud, from the very boards of the buildings that lined them, rose an odor of rotting-sweet garbage and excrement that filled her nostrils as if it had physical mass. Finally, when she feared she would retch, Jeanne stopped and said, "Here. I was born and lived here with my family. We were ragpickers."

Gabrielle looked blankly at sagging doors green with mold. Once or twice, returning from a soirée that lasted until dawn, she had seen bands of ragpickers shuffling along with their hooks and bundles, but she had never considered how or where they lived—or even that they lived at all. She turned her gaze, still blank, on Jeanne, who went to one of the doors. After she knocked on it, a long time after, it opened. A gray face appeared, and gray lips said, "What?"

"I am looking for the Sorel family," Jeanne said. "Do any of them still live here? Pierre or Bertrand?"

The face turned away and called something. After some moments a man came to the door, tall, pale, and so gaunt his wrists were knobs. "Who is looking for me?"

"Hello, Bertrand."

The man squinted. "What you want? Who the hell are you?"

"I am Jeanne."

"Who?" She said it again. Recognition dawned on him so slowly that it might have been the reaction of a comic in the theatre. "Sweet loving God. Jeanne?" She nodded. "Shit," he said. "Shit! What the hell you want?"

"I have brought my daughter to meet her relatives. Gabrielle"— Jeanne took her hand and pulled her forward—"this is your uncle Bertrand."

Gabrielle managed, "How do you do?" The man did not respond, only stared at her as rudely as if she were naked.

"May we come in?" Jeanne said.

He opened the door all the way. The room, which had only the most rudimentary furnishings, smelled like a cellar unopened for years. A gray-faced woman sat at the table, with two children on the floor beside her. Their cheeks and lips were so thin that their eyes seemed as large as goblins'.

"Where is Maman?" Jeanne asked.

"Died," Bertrand said. "The cholera."

Jeanne sighed deeply. "And Papa?"

"The same."

"Pierre?"

"He left. Went south. We heard he was in prison, but who knows?"
It might have been "Who cares?"

"Is this your family?" Jeanne said.

"Yeah. Marie, and the kids are Pierre and Louise. Marie, this here is
Jeanne, my sister that run away with the dwarf."

"Gabrielle," Jeanne said, "meet your aunt Marie and your cousins
Pierre and Louise."

The woman nodded incuriously. The children's huge eyes fastened on
Gabrielle. She tried to smile at them but failed.

For the first time Bertrand focused on Nandou, who stood quietly
just inside the door. "By God, Marie, there he is. There's the dwarf.
Look at him, kids. A dwarf! Look how short his legs is, and his arms."
He snorted.

"Jeanne," Gabrielle whispered, "why don't you stop him?"

Jeanne seemed not to hear. "Are you still a ragpicker, Bertrand?" He
nodded. "Kidnapping did not work out for you, then?"

"What the pissing hell you saying?"

"You know very well. Gabrielle is the daughter you and Pierre once
took from me. Please tell her how it happened."

Bertrand folded his arms. A crafty look slid over his face. "Why the
hell should I? What's in it for me to tell?"

Jeanne took some coins from her purse. Bertrand snatched them,
studied each closely, then dropped them into his pocket one by one.

"Now tell her," Jeanne commanded.

Bertrand glanced at Gabrielle but looked into space as he talked.
"Long time ago, it was. Me and Pierre, a man sent for us. A rich man.
Said our sister had his kid. Said he'd pay us to get it away from
her. So we did. He paid us enough to stay drunk for a week. But
then . . ." He faltered.

"Then someone far cleverer than you retrieved her for me," Jeanne
said. "Gabrielle, no doubt there are questions you would like to ask your
uncle?"

"I do not think so," she said.

"No? Perhaps you would like to sit down and chat with your aunt?
Or sing a song for your cousins?"

Gabrielle shook her head, feeling she would choke. "I think I should
like to leave."

"So soon?"

"Yes. Please."

"Hey, wait," Bertrand cried. "You can't go without—You turned out rich, Jeanne. We're hungry, me and the kids and Marie. Give us some more money. We need it." The boy and girl began to wail thinly.

Jeanne opened her purse, took out more coins, went to Marie, and pressed them into her hand. "Use them for the children, if you can, not for him," she said. She hesitated, her hand still on Marie's. But the woman neither moved nor spoke. Jeanne walked away. "Come, Gabrielle, let us go." Nandou opened the door for them.

"Damn it," Bertrand said. "What about the girl's purse? She's got money too. Give me her purse!" He started toward them. But Nandou raised a hand and said, "Stop" in a voice so commanding that not only did Bertrand do so but Gabrielle herself stumbled and Jeanne had to pull her along.

"You fucking little dwarf!" Bertrand screamed after them. "Runt! Dwarf!"

The words ricocheted through the alleys as they retraced their steps and, when they reached the cab, hovered outside it like angry birds. Gabrielle sank onto the seat; mud streaked her skirt and shoes, and she was shivering, though not from external cold. Ice seemed to be breaking and shifting within her.

When the cab started to move, Jeanne folded her hands in her lap and said, "That was my world, Gabrielle. That is why your father was not allowed to stay with me, because I was a ragpicker's daughter. Can you still want to ally yourself with his family? Do you not see that they would refuse your marriage if they knew you had in your background the place and the people I have shown you?"

"But Marc is not like that. He would not care how poor I was, even if I had been a ragpicker too. Truly. Such things do not matter to him. He cares for nothing except painting and . . . except painting. You must believe me."

The cab rolled on for a time in silence.

Jeanne began to speak again, slowly, as if to herself, though her eyes rested on Gabrielle's. "I would still be in that world—or dead of the cholera—if Nandou had not taken me from it. One day when I was thirteen, I looked up from the garbage heaps and saw him, against the dawn sky, with his eyes glowing. I had never seen anyone like him. I never shall. He walked away that day, but I knew he would return. When he did, he asked me to come live with him. My father tried to sell me to him, for fifty francs. My oldest brother cut him with his hook—it left that faint line on Nandou's cheek—but he stopped them all, with no weapon but his magic and the power of his voice and spirit. He took me to his room near the Boulevard of Crime and taught me how to read and write and think, how to speak properly, how to love the theatre and liberty. He never asked anything of me but that I learn well." Jeanne raised her hands and folded them in a steeple below her chin. "When I met your father, he seemed to love the things Nandou had taught me to love. I thought he had a soul like Nandou's, and I fell in love with him. Perhaps there was a time when he truly loved art and liberty—for his sake I hope there was—but it was soon over. He left me before you were born. His mother offered me money to stay away from him. I refused it, but I stayed away." Her chin lifted. "One day I was so hungry I was going to return to the ragpickers' life. I was in the streets when I felt you ready to leave my body. I would have died, but Nandou found me and cared for me. For both of us. And when Louis decided he wanted you after all and paid my brothers to steal you from me, it was Nandou who rescued you—from under Louis's nose." She smiled at the memory. "He has saved you twice, and loved and cared for both of us with more devotion and passion than anyone has a right to expect in this life. If I allowed and encouraged you to believe you were his child, it was because I wanted you to think you had the most splendid man in the world for a father."

"Why do you tell her this?" Nandou said softly. "I thought you meant to speak of the Vollards."

"You are right." Jeanne looked surprised. "I tell her because it is true." She put out her hand to him. He took it.

"You love him, don't you," Gabrielle said. It was not a question.

"Yes," Jeanne replied. "And so do you."

"I know," Gabrielle said hoarsely.

The cab rolled on for a time.

Jeanne put her free hand on Gabrielle's arm. "I want you to find a man to love with all your heart and mind and body. I do not care if you marry him, but I want you to find him. However much you care for Marc Vollard, he cannot be such a man. You say it yourself. Are you not willing to wait until you—"

"I cannot love any man in the way you describe!"

"What do you mean?"

"I sing of love in a hundred arias and songs but I cannot learn what it is, how it feels. I want to love a man, I have tried, but the men I meet seem foolish to me, if not despicable." The words were coming without Gabrielle's will or consent. "They only want to use and exploit me. Marc does not want to do those things. He is kind and understanding. He will let me live as I want . . . We can help each other. Why should I not marry him? Should I spend the rest of my life having supper with fools . . . or living in rooms alone with my . . . " She put her head in her hands and surrendered to tears.

She felt a touch on her knee; Nandou was holding out a handkerchief, his dark eyes moist. Jeanne was rocking back and forth, her face stricken. "What have I done to you?" she whispered. "What have I done to my darling daughter?"

"Jeanne . . . Nandou . . . " Gabrielle sank to her knees on the floor of the cab, arms out blindly for both of them. They reached down and pulled her up against them; she felt enveloped by them, Jeanne's wet cheek and Nandou's muscled arm, Jeanne's thin fingers on her back and his coarse hair tight against her forehead. The motion of the cab sealed them even tighter against one another, until the three of them seemed to make one body.

At length noise from the boulevards began to penetrate Gabrielle's awareness; they were back in the heart of Paris.

Slowly they disentangled themselves, laughing as awkwardly as strangers who had been forced into physical proximity. Yet when Gabrielle was back on her seat, facing them, their eyes clung to one another's faces.

As calmly as she could, she said, "I am going to marry Marc Vollard. I do not believe I am making a mistake, but if it turns out that I am, I shall have to pay for it."

"I cannot even go to your wedding," Jeanne said. "You have told them I am dead. Perhaps you are right."

"Shall we never see you again?" Nandou said. "Do we find you only to lose you once more?"

"I . . . I am not lost. We shall see each other. It will be difficult, for I cannot bring you into my life as a Vollard, nor would you wish to come, but we shall see each other. I promise."

"Promise me one thing more," Jeanne said.

"What?"

"Call me Maman. Never Jeanne again, only Maman."

"Maman," Gabrielle said. "And Nandou. My father."

. . .

It was dusk when they returned to their apartment, a dozen shades of blue and purple folding slowly into one another before fusing into darkness. They went up the stairs, Jeanne before Nandou, as if they carried something delicate between them, stretching from her shoulders to his. Once inside, they sat at the dining table in the fading light, silent for a long time, as if speech might break the spell they had brought home with them so carefully.

Finally she spoke. "Edmée will be wanting to know what happened."

"We shall tell her. Soon enough."

After more silence, he asked, "Did it disturb you to learn of your parents' deaths?"

"No. For me, Papa died on the day he tried to sell me to you, and Maman on the day we went to her searching for news of Solange. Do you remember?"

"Of course."

"You remember everything."

"It is my curse. Or my blessing."

"How strange," she said, "that neither of us loved our parents, yet we could not bear it if Gabrielle did not love us."

"Perhaps that is why."

"And she does love us."

"Yes."

They were silent again, looking at each other in the dim, bluish light.

"We must accept the marriage, I suppose," she said.

"We must always accept what we cannot change."

"I feel she is doing it to defy me, yet, in some way, also to please me."

He nodded.

"How can she be doing it for both those reasons?"

"Are we not all creatures of contradiction?" he said.

She sighed.

He said, "I think there is another contradiction—she wants the life that her position as a Vollard will give her."

"The life I have taught her to despise since she was a baby."

"Yes."

"The life into which I have now driven her."

He sighed.

"I turned her against men," she said. "Now she cannot love a man, as a normal girl would. The only marriage she can accept is this twisted one. I have driven her into the very life I told her to despise." Soundlessly she began to cry.

He got up, with his tiny unconscious sound of effort, and went around the table to her. He laid his thumbs on her face to smooth away the tears and then put his arm around her shoulder.

She leaned against him. "What have I done to her?" she said. "I, her own mother."

"No more than what I have done to you."

"What do you mean?"

"Who gave you a life so unnatural that you could not become a normal woman, with a normal woman's emotions? I did. I the dwarf. I fastened your soul to mine with every hook and chain I could devise, until you could not break free even when I would release you." He confessed his crime softly, stroking her hair.

"Then you are not free either," she said, looking up at him.

He bent to kiss her forehead. She moved, and the kiss moved as well, to her lips. She put her hands on his muscled arms, to hold him, and because he had no intention of allowing it do so, his mouth moved against hers. She made a sound of content, rose slowly to her feet, and let her body rest against his. He thought sadly of the loss of his desire, and found that it was returning.

She guided his hands to the cloth over her breasts. "I want you to make love to me," she whispered.

In the most extraordinary moment of his life, he found that he believed her.

"For this once," she said, "can you do as I do and forget you are a dwarf?"

"I do not need to," he said, "because I remember I am also a man."

They went to her bedroom. Purplish light filled it, from the open window. He looked at the shutters but did not close them. They lay together, whispering, holding each other in wonder. They did not hurry; nothing was done in shame or darkness or haste. He discovered a new magic in his hands. She found a new power in words. Her body had never seemed so beautiful to him, because his own did not seem ugly; it could not, when it was giving both of them such pleasure. She had never felt such tenderness for him, because at last he was stirring her to more than tenderness. To both of them, what was happening seemed miraculous: the joining, finally, of flesh where spirit had always been joined.

For the first time, she was happy that he loved her. For the first time, he loved her because he was happy.

On the fifteenth of September, two days after the civil ceremony, Gabrielle Corday was married to Marc Vollard at the church of Saint-Sulpice.

Having reconciled themselves to the wedding, the Vollard family, and the Tissots, determined to make it a splendid one. Guests were sent entry cards to the church along with their invitations. A hand-painted curtain draped the main door, flowers banked the altar, and several of the bride's colleagues from the Théâtre-Italien sang music by Bach and Monteverdi. The size and order of the wedding procession, the black-and-white crispness of the men's clothing, the satin, lace, and tulle glory of the women's gowns—all were in accordance with the latest custom and fashion, as determined by the Vollards, acting *in loco parentis* to the bride, who had lent herself to the deliberations with a fervor that surprised their chief engineer, Joséphine. The most difficult question had been who would lead her to the altar; several musician friends were considered and even Louis Vollard—an idea abandoned in the face of his unexpectedly strong opposition, backed by the bride's and the groom's. At length it was decided that she should appear on the arm of her uncle-to-be Nicolas, for whom she had developed a fondness that seemed reciprocal.

An hour before the ceremony, a cab stationed itself across from the church. From within, its three occupants watched the arrival of the guests and the wedding party. They said little, but their eyes never left the church doors.

"Half the bankers in Paris are here," said Edmée, who wore her spectacles and a veiled hat. When Marc alighted from a carriage, she put her hands to her cheeks and stayed that way for some minutes.

When Gabrielle appeared, Jeanne said, "She is beautiful, isn't she?" and Nandou, taking her hand, said, "Like her mother."

Inside the church, Nicolas led Gabrielle to the altar. Behind him he heard the sound of her train, like a wave hissing into foam, and his nostrils filled with the scent of her orange blossoms. He had liked her since the night the family met her, more than he could explain by noting that the propriety of her behavior hid sparks of independence. He had wondered then why she and Marc wished to marry; he wondered still, in spite of the obvious affection between them. Something about the marriage seemed odd, though he could not quite say what. As long as it made his nephew happy; as long as Gabrielle did not discourage Marc from painting. He had asked her pointblank, and she had said, "Do not worry, Uncle Nicolas. I understand artists, you know. The thing I do not understand is why a banker like you would care about Marc's painting." He had liked that. One day he might even explain it to her. He cast a glance at her as they moved sedately down the red carpet. She looked very calm—perhaps even numb.

Louis turned to watch them coming. His gaze swept over the rows of guests, rustling with anticipation, and the banks of flowers and candles. Everything was beautiful, fragrant, perfect. Everything was a sham. The glowing bride and the handsome groom, who were at once so much more than husband and wife, and so much less. The proud father, whose heart was sick for his children, both of them; for the tragic union which his weakness was not only allowing them to form but to which it had helped bring them. The wedding was a sham, worse than his own had been, *because* his own had been. He fought down the desire to stand up and shout the truth to all those captains of finance and industry and their wives. Perhaps everything in their lives was hypocrisy as well; perhaps nothing anywhere was what it seemed, or what it should be. Only one thing was certain: This wedding was the last act of sham to which Louis Vollard would lend himself. His children had done more for him than he ever had for them, for they had made him see, finally and forever, that he could no longer tolerate the life into which he had slipped like quicksand on the day he had been carried to his parents' house with a gash in his thigh. He blinked, and saw Marc and Gabrielle standing together before the priest. As they took their vows, he swore his.

They said the ritual words and looked at each other. A flare of doubt and fear went off in the gaze of one of them; neither could have told whose. For a timeless moment their eyes steadied each other. *It will be all right,* one of them thought; neither could have told which one. They exchanged a chaste kiss, the thought passing between them.

When the church doors opened, the three in the carriage leaned forward. The guests congregated outside the doors, waiting, until the bride and groom emerged to a shower of applause and flowers.

"Our children," Edmée said, her voice catching. "What kind of life can they hope to have?"

Nandou groaned. Jeanne put one hand on his arm and with the other clasped Edmée's. "Let us leave now," she said.

As the carriage started to move, Nandou thrust his head out its window. "She is my daughter!" he cried. "Mine! Gabriel Corday's!"

"Hush," Jeanne said, pulling him back to his seat. "Hush, Nandou, my dear, my love. She has chosen her life, and we have chosen ours."

The two of them leaned against each other. Edmée looked at them, dried her eyes, and managed to smile.

PART THREE

1870–1885

In recent years we have heard in a thousand different ways: "Copy nature, only nature. There is no greater joy or triumph than an excellent copy of nature." And this doctrine, which is an enemy to art, was said to apply not only to painting but to all the arts, even the novel, even poetry. To these doctrinaires who are so satisfied with nature an imaginative man would surely have had the right to reply: "I find it useless and tedious to depict that which exists, because nothing that exists satisfies me. Nature is ugly, and I prefer the monsters of my imagination to the triteness of actuality."

—CHARLES BAUDELAIRE,
"Salon de 1859"

Chapter Twenty-One

*S*he was born into the Second Empire, with its peace and prosperity, its balls and receptions, its glittering displays of military pomp and strength. She had nearly everything money could buy a child of that empire: a nursemaid, a governess, a pony to ride in the Bois in summer, suits of fur-trimmed velvet for ice-skating there in the winter. She had dozens of frocks—especially yellow and pink, in which her mother loved to dress her, all lavishly trimmed, so that as she ran about the house and the garden, she was like a flower shaking petals of ribbons and lace. She had dolls with sweet porcelain faces and frocks as beautiful as her own, a toy theatre with Guignol and Polichinelle, a little dog named Bijou. Her mother read the most authoritative books on child care and worried about spoiling her, but there was no sign of willful behavior developing. Besides, her parents found it an irresistible pleasure to buy her pretty things. But two of the things she loved best cost no money at all: to curl on the window seat in her bedroom and read, and to be taken by each of her parents, separately, into worlds quite unlike the one in which they were raising her.

Her father sometimes let her be with him as he painted or sketched, either in the Bois or the Jardin des Plantes or in his special room on the third floor of their house. She was aware that he often went to something called "the firm"—wearing a black suit and seeming as stiff as a brush he had forgotten to clean—but for her the reality of Papa was the man who set her on a chair and painted her or else let her sit beside him on a stool and watch while he worked.

The brush fascinated her, diving into the palette and coming up with color, like Bijou with a ball in his teeth, then rising to the canvas to dab and dig away at a spot until it became a flower or a piece of fruit that grew richer and more beautiful with each trip. Her father's face fascinated her too, for it changed when he was at the easel, until he was no longer the dear, familiar man who bounced her on his knee and peered around his newspaper to wink at her but a stranger, whose deep, hot gaze bored into something she could not see and whose lips clenched and pursed and worked on each other in a silent dialogue she would not dare interrupt. He was in some place where she could not follow, from which he made the brush perform its magic. She would twist her feet around the legs of the stool and her long chestnut hair around one finger, watching the journeys of the brush and the intensity of the face, and wonder, *Where does Papa go?*

Eventually he would shake his head in a slow, half-angled way, put down his brush, and become familiar again. "Well, Simone," he would say, "what do you think?" regarding her as gravely as if she were some adult authority. She held his gaze as long as she could—that was part of the ritual—until finally, helplessly, she had to giggle. When he heard it, a smile burst across his face; he would lift her off the stool into his arms, give her a kiss, and say she was the best art critic in France.

Sometimes he took her to places he told her never to talk about. In one of them lived a woman about whom Papa said only, "Here is a lady who loves you very much." Simone named her the Rose Lady, for she smelled of roses. Her embrace was so tight that it sent the breath right out of Simone's body. The lady sewed on a magic machine operated by her foot. Bolts of cloth and laces sat everywhere, dressmaker's dummies stood smooth and naked, and pins stuck up from the carpets. While the lady and Papa talked, Simone tried on some of the clothes she made, grown-up dresses with pearls and sequins and feathers. Sometimes she played her piano while Simone sang. When they got ready to leave, she would cry and cover her eyes with a rose-scented handkerchief.

Next they would go to a strange, untidy room where lived a giant named Belloc. "Mademoiselle Simone!" he shouted when Papa brought her in. "Clear a space for Mademoiselle Simone"—and, as if he had given the order to them, his huge hands flew through the air, tossing aside rags and shirts and orange peels and making a clean place for her to sit on the table while he and Papa talked. In Belloc's room were things to stare at and let one's mind play with: a stuffed owl with glass eyes that seemed to move inside their rings, a coal stove with a fat pipe bent like an elbow, a pile of embroidery fabrics and straw hats, a violin missing a string, a clay pipe so long and thin its smoke must surely come out in threads. When Belloc brought out wine for Papa and him to drink, there was lemonade for her, in a blue glass the shape of an upside-down bell; when she finished it, Papa sat her on one knee, his hand playing with her ringlets while he talked. Just before they left, the giant Belloc lifted her to the ceiling and brought her down slowly for a kiss full of wine and beards.

On the way home Papa said, "We do not tell Maman where we've been today. Let's just say we went to the Bois." Or the Louvre or the booksellers or some other place they went after leaving Belloc, so they never told Maman a lie.

It was funny, because her mother also took her on Secret Visits. "Not a word to anyone about where we have been, Simone, my love."

"Why not, Maman?"

"Oh, dear . . . because we would get into trouble, all of us, and you do not want that. When you are older I will be able to explain it better, but for now, just give me your promise, or else I won't be able to take you back again."

Naturally Simone promised. She would have done so in any case, just to make the worry-lines vanish from her mother's beautiful face, but never to visit Jeanne or Nandou again—that was a terrible prospect. Whenever she and her mother went there, Jeanne would smile and hold out her arms so invitingly that one simply had to run into them. Then Jeanne would ask all about what one was doing and thinking and feeling, in a way that made it impossible not to tell her everything, and as Jeanne listened, things would emerge from various pockets and folds in her dress: chocolates or a bag of nuts or a figurine of Harlequin.

As for Nandou, he was the most magical person Simone had ever met.

"I am a dwarf," he explained when she wondered why he did not look like her father or any other man she knew. She had not asked the question; she was only thinking it, but he seemed to have heard. "Dwarfs are people whose brains grew more than their bodies," he said. "Once upon a time the earth was full of dwarfs and giants, you know. The giants were very cruel and also very strong, so the dwarfs had to become exceedingly clever to outwit them. How did they do it? They learned to ride upon the wind. Yes, it is true. They sailed above the giants' heads, and leaned down and whacked them off. Then they made friends with the birds and learned their language. That done, they came back to earth and hid themselves away in the mountains. But no dwarf ever forgets there was a time when his people sailed the air, and every dwarf, in his soul, is still king of the wind."

He could do wonders of all kinds: make voices come from places where there were no people, push a yellow scarf into his fist and pull it out green, create shadow-animals on the wall with his fingers, tell a tale like "Puss 'n Boots" so that the scheming cat was right there in the room, doing his tricks. Before one's eyes, he could turn himself into an old woman, a dragon, a horse, and—most miraculous of all—a giant. "Is Nandou very old?" she asked her mother, for gray ran through his thick hair and wrinkles nested in the corners of his eyes. "Rather old," her mother replied. "But it does not matter because he is also very young." Simone nodded.

While Nandou told her stories, her mother and Jeanne sat across the room chatting and smiling. Then the four of them would gather around the table, to eat and talk and laugh. Simone would feel she was in an enchanted circle.

On the way home, her mother would always say, with a little catch in her voice, "Now we shall go for a nice drive through the Bois. And remember, not a word to anyone about where else we have been."

Simone would nod and say, "Yes, Maman," and slide back into a corner of the carriage. By the time she was eight, she was thinking, above the rhythm of the horses' hooves, how strange it was that Papa took her on secret visits to a giant and Maman to a dwarf.

Things collapsed with the speed of electricity. In June of 1870 everything was normal: The Grand Prix de Paris was run at Longchamp in the Bois, with competitors from England and all over Europe. The sun shone on the gold braid of cavalry officers, beat on the swan-feather parasols held up against it by women in brilliant silk and taffeta dresses, and flashed on the champagne bottles that opened and foamed when the first four horses turned out to be French ones. But in July, what had begun as a trivial argument between France and Prussia ended with Louis Napoléon's declaring war, goaded by a public indifferent to reports of Prussian military might and certain that victory would drop into French hands as easily as it had at the Grand Prix.

Smiling bravely—for he had a gallstone the size of a pigeon's egg, which pained him so much he had to take opium and wear makeup to disguise his haggardness—the emperor rode at the head of the resplendent and glittering Imperial Army. It met the steel cannons and brutal efficiency of the Prussian forces like pastry meeting a knife; on September 1, the emperor surrendered.

Overnight, Paris turned against Louis Napoléon and his empire, shouting *"Vive la République!"* The royal family escaped with its dentist, while servants in the Tuileries looted the silver and jewels and the gilt N's on the gates were covered with old newspapers. Three days later a republic was proclaimed at the Hôtel de Ville, and crowds filled the streets, singing, shouting, overturning statues, destroying everything they could that symbolized Empire.

"It is more like carnival than the fourth of September," Jeanne said.

"How can the people know the power is in their hands," Nandou asked, "if they do not experience it by acting without restraint?"

"I have never seen anything like this," Edmée said. "In '30 and again in '48, I was kept inside, away from everything."

Dressed in old clothes, the three of them went into the streets in the late afternoon and joined the throngs on the boulevards, cheering when news of the Republic came, embracing one another and everyone in sight. Eventually they had to sit down in a café—especially Nandou, whose feet had been hard used by years on the nocturnal streets and the *Dwarf Lord* stilts. All around them, people grinned as if France had won a great victory instead of suffering a humiliating defeat, and waiters flourished their trays like tricolors. From a table in the corner erupted cries of *"No more Louis Napoléon!"*

"How ephemeral it all is," said Edmée. "Three months ago most of Europe and much of France were hailing him for bringing us prosperity and making Paris the most modern and beautiful city in the world."

"Underneath her paint, a whore is a whore."

"Nandou!" Jeanne said. "Don't call Paris a whore. You love Paris."

"True. A mistress, then." He smiled at Jeanne and raised his voice above the chatter around them. *" 'Allons enfants de la patrie'. . .* After eighteen years, we sing it again!" He lifted his hands in sweeping gestures until he had roused the whole café to join him. The "Marseillaise" had been forbidden under Louis Napoléon; now people burst into it with gleeful defiance. Jeanne sang lustily, giving herself as completely to the moment as a moth to flame. Nandou clutched her hand, his face flushed, his eyes snapping.

He was happy, Edmée thought, in a way he had never expected to be. He had not told her so; he did not need to. She saw it in the look that sometimes crossed his face of belief and disbelief at the same time, as if he had never thought happiness was his lot and therefore had been a fool, and was now glorying in admitting his folly. From the first time she met him, when he had been trying to steal back the child, Edmée had known what was in his heart because, until Louis killed it altogether, it had been in hers as well: the torture of loving more than one was loved, of each day damming the passion one felt lest it drown its object. She did not know how release finally had come for Nandou, only that it had. The retraction of a sharp edge in Jeanne's voice and manner said that she was happy too, although in a different way—as if Jeanne knew the happiness of accepting love and Nandou of being able, finally, to give it.

How, Edmée wondered, had she become an expert reader of the silent language of other people's love and desire? Perhaps because she herself no longer spoke it. The needs of the flesh had brought too much grief; she had shed them along with "Edmée Vollard." Doing so gave her a silent bond with Marc.

She was quite used now to being Aimée Sorel. Dyeing her hair and making up her face differently were second nature, and the glasses, which had once been only for disguise, had become a necessity after so much close work with her needle. Even the invention of a machine for sewing had not helped her eyes, although it had shortened the time she spent on each costume by at least half. Managers and performers demanded her services steadily. She had other friends in the theatre now, although Jeanne and Nandou would always be the closest, and had moved to a larger apartment in a building near them, in which she lived comfortably but simply, her chief luxury the installation of a piano. She played only for herself, surrendering to the sound with a pleasure as keen as any she had known, and for Marc. She had finally decided it was safe to let him know something of her new life, and when he came to visit, after they had talked over tea or perhaps lunch, she would play for a while, happy because the music gave voice to something otherwise voiceless, which she needed her son to know: something in her hands that was parent to the great gift lying in his, although so much lesser than his gift.

"That was beautiful, Maman," he would say when she finished, and the words would linger in her heart for days. When he brought the child with him, and she sang in her piping little voice, the music bound the three of them together so closely that Edmée had trouble catching her breath.

All around her in the café, as the "Marseillaise" finished, there were laughter, cheers, more gibes at the departed emperor. "We do not know what will happen tomorrow," Nandou said, "but tonight we can assume it will be splendid."

The three of them lifted their wine and toasted—one another, the Republic, the future.

"To our children," Edmée said. Their eyes met and grew darker, acknowledging the secrecy in which they had to keep the existence of the family they now shared.

"Where do you think they are tonight?" Jeanne said. "On the streets with the crowds?"

"If so," Edmée said, "Marc is probably sketching them."

Nandou pulled a watch from his pocket. "Ten o'clock. Simone has been put to bed."

"To Simone," Jeanne said. They drank again, each visualizing her sturdy little person, her determined jaw and brown eyes that could study things gravely one moment and, the next, spill with laughter.

Although they never put it into such words, they thought of her as their collective grandchild. She seemed to have inherited something from each of them, even Nandou—his quickness of wit, Jeanne's direct-ness, Edmée's gentleness—as well as a practicality all her own: One day at Jeanne and Nandou's, a doll she had brought with her fell from the table and its face cracked. When Jeanne exclaimed and fussed, Simone had said, "Do not worry. I am sure there is glue in your cupboards. And if not, I shall tie a scarf under her chin and say she has the toothache."

But Simone was not their collective granddaughter; only Jeanne's for certain. She could not possibly be of Nandou's blood, and as for Edmée, she could not tell, because Marc would not explain. "Gabrielle is preg-nant," he had told her, his smile at its widest but his eyes defiant. Before her thoughts could settle into words, he had added, "Please do not ask me questions, Maman. Just accept that I shall be delighted to be a father, and that there is no need for you to worry."

To Jeanne and Nandou, Gabrielle had been equally enigmatic: "I am going to have a child. I did not expect to, that it true, but it has happened, and Marc and I are both well pleased. I assume you will be happy for us, and will not inquire into things we do not intend to discuss."

"How can I remain silent?" Jeanne had cried.

"You must," Nandou had said.

As far as the three of them knew, Gabrielle still believed Marc was her half-brother. Would she have entered into a physical relationship with him, believing it to be incestuous? Or had Marc decided to tell her the truth, that he was not Louis's son, so that if physical desire had grown between them, they could accept it? But could Marc really have changed that much? And if not, who had fathered Simone? And under what circumstances? The three of them had been over and over the questions without ever deciding on the answers. It had been years since they asked them aloud, but the questions hung in their thoughts of Simone like hawks above an aviary.

"Nandou!" cried a voice. "Jeanne!"

A man was heading toward them, angling around the café's crowded tables and rushing waiters. He had gray hair and bronzed skin, and as he came closer, Edmée suddenly ducked her head and clutched her glass with both hands. He reached the table. From beneath her lowered lids she saw the gray fabric of his jacket and the bottoms of his gestures.

"What a homecoming," he said. "I return to Paris for the first time in years and walk straight into a revolution."

"In France that should make one feel at home." Nandou's voice was cool.

The man laughed, too briefly. "Do you think this Republic will last?"

"We are gathered to pray that it does."

A pause. "Are you performing these days, Nandou?"

"Not at present. I do less and less as I grow older."

"How do you keep yourself busy, then?"

"I give advice to managers and allow them to pay me for it. The rest of the time I study life, and enjoy its lessons."

Another pause, awkward. "Jeanne, I understand you have become something of a Realist in your plays. Do you lecture your audiences from the stage?"

"I write of what I see around me. If the public takes it as a lecture, that may say more about them than about the plays." Jeanne's voice was tight.

"You concern yourself with the rights of women, I am told."

"Do you not agree they are worthy of concern?"

"You must let me come and speak to you soon, Jeanne. There are things I wish to discuss and . . . explain."

Edmée lifted her head. She felt dizzy.

"Will you introduce me to your companion?" the man asked Jeanne.

"I have the honor to present my cousin, Aimée Sorel," Jeanne said. "Aimée, Monsieur Henri Foucher."

There was noise around them, chatter and shouts, but Edmée felt as if the four of them were encased in a bubble of silence. "Aimée is my cousin," Jeanne went on. "Since coming to Paris, she has become a designer of costumes."

"When did she come to Paris?" Henri said, staring.

"Many years ago," Jeanne answered blandly.

The sounds of the café receded to ghost voices. *"Enchanté,"* Henri said, taking Edmée's hand. But instead of bending over it, he held it for a long moment. "We have met before," he said.

"I am sure you are mistaken," Jeanne said.

He paid no attention. "I would know you in any guise, Edmée— despite the glasses, the hair, the years. If you could know how many letters I wrote you, with nowhere to send them, so they rose in piles of reproach on my desk. If you could believe how I have wanted to beg your forgiveness. Is it possible I have found you again?"

"Allons enfants de la patrie . . ." sang a crowd surging past the café. Was it to be a new world, then?

The euphoria over the end of the Second Empire faded, for the Prussians laid siege to Paris, expecting to prevail over such a morally degenerate place in six weeks at the most.

But the city had its defenses: seventeen forts, a garrison of two hundred thousand plus three hundred thousand reservists, and a patron saint, Geneviève, who had protected Paris since the time of Attila. The new government acted to guarantee the food supply and essential services: The lower reaches of the new Opéra house, not yet completed, were made into a reservoir; above it were installed a bakery, a hospital, a clothing depot. Cattle, sheep, and lambs bawled and grazed in the Bois and the Luxembourg Gardens.

The Vollard family made plans to leave the city: Joséphine, most of the cousins, Gabrielle and Simone.

"I would not mind staying," Gabrielle told Marc. "It may be exciting."

"It may also be dangerous, and we must think of Simone."

"I know. But you are staying, and Nicolas and Denis." Although Denis was twenty-five, Joséphine had secured him an exemption from military service.

"We cannot abandon the firm," Marc said, "or Grand-mère. Just this

morning, she repeated that she will not allow Prussians to drive her from
Paris."

"The others may be staying for the firm, or for Henriette, but you
are not," Gabrielle said. At thirty-nine she still had a vivid beauty made
of contrasts: pale skin, cheeks and lips rouged by Nature, hair as black
and soft as soot. But if she had still been singing professionally, she
would not have been as easily cast for the "nightingale" roles. Something in her manner had tightened, imperceptibly if one examined her
feature by feature, but the effect as a whole seemed to be one of holding
herself back from close, invisible walls. "You are staying in Paris," she
said, "because you will enjoy being alone."

"I have no such thought! I shall miss Simone. And you, of course."

"Nonetheless, you would like to be free for a time of the role of
loving spouse." Before Marc could protest further, she added, "So
would I. Did we not agree to keep our pretenses for the world and use
none on each other?"

"True, but other matters are involved. I am too old for military
service, but not for the National Guard. I must do what I can to help
defend Paris."

He took her and Simone to the Gare du Nord, where a week before
Victor Hugo had returned from exile to the cheers of thousands. Now
the train was uttering metal sighs and groans, as if the load of humanity
it carried would make it burst. Marc kissed Gabrielle on both cheeks.
"Keep yourselves safe."

"And you. I shall worry about you constantly."

Clutching Bijou, Simone threw herself tearfully into Marc's arms,
and said he must write every day. "I do not think I can, little cabbage,"
he said. "There may not be mail delivery much longer."

He was right. Within days there were no more trains or mail. Carrier
pigeons and balloons were called into service. The Prussian cannons,
ringed around the city, began to shell it, one arrondissement after
another.

The theatres, which had been closed at first, opened again to give
benefits for orphans and wounded. To raise money for cannons to
defend the city, Victor Hugo gave permission for public readings from
Les Châtiments, poems written in exile, which Louis Napoléon had
banned because they not only satirized his regime violently but called
it a crime. Nandou was asked to be one of those who read—and who
would rehearse at Hugo's home.

When he returned, his eyes were dazed, as if he had been staring at the sun. "Hugo remembered me, Jeanne, from forty years ago. He thanked me again for saving him from the footpads. And he said . . . I would do honor to his verse."

The next night, dimly lit and without scenery, the actors recited before the curtain, while in the theatre's foyer wounded soldiers lay on straw mattresses. Nandou stepped out and began a poem about an insurgent finding the body of a young boy who has been shot in the temple. From the audience Jeanne watched Nandou disappear, his place taken by an exhausted fighter, streaked with powder, dark with rage, who cried, *So they are killing children now?* He had never been more inspired, she thought, with every gesture and inflection aimed surely at the heart. When he finished, the audience howled its admiration.

Later that night, she went to his room and his bed, called not by desire but, as sometimes happened, by the pleasure of lying together without it. "Do you realize," he said, "that tonight was the first time I performed in public simply as a man, not as a dwarf?"

"I had not thought of it."

"Sometimes I truly believe you forget there is a difference."

"No," she said, settling against him, "I just do not think of it."

He stared into the darkness. "I do not think I will perform in public again. But I have finished with the best, have I not, Jeanne?"

"The best," she said.

In the streets, as the shops grew emptier, the voices of revolutionaries grew louder: workers in their smocks and caps, Socialists, Communists—all denouncing the new government. The theatres closed again, for lack of heat and fuel. In the house on rue du Faubourg Saint-Honoré, Henriette Vollard lay under hills of blankets, her arthritic joints holding her nearly immobile, her fireplace smoking because the servants had only green wood to burn. Nicolas or one of her grandsons looked in on her briefly but often. She did not always seem to know which of them it was, if any. One day she called Marc "Louis" and asked why he had left and if he would ever return.

"I don't know," Marc said, as kindly as possible. What other reply was there? He had never shown her the letter he and Gabrielle had received a week after their wedding: *Dear children, I am leaving your lives, to which I have brought nothing but sorrow, and abandoning my own, which*

I have lived without distinction. I want to live in new places, with new people, to try to recapture the dreams I had when I was your ages . . . At the time Marc had wept with the pain of Louis's absence. Now, when he thought of it, there was a touch of envy.

Marc had become a rifleman in the National Guard. Everyone was allowed to live at home and do as he liked when not called up for training or a tour of duty, so Marc was able to go to the House of Vollard, where caution and concern were thick in the air, or visit Edmée. For the first time in his life he did not want to paint constantly; experiencing the strange new reality of the siege was all he could handle. He walked great distances, sometimes sketching what he saw, more often merely seeing and disbelieving the state to which Paris had been brought. His life and creativity were in a restless suspension.

His way to and from his assigned fortification took him through Montmartre. The village had been incorporated into Paris ten years before when the old city wall was pulled down, and the new painters, those who rejected the academic approach and were derided by the art establishment, had begun to gather in the cafés there. Marc took to stopping in to listen, sometimes to add his voice. The arguments over Ingres and Delacroix, the debates over the social function of art, the discussions of *Where does beauty lie?* could go on until two in the morning. Edgar Degas was often there, and Manet—men for whom Marc felt a kinship beyond art, for they too were the sons of prosperous families, with whom they stayed on good terms. At the special showing in '63 of works refused by the Salon jury, when Marc had first seen *Le Déjeuner sur l'herbe,* he had felt as if a wind were rushing through his brain, blowing away his previous ideas. There were no halftones, no lines separating the shapes, in the prescribed manner—only flat areas of color, so the whole composition seemed made of coloured shapes, not of the male and female figures it contained. What was the meaning of such a technique? Why use it on such a subject—to be shocking? People had stood before the painting, blind to its brilliance, snorting and jeering because it was something they had never seen before, but Manet had not rejected the world to which they belonged—only their manner of seeing. He rebelled without being a rebel.

There were writers present in the Montmartre cafés as well. One of them was the most attractive young man Marc had ever seen: a poet named Octave. When Octave read some of his verses, their images would bloom in Marc's mind as if they had been painted. *Dawn comes over Paris in a rush of white birds; the rooftops reach up to pull them down; the yellow picks of their beaks hunt for pieces of heart left by the Night* . . . He and Marc exchanged only impersonal sentences, but they looked at each other in the same way.

The new and chronic hunger caused by the siege, which left a rodent gnawing in Marc's gut day and night, weakened his defenses and made him confront a deeper hunger: a void in his life that not even art could fill, nor Gabrielle's companionship nor Simone's love. Over the years, when physical desire tortured him, he had occasionally tried to appease it with women like Arlette, but reliving the experience of his boyhood opened a hollowness below his breastbone that he could not bear and left him with only the two evils. He could permit himself only the lesser of them. Always, the instant he finished, self-loathing would invade him, making him wish he could cut his capacity for desire out of himself, like a bullet out of flesh. Later, when he was painting, he would look at the hand holding the brush and remember how he had allowed it to sate the inner Darkness, and wonder if that was why it too often failed to do his bidding with the brush; why there was some vision within him he could never fully bring to the canvas. Now, in the otherworldliness of the siege, the Monk of Art was growing weary of his struggle against the Darkness. Sometimes the Monk could make Marc leave the café and Octave's presence. More often he would fail, and Marc would remain, helpless, until Octave left or the café closed.

The weeks wore on. Heat and light became problems, then food. Volunteers from the Army of Paris went through the city gates at night to pick vegetables, under the fire of enemy snipers, but returned with meager rewards. The cattle that had blocked the boulevards, bawling in distressed confusion and butting against trees and buildings, thinned in size and number and finally disappeared. Suspicious-looking ragouts of "lamb" and "rabbit" appeared on restaurant menus.

"We shall be all right," Jeanne said grimly. "I know how to cook without food. I learned in a good school." When there were no vegetables at all, she made soup from boiled weeds and leaves, which Nandou called "the devil's piss," and cooked horsemeat, boiling it, then piling it with so much horseradish sauce they could taste nothing else. Nandou absolutely forbade cat or dog: "I will cut up and chew every tree in the Bois before I will do that." They determined to keep up the salons for their theatre friends, who were out of work. The guests tried to bring something, if they could. The first time one of them brought a rat, available in the shops for one franc, everyone turned rather pale, except Jeanne. She went into the kitchen and, swearing loudly the whole time, chopped the rat till it looked like minced beef and made a meat pie. Each week they found new names for the disgusting fare: "Pâté of Prussian Private Parts" and "Soup without Honor or Glory or Taste" and "Pie of the Right Psychological Moment"—after the fact that Bismarck was reported to be waiting for the "psychological moment" before launching a decisive bombardment.

Edmée asked them to invite Henri Foucher. "Have you forgiven him?" Jeanne asked sharply.

Edmée flushed. "Did you not tell me long ago that one should not lean on hatred for support?"

In the segment of the fortification ring to which Marc was assigned, there was not a great deal to do. But one gray, cold day in November, when his company was sent on one of the periodic sorties that tested enemy lines, they ran into unexpected, heavy fire. In an instant the world filled with smoke and oaths and cries of pain, and the confused shouts of officers, which Marc could barely decipher above the crazed pounding of his heart. He fired his rifle blindly, loaded, fired again. The spikes of Prussian helmets reared into his vision, out of the smoke, like snake tongues. When the air finally cleared, the man who had sat next to Marc all morning was lying two feet away, his eyes as vacant as his chest, where there was only a huge hole.

That evening Marc stopped in Montmartre. The front room of the café, all white and gold and mirrors, held few people, and in the back room were only some old men playing cards. Marc sat alone, drinking beer so weak it seemed to contain no alcohol, watching the light of some candles make and then erase shadows on the men's faces and bald pates. In his mind, blurring what he saw, hung the image of his dead fellow rifleman.

Something made him look toward the doorway. Octave came in, shivering from a cold rain that had begun to fall. He hesitated, then came to Marc's table.

"Do you not sometimes wish," he said in his soft, melancholy voice, "that you had left Paris?"

"Yes." Something made Marc add, "I sent my wife and daughter away on one of the last trains."

"Ah. Why did you stay?"

"To do what I could. And to . . . see."

Octave nodded as if he understood. "For three nights now I have had a dream of bread. Fresh bread, with a crust you can knock upon like a golden door. Have you ever been hungry before?"

"For food—no."

"For what, then?"

Marc heard himself say, "Happiness."

"Do you think happiness is possible?"

"I do not know. But tonight I must believe in it."

"Why?"

"To blot out the sight of death."

Octave nodded again. "What else do you believe in?"

"The truth that lies at the heart of things."

"Have you ever found it?"

"Not yet."

"Is that why you never show your paintings?"

"Yes. They are not truthful enough."

"I believe in language," Octave said. "And bread. And love."

It was the strangest conversation he had ever had, Marc thought. He seemed to have no more control over his own words than over Octave's. When Octave put a hand on his arm, he had no control over that, either. But he did not care, for the vision of the dead man was fading, and so was the specter of the Monk.

In the morning there were knives of remorse, one after another, and a vow never to permit himself to do it again.

Each time, it was that way.

In December the temperature fell below freezing and stayed. Coal stocks were soon gone, and firewood thieves roamed at night, chopping down trees in the squares and on the Grands Boulevards. Gray, pocked snow covered the ground. There was virtually no transportation, for the omnibus company horses had been slaughtered for food. The zoo did the same with its animals; those who could afford to do so bought antelope steaks and filet of boa constrictor.

On January 28, after an intensive Prussian bombardment of the Left Bank and a sad retreat of the garrison that tried to push back the enemy, and despite violent protests from much of the National Guard, the city capitulated. Bismarck insisted that a government be elected, to surrender to him officially, and he dictated to it the harshest of terms: five billion gold francs in indemnity, and the ceding of two provinces, Alsace and part of Lorraine.

Marc sent word to Gabrielle not to return until the city was normal again, telling himself he had nothing but his family's comfort in mind. He spent every night in Montmartre, talking in the café for several hours—fuming, with the others, over the peace terms and the Assembly's disgraceful acceptance of them—although part of him did not care a damn and simply counted the minutes until he could leave with Octave. Soon it would be finished, he knew; he, and Paris, would return to normal life. He hated the signs of that returning life, even as he welcomed them: the loaves of wheaten bread, the clop of hooves, the mail delivery that finally let him send a daily letter to Simone.

On March first a token Prussian army of occupation entered the city. Marc watched from the House of Vollard, with Nicolas, Denis, and cousin Blaise. Black flags hung before the city hall in each arrondissement; all the shops and cafés were shuttered, with signs that read *Closed for national mourning.* "Bastards," Nicolas muttered, looking down on the spiked helmets. Denis, who had his father's build and his mother's features, said, "It is very unpleasant, but even a bad peace is better than war." Blaise sighed. When Marc began to hum the "Marseillaise," Nicolas clasped his shoulder.

They heard a commotion in the hall, then a knock on the door. A maid from Henriette's entered, panting from running, and said they should come; Madame was ill.

The doctor said it was her heart. She, with a ghost of imperiousness, said it was the Prussians: "I do not care to live in a Paris they claim to rule."

"I think we had better bring our wives home," Nicolas said. Marc nodded.

He did not think he had the strength to see Octave; he sent a note. *Like the siege, it must end. We always knew it would. Now it has. With gratitude, forever.* He did not expect an answer, but several days later, on the day that Simone and Gabrielle arrived, he received a single sheet of paper, unsigned, with a poem on it. He read it half a dozen times, then hid it in a drawer in his studio.

. . .

Simone flung herself into her father's arms and kissed him so many times that, laughing, he told her he felt as if he were being sponged. She clutched him again and whispered in his ear, "Are Belloc and the Rose Lady all right?" "Yes, yes," he said hastily, and put her down. She had grown at least an inch, and there were a dozen marvelous tones in her skin, all of which he seemed to have forgotten; he wanted to set her on a chair, in her yellow dress, and start painting her at once. Gabrielle embraced him, then pulled back and looked into his eyes. "You are different," she said.

"How?"

"I do not know. You are thinner, of course, and you seem tired. But you also look . . . younger."

"I assure you I am not," he said lightly.

She changed the subject, but a number of times he could feel her studying him. He wanted to ask her what she saw; he wanted to tell her everything and, also, to keep his secret forever. He said nothing.

In the streets, people were rumbling and demonstrating, infuriated by the disgraceful peace that had been achieved. On March 26, defying the provisional national government that Bismarck's orders had brought into existence, they held their own elections and produced a radically Republican municipal council, which called itself "the Commune of Paris."

On March 27 Henriette weakened still more. The entire family gathered in her bedroom and, one by one, went forward to kiss her and murmur a few words.

"Never wish you are not what you are," she said to Marc, who stared at her face, where gray and white and yellow lay in blotches, as on a palette. Then she added, "Never forget you are a Vollard."

To Gabrielle she said, "Raise your child as a Vollard. Please."

Gabrielle hesitated only a moment. "But I am doing so, Grand-mère."

Henriette sighed. "I never learned to like you, but you have done things correctly, and for that I thank you."

She beckoned Nicolas to lean closer. "I have loved you," she said. "Do you believe that?" He stroked her cheek. "But I have never understood you. If you have done what I asked, it was always for your own reasons. I should liked to have understood you."

In a moment she added, "I should have liked my sons to be happy."

They all marveled that she, who had always wanted to preserve decorum in life, should abandon it for truth in the face of death.

Suddenly she fretted at the covers with her swollen hands. "Where is Louis?" she said with surprising strength. No one answered. No one knew. "He must forgive me. I did what was best for Louis. Tell him that. Find him, tell him, make him forgive me . . . " She took a breath that rattled in her throat like peas in a shell, and died.

Nicolas's eyes were wet, but Joséphine was the only one who wept, covering her tight mouth with a black handkerchief.

Chapter Twenty-Two

Paris was red. Red with the flag of its Commune government, red with the increasingly left-wing fervor of those supporting that government, and for one week in May, when the conservative government in Versailles sent its troops to confront the communards, red also with fire and blood.

"We should not have come back," Joséphine said, pacing her drawing room. Although it was warm, the double velvet drapes were pulled tight, struggling to silence the sounds of rifle shots and screams but able only to muffle them. "Mother Vollard would not have wanted her death to bring about our own."

"We are not going to die," Nicolas said.

"How can you know? Those madmen in the streets, shouting for a new social order, burning the Tuileries—the palace, Nicolas, they have burned the palace!—what will stop them from tearing down our door and burning this house?"

"We are not grand or symbolic enough. They prefer public structures."

"But we have wealth and position! They call us the enemy. Oh, this is much worse than '48, much. How can you be calm about it?"

"I am not," Nicolas said. "But there is nothing to do."

"You are the man of action. You must be able to think of something."

"When it comes to money, yes. Not when it is a matter of passions."

Joséphine darted a look at him and went on pacing. "Thank heaven Denis is at home. I hope Marc is too. The National Guard has become a hotbed of radicals. I cannot understand why Marc joined it, or how you allowed him to."

"He did not ask my advice."

Joséphine's eyes beseeched the ceiling. "If he is out there now with the Guard . . . if he has become one of those communards, who oppose all that this family has achieved . . . His painter friends encourage him, of course. He should stay away from such people." She stopped. "Did you say something?"

"Only that the more things change, the more they stay the same."

"If only they do stay the same! If only we are not destroyed!"

"It serves no purpose to agitate yourself this way, Joséphine."

"How can I help it, with gunfire outside the windows?"

"True." Nicolas gave her his full attention, as he seldom did, and watched the pacing that swayed the bustle of her dress, the clenching hands, the teeth tugging her lips. "But you seem to grow more and more nervous with the years."

"I am concerned for the future of this family. With Mother Vollard gone, and you indifferent to every kind of social consideration, a great deal of responsibility falls upon me."

"Isn't that what you wanted? Isn't that why you married me?"

She stopped and looked at him, her neck and forehead turning red. "Oh, you do not understand such things. You never will."

"I pray you are right."

She started to speak, but through the muffling of the drapes came a volley of shots, eerily like the popping of champagne corks. She gave a little scream. "Go and make sure all the doors are properly locked. Please, Nicolas, do this for me. I do not ask for many things, but I beg you to do this, so we are not all murdered in our beds."

Nicolas frowned and would have refused, but there was real panic in her eyes. And it was true: She never asked him for anything, except money. He put down his paper and left the room.

On the streets, pressed ruthlessly by the Versailles regulars, the communards fought like the savages they had been called all along. They took hostages, executed them, shot down monks, killed the archbishop of Paris, burned the Hôtel de Ville.

One morning, as a band of them was trying to regain control of a certain street from the regular army, a man emerged from a café and stood blinking in the sunlight. For several minutes he watched the action intently, as if it were a lamppost against which he could steady his vision. Then, with a cry of "Liberty! I shall fight for liberty again!" he stepped into the street and joined the communards. They were too busy firing and dodging fire to notice or care that his gait was unsteady or that, despite his peasant trousers and smock, his demeanor revealed he was not a worker like them, and never had been. He had no rifle, but someone plucked one from a fallen man and put it into his hands. He carried it oddly, more like a broom than a gun, but fired it nonetheless. Once he hit an enemy soldier in the leg and shouted, "Long live the Charter!"

As the fighting grew more desperate, the communards were driven from one street into the next and reduced to fewer than a dozen men. The regulars from Versailles moved into the center of the street, rifles spraying. The man was crouched behind a barricade. A younger man beside him raised his head to peer around, then jerked back violently, blood welling from his eye. He started to groan, the sound like a rusty hinge in the wind.

The regulars, who had won the street, began rounding up survivors. Fear lunged at the man like an animal out of the brush, and released his bladder. He began to shake. Beside him, the young communard with the bleeding eye ceased groaning and lay still. The older man crawled partway under his body, as one might burrow beneath bedcovers, and tried to lie without moving, but the uncontrollable shaking of his own body agitated the dead man's as well.

Two regulars came by, testing corpses with their bayonets. "That one is moving," said one of them. "Over there, lying atop the other."

The man thought his heart would give out, but only his consciousness did; he fainted. The bayonet plunged all the way through the corpse's chest and several inches into his own forearm.

When he revived, the pain was as sharp as fire. The street was silent, although gunfire and shots could be heard nearby. At length he extricated himself and stared around, dazed. "Long live the Charter?" he whispered, beginning to realize where he was: in 1871, not 1830. Clutching his bleeding arm, he started toward the only place he could think of to go. It took him two hours but seemed a lifetime, for everything he had lived through swam disconnectedly in his mind, like leaves and twigs in a swollen river: his children, his wife, the mistress he had loved, the unknown woman who, at some unknown time, had given him the disease that now caused his headaches and fevers, and all the sights he had seen since leaving Paris—Italian villas and lakes, vineyards along the Rhine, plantations, New England churches. He wept as he moved along.

Finally he reached the street he wanted, and the door, but could not make himself walk up to it. He slumped to the ground against some bushes and sat staring at the knocker as the fresh blood welling from his arm joined the mass already caked on his sleeve. When the door opened and a figure appeared in the light, he thought he was dreaming. But he called anyway, "Nico . . . "

"What a shock you gave me," Nicolas said the next morning, when Louis's eyes opened and gazed at the flowered hangings of the bed they had put him in. "Joséphine sent me to check if the doors were locked. I opened them and found you."

"If she had known what you would find, I doubt she would have sent you."

Louis smiled, and Nicolas smiled back, feeling the identity of that gesture stretch between them as it always had, even though with age his brother's face had grown still more unlike his own; even though Louis's skin was as rough as if he had been working at it with ragged fingernails, and his lips were redder by contrast with a short, pointed beard in which gray and black mingled.

"Twelve years, Louis," he said. "I feared I would never see you again. What has brought you back?"

"In Florence I saw some Paris journals. I read that Mama had died. Suddenly I had to make sure the rest of you had survived all that has been happening. I have been here for two weeks, trying to find the courage to see you."

"Why would you need courage?" There was no answer.

"The last letter I had was nearly two years ago, from London," Nicolas said. "Where have you been since then?"

"I went to America for a while. You should go, Nico. The South needs rebuilding, now that the War Between the States is over. And they are covering the whole country with railroads. Nico . . . how is Marc?"

"He is well. Gabrielle too."

Louis sank back into the pillow. A spasm of longing twisted his face. "I must see him . . . once . . . But I shall not stay. Do not let Joséphine or Denis tell anyone about me. As soon as I have recovered, I shall leave again."

"For where?" Louis was silent. "Do you need more money?"

"I lived all last year year without touching my allowance."

"Don't call it that. It is money you earned."

Louis raised a sardonic eyebrow.

"Are you earning money from your paintings, then?" Nicolas asked.

"I value them at their worth, which is to say I throw or give most of them away. Do not frown, Nico. I am not very good, you know."

"You are certainly not bad."

"True. But for a painter, to be not bad is to be . . . nothing."

"You evaluate yourself too harshly."

Louis smiled without mirth. "Surely that is the last thing to be said about me."

"Are you going to tell me how you got that wound in your arm?"

Louis sighed. "Fighting for the communards."

"Good God, Louis! They're out to destroy the city. They even tried to burn down the Louvre! Have you become a Red and don't give a damn?"

"I am no more Red than you are," Louis said. He turned away. "It was only a . . . misunderstanding."

Nicolas leaned forward. "Are you all right, Louis? I must know."

"I am fine. Well, I have the sickness. The syphilis. But I have seen doctors and taken their damned mercury, so perhaps . . . " Louis shook himself. "I am fine. You see . . . I have fallen in love."

"Have you? I am glad for you." Nicolas said it automatically, over a spurt of the feeling he had not known for years: the envy of Louis for his passions, however misguided or destructive they turned out to be; for his willingness to surrender to them. "Are you happy, then?" Suddenly it was the most important question in the world. Louis had put behind him all his mistakes, everything that tortured him; he *must* be happy, for both of them.

"Sometimes I am," Louis said. "I am in love with . . . absinthe. It is so cool and green and beautiful, like the sea. You slide down into it, and you lose . . . Do you remember the summer when Papa and Maman took us to the sea?"

Nicolas had not thought of it in fifty years, but now the scene was as clear as yesterday: the pale green water of the bay, he and Louis churning it to foam and laughing until their bellies hurt, then running back to the beach to build a huge structure of sand. He closed his hands and felt the cool, wet grittiness beneath his palms, which stung with the pleasure of smacking against it . . .

Louis said, "I was with the communards because I had been drinking. In my mind it was . . . long ago. I went into the streets because I was going to fight for . . . something, and this time I was going to do it right. But I didn't, Nico. I was terrified. So terrified . . . "

The brothers were silent. Then, as if the connection were so clear it needed no statement, Nicolas said, "Maman's last words were about you. Find Louis, she said, and make him forgive me."

"All my life I did what she wanted. But I do not think I can do that."

"I think you will have to forgive yourself first."

Louis's eyes filled. "No one will ever understand me as you do, Nico."

Nicolas covered Louis's hand with his own, and the brothers' gaze locked in the ship-to-lighthouse look of their youth.

"What will you tell him?" Gabrielle said. "You know he will ask."

"Perhaps not." Marc pulled on an old jacket he wore when he went sketching. "Papa and I are old hands at not asking about the things we want to know."

Gabrielle, in a green dressing gown cascaded with lace, sat on the chaise in her boudoir.

"If he does ask," Marc said, "I shall say she is our daughter, and nothing more. Would you have me say anything else?"

"No." Gabrielle's body twisted, as if with a sigh she could not release.

Marc sat beside her. "From the moment you said you were pregnant, I have had no regrets. Have you?"

After a moment she said, "No." She dug her hands into the cushion of the chaise.

"Why did you hesitate?"

"No reason." She could tell Marc many things, Gabrielle thought, but not that there were days when she felt like a mouse in a velvet trap, which got softer and tighter each time she tried to lift out a paw.

He said, "Do you sometimes want to leave, Gaby?"

"Leave?"

"Are you not tired of being the beautiful, respectable Madame Vollard, who gives the most knowledgeable musical evenings in Paris and has a perfect life?"

She looked directly at him and pushed her nails deeper into the chaise. "Sometimes. But where could I go? Back to being one of those sopranos who depend on people like me to engage them for an evening?" Or back to Jeanne and Nandou, she thought, after the warnings they had given her about her marriage? Back to admit they had been right about so many things? Never. "And even if it were possible to return to the stage," she said, "how could I leave Simone?"

Marc sighed and squeezed her shoulder.

When he was at the door, she said, "You don't look as you did when we first came back. During the siege you were happy. Can you not be happy again?"

He hesitated. "You imagine things, Gaby," he said and left.

She stood up and began to pace between the chaise and the fireplace, eight steps, back and forth. She and Marc were good friends, but in her life—as in his, she presumed—were large tracts of privacy. What had he done during the Terrible Year of the siege when she was out of the city? What did she know of his desires, which had no outlet in their marriage? She knew what happened to her own, the things they had led her to do, the tensions they strung along her veins, but what of his?

She reached the fireplace and spun sharply, swinging the skirt of her dressing gown; if the lace had been bells, she would have rung in a dozen tones. How could one know a man's heart without the closeness of physical intimacy? Or even with it? The one man who had made her feel passion, whose embrace she could recall in every detail if she allowed herself to, but she would not—what did she truly know of him? She thought of the communion between her mother and Nandou, which had intrigued and puzzled her when she was a child; she still did not understand it. What did one have to do or know in order to be certain one understood another human being?

Order had been brutally restored to the streets. The Bloody Week was over. Government troops had taken the last of the communards to Père-Lachaise, lined them against the walls, and shot them. The forty thousand captured earlier had been marched to Versailles, to meet God only knew what fate: at its kindest, deportation to the penal islands.

Order at all costs, Marc thought. He felt sympathy for the communards—not because of their goals and methods, which alienated him, but because of their savage suppression, which mirrored his own private struggle: crush and break the uprising of feeling he had known with Octave, exile it, execute it. Restore everything to respectability, put out all fires, so not a wisp of smoke hung in the sky, not a scrap of charred paper blew in the wind. He had allowed himself to go to the café in

Montmartre only once, and then only to peer in and see that Octave was there, unharmed. He left before Octave could turn and see him.

When he reached his uncle's house, Nicolas was not there. His aunt Joséphine, her mouth a radish of disapproval, took him upstairs. As Marc followed, he looked at the thin blades of her shoulders and the resolute motion of the bustle on her brown print dress, and wondered what gave her joy: her house? her son? her social position? Even at a party, even when she was laughing, a strong vertical line lay at the bridge of her nose like a pin anchoring the wings of her brows. She seemed to live with the imminent possibility of some further uncertainty or scandal, which only her vigilance could fend off. Why was respectability so crucial to her? Marc wondered. Could she too have an inner Darkness? For a moment he felt a surge of pity for her, but they had reached the door of a second-floor room, where she stopped and said, "It would be more convenient if Louis had gone to you and Gabrielle, but he insists on staying here. He says he does not want to trouble your family, but what about this family? And he won't have a doctor in, although that may be just as well. Nicolas and I have had to do all the nursing. Perhaps you can persuade him to go with you."

Marc shrugged and opened the door.

His father sat in one of two chairs by the window. He was dressed but held his right arm outside his shirt sleeve. Despite all that Nicolas had told Marc, he was unprepared for how the elegance had crumbled, the handsomeness raddled.

"My boy," Louis said. He rose and held out his good arm.

Marc went to him. They embraced with an awkwardness due only partly to Louis's wound and then sat down.

"You have a beard, Papa." A foolish thing to say, but it was a small plug with which to begin filling the gap of twelve years.

"My dear son . . . " Louis blinked and looked at him as if picking his way among a dozen thoughts. "Every year I hoped to read that something of yours had been selected for the Salon."

"I have not submitted anything."

Louis's brows rose in his high forehead. "You did not even show in '63, at the Salon des Refusés? Why not?"

"Because I had nothing good enough."

"What do you have, then? Tell me."

Even as the answer came from him, unplanned, Marc thought how like the two of them it was, that they should be speaking of painting first, as if nothing else mattered as much. "I am more skillful than I was when you left. Composition and modeling—I can now manage them to my satisfaction. But the color—there is some mystery at the heart of the color that I cannot solve, cannot reach. I feel as if my brain and my brush are trying to go deeper, deeper—almost through the canvas, but they never get there. Something always lies just beyond their grasp. Sometimes what I do is close to what I want, but never close enough. I throw much of it away."

Softly Louis said, "You would not come without something to show me?"

Marc smiled; he might have known his father would guess. He went into the hall for the case he had brought, which held three canvases. Two of them he propped on the floor against the armoire: one of a pensive old woman who wore a red scarf and was about to bite into an apple, the other of a younger woman, laughing, pulling ribbons from a box and running them through her fingers like water. Louis's eyes, darker and brighter than when Marc had come in, went from one to the other in a long silence. Then he began to talk of technical matters: the brushwork, the use of cadmiums, the lack of varnish, the skill with which the figures dominated the space. Marc responded impersonally, though he felt the pulse building up in his neck. Finally Louis sat back. "I have seen nothing quite like them. They are unique. And good."

Marc felt the color flood his face in relief.

"But you are right, they are struggling. Like a horse at a crossroads, reined in while the rider peers about for direction."

"It is good to talk to you, Papa," Marc said slowly.

"I think you have brought something else in your case. What is it?"

Marc took it out and put it in front of the others: a small canvas of Simone, her hair a mass of curls, gazing out at the world as if she could not wait to grow up into its wonders.

"Ah," Louis said and smiled. "The light on the hair is splendid. And on the skirt, there, the way you have—"

"She is your granddaughter," Marc said.

Louis's hand stopped in mid-gesture, then fell back to his lap. "I don't understand. You and Gabrielle said there would never . . . I have been able to live with the fact of your marriage only because . . . How can I take joy in the existence of this child?"

"Papa, I swear to you she is not the child of incest. I swear it, and then I beg you to ask no more questions."

Louis closed his eyes. The sun had crept across the window and now struck his face, glittering on the faint stubble on his cheeks. He blinked and shook his head. "I must ask one thing more. Are you and Gabrielle happy?"

"We live . . . contentedly. And you, Papa?"

It was some time before Louis answered. "I have accepted what I am, and what I am not."

"Then you are fortunate," Marc said.

When Henriette was alive, the Vollard clan had gathered to celebrate the anniversaries and birthdays that marked its passage through the years and to figuratively close ranks over the chairs where first Edmée, then Louis, had used to sit. After Henriette's death Joséphine insisted that the tradition be kept up, so on each occasion they gathered at the home of the relevant member. On holidays they went to Joséphine's, where Nicolas presided over the table with a detached, ironic smile.

On a May Sunday in 1872, Simone's tenth birthday, they were all at Gabrielle and Marc's, nearly twenty of them. The day was warm and the sky cloudless, so the children played in the walled garden while the adults, except Marc, who wandered off by himself, sat on chairs and benches beneath a chestnut tree, talking desultorily of the political stalemate that had followed the repression of the Commune. While the monarchist groups in the National Assembly fought each other bitterly and the Republicans hoped for the balance of power to fall to them, the country was in limbo. "They are starting to laugh at us in London, I can tell you," said cousin Blaise, who had just returned from a trip there. "Nearly two years without a responsible government!"

"Think what we are thus doing for the English sense of superiority," said Nicolas. He sat with his legs outstretched and his hands behind his head and seemed totally relaxed, but his eyes moved back and forth over the party, settling often on Gabrielle, who was dressed, like Simone, in lacy pale yellow.

The older child of Sophie and her husband Victorien ran past the adults, chased by her brother and Simone, all of them shrilling with laughter.

"Where do they find the strength?" murmured Blaise's wife, Florine. She suffered from a series of odd ailments, vaguely diagnosed as "nerves," and was currently being treated by hydrotherapy.

The conversation continued languidly. Even Joséphine relaxed, until Victorien made a passing reference to the communards. Then her eyes narrowed and she said, "They ruined Paris! Have you forgotten the streets churned up as if an earthquake had hit, the telegraph wires hanging like strings, the place de la Concorde turned to rubble? God knows what would have happened if those radicals hadn't been stopped!"

"I believe the more accurate word is 'crushed,'" said Nicolas.

"All of that is behind us," said Sophie, ever a conciliator.

"The fighting, yes," Joséphine said, "but Paris is more full than ever of people with radical ideas."

"Surely ideas never hurt anyone, Aunt Joséphine."

"My dear Sophie, ideas can send people to the streets, to the barricades. The wrong ideas will undermine society if we are not careful."

"I am sure you will keep us from exposure to all ideas," Nicolas said mildly, "except the correct ones."

Gabrielle looked over at him and smiled.

"You may be as ironic as you like," Joséphine said, "but there are hotbeds of radical thought everywhere. I am sure Marc hears Communist ideas all the time from his painter friends."

Gabrielle said, "Painters discuss painting, Aunt Joséphine."

"Then why is that Courbet person in prison for fighting on the side of the communards? And look what kinds of aesthetic ideas such people have. They place the most disgraceful subjects on a canvas—sweaty peasants in a field, a naked woman lunching on the grass . . . "

"Oh!" cried Sophie in relief, "Here are the drinks!"

As two servants came out with trays of lemonade and tea and ice in coolers, Joséphine patted her mouth with a handkerchief and sat back. The children emerged from the paths as if the clink of glasses had been gongs. They sat to one side on the grass, eating little sugared cakes and drinking thirstily, at first looking to the adults for amusement and then resuming their own conversation.

"Maman took us to the circus," said eight-year-old Annabelle importantly. "There was a huge bear who stood on a little ball and didn't fall off."

"Maman is going to take me to the theatre to see Sarah Bernhardt," Simone retorted.

"We went to the theatre," said Annabelle. "We saw fairies and dwarfs."

"What are dwarfs?" asked six-year-old Maurice.

"Don't you remember anything?" Annabelle said. "Dwarfs are people who look as if part of their legs and arms have been cut off.

"Cut off?" Maurice squealed. "CUT OFF?"

"Not really," Annabelle said, "but it looks that way. Dwarfs are funny-looking. They walk like this." She jumped up and began walking exaggeratedly, rocking from side to side. "I am a dwarf," she said, "Dwarf, dwarf, dwarf!" Maurice rolled on the grass laughing.

"Stop that!" Simone cried. "You don't know anything about it, Annabelle."

"Yes, I do. We went to the theatre and saw a dwarf, a dwarf!"

"You don't know ANYTHING! I'll pull your hair if you don't stop!"

Joséphine turned to Gabrielle to protest, but Gabrielle's face held such an odd expression that Joséphine said nothing.

"Annabelle, dear, come sit down," said her mother Sophie, but the child continued her chanting and lurching. "Dwarf! Dwarf! Dwarf!"

"Stop!" Simone cried wildly. "Dwarfs are smart and clever. They rode on the wind and killed the giants! I know! I go to visit a dwarf and you don't!"

"Simone!" Gabrielle said. She went to her daughter and grabbed her hand. "Sit down at once and be silent. And you, Annabelle, stop that."

"What tales you tell, Simone," said Joséphine. "It is all those books your mother allows you to read. I am sure you have never gone to visit a dwarf."

"I have too," Simone said passionately. "His name is Nandou. He is the king of the wind, and he knows how to—" She stopped, looking stricken, then closed her mouth and bit her lips. Her face turned red; she buried it in her mother's skirt.

"It is not a tale," Gabrielle said calmly. "I took her to visit some old theatre friends who seem to have made quite an impression. Would anyone like more tea with ice?"

Amid the murmurs of "No, thank you," Nicolas's eyes remained fixed on her.

"I dreamed of ragout last night," Jeanne said.

Edmée, Nandou, and Henri nodded in understanding. The deprivations of the siege lay over a year behind them, but they were still not quite able to take the phenomenon of plenty for granted. The four of them were dining together for the first time, in Edmée's apartment. She had prepared a ragout of veal, and Henri had brought wine and beer.

For a few moments they all ate in silence, savoring the food. Then Jeanne returned to the theme she had been sounding. "It is over fifteen years since I wrote *Louise Bernier*," she said. "Since then I have written four other plays, every one of them dealing to some extent with the hypocrisies to which women are subjected. But I see virtually no improvement in women's lot. They still cannot attend a lecture at the Sorbonne or get a *baccalauréat*."

"My dear," Nandou said, "the theatre cannot change the world. It can only make living in it more exciting."

"What about *Hernani?* Didn't that change the world?"

"It changed only the theatre," Nandou said, "and only for a while. In some respects the world will never change, especially its hostility to whatever is new and different. Remember when Romanticism was the shocking and hated thing? Then it was Realism, and now it is Monsieur Zola and his Naturalism."

"Are you trying to tell me the only reason people hate his sordid stories about wretched creatures is because they are new and different?"

"My love," Nandou said, "would I ever try to tell you anything?"

Jeanne sniffed. "The ragpicker's daughter did not learn to read in order to read stories about trash."

Nandou merely smiled.

Jeanne ate more ragout. "The law about secondary education for girls was passed four years ago, but how many such lycées are there today? Perhaps it is time to do something about these situations other than play-writing."

"What would that be?" Henri asked.

"Do you realize that if a woman does not wish to reside where her husband dictates, he can legally compel her to do so? That even if they separate, she needs his signature for all her business affairs?"

"Good heavens!" Edmée's fork clattered to the table. "If Louis knew where I am, he would be able to control the way I manage my money. Not," she added, "that I think he would want to."

"But he would have the right."

"Careful, Jeanne," Henri said. "You will crush any hope I had of persuading Edmée to marry me."

"Marry!"

Edmée retrieved her fork and shook it at Henri. "I have told you many times that even if the complications of my identity did not exist, and even if divorce were legal, I would never marry again."

"Here, here," Jeanne said. "Why should a woman be the property of a man?" She turned to Nandou. "Would you want to own me?"

His upper lip twitched. "The idea has a certain attractiveness, I find."

She made a face at him and turned to Henri. "There are clubs that work for women's rights. One might join them or write for their journals. You could write for them too. That is, if you believe in the cause."

"Have I not established my credentials," he said wryly, "by providing part of the inspiration for *Louise Bernier?*"

"I should like it," Edmée said, "if neither of you ever again mentioned what happened all those years ago. I no longer think of it, so why should you?"

"You were the victim," Jeanne said, "not one of the executioners."

"For heaven's sake!" Edmée said. "Do we not have enough to worry about—the future of our poor children—without reliving the past? If you two do not take a vow this moment to forgive and exonerate each other . . ."

"Yes?" Henri touched her hand.

"There will be no dessert."

"Swear, Foucher, swear!" Nandou said in a tragic voice.

Henri laughed. "All right. I swear it."

"Jeanne, you must swear as well," Edmée said, smiling, but not joking.

When Jeanne was silent, Henri pushed aside his plate. "Very well. Let us say what needs to be said. Jeanne, you once conceived a plot, which I executed. For each of us there were unintended consequences. I fell in love with my victim, and when she was arrested, I believed I had destroyed the happiness I had only begun to realize I wanted. I went to Italy, thinking it would be easier for her if I were not here. I never expected her to be sent to prison, you see. In any case, I could not have pressed my suit without confessing that I had approached her in the first place at your behest, Jeanne. If she knew that, how could she love me? Still, I could have stayed in Paris and tried to help her." Jeanne nodded. "You are right, of course," Henri said. "I have had years in Italy to accuse myself in exactly those words. But I accused you, too, Jeanne. You should have told me you intended to betray us to her husband."

"I should never have done any of it!" Jeanne cried.

"Stop!" Edmée said. "Give me your hand, each of you. There. Now clasp those hands and swear to each other, and to me, that you will allow the past to lie in peace, as the dead should."

Jeanne looked at Henri across the span of their extended arms. "Why is it so damned hard to forgive?"

"Because it is not each other you are trying to forgive," Nandou said. "It is yourselves."

Jeanne's gaze swung to him. How did he know, when she had not said a word to him about it for years? She had simply accepted the silent burden of regret for actions that could not be undone.

Henri smiled ruefully. "In the name of the love I feel for Edmée, I promise to look only to the future."

"I share that love," Jeanne said, "and shall try to share the promise as well."

"Let us drink to that," Edmée said. She was beaming.

How strange, Jeanne thought, that it was she who, in effect, had chosen Edmée's life partner.

Henri put down his glass and looked from her to Nandou. "May I ask whether the two of you ever considering marrying?"

Jeanne shook her head. "No."

For a moment it appeared Nandou would not answer. Then he pulled a hand through his hair, still long and coarse but now quite gray, and said, "In the beginning I would no more have dared to think of it than of playing Rodrigue in *Le Cid*. And when I began to wish it were possible, I saw that the only hope of keeping Jeanne lay in forswearing all claim to her." He leaned forward, clapped his hands, and said, his voice closing the subject, "Now, Edmée, where is that cake you have been promising us?"

Later, when they were back in their own apartment, Jeanne came from her room, brushing her hair, and stood before him as he sat in the dining room, reading. "Nandou, did you mean it? You wanted us to marry?"

"For a long while, yes. I told myself it was for Gabrielle's sake, but that was only part of the reason."

"Why did you never say anything to me?"

"To avoid the pain of hearing you say no."

She sighed. "And the other part of the reason?"

"I wanted the very thing you would object to most—to make you legally mine, to own you so that the chance of your leaving me might be diminished."

She looked at him, pulling the brush through her long hair, sending tiny points of light crackling into the silence. "I think I understand you as much as one human can understand another," she said at last, "but there is always something I never knew."

He smiled. "A magician must continually have new tricks."

An hour later, lying beside him, she said into the shared, sleepy warmth, "Do you still want to marry?" There was no answer. "Because if you do . . ."

He shifted against her. "No."

"Why not?"

"There is too great a pleasure in holding you by no means other than your wish to stay."

She smiled. They drifted into sleep.

It was the thirtieth anniversary of Nicolas and Joséphine's marriage, and they were giving a party that Joséphine had spent weeks planning. The floor of their large salon shone beneath the feet of dancers, the women making brilliant, oddly shaped sails that swung out from the black-and-white masts of the men. People played at cards in several smaller rooms, and tables of food and drink seemed to be everywhere. Joséphine's doll-face was flushed beneath the mass of curls at the back of her head—her own plus a pound of someone else's—and her hands made constant nervous journeys over the brilliant blue silk of her dress, trimmed with yards of ruching and white rosettes and draped in back over a bustle, which mimicked and magnified the shape of her hair. She darted from one group of guests to the other, but after a few minutes' conversation she would look around asking, "Where is my dear Nicolas?" He, his sandy brows thicker and his square jaw more pronounced than when they had married, was wearing formal dress, with a white brocade waistcoat. He too circulated, listening more than speaking and seldom staying long with any one group, excusing himself with polished skill. Sometimes he danced, as expertly as any man in the room, partnering the wives and daughters of men with whom the House of Vollard did business and also his female relatives—except Gabrielle, who refused him three times, saying she was already engaged.

She was the most beautiful woman present, slim and graceful in yellow satin, black hair swept up behind a fan-shaped comb of pearls and ivory that Marc had given her on her fortieth birthday, the previous year. As he had done at so many other affairs, Marc watched with equanimity while admirers clustered near her. She had a way of holding back from them even as she seemed to be inviting them closer, and they responded to the contradiction as if to a challenge they must resolve, but never did. Sometimes her laugh could be heard above the chatter in the room: clear and musical yet not quite natural, like a glass harmonica.

Around eleven o'clock she felt the pressure of a strong arm on her elbow and turned to see Nicolas. "My dear," he said, "I am sure your friends will allow your uncle to take you away for ten minutes if he promises to return you in the same beautiful condition in which he finds you." If she wanted to protest, she had no chance, for he guided her smoothly and firmly toward a windowed alcove and onto its velvet seat.

"I needed fresh air," he said.

"This window is closed," she said, not quite looking at him.

"I mean the fresh air of a kindred spirit who is not dazzled by surfaces but recognizes the emptiness they can hide."

"Why do you give this party if you feel that way?"

"Perhaps for the same reason you attend it."

Gabrielle lifted her fan but said nothing.

"You have been avoiding me since Simone's birthday," Nicolas said.

"We have seen each other at half a dozen dinners and parties since then."

"At all of which you avoided speaking to me alone."

"Why on earth would I do that?" She rested her chin on the folded fan.

"Why indeed," Nicolas said, "when we are such friends."

They were silent. In the distance the small orchestra played a waltz from an Offenbach operetta. "I sang in that once," she said with a touch of wistfulness. "Years ago."

"Yes, let us speak of the past. Gabrielle, I heard what Simone said that afternoon. Others heard it, too, but I believe I am the only one to whom it meant anything. You know Jeanne Sorel and Nandou, do you not?"

She shrugged. "Yes. I never mention it in this family, knowing how you all feel about the author of *The Trial of Louise Bernier*."

"Are you sure you know how I feel?"

"What do you mean?"

"I have met Jeanne Sorel and admired her greatly. I still do, although I have not seen her in many years. I have always liked you," he added, as if it were not a non sequitur. "I like you not only for yourself but because in a way, at times, I have seen in you touches of Jeanne Sorel. Until the afternoon of Simone's birthday, I assumed those touches of similarity to be accidental."

"I don't understand," Gabrielle said.

"How do you know Jeanne Sorel? What is she to you?"

"She is . . . a friend."

"No more? Gabrielle, take that damned fan from your face and answer me."

There was no disobeying Nicolas's voice when he chose to be authoritative. Gabrielle lifted her chin and looked at him.

"Ah," he said. "The chin . . . " He stared at her. "Jeanne Sorel and Louis were lovers. They had a child. Are you that child?—the Solange I met so many years ago? Am I your uncle by blood as well as marriage?"

Gabrielle's eyelids flickered as if a bright light were hitting her. She put up a hand to smooth her hair, then let it fall to her lap, palm up.

"You are that child," Nicolas said. "Do not be afraid to admit it. I will be more sympathetic than you can have any reason to imagine."

He put his hand over hers. She looked down at the squared fingers, then up into the gray eyes. "Yes," she whispered. "I am."

Without moving, they sat for several moments looking at each other, he absorbing the confession, she trembling with the relief of making it. Finally she opened her mouth as if to say something. But she was stopped by the figure now in her line of vision.

"Nicolas, dear," Joséphine said. "I have been wondering where you were." She spoke too brightly, and her cheeks were as red as if a madwoman had applied her rouge.

Chapter Twenty-Three

The woman had known better times—she had even been the mistress of a government official once—but for several years she had lived by her wits, which were not the keenest. Possessing a pretty face and neat figure, she tried to take up with some of the students who filled the Latin Quarter and also to find work as an artist's model, hoping a liaison would result—if she were lucky, even a marriage. But often she was forced to work in brothels. Her name was Albertine Fossey, but she called herself La Grande Carlotta in the hope that, although she barely spoke the language, painters would take her for an Italian.

She arrived early at the model market and stood in poses she hoped would attract attention: hands on her hips, clasped beneath her chin or behind her. But no one singled her out, so she gave up and wandered slowly back to the street where she lived. The cafés were full and noisy, but she was starting a headache, so she decided to go to her room and lie down. As she climbed the stairs, past Belloc's studio, she hesitated but decided he was probably away. He had hired her several times. Once he sent her out afterward to buy chops and bread and wine, and she had stayed the night. He was not interested in liaisons, at least not with her, but he was amusing and not unkind.

By eight she was asleep on her narrow bed. When a knock came, she struggled out of unconsciousness as if it were deep water. Throwing on an old shawl, she opened the door. "My God," she said. "You? What do you want?"

The man came in quickly and shut the door behind him. They talked for a few moments, until with a swift, sudden motion, he twisted her arm behind her. He pushed her to the bed and shoved her onto it, facedown. He pulled a scarf from his jacket and managed to tie it over her mouth. A long, muffled moan came from her, but he seemed not to hear it. He lifted her skirts from behind and undid the buckle of his trousers. She lay still, except for a trembling she could not control, while he satisfied himself.

When he had finished, he untied the scarf and wrapped it around her throat, pulling it tighter and tighter. Her arms and legs flailed wildly and uselessly. Once they stopped, he retrieved the scarf and put it in his pocket.

After his breathing slowed, he went to the single window. He sat there for several hours, looking out, never back at her body, which remained face down, bare buttocks gleaming beneath the raised skirt. When the sky was completely black and the noise on the street had lessened, he opened the window wider, stepped out, lowered it behind him, and made his way over the roofs.

"My dear," Nandou said, regarding Jeanne across the breakfast table, "a look comes over your face sometimes that, as unfailingly as the cock heralding the day, signals your launching some course of action. I imagine you had that look on the day you went off to the theatres by yourself to find a job as a callboy, but I hadn't seen it enough to recognize it. Now I have lived with it for many years, and I see it again this morning. What are you contemplating?"

Jeanne tapped her paper, a small journal issued sporadically by a society devoted to women's rights. "I am contemplating this article. Two months ago a woman—a grisette at her best, a prostitute at her worst—was raped and murdered in the Latin Quarter. Not only have the police failed to find the man who committed the crime, they barely made an effort to do so. Because she is poor and female, her death merits no attention."

"It is reported in that journal," Nandou said.

"Which neither the police nor the general public reads."

"So, what do you plan? An assault upon Sûreté headquarters? A new play to dramatize the lot of this poor victim?"

"No. An article about her, perhaps. If I take it to one of the better journals . . . the one that printed my pieces on divorce . . . Or should I approach one of those gossipmongers who like to chronicle my eccentricities? . . . 'J. Sorel takes up cause of murdered prostitute' . . . ?"

"Your day will be full, then. I shall spend mine at the theatre. The

Divine Sarah is rehearsing, and my old friends will let me sit in the back and watch."

"What kind of look?" Jeanne said.

"What do you mean?"

"What kind of look comes over my face?"

"Ah." Nandou folded his arms. "It lies somewhere between attack and ecstasy. The eyes narrow like an archer's sighting prey, and the mouth grows fuller and more ripe, as if to be kissed or bitten. Or perhaps to bite."

Jeanne laughed. "I do not think I like it."

"I do. But to whoever is its object, I say, beware."

Jeanne leaned forward. "And there is a look I have come to recognize on your face—it appears when I speak of working for the rights of women."

"What kind of look?"

"As if you share my views but have a reservation you keep to yourself."

"It is not a reservation."

"What, then?"

"An observation." She waited expectantly. "My love," he said, "I believe you are trying to do more than make the public aware of the inequalities of women's lot. I believe that in some way you are still seeking atonement for what you have done to two women you love very much—Gaby and Edmée."

Jeanne rocked back in her chair.

"I may be wrong," he said.

"And if you are right? Do you suggest I should not write the kind of plays I have written, or do the things I am now planning?"

"Not at all," Nandou said. "I only wish you to be at peace with the past."

Deputy Chief Labat of the Sûreté looked from a pile of journals on his desk to the faces of three inspectors. "The situation has passed beyond annoyance," he said. "For weeks the vultures of the Republican press accuse us of neglecting our duty. Now they claim we abandoned the case because of its victim." He lifted a journal. *"Is Fossey's Death Unavenged Because of Her Life as a Woman?* Such charges are ridiculous, erroneous. They must not go unchallenged."

The three inspectors nodded, as if it were a common occurrence to devote the full resources of the Sûreté to the death of an obscure prostitute.

"Advise me what has been done to date," Labat said.

One of the inspectors took out a folder. "Fossey, or La Grande Carlotta, was not seen in the cafés for several nights before her body was discovered. That was on June 3. Clearly she had been raped and murdered in her apartment, several days before, but there was no evidence to indicate by whom. The door had not been forced, and the room held nothing but the woman's own paltry effects. The concierge had seen no suspicious strangers entering the building."

"What of the other tenants?" Labat asked.

"On the ground floor is a sculptor who was away for several weeks during the time of the crime. On the second and third floors are a retired wine merchant and his wife, two sisters who sing at the *café chantant* in the next street, three students, and a waiter. Above them is a painter who went to Provence for the summer and is still there, and on the fifth floor, besides the victim, live two other prostitutes. Not a promising field of suspects."

"Hmmm," Labat said. "Two artists in the building."

"Didn't the victim work as an artist's model?" asked the second inspector.

The first consulted his notes. "Sometimes, according to her friends."

Labat brightened. "Did she ever pose for either the sculptor or the painter in the house?"

"That information is not in the file."

"Then get it. That is the line to pursue, gentlemen. Find out if either of the artists belongs to these new radical movements or has friends who do. Such people are a dangerous lot, who might well have committed our crime."

"If so," said the third inspector, "the journals clamoring for justice will not be pleased. They do not want the guilty man to be a radical, like them."

"Justice does not permit us to pick and choose," said Labat righteously. "The case has been assigned to an examining magistrate, and we will work under his orders. Use your best men, and bring me results soon. Soon!"

For several days teams of officers questioned the tenants of the victim's building again and canvassed the cafés, shops, and buildings surrounding it. By the end of the week the inspectors could offer Labat a more encouraging report:

"Fossey, who incidentally had a reputation for embroidering the truth, never worked for the sculptor, according to her prostitute friends. However, they say she did pose several times for the painter, one Jules Belloc."

Labat tapped his desk. "That is of little consequence if the painter was in Provence when the crime was committed."

"True, though we do not know just when he went to Provence. In any case Belloc has artist friends, at least one of whom has keys to his studio. The concierge believes the friend was in the building the day of the murder."

"Believes? Is she not certain?"

"She has arthritis and drinks brandy for the pain. But she says the friend was in the building that day, and will so swear to Magistrate Foucault."

"Very good," said Labat. "Now tell me more about this man."

"Look, Maman!" In their carriage Simone and Gabrielle were passing a pile of blackened walls that, before the Commune, had been the Tuileries palace. Unlike the rest of the devastation, it had not been cleared or restored. A laurel tree stood near the rubble, and on the grass a bird-charmer had set up his cages and was taking out his flute. "Maman, can we not stop and see the birds?"

"No," said Gabrielle edgily. "I do not care for birds."

"Do you know, Maman, I have noticed that. Why don't you care for them?"

"I lived with one for many years, that is why. And don't ask me about that, Simone, not this afternoon, please. Besides, there is no time to stop."

"Are we in a hurry? Where are we going shopping?" When her mother did not reply, Simone sat back. At thirteen, she had a curiosity she could not control—she always saw and heard things that made questions pop into her mind—but she had learned to keep them to herself if her mother was impatient or her father busy or her governess unable to answer. Nandou always answered her questions, no matter how many, but she didn't see him that often. The same was true of Great-Uncle Nicolas, now she thought of it. Once when she was at the firm, he had taken her into his office and explained what they did at the House of Vollard and answered every question she asked. He told her she could have a head for business, if she liked; why had he said that? She looked out the carriage windows and wondered why men dressed in the same black coat and trousers whereas women abhorred to look like one another; why her mother was not interested to hear her play the Mozart sonata she had learned, or anything else, for that matter; where a bird-charmer kept his birds at night; why some people got excited when they said France should have a king, not a president; why her father had looked so odd that morning, as if his face were a mask being pulled too tight.

As the carriage turned a familiar corner, her eyebrows and her spirits rose. "Maman, you did not tell me we were going to visit Jeanne and Nandou."

"I just decided it," Gabrielle said, still edgy. "We will not stay long."

Simone smiled, despite the twinge of guilt she still felt for having spoken of Nandou at her birthday celebration three years before. That evening her mother had scolded her harshly and threatened not to take her again. She had had to plead tearfully and swear never to repeat her mistake—and she had not.

Jeanne was wearing an old red *robe de chambre* and smoking a small black cigar. "Good heavens," she said when she saw them, and began waving the smoke away. Simone could not help staring: Why would a woman smoke cigars?

Jeanne stopped her waving in mid-air. "Ah, what does it matter? Let the child know my vices. How are you, Simone dear?" She held out her arms, but before Simone could go to her, Gabrielle took Jeanne's elbow and steered her away, across the room, saying, "I must talk to you, Maman. Something has happened."

"So," Nandou said to Simone. "We are abandoned, you and I. No matter. It will be easier to discuss important matters this way."

He reached over as if to adjust the ruching at the neckline of her dress; instead he produced a small red flower and handed it to her with a low bow that was exaggerated but elegant. "Now tell me," he said, "what is important to Simone Vollard on this glorious September twentieth of 1875?"

She regarded him happily: the dark, brilliant eyes in the nests of fine lines her father would call "cross-hatching," the head too large for its body—or was the body too small for its head?—the high brow that was smooth although the hair falling over it was gray. She had questions for him, but the one that came blurting out was nothing she had been thinking on the ride over. "Why must I never tell anyone that I visit you and Jeanne?"

He pursed his lips. "Best if you ask your mother that question, I think."

"I have. She said there will be trouble if people find out. But what sort of trouble? Would people not like it because you are a dwarf?"

Nandou gave a little grunt and crossed one leg over the other. "Perhaps. Some people never want anyone or anything to be too different from themselves."

"But if things are never different, how can they be new and exciting?"

Nandou laughed, his skin crinkling like a strange, wonderful fabric. "An excellent question, which many adults lack the sense to put to themselves." Simone flushed. There were two people whose praise always made her cheeks tingle: her father and Nandou. "However," he went on, "do not assume that everyone wants things to be exciting. Many prefer them to be familiar and safe."

"I do like some things to be familiar," she admitted, "like Bijou and pear tarts and my room. But I should also like one exciting thing to happen every day. At least in a book."

"Now you have said something wise. Why do we read and go to the theatre, except to have excitement as a constant in our lives?"

"What is the most exciting thing you have ever read or seen on stage?"

"There you ask a difficult question," he said, "for so much depends on one's age, the state of one's life, even one's country . . . When I was young, it was the English playing Shakespeare and the opening night of *Hernani*." She nodded, for he had told her of the battle of *Hernani*; Jeanne had joined in, the two of them yelling and hurling bits of bread and cheese around the room. "When I was older," he said, "to tell you the truth, it was being onstage myself, in *The Dwarf Lord*. But now . . . " His eyes began to glow. "Now it is to see Sarah play *Phèdre*. There is greatness for you. She acts with her whole body. I have never seen a *Phèdre* like hers. No one has! The desire she feels for her own stepson, which racks her in every gesture, the guilt over that desire— they are so real they tear out your heart, and at the same time they are so grand, so far beyond the ordinary emotions . . . Look, the gooseflesh appears on my arms just at recalling the performance. To see greatness, Simone, to be drowned in it, is one of the most precious things life can offer. If you ever—"

There was a loud knock at the door. Simone jumped, and Nandou's eyes came back to the room with a sharp blink.

Without waiting to be answered, the door swung open and in rushed the Rose Lady. Simone gaped at her.

"Jeanne!" the Lady cried. "A terrible thing has happened!"

"I know," Jeanne said. "Gabrielle has been telling me."

The Rose Lady stopped and stared almost comically at Gabrielle, then looked around the room and saw Simone. "Simone . . . " she said, her voice fluttering like birds' wings. Then she took a grip on it and went toward Maman. "Gabrielle," she said, "I am delighted finally to meet you. I have heard about you for many years. I am an old friend of your mother's, a distant cousin, Aimée Sorel . . . "

Beside her Simone heard Nandou give an explosive "Pah." She struggled to understand what was happening. Did the Rose Lady know Jeanne, then? Was she herself to pretend she did not know the Lady? She heard her mother uttering the sort of polite phrases she used when there were guests for lunch or tea.

But Jeanne's voice interrupted. "Enough, Gaby! Isn't it enough for all of us? Haven't we lived enough years with secrecy and sham?"

"Bravo," Nandou said.

Gabrielle stood as if a magician had struck her into lifelessness.

Jeanne said, "Can we not acknowledge the connections that exist among us and join us? Can your disastrous news not free us to speak honestly?"

"What news?" Nandou said.

The Rose Lady gave a sob and covered her mouth with a handkerchief.

Jeanne said, "Marc is under suspicion for the murder of Albertine Fossey."

"Dear God," Nandou whispered.

"Why did we ever seek justice for that woman?" the Rose Lady said. "Is God punishing us, Jeanne?"

"Please!" Gabrielle cried. "Remember Simone."

Four pairs of adult eyes turned on her. Four mouths trembled with words they seemed unable to say.

Finally Nandou spoke. "Simone is not a rare plant in a hothouse. She is a sensible girl, who should not be protected from the reality of things by adults who do so in an effort to protect themselves."

"Nandou, she is only thirteen," Gabrielle said.

"When your mother was that age, she left everything she knew and came with me into a strange new world. Thirteen is an age when a child can be a woman, if she has to."

"Please," Simone said, feeling as if she were in a carriage with a runaway horse, "please, Jeanne, what did you say about Papa and murder?"

Silence. Her mother came to her, swung the long train of her dress aside, knelt, and embraced her. "A woman was killed in a place where Papa sometimes goes to paint. The police think Papa killed her. They are wrong, of course, and soon they will realize it. But in the meantime, we are all very upset."

"How can they imagine Papa would do such a thing?"

"Because they are desperate to say they have found the guilty person, even if they have not."

"But that is stupid," Simone said. "How can they be so stupid?"

No one answered her.

"I cannot bear it," said the Rose Lady. "How can I have helped to bring such a disaster on the head of my own son?"

Gabrielle released Simone and rose slowly to her feet. "Your own son?"

"Yes," the Rose Lady cried. "Jeanne is right—let us speak honestly for once. I am, I was, Edmée Vollard. You are the daughter-in-law I have never been able to claim, and Simone is . . . Simone, I am one of your grandmothers."

"And I am the other," Jeanne said.

Simone could not speak or even gasp; no breath would come.

Beside her Nandou said quietly, "Perhaps there can be too many exciting things in one day, eh?"

The news of a suspect in the Fossey killing pleased nearly the entire spectrum of opinion in the press, although for different reasons. The gossip writers reveled in the discovery of yet another scandal in the family that had inspired *The Trial of Louise Bernier*: more rot in the same pillar of society. The literary journals saw in the whole sordid affair further proof of the decadence of the times and the nation. The radical papers applauded because the suspect was a member of the wealthy bourgeoisie—quintessentially, of a banking family. The liberal journals approved because justice was seen to be impartial and even-handed. The conservative press, however it disliked seeing the name Vollard linked to such an unsavory crime, turned the issue to the support of its own causes: The suspect was, after all, an artist—not one who had studied at the Ecole des Beaux-Arts and painted in the academy style but, rather, a friend of the modernist painter whose studio he had used on the day of the crime. If Vollard had not come under the influence of such men—whose politics were radical and whose "art" consisted of the incomprehensible, crude, and immoral daubs parading under the rubric "Impressionism"—he would in all probability have lived a completely respectable life and never committed such a crime.

As part of the process of *instruction,* which combined investigation and interrogation and could culminate in arrest, Examining Magistrate Foucault had not only weighed the evidence but gone to inspect the building, the victim's room, and Belloc's studio. He had observed the ease with which one could move between that studio and Fossey's room, and the presence in the studio of fabrics and scarves that would fit the physical evidence of the strangling. He had questioned the concierge, who said Vollard came often to the building, sometimes bringing a female model with him, occasionally even a child. She swore he had come on the afternoon of the crime, and she had not seen him leave. Magistrate Foucault had arranged for Belloc to be questioned in Provence. According to the report, he had been reluctant to discuss Vollard except to say, in "a loud, unconvincing tone," that only an idiot could think Vollard capable of either rape or murder, let alone both. Finally, Foucault considered two additional facts: Vollard had not arrived home until nearly ten that night and could produce no one to substantiate his claim of "walking the streets" until that hour; and, most interesting, a prostitute in a brothel where Fossey worked said a man of Vollard's description had been there some years before. She remembered him because he had "talked so oddly" and had been taken ill in the middle of the act.

On Foucault's orders, Vollard was brought to the interrogation room of Sûreté headquarters. Accompanied by his lawyer, he admitted meeting the murdered woman several times in Belloc's presence and insisted he had gone walking after leaving Belloc's studio on the day in question. But he gave few specifics of where he had gone, except "To Montmartre, to watch the lights come on at dusk." He was shown the shawl and skirt Fossey had been wearing when she died but exhibited no reaction. Without warning, he was confronted with the victim's corpse, which was disinterred after several months in the paupers' cemetery. Observed keenly for signs of guilt by Foucault, Labat, and two inspectors, he looked down at the bloated, faintly greenish skin, the dead-white nails that had grown too long in the grave, and the jellied eyes. He was silent and immobile for some moments. Then he shivered, put his hands to his face, and began to retch.

Nicolas and Joséphine waited in the drawing room, on a dark-green velvet sofa. She smoothed the skirt of her dress as if its stripes were crooked; he sat quietly. When the door opened on Marc and Gabrielle, Joséphine made as if to rise but sank back.

Nicolas went to them. "My dears," he said. He kissed them both and embraced Marc.

Despite the warmth of his greeting, when Marc and Gabrielle took the two tapestry chairs facing the sofa, the arrangement had about it an air of the courtroom.

"Thank you for coming," Marc said. "We wanted to prepare you for what may happen. It will affect the whole family, but I could not face everyone, not tonight."

"What is it that may happen?" Joséphine said.

"Maître Durand thinks they will arrest me, perhaps as early as tomorrow."

Joséphine cried, "Dear, sweet Lord."

Nicolas winced. There was a long silence.

"How can they do it?" Joséphine said. "Merely because you had met that . . . that creature and were in the building on the day she was killed?"

Marc said nothing. He was very pale, with dark patches under his eyes like chalk smears.

"Where *were* you that night?" Nicolas asked. "Why didn't you come home until ten?"

"I was in Montmartre."

"Doing what? Someone must have seen you, somewhere."

"I only went up to find out if someone I had once met was . . . still there."

Joséphine leaned forward. "Do you mean some woman? Some . . . prostitute?"

"No. A man." Marc looked at Gabrielle, who compressed her lips.

"I see," Joséphine said. "One of your artist friends, I suppose. If only you had never become involved with such people!"

" 'If only' could be said of many things, Aunt Joséphine." Marc was calm, like a man who has accepted his last meal.

"Was the man there?" Nicolas said.

"Yes."

"Then you must get him to tell the police, for God's sake!"

"I never spoke to him. I simply saw that he was there."

"You talked to no one else? No one will remember you?"

"I was . . . making an effort to keep to myself."

Nicolas looked puzzled but said only, "Whatever happens, I shall stand with you."

"Thank you, Uncle Nicolas. I am very grateful for your support."

"How should I not support you? You are my nephew, my brother's child. In his absence, I regard you as my son."

Joséphine started to speak, smoothed her skirt, then said, "There must be a way to clear yourself of this monstrous, unfair charge."

Marc smiled faintly. "You believe I am innocent, then?"

"How can you suggest I would think otherwise?"

"I am sorry, Aunt Joséphine. I do not mean to do you an injustice."

"We must find a way to clear you. We must! No matter the cost. If Louis Napoléon still ruled France, I am certain a way could be found. But now . . . " Her mouth worked and tears beaded in her eyes.

Marc breathed deeply. "If all else fails, there is a way that might convince the police of my innocence. But I could not take it, or even mention it to Maître Durand, without advising you, for its effect on the family could be . . . unfortunate."

"What is it?" Joséphine said.

The gaslight reflecting in Marc's eyes made them burn yellow, like a cat's. "If the police were to learn that I am . . . that I . . . "

"What is it?" Joséphine rose and fixed her eyes on him.

". . . that I am a man who would never commit the crime of rape because . . . "

"Of course you are not. But what will convince them?"

Gabrielle leaned forward. "This is very difficult for Marc to say.

Perhaps I can explain for him. He could not commit the crime of rape because—"

"No, Gaby," Marc said sharply. "It is for me to explain. We agreed on that." He gripped the arms of his chair. "The facts is . . . I am unlike other men. I do not engage, or wish to engage, in physical intimacies with women. I have no desire to do so."

Nicolas gave a long sigh, sad yet relieved, as if he had finally grasped the key to a cipher.

Gabrielle said, "I would confirm to the police that what Marc says is true. They must accept the word of a man's own wife, must they not?"

"I do not understand," Joséphine said, as if she did. Her face went red, not in circles of color on her cheeks but all over, as if blood was rushing to every possible portal.

"I am the kind of man," Marc said, "for whom the name is . . . sodomite."

Joséphine fell back onto the sofa as if she had been struck.

"I am most desperately sorry," Marc whispered. "You cannot loathe me more than I loathe myself."

For some moments they were silent, Marc's eyes moving wretchedly among the three of them, who were each deep in inner contemplation.

"I am sorry too," Nicolas said at length. "Tell me, did your father know?"

"Yes."

Nicolas sighed again.

"If you knew what a relief it would be to confess," Marc said softly, "to stop pretending . . . "

"You cannot tell that to the police." Joséphine's voice was loud and sharp. "You cannot tell it to anyone, Marc, ever."

Gabrielle said, "He will not do it unless there is no other way to prove he would not commit the crime of which he is suspected. We would hope Maître Durand could then persuade the police to keep the matter in confidence."

"You would hope!" Joséphine cried. "The journals have reveled in the fact of Marc's being a suspect. If they should learn this, the family's reputation would never recover. Think of what your grandmother would say. In her memory, if for no other reason, you cannot do it. Nicolas, tell him he cannot."

Nicolas put his hands to his eyes. "It is not my decision to make,

Joséphine, or yours. It is Marc and Gabrielle's. However," he said to them, "I am bound to point out that if you do tell the police, they still may not accept Marc's innocence. Because a man does not prefer women, it does not necessarily follow that he could not commit the crime of rape."

"It does if the man is me," Marc said with uncharacteristic savagery.

Nicolas hesitated. "Do not forget, the police will consider that you have fathered a child, which fact they will take as proof that your disinterest in women is not total."

Gabrielle and Marc turned to each other; neither spoke.

"Unless," Nicolas said, "and pardon me, but I can find no other way to put this . . . unless you mean to tell the police that you have never engaged in conjugal relations?"

"No," said Marc, at the same time as Gabrielle said, "Yes."

"Stop, stop, stop," Joséphine said. Her hands ran along her skirt like frightened animals. "You cannot tell the police. If you tell them, if you tell anyone this, this unspeakable thing about yourself, I shall tell Simone the truth about her parents. I shall tell her she is the child of incest. Yes, look at me as if I were a viper, all of you, but the viper is you, Gabrielle, because you are the daughter of Jeanne Sorel, who has brought so much damage upon this family. I have known it since the night of our thirtieth anniversary party, when I heard you admitting the truth to Nicolas. For three years now it has been stuck in my throat, like a dreadful bone I can neither swallow nor spit out. Now I see that God gave me the knowledge so I might make use of it one day, and I shall. I swear it. I shall tell Simone. Consider what the knowledge will do to her, to her future and her prospects. Do not imagine I will not do what I threaten. If you declare yourself to be that . . . that dreadful thing, I shall see that the Vollards sever all connection with you and your unnatural wife and child. We shall tell the world that we renounce you utterly, and the world will welcome our action. Yes, I would do it, make no mistake."

"Joséphine!" Nicolas said, his voice a sword.

She turned on him, tears leaking down her cheeks. "I know what you think of me, Nicolas, what you have always thought. To you I am only a foolish woman whom you tolerate and smile at behind her back. But what is so terrible about wanting a decent, respectable life for my son and myself? Why do you damn me in your heart, for I know you do, merely because I want to be accepted by society and thought well of? What is wrong with a life of order and peace and respectability? If you knew what it was like to be the child of poor relations, to get your clothes, your food, your piano lessons, your very breath it often seemed, from the charity of the Daudets . . . your own father's people, yet they looked down their noses at you and your mother . . . If you had sworn every day of your childhood that when you were grown, no one would ever again look down on you or on anyone you loved, that your son would never feel as you had felt, that you would become more respectable and well regarded than any of the Daudets with their sneers and their noses, their long noses . . . " She put her head on the arm of the sofa, sobbing.

Nicolas looked down at her, helpless for once. "Come," he said at length. "I shall take you home." He turned to Marc and Gabrielle. "My children, I truly do not think it wise for you to tell the police what we have been discussing. I do not think it will help you, Marc. There will be another way to clear you. We will find it. I swear we will. Maître Durand is an excellent man. Come now, Joséphine," he said, lifting her to her feet. She sagged against him like a bag of sticks.

After they made their way out, Marc sat heavily on the sofa. "What irony," he said. "Aunt Joséphine thinks it is worse than incest—this thing that I am. No doubt most of the world would agree with her."

"We could have told her there is no question of incest," Gabrielie said slowly.

"And have to tell her the entire story? Which she would then threaten to tell Simone?"

Gabrielle sighed.

Marc put his head in his hands, thinking of the deeper irony that Gabrielle still did not know: He could have said to Joséphine, "But Gabrielle and I are not half-sister and brother. She is the daughter of Louis Vollard, but I am not his son." He could not bring himself to say it, however. He never had been able to.

"Marc," Gabrielle said hesitantly, "what Aunt Joséphine said . . . about my mother . . . You must have been shocked." He lifted his head. She was twisting her hands together. "I wanted to tell you so many times," she said. "But your family hates her so bitterly . . . how could I . . . I thought you might feel . . . "

"It doesn't matter, Gaby," he said. "I might have been shocked, once. But not now."

"No? No, you are right. But how strange—something I have worried about all these years, so much, and now it simply . . . does not matter."

"Nothing matters except tomorrow, and the police."

Gabrielle went to him and embraced him as if he were a child, stroking his curly, light-brown hair. There were hints of gray in it, she saw. She leaned against him, and they sat for a long while, supporting each other.

Chapter Twenty-Four

Nandou walked along the boulevard Prince-Eugène, looking at ghosts.

There, where a new apartment building stood, had once been the theatre in which he had made his first appearance, as an elf. A little farther along, what was now a tobacconist's had used to be the stage on which he had performed his magic act so many times. Two doors down—or was it three?—had been the site of *The Dwarf Lord*. Surely, if he turned his head, he would see the plebs queuing up for tickets, or the actors rehashing everything at the foot of the fountain in the square and then trooping to the little bistro around the corner for supper at two in the morning; or, if he faced the boulevard itself, he would hear the cacophony of vendors' cries and see a dwarf standing beside a pan of sizzling fritters. *Oh buy them hot, eat them sweet . . .*

Years before, in 1862, it had all been leveled to make room for the new Paris. On a mid-July day he and Jeanne had joined the crowds of plebs to watch an impromptu Farewell to the Boulevard, to see the great mime Deburau's son play Pierrot dressed in black, and simply to stand on the street and feel its raucous, bursting vitality. *This is my home,* Nandou had been thinking, when Jeanne turned to him and said, "I shall always remember it as the most exciting place on earth." Some people had recognized him; they had shouted "Hola, Nandou!" and *"Vive* the Dwarf Lord!" A lump had come into his throat and refused to be cleared away. The next day there were auctions; he had purchased a property sword and a gilt chair. Then the demolition had started. By Christmas there had been only level ground, over which Napoléon III and Empress Eugénie had driven in state and renamed the boulevard after their son Prince Eugène.

In truth, Nandou thought, he had hated Louis Napoléon as much for his destruction of the Boulevard of Crime as for his tyranny. True, the theatre flourished elsewhere, but for him its heart had been cut out. He sighed, contemplating the passage of time. Now the man who wrote a militant preface to a new play, throwing down the gauntlet to his critics and demanding truth in the theatre, was not Victor Hugo but Emile Zola—who said Romanticism was false and the drama should reveal the beast in human beings and portray the drab life of every day. "Naturalism," he called it, and said it was "scientific." But what did science have to do with the truth of the heart, which wanted glory and beauty?

"Do you need some help?" said a voice.

Nandou looked out of the past and saw a youngster, no more than Simone's age, regarding him with interest and concern.

"What do you mean, help?" he said as forcefully as he could, although in fact he was leaning heavily on his stick, aware of another sign of the passage of time: finding it difficult to catch his breath because the pain was flickering in his chest. It came every now and then; his heart would boom in his ears more loudly than ever, protesting. But who didn't have pains, with age? Whenever this one started, he faced it down by going out for a walk, to prove who was master. His legs didn't like that, but they could not be allowed to dictate, either. All his life he had fought the limitations of his body. He would not stop just because he was seventy-two.

"You look as if you should sit down," said the youngster.

"If I need to sit down, I will," Nandou said. But it was wrong to be sharp with a boy who had a kind smile. "I thank you for asking," he added.

The boy studied him with a curiosity unmarred by meanness of spirit. It reminded him of the way Jeanne had looked at him from the garbage heaps, and of Simone, who in ways was so like Jeanne at thirteen that his heart quivered with the memory of being captured. "Have you not seen a dwarf before?" he asked.

"Yes, I have," said the boy. "In the theatre."

"Is that so? I was in the theatre."

"Were you?" The boy's green eyes lit up. "My brother is second leading man and my uncle is grand first comedian in all categories."

"Ah. Where do they play?"

"Why, in our theatre in Belleville."

"What theatre is that?" The boy looked amazed. "Suppose we sit on that bench," Nandou said, "while you tell me about it."

When they were settled, the boy talked of plays that sounded like those of Nandou's youth, and of a theatre where they were enacted by the old hierarchies of performers. The boy said he knew of similar theatres in other suburbs but believed his own to be the best; in his naïveté, he assumed that all Paris must know of it. Questioning him, Nandou felt his breath grow stronger and the pain in his chest flicker out. He began to feel not only normal but splendid, for the boy's words meant that the Boulevard of Crime, although dead, had been migrating into the suburbs, that neighborhood theatres were springing up to perpetuate the old melodramas. He cursed himself for not having known it—he who always knew everything about the theatre; he must be getting lax and foolish with age. He smiled as the boy chattered on about an old play that fashionable Paris would consider hopelessly out of date. In many respects it was, but somewhere, up in the hills of Belleville, people were still being excited by it.

"So old things can still stir the blood?" he said to the boy, who looked at him quizzically. Nandou laughed. "You do not understand because you are young, and the young do not have to understand. Go home and ask your brother and uncle if they have heard of the dwarf Nandou, and if so, say that he presents his compliments. Say he presents them even if they have not heard of him, for all of us in the theatre belong to the same great fraternity."

"Nandou," the boy said reflectively. "I'm sure I have heard your name."

"And yours?" When the boy gave it, Nandou shook his hand, and from their grasp he pulled a coin. The boy gaped. "It's yours if you bring me a carriage," Nandou said. The boy flew off.

He should walk, Nandou thought, but he wanted to be home at once, telling Jeanne the strange, wonderful fact that, no matter how the times and the theatre had changed, no matter how "scientific" it might be to change with them, the boulevard of their youth was being kept alive by the plebs on the outskirts of Paris. He imagined how she would laugh and clasp her hands, how the net of little lines in the corner of each eye would tighten as if it had captured a fish. The events of his life, great or small, were savored best by their reflection in her eyes and on her face. The two of them would have dinner and talk and talk, and lie in bed in the warm and wordless communion that was stronger than language and, sometimes, even than desire.

The boy returned with a carriage. Nandou climbed in without too much difficulty, ignoring the driver's stare. "Remember the camaraderie of theatre," he said, saluting the boy, and sank onto the cushions. The boulevard Prince-Eugène and its ghosts receded, and he rocked along, smiling with an inward look, wondering how the young dwarf beside the fritter-pan would have felt if he could have known how full and rich was the life ahead of him.

After a few blocks he shook himself. One must not become an old man who nodded in the sun and looked nowhere but behind him. "Stop at the next news-vendor," he told the driver. He would read the latest about the Third Republic, which finally had tottered into a proper existence after nearly three years of wrangling in the Assembly; one could only pray it would last longer and do better than its predecessors. Why was liberty so easy to lose and monarchy so hard to dislodge? Because men too easily grew accustomed to being told what to do.

As the carriage slowed, he heard a news-vendor crying, "Son of House of Vollard Arrested for Murder of Prostitute!"

He thrust out a coin, grabbed two of the journals, and took out the spectacles he had been forced to adopt. The motion of the carriage made reading difficult. "Can we not go any faster?" he asked the driver.

Twenty minutes later he climbed the stairs, panting, and flung open the apartment door. Jeanne and Edmée sat grim-faced, a journal on the table between them. "You know, then," he said.

Jeanne nodded. "We are trying to decide what to do."

He went toward them. "You have already done so much."

"Yes, have we not?" Edmée said. "We have ruined our children's lives."

"I don't mean that." Nandou sat between them. "Since you heard Marc was a suspect, you have been working hard to make your own inquiries into the crime."

"Without success." Jeanne's eyes glittered, yet were dull. "If you are right, if I was still trying to atone for the past, I have succeeded only in destroying the future."

"Do not say such things! Neither of you is at fault. You sought justice for a fellow creature. You could not have known Marc would become involved."

"I should have known!" Edmée cried. "It happened in the building where the painter Belloc lives, and Marc used to go there frequently."

"Did you know he was still going there?"

"No, but I—"

"When was the last time he mentioned Belloc to you?"

"Oh . . . not for years, that is true. But . . . If only Jeanne had never started a crusade for that woman, if only I had not joined in!"

Today there would be no reasoning with them or comforting them, Nandou saw.

"We must do something," Jeanne said. "We must and we will!" Over her face came the look Nandou knew well.

It took Gabrielle only three minutes to mount the stairs, but it had taken her a week to decide to do so.

Dressed in a simple dark skirt and yellow shirtwaist, she told the concierge, who was new to her, that she was going up to work as a model. As she climbed, her heart pounded, and knocked so loudly when she stood before his door that it hardly seemed necessary to use her knuckles on the wood.

Silence. She raised her hand to knock again, but suddenly the door was pulled open and he stood there, in a paint-stained smock and rumpled trousers.

His eyebrows rose. So politely that she could not tell if he was mocking or sincere, he said, "Madame Vollard. I wondered if we should ever meet again."

"Hello, Belloc. May I come in and speak to you?"

He pulled the door wide. "You find my quarters in their usual state of chaos. I have been working since the light came. What time is it?"

"Nearly two," she said.

"No wonder I am starving." He went to a cupboard, rummaged, and produced a half-loaf of bread, some cheese, and a bottle of red wine. He cleared space on a small table and said, "Want some?"

"No, thank you." She sat on the corner of a bench and looked around at the clutter, which seemed not to have changed in the years since Marc had first brought her there; even the stuffed owl, she would swear, sat in the center of the same shelf. On the easel was a portrait, in its early stages, of a black-haired woman in a red hat. The strange thing, Gabrielle thought, was that she had never particularly liked Belloc's work. When she turned to him, he was chewing slowly on a piece of bread, watching her. He was older, of course; so was she. His presence, as forceful as ever, had not changed. Had hers?

"A man could paint you in that outfit," he said.

"No. He could not."

He smiled. "You are still the most beautiful damned woman in Paris."

"You must know I didn't come to talk of such matters."

"Yes. But a painter cannot help seeing what he sees."

"He need not speak about it."

Belloc poured wine into a cloudy glass. "Perhaps you are right."

"In any case," Gabrielle added in spite of herself, "you see beauty in every woman, don't you?"

"Some more than others." He laughed at her discomfiture.

After a moment she said, "You know that I came to speak of Marc."

"Of course."

"I'd like to know . . . I need to know what you told the police."

"Not a great deal. I told them what little I knew of Albertine Fossey—that she was a sad little thing, not too bright, trying to portray herself as more than she was but only making herself seem less. I said that I have known Marc for over twenty years and that the idea of his killing her is absurd. I did not go into the details of my friendship with him. I could not see that doing so would advance the case for his innocence. Would you have wanted me to?"

"I don't know. Sometimes I think . . . No, I suppose not."

"Besides, a fellow artist is not a particularly good character reference. The police, like the public, think we are all ex-communards or decadents, or both. I could do Marc more harm than good."

"Can't you find some way to help him? They may very well find him guilty of something he could not possibly have done. And if they do . . . "

"It will be the greatest injustice I know of."

"Then can you not stop it?"

"How? If there is something you want me to do, Gaby, tell me and I shall do it at once."

She closed her eyes. What she wanted was for him to know what to do. Everything had seemed to come unraveled with one sharp tug. Marc was in prison. Jeanne and his mother were desperate. Joséphine believed Simone to be the child of incest. The one good thing was that Gabrielle's years of hiding her own heritage were over: She had told Joséphine—in a loud and angry conversation—that she would visit her mother and Nandou as often and openly as she liked. But for once they were no comfort. And Simone, poor Simone . . .

She opened her eyes. "Marc told me the police know he brought a child here sometimes. He admitted it was Simone."

"I wanted to see her," Belloc said, as if his wish were all that mattered.

"No more," she said sternly.

"How is the child?"

"She is bewildered and upset by all that has happened. Supposing she had come with Marc on the day of the murder? That would have been disastrous."

Belloc reached across the table and cupped a giant hand around her cheek and chin. "Don't be angry, Gaby. Gabrielle the beautiful."

She felt herself trembling. "Let me go, Belloc."

"You ask difficult things of me. You always did."

"I should not have come."

"A pointless thing to say, since you are here." He stroked her cheek. "You came solely in Marc's behalf?"

"Belloc . . . please let me go."

"I exert no pressure."

"I am a woman who has made foolish choices in her life and does not wish to compound them."

Belloc looked at her for a time, then took his hand away and said lightly, "As always, I obey your wishes." He finished his wine in a gulp and rose. She could see that his eyes, and his mind, were already returning to the easel.

"So you can do nothing to help Marc?" she said.

"Beyond what I have done, no. I wish I could."

"I shall say good-by then, Belloc."

"Good-by, Gaby."

"Don't show me out," she said. "I know the way to your door."

He inclined his head in silence. Just before she left, she looked back. He was already in front of the easel, lifting his palette, sinking into the oblivion of the painter, where the world was bounded by a rectangle of canvas and his own inner visions.

On a crisp October day, Edmée put on the dress she had made just for the occasion—silk moiré, in the peach color that she loved but that "Aimée Sorel" had never worn. She made up her face, with the eye-brows and lip-lines she had nearly forgotten how to draw, and arranged her hair, which she had dyed back to blond the night before, completely off her face. The person looking from the mirror was someone she no longer quite knew: an Edmée Vollard who was older, certainly, but also something else. Stronger? Wiser? Happier? She thought that she simply looked . . . *more,* as if she had acquired greater substance, but not weight. She put on her eyeglasses, not only to see better but to give her a last tie to safety, and went out to get a cab.

"To the Sûreté, please," she told the driver. *I have no choice,* she told herself. She had been saying it ever since Marc's arrest.

If she had told anyone what she was about to do, they would all have tried to stop her. Jeanne would have marched around the room in agitation, warning her that she was placing herself in terrible jeopardy. That was true, but, as Edmée had argued to herself many years before, in the church of Saint-Sulpice, a mother had to do what she could for her child, no matter the consequences. Nandou would have scowled and said that what she was planning was by no means guaranteed to convince the police of Marc's innocence. Also true, perhaps; but how could she fail to try as long as there was any chance at all?

And Henri—if she had told Henri, she might not have been able to withstand him, for he had the greatest power to dissuade her. Having him in her life was a pleasure so keen, and so unexpected, that relinquishing it even for a short while seemed impossible. She could see the scene as clearly as if it had actually occurred: Henri putting his arms around her and saying she must not go to the police because he loved her and could not bear to lose her again, now that he had found her. "But I have no choice," she said to him in her imagination, over and over, as the carriage rolled down the asphalt streets.

There might have been a choice if she and Jeanne had been able to find the real killer of Albertine Fossey.

Assuming that Fossey must have known the man, because there had been no sign of forced entry into her room, they had gone to talk to the two prostitutes who lived on her floor, trying to find out about the men in Fossey's life. At first the women had been sullen and suspicious, but Jeanne had spoken to them in sympathetic, rather coarse words that had loosened their tongues. They said Fossey liked to hint that she had important lovers; she had even boasted of being the mistress, for a while, of an official in the Second Empire, someone in the bureau of the censor. He had been "crazy for her," but she had tired of him. When he refused to leave her alone, she claimed, she had stopped him by threatening to tell his wife of the affair.

"A censor is sure as hell no one to boast about," Jeanne had muttered, and then asked the two women, "Did you believe her?" One had raised an eyebrow, while the other shrugged and said, "Who knows? She liked to tell tales. Made her feel better. But it might be true." It emerged that Fossey had referred to the man only as "César" and had claimed she didn't dare mention his surname.

It was little to go on, but Jeanne and Edmée had marshaled what connections they had, through the theatre and the movement for women's rights, and learned that in fact there had been a minor personage in the censor's bureau named César, a man whose wife's family connections gave her the power to advance or destroy his career—a man who had survived into the Third Republic and become a well regarded middle-rank official in the Ministry of Justice. They had even gotten in to see him, on a pretext, but had left with nothing that would convince the Sûreté to investigate an official of its own ministry. Not on the second-hand account of a flimsy tale told by a woman known to embroider the truth. Not when they had Marc Vollard in hand.

There had been one last thing to try. The two prostitutes had given them the names of several brothels where Fossey had worked. Jeanne had gone to them—"No, Edmée, you must let me do it, for despite your intentions to the contrary, you would be so ill at ease that no one would tell you a thing." She had learned nothing useful.

No, Edmée thought, she had no choice, except to do what she was doing.

The carriage stopped at the Ministry of Justice.

Edmée presented herself at the office of Deputy Chief Inspector Labat but refused to give her name, saying only that she had important information about Marc Vollard. Soon she was facing a large, untidy desk and its occupant, a man with ginger hair and beard. She told herself to think of Simone, of the fact that the secrecy of all their relationships had been cast aside at last; that would give her strength. "I know something about Monsieur Vollard," she said, "that will indicate the extreme unlikelihood, if not the impossibility, of his committing the crime for which you arrested him."

"You have some new evidence, madame?"

"Yes. Well, it is not physical evidence. It is evidence of the spirit, I suppose one might say."

"Indeed?" Labat's voice was like the ice on the rink in the Bois.

"Before I share it, however, I require your assurance that it will be kept confidential."

"Madame, the Sûreté cannot give such an assurance, especially not before knowing the evidence that would be its object. I can say only that we do not release information unless it is in the interest of other parties, including the public, to know it."

That seemed as much as Edmée could hope for. She moistened her lips and began the speech she had rehearsed. "The truth, monsieur, is that Marc Vollard involves himself with women as little as possible. I speak of the . . . physical sense. The fact is that by temperament he is not interested in women."

"Vollard is a married man, madame."

"I believe his wife will confirm what I am saying, should you find it necessary to ask her. They have an . . . arrangement, he and she, and are certainly not the only married couple in Paris whose outward appearance belies the truth of their relationship."

"Indeed?" Labat said the word exactly as he had before.

"Monsieur, if Marc Vollard ever permitted himself to act on his inclinations, they would be toward the . . . toward his own sex. However, I can assure you that he does not act on them. He is far too honorable a man. He has committed no crime of . . . sodomy, but neither is he guilty, or even capable, of the crime of raping a woman. He is simply a man whom nature has condemned to an unhappy life, and if you are a good man, monsieur, as I believe you must be to hold so high a position in the administration of justice, you will wish to release him now that you know the truth of his nature, which I beg you to hold in confidence, the deepest confidence."

Labat made a spire of his fingers and regarded her above it. "How, madame, do you come to know what you are claiming?"

This was the most difficult part. Edmée shifted her legs; a moment of pride in their shapeliness came into her mind with mad irrelevance, followed by the stabbing thought that Henri might never again want to see them and run his hands along them. He would never accept her returning to prison, even for a day, to serve a sentence that his own action had helped bring about; the thought would drive him mad.

She removed her glasses, blinked, and said, "I think you will believe me when I tell you I am the mother of Marc Vollard."

There was some comfort in seeing that she had cracked Labat's impassivity. Amazement spread from his eyes across his other features. He leaned forward as if she were under a microscope, then sat back stroking his gingery beard. "Edmée Vollard," he said slowly, and after a moment, "I was a sergeant when you escaped from Saint-Lazare. You served only two months of a one-year sentence."

She nodded, although her fingers had gone so cold and numb that she could not feel the stems of the eyeglasses they held.

An expression crossed Labat's face that she could not decipher because it seemed like admiration, which it surely could not be. But he was saying, "Madame Vollard, I salute you. To place yourself within the reach of the law in an effort to save your son—one can only admire such devotion." He shook his head. "In this instance, however, one must regret the exercise of such devotion and wish that you had been able to devise a tale more convincing, and more useful."

"You do not believe me?" Edmée feared she might choke. "You think a mother would tell such a lie about her own son?"

"No, madame. But I think a son might tell his mother such a lie, in a desperate and futile hope that she would carry it to the police." Labat held up a hand to stop her protest. "Even if it were true, madame, I would not find it compelling proof of innocence. Rather, it seems further indication of a depraved nature, for a man capable of wanting to commit vile acts with someone of his own sex is surely capable of committing a vile crime against a woman."

Somewhere, someone was doing what Edmée wanted to do: scream. She turned her head to look, and realized the sound had come from her.

"Madame," Labat said, "it distresses me that you have come here, and that I am now obliged to reclaim for French justice one of its escaped fugitives, who has just given one of the finest demonstrations of French motherhood that I have been privileged to witness."

In his small rooms on the fifth floor of a building in the Latin Quarter, Louis Vollard drank bitter coffee and read the journals he had just gone out to buy. For days—perhaps weeks—he had had a fever and a headache so severe that one night he found his hands digging so deeply into his left eye that he feared they might rip it out, and did not care. But on this day the agony had cleared, leaving him with only a dull ache in the temples, so he had washed and gone out for some food and the journals.

As he read them, he almost wished to be back in the black state of fever and pain, for the news was dreadful. While he had been tossing on his bed, both his son and his wife—Edmée, after all these years!—had been taken to prison.

He pushed the papers aside, ran his hands over his beard, which had become chronically itchy, and looked around his rooms. They were cluttered with canvases and painting paraphernalia, which he seldom touched any more. He could have put it all away—should have done, perhaps—but it stayed out in full view. On some days it gave him hope; on others it reproached him. Four years earlier, after the debacle of his day with the communards—after his arm had healed, if not his spirit— he had left Nicolas and Joséphine's home, intending to go to Germany and then to Spain. But first he had gone to a Left Bank tavern famous for its forty casks of liquor, and the longer he had sat there, the more strongly Paris had called to him, as if whatever else he might have to prove or to learn about himself could be done only on her streets. To be in exile, yet still in Paris—that was a pleasing prospect. He had found the rooms the next morning and had seldom left the neighborhood since. For a while he had painted nearly every day and gone to a café at night. But the patrons were all younger than he, and better painters than he; and then the dreadful headaches had begun. He had the strange idea they were related to the syphilis, but he would not go to a doctor. Absinthe was better medicine than any they prescribed. He had not consulted one since a long-faced quack in London had given him mercury. True, the sores had disappeared after one recurrence, but doctors were a useless lot, masking their ignorance with a knowing manner. They had once told him Edmée would never have a child, had they not?

The knowledge that Marc was in prison knifed into Louis like one of the headaches. He thought of the granddaughter whose portrait Marc had showed him: the wonderful mass of her hair, so expertly rendered, the excited and innocent eyes, the smile curling her fine red lips. What would her future be?—with a father in prison and a grandfather whose only distinction had been to fail in two separate worlds, art and com- merce.

How had everything gone so badly wrong?

Slowly, like the lifting of a headache, like a gift from God, came the idea of how he could make everything right.

At the Quai des Orfèvres they made him wait while they summoned an official named Labat. Louis did not mind waiting; he had time, and now that he knew what he was doing, sitting for nearly two hours did not matter.

When he finally spoke to Labat, the man told him he would have to wait still longer, while various papers were signed and filed with the appropriate authorities. He passed the hours by walking slowly along the Seine, looking into the booksellers' stalls without seeing any of the titles. For a long time he stared down into the gray-brown water. The surface shivered with hundreds of tiny motions, but the depths seemed steady and calm.

At six o'clock he stood outside the gates of the prison.

At a quarter past six they opened and Edmée came out. Beneath her shawl he saw a dress of the peach color she had always favored. She looked around, blinking as if emerging into strong light, although in fact the sun was setting behind the prison with a cool orange glow. Louis was in her line of vision, so her gaze had to come to him. When it did, she angled her head, frowned, and said, in the kind of voice that hopes incredulity will cancel its object, "Louis? Is that Louis?"

"Yes," he said.

"They told me you had rescinded the old charge against me, but I don't think I believed them."

"It's true."

"But . . . why?"

"It was long ago, Edmée. I didn't want you to keep paying for it."

"Do you mean," she said slowly, "that the only thing required was for you to tell the police you were withdrawing the charge?"

"There were some bureaucratic procedures," he said, a bit defensively, "but Labat was anxious to cut through them for your sake."

She nodded. "He didn't want to put me back in there." She came closer to him. She was still lovely, despite her sixty-odd years. The lines in her face only made her skin seem like crushed ivory velvet. "Why did you come here now?" she asked. "Do you expect me to thank you?"

"No."

"Strangely enough, I could. What you did changed my life in ways that turned out to be for the better."

"Have you been happy, then?"

"Yes. I have. And you, Louis?"

"No." He hesitated. "Do you hate me, Edmée?"

"Why should my opinion matter to you?" Looking at him closely, she said, "Where have you been, Louis? What has happened to you?"

"I have been all over the world, learning that it is too late."

He hadn't intended to put things that way, but she looked at him as if she understood. "Do you know what has happened to Marc?" she asked.

"I do. I think I may be able to help him, Edmée."

"What do you mean?" she said sharply.

"If I am successful, you will learn of it. And if I am, perhaps you will hate me a little less."

"If you can help him, I would forgive you everything."

He felt tears start to come, and cleared his throat. "May I get a cab and take you wherever you wish to go?"

"No. A friend is coming for me. He will be here in a moment."

"Shall I stay until he arrives?"

"I would prefer it if you did not."

"I understand."

Edmée took a half-step toward him. "I loved you once, Louis. I truly loved you."

"I know. I am sorry I killed that love."

"Well . . ." she said uncertainly. "Good-by, then, Louis."

"Good-by, Edmée. Be happy."

He found a cab and gave it an address he had known for years but had never even said aloud.

At eight o'clock he climbed a flight of stairs and knocked on a door.

When it opened, he watched the slow change in her eyes: puzzlement surrendering to recognition, then to bewilderment. "You!" she said.

"Hello, Jeanne."

"I never expected to see you again in this life."

"Yet here I am."

"So I see. Why?"

"I came in the hope that you do not hate me."

She lifted her chin; he had forgotten the gesture, until it swept away the years, making her eighteen again and calling his own youth from the depths where it was buried.

"You appear at my door after more than forty years to find out whether I hate you?" she said.

"In part, yes."

"Very well. The answer is, I have learned that hate is exhausting. It leaves one no room for anything but feeding it."

"What do you feel then, Jeanne?"

"Astonishment at seeing you here."

"Jeanne, I am here because I wanted you to know . . . to believe . . . What I did all those years ago, the way I allowed things to end—that was foolish. It was a great waste of my . . . life."

From inside the apartment a voice called, "Who is it, Jeanne?"

"It's no one," she called.

Suddenly, terribly, her words struck Louis as true.

"Jeanne," he said, hearing the pleading edge in his voice, "I only came to say that you were the best thing, the one good thing, in my life. If I had had the courage to stand by the love I felt for you . . . " The sentence hung in the air, a sail on a windless day.

"But you did not," she said softly.

He bowed his head. After a moment he lifted it and asked, "Are you still with Nandou?"

"Yes. We are faithful to each other." He said nothing. "Have you been painting, Louis?"

"Yes, but too little, too late. I left Paris to recapture a dream and to make life easier for Marc and Gabrielle. But neither of those things happened."

She sighed. "Why did you allow our children to marry?"

"I did not think I had any choice."

"Poor Louis," she said, as if he were not there. "You never liked making choices."

"But I shall make up for whatever wrong I have done them."

"What do you mean?"

"Jeanne!" called Nandou's voice. "What on earth are you doing?"

"I shall be finished in a moment," she answered.

"I'll go," Louis said. "I only wanted to . . . to see you again, and to tell you that I did love you, Jeanne . . . I truly loved you."

"I know that. I am sorry for you, Louis," she said, as if amazed to realize it.

Of all the things she might have said, that was the most chilling.

"Good-by then," he said.

"Good-by, Louis."

. . .

At ten o'clock he rang the bell at Nicolas and Joséphine's.

As soon as he was announced, Nicolas came striding down the hall, arms held out in welcome. The brothers embraced each other wordlessly, for a long time.

Then Nicolas pulled away, full of questions—"Where have you been? Are you back in Paris for good? Have you been well?"—but Louis waved them off. "Not tonight, Nico. Tonight I am very tired. Give me just one glass of your best brandy and a bed, and tomorrow everything will be settled."

Joséphine hovered in the background, trying to put a good face on the fact of her disapproval, and then hurried off to have a room prepared for him. The brothers went into the library and sat before a fire that leapt and crackled yet was steady at its heart—like the Seine. The brandy was fire in Louis's throat but calm in his stomach. The two men talked a little, mostly of Marc's arrest and what the lawyer was trying to do for him. "It will be all right, Nico," Louis said. "I know it will be." But when Nicolas tried to bring up other subjects—when he said, "Marc has told us the truth about himself, which I understand you have known for years"—Louis shook his head and repeated, "Tomorrow, Nico. Tomorrow. I must go to bed now. Come and wake me in the morning early, before you go to the firm. Will you do that for me? Will you promise?"

"Yes, if you like."

"Thank you. Nico, do you know that I love you?"

"Yes, Louis. I too."

In the bedroom Louis sat writing for a long while. When he had finished, he wrote another, much shorter letter:

Dear Nico,

Your nature is so different from mine, praise God, that you will not understand what I have done until I tell you that it is for Marc and that I do it with a heart that is not only willing but, for the first time in many years, happy.

The enclosed letter is for the police. It contains my confession to the rape and murder with which Marc is charged. Whether it was prescience or merely luck that made me settle in the Latin Quarter, the fact is that I was there on the night of the crime, which will add credibility to the confession. As the brother I love, make it your sacred trust to see that the police get it.

Some day, when this dreadful business is behind Marc, tell him how much I loved him and how glad I was to be able to do this for him. Brother, forgive me, and think kindly of me sometimes.

L.

He addressed the note to Nicolas, enclosed the confession, and placed the envelope on the mantel. As he turned to his next task, a look of fear shivered on his face, then dissipated, replaced by calm and by the knowledge that there would be no more of the terrifying headaches. For almost the first time in his life, he realized, he had complete certainty that he was doing the right thing.

The next morning Joséphine rose early, determined to speak to Louis privately and urge him to help ensure that Marc told the police nothing of his perverted nature. She knocked at the bedroom and, when there was no answer, turned the knob. The door was locked, but she took out her keys and let herself in.

At first she did not realize that the object swaying lightly in the wind of her entrance was Louis's body, hung from one of the ceiling joists by a knotted sheet.

When the knowledge struck, her mouth opened in a soundless scream. She sank onto a carved chair and tried to keep her thoughts from sliding away unfinished as if each had hit a patch of ice.

At length she was able to steady herself. Averting her eyes from the body, she looked around the rest of the room. Her gaze fell on the envelope on the mantel. She went to it, hesitated only for a moment, opened it.

She read its contents three times, both notes, her back to the swaying body, her mind racing and her hands growing as cold as Louis's must be. At length she put the notes in her pocket and crept out of the room and down the hall to her boudoir.

Chapter Twenty-Five

The secretary looked up from her typewriter and saw her employer coming through the firm's outer offices toward his own room. His expression was tight and set, as if in wax.

"Good morning, Monsieur Vollard," she said. He nodded. "May I say," she went on, "that, like all of us here, I am saddened by the tragic news?" He nodded again. She hesitated because she found him a formidable man, but continued because she also admired him and responded to his fairness and firmness with a feeling that outside the environment of the firm might have been described as "fondness." Inside the firm such things were never named. "I saw how deeply you cared for your brother," she said. "I am truly sorry for your loss."

Nicolas stopped, closed his eyes for an instant, and said, "Thank you" before disappearing behind his door.

He took off his coat methodically, laid it over a chair, and got to his desk and into the chair before he began to cry. His body shook but no sound emerged; he was like a statue rocked by wind. For weeks—ever since he had gone to wake Louis and found he could never be waked again—he had kept himself both busy and controlled by personally taking charge of the details that accompany a death. The most crucial had been persuading the doctor and the relevant officials not to publicize the fact of suicide. Then there had been the decision about the kind of funeral: for the obvious reason, no religious ceremony, a lack Henriette would have deplored. Of course she would have deplored everything. Nicolas had opted for the simplest rites consonant with decency and the family's position, and Louis had been laid to rest in the family chapel with an inscription that Nicolas wrote himself: *Here lies Louis, younger son of Henriette and Olivier. 1810–1875. In life, struggle; in death, peace.*

Why had Louis left no word of explanation? How could he have killed himself without leaving even a note? Why had he said nothing when the two of them had talked the night before his death, except to mention that he had rooms in the Latin Quarter? "I am sorry, Nicolas," Joséphine had said, not unkindly, "but it is typical of your brother, do you not think?"

Nicolas had put aside his feelings and settled Louis's affairs. He had gone to the Latin Quarter rooms and retrieved his effects, then tried to sort out financial matters. What remained of Louis's estate would go to Marc—if Marc were ever in a legal position to inherit. As far as could be determined, Louis had left no debts, but that had taken a good deal of determining. Nicolas had felt like a detective, trying to piece together the trail of his brother's life for the past eighteen years. All the while he had tucked his grief away in a hundred separate compartments and sealed them off, as a man might pick objects from his dresser in the morning and slip them into different pockets. He had never taken them out again until, somehow, the secretary's words had called them forth without his will or consent. *I saw how deeply you cared for your brother.* Had she? Had anyone—including Louis himself—known how much he loved that handsome, indecisive, unhappy man, about whom he had no illusions and whose behavior had often made him angry? Sometimes loving Louis had seemed the most rewarding thing in his life; sometimes, the hardest.

Why did Louis kill himself? Despair over Marc's situation? Or a sadly Romantic gesture—a misguided attempt to return to the passionate time of his youth? Or cowardice—unwillingness to face the disillusions and desiccations of age? Even as he mourned his brother, Nicolas realized, he was still angry with him and bewildered by his behavior. Louis's death had been like his life.

A fresh bout of weeping shook him. When it let go, he leaned back in his chair and put the heels of his hands over his eyes. Finally he sat up and restacked the papers on his desk. There was the projected establishment of a new branch bank in lower Languedoc, where the financial health of the wine producers was at issue; there was an upcoming important meeting of the founders of the credit association to which Nicolas had committed the House of Vollard in the early sixties; there were dozens of other considerations in the work of keeping money in ever faster and wider circulation in order to support the economic growth on which the future of France, and the House of Vollard, rested. Try as he might, Nicolas could not make his mind stay with them.

Why had Louis come to Nicolas's house to kill himself? Even in his final act, had Louis lacked the courage to undertake it on his own, in his own surroundings? Or had he meant that final act as a reproach: a last, horribly mute cry, declaring that Nicolas had withdrawn too far from the life around him, had done too little to help not only his brother but also Marc and Gabrielle?

As soon as the thought came to him, Nicolas recognized it as the one he had been refusing to allow; as the reason he had kept his grief squirreled away in separate pockets. He pushed aside the papers in front of him, put his arms on the desk, and rested his forehead on them.

An hour later he was at Gabrielle's house, in the library, facing her across a small table laid with coffee and *gaufrettes*. She tilted her head and asked, "What do you have in mind to do?"

"I do not know yet," Nicolas said. "I only know that I must do something—anything, legal or otherwise—to save Marc from a life of imprisonment."

"Why must you?" she said.

Nicolas pushed aside his coffee, untasted. "I can do nothing for Louis now, except mourn his loss. But if there is still some action I can take for his son, then in Louis's memory, and for his sake, I must take it, so his spirit may rest in peace." Silently he added, *And my own may live in the same state.* When Gabrielle frowned, he said, "I tell you in advance in hopes you will approve my efforts and back them to the rest of the family, if necessary."

"You have never needed anyone to approve what you do."

"Very well, that is not the reason. I come to you because . . . because I want to feel I have your consent and moral support."

She was silent, then said, "You have them. But what are you going to do?"

"I thought I might try to bribe the guards to let Marc out. I may even have to hire people from the underworld to take him from prison by force."

"You will not find it easy."

"No doubt you are right.

"What does a man like you know about bribing guards and hiring criminals?"

"Nothing, yet. But a man who has spent half his life courting ministers of finance and their kings and emperors and battalions of toadies and functionaries—he is not so far from bribery as you might think, or as he might wish."

"But you are contemplating entering a strange world, Uncle Nicolas. Do you not think . . ." Gabrielle's voice trailed away as an idea turned her eyes even darker. "You should go to Nandou. He knows how to do these things. Once, when I was a child and my father had me kidnapped, Nandou came and rescued me. And only recently I learned that when Marc's mother escaped from prison, it was Nandou and Jeanne who arranged the escape. Did you know that?"

"No. It seems Monsieur Nandou is an even more amazing man than I thought. As your mother is an amazing woman."

With no warning except a shiver across her features, Gabrielle's eyes filled with tears.

"My dear," Nicolas said, "what is it? What is wrong?"

She put her hands to her mouth and said through spread fingers, "I used to be ashamed of Nandou. All my childhood. It made me ashamed of myself, but I could not seem to stop. I hated both of us, me for what I felt and him for making me feel it. But I loved him too, more than anyone."

How on earth, Nicolas wondered, was one to respond to such a confession? "Perhaps Nandou understood how you felt," he said.

"I hope not," she cried. "I hope he never knew any of it." She took up a linen napkin and dabbed at her eyes. "Come, let us go and see them. Nandou and Maman."

"Now?"

"Yes, now. Did you not say you were anxious to take some action?"

Forty minutes later Nicolas was mounting stairs he had never thought to climb again. He looked up at Jeanne's daughter, and Louis's—at the train of a burgundy dress advancing ahead of him, at the straight spine, the curls of black hair visible around the back of a beribboned and flowered hat—and felt as if some invisible bond tied him, through her, to both her parents.

When they arrived at the apartment door, Gabrielle knocked. In spite of himself, Nicolas knew an instant of near-panic; all his emotions seemed close to the surface today. Gabrielle turned to him. "How long did you say it had been since you saw Maman?"

"Twenty-one years," he said. The door opened.

"Hello, Maman." Gabrielle kissed her cheeks. "Simone is not with me today. Instead I have brought Uncle Nicolas to see you after all these years."

From her daughter's embrace, Jeanne looked up at Nicolas. He felt as if no time had passed since he last appeared at her door. Some part of him registered that she was older and graying, but did not interfere with what he saw: skin as pale and fine as ever, eyes as direct and dark, a mouth as intriguingly shaped.

"Nicolas," she said faintly. Then she slipped from Gabrielle's grasp. "I did not think to see you again. It is good to do so, though I confess it is also strange." She put out her hand.

He lifted it to his lips, knowing it would be warm. "It is good to hear that you are as straightforward as ever."

"Louis's death will have saddened you greatly. May I offer my sympathy?"

"Thank you," he said.

"Please come in," she said. In the dining room Nandou sat at a large table, a book open before him. The hair that hung to his shoulders was still thick but grizzled, and deep lines ran from his nose to his mouth. It occurred to Nicolas that he had never seen a dwarf as old as Nandou. In fact, the only other dwarfs he had seen had been young ones.

Gabrielle said, "Nandou, you have met Nicolas Vollard?"

"I have." Nandou rose slowly and bowed.

"Monsieur Nandou. The memory of your artistry remains bright for me."

Nandou inclined his head and motioned Nicolas to sit.

When they were all seated, Gabrielle said, "I like our being together at one table. I hated keeping my two families in separate and secret compartments."

"Nandou and I were the only ones you kept hidden," Jeanne said tartly.

Nandou put a hand on her arm. "Where is the point in saying such things?"

Gabrielle spoke before Jeanne could. "Maman fears I will forget the truth if I am not reminded of it."

"Is she right?"

"I am nearly forty-five, Nandou. I hope I have learned not to repeat my mistakes."

"Oho! You think there is some age at which one is cured of that disease?"

"I certainly hope so."

"Gaby, my dear," Jeanne said, "I must regretfully inform you that one can be a fool at forty-five as well as at any other age."

She did not glance at Nicolas, but he wondered if she could be referring to the night when they had fallen on each other and rolled about this very floor in ecstasy. If so, he did not know which was the folly—to have done it, or to have done it only once. That night he had felt propelled by a force that was outside him yet expressed his deepest desires. Afterward he would not permit himself to reflect on what had happened, even to recall it. He had tucked it into a secret pocket and gone on with his life, plunging deeper still into business affairs while increasing his distance from everything and everyone else, except Gabrielle, whose company he had enjoyed from the first. Only on the night he learned she was Jeanne's daughter had he allowed himself to think of those hours with Jeanne: to recall the glorious abandon of their behavior, to wonder what his life would have been like had she agreed to his offer.

Gabrielle was leaning across the table and saying, "Maman, Nandou, are you not certain that I would never again try to hide my relationship to you?"

"I am certain," Jeanne said. "But do you not know that even when it is healed, a wound can still throb in the rain?"

Gabrielle flushed. "I do know that."

Nicolas listened, fascinated. The spirit and independence he liked in Gabrielle seemed muted here, as if he had suddenly seen the original after looking for years at a copy. He wondered how she could have left, why the world of the Vollards had seemed more attractive than Jeanne and Nandou's. He had used to assume she married Marc because she loved him, but once he learned what she and Marc were to each other, and what family she had abandoned, he had been puzzled. Perhaps she had given him the answer—*I used to be ashamed of Nandou.* Perhaps the price she had paid for that weakness of spirit had been to cut herself off from the people who might have strengthened it.

"It is not only for my sake that I am glad we are all here together," Gabrielle was saying. "It is for Marc's. Uncle Nicolas wants to get him out of prison. I want him to succeed, but, with respect, I do not think he can do it alone, so I insisted that he come and speak to the two of you. I know you can help him if you are willing."

"Gabrielle has great faith in both of you," Nicolas said.

Jeanne's gaze moved to him. "What kind of help do you seek?"

"If I knew, perhaps I would not need to seek it. I know only that I cannot allow my nephew to be imprisoned for a crime of which he is innocent."

Nandou said, "Do you not believe that a trial will acquit him?"

"In the climate of public opinion that has been created, the likelihood of acquittal—even of a fair trial—diminishes every day. In any case, Marc has months to endure in the Conciergerie before the trial begins. I want to get him out of prison by some means, *any* means, for which I am willing to pay any cost."

"Money alone will not achieve that end," Nandou said. "The case is too public for guards and wardens to accept bribes to release him."

Jeanne said, "Can no witness be found who will swear he was elsewhere on the night of the crime?"

"Marc says there is no such person," Gabrielle replied.

Jeanne regarded Nicolas blandly. "Can one be invented?"

Gabrielle looked at her mother in amazement.

"I am unwilling to hire a lie," Nicolas said. "Even if my business experience had not shown that it rarely is practical, my nature balks at suborning perjury. I prefer to outwit the legal system rather than show my contempt for it." When Jeanne smiled, he felt an unreasonable pleasure.

"Then we are speaking of an escape," Nandou said. Arms folded, he sat back. His mouth curved up as if he could not control it. "There are ways. In fact I have thought of one, purely as a mental exercise, you understand, for I could not undertake it on my own."

Nicolas forgot he was not in his office. "Tell me at once," he commanded.

Nandou smiled broadly and told him.

Nicolas said, "Yes. We could do that. Together. I will do it with you."

Jeanne shot to her feet. "I will not allow it! Nandou, you are not young, not even middle-aged. You cannot do such things any longer. You do not have the strength!"

"Then I must find it." Nandou's eyes glowed, a tiny sun in each.

"If something happens to you, what shall I do? I cannot live without you!"

The bond between them was suddenly palpable in its reality. Gabrielle gave a little sound, as of recognition.

There had never been a chance for his own relationship with Jeanne, Nicolas thought. Her flesh had met his hungrily, but her spirit had never belonged to anyone but Nandou. Not even to Louis. How had the strange dwarf, now grizzled with age, won and held her forever?

"One more chance to perform, my love," Nandou said. "One more."

They looked at each other for a long time. Finally Jeanne nodded and said, unhappily, "I understand. I accept."

Nandou kissed her hand.

"Good-by then, my dear," said Joséphine. She kissed the cheeks of Edith Pasquier, whose husband was involved in some kind of business with Nicolas. "The tea was lovely."

"Good-by," said Edith. "Tuesday I am going to Baccarat to find my daughter-in-law a gift. One of the engraved bowls, perhaps. Would you care to come?"

"That would be delightful," Joséphine said. "I may find something for my Denis's Charlotte."

Again they kissed the air beside each other's cheeks, and Joséphine was shown out along the elegant hall lined with statuary and through the carved front door to her carriage. Her head stayed high and her back erect until the carriage started off. Then she sank against the seat. Her cheeks burned, as they had all the time she was drinking tea, eating exquisite little cakes, and chatting with Edith and three other women as if the world held no matters more pressing than Worth's latest dress designs and the Pasquiers' upcoming reception. No doubt they had started gossiping about her as soon as she left.

My dear, imagine, a nephew arrested for murder!

They say his father came back to Paris and died of the disgrace—not that Louis Vollard was any stranger to scandal.

At least he cleared his wife before he died.

Yes, but have you heard—Edmée refuses to return to society, not that society wants her, but still, to claim she would rather live by herself in some building filled with actors and the Lord knows who else . . .

Can you blame her? With a son arrested for murder?

The words rang with the heightened reality of imagination, more clearly that if Joséphine had actually heard them. Sometimes she thought her friends still invited her to their five o'clocks only to watch her struggling to act as if nothing were wrong, a struggle she would die before losing. Head high, back a plumb line to the ground, smile flicking on and off as needed, like an electric switch. They would not look down on her, ever. But she ached for someone sympathetic to talk to. Blaise's wife, Florine, was too absorbed in her illnesses. Her niece Sophie never wanted to hear about troubles. Her daughter-in-law, Charlotte—whom Denis had married three years before in one of the season's most beautiful and expensive weddings, attended by everyone—had a haughty manner that would not lend itself to sympathy or confidences. One had to keep up appearances with Charlotte almost more than with strangers. And talking to Gabrielle was out of the question.

Joséphine reached her own door, gave the butler her things, and went up the stairs, lined with statuary grander than the Pasquiers', thinking how she missed Henriette. Henriette would have understood what she was going through.

In her boudoir a fire had been laid. She warmed her hands before it, touching the sapphire ring Henriette had bequeathed to her, then took off her bonnet, set it on its stand, and looked into a mirror with a heavy, carved frame. She was sixty: too old for such racking of the spirit. As if they were outside her control, her feet moved across the room to her *écritoire* and her fingers touched the panel that opened one of its secret drawers. She took out an envelope addressed to "Nico" and read the contents for at least the hundredth time.

How tempted she had been to leave the envelope where she found it that morning: to let Louis be blamed for the crime. He had not committed it, but he had done so much else that caused grief to the Vollard family: forming a liaison with the Sorel woman, fathering Gabrielle, allowing Marc to marry her . . . But it would hurt Nicolas to have his brother publicly shamed in that manner.

Initially she had taken the envelope back to her own room just to give herself another half hour in which to think. But Nicolas had gone to Louis's room and discovered the body. It still had not been too late; Joséphine could have said she had found the envelope and been too shocked to know what to do. But then she would have had to explain why she had opened it . . . Another hour had gone by, the rest of the day, then weeks, now months. October to January, with the envelope and its two notes lying in her *écritoire,* burning in her brain.

Even now it was not too late to go to the police and say she had held the confession so long out of a desire to protect her husband's feelings. Nicolas would never believe that she cared for his peace of mind, but she did. It was a wife's duty to care.

But would the police believe the confession? They might know it for what it was—a father's lying attempt to save his son. Marc would remain charged with the crime, and nothing would have been accomplished save to blacken two Vollard reputations, father's as well as son's.

And if the police believed the confession? Then Marc would be released . . . free . . . free to express the perverted side of his nature to which he had confessed, to commit acts Joséphine could not bear to imagine, let alone to contemplate others' hearing of them. To have a Vollard known to the world as a . . . as a . . . She could not even say the word. How could she bear it to be on the lips of every five-o'-clock tea-drinker in Paris?

Louis had brought so much dishonor on the family; why should he have the chance to bring more?—to clear his son's name and, in so doing, free Marc to create the worst scandal of all.

She stared down at the two letters. Not giving them to Nicolas, keeping the confession from the police—that had been the right decision, hadn't it?

Henriette would tell her it was. Henriette would have done the same. But Henriette would not allow herself to be tortured by her action: to keep the evidence in a drawer, where it could call to her any hour of every day and night.

Joséphine rose, motionless for a moment, then darted across the room as if pursued by an animal, and threw the two notes on the fire.

"He doesn't look much like a footman," Nicolas said dubiously.

"He is a good actor," Nandou said, "and, what is more to the point, as strong as an ox."

"True, that is critical. Your own energies must be safeguarded."

The object of their comments, a man of forty, heavily muscled, nearly six feet tall, bowed to Nicolas and said grandly, "Monsieur, as utility actor for the Théâtre de Belleville I have played first dotard, cloaks, financiers, jovials, and for the past year I have been grand first comedian in all categories!"

"Financiers, eh?" said Nicolas. "How do they behave?"

The man thrust out his stomach, patted it, pulled in his chin, and contrived to look both menacing and sly.

"Remember," Nandou said quickly, "that Fernand will be the footman. It is his nephew Charles here who will play Marc's fellow banker and friend."

"Monsieur," said the other actor, bowing.

Nandou clapped once. "My friends, let us return to work."

He had gone to Belleville, found the theatre the young boy had told him about, and in fact hired the boy's brother Charles and his uncle Fernand. It was part of his plan that, before leaving Paris, perhaps the country, Marc should temporarily hide in Belleville with the theatre people. They were a world unto themselves, as he explained to Nicolas: part of a wraparound, working-class community outside the city whose ways and means were unknown to bourgeois Paris. Nicolas nodded; certainly he had known nothing of them.

They were rehearsing in an empty apartment on the Left Bank, which Nicolas had rented for the purpose. He wanted to watch and did so wearing a half-mask, so that if the rescue should fail and the players be caught, they could not identify him to the police. But Nandou was not disguised. "These men are loyal to the theatre and will not betray us," he said. Nicolas could not decide whether his confidence was admirable or foolhardy.

Nandou's plan was simple but dangerous: Charles, posing as a friend of Marc's from the financial world, would pay the guards to let him spend part of an evening in Marc's cell having dinner with him. The request was not unusual; despite the squalor of the Conciergerie, where during the Revolution people had lived in a hell of vermin and ordure before being taken out to be separated from their heads, wealthy prisoners could pay for luxuries, and sometimes even for extended visits. Charles would say he wished to bring in a true gourmet's dinner and two footmen to serve it: Nandou and Fernand. They would carry the viands and wine in a special, lightweight chest that had been carefully chosen: It must be visibly too small to hold a normal-size man, so the guards would not suspect that Marc was being smuggled inside it when it was taken away. In fact, he would not be. Rather, in disguise, he would help to carry the chest away.

Jeanne said little while the plans and rehearsals went on. A protest lived on her tongue—*You cannot do it, Nandou, to use the Dwarf Lord stilts is madness*—especially when she heard him in his room working on them, grunting and groaning. But when she looked at his face, she swallowed the protest, for new fires burnt in his eyes, he smiled often and easily, and he bustled about with the energy of a stagehand, albeit not a young one.

Perhaps it would be all right, she thought; perhaps the plan would work perfectly and no harm would come to anyone. Hadn't much of Nandou's life consisted of doing things she would not have believed he could do? Was that not part of why she loved him? Still, when she went to his room at night and slipped into the bed, she lay against him with more urgency than languor, staying awake to cherish the feel of his solid chest, matted with hair, against her naked back or breasts.

"My love," he said to her, "you would not worry so much if you stopped blaming yourself. For the hundredth time, it is not your fault that Marc is in prison, so it cannot be your fault that I am going to rescue him." She smiled ruefully and went about as before, castigating herself, worrying about him, and marveling at the irony of it: Nandou and Nicolas working together to save Louis's son—that is, the man everyone, including Louis, believed to be his son. And all of it called into being by her need to vanquish the past.

Nicolas worried for different reasons. By his code, it was not right to initiate a dangerous, illegal venture and then take no active part in it. But his hands were tied. He had wanted to join the rescue as himself: the prisoner's uncle who paid the jailers so he could have an elaborate dinner with his nephew. "Never!" Nandou had said. "The jailers would know who you are, and you would be guilty of arranging the escape of a felon. What is the point of rescuing the nephew only to implicate the uncle?" Nicolas had to bow to the logic of the argument: to sit through rehearsals in his half-mask and be satisfied with the innocuous assignment of visiting Marc to win his consent to the rescue, which he gave eagerly, and explain the plan to him.

"You do not like to be the bystander, do you?" Nandou said.

"No more than you would."

Nandou smiled and nodded.

The two worked easily together, finding that their minds approached problems similarly. Nicolas's sardonic comments made Nandou laugh; Nandou's flamboyance and wry humor made Nicolas smile. Their camaraderie surprised them—privately each suspected it came from their mutual feeling for Jeanne—and made each more curious about the other. Why, Nandou wondered, noting the cynicism that lifted Nicolas's eyebrow and sharpened his voice, had the man become a pillar of society if he despised its hypocrisy and most of its conventions? Why did he hold himself aloof from others, indeed from himself as well? How, Nicolas wondered, watching Nandou on the stilts, sometimes biting his lip in pain, had the dwarf achieved such satisfaction in his life? What gave him a weight of character and personality that belied his stature?

At length all was ready. Charles, as Marc's friend, was dispatched to the prison and reported success: The dinner was arranged for two nights hence.

The night before, Edmée joined Nandou and Jeanne for dinner in their apartment. By mutual agreement, Henri had not been told of the rescue attempt. The friends kept urging one another to eat and ignoring the advice; a platter of roasted squab sat untouched. In the light of three red candles they talked, sometimes with too much animation, sometimes with too little, of another rescue: how brilliantly Nandou had played a woman and Jeanne a man, how convincing Edmée had been as a medium.

Edmée took some squab, picked at it, then said, "I am afraid, Nandou, for my boy and for you. If anything happens . . . "

He patted her hand. "Dear friend, I assure you we are taking less risk than Marc would face before a judge and jury." He poured wine into her glass. "Try to leave the fear to us actors. To us, stage fright is an old companion."

Jeanne stifled a sound.

"When you saved the mother," Edmée said, "who could imagine you would one day do the same for the son?"

"No one could imagine it," Jeanne said. "If it happened in a boulevard play, the critics would complain of coincidence." She tried to laugh, then gripped Nandou's hand. "I still cannot believe you are going to do it. Twice in one lifetime."

"It is not a coincidence," he said, "that society is always eager to imprison those who do not accept its codes. A woman who dares to venture outside marriage, an artist who makes an easy suspect because he does not paint in the approved manner . . . As long as our world is what it is, one must respond to its nature."

"But why must you be the one who responds?" Jeanne cried.

"Like the world, I too have a nature." He smiled at her. "Now, ladies, let us try to eat something."

In the carriage he had hired under another name, Nicolas drove them onto the Île de la Cité. "Where is your mask?" Nandou asked him in surprise.

"Damn the mask. It suits a man who is only half involved. I no longer wish to be such a man. Even without the mask, I take far less risk than any of you."

Nandou smiled.

When they all stepped out of the carriage, Nicolas shook the hand of each. "Good luck," he said, and to his surprise added, "my friends."

Nandou grasped his arm. "It will be injudicious for us to remain in touch when this is over, but let us do so anyway."

Nicolas saluted him, and drove off to wait at the appointed place.

Charles presented himself at the Conciergerie. Behind him, dressed as footmen, came Fernand and Nandou, carrying the chest between them. Fernand supported most of its weight while Nandou, on the stilts, used his grip on it primarily to steady his balance. The path to Marc's cell required him to negotiate a flight of stairs. It had been their greatest worry, but he managed it well.

In the cell—one of the larger ones, fifteen feet square—Marc greeted Charles like an old friend. Fernand and Nandou unpacked the chest and laid out supper. With a supercilious manner Nicolas would have winced at, Charles offered the guard two bottles of the wine they had brought and told the man to be off: "I did not pay you in order to dine with my friend under a jailer's eyes."

The guard grumbled, peered into the now-empty chest, locked the cell door behind him, and said he would return in three hours.

The most difficult part, Marc said later, was to choke down the food while trying to make conversation with a stranger. The most dangerous part was the change—making Marc resemble the footman Nandou had played—which had to be done while one of them kept watch. After they exchanged clothes, Nandou made up Marc's face to look as much as possible like his own and helped him put on the gray, shoulder-length wig they had brought. When the change was finished, they rolled the empty plates and silver in the bedding and arranged the roll to look like a sleeping figure. To the back of its "head" Nandou attached the other wig he had brought, which resembled Marc's hair. He took off the stilts, rolled up Marc's trousers to fit his own short legs, and got into the chest. Marc and Fernand arranged the tablecloth over him and knocked on the bars to call the guard.

When the man came, Charles gave another high-handed performance: "I do not know what you have done here in prison to my friend, but he can no longer hold his wine like a gentleman." Imperious wave of Charles's hand toward the cot. "He has fallen into a drunken sleep. I have no wish to remain with an insentient creature. Lead us out."

Looking long and suspiciously at the "figure" on the cot, the guard started toward it. Charles, Fernand, and Marc froze.

A moan came from the cot, followed by muffled words: "Go away, Charles. All of you. Leave me alone." The voice was Marc's.

The guard stopped.

Behind his back Marc shot puzzled glances at Charles and Fernand, who returned them in kind.

The guard shrugged. He turned and regarded each of them with narrowed eyes but seemed able to find nothing wrong: Three men had entered the cell, and the same three were apparently leaving it. The guard signaled them to take up the chest and follow him out.

When they emerged from the prison, euphoria gripped them, so that they could barely walk in character to the corner where Nicolas waited in the carriage. He flung open the door. They pushed in the chest, climbed in behind it, and cried in one voice, "Success!"

Nicolas embraced his nephew. Charles and Fernand clapped each other repeatedly on the shoulders. It was some minutes before any of them realized that Nandou had not emerged from the chest.

Fernand lifted its lid and pulled the tablecloth off him. In the light of a streetlamp they saw that his eyes were closed. One arm clutched the stilts, the other fist was pressed against his chest, and his forehead was carved by deep lines of pain.

Chapter Twenty-Six

*I*t was wonderful in Belleville. Wonderful.

No prison dogs barking when the bells chimed the hours. No moaning or cursing coming from the other cells. No doors clanging with hollow metal sobs. Instead, the huge sky shifting its palette of colors from moment to moment, and the sun throwing ever-changing shadows on the angles of the roofs and the paving stones.

Dressed in a workman's blouse and trousers, his beard untouched by a razor, a cap low on his forehead, Marc roamed the streets of the working-class community. It did not matter if a building was ugly or charming, a face forgettable or arresting; he pulled a notebook from his pocket and sketched it for the sheer pleasure of being able to choose to do so. It did not matter that the food and bed offered by his hosts, Charles and Fernand and their family, was of the plainest, or that their house was little more than a cottage, with no plumbing. He reveled in the tones and shapes of the sooty walls, the crumbling outside staircase, the hearth where three dogs, a cat, and sometimes the goat all slept. The physical world, which had fascinated him since childhood, was now a source of pleasure so intense that at times it resembled pain. A wheel of cheese in the market, as pale and full as the moon, or the Oriental asymmetries of bare branches against the winter sky could make him want to weep for the joy of their existence, and of his own.

It was not merely that he cherished his liberty as only one who has lost it can do; he was experiencing a freedom beyond freedom. He had known pleasure in his life, even happiness—sometimes in fleeting moments at his easel, always in the presence of Simone—but now when he looked back, everything seemed to have taken place within close walls. When he thought of his cell in the Conciergerie, it was a cave at the end of an ever-narrowing tunnel, and the rest of his life was that tunnel, leading him to the cell as surely as if he had committed the crime he was accused of, and ending in his farewell to Gabrielle.

She had come to see him in prison once the escape plan was underway, wearing a somber dress that made her eyes look black and no jewelry but her wedding band. "So, husband," she said, coating the word lightly with irony, "I never thought we would be driven apart in this manner."

"Nor I. But no matter how it transpires, perhaps it is better that we be apart. You have not been happy, Gaby."

"We did not marry for happiness, did we? You married for protection, and I . . . Do you know, Marc, I have nearly forgotten why I married you."

"Security. Respectability. And safety," he had added, thus calling a mirthless smile from her.

If he were ever going to tell her the truth, that would have been the time to do it—to confess she was not his half-sister, to say his mother had told him that Louis was not his natural father. But he had not been able to make himself tell her. He had kept the secret for so long, for Louis's sake, and even though Louis was now dead, the secret was still his mother's to divulge, not his.

Instead, they had talked of Simone, of what she should be told and when, of the wisdom of their decision not to bring her to the prison and let her see her father in such a setting.

He had made Gabrielle promise never to let Simone forget that he loved her. When she had sworn it, she looked at him with the trust and affection he remembered from their youth but had rarely seen in recent years. "You have been good to me, Marc. Better than any man I know. I shall always be grateful for that."

"Remember that I loved you, Gaby," he had said, "as much as I can ever love a woman."

Their hands had clasped, hers cool and small in his. Then she had risen and left, and the first forty-one years of the life of Marc Vollard had ended.

On the second morning after the escape, when he was out walking, recalling that farewell, a disturbing realization came to him. If he had never told Gaby they were unrelated, he had been silent not for his father's sake or his mother's, but his own. He had been protecting himself from the possibility, however unlikely, that Gaby would then want him to act as a normal man. His cheeks burned in the cold. He jammed his hands in his pockets and walked on.

The next morning, when he was following the frosty patterns of his breath down a new street, another thought came to him. He let out such a cry that an old woman who had stepped from her cottage to empty a basin dropped it instead. He saw that if he had never been able to paint as he wanted, to make his fingers fully execute his vision, it was because he had never lived as he wanted. He had been the Monk of Art, but Art was not well served by monks. Art needed those who lived fully and joyously in the world.

He helped the woman pick up her bits of crockery and pressed some coins into her hand. He told her to buy a new basin—three new basins—and walked off, his mouth as slack with astonishment as hers. It was all so simple, once he saw it; how had he lived forty-one years without seeing? The answer came as he was asking the question: To live within the confines of narrow walls meant adjusting one's vision to those walls.

Even so, he was amazed that he had done it. Why should a man live in a self-made prison? he thought. The question itself seemed so wonderful that as he walked along in the chilly, bright morning, he repeated it to himself again and again before trying to answer it. When he did try, the answer came swiftly: the inner Darkness. Darkness needed tunnels and caves.

He sighed and walked on. It was difficult to think of darkness when the world was so free and full of light.

Four days after the escape, as arranged, his uncle Nicolas came to the cottage to see him. Charles and Fernand waited to greet him. "How is Nandou?" Fernand asked at once.

"The doctors say he must remain absolutely quiet. It is his heart. There must be no exertion of any kind."

Charles struck a fist against his thigh. "The man exerted himself all during rehearsals and the escape."

"Exactly," Nicolas said. "No doubt those exertions caused his collapse."

"Do you think he knew what he was doing?"

"My friends, I think Nandou is a man who always knows what he is doing."

Marc said, "When my voice seemed to come from the cot while I was in fact standing beside Fernand—was that Nandou?"

"I learned from Jeanne Sorel," Nicolas said, "that he is a ventriloquist as well as an actor."

"He saved me, and all of us, by such difficult means while he lay cramped in the chest and may already have been feeling the pains of the heart attack?"

"Yes," Nicolas said.

The four of them stood in silence, remembering the gray of Nandou's skin and the rasp of his breathing when they had lifted him from the chest and carried him up the stairs to his apartment.

"Tell him," Marc said, "that I shall thank him every day of my life, which he saved in more ways than he can know."

Fernand said gruffly, "Tell him we pray for his health." Nicolas nodded.

"Now," Charles said to Fernand, "we must leave Monsieur Nicolas and his nephew to say what they need to say to each other."

When the two men had gone, Marc and Nicolas sat at the table near the hearth. The air was smoky but also held the aroma of a large pot-au-feu.

Nicolas unbuttoned his greatcoat. "Have you seen any of the newspapers?"

"I have avoided looking at them. What do they say?"

"They make much of the fact that now both mother and son have escaped from prison."

"Oh, dear. I suppose Aunt Joséphine is very upset?"

"No doubt, but she has said very little."

"And Maman?"

"I believe nothing can upset her, now that she knows you are safe."

"That is good to hear." Marc had said his good-by to her when she visited him in the prison. She had held a handkerchief to her mouth nearly the entire time, but sobs worked their way around its edges. "We have lost so much of our life together," she had said.

"We made up for much in recent years, Maman."

"Now we shall be apart for the rest of our lives."

"We cannot know that, Maman. One can never predict with certainty."

She had lifted her hand, run it over and over his cheek, and said, "Wherever you go, whatever you do, promise me to be happy, will you, my dearest boy?"

"I promise to try, my darling Maman."

Marc looked at his uncle across the crude table. "I wonder if I shall ever see Maman again, or any of you."

"I would say no, but life likes to take unexpected twists."

"So I have noticed," Marc said wryly. "Look after Gaby and Simone, Uncle Nicolas."

"I swear it on your father's memory. You know I am devoted to both of them." Nicolas smiled. "If she cared to, Simone might be a better banker than you ever were."

"That would not be difficult." Marc shook his head. "It is best for all of us if I disappear from their lives forever. They will be happier for it."

"And you, my boy?" Marc did not answer. "If your father could know you are free," Nicolas said, "he would be at peace. His love for you was the one thing in his life he felt he had never betrayed."

The smoke from the hearth blurred Marc's vision. He rubbed his eyes and said, "Have you sometimes wondered, as I have, whether Papa took his life because he was in despair over my arrest?"

Nicolas nodded. "Yet the night before, he seemed confident you would be all right." He shook his head. "If only we could know . . . But, even knowing, could we have stopped him?"

The fire popped in the silence. Nicolas reached into his greatcoat pocket. "Here is money. Get word to me if you need more. I'll find a way to send it."

"I shall not need more, Uncle Nicolas."

"How can you be sure? Have you decided where you are going, then?"

"No," Marc said, pushing aside the thought that came to him. "No. But wherever it is, I must live there on my own resources."

Jeanne stirred the pot, then tasted her handiwork. Carrots, potatoes, turnips, and leeks, simmered for hours with a beef bone. Nourishing, and as flavorful as could be expected given the doctor's warning against using salt. She reached into a dish of dried herbs, added several pinches, and stirred again.

There was relief in the stirring, in any motion. Since the nightmare time of the rescue, she seemed to have been on a constant search for physical tasks. None of her usual concerns were relevant. Writing a piece for the journal on women's rights, brooding over a possible new play—such matters were as unimportant as old clothes hung at the back of a cupboard. She went to the markets each morning, cooked, changed the bed linens, sometimes even scrubbed the floor while the *bonne* stood by awkwardly. At night she slept, very little, on a cot she had had brought into Nandou's room. Everyone wanted to help—Edmée, Henri, Gabrielle, theatre colleagues by the dozens. "Don't you understand?" she told them. "If I don't have things to do, I shall go mad."

"You will wear yourself out," Edmée said. "That is what I want," Jeanne replied.

She was trying to do sleight of hand, to distract her mind from everything but the immediate moments and their tasks. Nandou would be better at it, she thought; he was wonderful at sleight-of-hand. Suddenly, though she stared down into the soup, her mind filled with an image of Nandou walking to a garbage heap and plucking a white rose from it. Tears ran down toward the pot. She caught some with her tongue. *Salt,* she thought. *There must not be salt in his soup.* She smiled at the prospect of sharing the thought with him, decided against it, and wiped her eyes.

She put a bowl of the soup and some bread and butter on a tray, added the morning papers, and went to his room. The worst of the pain was over, so the doctor was no longer giving him morphine, but she had to paste a smile over her concern each time she went in because he looked so weak and pale. And small; for the first time in his life he seemed small to her. "More haute cuisine from the hands of Jeanne Sorel," she said as cheerily as she could.

For an instant the old Nandou came alive in his face, then faded. "I am not hungry for food," he said. His voice was not strong.

"I found such good vegetables in the market, and the bread is—"

"I shall eat in a moment. Put it down and sit beside me."

"Do you want the papers?"

"Read me what is interesting."

Jeanne unfolded the journal and read to him: a little about the Third Republic, which was growing less shaky despite the attacks of the monarchists on one side and the Socialists on the other, and much about the theatre, where there was word that the Comédie's next season might contain a revival of *Hernani,* starring Bernhardt.

Nandou's eyes shone, making the skin around them look waxier than ever.

"We will be there on opening night," Jeanne said.

"Take Simone," he said gently.

"That is a good idea. The two of us will take her."

When he did not reply, she reached for the bowl of soup and handed it to him. He ate half of it, chewed some bread, then waved it all away and settled against his pillows.

"Do you want something else?" she asked.

"Only to look at you."

He dozed almost at once, but soon his eyes opened again and he said, "Do you remember how Simone loved the rooster I carved for her?"

"I do, but it was Gabrielle you carved it for."

"Was it? Yes, you are right. Simone is like her mother in some ways, but like you in more. A mind filled with questions, eyes ready to catch fire."

"Then it is you she resembles most of all."

He smiled. "Except that she is tall." He dozed again, then said, without opening his eyes, "If Edmée and Henri go to live in Italy as they are planning, you could stay with them for a while."

"What are you saying? I have no intention of leaving you."

"I mean when I am gone."

"Do not go!" she cried before she could stop herself.

His eyes opened. "My love, do not pretend that things are not as they are. Have you not learned to appreciate Realism?"

"I renounce it. I want the impossible."

He smiled again. "I think that is the story of all our lives—Romanticism in youth, Realism in later years, and finally the yearning for fantasy."

She could say nothing. Soon he was asleep again. She sat for some moments looking at the hand that rested on the coverlet, thinking of all the magic it had performed on stage and off, with cloth, wood, beads, metal, and flowers. And flesh, her flesh. Then she rose, took the tray, and went to find new tasks.

The next afternoon brought an unexpected visitor.

"I want to assure him that the last stage of the rescue has been satisfactorily completed," Nicolas Vollard said, "and to tell him . . . I have nothing else to tell him. I simply would like to see him again."

"I understand," Jeanne said.

She saw that Nicolas looked at her guardedly. The night he came with Gabrielle to broach the subject of the rescue, she had known that for him the memory of the hours they once spent in each other's embrace was still alive. The knowledge had been pleasurable—why deny it?— and, strangely, had made her feel even more loved and desired by

Nandou; it was as if each man's regard for her enhanced the other's. But now such thoughts, and such pleasure, were in the cupboard with everything else that had once comprised her life. Far at the back.

Even so, when she took Nicolas to Nandou's room and left them together, she was unable to keep herself from standing near the door, listening.

"My friend," Nicolas said. "How are you?"

"As you see me—an invalid."

"I come to tell you that your success is complete. After hiding for several days with your colleagues in Belleville, Marc executed the last step of the plan and left Paris. As agreed, none of us know where he went, so the safety of his destination is assured. I congratulate you, and assure you my gratitude could not be more deeply felt if it were my own life you had saved."

"We did it together, all of us," Nandou said. "Success is the finest meal in the world." There was a low sound, as of the bed shifting.

"What is it?" Nicolas asked. "Are you in pain?"

"No. This body of mine seems to have grown heavy and slow. It does not wish to move as it should."

"You must give it rest."

"I have no choice." Nandou grunted. "That is the hardest part, you understand—to have no choice."

"If you had not chosen to undertake the rescue, you might not be lying here now." Nandou was silent. "Truthfully, my friend," Nicolas said, "did you know you were ill?" Silence again. "I think you did. I think you knew or suspected for some time that your heart was in bad condition. I think you had been having pain and perhaps other symptoms as well."

After another silence Nandou said, "No other symptoms, only pain."

Jeanne looked down and saw her hands clenching so tightly that they were turning white. Her suspicion had been confirmed: Nandou had indeed been ill for some time, had known it, had ignored it. Her shoulders shook with fury at him. Then tears came because she could not bear to be angry at him.

Nicolas was speaking again. "You undertook an adventure that was not only physically strenuous but certain to cause mental stress." His words were neither critical nor accusatory, merely statements of fact. "Why did you do it?"

The bed shifted again. "Because I hate prisons of all kinds—of the soul, the mind, the body. Because Marc is innocent. Because he is Gaby's husband and Edmée's son. And because I wanted to do it." After a moment Nandou added, "My life has been so good that I was not afraid to risk it. I have played more and better roles than any dwarf in history. I have seen France declare herself a Republic three times, this last one, please God, forever. I have known the genius of Hugo and Bernhardt. And I have loved and been loved by Jeanne Sorel. Who has been luckier than I?"

"You attach too great a role to luck. Let me tell you what I understood on the night of the rescue—that you have been a happy man, that you have earned and held the love of one of the most worthy and beautiful women in Paris, because you have not hidden from yourself, or the world, the things that you wanted. You have gone about getting them. You have not lived your life wearing a half-mask."

Silence. Then Nandou said gently, "You did everything you could in regard to the rescue. I have no doubt the same is true of your whole life."

"Of my work perhaps. But only of that."

Jeanne turned and walked quietly away. It was not right to listen without his knowledge to a man baring his soul.

When Nicolas emerged, she was sitting at the large dining-room table, making a list of items she needed from the shops.

They looked at each other. He said, "Are you angry with me for coming to ask his help in the rescue?"

"Yes. But I do not find it reasonable of me. And I know that Nandou himself is not angry."

"The Vollards have never brought you any luck, have they?" She was silent. "If you need anything," he said, "anything at all, please send word to me."

"Thank you, but the only thing I need is his health."

Nicolas took his hat from the chair where he had laid it and turned it in his large hands. "I would like you to know that I am deeply fond of your daughter and Simone. In fact I . . . love them. More than my own son, if that does not shock you."

"No. But your saying it surprises me."

"Now that Marc is gone, I shall do everything I can to make Simone's and Gabrielle's lives comfortable and happy."

"I do not think Gaby knows how to be happy. But Simone . . . "

"Yes. Simone." He smiled, then put on his hat with a quick, efficient motion. "Good-by, Jeanne. I shall be wishing every day for his recovery."

"Thank you. Good-by, Nicolas."

When she went into Nandou's room, he said, "I am glad it was not Nicolas you met at the battle of *Hernani*. I do not think he would have been fool enough to let you go, like his brother."

"I am the one who decides where I go," she said indignantly, and was rewarded with a faint smile.

In a few moments he was asleep. She sat for a long while looking at him, at the bones now jutting up in his cheeks and the high slope of his brow. Suddenly his eyes opened, large and black, and he said, so softly that she had to lean forward to catch the words, "I miss the sound of my heart. I do not hear it any longer. All my life I have heard it beating in my ears, sometimes faint, sometimes like a drum. I have always imagined it was larger than normal—in compensation for the body that was smaller. It was a comfort. The sound of myself. I miss it. I do not like silence in my ears."

"Then I shall talk to you," she said. "I shall tell you a hundred times, and then a hundred more, that I love you as I love my own life."

"Maman," Gabrielle said, "you must let me come and stay with you until . . . "

"Yes? Until?"

"Until he is better."

"I am managing very well."

"You are not. There are rings under your eyes, and you have lost weight."

"Who would look after Simone?"

"She has a governess and a house full of servants, and she is a self-sufficient child. With a book and her little dog, she is quite content."

"I do not think she is content. She misses her father."

"Certainly, but all the same, she is self-sufficent."

"What have you told her about him?"

"The truth. That Marc was accused of a crime he did not commit and managed to escape from prison but has had to leave Paris, perhaps forever, in order to be safe."

"What does she say to that?"

Gabrielle sighed. "Nothing. It is the one subject in the world on which she does not ask questions. Now, Maman, do not try to distract me. Let me come and stay with you and help you, at least for a while."

They were drinking tea in the dining room while Simone talked with Nandou in his room. Jeanne studied her daughter. "We are so different, you and I."

"How do you mean?"

"Look at you, in your beautiful flowered green silk and me in this old, torn black skirt." She poked a finger through a hole in the pocket.

"It gives me pleasure to look as elegant as I can."

"I am not criticizing, Gaby, merely observing one of our many differences."

"What else do you observe?"

Jeanne spooned sugar crystals into her cup. "To me you always look beautiful, smartly dressed, wealthy, and unhappy."

"Unhappy?" Gabrielle's voice lifted and thinned, like a string suddenly pulled tight. "Unhappy?"

"Yes."

"I am certainly not . . . " Gabrielle's mouth wavered. "Oh, I am tired of pretending, Maman, to you and to everybody, but especially to you because you warned me it would happen." She tried to smile. "It is hard to admit that one's mother was right."

"It may help to remember that she was wrong about other things. But let us forget who said or did what in the past. Nandou tells me I must do so."

"I do not think one can. Do you not remember that I abandoned you, that for years I let people believe my mother was dead?"

Jeanne folded both hands around her cup; they were roughened by the physical work she had been doing, and three of her nails were broken. "What I remember even more is that I helped push you into the very life I thought I was teaching you to despise. I cannot cut the memories out of me, but I hope I have learned something from them."

"What, Maman?"

"That you cannot force people to become something they are not willing to become. Twist the sapling, and you only make a crooked tree."

Gabrielle sighed. "I was so afraid of pushing Simone to become a singer that I refused to allow her music lessons. Then I learned that for years she has been singing and learning piano every time Marc took her to his mother's."

"Would you have been happy if you had remained on the stage, Gaby?"

"Sometimes I think so, but I cannot tell. The trouble, Maman, is that I have never been sure what would make me happy. I used to look at you and Nandou and wonder, What is their secret? How can they always know what to do? For a while I tried to do exactly as you did. Then I ran away and tried to do just the opposite. Neither worked, I found." Gabrielle pushed her cup away. "Why do I burden you with these things when you have so much else to worry about?"

"Because I am your mother. Because I asked you. And since you are answering me frankly, I must ask you something else. My deepest fear is that I have made you forever unable to love a man as you would wish, as any woman would wish. Is my fear justified?"

"No, Maman," Gabrielle said slowly. "I have loved a man. I loved him passionately. But it did not make me happy."

"Oh, Gaby, my darling . . . "

Gabrielle shook her head impatiently. "I sound like a child. No, not even a child, for I sometimes think that Simone at her age is more self-sufficient than I. Do not worry about me, Maman. I shall be fine."

"As a wife whose husband is gone, probably forever, and to whom the law forbids divorce?" Jeanne began to tap two fingers on the table. "When Nandou is well again, I must write another article on the need for divorce. Or would a play be more effective?"

"Maman," Gabrielle said. "Dear Maman." She reached across the table and covered Jeanne's hands with one of her own.

Jeanne squeezed it hard. "He will be well again. No, he cannot go walking all over Paris, and he can never again put on the Dwarf Lord stilts, for if he does, I shall kill him, but he will be well again. I am certain of it."

"He has made you very happy, hasn't he?"

"If I could give you half the happiness we have known, and I would if I could, my dear girl, enough would still remain to fill my life. Gaby, now that you are alone again, now that this strange marriage of yours is ended in fact if not in law, you are free to find someone to make you happy as well, to love you with his heart, his mind, and his body . . . " Jeanne pulled her hands away and buried her face in them.

Gabrielle stroked the hair that hid those hands and made sounds of comfort, as if she were the mother and Jeanne the child.

"Grand-mère Jeanne, why are you crying?" Simone's voice startled both women; the girl had come along the hall from Nandou's room to stand between them.

Jeanne lifted her head and wiped her eyes with two sharp motions. "I cry, child, because I cannot make the world run as I would wish it to."

"Nobody can do that."

"True. Not even kings and emperors and all their armies. You are a wise child."

"I don't believe I am still a child, Grand-mère. I am thirteen now."

"True again." Jeanne leaned her head far back and stared at the ceiling for a moment. Then she straightened. "Your visit with Nandou was short."

"He gave me this." Simone held out a book: *Preface to Cromwell.*

"Ah. Did he tell you how he came to have it?"

"Yes. And he showed me the writing: *Victor Hugo to the dwarf Nandou.* He was reciting me a passage from it, about the harmony of opposites, but then he said he was very tired and leaned back. And he . . . I wondered . . . Should he be lying there like this?" Simone closed her eyes and put a fist to her chest.

Jeanne cried out as if something were ripping in her throat and ran down the hall.

The doctor came with his needles and his morphine and his long face.

Edmée came, and Henri, and friends from the theatre, who stood about the dining and sitting rooms in anxious clusters. Some of them went in briefly to speak with Nandou; others simply waited to hear their reports.

Edmée sat beside him for a while. "My good friend," she said softly, "what is there that I do not owe to you? The best part of my own life, the safety of my son's—everything that matters to me has been touched by your courage and cleverness and generosity. Sometimes when I am saying my prayers, I feel it is you I should be thanking ahead of God."

He smiled and whispered, "Blasphemer."

She leaned closer; his breathing was not easy.

"Many wonderful evenings together," he said. "Have many more in Italy . . . with Henri." She nodded. "Good friend," he said. "To me and to Jeanne." He closed his eyes and added faintly, "Best friend. Thank you."

Edmée's hands went to her mouth. She left the room. Jeanne moved from the shadows and slid back onto the chair.

Gabrielle and Simone came in a little later. His eyes opened, saw them, grew brighter.

"Oh, Nandou," Simone said, "you are so sick, and I love you so much."

"To see you . . . makes me better."

Gabrielle fell to her knees beside the bed, crushing her skirt, not noticing. "I love you too. I always did, even when I . . . I always did. Do you know that? Do you believe me? Papa?"

"Ah." It was as long as a sigh, but without melancholy. "I believe you. Always did." He lifted a hand and touched her cheek. "Love your mother. Be good to her."

Jeanne came up behind her, and the three of them looked at him. "My ladies," he said, and smiled.

"Dou," Gabrielle said. "Oh, Dou . . . "

After a time they left Jeanne alone with him. She sat beside him and took his hand. It was cool and damp, and the nails bluish. He seemed to be asleep, but then he began muttering something: his final lines from *The Dwarf Lord*. His eyes opened. "When I first saw you . . ." he said, " . . . pierced my heart. I die with you . . . still there."

His body shuddered as if a giant hand were shaking it free of life, and fell back into stillness.

They buried him in Père-Lachaise, on a raw, bright day early in March.

The coffin was larger than a child's but smaller than a man's. Stage-hands and actors carried it, not professional pallbearers. The word had gone out, not only in the journals but on the tongues of those who had seen him perform, and as the procession moved along, winding its way up from the old Boulevard of Crime, through Belleville, it gathered onlookers on all sides, some hanging from their windows, others standing on the sidewalks, so that the coffin seemed flanked by a continuous audience, orchestra and gallery. The men took off their hats, the women waved their handkerchiefs slowly, and voices called, "Nandou!" or "Dwarf Lord!"

In the large coach, dressed in black, Jeanne sat stiffly with Gaby and Simone on either side. Henri and Edmée faced her. Edmée pulled aside one of the curtains. "Do you see the people?" she said. "Do you hear how they remember him?"

Jeanne looked to the window. The corners of her mouth lifted, then collapsed before a smile could form.

Simone peered through the curtain on her side. The sun dazzled like a spotlight, and a breeze snapped the black silk tied to the saddles and bridles of the horses. The world seemed amazingly, cruelly bright; she felt unable to breathe, so great was the disparity between the beauty of the day and the sadness of the ceremony. Then some words came into her mind, healing words that Nandou had recited to her on the day he died. *For true poetry, complete poetry, resides in the harmony of opposites.* "That," he had added, "is also the secret of a true and complete life."

She looked out at the crowd. For an instant, no more than the catching of her breath, she saw a face she thought was her father's. But of course she was mistaken. *Where does Papa go?* she wondered, echoing the line from her childhood. Wherever it was, he was gone. Like Nandou. Everyone in the coach would be gone one day. She thought of Bijou, waiting at home, who would lick her face and make her feel better; but Bijou could barely run to meet her any longer. A dreadful sense of the impermanence of life gripped her.

There was no priest at the cemetery. One by one actors came forward and recited or read: passages from Racine and Corneille, Musset and Molière, Lamartine and Hugo. There was the pain of Grand-mère Jeanne's face, and of the coffin sliding into darkness forever. Yet the words and voices were so beautiful that the wind whipped them away to keep, the sky was a vast bolt of blue silk, and not far away was a rise from which all of Paris spread out below them. *A harmony of opposites,* she whispered.

The wind touched her face. She lifted her head to the sky and looked as high as her gaze would reach. She smiled, knowing it with certainty: He was up there, a king, riding the wind at last.

The parcel came a month later.

A young man brought it to the house, the butler said, but no one had paid attention to what he looked like, and by the time the parcel was taken up to Simone and she finished her lessons and unwrapped it, there was no hope of tracing the deliverer.

It was a small painting, unsigned. Simone was sure she had never seen it before, or anything like it, yet something about it was familiar. It was of yellow lilies in a green vase, on a table before an open, sunny window, where a white curtain was blowing. The brushstrokes were fluent, and the colors brilliant, exuberant; Simone almost wanted to squint, as if looking into the sun, yet at the same time the colors drew her into them, so that she felt she must look deeper and deeper into the lilies and longer and longer at the vase. The white curtain blew in a motion both elusive and compelling, so that she could not stop looking at it and trying to catch the exact feeling it meant her to catch, which seemed always beyond her grasp, but only just beyond.

It was many minutes before she thought to turn the painting over; when she did, she gave such a cry that her governess came running. A paper was pasted to the back of the canvas: "To my darling Simone, so she may remember that her Papa loves her wherever he goes."

She hugged the painting and walked around the room holding it, Bijou following on stiff old legs. When Gabrielle came home, she showed it with a flourish: "I told you he would not disappear without a word to me. I told you!"

"I know you did, my sweetheart. I am very happy for you."

"Do you think he is in Paris, Maman? Do you think we can find him?"

"He would be a madman to be in Paris. And I do not think he wants to be found, or he would have given you some means to find him."

But I shall find him one day, Simone thought. *I shall!* The words were comforting. They made her feel that all would be well—that one day she would understand the strangeness of adults, who filled their lives, and hers, with secrets; who made one love them and then disappeared or died.

She took the painting to her room and hung it directly opposite her bed. When she turned her head, she could see the bookshelf where her gift from Nandou, the *Preface,* held a special place.

Her gaze went often from one to the other: from memory to hope.

Chapter Twenty-Seven

For nine years she looked at them, book and painting, in the morning when she woke and at night before she slept:

On the night she attended the revival of *Hernani*, starring Sarah Bernhardt; Jeanne sat beside her, dressed in black velvet and red silk, the emotions of the play striking her small frame so strongly that Simone could feel it reverberating beside her; or was it her own body that shook, and for the same reasons?

On the night after Great-uncle Nicolas took her and Maman to the latest exhibit of the painters who now publicly called themselves Impressionists; some people scoffed but others' faces held the look Simone felt on her own—as if she had been peering through the slats of a garden gate for years, but now the gate was open and she could enter and be part of the garden.

On the morning after she fell in love; she had gone to a party with Maman and danced with a certain Frédéric, youngest son of a banking dynasty, whose smile and a particular way of turning his head connected directly to a place beneath her breastbone.

On the morning after she fell out of love, realizing that, despite the sensations beneath her breastbone, she was turning herself into a mute, who smiled but could not speak of what interested her because doing so made strange expressions cross Frédéric's face, as if some unpleasant odor were wafting to him from the far side of the ballroom.

On the night she was in bed reading a collection of poems by Verlaine and her mother flung open the door to tell her that, quite suddenly, Great-uncle Nicolas had died of a heart attack.

Her mother sank onto the bed beside her, pale, tear tracks in her rice powder. The two of them embraced. Images of Nicolas crowded Simone's mind: his brow lifted ironically at family dinners, his smile broad if she dropped in at the firm and asked to be taken to lunch, his gray

eyes brightening if she asked about the financing of railway development or the operation of a stock exchange.

Gabrielle pulled away and looked at Simone indecisively. "I could
not have stayed here without Uncle Nicolas, after your father left. He
was the only Vollard I really liked. Does that shock you?"

"No. I think I have always known it. Does that shock you?"

"A little. A mother does not like to be obvious to her daughter."

"You are not, for the most part. Sometimes you seem almost a
stranger."

"Oh my dear Simone. Must you always say what is on your mind?"

"But I do not do so, Maman. I keep a great many things to myself."
It was strange to Simone that in the moment when she was confessing
to feeling sometimes distant from her mother, from that beautiful,
perfectly dressed lady whose manner could be a clear, impenetrable
glaze, she should also feel protective of her, and so loving that she
wanted to embrace her again, to feel Gabrielle's hair springy against her
cheek and inhale the jasmine scent she always applied to its upward
sweep at the back of her head, and promise her everything would
be all right. Instead, she took her mother's hand and said, "Why do
you . . . did you . . . like Great-uncle Nicolas so well?"

"*Did.* Already he is part of the past." Gabrielle shivered. "And what
of the future? Our future? Uncle Nicolas made it possible for us to live
as we liked, but now . . . " Her hands ran quickly over her hair. "I
appreciated the way he looked after our affairs after your father left,
but I liked him long before that—from the moment we met. Looking
back, I suppose I could say we shared a certain . . . inability to know
what would make us happy. Nicolas seemed to understand me without
my having to explain myself. Perhaps that was why I did explain. I used
to tell him things I told no one else. Does that surprise you?"

"No. But if he was the only Vollard you truly liked, what of Papa?
Did you not like him?"

"Of course. We were good friends, which, as you must have noticed,
is not a common state of affairs between husband and wife. But . . . isn't
this odd . . . I seldom thought of your father as a Vollard. He and I
were the outsiders. The rest of them were the Vollards."

"What was I?"

Gabrielle took her gaze from the past and her hand from Simone's.
"You are my lovely, intelligent daughter, who can be too grave for her

own good." When Simone did not reply, she said, "Do you think of him often? Of your father?"

Simone's eyes went to the painting across the room. "Every morning and every night." She turned back to her mother. "Do you think of him? Ever?"

"Yes, sometimes. But he and I were not . . . " Gabrielle compressed her lips and shook her head so sharply that a pin slid from her hair onto her lap. She picked it up and twisted it open with both hands. "He is not part of my life any longer. He cannot be. I may as well tell you, I have been thinking of trying to get a divorce, now that it finally is legal to obtain one, thank God."

"Better to thank people like Grand-mère Jeanne, who crusaded so hard for it. But could you get a divorce without Papa's being here?"

"I do not know. The law is so complex, and my circumstances so strange . . . Nicolas was going to help me learn what to do, but now . . . " Gabrielle had straightened the hairpin; she held it between her thumb and forefinger. "Now Nicolas is gone, and under the law you and I are in Denis's hands. Like this." Her fingers bent the hairpin into an arc. It shot from her grasp and *ping*ed onto the wood at the edge of the carpet, where she regarded it woefully.

Simone looked at her mother, whose dress of pale blue silk was draped over the latest, exaggerated version of the bustle. Her small waist was made smaller by a corset that began below her armpits and extended nearly to her knees, hollowing her stomach and pushing her breasts high. She was absolutely in fashion, but to Simone, her clothes expressed not only her elegance but also a constriction in which she seemed to live. Something about her was like Great-aunt Joséphine, though no love was lost between the two of them; though Gabrielle had none of the mannerisms that punctuated Joséphine's behavior like the scurryings of small animals, nor the sense of apologia that crept deeper each year into Joséphine's manner. They were in fact quite different, yet in each of them, Simone felt, something was locked too tightly. Into her memory came a long-ago summer day in the country, when she and her mother had gone running in an empty field, Gabrielle's skirt and petticoats flying in the wind, her black hair and her laughter streaming behind her. How long since she had done, or been, anything like that?

"Mother," Simone said, "I have decided I am going to do something. Perhaps you would like to come with me while I do it."

Gabrielle turned to her. "What is that, my dear?"

"I am going to go looking for Papa."

Gabrielle's color returned suddenly in irregular patches. "What do you mean?"

"I have always intended to find him one day. Now I am ready to start."

"But . . . how on earth will you do it?"

"I shall have to figure it out. Perhaps I shall begin by speaking to some of his former friends, his fellow painters. You must know who they were."

Gabrielle looked at her steadily. "I am afraid I do not. That was a part of your father's life I did not share."

Carefully, because even after so many years she was reluctant to breach the promise of secrecy she had once given her father, Simone said, "What of the painter in the building where the woman was killed? The man to whose studio Papa had a key? If I remember, the newspapers said his name was Belloc."

Her mother blinked, then lifted her chin and said, "I should never have let you read those old newspaper reports."

"How could I spend my life with a thirteen-year-old's understanding of what had happened?"

"Paris is filled with mothers who would not allow their daughters to read such articles—who never allow them to read anything without a chaperone." Gabrielle tapped the volume of Verlaine's poems lying on the bed.

"I am lucky you are not one of them. But what of that man, Belloc? Did you know him?"

"I have not seen him since the time of your father's arrest. I doubt that he is still in Paris. He always spent much time out of the city. As I recall."

"I shall go to his studio and find out."

"You will make me very unhappy if you do that."

Simone raised her eyebrows. "Why?"

"I do not want to live with ghosts. Your father's arrest was one of the most terrible things that has happened to me, and I prefer not to dwell on those times or the people involved in them."

Simone said nothing more on the subject until they returned home after Nicolas's funeral, days later. "Maman," she said, undoing a black hat and shaking out her chestnut hair, "I think I shall start looking for

Papa by going to Venice to see Grand-mère Edmée and Henri. He may have visited them at some time."

"You take away my breath. A young girl simply announces that she will travel to Italy? Who will go with you? Where will the money come from?—for you know Denis will not pay for such a trip if he has any idea of its purpose."

"First, Maman, I am not a young girl. I am nearly twenty-three, well educated, with no employment or husband to hold me back. Second, if you don't care to join me, I shall find someone else. And third, as to the money, I had intended to get it from Great-uncle Nicolas. But now . . . if no Vollard will give it to me, I shall ask Grand-mère Jeanne for it."

Gabrielle took off her gloves, one slow finger at a time. "Why not let the past settle quietly into the earth? Why try to find him when he does not wish to be found, when he has made no effort to contact us in nine years? I cannot understand why you are so determined."

Answers hesitated on Simone's lips: *Because I loved him so much. Because I want to know why he remains silent, if he truly loved me.* But she knew that, however true, they did not fully explain the strength of her feeling, which dug back into her childhood like the roots of an ancient chestnut into the soil. All she said, with a faint smile, was "I want to see what he is painting."

It was an odd sensation, to be locked in a rocking cage of wood and metal as the countryside passed before her through the unmoving frame of the train's window in a series of changing paintings. A field of haystacks like huge hats tossed neatly into a ring. A farmer and his wife, leather-brown, looking up at the train as if it hurt their eyes. A spread of tall grasses—wheat? barley?—like an army of little spears raised to the sun. A brilliantly green tree hanging over a bend in a river, in love with its own reflection.

Within each painting that passed, like a ghost presence, Simone's reflection hung in the glass of the window, with two others flickering in and out of the frame as the train swayed: Jeanne, who sat across from her, wearing a dark-red bonnet, and Gabrielle, who sat beside her, a sculpture of blue and cream feathers rising from her hat—all three of them in one plush-seated cubicle, plunging southward to Italy.

Gabrielle had not been going to come. Steadily she had declared her lack of interest in, and disapproval of, the trip. The day before they left, she had announced she was coming. "How can I leave you and your grandmother alone? You are too much alike." Jeanne had smiled and said, "That is true, Gaby. You are the odd woman out." It had been a light exchange, but Simone had known there was truth in it: The strongest bond among the three of them was hers and Grand-mère Jeanne's.

Simone thought of Jeanne as someone who had fought a long battle and finally won. The enemy was grief, which had attacked her when Nandou died, squeezing her in a grip so tight that she seemed always hunched in submission. Gabrielle had offered many times to stay with her for a while, or to find her another apartment closer to their home. Edmée and Henri had begged her to come to Venice with them. Theatre friends had offered their company, their homes, at any time. But she stayed alone in the apartment she had shared with Nandou for over forty years. "You don't understand," she told them all. "I want to have my tea at the table I am used to, and look out the window at the same *boulangerie,* and put my feet up on the same little stool."

Simone said to her one day, "I don't think it is truly the furniture or the view. I think you feel he is still here, and you don't want to leave him."

"But he is here, my wise child. Do you not feel him?"

The two of them had sat in silence, with the faint whirring of the gas and the occasional sigh of a floorboard or a cupboard. Gradually Simone had begun to hear other things: the little grunt he made when he got up or sat down, the "Pah" of his disbelief or displeasure, and underneath those sounds and all others, the cadences of his speech, not actual words but the rolling music of his voice, which filled the corners and spaces of the apartment. "I can hear him," she had said wonderingly.

"So can I. As long as no else is here but you. Not even your mother, whom he loved so much. Sometimes, when she was a child, I used to think he loved her more than I did. Certainly he was wiser about her. But when she was older, there were troubles . . . No, you are the only one he allows to be with us now."

That was the moment when Simone's relationship with Jeanne had begun to shift into adult exchanges. "I need to speak of him," Jeanne said. "People do not understand. They come in and tell me to look to the future, to go back to work. But I am so filled with him, with our life together, that if I do not speak of him, the words rise inside me into great piles and crush my heart."

"I understand, Grand-mère."

Many afternoons, finishing her lessons, Simone had gone to sit with Jeanne while she talked of life with Nandou: of how they had met and come to live together; of the theatre and *Hernani*; of a child called Solange and a kidnapping; of poverty and struggle; of a love slow to find its physical expression, which was therefore even more precious. Jeanne laughed as she told her tales, and wept, and Simone laughed and wept with her. From the telling she began to realize things that her mother had only hinted at, or glossed over: that Gabrielle was the child of Louis Vollard and had run away from Jeanne and Nandou when she learned they had not told her the truth of her parentage.

Questions had leaped into Simone's mind, foremost among them how her mother and father could have married if they were half-brother and sister. But she didn't ask, knowing the questions would break the spell; knowing that although her presence was crucial to her grandmother's reminiscing, at the same time Jeanne spoke as if she were not there.

"What do the two of you talk of for so many hours?" Gabrielle would ask, a bit uneasily.

"The past," Simone told her. "How things used to be with her and Nandou."

"It's not good for a young girl to spend so much time in the past."

"I like it, Maman. I like to hear about the way things used to be."

Gradually, as if emerging from a deep, restless sleep, Jeanne had begun to lift her head and look about her, rather than within. She had remarked on the new theatre season and commented acidly on the anti-Semitism inherent in the president's latest actions; and one day, after marching around the table in her old way—arms folded, eyes narrowed, mouth busy—she announced that since an international congress on women's rights was going to be held in Paris at the same time as the next international exhibition, she would be part of it. From that day, she had begun to rejoin the world.

She turned from the train window and smiled at Simone. She was seventy-one now, her hair as even and handsome a shade of silver as if an alchemist had worked its change, her skin soft but lined, like unironed damask. Once the years of her terrible grief were over, she had never referred to the hours Simone had shared with her. Sometimes Simone wondered whether she even recalled them, but when she smiled in a certain slow and loving way, as she was doing at the moment, Simone would know the imprint of those hours was permanent, even if buried.

"If you learn that Edmée and Henri know nothing of your father," Jeanne said, "will you conclude that he does not wish to be found?"

"I have already concluded that, Grand-mère."

"So you act against his wishes?" There was no censure in Jeanne's voice, only curiosity.

Gabrielle leaned forward. "I have told Simone she would best honor him by leaving him at peace in her memory."

"My memory is not at peace, Maman. It must know what has happened to him."

After a silence Gabrielle said, "Most mothers would not permit a daughter of theirs to make this trip. Joséphine Vollard would not."

"Is it not interesting," Jeanne said, "that you did not raise your daughter to be like the rest of the Vollard women? Perhaps you are still something of a rebel. Perhaps this railway carriage holds three generations of rebels."

Gabrielle looked pleased, then shook her head. "When the women travel in luxury because the railroad is financed by a family into which one of them has married, I do not think that one can be called a rebel."

Simone turned back to the framed beauty streaming past in the window, and toyed with the notion of her mother as a rebel. It was a strange perspective to take on the woman who, while seldom prohibiting Simone's actions, issued so many cautions about them. *I cannot prevent you from aping the English and their Rational Dress movement and abandoning fashion and the corset, but you realize your waist will never be trim. And people make fun of those Aesthetes you admire. . . . If you have decided Frédéric Lacroix is a fool, of course you cannot marry him. But you realize you may never again have the chance for such a match, or any match at all if you wait much longer . . . I am not trying to find a husband for you, as Joséphine and Sophie are. I do not want you to marry for the sake of being married. I only want you to realize that life is not simple for a woman who lives by her own rules . . .* Maman a rebel?

Perhaps it was not only impossible but also undesirable to see one's parents as others did. Perhaps one could love them only by holding them tightly within a frame, in which their sole passions centered on their children.

Jeanne leaned over to put her hand on Gabrielle's. "Shall I tell you something, my dear Gaby? You chose a path more difficult than being simply a rebel. Part of you wanted to be secure and accepted, and succeeded in so being, but the irony is that you have finished by defying society's rules as much as I ever did, perhaps more. You have done things, and faced things, I would have found too difficult. To write what I wanted, to live as I wanted—that has been easy, for I have had only my own wishes and demands to satisfy, not the rest of the world's. Halfway measures are hardest, for neither part of you can fully accept the other. Yet you have never complained of your choices, ever, and for that I respect you."

Simone watched her mother's eyes fill with tears and her hands grip Jeanne's tightly.

Venice seemed to have been sketched up out of the water in pastel chalks.

Edmée and Henri had a large apartment in an ancient pink-and-gray building that looked as if it might crumble softly into the water chuckling and licking at its blackened base. From the half-round windows of Simone's room she could see boats making their pointed way along the canals, their carved black feet lifting and rocking. She could barely wait each day to get out onto the narrow streets, where the very act of walking seemed different, muted by the liquid presence beneath the cobbles. Water was the law of gravity, drawing everything toward it in the curves and semicircles of bridges and leaning trees, anchoring the heights of the spires in its mirror, poking thin fingers into ancient corners, making the days a running green and the nights a liquid black.

A dozen times a day Simone thought how much her father would love to paint there. In every courtyard, before each bridge, someone seemed to be working at an easel; she could not pass without checking the person's face.

But Edmée swore that Marc had not been there. "My dear, he has never come to see us. I do not even know whether he knows we live here, for I have not heard a word from him since the day we said good-by in the Conciergerie."

"Do you have no idea where he might have gone, Grand-mère Edmée? He must have said something to you at some time that would give you a hint."

Behind the spectacles she now wore constantly, Edmée's brown eyes grew moist. "We had so little time together," she said. "So little."

"Do not upset yourself," Henri said, stroking her hand. "Let me bring you a fresh cup of chocolate. Simone, you should not ask her such questions."

Henri looked after Edmée as if she were helpless, and she, who had lived on her own for so long, accepted his protectiveness with equanimity. "Why does she do it?" Simone asked Jeanne in private. "Because she loves him," Jeanne said. "It allows him to forgive himself for what he did to her years ago."

"So they play a kind of game with each other? I do not think adults should have to do such things."

"No doubt you are right," Jeanne said calmly. "You never played any kind of game with Frédéric What-was-his-name?"

"Not with him. Only with myself."

Jeanne smiled and patted her arm.

They went every day to a church or museum, where Henri gave informed commentaries on Titian, Leonardo, Giorgione, Tintoretto— he supplemented a meager inheritance by writing articles and travel guides on the city—and shopped for glassware and leathers. Simone was aware of men looking appreciatively at her and her mother, rolling their eyes and uttering liquid phrases. Most of the attention, she noted wryly, was directed at Gabrielle. On those exotic streets she realized something she had never noticed in the familiar settings of Paris: Not only was her mother beautiful, she carried herself with a seeming indifference to her beauty that heightened men's response to it. In the late afternoons they all sat in the Piazza San Marco drinking bitter coffee while the sun struck the golden chipwork of the basilica and the strutting pigeons flung themselves into the air. In the evenings, after splendid dinners, they attended concerts, whose notes resonated against vaulted stone ceilings. The whole experience of the city was so mesmerizing—like being transported into the world of a fantastical book, which one dared not put down for fear of breaking its spell—that it was two weeks before Simone set out to do what she had come for.

On a Sunday morning when the others were chatting lazily over breakfast, she excused herself, went to her room, then slipped out the door, down the crumbling marble stairs, and into the street. All the bells in the city were ringing; the air, which shimmered with a thousand reflections from the water, parted to let through the rich-throated calls.

She strode along the cobbles, consulting her map frequently, feeling slightly drunk on beauty and anticipation. But when she reached the address they had given her in Paris, an old woman sweeping the stairs told her that no, no, no, the *signor* was not there; he was out painting, as he was every morning, even on the Lord's day, may his soul be spared, for he was not a bad *signor*.

It took Simone over an hour to find the square where the old woman had said he was working. By then the linen of her blouse was sticking to her shoulder blades and strands of chestnut hair had slithered from their moorings. She had not known whether she would recognize him, but as soon as she saw the broad back, she knew who it was. Quietly she moved up behind him. His outdoor easel was shabby, and there were two holes in the back of his shirt. He muttered to himself as he worked on a canvas of a bridge and the statue of a lion near it. It seemed expert to her, but rather flat. She was about to say his name when he stepped back to check his perspective and knocked into her.

He spun around, clutched her arm to keep her from falling, and spoke angrily in Italian until she said, "Monsieur Belloc?"

He stared and released her. "And who in hell might you be?"

She had meant to be artful and not reveal her identity at once, but his gaze was a demand for directness. "My father used to bring me to visit you in Paris," she said. "I am Simone Vollard."

"By God," he said. "By God. Mademoiselle Simone." He ran a large hand in circles over his beard, which was a salty mix of blond and gray. "What are you doing here?"

"Looking for you."

"By God." He laughed. "I think we have heard that enough for one morning, even if it is Sunday. So you are the little girl who used to sit on my table with her brown eyes as big and wise as an owl's." He laughed again; the sound rolled in the air like a bell's. He put his hands on her arms and looked at her searchingly. "It is good to see you, Mademoiselle Simone. But why do you look for me? How did you find me?"

"At your Paris studio, they told me you lived in Venice now and gave me your address. Someone there directed me to this square. I wanted to see you because I am trying to find my father."

Belloc was still gripping her arms; there was a sudden stillness in his energy. "Why do you come to me?"

"Because you and Papa were good friends, were you not?"

"Yes." She sensed that he was relieved, for some reason. He released her.

"You are the only painter friend of his I ever met," she said. "I thought he might have contacted you after he disappeared."

"He did not," Belloc said. "I am sorry."

He knew things he was not telling her; Simone was sure of that. "Will you talk to me about him?" she said. "Will you tell me everything about him? We could go to that little restaurant over there."

"No man would want his daughter to know everything about him. But yes, all right, I will talk to you." He began to get ready, cleaning his brushes, emptying and wiping his oil cup, folding his palette down into a rectangle and tucking it into the paint box that fitted so cunningly beneath the picture rest on the easel. "You go about the streets alone, do you?" he said.

"If I find it necessary."

When they were seated at a table outside the trattoria, with wine and bread before them, Simone said, "Did you believe Papa was guilty of the crime they charged him with?"

"Never for a moment. Marc Vollard loved light and color and beauty with a passion that is simply not compatible with blood and brutality. I told the idiotic police at the time, but they do not seem to consider issues of a man's soul relevant. In all the years I knew Marc, I never even heard him express anger at anything besides his inadequacies as a painter."

"Was he inadequate, then?"

Belloc drank off a large quantity of the wine. "No. He was the best pupil I ever had. In the early days, my studio was quite a going concern—until I decided to spend every moment of good light on no one's canvases but my own. I suspected I had a divine gift, you see." His laugh boomed out. "By the time I realized that my true gift was for teaching, that I was a perfectly good painter but nothing more, perfectly good . . . " He lifted the wine and grimaced, as if it had gone rancid. "By that time I did not want pupils any longer, with their careful little compositions and their boring little palettes. Your father was different, though. We became friends. He had a vision, by God he did, but I do not think he could ever surrender himself to it completely. Something always held him back—that damned bank, I believe, which hung like a chain around his neck. I told him a painter cannot be pulled between two lives. He knew it, but . . . For reasons I never grasped, he could not cut his ties to that damned bourgeois existence . . . " Belloc stopped and looked at her. "Do I speak of a way of life that is sacred to you?"

"Not sacred," she said. "I find the world of business intriguing, but I do not feel I belong to it."

Belloc's gaze went over her like a probe. She was suddenly aware of his energy, his maleness. He must be sixty or more, she thought, but she would wager he had no shortage of female companionship. "Are you married, Simone Vollard?" he asked.

"No."

"Why not?"

"I have not met someone with whom I wished to spend the rest of my life. And you, Belloc? Have you a wife?"

"No. For much the same reason." He laughed; she could see that the wine had darkened his tongue. "So the Vollards—your mother—allow you to make your own decisions about such matters?"

"My mother is a modern woman. She does not force me to do anything, least of all to marry." Belloc was silent, but his eyes went a shade more blue. Simone leaned over the table. "Please. Is there anything at all you can tell me about my father that would give me a hint where he has gone? Did he never say, 'If only I could go to Germany or America to paint, or Florence or the Auvergne?' "

"No."

"If you did know where he is, or suspect," she said, "would you tell me?"

The clangor of the bells had stopped. Belloc poured himself more wine, then leaned back and looked up to the sky. "Such extraordinary light here. It is filled everywhere with reflections of the water." Simone waited, looking at the slant of his beard and the leathery skin of his cheeks. Head still lifted, he said, "What do you want of your father? If you were to find him, what would you say to him?"

"I would say that I love him and ask him to come back into my life, at least a little bit, if that is possible, enough so I can feel he is not dead to me." She waited. "If that was a test, Belloc—if you do know where he is and are trying to decide whether I can be trusted with the information—I should like to know whether I have passed."

He brought his gaze down to hers. "Simone, I cannot say where he is."

Cannot say, not *do not know.* Simone was ready to push him further,

as far as she had to, when she saw astonishment seize his face. She heard
her mother's voice: "Simone! What are you doing here?" A moment
later Gabrielle was at the table, standing between them, holding a green
parasol, blocking the sun.

"I am talking to Monsieur Belloc, Maman," she said. She saw that
his astonishment was giving way to wry amusement and that her
mother's color was as high as if she had fever. "I have been asking him
if he knows anything about Papa."

"This is what you came to Venice for, isn't it?" Gabrielle said.
"Wanting to see Edmée and Henri was only a ruse."

"No. I did want to see them. But when I learned that Monsieur Belloc
was here as well, it seemed only natural to try to speak to him." That
explanation, Simone thought, was not far enough from the truth to
qualify as a lie.

"Why did you creep away from the apartment like that?" Gabrielle
said. "You deliberately did not tell us where you were going."

"I feared you would object. It seems I was right. Did you have
someone follow me? The maid, was it, or one of the concierge's boys?"

Belloc pulled out a chair, and his voice curled into the tension rising
between them. "Join us, Gaby. It is Sunday, it is beautiful, it is Venice,
and the wine is not bad at all."

She turned to him for the first time, as if reluctantly. "I do not want
to join you. I want Simone to come back to the apartment with me."

"But I have not seen you for many years," he said. "How have you
been?"

"Splendid."

"That is all? One word?"

Gabrielle gripped her parasol tightly. "After Marc's disappearance I
had a life to rebuild for Simone and myself. In the main I have been
successful."

"I would expect nothing less from a woman of your abilities and
charms." Belloc folded his arms and smiled up at her. "As for me, since
you do not ask, I have been enjoying a life of modest failure and
intermittent pleasure. The latter would increase if you would sit down
and join us."

"What have you been telling my daughter?"

"That I do not know where her father is."

Gabrielle's gaze ricocheted between the two of them, then settled on
Simone. "You will come home with me now, please."

"I was just telling Monsieur Belloc of my good fortune in having a mother who does not force me to do anything."

Gabrielle pushed back a lock of her hair, which was still thick and black. "I am not forcing you, Simone. I ask you to do something that is of particular importance to me. Please."

"You will make her wonder why it is so important," Belloc said. "Joining us would be simpler and wiser, I think."

"I did not ask what you think. I do not care what you think. I do not want or need advice from a man like you." It was as if a coiled rope had suddenly risen into a whip. Simone regarded her mother in amazement.

"Ah, well," Belloc said, as lazy as honey, "no reprimand is too painful when delivered by a beautiful woman."

"No doubt you speak from as vast an experience of reprimands as of women."

"No doubt you are right."

"You are a completely selfish creature, Belloc. Do you ever think of anything except your own pleasures?"

He grinned. "Why should I?"

Simone watched Gabrielle reassert her customary control with effort; only a tiny jaw muscle escaped. She turned to Simone. "Shall we leave now, dear?"

"How nice it would be," Belloc said, "to sit here with you in the kind of light your father would love and reminisce about him."

Simone did not know how she suddenly had become a pawn between them, or why. She felt as ignorant as a child, except about one thing: If she defied her mother now, however badly she wanted to do so, something in Gabrielle would be destroyed, and she, Simone, would have done it. She looked at the vagrant muscle dancing in the rigidity of her mother's jaw, then took from her purse the small notebook she always carried, scribbled something on a page, and got to her feet. The sun flashed up in a hundred pieces from the water of the canal. "If you think of anything you wish to tell me about my father, Monsieur Belloc," she said, "please send the information around to this address." She gave him the piece of paper. "Very well, Maman, let us go."

As they walked away, Gabrielle took her arm; she felt her mother's body trembling against her own and Belloc's gaze on her back.

They were in a gondola, halfway to the apartment, before either spoke. "Why do you hate him?" Simone said.

"It is not a question of hatred. I do not trust him."

"Why?"

"Dear Lord, Simone, must you always ask *why* about everything?"

"About this I must."

"Yes, yes, I suppose so. Well, then, the truth is that Belloc did not do everything he might have to help your father when he was arrested. In my opinion he would be quite capable of telling you a lie if it suited him."

"Why should it suit him? Ah, sorry, Maman. But when I was a child, I thought Papa liked Belloc a great deal."

The prow of the gondola lifted and fell like a sigh. "Do not speak to him again," her mother said. "Promise me. Please, Simone. Please."

Suddenly Simone was not in a gondola in Venice but in a carriage in Paris, riding away from a secret visit, being made to promise one parent she would never tell the other where they had just been. Stuffed with secrets and cautions, implored to be silent . . . *No more,* she wanted to say. *Let everything be as open and bright as the sun striking this water . . .*

She looked at her mother's tight face. "Very well, Maman. I promise."

Two days before they left—at a long lunch when Jeanne and Edmée and Henri were talking so vividly of the past they had shared that Nandou seemed to be at the table with them—the maid handed Simone a note a boy had just brought for her. She excused herself and stood by the windows that looked over the canal while she read it:

Simone Vollard,

I liked the color of your eyes and the angle of your chin. I have decided to tell you something. There is reason to believe two things about Marc Vollard: He will never again be known by that name, and he is living in Paris. If you ever find him, and I do not know whether to hope you will, you may tell him that, despite promises made to the contrary, you received the above information from your devoted servant,

J. Belloc

Chapter Twenty-Eight

*V*ictor Hugo was dead.

The president designated a national day of mourning. Government offices, factories, business, schools, shops, restaurants—all were to be closed. The House of Vollard was no exception, although Denis, who had assumed his father's guiding role, remarked at a family dinner that, great man though Hugo undoubtedly was, he did not merit the adulation due a king. "To me," Simone said quietly, "France's glory is that she will honor a poet above a monarch."

The Arc de Triomphe was swathed in crepe, and Hugo's coffin was taken there to lie in state guarded by horsemen and surrounded by flags bearing the titles of his works. Simone went out early in the morning, wearing a simple dark dress that gave her tall figure the freedom to breathe and move easily. She needed every bit of her height and mobility to fight her way to the Arc, for all night it had been flooded by waves of people calling out Hugo's verses, weeping, laughing, drowning the coffin in wreaths and flowers. She had to be there, not only for her own sake but for Nandou's, and for Jeanne, who said regretfully that she lacked the strength to contend with crowds and would watch the procession from her window. Simone wedged herself between a man with a child riding his shoulders and a woman clutching a worn copy of *Notre Dame de Paris,* just in time to see the arrival of the pauper's hearse in which Hugo had requested to be carried, adorned with nothing but two small wreaths of white roses. When the speakers, who included the presidents of the Republic and of the French Academy, had finished, the hearse began its journey to the Panthéon, accompanied by regiments of calvary and infantry, followed by a heavy swell of humanity. Overhead were both the clear, bright sky and the gas lamps, flickering with a twilight pallor because they were covered in crepe. *A harmony of opposites,* Simone thought. She smiled, and a young man marching beside her smiled back. He had very brilliant brown eyes and pale gold hair that the breeze blew back from a high forehead. "Are you alone?" he said, and it seemed to her that he asked half in admiration and half in concern.

"Today no one in Paris is alone," she replied.

He nodded. "My father has read *Les Misérables* a dozen times," he said.

"My grandmother was at the battle of *Hernani*."

They smiled at each other again before their gazes returned to the scene around them.

The population of Paris had grown to two million; the throngs following the procession and watching its passage easily totaled that many people. As she moved along, Simone looked into the crowd lining the streets. The faces were as varied as the humanity about which Hugo had written, she thought, glimpsing a patch over an eye, a schoolboy-smooth chin, a heavily rouged cheek. Words had reached them all, gone to their hearts and minds as directly as arrows to a mark—but carrying life with them, instead of death. A fantastical idea began to come to her: She was marching in tribute not only to France's great poet but to language itself, to the power and glory of words, which opened people's minds to one another and allowed the profoundest of thoughts to reach the simplest of men and women. Nothing was more important, she thought, and if she was to do anything with her life, if she was to find something to absorb her restless energies, it must have to do with words: not the creating of them, for she knew she was no writer, but something more than merely admiring them and surrendering, as a spectator, to their power. She swore it to herself, on the day of Hugo's funeral and in his name . . . She gasped and swung back to the crowd she had been only half-seeing. There had been something in one of the faces—eyes, an architecture of nose and cheekbones—that was agonizingly familiar. But she could not find it again. He had moved, or she had been swept past him. She tried to push back through the forward surge in which she was caught, but it would not give. Brows frowned at her, eyes glared, bodies refused to yield. She cried out in frustration, and felt the man beside her take her arm. "What is it?" he said. "May I be of help?"

"My father!" she cried. "It was my father, I know it. I have been hunting for him for weeks, all over Paris. I must go after him!"

She would always remember that the man asked no questions, merely shouldered his way into the people around them. "Let the lady through, please, let the lady through!" With his help she managed to break free; she stood for an instant on the edge of the marching crowd, shouted "Thank you" at him, then began to make her way back to the spot where she thought she had seen Marc.

But if she had, he was there no longer.

She redoubled her efforts: roaming the Latin Quarter, sitting for hours on the terraces of cafés to watch the passing traffic, visiting the places in the Bois and the Jardin des Plantes where she could remember being with Marc while he painted, sometimes taking a carriage back to the Right Bank and venturing far up to the maze of streets that was Montmartre. Twice she was approached by a painter and asked to model, and more than once she was regarded askance by fashionably dressed figures whose eyebrows lifted at the sight of her uncorseted figure, loosely arranged hair, and heelless shoes. But she never caught a glimpse of anyone who even resembled her father.

One night she sat on the bed in her room, between the book and the painting, wondering whether it was hopeless to roam a city of two million people armed with nothing but hope, when there was a knock at the door.

Her mother came in, flushed. "Dear Simone, I must speak to you about what you are doing, this crazy search that takes you out all day every day."

"Maman, you cannot tell me anything I have not already thought—"

"Please let me say what I came to say. I am not here to argue, only to give you something I never meant to give you. But now I must do so, in the hope it will persuade you where my own arguments have failed." While Simone looked at her quizzically, Gabrielle produced a small envelope from the pocket of her dressing gown. "After your father left, when I went through his effects, I found this in a drawer in his studio. I dislike showing it to his daughter, and I cannot imagine he would want you to read it, but if it is the only way to keep you from wasting your days and your spirit looking for him . . ."

Simone took it with hands that wanted to shake: What could it be that her father would have never meant her to see? Grotesque possibilities loomed in her mind—a confession to the rape-murder he had been charged with, a suicide note—so that she felt relief, not shock, when she saw what it actually was: A poem. An erotic poem of love. It was unsigned but clearly meant for her father; his name appeared several times.

She read it twice before looking up. "Do you know who wrote it?"

"You are not shocked? Somehow I knew you would not be . . . I have no idea who wrote it, nor do I care to learn. The point is that your father had a life apart from his life with me, with us. I am glad he did—does that, at least, surprise you?—for he was not happy with me. Nor I with him. We were good friends, but we . . . lacked the capacity to make each other happy. When we were young, we did not think that would matter. But it does, Simone. It does." Her mother brought her palms together slowly, as if holding a moth between them. "I feel certain that when Marc escaped, he would go to this . . . lover, if possible. So, you see, not only would he be afraid of revealing his whereabouts to us for fear the police would learn of them, he would have this additional, powerful reason not to be in touch with us. He would want to put this life behind him and leave it there."

"Including me, Maman?"

"I know it is difficult to accept, but do you not see that if your father is living somewhere with a new lover, he would want to make a clean break with his past?—for your sake as well as his own."

"No, I do not see that. He might have been reluctant for me to know when I was younger, but now I am an adult. I am not going to be shocked by a mistress, especially if she makes him happy. Papa would know that. I am sorry, Maman," Simone added gently, "but I cannot see that this poem is reason for me not to try to find him."

Gabrielle stared at her cupped hands as if the moth were struggling inside them. "You force me to tell you things you have no need to know."

"I do not mean to force you in any way, Maman."

"I know that. It is not you . . . When one is young, one makes a decision. It seems safe. It seems to be an end of things, to problems. One feels such relief. One does not see that the decision is only a beginning, that other things will flow from it, dozens of them, in directions one did not foresee . . . " Gabrielle shivered. "Because of something I have always known about your father, Simone, I believe that his lover, be it the person who wrote him that poem or someone new, is . . . is not a woman. Ah. I see you are shocked at last. Now perhaps you will understand why he would hate to be found, by his daughter above all.

Do this last thing for him, for his peace of mind as well as his safety. Leave him alone, wherever he is. Whomever he is with."

Finally Simone was able to reply. "Are you sure, Maman?"

"How could I not be? I am so sorry, my dear. I did not want you to know, but you . . . "

"I made you tell me." Simone shook her head. "So Papa is one of those men who are despised . . . vilified . . . " Her eyes widened. "What a sad life you must have had together, Maman."

Her mother looked startled, then grateful in a pathetic way, as an animal might do if one released its paw from a trap. Simone embraced her. "I expected to be comforting you," Gabrielle said.

That night Simone looked long at the painting: the lilies that pulled her into their yellowness, the white curtain that was always blowing yet never moved. Her mother was right: She was shocked—by what she had just learned, but even more by the realization that she did not, and could not, know her father the adult. When she thought of finding him again, she always pictured the man whose smile held only love for her: the man who came to kiss her good-by before the police took him away. But he was not that man now, if he ever had been. In him were gates he had never unlocked to her. Had Belloc known about them? Is that why she had been told never to speak of the visits to Belloc? She felt the cloak of secrets from her childhood slipping around her again and lifted her shoulders to shake it off, to be free of it, to live in the sun, as the lilies did, bathing their faces in the light. . . .

Her father thought she would be ashamed of him, even hate him. Maman believed that was why he had never tried to contact her. But was it so dreadful to be the kind of person who loved those of his own sex? Admittedly she knew nothing about it. Perhaps it was an admission of ignorance even to assume there was such a thing as "the kind of person." All she knew was that the law, and society, regarded such men—men like Rimbaud and Verlaine—as criminals and made their names synonymous with depravity. Aunt Charlotte had paled with outrage when she chanced one day to find Simone with a volume of Rimbaud's poems. What would she do if she knew of Simone's vow?— to find a way to be part of the world of such writers, of all writers, once her father was found.

She would never believe he was depraved, Simone thought, or a criminal. When she found him, she would tell him so. If he had chosen to live in a way she did not understand, she would simply . . . learn to understand it. Then they would be free to love each other as they had done when she was a child.

Her mother's revelation, she thought, had been intended to stop her search for him, but, ironically, it had strengthened her resolve.

She picked up the poem and read it again. Clearly influenced by *Les Fleurs du Mal,* it was not the equal of Baudelaire, to be sure, but it had been written by someone of talent. She read it over and over, no longer trying to connect it to the father she had known, but pretending it was written to a stranger: a stranger about whom she might learn something. Before long she began to see that the allusions could refer to actual places; that possibly she could extract some kind of clues from them.

The Vollard family had gathered for one of its occasions: Joséphine's seventieth birthday.

In a pearl-gray dress of lace, chiffon, and velvet, she sat at the head of the table in the chair that had been Nicolas's, darting tight smiles around the long oval as if ladling them out with a spoon. When Nicolas died, she had surprised the family by virtually collapsing and taking to her bed for many weeks. Despite their obvious mismatch, it was as if his existence had been necessary to maintain her in an upright position. "Maman, you must pull yourself together, for all of our sakes," Denis said. But she merely shook her head. There was no one to whom she could have confided the truth: Without Nicolas's wealth and power to make her feel safe, she could not shake her fear, a literal fear of stepping out of the house, where she would be easy prey for the haughty eyes and lifted noses of the women she had always called friends but who she knew had as little affection for her as she had for them. They had tolerated her, despite all the scandals that had racked the Vollard family, only because of the barrier of money and influence that Nicolas built around her. She had not been aware of its existence until the night when, perfectly healthy during dinner, he had collapsed an hour afterward; not until the doctor, bloodless lips parting, had said that, despite all efforts, he had failed to save her husband. Then she had seen it all too clearly: herself protected from an army of jeering faces by a ring of fire, like that female in the opera by the new German composer she disliked, and the fire that held everyone at bay was created and fed by Nicolas. Within days of his death a new thought had seized her: If she had not burned Louis's suicide letter—if she had at least told Nicolas about it—Nicolas would not have died. Many times she had been on the verge of telling him but had always been stopped by fear of his anger. Now it was too late, forever too late. She had confessed her act to a priest but found only temporary relief in his whispered absolution. The weight of the letter would go to the grave with her, crushing her like a coffin lid, forever reminding her that she had not been a good wife. She had done her duty by Nicolas but nothing more. Now her punishment was to be left alone, unable to hold her head and spine straight, trembling at the idea of stepping out her front door, needing all her strength merely to sit at the head of the family table.

It had not taken her daughter-in-law Charlotte long to realize that the reins of family power were loose and to pick them up. It was Charlotte who had summoned all the clan to the birthday dinner: "Very well, Maman Joséphine, if you do not wish to come to our house, or anyone else's, we shall have the celebration here." Charlotte had decided on the menu and supervised its cooking, and now, her chin at an imperious tilt, she guided the conversation away from Denis and Blaise's discussion of how the price of steel continued to lower, thanks to the Bessemer process, and toward subjects of more general interest, such as the huge metal tower Monsieur Eiffel was talking of building for the next Universal Exposition, the obvious supremacy of César Franck's music over Richard Wagner's, and the fact that Blaise and Florine had attended one of the splendid Tuesday evening receptions at the home of the celebrated Dr. Jean-Martin Charcot, who had turned the old poorhouse and asylum, the Salpêtrière, into one of the most famous centers of neurological research in Europe.

Charcot was apparently prepared to take an interest in Florine's illness, which finally had been given a name: hysteria. Pale as ever, she had just endured another series of the treatments that left her virtually unchanged, prey to spells of fainting and debilitating weakness. She talked in her soft voice of the furnishings of the Charcot home, the impressive list of other guests, and the penetrating, even frightening gaze of the doctor himself.

Simone, who had said virtually nothing throughout the meal, leaned forward. "Do you know what treatment he will suggest for you?"

"No, not yet."

"Will you go to the Salpêtrière?"

"I believe I should do so, to the special ward for cases like mine."

"I am not sending my wife into a lunatic asylum," Blaise said firmly.

"Are there still lunatics in some of the buildings, then?" Simone asked.

"My dear Simone," said her cousin Victorien, "do you not see that such a question is upsetting to Florine?"

"Is it? I am sorry. I was merely curious."

"I am not upset," Florine said.

"We do not wish to intrude such subjects into a birthday dinner," Charlotte said. "Do we, Maman Joséphine?"

Everyone turned to look at Joséphine, who flushed, looked rapidly around the table, and said, "No, no. Quite right. Quite right."

Simone lapsed into quiet again, and as soon as the cake had been brought in—three tiers, lacy icing, and candied violets—and she had taken several bites of her slice, she stood and said, "My apologies, Great-aunt Joséphine, but I am unable to stay. I wish you every joy on this occasion, and hope to be present at many more."

"What do you mean, you are unable to stay?" Charlotte asked.

"I have another engagement."

"Excuse me, Simone dear, but I do not find that acceptable. On an occasion such as this, you cannot be disrespectful to our dear Joséphine."

"I am not disrespectful, cousin Charlotte, merely otherwise engaged."

"At what, may one ask? If a suitor has finally appeared, I shall be the first to applaud, even though I do not condone your leaving an important family occasion."

"I am sorry, cousin Charlotte, but the nature of my engagement is private."

"Gabrielle!" Charlotte said. "Can you not discipline your daughter?"

Gabrielle's chin rose until its angle equaled Charlotte's. "Simone is a grown woman, no longer subject to my discipline and certainly not to yours."

"No doubt that is the reason she is unable to find a husband to give her a proper place in society."

Do not do this, Simone told herself, even as she began to do it: "If you insist on knowing my destination, cousin Charlotte, I am going to Montmartre."

"Montmartre!" The eyes of the entire family joined Charlotte's and fixed on her. "I think we deserve some explanation," Charlotte said.

"I do not agree," Simone replied. "This is 1885, and I am a modern woman. But I shall explain, nevertheless. I am going to Montmartre because I have a job there, and I must not be late."

She had already been going to Montmartre periodically, but the poem—two passages in particular—had convinced her to search nowhere else, to abandon the Latin Quarter and all other possibilities. One passage was a description that could well be Paris viewed from the Butte: "At dusk, prone below us, the huge body starts to tremble with light; from the star of its navel, the veins fill with slow fire." The other was a verse that could be describing the streets canting up sharply from the place Blanche and the tranquillity of the little houses and fragrant gardens that made Montmartre seem like a country village, and must have done so even more years earlier, when the poem presumably was written. For several weeks she had gone there nearly every day, dressed simply and unobtrusively, to wander amid the fairy-tale charm of the windmills and street fountains, the orchards and old wells, the finches nesting in the acacias. Paris, with all its steel and bustle and smartness, seemed as distant as another country. But she had not dared to go into any of the shops or cafés and ask after her father, for Marc Vollard was a fugitive from justice. In any case, Belloc had said he no longer used that name.

She stopped in various cafés for lunch, to study the sketches and paintings adorning their walls. Some of them struck her powerfully, but she could not swear that any of them had come from her father's hands, and the ones she liked most were signed with an Italian name. After lunch she would stay for several hours to observe the parade of artists, models, writers, journalists, and demimondaines, and the people who in growing numbers came up from fashionable Paris, attracted by the radicalism and decadence that clung to the name of Montmartre; in fact, Simone had begun to feel a bit nervous that someone might recognize her. In addition to older establishments like the Dead Rat and the Black Cat, new cafés were opening, vying with one another in creating exotic atmospheres: Italianate, medieval, countrified. One even created the ambience of the Commune, dressing its waiters as convicts.

But in none of those cafés was there a glimpse of her father, and on none of the streets had the men working at their easels turned to her with his face.

One day, when she was gloomily watching a painter in the square across the road and wondering whether it would be more profitable to visit the cafés at night—and whether she had the courage to do so alone—the idea had come to her, outrageous and tantalizing.

The next day, instead of lunching at the café she had chosen, she had approached its owner and asked for a job as a waitress. He had looked her up and down, as if appraising the value of her brown skirt and white blouse. "Never worked any place else, have you?"

"No."

"Why should I take you on, then? I'll wager you never worked hard at all."

"I will learn quickly and work as hard as anybody." With sudden inspiration, and a measure of truth, she had added, "I have been a model, but the work isn't steady enough. I need something more dependable. Please, monsieur. You will not regret it."

Later he had told her he didn't know what quixotic impulse made him agree—sheer curiosity, perhaps. She had started with two afternoons and nights a week and been promoted to three, and it was indeed harder than anything else she had done. Racing across the sawdust-covered floor with trays of soup and chicken and sausages and glasses of beer, wine, and absinthe. Wading through clouds of cigar smoke and ducking below people's line of vision when a singer was performing at the front of the room. Keeping orders straight and bills correct. Ignoring the sniping of the older male waiters, some of whom still could not accept the idea of women serving beer. Trying not to be distracted by the conversations boiling up from the tables: denunciations of the Ecole des Beaux-Arts and the Republic, claims that only Communism would save the country and the world, discussions of the best places to buy paints and brushes, arguments over whether "symbolism" or "decadence" was the best word to express the nature of the new poetry. There was no sign of her father, but she saw Zola several times, and Degas, and one evening Verlaine himself. Sometimes she would stop in the middle of the floor simply to breathe in the yeasty, dusty, smoky smells and the pungency of ideas; but in moments one of the male waiters would snap her back into action. "I feel that everything there is in a wonderful ferment," she had told Jeanne, to whom she had confided the secret of what she was doing. Jeanne had clapped her approval and demanded detailed accounts of all that happened.

After considerable hesitation, Simone had also told her mother, who rolled her eyes toward heaven, argued for over an hour, and then subsided in defeat, demanding only that Simone hire a cab to take her home from the café each night. "But if the family ever learns what you are doing . . . They believe there is nothing in Montmartre but Socialists and prostitutes. And are they so far wrong?"

Yet her mother had defended her at the family dinner, Simone thought, as she tied on her white apron in the bare little room behind the café's kitchen and twisted her hair into a high knot at the back of her head. She should not have said what she had at the dinner; it had been foolish, if satisfying, and they would find ways to make her pay for it. Her mother would have to pay as well, which was not fair. Poor Maman, Simone thought. If she found her father . . . *when* she found him . . . she would ask him to help her mother get the divorce she wanted. She peered into a small, cracked mirror, stuck a last pin into her hair, and smiled, thinking of the looks on Aunt Charlotte's and Uncle Denis's faces. Then she heard the owner calling her, and dashed into the kitchen.

It was a busy, lively night. Apart from the regulars who began drinking absinthe before five o'clock and grew quieter each hour, staring down into the green liquid with waxed expressions, everyone seemed in a happy but disputatious mood; the air was thick with laughter, shouts, and smoke. Before the cabaret began, there was a rush of new arrivals: "society" coming up from the wealthy drawing rooms far below the Butte. Simone raced about, replenishing drinks, barely able to notice whom she set them before. The man had to wave his hand wildly and finally catch at her apron before she realized he wanted to do more than place an order. Assuming he was one of those with after-hours assignations on their minds, she said tartly, "I serve food and drink, nothing more."

He smiled. "I only wanted to ask if you ever found your father."

"Oh," she said. "Hello." It was the man who had walked beside her in Victor Hugo's funeral procession and helped her fight her way out of the crowd. "No, I did not find him," she added, conscious of the hair that had escaped from its knot and the fresh beer stain on her apron.

"I am sorry. You seemed so distressed that day."

"I was. Thank you again for your help."

It was difficult to hear; the cabaret had begun, and the singer was spitting out satiric words in a piercing, smoky voice. The man motioned

Simone to take the chair next to him, momentarily vacant. "Somehow," he said, "I did not think you were a waitress in Montmartre."

"What did you think I was, then?"

"A patroness of literature. A *pensionnaire* of the Théâtre-Français."

"I thought you were probably a poet."

"Alas, no. I have just finished law studies at the Sorbonne."

"And I am . . . " She made a decision. Leaning closer, she said, "I work here because I am still trying to find my father, and believe he is in Montmartre."

The man was silent for a few moments, his brown eyes searching her face as if it contained something he had lost. "What is your name?" he said, so quietly that she had to lean closer still.

"Simone Vollard."

"I am Paul Renaud."

They smiled at each other as they had in Hugo's funeral procession.

"What do you do when you are not working here?" he asked.

"I think of the publishing company I would like to start," she said and then blinked, astounded by three things: the idea itself, which she had not even known was in her mind; the complete rightness of it; and the strangeness of learning it in this stranger's presence.

He said, "I should like to continue our talk some time when you are free."

"I should like that, too."

"Would you lunch with me tomorrow?" He named a modest, pleasant restaurant near the Sorbonne.

"Yes. One o'clock? Now I must get back to work."

"Until one o'clock."

She walked away, aware of moving in a subtly different rhythm because he was watching her. When he left with his friends, she was surprised at the degree of her disappointment, and as she ran about with her trays of drinks, she kept recalling the way his blond hair slanted off his forehead. She was not scanning the crowd with her usual keenness, so she did not see the two men come in. When she glanced at their table, she knew only that, despite a full beard and longer hair, the angle of the shoulders on one of them and the set of his eyes reached into her memory and declared themselves to be her father's.

The noise and bustle of the café receded to distant surf. Only when one of the waiters nearly crashed into her did she realize she had stopped in the middle of the path to the kitchen. The waiter's hiss jolted her back into action. She moved about the floor mechanically, aware not of what she was saying or doing but only of the booming of her heart and the oddness of the muscles near her mouth, which seemed to have been glued into a smile.

She did not recall going toward the table; she simply found herself standing there, looking down at him.

His beard, thick and brown, had altered the shape of his face, but the eyes were the same. "Yes?" he said. "We gave our order to the other waiter."

In all the times she had imagined finding him again, he had looked at her, smiled the beautiful smile that was his alone, and embraced her. It had never occurred to her that he might not recognize her. Had she changed so much between thirteen and twenty-three?

"Hello, Papa," she said.

His face went as still as if she had struck it. Then he blinked three times, slowly. "I am sorry, you mistake me for someone else."

"Please, Papa, it's me—Simone. I have been looking for you for so long."

His glance went briefly to the man sitting with him. A look of discomfort flashed across his face like a bird streaking past a window. "I do not know any Simone," he said.

"Are you angry because I have found you?" she said. "Is that it?"

"I tell you, I do not know you," he said firmly. "Please leave us alone, or I shall have to speak to the owner."

When she turned and walked away, he thought his heart would leap from his chest and go after her.

"Are you all right?" Octave said.

"Yes. No. No, I am not. I never imagined she would come looking for me. How did she find me?"

"She is a handsome woman. She must be clever as well."

"Certainly she is clever. And determined and lovely . . . " Marc put his head in his hands. The cabaret singer launched into a verse that everyone knew; around them people rocked and sang,

> *"There was a big white wall—bare, bare, bare,*
> *Against that wall a ladder—high, high, high,*
> *On the ground a red herring—dry, dry, dry . . . "*

"I did not think you would turn her away," Octave said.

"Haven't I always said that if I chanced on anyone from the old life, I would claim not to know them?"

"Apparently I never believed you, or I would not be so surprised." In spite of the turmoil that gripped him, Marc smiled.

"Would you like to leave?" Octave said.

"Soon. When I have reassembled my wits. When I have had the chance to look at her a few more times."

They sat quietly until Octave said, "She moves like a beautiful big cat. If it were not so noisy in here, we could hear the silence of her walk."

"When I painted, she used to sit beside me on a stool with her legs twisted around it, watching my every move. I would feel her eyes going from the brush to the canvas to my face. Sometimes I would have the crazy idea that she could see the images I had in my mind." He looked at her across the café, memorizing the planes of her face and the curves of her movements, praying she would never learn the truth about him. After a while he said, "We had better go."

Outside, the cabaret music drifted after them and the moon washed everything in white light, through which the roofs and streets cut slanting black lines. Marc found it hard to believe that only an hour earlier he had come down the same steep incline with his old life as far from his mind as a foreign land; he had walked in the freedom of mind and body he had begun learning on the day he left Belleville, which finally had let him approach Octave's door and which he had come at last to take for granted. The two of them had gone abroad for several years—Italy, Switzerland, Germany—but he had always known they would return to Paris and Montmartre, which was part of Paris yet existed in defiance of the values of the city below it; where the light and language were French; where no one looked askance at two men sharing rooms, or cared to search behind the beard and name for signs of Marc Vollard. He had thought there were none to find. Then Simone had stared down at him with eyes that made him remember everything.

"I feel like Judas," he said.

"Betraying her?" Octave said. "Or yourself?"

"Does it matter?"

They had gone only a short distance farther when Marc heard someone running behind them up the steep street. He turned and saw her coming after them, holding up her skirt so she could run freely. He watched her approach.

She let her skirt fall, caught her breath, and said, "If you are not my father, who are you? What is your name?"

He hesitated. "Marcello Vianello."

"Oh! Two of your paintings are on the café walls. That is why I wanted to work there—I liked them best of any I saw. I thought, something about them is like my father's paintings, but his were never so brilliant and so free."

"I tell you I am not your father," Marc said. He feared his voice would strangle him, because it was speaking the truth.

The moon reduced half of Simone's face to shadow and made the other half preternaturally clear and pale. "I see," she said. "Very well, I shall not trouble you further. I shall only wish you happiness." She started to leave but looked back. "I shall not stop loving you, no matter how your feelings for me have changed."

She set off, her shoulders broad and straight. The breeze carried up a strain of song. *"Against that wall a ladder—high, high, high . . . "*

"Simone," he said softly. "Simone!"

She turned and came running. He put his arms around her and wept.

She refused to hear of leaving now that she had found him, no matter what the hour was, so they went to the apartment, the three of them, walking up and up in silence except for the clicking of their steps and the deep pulls of their breathing.

Once inside, Octave lit the lamps and offered to leave the two of them alone, but Marc asked him to stay.

"This is my friend Octave Guilbert," he said, "who shares these rooms."

"How do you do?" Simone said formally.

Octave brought out wine and glasses, and they sat around the plain pine table in awkward silence while Simone's gaze went around the room. It seemed to Marc that she was a stranger now; he had felt closer to her while pretending not to know her.

"This is the way I live," he said, half in apology, half in pride.

Simone said nothing.

"How can your mother let you come up here and work at night? A young woman alone . . . "

"She could not stop me. I am twenty-three row, and I am not one of those hothouse women who faint at the smallest thing and need a chaperone to go outside their own doors. Maman understands. She would not want me to be such a creature."

"How is your mother?" Marc said.

"She keeps busy planning her musical soirées and going to the opera." Simone lifted her glass but put it down untouched. Her fingers were rather short and square, Marc noted. "Do you paint every day?" she asked.

"Yes. Sometimes all day long."

"Sometimes all night as well," Octave said, then looked as if he regretted speaking. It was impossible, Marc thought; how was he going to explain Octave to her? Or anything else, for that matter?

"I want to look at those paintings," she said. She took up a lamp and went to one of the many canvases that sat about the room. She held up the light and looked at it long and closely. Then she went to the next one, and the next, until she had examined them all. Marc was aware of Octave watching her in the quiet, focused way that always made it seem he was composing words to describe what he saw.

She came back to the table. Despite himself, he could not help using the sentence from her childhood: "Well, Simone, what do you think?"

She smiled. "They are wonderful, Papa. Magnificent. You have not abandoned Impressionism, have you?—and become 'scientific,' with Seurat." He said nothing; it was odd to hear her speak of painting as an adult. "But even so," she added, "these canvases are quite different from what you used to do. Are you yourself different too?"

"Yes," he said softly. "I have given up doing things I do not wish to do and pretending to be what I am not."

She sipped her wine. "Why did you keep saying you did not know me?"

"I thought it would be easier that way."

"For whom?"

"That is the question, isn't it? For me, yes. But also for you. I wanted—I still want—you to have a life uncomplicated by me and my difficulties."

"I know what you were charged with. I know you were not guilty."

"Bless you. But I wanted the shadow of my arrest to fall over you as little as possible. I wanted you to forget me, put me out of your mind and life. I am Marcello Vianello now, and have been ever since we . . . I . . . came back to Montmartre. As far as the world is concerned, I am a painter who was raised between his father's Florence and his mother's Paris and now prefers to live in the latter."

After a pause she said, "Why did you keep your same initials?"

He shrugged. "I don't know. Force of habit, perhaps."

Another pause. "Do you know that Uncle Nicolas died?"

"I read it in the papers. He was a good man, who was always good to me."

"And to Maman and me. He was your surrogate. But now we are in Denis's hands. You know that the law does not permit a wife or daughter to spend money without a husband's or father's consent. With Nicolas gone, that consent must come from Denis. Do you want us to be in that position?"

"I regret it more than you can know. But I can do nothing about it."

She lifted her chin. For a moment the face he saw was Gabrielle's, and he wondered if Gaby were still lifting her chin at Joséphine and the cousins. He shook his head; they were ghosts, crowding into his mind without permission.

"When we embraced on the street," Simone said, "I could feel that you still loved me."

"I do. I always will. But that does not mean I am the man you once knew as your father. I cannot be that man, for reasons I am unable to explain to you. So is it not better, and kinder, for that man to cease to exist?"

"You do not have to explain your reasons to me," she said. "I understand them."

"No, Simone. You cannot."

"Yes, I do, Papa." She turned to Octave. "Are you a poet?"

He inclined his head. "Perhaps I am more of a soldier. I spend my time battling with words. Too often I lose."

Simone hesitated. *"I am left alone with dreams of bread and fire . . ."* Did you write that line to my father years ago? I find it very haunting."

For once Octave was speechless.

"How do you know the line?" Marc's voice seemed as harsh to him as a seabird's cry.

"Maman found the poem among your things. She gave it to me."

"She had no right to do that!"

"She thought that by telling me what it meant about you, she could stop me from searching for you. She said you would not want me to know such a thing about you, and it would be cruel of me to find you. Was she right?"

"Yes," he said, hating the truth of Gabrielle's words. "Yes!" Hating the fact that his daughter was not an adoring child but an adult, capable of knowing what he had become and looking at him with unsettling directness. "Yes, it is cruel. *You* are cruel." Above all, hating what he was feeling for the first time in many years: the loathing of himself, the Darkness, and hating her for making him feel it. "Leave me in peace to be what I am," he said, making each word the lash of a whip, watching for the marks it would cut across her face. When they did not appear, when she merely kept gazing at him, he cried, "Leave me alone!"

"But Papa," she said, "you must live in a way that makes you happy. I can accept that you do so. Can you not believe me?"

He felt the skin prickle on his face, then all over his body. What right had she, so young, to be so calm, so tolerant, when he had wasted forty years of his life enslaved by fear of the Darkness? How dare she speak as if the agony he had known had no more weight than a schoolboy prank? He had struggled to put her out of his life and his memory because of the shame and pain he had been certain she would feel—what right had she not to be feeling it? How dare she look at him as if nothing mattered, nothing, except the fact that she loved him?

"Damn it, I am not your father!" he cried, hearing the sharp intake of breath that followed his words, unsure whether it came from her or Octave. "If you understand what kind of man I am, then you know I was never a true husband to your mother. I am not your father!"

The marks appeared on her face at last.

By God, it was good to see them. His whole body flushed with satisfaction.

Then the satisfaction rolled away as quickly as it had come.

"What do you mean?" she said. "How can you not be my father?" Even in the gaslight he could see that she had gone quite pale.

He remembered a Christmas when she was seven or eight and had caught him filling the shoe she had left in front of the chimney. "Are *you* le Père Noël, then, Papa?" she had asked plaintively. He had had to admit that he was.

Octave said, in his soft, melancholy voice, "You cannot stop now, Marc. You must go on."

"Yes. I suppose I must." He ran his hands over the comforting thatch of his beard and fixed his gaze on Simone's face. "Your mother fell in love with someone. I did not mind, for I could not make her happy, not as a woman. When she became pregnant, I agreed to accept the child as mine. I did. I loved the child as surely as if she were my own—perhaps more, for I knew I would never father a child myself."

He watched tears fill Simone's eyes—her brown eyes, which he had sometimes pretended were like his own. Which *were* like his own, by some trick of fate or biology, if those were in fact two different entities. He put his hand over hers, but she pulled away. "If knowing I am not your father can make it easier for you to accept the other things I have told you, then it is good you have learned the truth."

She wiped her eyes with both hands, a child's gesture that made his throat close. "It may be better to know," she said in a thin voice. "But it is not easier." She lifted her wine and drank. Marc watched the liquid's passage along the smooth column of her neck.

When she set the glass down, she said, "I think perhaps I can guess who my natural father is. I promise you that if it had been in my power to choose between the two of you, I would have chosen you. Even now, even when I learn you did not tell me the truth, I would still choose you."

She was tearing him in two, Marc thought. Why had she come—to confront him with things he had buried, and force him to make the same painful choices all over again? He put his head in his hands.

Chapter Twenty-Nine

"I do not believe it," Gabrielle said. "You actually found him?"

"Yes, Maman."

"Well. My God. I do not know what to say to you."

"You could say you are proud of me, or furious with me. It must be one of the two."

Mother and daughter sat in the little study where Gabrielle did her correspondence and planned her musical events, invitations to which became more eagerly sought every year. She had been doing her schedule for the fall and winter when Simone, who had not appeared for breakfast, had knocked at the door. Simone was dressed with her usual indifference to fashion, and her expression, although struggling to be neutral, kept skewing toward triumph.

"Must I choose between proud and furious?" Gabrielle said. "It seems to me that I am something of both."

Simone looked startled, then smiled. In that smile, although it was not possible, Gabrielle often felt there was something of Marc's: transforming the seriousness of the face by seeming to lift its center of gravity. "I presume you found him in Montmartre," she said. "How is he? What is he doing?"

"He is painting, under a new name. He says he is happy, at least as much as is possible for him, and I believe him. I saw it in his work, which is powerful, Maman, quite brilliant and powerful."

"Is he alone?"

Simone hesitated. "No. He lives with the author of the poem."

"I see," Gabrielle said. What she saw was Marc's face, more clearly than she had for years, across the breakfast table they once had shared. Without naming the action in words, she had used to watch that face push away the vulnerability of sleep and tighten itself for another day, like plaster hardening into a death mask. *"Requiescat in pace,"* she murmured.

486

"What?" Simone said.

"Nothing. He must have hated you to see him . . . that way."

"It was difficult for him, yes."

"And for you?"

Simone did not reply. She looked at Gabrielle as she had never done: her lips tight together, her eyes motionless in the grip of the muscles around them.

"What is it?" Gabrielle said. "What is wrong? Did Marc hurt you somehow? I cannot believe he would. He loved you so much . . . What on earth is it, Simone?"

"He said he was not my true father."

"Oh, my God." Gabrielle felt she was sinking into a chair, but she was already seated; her blood seemed to be draining down to her feet and the tips of her fingers. She made herself look at the writing on the paper on her desk: *October 20. Sonata by Liszt. Arias by Verdi?* Had she written those things? Would she ever write any such words again?

"Is Belloc my natural father?" Simone said.

"Did Marc tell you that?"

"No. But I'm right, am I not?"

She could leave the room, Gabrielle thought; she could walk across the carpet roses, out the door, down the stairs, into the street. She could begin running, all the way to Jeanne and Nandou's. But Nandou was not there. She could keep running east, to Père-Lachaise, to sink before his headstone and ask again for the forgiveness he had long ago granted her but she could never fully accept. *How could you have believed that lying to me would be best for me? You who say the truth means everything?* She had said those words to him, and been angry with him for not being tall and handsome, like Louis Vollard. She had told him *I do not wish to see you . . .* Simone's question was retribution, put off all these years, no longer evadable.

"Maman," Simone said, "I must know the truth."

"Yes." Gabrielle's voice was as heavy as her body felt.

"Yes what?"

Gabrielle forced her gaze not to pull away; she must have the courage to look directly at her daughter. "Yes, you must know. Yes, it is Belloc."

Simone closed her eyes. Hours went by before she opened them and said, "Why did you lie to me?"

"We thought it was for your own good. And it was, Simone, believe me, it was!" The words would choke her, Gabrielle thought—those words for which she had once damned her mother and Nandou. She coughed and went on. "To tell you the truth of our relationship, to let you know that you existed only because I had had an affair with, with someone . . ." There was a strange pressure in her head, in her mind, as if other words were struggling to get to her lips. "It was a painful situation," she said. "Painful and not simple. I hope you can understand that. We decided . . . We tried to do the best thing for you . . . " The other words found their way. "Marc and I lied for our own good, too."

She realized where the words were coming from: Nandou. He had said them to her once. He had been honest with her. Now he was telling her to be honest with Simone; she could feel him in the room, almost see his eyes glittering.

"My darling," she said to Simone, "however much we wanted to protect you, we were protecting ourselves as well. If you had known Marc was not your father, then every time he looked at you, he would have had to face *why* he was not. I . . . I would face the hollowness of my marriage, which I would have left in a moment if Belloc would have had me . . . And once we had begun lying to you, we kept on, to protect ourselves from having to tell you that we had lied." Gabrielle felt the heaviness lifting from her voice and body. Nandou was lifting it, she thought; he was finally forgiving her for the way she had rejected him. No, that was not fair: He had forgiven her long ago. But she was finally able to accept his forgiveness.

"Tell me about Belloc," Simone said softly.

The temptation to speak of it, once if never again, should be resisted. But it was so strong. And wasn't Nandou's spirit with her, telling her to speak the truth? She looked into Simone's face—the face in which, ironically, she had never been able to see traces of Belloc's—and took a breath so deep it seemed bottomless. "I used to go with your father sometimes when he went to Belloc's. We would have dinner, the three of us. Belloc always flirted with me. He flirted with every woman, but I could not stop myself from believing he looked at me differently. I began to think of him all the time. I was like a child impatient for Christmas—I could not wait for the next time Marc and I would go to see him. Belloc knew what I felt. Perhaps men always know such things. He asked me to come alone to the studio. I refused at first, even though Marc and I had an understanding that I could do as liked in regard to men. But I had never liked. I had never fallen in love, you see. I had wanted to, God knows, but somehow . . . That was one of the reasons I felt it appropriate to marry your father. I believed I was a woman who did not have . . . normal passions. Perhaps I was right, for was it normal—what I felt for Belloc? Nothing mattered but him. Nothing. I would have lied, stolen, walked into fire to be with him. When I was not, I went home and stayed in bed and said I felt ill, so I could think of him without distraction. And he . . . he was merely enjoying himself. One day, after I left him, I stayed in the Latin Quarter to watch what he did. I sat in a dark corner of his favorite café, and around eight o'clock he came in, alone. I was exuberant. He wanted to be with no one but me! But half an hour later he was laughing with one of the models, and at ten they left together and went up to his rooms. I knew then that he was a man with no capacity to love anyone but himself. I knew something else—that what I felt for him was my punishment for having married as I did. I walked up to the Seine. I decided to throw myself in. But I couldn't because then I could never be with Belloc again. . . . Several weeks later I realized I was pregnant. I told Marc. We went to Belloc. Marc said, 'Gabrielle will leave me, with my blessing, if you will swear always to take care of her and the child.' I looked at Belloc. The answer was on his face. Before he could speak, I said to Marc, 'I have changed my mind, I do not want to leave you. I want to raise the child as your child. My only condition is that Belloc never be allowed to see it.' We agreed, the three of us. We filled our wineglasses and sealed the vow. From that night, as far as Marc and I were concerned, the child was ours. You were ours. If I had known Marc took you to see Belloc sometimes, I would have killed him. But I would have understood, for when Belloc asks for something, he is the most charming, persuasive man on earth. I never went to see him again, except once when your father was charged with the crime. I have never again felt as I did for Belloc. God knows I do not want to. Yet if he came to me now, even now, and asked me to go with him, I would not even look backward."

Simone was staring at her as if seeing her for the first time.

"Are you angry with me?" Gabrielle said. "But that is a foolish question. Of course you are. I—Marc and I—lied to you. You want to leave, run away, never see me again. I understand. God knows, I understand. But I do not think I can bear it." She fumbled for the handkerchief in her pocket and lowered her face into its perfumed softness.

"I suppose I can understand what you did," Simone said, "even if it makes me feel . . . I am not so much angry as numb. Nothing is what I believed it to be—not Papa, not you, not all the years the three of us were together. I am like a tree that has been yanked up by the roots and does not yet know where it will be transplanted."

"I am so sorry," Gabrielle whispered.

"I am sorry too, Maman, for what you have suffered."

"Oh God," Gabrielle said. "I can't bear you to be kind! How can you be?" She started to weep. She felt Simone put an arm around her shoulders and hold her tightly. For the first time she thought she might be able to forgive herself for the mistake of her marriage.

"I know it is here somewhere," Jeanne said. She took another box from the armoire in her bedroom and handed it to Simone, who placed it on the bed. "Unbelievable, the number of things one collects in a lifetime. After Nandou died, I vowed to throw most of it away, but I could not. I would have been throwing away pieces of my life. So I piled everything in boxes instead."

She opened the lid and spilled a pile of papers onto the duvet. "Ah," she said. "The last play I started to write. 1879, was it? About a woman who ran away from her husband. It was not good, so I gave it up. Besides, I am old-fashioned now, you know. Even if I wanted to write one of these Naturalistic plays, which I do not, I would be no good at it. Leave that to Zola, who is so enamored of 'the banality of everyday life,' to use his phrase. And let us give him his due, he portrays it well. But I cannot understand why one should want everyday life to be banal. No, I am just an old Romanticist at heart, who had to write in prose because she had no gift for poetry. . . . Ah, why do I pretend? The reason I have not written a play for over ten years, and never will again, is because I cannot write without him. What is the pleasure of staying up all night to finish a scene if I cannot wake him at dawn and make us coffee and sit down at the table while he reads what I have written?" Jeanne lapsed into silence, hearing his voice, then shook her head. "But you did not come for such talk, did you, my dear? Let us be disciplined! Let us move on! Let us open another box!"

Simone laughed, but her whole demeanor, Jeanne noted, was tense with purpose. Even her chestnut hair seemed to chafe at the ribbon that tied it back. One could almost pity the Vollards; if they had hoped to turn Gabrielle's daughter into a dutiful, fashionable young woman who occupied herself by waiting to be called to matrimony, they had been defeated. By Gabrielle, Jeanne thought, for however much Gaby had wanted the security of that world, she had allowed, even nursed, the flame of independence in her daughter. Perhaps Nicolas had helped as well. Poor Nicolas. A prisoner, not of respectability but of taking a part of himself for the whole. Had he died without ever again succumbing to the passions of the moment? Doing so was dangerous but also liberating, for it made one know directly the needs of one's soul. Edmée had learned that in the hardest way possible, but if she had not had the affair with Henri, would she have known how deeply she desired another kind of life? Would she ever—

"Grand-mère," Simone said, "what has happened to the discipline?"

Jeanne patted her cheek and went to the armoire for another box. "This one is promising," she said as its contents slid onto the bed. "Playbills from 1874, so the time is close. A piece in *Le Figaro* about Monsieur Zola and his unsavory characters—Nandou wanted me to write a response, but I never did. . . . Tell me, this desire to clear your father's name—does he want it cleared?"

Simone blinked but did not look away. "I do not know. But he must want it. After all, he has kept his same initials—M.V. He was not willing to let Marc Vollard go completely."

"People often retain their initials, I believe. I would not make too much of that."

Simone lifted the tail of hair off her neck and let it fall back. "Besides, if his name were cleared, he could resume responsibility for Maman's and my affairs. He could make Uncle Denis give me the money to start my publishing company. And Maman could get a divorce."

"Yes, those are all good practical reasons. But I sense in you a depth of feeling that practicality alone cannot explain."

"Do you think I should cease to feel strongly because I have learned he is not my father?"

"No, no, I do not say that. But I wonder . . . If you could clear his name, perhaps you think he would love you even more—enough to live with you again."

"What a foolish hope. One cannot buy people's love in that way." Simone said it so sharply that Jeanne knew there had been truth in her guess. But one could not make people accept the truth merely by stating it to them. Had Nandou not seen things about her that she denied when he named them? Had she not insisted that she did not want to learn to read; that Louis Vollard would marry her? And when she told Nandou she would never leave him, had he not refused to believe it for years? It was hard, she thought, to be old and to see clearly the deceptions people practiced upon themselves. Perhaps that was what it meant to be old: to see clearly but to be alone in one's vision, which could not be passed on to the young. If it could, they would no longer be young.

She took Simone's chin in her hand. "You must follow your convictions. If they demand that your father's name be cleared, then you must try to clear it. I do not see how you will manage, but I see that you must try."

"Nandou would have found a way, wouldn't he? No matter what."

"What a dear child you are!" Jeanne put out her arms and laid her cheek against Simone's, which was as fresh as petals.

"I am twenty-three, Grand-mère. I am not a child."

"Of course not. I must flagellate myself for my stupidity."

Simone laughed and pulled away. "Let us move on, Grand-mère."

"Yes, yes." Jeanne pushed aside a wad of papers. "This is the right box. Here is an envelope of pieces I wrote about Fossey for *Le Droit des Femmes* . . . And yes, here!" She picked up a fat envelope and removed a pile of clippings and a green notebook. "News articles about Albertine Fossey and her death. At first the journals barely mentioned it, but your grandmother Edmée and I set to work. I wrote about Fossey, we appealed to people we knew in the theatre and in the movement, and we called forth this sea of ink from the journals. We had no idea your father would be drowned in it." She sighed. "This is the notebook in which I recorded everything we learned." She began to leaf through it. "We went to some of Fossey's women friends. They spoke of a lover she had claimed to have." Jeanne squinted at her faded handwriting. "Here. 'Fossey bragged of a certain César in the bureau of the censor, who was mad for her. Said she tired of him but he would not leave her alone, so she threatened to tell his wife of their affair.'" Jeanne turned more pages. "Leroux, that was his name. Why could I not remember it? Because I am getting old. No, because he was a censor. Such men should be forgotten. César Leroux. Edmée and I investigated. His wife was from a family with some connection to the duc de Morny, so she probably did have the power to ruin his career. With her influence he left the bureau of the censor and got a position in the Ministry of

Justice. We learned that he had a reputation for outbursts of temper and that his colleagues regarded him as efficient but strange. Edmée and I got to see him by pretending to solicit funds for destitute women. I managed to work in a mention of the Fossey case, and Leroux grew quite unnecessarily vitriolic about what he called 'grisettes of the Latin Quarter.' And that is it, my dear. Hardly a court case against the man, but he was the only possibility we could come up with. If he hadn't been a ministry official, the Sûreté might have been persuaded to investigate him, but we did not see any hope, not when your father made such a convenient suspect." Jeanne handed the notebook to Simone. "Here it is, my dear, for whatever it is worth. Before you do anything, perhaps you should check out its legal implications with this new friend of yours, this lawyer named Paul."

"Yes, perhaps I will." Simone spoke evenly, but her eyes went to some private inner place and gazed hungrily. There was such conflict to being in love, Jeanne thought: the thrill of secrecy, yet the desire to tell the world.

Then, brisk again, Simone said, "First I must have a plan."

"Do you have any ideas?"

Simone laid the notebook against her chin and drew her brows into a V. "I must know where César Leroux is. I shall find his address and go there to see what I can learn. Perhaps I can pretend to apply for a position . . . a cook's helper? But they might ask me to cook something. If only I hadn't been such a poor student in the kitchen. Ah! I shall pretend to be a maid. Why not? I have been a waitress in Montmartre. Why do you grin?"

"It is like listening to Nandou hatch a plan."

"Or yourself, perhaps?"

"Perhaps. So I know plans can be dangerous. Promise me to be careful."

"There is absolutely no need to worry, Grand-mère."

Jeanne shook her head. Believing that, she thought, was another part of what it meant to be young.

In the Luxembourg Gardens, where students and scholars and nurse-maids wandered casually along the formal rigidity of the paths, Paul and Simone sat on a bench beneath an alley of clipped lime trees. "Once you got in the door and into the kitchen," Paul said, "I suppose the rest was simpler. Still, how did you manage to work the conversation around to him?"

"I said I had heard that Monsieur César Leroux was a difficult man to work for, and was that truly so? The footman rolled his eyes, and the butler said grandly that the elder Monsieur Leroux no longer lived there. 'Oh, really?' I said, all innocence. 'What happened to him?' The butler said it was not my place to ask such questions, so I knew something *had* happened. After surviving my interview with Madame Leroux, I managed to stay around the kitchen for coffee with the cook and the footman, and I got it out of them. César Leroux's behavior had grown very strange—and imagine when? Not long after the Fossey murder! Eventually he had to leave the Ministry of Justice, and two years ago he was put away in the Salpêtrière. It was all quite easy, Paul, easier than I imagined."

"Still, you took a risk," he said. "Going with your forged letter of reference, letting Madame Leroux think you were seeking a position . . . If they had suspected something, they could have called the police."

"But they didn't, did they?"

Paul narrowed his eyes against the sun and looked at Simone prosecutorially. Then he laughed, the sound rumbling easily from his chest. "Why are you laughing?" she asked.

"Because you are quite wonderful."

"Yes? Well, so are you," she said. They regarded each other and suddenly began to laugh so happily that two passing nursemaids interrupted their measured pace to turn and stare.

At length Paul said, "Very well. You have learned the gentleman's whereabouts. What do you plan to do next? Steal into the Salpêtrière by pretending to be one of the inmates?"

Simone looked thoughtful. "No, no, no," he said. "I am joking!"

She smiled. "So am I. I would never do anything like that, Paul. I am quite realistic, you know. I may like to take risks, but I do not believe in reckless endangerment."

He put a thumb on her forehead, pushed back a lock of her hair, and said, "I cannot decide which of you I prefer—the risk-taker or the realist."

"Must you choose?" she said, studying his face, which was slightly, endearingly crooked in a way she could not quite identify. Therefore she was obliged to study it often and at length.

He was the youngest son of a baker who lived in the Marais and always had more mouths than money to feed them: an old communard who barely escaped execution in '71 and believed that only communism could free the working classes and make them prosperous. He was proud that Paul was a lawyer, enraged that Paul had had to work at so many extra jobs to pay the tuition, and uneasy over the clients Paul might one day serve. He would be apopletic, Simone gathered, to see Paul gaze tenderly at a female member of a banking family like the Vollards. Paul himself was not a radical, but he had a keen sensitivity to the inequities of Parisian life, although his reactions differed oddly from Simone's. That very morning they had passed a beggar covered with sores holding out his bowl. As Paul dropped a coin into it, a carriage sped past with two elegant, laughing women, feathered hats bobbing above them like tiny swans. Paul had stared after it and said, "Is it fair? Yet are the women to blame for their wealth? Does it cause the beggar's misery? If we took it from the women and gave it to him, we would simply have exchanged his misery for theirs, which does not seem to be justice." By contrast, Simone felt uneasy confronting the spectacle of poverty, as if she should be doing something to eradicate it. "Guilt is the curse of wealth," Paul told her. "But I am not wealthy," she retorted. "My male relatives control all the family's money. They treat Maman and me, and their own wives and daughters, like children, incapable of making such decisions. And both society and the law sanction them in such a practice."

"I don't," Paul said.

One of the first things Simone had learned about him was that the year before, when the Faculty of Law at the Sorbonne finally admitted a woman, Paul had been one of the few males to speak to her. "If she has a good brain and works hard," he told Simone, "welcome to her. If she does not, then she can suffer the same fate I would in the circumstances."

"I knew you would feel that way," Simone had said.

The sunlight filtering through the lime trees struck Paul's eyes. He blinked, took his gaze from Simone's, and said, "Shall we have lunch?"

She nodded. They rose and wandered off hand in hand along the precise paths, toward the small restaurant they had come to think of as their own.

The next morning Simone called on her cousin Florine. Florine lay on a chaise in her boudoir, beneath a crocheted coverlet; her fingers worked in and out of its holes as she answered Simone's questions about her health.

"Florine," Simone said, "I know the family does not approve of me in many ways. I know they think that my idea of starting a publishing company is mad and that I must give it up, along with any similar ideas, and marry as soon as possible. Do you think they are right?"

"I don't know," Florine said cautiously. "Why ask me such a question?"

"Because I think that if you wanted, you could help me do something."

Florine gestured at her body as if it were a useless appendage. "All week I have barely been able to get off the chaise. I could do nothing for you."

"You could help me learn where a certain patient is in the Salpêtrière and then get in to see him."

Florine raised pale hands to her mouth and stared above them like a child peering over a fence at forbidden things. "You know Blaise does not want me to go into the Salpêtrière."

"I don't mean to ask anything impossible," Simone said, "but I have always thought you were more clever and adventuresome than you were allowed to be."

Florine's hands came down slowly. "Blaise says there is too much in you of Jeanne Sorel for the Vollards ever to trust you."

"He may be right. But I have no wish to hurt the family, Florine. I simply have certain things I want to do. Have you never felt that way?"

Florine's eyes, the pale, flat, blue-gray of cobblestones, grew moist. "Every day."

Into what thicket of emotions, Simone thought, had she blundered?—with her blithe assumption that by uttering a few provocative sentences and outlining the plan she had conceived, she could get Florine's help. "I am afraid I have upset you," she said. "I had better go and leave you to rest."

"I rest all the time."

"No doubt because that is what you need." Simone stood, tucking her blouse into her suit skirt.

"You never wear corsets, do you?" Florine said.

"No."

Florine pulled a lacy bedjacket more tightly around her shoulders. "Why do you want to get into the Salpêtrière?"

Simone hesitated. "To speak with someone who may make it possible to prove my father is innocent."

"Marc . . . ? There is no way I could help. What could I possibly have done?"

Despite her misgivings, Simone was ready to explain. But something stopped her tongue. "I had no plan, Florine. I was hoping you could . . . I was depending on you to figure something out."

"On me?" Florine said. An automatic demur started across her face but halted, and one corner of her mouth lifted, like a cat's ear pricking cautiously.

Louis XIII had built it as an arsenal for storing saltpeter. Then it had become an asylum for beggars, whores, and the insane, who were locked away and chained like beasts; then the biggest women's poorhouse in Paris. By now its many structures, haphazardly laid out around squares and amid gardens, housed nearly five thousand patients. Charcot might have made it a renowned research center, but in wards like the one where César Leroux was kept, the air of a lunatic asylum had not been dispelled. Patients moaned on their beds, or leaned against the walls like sculptures of misery, or moved about with a briskness that had no purpose or end. Scraps of speech rose and fell, sometimes without reference to any discernible reality. The only thing more unsettling than their eruptions was the vacant silence that followed.

Now that she was actually in the Salpêtrière, Simone was terrified. She had waited six weeks, impatiently but unavoidably, because what Florine had suggested, while her fingers twisted the coverlet, was that she herself should enter Dr. Charcot's special ward and from a position inside the hospital learn what she could about Monsier Leroux's condition and whereabouts. "Oh, no," Simone had cried. "I cannot be responsible for sending you into hospital."

"I want to go," Florine had said. "I am weary of this house and this chaise. I have been to hospitals in London and Vienna—why should I not go to the one right here in Paris? Dr. Charcot may be better able to help me in his special ward. Besides, why should Blaise always be the one to decide where I go, and when?" Simone saw that the spark of rebellion she had unwittingly ignited in her older cousin was coloring Florine's cheeks and stiffening her voice. Despite Blaise's objections, Florine's admission had been arranged.

Simone had visited her several times, explaining to Gabrielle that her sudden attention to Florine was fed by curiosity about this disease, hysteria, that seemed to strike so many women. There was truth in the explanation, but even so, she had to struggle to control her impatience. "You cannot have everything at once," Jeanne told her. "Why not?" she replied. And when Paul said, "There is no rush. It is better to proceed on a solid foundation," she had made a face and told him he sounded like a lawyer.

Most of the time she had kept herself busy by planning her publishing company: making lists of the works she would try to carry, investigating the costs of paper, ink, labor, and facilities. She even went to the House of Vollard to raise the issue with Denis again, as dispassionately and rationally as possible.

He listened, smiled tolerantly, and said, "It would not be appropriate, Simone."

"Why not, Uncle Denis? When you were my age, you were actively working for the House of Vollard."

"I am a man. The women of this family do not engage in behavior for which they are ill-suited by nature."

"It is my nature to love books. Why is it not also in my nature to publish them?"

"I have more judgment than you in such matters. Even if I were disposed to consider your request, which I am not, the kind of books that you admire would militate against my consent. No Vollard is going to be associated with authors the likes of Paul Verlaine and Arthur Rimbaud, and certainly no Vollard woman."

Fortunately, the day after that meeting she had visited Florine, who announced success. By putting innocent-seeming questions to various staff members, Florine had learned the whereabouts of the male patient César Leroux. She had confided to an attendant that she and her family suspected M. Leroux might know something about a long-lost relative; could it be arranged for a member of the family to see Leroux and try to speak with him? The attendant had been reluctant—for one thing, Leroux had said almost nothing intelligible since his admittance—but the promise of certain monies had changed his attitude. On Simone's next visit to Florine, she was escorted to a distant building and a large room; in one corner, with other patients frozen or wandering past him aimlessly, an elderly gentleman sat muttering to himself.

The reality of his presence made the impossibility of what she hoped to do sweep over Simone like a shower of ice. Of all the poor creatures in the room, she thought, she was the maddest. She swallowed hard three times, pushing down the urge to run away, put her hands solidly together to prevent their shaking, and said, "Monsieur Leroux?"

Silence. Only after she repeated his name twice did he turn to her, and then she wished he had not, for she had never had such a gaze directed at her: piercing yet empty, as if he saw everything but understood nothing. "How are you?" she faltered.

"Ha!" he said. The long locks of gray hair that framed his face swung like ropes. He got up and walked away, across the room, where he stood against the wall, arms folded, glaring into space.

Simone gave the attendant a beseeching look, but the man merely shrugged and folded his arms. It was that echo of Leroux's gesture, the duplication of indifference, that made her angry and gave her the courage to cross the room and stand beside Leroux. "Monsieur," she said, "will you permit me to ask you some questions?" Silence. "I wonder if we might speak of the time when you were still with the bureau of the censor." Silence, except for a moaning coming at intervals from an unseen room.

For fifteen minutes she tried to get him to acknowledge her presence, let alone to speak of the past. She felt eyes on her from all directions: the attendant's, the other inmates, everyone's but Leroux's. A ribbon of perspiration ran down the back of her neck and inside her collar. The moaning faded, but someone began marching up and down the center of the room, uttering with perfect clarity and deep conviction phrases that made no sense at all.

It was time to leave, Simone thought. She had been deluded to imagine she could achieve anything with such a visit. She looked at Leroux again. His lips, thin and dark, were clamped together. The madness in the room seemed to invade her brain. She leaned closer to him and said, "I am Fossey. Albertine Fossey. I can be killed but I do not die. I live on, to disturb the dreams of all who were cruel to me."

She was so cold that the ribbon of perspiration burned her neck. Now she was not involved in a simple, even amusing, deception, like pretending to be a waitress in Montmartre or a maid applying for a position. Now she was misrepresenting herself to a mental patient, with what consequences she could not imagine, should his family ever learn of it. Her jaws began to jerk with cold. She stared at Leroux, but he remained silent, unmoving.

She forced herself to breathe deeply and walk away, concentrating only on putting one foot before the other. The attendant shrugged and began walking with her to the door.

They had nearly reached it when the word came: "Whore!"—like a saw blade biting into a log. "Dirty whore! You deserved to die!"

Simone turned. One of Leroux's hands was outstretched, pointing at her, and the cords in his neck bulged when he spoke, but the rest of him was still immobile, as if he were a corpse whose arm and throat had been commandeered by an agonized spirit.

Chapter Thirty

*O*ctave had been up most of the night, polishing a verse for one of the journals that many cafés published regularly and sold to their customers. Marc planned to spend the day painting higher up on the Butte, and between Octave's going to bed and his own going out, the two of them were having coffee and rolls at the table. When their schedules diverged in that way, the breakfast that was also a nightcap often stretched into more than an hour's worth of talk.

Marc read over the poem Octave had revised. Called "Five o'Clock," it contrasted the hour of absinthe in the cafés and the hour of dawn in the village that surrounded them: one an awakening to oblivion; the other, to life. The images were splendid and melancholy. Through all of Octave's writing ran a dark, sad streak that never failed to stir Marc and also to puzzle him. In his own work he was mesmerized by light and its brilliance; why should he find his heart stirred by verbal images of night and misery and decay? For that matter, why should the reverse be true for Octave? The two of them had discussed the paradox many times but never come to a satisfactory answer—unless they accepted that they were two opposing and complementary halves of a single being. Octave had in fact accepted that explanation, even reveled in it, but Marc had always been reluctant to do so.

"I know why," Octave had said. "You think you have freed yourself to live this life with me, to accept being the kind of man you are, but in spite of all the changes in you, part of your soul is still chained to the old life." When Marc protested, Octave said, "I do not mean to the life itself, but to the shame you accepted for so long. We can never cut free of the shames of our youth."

Marc crumbled a last piece of roll, finished it off with the cold remains of his coffee, and rose to prepare for the day. He was working on a canvas of a street fountain with young girls standing near it, stretching out their fingers to the water. The water and their long hair and the ribbons in it were one kind of motion expressed in three textures and lit by the mellow November sun, and their bare, rounded arms had to gleam with life. Everything must be simple, unaffected: a composition arranged by Nature. He was, with luck, perhaps halfway toward what he wanted to achieve. As he took out his easel and the case that held his brushes, paints, and rages, the familiar sensation began in his solar plexus: the mix of tension, exhilaration, and doubt that was the continuo of his work.

Octave went to the cupboard and lifted the lid of the yellow crock on the second shelf. "Getting low," he said. "They had better pay decently for 'Five o'Clock.' "

"They will," Marc said.

The two of them seldom had enough money. The café journals bought Octave's poems and sketches by Marc, and occasionally he sold a canvas from a café wall, but no dealer had had success with his work. When the yellow crock was empty, he hired out as a day laborer, and Octave worked in a printer's shop.

"I must go to bed," Octave said, stretching, but the yawning reach of his arms was interrupted by a knock at the door.

Even before Marc opened it, he knew who would be standing there, her hair almost red in the light. "Hello, Papa," she said. "May I come in?"

When he did not answer, she simply walked into the room. "Good morning, Monsieur Guilbert," she said. Octave inclined his head.

She had not been back since the night of their conversation, four months before. At the café Marc had learned that she had quit her job that same night. He had decided she was going to leave him alone. Each day he had told himself he felt relieved.

"Papa," she said, "I have something important to tell you." Her voice was solemn, but excitement leaked around its edges like smoke beneath a door. "Today the charge against you for the murder of Albertine Fossey will be formally dropped."

She waited for Marc's response, her eyes snapping with eagerness. But the statement was too amazing to absorb. It hung outside his comprehension like the moon outside a barred window.

"What do you mean?" Octave said. "I do not understand you."

"The police have a much more likely candidate," she said. "A man named César Leroux, who is now in the Salpêtrière. In his ravings he talks of a woman he strangled with a scarf. He calls her a prostitute, abuses her with dreadful names, and says she forced him to desire her against his will and finally to kill her. He seems haunted by her and by what he did—at least that is the substance of his disjointed words, which are buttressed by the testimony of two of Fossey's women friends. She used to boast to them of being the man's mistress."

"Why was none of this known at the time of Marc's arrest?" Octave said.

"Leroux was then a government official who was behaving normally. He was sent to the Salpêtrière only two years ago, and no one deciphered his raving. Besides, Fossey was known to invent tales, so little attention was paid to what she might have told her friends, who are prostitutes."

"Who unearthed all of this?" Marc said slowly. "Was it you?"

"I had a great deal of help, Papa. Your mother and Grand-mère Jeanne had learned about Fossey's tale at the time, and Grand-mère Jeanne gave me the information. I discovered where Leroux was, and then cousin Florine worked out a scheme that got me into the Salpê-trière, where I talked to him and—"

"Florine?" Marc said. "Florine, with her vapors and her constant illness?"

"She seemed to come to life when I asked her to help me. Perhaps no one has ever asked her for such a thing. Then, once I had seen Leroux and managed to get him speaking, a good friend of mine, a lawyer, helped me take the information to the Sûreté. At first they were not very sympathetic, but he—Paul—knew how to persevere." She looked at Marc; her whole body seemed to tremble as if waiting to be embraced.

He could not move. He had told her a terrible thing—that she was not truly his daughter—but despite that rejection, she had gone out to clear his name. He felt awed by her defiance, and angry at her, and filled with love for her because she was *his*. Belloc had nothing to do with her, just as the unnamed stranger with whom his mother once had an affair had nothing to do with him. She was truly his daughter, as Louis had truly been his father. *Papa,* he thought, *was it this painful for you to love me?*

"Papa," Simone said, "I realize you no longer think of yourself as Marc Vollard, but I still believe you will be glad to know that, as of today, his name is no longer dishonored."

He sank into a chair. Did she not know what conflict she was now forcing him to face? No longer could he put it off, as he had been doing ever since the night he looked up from his beer to find her staring at him. He put his head in his hands.

"Papa, please do not weep. I thought the news would please you."

He looked up into her concerned face. "I am not weeping. I am afraid. Your news tells me how clever you are, how courageous and determined. Yet it lays a trap for me, and I am frightened."

"Papa!"

"What do you expect of Marc Vollard, now that you have resurrected him?"

"I do not know what you are asking,"

"Do you expect me to return to the old life now?"

"Well . . . yes," she said, as if the answer was both self-evident and surprising. "At least part of the time."

"You ask me to give up my happiness with Octave and return to a world that calls my happiness a crime. What does it profit me to be cleared of a murder I did not commit, if I must then be charged with depravity of my very nature? The world was willing to call me a murderer—do you think it will hesitate to call me evil?" He stopped, watching her face change. "I see you did not consider such matters. I do not blame you. Thank God you have a life in which such matters do not have to be considered. But how can I share that life again, Simone? You have done a wonderful thing for the father you remember, but he has ceased to exist. He is . . . no longer my concern." Marc spoke as gently as he could, trying to keep bewilderment and hurt from her eyes, but failing. "Now you see why I thought it better never to contact you again—because I would have to tell you things you find difficult to hear."

She bit her lips. "Why did you come back to live in Paris?"

"Because the art and the artists I admire and feel part of are here. I have become a selfish man. For ten years I have had the luxury of thinking of nothing but painting and doing only what is needed to make my eyes see more clearly and my hand move more surely. Nothing could induce me to give up that way of life. Not even my love for you."

She locked her hands together tightly. "Why did you send me the painting, then, and tell me to always remember that you loved me?"

"Because I do love you! But I cannot live in the same world as you! If I do, it will choke me, kill me. Can you not understand that?"

She lifted her hands and pressed them against her mouth.

"Poor Simone. She has two fathers, and both of them are selfish bastards."

"I have only one father," she said, "and I need him back. Maman and I both need him." A tear leaked down to the corner of her mouth; she licked it away.

"My dear," Octave said, "would you like to sit down and have some coffee?"

"No, thank you, Monsieur Guilbert. I will stand." She put back her shoulders.

The gesture knifed into Marc. "Only a monster would ignore what you have done, the love for me that your action expresses. Marcello Vianello of Montmartre *needs* to be such a monster. But can I?"

He turned to Octave, who said, with a melancholy smile, "You can wish things to be as they were before your daughter found you, but you cannot make them so."

Marc rose slowly. "If your mother wants a divorce," he said, "I can make whatever appearance is necessary. I owe her that, for never having told her that we are not . . . " He sighed. "I owe her that. As to Denis, I can tell him that you and she are to be given my inheritance, my share of the family fortune, to use in any manner you see fit. I can sign whatever papers are appropriate and necessary. But I cannot make Denis do what I ask unless I remain and enforce my wishes. If Marc Vollard reappears, it will have to be permanently."

"If he does," Simone said, "will he still love his daughter?"

She walked to the place du Calvaire and stood for a time looking down at the panorama of Paris. An odd feeling began to grow: that it all unrolled from her person; that the hundreds of skeins of streets, the broad strokes of boulevards, the curving metal of the Seine were all flung out from the core that was Simone Vollard. She remembered a day when Nandou had taken her to a bookstore and they had gone afterward to sit outside a café and watch the passersby.

Tell me, my dear, he said, *what is the center of the universe?*
Paris.

He smiled and said, *No,* and then, tapping the side of her head, *It is here. And here,* tapping the side of his own. *And out there, in each person passing by, in every bird in the chestnut trees and every cat who watches it.*

From its own perspective, every living thing is the center of the world. That is an important thing to remember sometimes, and sometimes to forget. I believe it is the secret of all man's glories, and the heart of all his troubles.

Simone smiled ruefully, then buttoned her jacket against a rising breeze and started down the incline.

"My dear!" Jeanne said. "What a happy surprise. I did not expect you today."

Simone embraced her and stepped into the apartment.

"Your mother is here, you know. It is Tuesday, when she lunches with me."

"That is part of the reason I came, Grand-mère. I want to speak with both of you."

Simone walked into the dining room, kissed her mother on a perfumed cheek, and sat at the table, where the plates held little piles of fish bones and the glasses were almost empty. "I went to see Papa this morning," she said without preamble. "I told him all that has happened."

"Ah." Gabrielle lifted crossed hands to her throat. "What did he say? Did he thank you for what you have done?"

"You knew how he would feel, did you not, Maman?"

"I told you many times he should be left in peace."

"He was not angry, was he?" Jeanne asked, disbelievingly.

"No," Simone said. "Well, yes, he was. A little."

"Surely he realizes what you did for him, how much you risked."

"I think he is proud of me, but in fact I have confronted him with a difficult choice. I did not see that at the time, but I do now."

Gabrielle said, "Did he tell you how he will resolve the choice?"

"If you need him to appear in order to obtain a divorce, he will do so."

Gabrielle lowered her hands to the table and studied them as if they were someone else's.

"He said he would come down . . . no, that's my phrase, not his. I think of him as coming down not only from the Butte but from another life. . . . He said he would come back and do whatever must be done to see that Denis gives you and me control over his money."

Gabrielle looked up. "He does not wish to claim his share of the Vollard fortune?"

"He does not *wish* to be part of this life at all."

Jeanne sighed. "I am afraid I understand quite well."

"But he will do it," Simone said. "For us."

"Darling," Gabrielle said to her, "you look so wretched."

"Why not? All I have done is to force Papa into a painful decision."

"You did what you thought should be done," Jeanne said.

"Yes. But I was thinking and acting from my own world. I forgot that his world is different. I think I forgot deliberately."

"In your world," Jeanne said, "he would say you are wonderful and he is thrilled to be coming back home. Isn't that so?" Simone nodded. "Instead he says he is not your natural father and does not wish to come back and live with you." Jeanne sighed. "It is hard to see one's father turn away from one."

"I wanted . . . " Simone looked down at her right hand, closed it, then opened it slowly, releasing words she had not known were waiting to be said. "I wanted him to embrace me and swear there would be no more secrets, to promise he would never hide anything again, or make me hide it. I wanted him to be the father I used to think he was, my true father, who loved Maman and me and would never disappear and leave us . . . " She stopped, listening to the echo of her words. "It all sounds so childish."

"Do the desires of childhood ever leave us?" Jeanne said.

"We loved you," Gabrielle said softly. "But we could not shield you from the consequences of our mistakes."

"And now I have made one, in turn, by forcing Papa to make this choice."

"Do not distress yourself," Jeanne said. "He knows you love him."

"So I should be thinking of him. And I am, finally. How can I ask him to give up a life in which he is happy, so I may have the pleasure of seeing him when I like and the ease of getting the money I need? I shall find some other way to get capital for my publishing company. I shall simply . . . do it. If I could find Papa and then track down the true murderer . . . " She swung her head. "I want your permission, Maman, to tell him not to come back to us, to remain Marcello Vianello and stay on the Butte and paint, and be as happy as he can."

Gabrielle ran her hands over her hair, then looked from her mother to her daughter. "You do not need my permission, Simone. I never expected him to come back. You are the one who found him. The decision is yours."

"Thank you, Maman."

"Besides," Gabrielle added, "if I am unable to get a divorce without him, I do not know that it will matter so greatly." She lifted an eyebrow in delicate self-deprecation. "It is not as if someone else is imploring me to marry him."

"I do not think you want a divorce at all, Gaby," Jeanne said tartly. "I think you are perfectly content with being Madame Vollard."

The two of them looked at each other, two pairs of dark eyes held in the combination of love and combat that had marked their relationship for decades.

"I feel no shame for what I am, Maman," Gaby said at last.

"That is good," Jeanne said.

Simone stood. "I shall leave you, then."

"Where are you going, darling?"

"Back to tell Papa."

"In a moment, Simone," Jeanne said. "Wait just a moment, if you please."

"But Grand-mère, I must find him and—"

"I am not asking you to stay, Simone, I am telling you. The impatience of youth is an excellent thing, but occasionally it must pause. There is something I wish to give you, and now is the time I choose to do it, so you can just sit back down and wait." She left the table and went toward her bedroom.

Simone looked quizzically at her mother, who returned the look in kind.

"Are you sorry now that you found your father?" Gabrielle asked.

"No. Never. But it does seem that the only people who will truly benefit will be the rest of the family. Uncle Denis and Aunt Charlotte and Great-aunt Joséphine will be delighted to have the scandal of Papa's arrest lifted from the family name. Such an irony. Isn't it?"

"If you think so, darling."

"And you—what do you think, Maman?"

"I think . . . that in the end, respectability often wins."

"I don't. I think rebellion has won more things for the world than anything respectable society could ever conceive."

"Perhaps you are right. But do not forget that it is the fate of the rebellious eventually to become respectable."

After a pause Simone said, "Now I see the true way in which Papa's name should be cleared—as a painter. People should know his work and appreciate how splendid it is. If I want to fight for him, that is the way to do it."

"Here," Jeanne said, coming back into the room. She carried a leatherbound box the size of a book, which she placed on the table in front of Simone with an air of ceremony.

"What is it?" Simone asked.

"In a moment you will open it and see. But first . . . " Jeanne ran her hands over the leather as if it were alive. "It is from Nandou, for you. He said to me, 'Give it to Simone when she has found something she truly wants and you are certain she could fight for it on her own. That is when it is best to have help.' " Her hands made a final circle on the surface. "You have shown how you can fight, my dear. Take it."

Simone raised her eyebrows, looked at the two women, then opened the lid. "It's some kind of papers . . . bonds?"

Jeanne nodded. "Nandou was clever, you know. He made a good deal of money from *The Dwarf Lord,* which he invested very prudently. And he also consulted your great-uncle Nicolas. He never amassed a fortune, but he was able to live very comfortably—we both were—and he put these aside for you. He did not know if you would ever need them, but he wanted them available if you did. And now I believe you do need them. They will not be sufficient to finance your publishing company, but they should give you a healthy start."

After a pause Gabrielle said softly, "I had no idea that he was doing—"

"Ssh." Simone lifted a hand. "If you are here, if you are listening in the shadows in the corner . . . thank you, my dear Nandou. Thank you."

"He is here," Jeanne said, and embraced her.

When they pulled apart, still looking at each other with love, Simone said, "I want to start by publishing poets—anything by Verlaine and Rimbaud, if I can convince them to let me do so, and poets no one knows yet, some of those who write for the café journals in Montmartre. I want to publish plays, wonderful old ones and brave new ones that are trying to tell the truth about life. I want to find someone to translate this new Norwegian author into French so Paris and I can read *Ghosts* for ourselves. I want—" She stopped suddenly. "Nandou would not like all the things I want to publish, any more than you will, Grand-mère. He might even hate some of them. Perhaps it is not right to use his legacy to publish such things."

"If he could, do you think he would order you not to publish them?"

Simone smiled. "He might try to convince me, but order me— never."

"Of course not. His whole life was devoted to the idea that art and artists—and all people—should be free. You should publish whatever you like, and not worry."

"I must be sure, Grand-mère, because, you see, in honor of his spirit, I intend to call my firm 'Nandou and Company.' "

"Ah." Jeanne sat back, her expression too serious for a smile but too happy for anything else. "Do you plan to publish anything that is boring or stupid, or simply repeats what other writers have already said and done?"

"Certainly not."

"Then you will be honoring his spirit."

"Thank you, Grand-mère."

"Besides, all artists, all who have anything genuine to say, are Romanticists in part, even when they rebel against everything the Romanticists did. I believe the very impulse to rebel is a Romantic one."

Gabrielle cleared her throat. "Simone darling, I am afraid that even though you have this money on your own, Denis will still have authority over how you spend it."

"No!" Jeanne said. "I would take it back before I allowed that to happen. I don't wish to alarm you, Simone, but I am serious. Nandou's legacy to be dictated by anyone other than Simone herself? Never."

"I understand, Grand-mère. If it came to that, I would want you to take it back. But it cannot come to that. There must be a way to make Uncle Denis leave me alone. I shall get Blaise on my side, somehow— perhaps Florine can help me. I shall think of something."

"You will not have to," Gabrielle said. "I shall do it. I have never waged a real war with any of them—unless you count telling Joséphine and Charlotte a hundred times that I would raise you as I saw fit, not as they wished—but if I chose to do so, I could create a scandal the threat of which would certainly make Denis pause." Jeanne and Simone looked at her questioningly. With one palm she smoothed the striped bodice of her silk dress. "I could simply tell the truth of what has happened in the Vollard family since I entered it, beginning with my own wedding."

"Maman," Simone said, "I cannot believe you want to do that."

"No, I do not. But if it is necessary to get you what you want, I shall."

Gabrielle lifted her chin. The three women regarded one another and smiled.

"Nandou and Company," Jeanne said.

Epilogue
December 27, 1897

The carriage pulled up to the Théâtre de la Porte Saint-Martin. "Are you all right, Grand-mère?" Simone said.

"Certainly. I told you I would be fine, and I am." Jeanne's voice was firm, in contrast to the slight tremor of her head, which had bedeviled her in recent years. She had a cold and had been confined to bed, but that morning she had risen and announced she was going to the dress rehearsal, she was extremely curious about this new play, and if Simone and Paul did not wish to accompany her as planned, she would go by herself.

"You must stop her," Paul had told Simone. "An eighty-four-year-old woman who is frail in the best of health and has now been ill for a week?" Simone replied, "You must have learned by now that there is no way to stop Grand-mère if she is determined. Remember how she insisted on riding to the top of the Eiffel Tower even though she was dizzy? Going to *Ghosts* only two days after she learned of Grand-mère Edmée's death?"

The three of them entered the theatre slowly, Jeanne supported by Paul's arm. When they were seated in a box, she carefully arranged the black lace of her bodice and leaned forward to study the audience. The white mass of her hair was pulled up and away from a profile as delicate as ever. Her cheeks were brighter with excitement than with rouge.

"I hope she will not be too disappointed," Paul mumured to Simone. Although the young author of the play had some reputation as a poet, the play itself was said to be so long and expensive, with a huge cast of characters requiring historical costumes, and so far from the Realism and Naturalism of the modern stage—it was actually written in verse— that even the management of the theatre was rumored to have little faith in it. The playwright had been forced to pay most of the production expenses himself, and his expectations of disaster had been whispered in theatrical circles for weeks.

"Grand-mère will accept what she has to," Simone whispered.

"As you do?" Paul took her hand and, in spite of their worry about Jeanne, they smiled, finding no less pleasure in each other than when they had married over ten years before. Paul had had difficulty convincing Simone, although his argument was perfectly logical: If she married him, she would not have to worry about circumventing her Uncle Denis in order to start her publishing firm, for Denis's legal hold over her would dissolve. "But yours would begin," she had retorted. Paul had countered by swearing that in practice she would establish and run the firm exactly as she saw fit. Still, she had resisted—until the day her uncle Denis told her she must stop consorting with a lawyer who had no money, no family background, and a Communist father. "Very well," she had said. "No more consorting. I shall marry him."

Jeanne turned toward the two of them. "A number of important people are here," she said with satisfaction. "At least they may hear some beautiful language tonight. Nothing like that *Ubu Roi* business last year."

"Dear Grand-mère, must I regret for the rest of my life that I took you to see that play?"

"Yes," Jeanne said, wrinkling her nose. *Ubu Roi* had opened the previous December. With "Shee-it" as its first word, and "bastard" in its second line, it had caused the biggest theatrical scandal in Paris since *Hernani.* Even the fact that the play attacked the bourgeoisie had not caused Jeanne, or most of the rest of the theatre world, to like it. "Too crude," she had said, and when Simone, playing devil's advocate, had suggested that, like *Hernani,* it was only struggling for a new freedom of language in the drama, Jeanne had rapped her knuckles on the table sharply and said, "Thank God Nandou is not alive to hear you say such a thing!"

Suddenly the prompter's three knocks sounded, the audience hushed, and the great red curtain rose.

Before the first act was half over, a fever of excitement was sweeping the theatre. Such poetry! Such glorious gestures and actions! And such a hero!—who composed elegant verse while fighting a duel! By the second act people were applauding so fervently that the actors could scarcely continue.

"I have never seen anything like this," Paul said during the intermission.

"I have," Jeanne said. "I was part of it once."

By the third act there was bedlam after many of the speeches. During the intermission people looked at one another in amazement, then burst into excited recountings of what they had just seen on the stage. The fourth act barely calmed them; the fifth act moved them to a solemn quiet. When the red curtain fell, a tidal wave of stamping and cheering and applauding began and gave no sign of ending.

"Grand-mère," Simone said after half an hour, obliged to shout into her ear, "perhaps we should leave now."

"Never!" Jeanne said, her thin hands beating together as if a supernatural energy possessed them. "Bravo Rostand! Bravo *Cyrano de Bergerac!*" She laughed and then sat down, crying, only to get to her feet again and again. Her eyes glowed, and curls of white hair escaped their pins and bounced alongside her ears and cheeks like a young girl's.

At two in the morning people were still applauding, crying, embracing one another in the corridors and the lobby.

At two-thirty, despite the gesticulating groups gathered in the street, Simone and Paul managed to locate their carriage and help Jeanne into it.

She sat on the edge of the seat as if she were still in the theatre. "It is the second most amazing night of my life, after *Hernani,*" she said. "I have not been so happy since Nandou was still alive. That I should live to see Romanticism reborn! Poetry in the theatre again—imagine it! Ah, this will put an end to dreariness on stage. Forgive me, Simone, I know you admire some of the new authors, and I do myself, for there are many ways to be truthful in art, but still . . . I always said the Romantic spirit could not be killed, and here is the proof of it, the magnificent proof. *Cyrano* will change the theatre, just as *Hernani* did, mark my words . . . You must try to publish this play, my dear. It would be a great success for Nandou and Company. . . . You know how he would have loved this night, don't you? I felt as if he were there. I could see him leaping onto his seat, crying 'Bravo, Hugo,' running out into the aisles . . . " Jeanne sank back against the cushion and closed her eyes. Their lids trembled, as if scenes were unrolling behind them.

If it were possible, Simone thought, for one human being to experience another's memories, such a thing had happened to her on this night, for even as she was swept along by the glorious verse and the thundering action, she had felt as if she too were reliving the past, the days that

Jeanne and Nandou had talked of so often, with such fervor. She reached over and took one of Jeanne's hands, thin and warm, which squeezed her own.

But was her grandmother right? she wondered. Would the new century, barely two years away, embrace the spirit of *Cyrano de Bergerac?* Or would it follow the lead of *Ghosts,* perhaps even of *Ubu Roi?*

She thought of her father's reply when, on one of her frequent trips up to Montmartre to see him, she had insisted that the work of the Impressionists would live and one day the paintings of Marcello Vianello would be properly appreciated. *I wouldn't try to predict the future of art, my love. The only thing we can be certain of is that artists will come along whom none of us have dreamed of, and if we did, would probably refuse to accept.* No doubt he was right—although she had done all she could to make her prediction about his own work come true. She had talked to dealers, even gotten one of them to take on some of his paintings, several of which had even been sold. For modest sums. *Do not distress yourself,* he said. *I am content. I am painting, and that is all that matters to me. Whatever else happens, will happen.*

Gently Simone released her grandmother's hand and sat back beside Paul. *I am content, too,* she thought. *Even Maman is, I think, in her own discontented way. And Grand-mère—look how she is smiling.*

"I am glad now that we brought her," Simone whispered to Paul. "If she had missed this night, I should never have heard the last of it."

The carriage rolled on through Paris, wheels singing softly. Paul whispered something in Simone's ear that made her laugh. The passing gas lamps flashed over Jeanne's face, over her closed lids and her smile, which went in and out of the light without losing any of its happiness.

At last the wheels stopped thrumming.

"Grand-mère," Simone said, "here we are. We are home."

There was no answer: only the smile that would never change now, and a wind that rose to greet it.

ABOUT THE AUTHOR

KAY NOLTE SMITH came to New York from Min-
nesota and Wisconsin to pursue a career as an actress
and writer. She won not only wide acclaim for her
first novel, *The Watcher* (1980), but also a Mystery
Writers of America Edgar Allan Poe award. *Catching Fire* (1982), which reflects her years as a professional actress, was followed by *Mindspell* (1983),
Elegy for a Soprano (1985), inspired by her lifelong
passion for opera, and *Country of the Heart* (1987),
about the conflict between artists and the state in the
Soviet Union. She is also the author of a new transla-
tion of Edmond Rostand's lyric drama *Chantecler.*
Art has been often the subject of and the inspiration
for her novels, and never more so than in *A Tale of
the Wind.* Her articles have appeared in such publica-
tions as *Vogue* and *Opera News,* and her short stories
have been anthologized and published abroad. She
lives in New Jersey with her husband, Phillip J.
Smith.